JAMES LEE BURKE
Three Great Novels

Robicheaux: Tales from Louisiana

Also by James Lee Burke

James Lee Burke

Three Great Novels

Robicheaux: Tales from Louisiana

A Morning for Flamingos

A Stained White Radiance

In the Electric Mist with Confederate Dead

ORION

A Morning for Flamingos © 1992 James Lee Burke
A Stained White Radiance Copyright © 1993 James Lee Burke
In the Electric Mist with Confederate Dead Copyright © 1992 James Lee Burke

1 3 5 7 9 10 8 6 4 2

This omnibus edition first published in Great Britain in 2005 by Orion,
an imprint of the Orion Publishing Group Ltd.

A CIP catalogue record for this book is available
from the British Library.

ISBN 0 75287 276 1 (trade paperback)

Typeset at The Spartan Press Ltd,
Lymington, Hants

Printed in Great Britain by
Clays Ltd, St Ives plc

The Orion Publishing Group Ltd
Orion House
5 Upper Saint Martin's Lane
London WC2H 9EA

www.orionbooks.co.uk

Contents

A Morning for Flamingos

To Martin and Jennie Bush

1

We parked the car in front of the parish jail and listened to the rain beat on the roof. The sky was black, the windows fogged with humidity, and white veins of lightning pulsated in the bank of thunderheads out on the Gulf.

'Tante Lemon's going to be waiting for you,' Lester Benoit, the driver, said. He was, like me, a plainclothes detective with the sheriff's department. He wore sideburns and a mustache, and had his hair curled and styled in Lafayette. Each year he arranged to take his vacation during the winter in Miami Beach so that he would have a year-round tan, and each year he bought whatever clothes people were wearing there. Even though he had spent his whole life in New Iberia, except for time in the service, he always looked as if he had just stepped off a plane from somewhere else.

'You don't want to see her, do you?' he said, and grinned.

'Nope.'

'We can go in the side door and bring them down the back elevator. She won't even know we've been there.'

'It's all right,' I said.

'It's not me that's got the problem. If you don't feel good about it, you should have asked off the assignment. What's the big deal, anyway?'

'It's not a big deal.'

'Then blow her off. She's an old nigger.'

'She says Tee Beau didn't do it. She says he was at her house, helping her shell crawfish, the night that guy got killed.'

'Come on, Dave. You think she's not going to lie to save her grandson?'

'Maybe.'

'You damn straight, maybe.' Then he looked off in the direction of the park on Bayou Teche. 'It's too bad the fireworks got rained on. My ex was taking the kids to it. Happens every year. I got to get out of this place.' His face looked wan in the glow of the streetlight through the rain-streaked window. His window was cracked at the top to let out his cigarette smoke.

3

'Let's do it,' I said.

'Give it a minute. I don't want to drive in wet clothes all the way up there.'

'It's not going to let up.'

'I'll finish my cigarette and we'll see. I don't like being wet. Hey, tell me on the square, Dave, is it delivering Tee Beau that bothers you, or do we have some other kind of concerns here?' The streetlight made shadows like rivulets of rain on his face.

'Have you ever been to one?' I asked.

'I never had to.'

'Would you go?'

'I figure the guy sitting in that chair knew the rules.'

'Would you go?'

'Yeah, I would.' He turned his head and looked boldly at my face.

'It can be an expensive experience.'

'But they all knew the rules. Right? You stuff somebody in the state of Louisiana, you get treated to some serious electroshock therapy.'

'Tell me the name of one rich man the state's burned. Or any state, for that matter.'

'Sorry. I'm not broken up about these guys. You think Jimmie Lee Boggs should have gotten life? Would you like him back around here on parole after ten and a half?'

'No, I wouldn't.'

'I didn't think so. I'll tell you another thing. If that guy tries anything on me, I'll park one in his mouth. Then I'll find his mother and describe it to her on her deathbed. How's that sound?'

'I'm going in now. You want to come?'

'She's going to be waiting,' he said, and grinned again.

She was. In a drenched print-cotton dress, sun-faded and colorless from repeated washings, that clung to her bony frame like wet tissue paper. Her mulatto hair looked like a tangle of gray-gold wire, her high-yellow skin as though it were spotted with brown dimes. She sat alone on a wood bench next to a holding cell, next to the elevator from which her grandson, Tee Beau Latiolais, whom she had raised by herself, would emerge in a few minutes with Jimmie Lee Boggs, both of them manacled in waist and leg chains. Her blue-green eyes were covered with cataracts, but they never left the side of my face.

She had worked in one of Hattie Fontenot's cribs on Railroad Avenue in the 1940s; then she'd spent a year in the women's penitentiary for stabbing a white man through the shoulder after he beat her up. Later she worked in a laundry and did housework for twenty dollars a week, which was the standard full-time salary for any Negro in South Louisiana, wherever he or she worked, well into the 1960s. Tante Lemon's daughter gave birth prematurely to a baby that was so small it fitted into the shoe box she hid it in before she put it in the bottom of a trash barrel. Tante Lemon heard the child's cries when she went out to use the privy the next morning. She raised Tee Beau as her own, fed him *cush-cush* with a spoon to make him strong, and tied a dime around his neck with a string to keep illness from traveling down his throat. They lived in an unpainted shack whose gallery had totally collapsed, so that the steps looked as if they led into a gaping, broken mouth, in an area people called nigger town. Each spring my father, who was a commercial trapper and fisherman, hired her to shell crawfish for him, though he could scarcely afford her meager salary. Whenever he caught mullet or gar in his nets, he dressed it and dropped it by her house.

'I ain't eating that, me,' he would say to me, as though he owed an explanation for being charitable.

I could hear the elevator coming down. A uniformed jailer at a small desk was finishing the paperwork on the transfer of the prisoners from the parish jail to Angola.

'Mr Dave,' Tante Lemon said.

'Tell them up there they already been fed,' the jailer said.

'There ain't anything wrong with them, either. The doctor checked out both of them.'

'Mr Dave,' she said again. Her voice was low, as though she were speaking in church.

'I can't help, Tante Lemon,' I said.

'He was at my little house. He didn't kill no redbone,' she said.

'Somebody's going to take her home,' the jailer said.

'I told all them people, Mr Dave. They ain't listen to me. What for they gonna listen an old nigger woman worked Miz Hattie's crib? That's what they say. Old nigger *putain* lyin' for Tee Beau.'

'His lawyer's going to appeal. There are a lot of things that can be done yet,' I said. I kept waiting for the elevator doors to open.

'They gonna electrocute that boy,' she said.

'Tante Lemon, I can't do anything about it,' I said.

Her eyes wouldn't leave my face. They were small and wet and unblinking, like a bird's.

I saw Lester smiling to himself.

'A car's going to take you home,' the jailer said to her.

'What for I goin' home, me? Be home by myself in my little house?' she answered.

'You fix something hot, you get out of them wet clothes,' the jailer said. 'Then tomorrow you talk to Tee Beau's lawyer, like Mr Dave says.'

'Mr Dave know better,' she said. 'They gonna burn that little boy, and he ain't done nothing wrong. That redbone pick on him, make fun of him in front of people, work him so hard he couldn't eat when he got home. I fix chicken and rice, everything nice, just the way he like it. He sit down all dirty at the table and stare at it, put it in his mouth like it ain't nothing but a bunch of dry bean. I tell him go wash his face and arm, then he gonna eat. But he say, "I tired, Gran'maman. I cain't eat when I tired." I say, "Tomorrow Sunday, you gonna sleep tomorrow, you, then you gonna eat." He say, "He coming' for me in the morning. We got them field to cut."

'Where everybody when that little boy need he'p?' she said. 'When that redbone roll up a newspaper and swat him like he's a cat? Where them police, them lawyer then?'

'I'll come over to your house tomorrow, Tante Lemon,' I promised.

Lester lit a cigarette and smiled up into the smoke. I heard the elevator motor stop; then the door slid open and two uniformed sheriff's deputies walked Tee Beau Latiolais and Jimmie Lee Boggs out in chains. They were dressed in street clothes for the trip up to Angola. Tee Beau wore a shiny sports coat the color of tin, baggy purple pants, and a black shirt with the collar flattened out on the coat. He was twenty-five, but he looked like a child in adult clothes, like you could pick him up around the waist as you would a pillow slip full of sticks. Unlike his grandmother's, his skin was black, his eyes brown, too big for his small face, so that he looked frightened even when he wasn't. Someone in the jail had cut his hair but had not shaved the neck, leaving a black wiry line low on the back of his neck that looked like dirt.

But Jimmie Lee Boggs was the man who caught your eye. His hair was silver, long and thin, and it hung straight back off his head like thread that had been sewn to the scalp. He had jailhouse pallor, and his eyes were elongated and spearmint green. His lips looked unnaturally red, as though they had been rouged. The curve of his neck, the profile of his head, the pink-white scalp that showed through his threadlike hair, reminded me of a mannequin's. He wore a freshly laundered T-shirt, jeans, and ankle-high black tennis shoes without socks. A package of Lucky Strikes stuck up snugly from one of his pockets. Even though his hands were manacled to the waist chain and he had to shuffle because of the short length of chain between his ankles, you could see the lean tubes of muscle move in his stomach, roll in his arms, pulse over his collar-bones when he twisted his neck to look at everyone in the room. The peculiar light in his eyes was not one you wanted to get lost in.

The jailer opened a file cabinet drawer and took out two large grocery bags that were folded and stapled neatly across the top. The name 'Boggs' was written on one, 'Latiolais' on the other.

'Here's their stuff,' he said, and handed the bags to me. 'If y'all want to stay up there tonight, you can get a per diem.'

'Lookit what you send up there, you,' Tante Lemon said. 'Ain't you

6

shamed? You put that little boy in chains, you pretend he like that other one, 'cause you conscience be bothering y'all at night.'

'I had that boy in my jail eight months, Tante Lemon, long before he got in this trouble,' the jailer said. 'So don't be letting on like Tee Beau never done anything wrong.'

'For taking from Mr Dore junkyard. For giving his *gran'maman* an old window fan ain't nobody want. That's why y'all had him in y'all's jail.'

'He stole Mr Dore's car,' the jailer said.

'That's what *he* say,' Tante Lemon said.

'I hope I don't have to pay rent here tonight,' Lester said, and brushed cigarette ashes off his slacks by flipping his nails against the cloth.

Then Tante Lemon started to cry. Her eyes closed, and tears squeezed out of the lids as though she were sightless; her mouth trembled and jerked without shame.

'Good God,' said Lester.

'Gran'maman, I be writing,' Tee Beau said. 'I be sending letters like I right down the street.'

'I got to go to the bathroom,' said Jimmie Lee Boggs.

'Shut up,' the jailer told him.

'That boy innocent, Mr Dave,' she said. 'You know what they gonna do. *T'connais*, you. He goin' to the Red Hat.'

'Y'all get out of here. I'll see she's all right,' the jailer said.

'Fuck, yes,' Lester said.

We went out into the dark, into the rain and the lightning that leapt across the southern sky, and locked Jimmie Lee Boggs and Tee Beau into the back of the car behind the wire-mesh screen. Then I unlocked the trunk and threw the two paper bags containing their belongings inside. At the back of the trunk, fastened to the floor with elastic rope, were a .30–06 scoped rifle in a zippered case and a twelve-gauge pump shotgun with a pistol stock. I got in the passenger's side, and we drove out of town on the back road that led through St Martinville to Interstate 10, Baton Rouge, and Angola Pen.

The spreading oaks along the two-lane road were black and dripping with water. The rain had slackened, and when I rolled my window partly down I could smell the sugarcane and the wet earth in the fields. The ditches on both sides of the road were high with rainwater.

'I got to use the can,' Jimmie Lee Boggs said.

Neither Lester nor I answered.

'I ain't kidding you, I gotta go,' he repeated.

'You should have gone back there,' I said.

'I asked. He told me to shut up.'

'You'll have to hold it,' I said.

'What'd you come back to this stuff for?' Lester said.

'I'm into some serious debt,' I said.

'How bad?'

'Enough to lose my house and boat business.'

'I'm going to get out one of these days. Buy me a place in Key Largo. Then somebody else can haul the freight. Hey, Boggs, didn't the mob have enough work for you in Florida?'

'What?' Boggs said. He was leaning forward on the seat, looking out the side window.

'You didn't like Florida? You had to come all the way over here to kill somebody?' Lester said. When he smiled, the edge of his mouth looked like putty.

'What do you care?' Boggs asked him.

'I was just curious.'

Boggs was silent. His face looked strained, and he shifted his buttocks back and forth on the seat.

'How much did they pay you to do that bar owner?' Lester said.

'Nothing,' Boggs said.

'Just doing somebody a favor?' Lester continued.

'I said "nothing" because I didn't kill that guy. Look, I don't want to be rude, we got a long trip together, but I'm feeling a lot of discomfort back here.'

'We'll get you some Pepto Bismol or something up on the Interstate,' Lester said.

'I'd appreciate that, man,' Boggs said.

We went around a curve through open pasture. Tee Beau was sleeping with his head on his chest. I could hear frogs croaking in the ditches.

'What a July Fourth,' Lester said.

I stared out the window at the soaked fields. I didn't want to listen to any more of Lester's negative comments, nor tell him what was really on my mind, namely, that he was the most depressing person I had ever worked with.

'I tell you, Dave, I never thought I'd have an assignment with a cop who'd been up on a murder beef himself,' he said, yawning and widening his eyes.

'Oh?'

'You don't like to talk about it?'

'I don't care one way or the other.'

'If it's a sore spot, I'm sorry I brought it up.'

'It's not a sore spot.'

'You're kind of a touchy guy sometimes.'

The rain struck my face, and I rolled the window up again. I could see cows clumped together among the streets, a solitary, dark farmhouse set back in a sugarcane field, and up ahead an old filling station that had been there since the 1930s. The outside bay was lighted, and the rain was blowing off the eaves into the light.

'I got something bad happening inside me,' Boggs said. 'Like glass turning around.'

He was leaned forward on the seat in his chains, biting his lip, breathing rapidly through his nose. Lester looked at him, behind the mesh screen, in the rearview mirror. 'We'll get you the Pepto. You'll feel a lot better.'

'I can't wait. I'm going to mess my pants.'

Lester looked over at me.

'I mean it, I can't hold it, you guys. It ain't my fault,' Boggs said.

Lester craned his head around, and his foot went off the gas. Then he looked over at me again. I shook my head negatively.

'I don't want the guy smelling like shit all the way up to Angola,' Lester said.

'When you transport a prisoner, you transport the prisoner,' I said.

'They told me you were a hard-nose.'

'Lester—'

'We're stopping,' he said. 'I'm not cleaning up some guy's diarrhea. That don't sit right with you, I'm sorry.'

He pulled into the bay of the filling station. Inside the office a kid was reading a comic book behind an old desk. He put down the comic and walked outside. Lester got out of the car and opened his badge on him.

'We're with the sheriff's office,' he said. 'A prisoner needs to use your rest room.'

'What?' the kid said.

'Can we use your rest room?'

'Yeah, sure. You want any gas?'

'No.' Lester got back into the car, leaving the kid standing there, and backed the car around the side of the station, out of the light, to the men's room door.

Tee Beau was awake now, staring out into the darkness. In the headlights I could see a tree-lined coulee, with canebrakes along its banks, behind the station. Lester cut the engine, got out of the car again, unlocked the back door, and helped Boggs out into the light rain by one arm. Boggs kept breathing through his nose and letting the air out with a shudder.

'I'll unlock one hand and give you five minutes,' Lester said. 'You give me any more trouble, you can ride the rest of the way in the trunk.'

'I ain't giving you no trouble. I told them all day I was sick.'

Lester took his handcuff key out of his pocket.

'Check the rest room first,' I said.

'I've been here before. There's no window. Lay off me, Robicheaux.'

I let out my breath, opened my door, and started to get out.

'All right, all right,' Lester said. He walked Boggs to the rest room door, opened it, flipped on the light, and looked inside. 'It's a box, like I said. You want to look?'

'Check it.'

'Bullshit,' he said. He unlocked Boggs's right hand from the manacle attached to the waist chain. As soon as Boggs's hand was free, he combed his hair back over his head with his fingers, looked back at the car, then walked inside the rest room with the short mincing steps that the leg chain would allow him. He clicked the bolt behind him.

This time I got out of the car.

'What's the matter with you?' Lester said.

'You're doing too many things wrong.' I came around the front of the car toward him. The headlights were still on.

'Look, I'm in charge of this assignment. You don't like the way I handle it, you write up a complaint when we get back.'

'Boggs has killed three people. He killed the bar owner with a baseball bat. Does that tell you something?'

'Yeah, that maybe you're a little bit obsessive. You think that might be the problem here?'

I unsnapped the holster on my .45 and banged on the rest room door with my fist.

'Open it up, Boggs,' I yelled.

'I'm on the toilet,' he said.

'Open the door!'

'I can't reach it. I got the shits, man. What's going on?' Boggs said.

'You're fucking unbelievable,' Lester said.

I hit the door again.

'Come on, Boggs,' I said.

'I'm going to get some cigarettes. You can do what you want to,' Lester said, and walked toward the front of the station.

I stepped back from the door, rested my palm on the butt of the .45, and kicked the door hard under the knob. It didn't give. I saw Lester turn and stare at me. I kicked it again, and this time the lock splintered out of the jamb and the door crashed back on its hinges.

My eyes saw the paper towel dispenser torn apart on the wall and the paper towels scattered all over the floor even before I saw Boggs, his knees squatted slightly in a shooting position, the links of chain crimped tightly into his body, one manacled hand frozen against his side like a bird's claw, his right arm outstretched with a nickel-plated revolver. His spearmint-green eyes were alive with excitement, and his mouth was smiling, as though we were in this joke together.

I got the .45 halfway out of my holster before he fired. The report was no louder than a firecracker, and I saw sparks from the barrel fly out into the darkness. In my mind's eye I was twisting sideways, raising my left arm in front of my face, and clearing my holster with the .45, but I do not think I was doing any of these things. Instead, I'm sure that my mouth opened wide in disbelief and fear as the round struck me high up in the chest like a fist that was wrapped in chain mail. My breath exploded out of my lungs, my knees caved, my chest burned as though someone had cored through sinew and bone with a machinist's drill. The .45 fell uselessly from my hand into the weeds, and I felt my left arm go limp, the muscles in my neck and shoulder collapsing as though all the linkage were severed. Then I was stumbling backward in the rain toward the coulee, my hand pressed over a wet hole in my shirt, my mouth opening and closing like a fish's.

Lester had a .38 strapped to his ankle. He had once told me that a cop he knew in Miami Beach carried his weapon in the same fashion. His knee came up in the air, his hand dropped towards his shoe, and in the light from the filling station front window his face looked absolutely white, frozen, beaded with raindrops, just before Jimmie Lee Boggs doubled him over with a round through the stomach.

But I wasn't thinking about Lester, nor in honesty can I say that I cared about him at that moment. Amid the pistol shots and the pop of lightning on the horizon, I heard a black medic from my outfit say, *Sucking chest wound, motherfucker. Close it, close it, close it. Chuck got to breathe through his mouth.* Then I crashed backward through a canebrake and tumbled down the slope of the coulee through the reeds and tangle of underbrush. I rolled on my back, my ears thundering with bugles and distant drums, and my breath came out of my mouth in a long sigh. The limbs of oak trees arched over the top of the coulee, and through the leaves I could see lightning flicker across the sky.

My legs were in the water, my back covered with mud, the side of my face matted with black leaves. I felt the warmness from the wound spread from under my palm into my shirt.

'Get in there, you sonofabitch,' Boggs said up in the darkness.

'Mr Boggs,' I heard Tee Beau say.

'Get the car keys and open the trunk,' Boggs said.

'Mr Boggs, they ain't no need to do that. That boy too scared to hurt us.'

'Shut up and get the guns out of the trunk.'

'Mr Boggs . . .'

I heard a sound like someone being shoved hard into a wall, then once again the report of the pistol, like a small, dry firecracker popping.

I swallowed and tried to roll on my side and crawl farther down the coulee. A bone-grinding, red-black pain ripped from my neck all the way down to my scrotum, and I rolled back into the ferns and the thick layer of black leaves and the mud that smelled as sour as sewage.

Then I heard the unmistakable roar of a shotgun.

11

'Try some Pepto Bismol for it,' Boggs said, and laughed in a way that I had never heard a human laugh before.

I slipped my palm away from my chest, put both of my hands behind me in the mud, dug the heels of my shoes into the silt bottom of the stream, and began to push myself toward a rotted log webbed with dried flotsam and morning glory vines. I could breathe all right now; my fears of a sucking chest wound had been groundless, but it seemed that all my life's energies had been siphoned out of me. I saw both Tee Beau and Boggs silhouetted on the rim of the coulee. Boggs held the pistol-grip twelve-gauge from the car trunk at port arms across his chest.

'Do it,' he said, took the nickel-plated revolver from his blue jeans pocket, and handed it to Tee Beau.

'Suh, let's get out of here.'

'You finish it.'

'He dying down there. We ain't got to do no more.'

'You don't get a free pass, boy. You're leaving here dirty as I am.'

'I cain't do it, Mr Boggs.'

'Listen, you stupid nigger, you do what I tell you or you join the kid up in the can.'

In his oversized clothes Tee Beau looked like a small stick figure next to Boggs. Boggs shoved him with one hand, and Tee Beau skidded down the incline through the wet brush, the branches whipping back across his coats and pants. The pistol was flat against his thigh. He splashed through the water toward me.

I ran my tongue across my lips and tried to speak, but the words became a tangle of rusty nails in my throat.

He knelt in front of me, his face spotted with mud, his eyes round and frightened in his small face.

'Tee Beau, don't do it,' I whispered.

'He done killed that white boy in the bat'room,' he said. 'He put that shotgun up against Mr Benoit face and blowed it off.'

'Don't do it. Please,' I said.

'Close your eyes, Mr Dave. Don't be moving, neither.'

'What?' I said, as weakly as a man would if he were slipping forever beneath the surface of a deep, warm lake.

He cocked the pistol, and his bulging eyes stared disjointedly into mine.

Some people say that you review your whole life in that final moment. I don't believe that's true. You see the fold in a blackened leaf, mushrooms growing thickly around the damp roots of an oak tree, a bullfrog glistening darkly on a log; you hear water coursing over rocks, dripping out of the trees, you smell it blowing in a mist. Fog can lie on your tongue as sweet and wet as cotton candy, the cattails and reeds turning a silver-green more beautiful than a painting in one flicker of lightning across the sky. You think of the texture of skin, the grainy pores, the nest of veins that are like the lines in a leaf. You think of your mother's powdered breasts, the smell of milk in her clothes, the heat in her body when she held you against her; then your eyes close and your mouth opens in that last strangled protest against the cosmic accident that suddenly and unfairly is about to end your life.

He was crouched on one knee when he pulled the trigger. The pistol went off ten inches from my face, and I felt the burnt powder scald my skin, the dirt explode next to my ear. My heart twisted in my chest.

I heard Tee Beau rise to his feet and brush his knees.

'I done it, Mr Boggs,' he said.

'Then get up here.'

'Yes suh, I'm moving.'

I remained motionless, my hands turned palm upward in the stream. The night was filled with sound: the crickets in the grass, the rumble of thunder out on the Gulf, the cry of a nutria farther up the coulee, Tee Beau laboring up through the wet brush.

Then I heard the car doors slam, the engine start, and the tires crunching over the gravel out on to the two-lane road.

It rained hard once more during the night. Just before dawn the sky cleared, and the stars were bright through the oak branches overhead. The sun came up red and hot above the tree line in the east, and the fog that clung to the bottom of the coulee was as pink as blood diffused in water. My mouth was dry, my breath foul in my own nostrils. I felt dead inside, disconnected from all the ordinary events in my life, my body trembling with spasmodic waves of shock and nausea, as though I lay once again on the side of a trail in Vietnam after a bouncing Betty had filled my head with the roar of freight trains and left me disbelieving and voiceless in the scorched grass. I heard early morning traffic on the road and car tires cutting into the gravel; then a car door opened and someone walked slowly along the side of the filling station.

'Oh Lawd God, what somebody done done,' a Negro man said.

I tried to speak, but no sound would come out of my voice box.

A small Negro boy in tattered overalls, with the straps hanging by his sides, stared down at me from the lip of the coulee. I raised my fingers off my chest and fluttered them at him. I felt one side of my mouth try to smile and the web of dried mud crack across my cheek. He backed away from the coulee and clattered through the cane, his voice ringing in the hot morning air.

2

Three months later I spent much of my day out on the gallery at home. The days were cool and warm at the same time, the way they always are during the fall in southern Louisiana, and I liked to put on a pair of khakis, a soft flannel shirt, and my loafers, and sit on the gallery and watch the gold light in my pecan trees, the hard blue ceramic texture of the sky above the marsh, the red leaves floating like rose petals on the bayou, the fishermen on my dock shaking sacks of cracked ice on their catches of *sac-à-lait* and big-mouth bass.

Sometimes after a couple of hours I would walk down through the grove of pecan trees and across the dirt road to the dock and bait shop and help Batist, the Negro man who worked for me, count the receipts, seine the dead shiners out of the aluminum bait tanks, or paint *sauce piquante* on the split chickens and links of sausage that we barbecued in an old oil drum I had cut longways with an acetylene torch and welded hinges and metal legs on. It was a good season that year, and I made a lot of money renting boats and selling bait and beer and serving barbecue lunches to the fishermen who came in at noon and sat around my Southern Bell spool tables with beach umbrellas set in the centers. But I would tire of my own business in a short while, and walk back up on the gallery and look out at the round shafts of light in the trees, and the gray squirrels that ran through the piles of leaves around the trunks.

My left shoulder and arm and upper chest didn't hurt me anymore when I moved around, or even when I turned on to my left side in my sleep. I was all right unless I picked up a lot of weight suddenly with my left hand. Sometimes I unbuttoned my shirt and fingered the round scar that was an inch and a half below my collarbone. It was the size of a dime, red, indented, rubbery to the touch. In an almost narcissistic fascination with my own mortality, I could reach over the top of my shoulder and touch the rubbery scar that had grown over the exit wound. The bullet had gone through me as clean and as straight as an arrow shaft.

On some afternoons I unfolded a card table on the gallery and took apart my guns – a double-barrel twelve-gauge, a .25-caliber hide-away Beretta, and the .45 automatic that I had brought home from Vietnam –

and oiled and wiped and polished all the springs and screws and tiny mechanisms. Then I'd oil them again and run bore brushes through the barrels before I reassembled them. I liked the heavy weight of the .45 in my palm, the way the clip snugged up inside the handle, the delicate lines of my fingertips on the freshly oiled metal. One day I loaded the clip with hollow-points, walked down to the duck pond at the back of my property, eased a round into the chamber, and sighted on a broad green hyacinth leaf. But I didn't pull the trigger. I lowered the automatic, then raised it and aimed again. The afternoon was bright and warm, and the grass in my neighbor's pasture was dull green in the sunlight. I lowered the .45 a second time, released the clip from the magazine, slipped it into my back pocket, pulled back the receiver, and ejected the round in the chamber. I told myself that the pistol's report, which was a deafening one, would be unsettling to the neighbors.

I walked back to the house, put the .45 under some shirts in my dresser drawer, and took no more interest in it.

I did not handle the nights well. Sometimes after supper I took Alafair, my adopted daughter, to Vezey's in New Iberia for ice cream; later, we would drive back down the dirt road along the bayou in the waning twilight, the fireflies lighting in the sky, and I would begin to feel a nameless apprehension that seemed to have no cause. I would try to hide my self-absorption from her, but even though she was only in the second grade, she always read my moods accurately and saw through my disguises. She was a beautiful child, with a round, tan face, wide-set Indian teeth, and shiny black hair cut in bangs. When she smiled her eyes would squint almost completely shut, and you would not guess that she had witnessed a massacre in her Salvadorean village, or that I had pulled her from a pocket of air inside a crashed plane, carrying illegal refugees, out on the salt.

One evening on the way home from the ice cream parlour I could feel her eyes watching the side of my face. I looked over at her and winked. We had bought some new Curious George and Baby Squanto Indian books, and she rode with them stacked on her knees.

'Why you always thinking about something, Dave?' she said. She wore her elastic-waisted jeans, pink tennis shoes, a USL T-shirt with the words 'Ragin' Cajuns' printed on it, and an oversized Houston Astros ball cap.

'I'm just tired today, little guy.'

'A man in Vezey's said hello to us and you didn't say anything.'

'I guess I didn't hear him.'

'You don't smile or play anymore, Dave. It's like something's always wrong.'

'I'm not that bad, am I?'

She looked straight ahead, her cap bouncing with the bumps in the road.

'Alf?' I said.

But she wouldn't turn her head or reply.

'Hey, Baby Squanto, come on.'

Then she said in a quiet voice, 'Did I do something that made you sad?'

'No, of course not. Don't ever think of a thing like that, little guy. You're my partner, right?'

But her face was morose in the purple light, her dark eyes troubled with questions she couldn't answer.

After I said her prayers with her and kissed her good-night, I read until very late, until my eyes burned and I couldn't register the words on that page and the darkness outside was alive with the cries of night birds and nutrias in the marsh. Then I watched the late show on television, drank a glass of milk and fell asleep with my head on the kitchen table. I woke during the night to the sound of Alafair's slippered feet shuffling across the linoleum. I looked up bleary-eyed into her face. Her pajamas were covered with smiling clocks. She patted me on top of the head as she would a cat.

He waited for me in my dreams. Not Tee Beau Latiolais or Jimmie Lee Boggs but a metamorphic figure who changed his appearance every night but always managed to perform the same function. Sometimes it was ole Victor Charlie, his black pajamas glued against his body with sweat, his face strung with human feces out of a rice paddy, one bulging walleye aimed along the iron sights of a French bolt-action rifle. When he squeezed the trigger I felt the steel-jacketed bullet rip through my throat as easily as it would core a cantaloupe.

Or I would see myself down a narrow, unlighted brick passageway off Dauphine in the French Quarter. I could smell the damp stone, the mint and roses growing in the courtyard, see the shadows of the banana trees waving on the flagstones beyond the piked gate that hung open at the end of the passageway. My hand tightened on the grip of the .45; the mortar between the bricks in the wall felt like claws in my back. I worked my way up to the courtyard entrance, my breath ballooning in my chest; then suddenly the scrolled iron gate swung into my face, broke two of my fingers as if they were sticks, raked the .45 out of my hand, and knocked me backward into a pool of rainwater. An enormous black man in a child's T-shirt, in lavender slacks at least three sizes too small for him, so that his scrotum was outlined like a bag of metal washers, squatted down with a .410 shotgun pistol resting on his thigh and looked at me through the bars of the gate. He was toothless, his lips purple with snuff, his eyes red-rimmed, his breath rank with funk.

'Your turn to beg, motherfucker,' he said. 'That's right, beg for your worthless shitass life.'

16

Then he smiled, lifted the point of my chin with the shotgun barrel, and cocked the hammer.

I would awake on the couch, my T-shirt and shorts damp with perspiration, and sit in a square of moonlight on the edge of the couch, my head bent down, my jaws clenched tight to keep them from shaking.

I was given full pay during my three months' leave, and when I returned to work I was assigned to restricted duty. I stayed in the office most of the time; I interviewed witnesses for other detectives; or sometimes I investigated traffic accidents out in the parish. I did a great deal of paperwork. I was treated with the deference you often see extended to a wounded and recuperating soldier. The attitude is one of kindness, but perhaps a degree of fear is involved also, as though mortality is an infectious condition that must be treated by isolation.

My life became as bland and unremarkable as the season was soft and warm and transitory.

Then, on a windblown afternoon, with leaves flying in the air, I drove to Lafayette in my truck to see Minos P Dautrieve, an old friend and DEA agent who was now assigned to the Presidential Task Force on Drugs.

He loved to fish, and because I didn't want to talk with him at his house, with his wife or children somewhere on the edge of the conversation, I asked him to bring his spinning rod and drive with me to the levee at Henderson Swamp.

I stopped at one of the bait and boat-rental shacks below the levee and bought two poor-boy shrimp sandwiches and a long-necked bottle of Jax for him and a Dr Pepper for me. We walked down to a grassy place on the bank, across from a row of willow islands that acted as a barrier between the channel along the levee and the swamp itself, which was actually an enormous wetlands area of bays, canals, bayous, oil platforms, and flooded stands of cypress and willow trees. He flipped his Rapala out to the edge of the willow pads that grew on the opposite side of the channel.

Minos had been All-American honorable mention when he played forward for LSU, and he still wore his hair in a college-boy crew cut, mowed so close that the scalp glowed. He was as lean, flat-stomached, and tapered-looking as he had been when sports-writers named him Dr Dunkenstein. He had been a first lieutenant with army intelligence in Vietnam, and although he was often flippant and cynical and defensive about his role as a government agent, he had a good heart and a hard-nosed sense about right and wrong that sometimes got him in trouble with his own bureaucracy.

I sat down on the incline and tore a long-bladed stem of grass along the spine. I told him about the strange sense of ennui that characterized my days. 'It's like being in the middle of a dead zone. It's like suddenly there's no sound, like all movement has stopped.'

'It'll pass,' he said.

'It doesn't feel like it.'

'You got two Hearts in 'Nam. You came out of it all right, didn't you?'

'That was different. The first wound was superficial. The second time I didn't see it coming. There's a difference when you see it coming.'

'I never got hurt, so maybe you're asking the wrong guy. But I've got a feeling that something else is bothering you.'

I dropped the torn grass blade between my knees and wiped my fingers on my pants.

'I feel like I begged,' I said.

'I don't understand. You begged Boggs before he shot you?'

'No, when Tee Beau climbed down into the coulee and cocked the .38 in my face.' I had to swallow when I said it.

'It sounds to me like you did just fine. What were you supposed to do? You had a round through your chest, you had to lie there in the dark with your own thoughts while a couple of guys talked about killing you, then you had to depend on the mercy of a black kid who'd already been sentenced to the electric chair. I don't think I would have come out of that altogether intact. In fact, I know I wouldn't.'

He flipped his lure out again and retrieved it in a zigzag motion just below the water's surface. Then he set the rod down on the bank, took our sandwiches and drinks out of the paper bag, and sat down beside me.

'Listen, podna,' he said. 'You're a brave man. You proved that a long time ago. Stop trying to convince yourself that you're not. I think what we should be talking about here is nailing Boggs. Like cooling out his action, dig it, like blowing up his shit. How'd he get the gun in the can, anyway?'

'He had a girlfriend in Lafayette, a dancer. She blew town the same day he escaped, but she left her fingerprints all over the towel dispenser.'

'Where do y'all think he is now?'

'Who knows? He left the car in Algiers. Maybe he went back to Florida.'

'How about the black kid?'

'Disappeared. I thought he'd show up by now. He's never been anywhere, and he's always lived with his grandmother.'

'Catch him and he might give you a lead on Boggs.'

'He might be dead, too.'

Minos opened the bottle of Jax with his pocketknife, put the cap inside the paper bag, and drank out of the bottle, staring out at the long, flat expanse of gray water and dead cypress. The sun was red and low on the western horizon.

'I think it's time to put your transmission into gear and start hunting these guys down,' he said. 'The rules of the game are kick ass and take names.'

I didn't say anything.

'It's pretty damn boring to be a spectator in your own life. What do you think?' he said.

'Nothing.'

'Bullshit. What do you think?' He hit me in the arm with his elbow.

I let out my breath.

'I'll give it some thought,' I said.

'You want any help from our office, you've got it.'

'All right, Minos.'

'If the black kid's alive, I bet you nail him in a week.'

'Okay.'

'You know Boggs'll show up, too. A guy like that can't get through a day without smearing shit on the furniture somewhere.'

'I think I'm getting your drift.'

'All right, I'm crowding the plate a little bit. But I don't want to see you sitting on your hands anymore. The lowlifes are the losers. They get up every morning knowing that fact. Let's don't ever let them think they're wrong, partner.'

He smiled and handed me a poor-boy sandwich. It felt thick and soft in my hand. Across the channel I could see the ridged and knobby head of an alligator, like a wet, brown rock, among the lily pads.

The next day I read all the paperwork on Tee Beau Latiolais and talked to the prosecutor's office and the detective who did the investigation and made the arrest. Nobody seemed to have any doubt about Tee Beau's guilt. He had worked for a redbone named Hipolyte Broussard, a migrant-labor contractor who had ferried his crews on rickety buses from northern Arizona to Dade County, Florida. I remembered him. He was a strange-looking man who had moved about in that nether society of people of color in southern Louisiana – blacks, quadroons, octoroons, and redbones. You would see him unloading his workers at dawn in the fields during the sugarcane harvest, and at night he would be in a Negro bar or poolroom on the south side of town or out in the parish, where he paid off the laborers or lent them money at high interest rates at a table in back. Like all redbones, people who are a mixture of Negro, white, and Indian blood, he had skin the color of burnt brick, and his eyes were turquoise. His arms and long legs were as thin as pipe cleaners, and he wore sideburns, a rust-colored pencil mustache, and a lacquered straw hat at a jaunty angle on his head. He worked his crews hard, and he had as many contracts with corporate farms as he wanted. I had heard stories that workers, or even a whole family, who gave him trouble might be put off the bus at night in the middle of nowhere.

Nobody doubted why Tee Beau had done it, either. In fact, people were sympathetic with his apparent motivation. For one reason or another, Hipolyte Broussard had made Tee Beau's life as miserable as he could. It was the way in which Tee Beau had killed him that had caused the judge to sentence Tee Beau to the electric chair.

It was misting slightly when I drove down the dirt road into the community of Negro shacks out in the parish where Tante Lemon now lived. The shacks were gray and paintless, the galleries sagging, the privies knocked together from tar paper, scrap lumber, and roofing tin. Chickens pecked in the dirt yards, the ditches were littered with garbage, the air reeked of somebody cooking cracklins outside in an iron kettle, which produces an eye-watering stench like sewage. On the corner was a clapboard juke joint, with tape crisscrossed on the cracked windows, and because it was Friday afternoon the oyster-shell parking lot was already full of cars, and the roar of the jukebox inside was so loud it vibrated the front window.

Tante Lemon's house was raised off the ground on short brick columns, and a yellow dog on a rope had dug a depression under the edge of the house from which he looked up at me and flopped his tail in the dirt. Flies buzzed back in the damp shadows beneath the raised floor. I knocked on the screen door, then saw her ironing at a board in the corner of her small living room. She stopped her work, picked up a tin can, held it to her lips, and spit snuff in it.

'They think they send you, I'm gonna tell where that little boy at?' she said. 'I ain't seen him, I ain't talk with him, I don't even know Tee Beau alive. That's what y'all done to us, Mr Dave. Don't be coming round here pretend you our friend, no.'

'Will you let me in, Tante Lemon?'

'I done tole them po-licemens, I tell you, I ain't seen him, me, and I ain't he'ping you, me.'

'Listen, Tante Lemon, I don't want to hurt Tee Beau. He saved my life. It's the white man I want. But they're going to catch Tee Beau sooner or later. Wouldn't you rather I find him first, so nobody hurts him?'

She walked to the screen and opened it. Her dress was wash-faded almost colorless, and it flapped on her body and withered breasts as shapelessly as rag.

'You going lie now 'cause I an old nigger?' she said. 'You catch that boy, they gonna carry him up to the Red Hat, they gonna strap him down, put that tin cap on his little head, cover up his face with cloth so they ain't got to look his eyes, let all them people watch my little boy suffer, watch the electricity burn up his body. I was on Camp I, Mr Dave, when they use to keep womens there. I seen them take a white man to the Red Hat. They had to pull him along the ground from the car, pull him along like a dog wrapped up in chains. Then all them people sat down like they was at the ballpark, them, and watch that man die.'

She raised the tin can to her lips and spit snuff in it again, then picked up her iron and began pressing a starched white shirt. She smelled of dry sweat, Copenhagen, and the heat rising from the ironing board. The walls of her house had been pasted with pages from magazines, then overlaid with mismatched strips of water-streaked wallpaper. The floor was covered with a rug whose thread had split like crimped straw, and the few pieces of furniture she owned looked as though they'd been carted home a piece at a time from the junkyard where Tee Beau used to work.

I sat down on a straight-backed chair next to her ironing board.

'I can't promise you anything,' I said, 'but if I find Tee Beau, I'll try to help him. Maybe we can get the governor to commute his sentence. Tee Beau saved the life of a police officer. That could mean a lot, Tante Lemon.'

'The life of that pimp mean a lot.'

'What?'

'Hipolyte Broussard a pimp, and he was gonna make Tee Beau do it, too.'

'I never heard that Broussard was involved with prostitution.'

'White people hear what they want to hear.'

'I didn't see anything like that in the case record, either. Who'd you tell this to?'

'I ain't tole nobody. Ain't nobody ax me.'

'Where was he pimping, Tante Lemon?'

'Out of the juke, there on the four-corner,' she said, and nodded her head toward the outside of the house. 'Out in them camps, where them farm worker stay at.'

'And he wanted Tee Beau to do it, too?'

'He make Tee Beau drive them girls from the juke down to the camp. Tee Beau say, "I cain't do that no more, Hipolyte." Hipolyte say, "You gonna do it, 'cause you don't, I gonna tell your PO you been stealing from me and you going back to jail." And it don't matter Tee Beau do what he say or not. Hipolyte keep making him feel awful all the time, sticking his thumb in that little boy seat, in front of all them people, shame him till he come home and cry. If that man ain't dead now, I go kill him myself, me.'

'Tante Lemon, why didn't you tell this to somebody?'

'I tole you, they ain't ax me. You think them people in that courtroom care what an old nigger woman say?'

'You didn't tell anybody because you thought it would hurt Tee Beau, that people would be sure he did it.'

It started raining outside. The hinged flap on the side window was

21

raised with a stick, and in the gray light her skin had the color of a dull penny. She mashed the iron up and down on the shirt she was ironing.

'I can tell lots of things 'bout that juke up the four-corner, 'bout the *traiteur* woman run that place with Hipolyte, 'bout them crib they got there. Ain't nobody interested, Mr Dave. Don't be telling me they are, no. Just like when I up in Camp I in Angola. On the Red Hat gang they run them boys up and down the levee with they wheelbarrow, beat them every day with the Black Betty, shoot them and bury them right there in the Miss'sippi levee. Everybody knowed it, nobody care. Ain't nobody care about Tee Beau or what I got to say now.'

'You should have talked to somebody. They didn't give Tee Beau the chair because he killed Hipolyte. It was the way he did it.'

'Tee Beau in this house, shelling crawfish. Right here,' she said, and tapped her finger on the ironing board.

'All right. But somebody drove the bus off the jack on top of Hipolyte. Tee Beau's fingerprints were all over the steering wheel. His muddy shoe prints were all over the floor pedals. Nobody else's. Then while Hipolyte was lying under the brake drum with his back broken, somebody stuffed an oil rag in his mouth so he could spend two hours strangling to death.'

'It wasn't long enough.'

'Where is Tee Beau?'

'I ain't gonna tell you no more. Waste of time,' she said, took a cigarette from a pack on the ironing board, and lit it. She blew the smoke out in the humid air. 'You a white man. Colored folk ain't never gonna be your bidness. You come round now 'cause you need Tee Beau catch that white trash shot you. You just see a little colored boy can he'p you now. But you cain't be knowing what he really like, how he hurt inside, how much he love his *gran'maman*, how much he care for Dorothea and what he willing to do for that little girl. You don't be knowing none of these things, Mr Dave.'

'Who's Dorothea?'

'Go up the juke, ax her who she is. Ax her about Hipolyte, about what Tee Beau do for her. You, that's gonna take him up to the Red Hat.'

I said good-bye to her, but she didn't bother to answer. It was raining hard when I stepped off the gallery, and drops of mud danced in the dirt yard. Down the street at the four-corners, the clapboard facade of the juke joint glistened in the gray light, and the scroll of neon over the door, which read BIG MAMA GOULA'S, looked like purple smoke in the rain that blew back off the eaves.

The inside was crowded with Negroes, the air thick with cigarette smoke, the smell of dried sweat, muscat, talcum powder, chitlins, gumbo, flat beer, and bathroom disinfectant. The jukebox was deafening, and the pool players rifled the balls into side pockets, shouting and slamming the rack down on the table's slate surface. Beyond the dance floor a zydeco band with an accordion, washboard, thimbles, and an electric bass was setting up on a small stage surrounded by orange lights and chicken wire. Behind the musicians a huge window fan sucked the cigarette smoke out into the rain, and their clothes fluttered in the breeze like bird's feathers. Two deep at the bar, the customers ate *boudin* and pickled hog's feet off paper plates, drank long-necked Jax and wine *spotioti*, a mixture of muscat and whiskey that can fry your head for a week.

I stood at the end of the bar, saw the eyes flick momentarily sideways, then heard the conversations resume as though I were not there. I waited for the bartender to reach that moment when he would decide to recognize me. He walked on the duckboards to within three feet of me and began lifting handfuls of beer bottles between his fingers from a cardboard carton, fitting them down into the ice bin. There was a thin, dead cigar in his mouth.

'What you want, man?' he asked, without looking up.

'I'm Detective Dave Robicheaux with the sheriff's department,' I said, and opened my badge in my palm.

'What you want?' His eyes looked at me for the first time. They were sullen and flecked with tiny red veins.

'I'd like to talk to Dorothea.'

'She's working the tables. She's real busy now.'

'I only want a couple of minutes of her time. Call her over, please.'

'Look, man, this ain't the place. You understand what I'm talking about?'

'Not really.'

He raised up from his work and put his hands flat on the bar.

'That's her out yonder by the band,' he said. 'You want to go out there and get her? That what you want?'

'Ask her to come over here, please.'

'Listen, I ain't did you nothing. Why you giving me this truck?'

The men next to me had stopped talking now and were smoking their cigarettes casually and looking at their own reflections in the bar mirror. One man wore a lavender porkpie hat with a feather in the brim. His sports coat hung heavy on one side.

'Look, man, you got a car outside?' the bartender asked.

'Yes.'

'Go sit in it. I'll be sending her,' he said, then his voice changed. 'Why you be bothering that girl? She ain't did nothing.'

'I know she hasn't.'

'Then why you bothering her?' he asked.

Before I turned to go outside, I saw a big black woman in a purple dress looking at me from the far end of the duckboards. Her hands were on her hips, her chin pointed upward; she took the cigarette out of her mouth and blew smoke in my direction, her eyes never leaving my face. In the dim light I thought I saw blue tattoos scrolled on the top of her breasts.

The rain clattered on the roof of my car and streamed down the windows. At the back of the juke joint, beyond the oyster-shell parking lot covered with flattened beer cans, were two battered house trailers. Two men who looked like Latins, in denim work clothes and straw hats, drove up in a pickup truck and knocked at one of the trailers, their bodies pressed up against the door to stay out of the rain. A black woman opened the inside door and spoke to them through the screen. They got back in their truck and left. I saw one of them look back through the rear window as they pulled on to the dirt road.

Five minutes later the bartender appeared in the front door of the juke joint with a small Negro girl at his side and pointed at my car. She ran across the parking lot toward me, with a newspaper spread over her head. When I pushed open the passenger door she jumped inside. She wore black fishnet stockings, a short black waitress's skirt, and a loose white blouse that exposed her lace bra, but she looked both too young and too small for the job she did, and the type of clothes that she wore. It was her hair that caught your attention, black and thick and brushed in soft swirls around her head, almost like a helmet that made her toy face seem even smaller than it was. She was frightened and would not look at me directly.

'You know I'm a police officer?' I said.

'Yes suh.'

'Tee Beau saved my life, so I don't want to see him hurt. The man I'm after is named Jimmie Lee Boggs. He killed two people and took Tee Beau with him when he escaped. You know all that, don't you?'

'Yes suh, I knows that.'

'You don't have to call me sir. If Tee Beau can help me find this man Boggs, maybe I can help Tee Beau.'

She nodded her head. Her hands were motionless on top of the wet newspaper in her lap.

'Did he tell you where Boggs dropped him off?' I said.

'Suh?' Her eyes cut sideways at me, then looked straight ahead again.

'When you talked to him, did he say anything about Jimmie Lee Boggs?'

'I ain't talked to Tee Beau.'

'I bet you have,' I said, and smiled.

'No suh, I ain't. Nobody know where Tee Beau at. Tante Lemon don't know. Ain't nobody know.'

'I see. Look here, Dorothea, I'm going to give you a card. It has my phone number on it. When you talk to Tee Beau, you give him this number. You tell him I appreciate what he did for me, that I want to help him. He can call me collect from a pay phone. I won't know where he's living. All I want to do is find Jimmie Lee Boggs.'

She took the card in her small hand. She looked out at the rain, her eyes quiet with thought.

'How you gonna he'p him?' she said.

'We can get his sentence commuted. That means he won't go to the electric chair. Maybe he can even get a new trial. The jury didn't hear everything they should have, did they?'

'What you mean?'

'About Hipolyte Broussard. Was he a pimp?'

'Yes suh.'

'Did he try to make Tee Beau a pimp, too?'

'He make him drive the bus with the girls out to the camp.'

'What else did Hipolyte do?'

'Suh?'

'Did Hipolyte do something to you?'

Again her eyes cut sideways, then looked straight ahead. I could see her nostrils quiver when she breathed.

'You don't have to tell me if you don't want to,' I said. 'But maybe Tee Beau had a good reason to kill Hipolyte. Maybe other people might think so, too.'

She squeezed her fingers and looked down at her lap.

'He say I got to get on the bus,' she said.

'Who?'

'Hipolyte. He say I got to go out to the camp. Tee Beau say I ain't going, even if Hipolyte hit him and knock him down in the dirt. Hipolyte say I going or I ain't working here no more.'

'So that's why he killed Hipolyte?'

'I ain't said that. I ain't said that at all. You ax me what Hipolyte done to me.'

I looked out at the trailers behind the parking lot.

'Is somebody bothering you now, Dorothea?' I said. 'Does anybody try to make you do something you don't want to?'

'Gros Mama's good to me.'

'Does she make you do something you don't want to?'

'I wait the table, I pass the mop on the floor 'fore I go home. She don't let no mens bother me. She pass for me in the morning, carry me to work, tell me not be worrying all the time 'bout Tee Beau, he gonna be all right, he coming back one day. Gros Mama know.'

'How does she know that?'

'She a *traiteur*. She got power. That's why Hipolyte scared of her. He got the *gris-gris*. That man you looking for, Jimmie Lee Boggs? You ain't got to worry about him, no. He got a *gris-gris*, too. He gonna die, that one.'

'Wait a minute, Dorothea. You knew Boggs?'

'I seen him with Hipolyte, back yonder by that trailer. Right there. Gros Mama say they both got the *gris-gris*, they carry it in them just like a worm. Suh?'

'What?'

'Suh?'

'What is it? And you really don't need to call me sir.'

'I wants to ax you something.' She looked at me full in the face for the first time. Her lipstick was on crooked. 'You ain't lying? You can really he'p Tee Beau?'

'I can try. If he'll let me. Do you know where he is, Dorothea?'

'Gros Mama want me back inside now. Friday a real busy day.'

'If you talk to Tee Beau, tell him I said thank you.'

'I got to be going now.'

'Wait a minute. I have an umbrella,' I said.

I popped it open in the rain and walked her to the entrance of the juke joint. Then she walked hurriedly past the men staring at her from the bar, toward her station by the dance floor.

I had promised to take Alafair to the open-air restaurant at Cypremort Point for bluepoint crabs, a weekly ritual whose aftermath made the waitresses cringe: Alafair, in a white bib with a big red crawfish on it, went about disassembling the crabs with wood mallet and nutcrackers and such clumsy intensity that the plank table had to be washed down later with a hose. I tried never to disappoint her, or see her hurt any more than she had already been hurt by the drowning of her real mother in the crashed plane, and the death of Annie, my second wife. But since I had been shot by Jimmie Lee Boggs, I had become an ineffectual caretaker in my own home rather than a parent, and I had no idea when I would put everything back in the proper box and see the worry and uncertainty go out of Alafair's eyes. And I knew absolutely that that moment would not come of its own accord.

So I drove down to a café on the blacktop, called the house, and asked Clarise, my mulatto house-keeper and baby-sitter, to give Alafair her supper and to stay with her until I got home. I talked with Alafair and told her I would take her out for ice cream later and we would go to Cypremort Point for crabs the next night. I sat at the counter and ate a plate of red beans, rice, and breaded pork chops, and drank coffee until over an hour had passed. Then I headed back to the juke joint.

It had stopped raining now, and the air was clear and cool, the sky dark except for a lighted band of purple clouds low on the western horizon. I drove through the parking lot to the back of the building, the flattened beer cans and wet oyster shells crunching under my tires, and through the big fan humming in the back wall I could hear the zydeco band pounding it out:

'Mo mange bien, mo bois bon vin,
Ça pas coute moi à rien.
Ma fille aime gumbo filé
Mo l'aime ma fille aussi.'

I parked by one of the trailers and walked up on the wood steps. Back under a solitary spreading oak tree was the pickup truck I had seen earlier: only one man was in the cab now. The trailer was made out of tin and had been covered with thick layers of green paint. Curtains were pulled across the windows, but a light was on inside. The inner door was closed and the screen was latched. I tapped on the screen with my knuckles and looked back over my shoulder at the man in the truck. He looked away from me.

'Sheriff's department,' I said, and tapped again.

There was no answer, but I heard movement inside.

'Open up,' I said.

Still no answer. I grasped the handle to the screen door firmly and jerked the latch out of the jamb, then opened the inner door, which was unlocked, and stepped into the trailer.

The musky, thick odor of marijuana struck at my face like a fist. The woman whom I had seen at the trailer door earlier lay on a narrow bed in a pink bra and pink panties, her head reclining on a pillow, one arm propped casually behind her head, her free hand holding a joint over an ashtray on a small nightstand. She put the joint to her lips, looked me straight in the face, and took a long, deep hit, ventilating the edges of the paper, until the ash was a bright red coal in the gloom of the trailer.

But the dark-skinned man in denims and work boots, his straw hat clenched against his thigh, his belt buckle still hanging down over his fly, was obviously terrified. His eyes were riveted on the badge in my palm.

'It's not a bust, partner. Rest easy,' I said.

He continued to stare wide-eyed at me. His hands were square with calluses, his fingernails half-mooned with dirt.

'Do you speak English?' I said. Then to the woman, 'Does your friend speak English?'

'You do it the same way in Mexican or English, honey,' she said.

'It's time for you to take off, partner,' I said.

But he didn't understand. I folded up my badge and slipped it in my back pocket.

'You can go now. We don't need you for anything. There's no problem. *No problema*. Your friend is waiting for you,' I said.

I took him gently by the arm and opened the door for him.

'*Adios*,' I said.

This time he realized what he was being offered and he was gone into the darkness like a shot. I closed the door behind him.

'You're a very cool lady,' I said.

She took a slow, easy hit on the reefer and let the smoke curl out of her mouth into her nose.

'I guess I just don't scare you too much,' I said.

She flexed herself on the bed and drew one knee up before her. Her toenails were painted red.

'You gonna do what you gonna do, ain't you?' she said.

'Possession can be serious stuff in Louisiana.'

'Honey, if you was interested in 'resting me, you wouldn't be tapping on no do'.'

'You're pretty hip, too.'

'Why don't you tell me what you want, sweetheart? Somebody tole you the black berry got the sweet juice?'

'Was Hipolyte Broussard your pimp?'

'That's a bad word. Like it mean I doing something I ain't suppose to.'

I turned a straight-backed chair around backward and straddled it.

'Let's understand something,' I said. 'I don't care what y'all do here. I'm after a white man named Jimmie Lee Boggs. I'll do just about anything to find him. I feel that way about him because he shot me. Are we communicating here?'

She smiled lazily in the smoke.

'So you the one?' she said.

'That's right. And let's get rid of this distraction, too.' I took the roach out of her fingers and mashed it out in the ashtray. 'Did you know Boggs?'

'I seen him.'

'Where?'

'He come see Hipolyte.'

'Why?'

'Where you been, honey? You ever see black folks who ain't got to give part their money to white folks? You ain't dumb. You just pretend, you. I think you just here to see me.' She smiled again and stretched both her arms over her head.

'Did Boggs come see Gros Mama Goula?'

'That white trash mess with Gros Mama, snakes be crawling out his grave.'

I heard the screen open on the spring; then the inside door raked back on the buckled linoleum floor, and the black woman in the purple dress with the scrolled blue tattoos on the tops of her breasts stood in the doorway, one hand on her hip, a flowered kerchief curled in her fingers.

'You taking up too much of people's time,' she said. 'You got jelly roll on your mind, or you think bothering my womens gonna clean that man outta your head?'

'What?' I said.

She told the woman on the bed to dress and get up to the juke and help wait tables. She picked up the ashtray with the roach in it and threw it outside into the darkness.

'Wait a minute, what did you say?' I said.

She ignored me.

'And tell that drunk nigger giving Al trouble when I be back up there his skinny ass better be gone,' she said to the other woman, who buttoned her jeans, pulled on her blouse, and went out the door.

Gros Mama Goula's face was big and hard-boned, like a man's, her eyes deep-set and dark, so that they had a cavernous quality under the broad forehead and thick brows. I had heard stories about her from other Negroes, the juju woman who could blow the fire out of a burn; stop bleeding by pressing her palm against a wound; charm worms out of a child's stomach; cause a witch to invade the marriage bed, straddle the husband, and fornicate with him until his eyes crossed and he would remain forever discontent with his wife.

'What did you say?' I repeated.

'Po-licemens after jelly roll just like everybody else. You want it, you come ax me first, don't be bothering my womens. That ain't what on your mind, though. You got Jimmie Lee Boggs crawling round in your head. Jelly roll ain't gonna get him out you. He lying there, waiting.'

'Is this supposed to impress me?'

She opened a cabinet over the stove, took out a jelly glass and a pint bottle of rum, poured herself three fingers, sat down at a small breakfast table, and lit a cigarette. She drank down the rum, inhaled from the cigarette, blew smoke out over her hand, and studied her knuckles as though I were not there.

'What you want?' she said.

'For openers take a break on the *traiteur* routine.'

'What you mean?'

'You talked with Dorothea. You knew I was looking for Boggs. You'd seen my picture in the newspaper, or you figured out I was one of the men he shot.'

'Think what you want. I ain't got the problem.'

'What I think is you're operating a place of prostitution.'

She smoked and flicked her ashes and waited for me to go on.

'I don't bother you?' I said.

'You want to carry me up to the jail, that's your bidness. They's people pay my bond make sure I stay open.'

'Was Jimmie Lee Boggs cutting into Hipolyte's and your action?'

'Darlin', they ain't nobody cutting into my action.'

'I don't believe you, Gros Mama. There's not a hot-pillow house in South Louisiana that doesn't have to piece off its action to New Orleans.'

She poured rum into her glass again, then as an afterthought looked at me and pointed her finger at the bottle.

'No thanks,' I said.

She screwed the top slowly onto the bottle.

'Lookie here,' she said. 'You don't care 'bout them dagos in New Orleans, 'bout what some niggers be doing down here on Saturday night. You want that man 'cause he hurt you, 'cause he walking round in your sleep at night. You wake up tired in the morning, cain't open and close your hands on the side the bed. You dragging a big chain all day long. Food don't taste no good, womens just something for other mens. You can tell the whole round world I lying, but me and you knows better.'

I stared at her woodenly. She continued to smoke idly.

'I ain't seen him since they 'rested him for killing that man with the ball bat,' she said. 'He in New Orleans, though.'

'How do you know?'

'He gonna die over there. In a black room, with lightning jumping all over it. Don't mess with it, darlin'. Come down see Gros Mama when you wake up with that bad feeling. She make you right,' she said, and squared her shoulders so that the tattoos on her breasts stretched like a spiderweb.

3

The next morning Alafair and I raked and burned leaves under the pecan trees in my front yard. It was a perfect blue-gold autumn day, and the smoke from the fire hung in the spangled sunlight and drifted out across the bayou into the cypress trees. A little over two years earlier my wife, Annie, and I had been seining for shrimp just the other side of Marsh Island when we saw a twin-engine plane trailing a column of thick black smoke across the sky. It pancaked into a trough, dipped one wing into a wave, and cartwheeled like a child's stick toy across the water. While Annie called the Coast Guard on the emergency channel, I went over the side with an air tank and weight belt and swam down into the greenish-yellow light to the plane, which had come to rest upside down in a trench. Through the window, among the drowned bodies undulating in their seats, I saw Alafair kicking her legs and fighting to keep her head afloat inside a wobbling envelope of trapped air. Her small mouth looked like a guppy's above the waterline.

Later, Annie and I would find the bruise marks on her legs where her mother had held her up in the air pocket while she herself lost her life.

I gave Alafair my mother's name, and after Annie's death I legally adopted her. But even now I still knew little of the Central American world which she had fled, except that memories of it had given her nightmares for a long time and she thought of manual labor almost as play. She loved to work in the yard with me. She held the rake handle midway down and scoured the ground bare with the tines, her elastic-waisted jeans grimed at the knees, her face hot and bright with her work. She wore her yellow T-shirt with a smiling purple whale and the words 'Baby Orca' embossed on it, but it was too small for her now and her arms looked fat and round in the sleeves.

It was too good a day to dwell on Jimmie Lee Boggs and Gros Mama Goula and a lot of mojo claptrap, so Alafair and I took the jugboat and headed out Southwest Pass onto the salt. It was called a jugboat because it had been used by a marine seismograph company to lay out and recover the long rubber-coated cables and instruments, or 'jugs', that recorded the vibrations off the substrata after an explosion was detonated in the drill hole. It was narrow and long, built for speed, with a low draft, a big Chrysler engine, two screws, and the windowed pilot's cab flush on the stern. I had outfitted it with gear boxes, ice bins, a small galley, a bait well, winches for my trawling nets, iron rod-and-reel sockets for trolling. In the middle of the deck I bolted down a telephone-company spool table, with a collapsible Cinzano umbrella set in the center hole.

The day was warm, the ground swells long and gentle and rolling, so that when they crested the wave broke into a thin froth and blew in the wind. I kept the bow into the wind and idled through the swells while Alafair set the rods into the sockets, spun out the lines behind us so the lures bounced in our wake, clicked on the drags, and threw chum overboard as if she were flinging shot. High up against the blue dome of sky, brown pelicans drifted in formation on the wind stream. Then suddenly their wings would collapse, cock into their sides like fins, and they would plummet with the speed of an aerial bomb into the water and rise from the foam with a menhaden or flying fish dripping from their pouched beak.

In the middle of a long green trough I saw a greasy slick on the water and smelled the fecund odor of speckled or white trout in a big school. I cut the engine, threw the anchor, and let the jugboat swing back against the tension in the rope. We reeled in our lines and rigged them with heavy teardrop weights, bait hooks, and big corks. Alafair's two-handed cast sent a lead weight and hook singing past my ear.

The clouds in the west looked like strips of flame above the green horizon when we headed back through the Pass into Vermilion Bay. The ice bin was loaded with gaff-top catfish and speckled trout, gutted and stiff and laid out in cold rows, their mouths hooked open, their eyes black and shiny as glass. Alafair sat on my lap and steered us between the buoys into the channel; when I touched her head with my chin I could feel the sun's heat in her hair.

'Let's take some to Batist tonight,' she said.

'That's a good idea, little guy.'

She twisted her head around and grinned up at me.

'Then maybe rent a movie,' she said.

'You got it, Alf.'

'Buy some *boudin* and fix some Kool-Aid, too.'

'That's actually been on my mind all day.'

'All right, big guy.'

We were happy and tired when we drove down the dirt road under the oaks toward my house on the bayou. Our clothes were flecked with fish blood and membrane, our skin salty and dry from the wind and the sun. It had been a fine day. I was determined that it would remain so, even though I saw Minos Dautrieve's car parked by my gallery and Minos sitting on my front step.

Alafair rinsed the fish in the sink while Minos and I went out in the backyard and sat at my redwood picnic table under the mimosa tree. The moon was up, and I could see my neighbor's sugarcane in the field.

'I've got a proposal for you,' he said.

'What's that, Minos?'

'You know I'm on that Presidential Task Force on Drugs?'

'Yeah.'

'It's an election year, and everybody wants to stomp the shit out of the drug dealers. Never mind the fact that we've had our budgets cut for years. But that's all right, it's all rock 'n' roll, anyway. We'll cripple up as many lowlifes as we can and let somebody else worry about the rest, right?'

'Minos—'

'Okay, take it easy. Have you tried to turn up that black kid?'

'It's all dead-end stuff. His grandmother and his girlfriend probably know where he is, but they're not saying. I ended up last night talking with a *traiteur* woman named Big Mama Goula in a hot-pillow joint. That's a long way from Jimmie Lee Boggs.'

'Look, I think your life's been too dull. So I talked with some people on the task force, then I talked with the Iberia sheriff. We want to put you inside the mob.'

'What?'

'You're the perfect guy.'

'Are you out of your mind?'

'Hear me out.'

'No. I went back with the sheriff's department to pay off some big debts. I got shot. You think I want to go undercover now?'

'That's why you're the perfect guy, Dave. It wouldn't be undercover. You resign from the department, we set you up in New Orleans, give you a lot of money to flash around the lowlifes. Then we put out the word with a couple of our snitches that you were encouraged to resign, you're a burnout, maybe you've been on a pad.'

I was shaking my head, but he kept talking.

'There's a new player in New Orleans we want to nail real bad. His name's Anthony Cardo, also known as Tony C. and Tony the Cutter. No, he's not a shank artist. He's supposed to have a schlong that's a foot and a half long, the Johnny Wad of the Mafia. He grew up across the river in Algiers, but he's got operations in Miami and Fort Lauderdale. In fact, we think he's a linchpin between the dope traffic in South Florida and southern Louisiana.'

'I'm not interested.'

'Look, it'd be a three- or four-week scam. If it doesn't work, we'll mark it off.'

'It won't work.'

'Why not?'

'They won't buy a cop who just turned in his badge.'

'Yeah, they will. They'll buy you,' he said, and tapped his finger at the air.

'I have a feeling you're about to say something else complimentary.'

'Let's look at your record, fair and square, podna. You were almost fired from the force in New Orleans, you have an alcoholic history, you've been in your own drunk tank, you were up on a murder charge, for God's sakes. All right, it was a frame, and that situation with the New Orleans PD was a rotten shake, too, but like I told you when I first met you, it makes socko reading material. How about your old Homicide partner, what's his name?'

'Cletus Purcel.'

'He didn't have any trouble going to work for the wiseguys, did he? They bought him, toenails to hairline.'

'He's clean now. He owns a club on Decatur.'

'That's right. But he still knows the greaseballs. They come in his place.'

'It's a free country.'

'You've got the conduit into the mob, Dave. They'll buy it.'

'Not interested.'

'It's no more complicated than a simple sting.'

'I told you you're talking to the wrong guy, Minos.'

'There's another factor. We think Jimmie Lee Boggs might be back in New Orleans.'

'Why?'

'A telephone tap. Last week one of Tony Cardo's people was talking about bringing in a mechanic from Florida to take care of a guy who held back twenty thou on a sale. Then yesterday somebody did this black street dealer with a baseball bat in Louis Armstrong Park. Sound familiar?'

'Why would he go back to a state where he's already been sentenced to the chair?'

'It doesn't make any difference where he is. There're warrants on him in three other states, and the FBI's after him as an interstate fugitive. Number two, he'll go where Tony Cardo tells him to go.'

'I'm not up to it. You'll have to get somebody else.'

'That's it, huh?'

'Yep.'

He looked at me reflectively in the moonlight. I could see his scalp glisten through his thin crew cut.

'How you feeling?' he said.

'Fine.'

'You're a good cop, Dave. The best.'

After he was gone, I sat by myself in the yard awhile and tried to put my thoughts into separate envelopes. Then I gave it up and went inside to eat supper with Alafair at the kitchen table.

So the days went by and I watched the leaves fall and my neighbor harvest his sugarcane, which was now thick and gold and purple in the fields. Each evening I jogged three miles down the dirt road to the drawbridge on the bayou, the air like a cool burn on my skin, and as the sun set over the bare field behind my house I did sit-ups and stomach crunches in my backyard, curled a fifty-pound dumbbell with my right arm, a ten-pound bar with my left, and sat down weary and glazed with sweat in the damp grass. I could feel my body mending, the muscles tightening and responding in my upper chest and neck the way they had before a bullet had torn through the linkage and collapsed it like a broken spiderweb.

But to be honest, the real purpose in my physical regimen was to induce as much fatigue in my body as possible. Morpheus' gifts used to come to me in bottles, Beam and black Jack Daniel's, straight up with a frosted schooner of Jax on the side, while I watched the rain pour down in the neon glow outside the window of an all-night bar not far from the Huey Long Bridge. In a half hour I could kick open a furnace door and fling into the flames all the snakes and squeaking bats that lived inside me. Except the next morning they would writhe with new life in the ashes and come back home, stinking and hungry.

Now I tried to contend with my own unconscious, and the dreams it brought, with a weight set, a pair of Adidas shoes, and running shorts.

Then one evening, a week after Minos had appeared again, a pickup truck with two cracked front windows, crumpled fenders, and a bumper that hung down like a broken mouth bounced through the depressions in my drive, the tailgate slamming on the chain, the rust-gutted muffler roaring like a stock-car racer. Tante Lemon's head barely extended above the steering wheel; her chin was pointed upward, her small hands pinched on the wheel, her frosted eyes pinpoints of concern as she tried to maneuver through the trunks of the pecan trees. Dorothea sat next to her, one hand propped against the dashboard.

'She wanta tell you something,' Tante Lemon said.

'Come in,' I said, and I opened the truck door for her.

'We ain't got to do that,' she said.

'Yeah, you do,' I said.

They both followed me up onto the gallery. I opened the screen door. I wondered how many times Tante Lemon had walked through a white person's front door. Once inside, neither of them would sit until I told them to.

'What is it?' I said.

'Ax her,' Tante Lemon said.

I looked at Dorothea. She wore an orange polyester dress and a straw purse on a strap, but her black pumps were scuffed and dusty.

'Tee Beau say maybe he can find out where that man's at,' she said.

'You talked to him?'

She looked at her hands in her lap.

'You got to promise somet'ing, Mr Dave,' she said. 'Tee Beau say you a good man. Tante Lemon say your daddy good to her, too. It ain't right if you try to trick Tee Beau, no.'

'What do you mean?'

'You tole me Tee Beau can call you collect. From a pay phone. But you can find out where he's at that way, cain't you?'

'You mean trace the call?'

'That's right. I seen them do that on TV. You gonna do that to Tee Beau, suh?' she said, and looked down at her lap again.

'If he'll call me, I'll promise not to do that, Dorothea. Look, I can't tell Tee Beau what to do, but isn't it better that he talk to somebody like me, who knows something about his case, who owes him a debt, than let some other cops hunt him down as an escaped killer?'

'Tee Beau say that man mean all the way through. He tell Tee Beau anybody stop them and Tee Beau open his mouth, he shoot everybody there and he shoot Tee Beau first.'

'Where does he think Boggs is?'

'He say he keep talking about the Italians, how they owe him a lot of money, how they gonna take care of him, how if Tee Beau smart he stay in New Orleans and sell dope. All the time Tee Beau sitting in back, scared that man gonna find out he ain't killed you in the coulee.'

'Tell him to call me at home. I'll write down my number.'

'He gonna find out where that man at first.'

'No, he shouldn't do that.'

'That little boy got courage,' Tante Lemon said. 'People ain't never see that in him. All they see is a little throwaway baby in a shoe box, him. Like when he took Mr Dore car. He ain't stole it. Our truck was broke and I didn't have no way to go to the Charity in New Orleans. Me going blind, couldn't see to light my stove in the morning. He come flying round the corner in Mr Dore car, couldn't even drive, smash right over the church mailbox. Policemens come out and put handcuffs on him, shove him in their car with their stick like he's a raccoon. Ain't nobody ever ax why he done it.'

'You tell him I said to stay away from Boggs. That's not his job.'

'That ain't what you said before,' Tante Lemon said.

'I didn't tell him to go looking for Boggs.'

'No suh, you say Tee Beau he'p you find that man, you he'p Tee Beau,' Dorothea said. 'That's what you tell me at the juke, out there in your car,

out there in the rain. When I tell that to Tee Beau I say I don't knows
what to think. He say Mr Dave a white man, but he don't never lie.'

Then both of them looked at me silently in the half-light of my living
room. Tante Lemon's frosted turquoise eyes were fixed on me with the
lidless glare of a bird's.

A therapist once told me that everyone has a dream box in his head. He
said that sometimes an event provides us with a rusty key to it that we
can well do without. Jimmie Lee Boggs had turned all the tumblers in the
lock, and I discovered that, like a perverse nocturnal demiurge, he had
taken my ten months in Vietnam from me, reactivated every fearful
moment I had lived through, and written himself into the script as a player.

*The sun is hot in the sky but I cannot see it through the thick canopy of trees
overhead. The light is diffused a yellow-green through the sweating vegetation, as though I am looking at it through water. The trunks of the banyan
trees are striped with moisture; the blades of elephant grass, which can leave
your skin covered with paper-thin cuts, are beaded with wet pinpoints of
light. I lie flat on my chest in the grass, and the air is so humid and
superheated I cannot keep the sweat out of my eyes – my forearm only rubs
more sweat and dirt into them. I can feel ants crawling inside my shirt and
belt, and ahead of me, where the elephant grass slopes down to a coulee, a
gray cloud of mosquitoes hovers over a dead log, and a red centipede, as thick
as a pencil and six inches long, is wending his way across the humus.*

*I can smell the sour odor of mud, stagnant water in the coulee, the foul
reek of fear from my own armpits. An eighteen-year-old kid nicknamed
Doo-Doo, from West Memphis, Arkansas, lies next to me, his bare chest
strung with bandoliers, a green sweat-soaked towel draped from under the
back of his pot.*

*His ankle is broken, and he keeps looking back at it and the boot that be
has worked halfway off his foot. His sock looks like rotted cheesecloth. The
whites of his eyes are filled with ruptured blood veins.*

*'They got Martinez's blooker. Don't go out there, Lieutenant. They
waiting for you in the tree line,' he says.*

'They'll bang him up in a tree.'

*'He at the bottom of the ditch. You cain't get him out. They waiting for
you, Lieutenant. I seen them.'*

*The rivulets of sweat leaking out of his pot and running down his face and
shoulders look like lines of clear plastic against his black skin.*

*I crawl on my stomach through the grass with the barrel of the .45 lifted
just above the mud. The under-side of my body is slick with green-black
ooze; my elbows, knees, and boots make sucking sounds with each movement
forward. My face is alive with cuts and mosquitoes. Behind me I bear Doo-
Doo easing a clip into his rifle.*

The grass thins at the edge of the coulee, and down the incline Martinez lies crucified in a half inch of water, his flak jacket blown off his chest, his face white with concussion, his dented pot twenty yards down from him. He has long eyelashes like a girl's, and they keep fluttering as he looks up at me; his mouth opens and closes as though he's trying to clear his ears.

The ground on the other side of the coulee is flat and clear for thirty yards back to a line of rubber trees. The sunlight here is bright and hazy, and I shield my eyes with my hand and try to look deep into the shadows of the rubber trees. The air is breathless, the reeds and elephant ears along the bank absolutely still. I drop over the lip of the coulee and slide erect down the embankment with my boot heels dug into the mud.

Martinez tries to speak, but I see the sucking chest wound now and the torn, wet cloth of his undershirt that flutters in the cavity from the release of air. He sounds like a man strangling in his own saliva.

I try to lift him on my shoulders and hold one of his arms and legs in front of me, but my knee folds and we both go down in a pool of muddy water that's hotter than the air. Then I see them walk out of the rubber trees against the sun. They look no bigger than children. Their black pajamas stick wetly to their bodies; their faces are skeletal and filled with teeth. One of them squats down and aims Martinez's blooker at me. A man behind him shakes cigarettes out of a pack of Lucky Strikes for his friends. They are all laughing.

My .45 lies somewhere in the clouded water, my boots are locked in mud. I hear Doo-Doo firing, but it makes no difference at this point. I stare at my executioner, my body painted with the tropical stink of his country, an unformed prayer wheezing like sand from my throat. The short, fat barrel of the grenade launcher recoils upward in his hands with a deep-throated roar, and a moment later I'm caught in an envelope of flame and I feel a pain in my chest like jagged iron twisting its way through tendon and bone.

Then I am on all fours, like a dog, vomiting blood on my hands, and in the smoke and the smell of burnt powder I stare up the embankment at where the small men in pajamas should be but are not. Instead, Jimmie Lee Boggs takes his package of Lucky Strikes from his blue jeans pocket and lights one. His mannequinlike head is perfectly still as he puffs on his cigarette and lets the smoke drift from his lips. Then he flips the butt in an arc out on the coulee, works his way down the embankment, and finds my .45 in the water.

He works the receiver and knocks the barrel clean of mud on his jeans. He casually points it behind my ear, lets the iron sight bite into my scalp.

'You thought the zips were going to get you, but I'm the one can make you cry,' he says.

I woke up with the sheets twisted across my chest, my body hot in the cold square of moonlight that shone through the window. Outside, the pecan trees were black against the sky. I lay awake until dawn, when the light became gray, then pink, in the flooded cypress on the far side of the bayou. Then I tried to sleep again, but it was no use. I helped Batist open up the bait shop, and at eight o'clock I drove to work at the sheriff's office and began processing traffic accident reports, my eyes weak with fatigue.

That afternoon, four days after Tante Lemon and Dorothea's visit, I drove to Minos Dautrieve's house in Lafayette. He lived in the old part of town on the north side, a neighborhood of Victorian homes, deep lawns, enormous live oak trees, iron tethering posts, gazebos, screened galleries, and cascading leaves. He had grown up in a shotgun farmhouse out-side of Abbeville, but I always suspected that inside his cynicism he had a jaded reverence for the ways of late-nineteenth-century southern gentility.

We sat on cushioned wood lawn chairs in his backyard and drank lemonade amid the golden light and the leaves that scratched across the flag-stones, or floated in an old stone well that he had turned into a goldfish pond.

'You already talked to the sheriff?' he asked.

'He says it's between me and you. I'll be on lend-lease to the Pres-idential Task Force, but my salary will still come from the department. Evidently everybody thinks this task force is big stuff right now.'

'You're not impressed?'

'Who cares what I think?'

'Come on, you don't believe we're winning the war on drugs?' He was smiling. He had to squint against the yellow orb of sun that shone through the oak limbs overhead.

'The head of the DEA says the contras deal cocaine. Reagan and the Congress give them guns and money. It's hard to put all that in the same basket and be serious about it,' I said.

He stopped smiling.

'But there's one difference,' he said. 'No matter what those guys in Washington do, we still send the lowlifes up the road and we trash their operation everywhere we can.'

'All right.'

'I'm not making my point very well, though.'

'Yes, you are. Look, I respect your agency, I appreciate its problems.'

'Respect's not enough. When you work for the federal government, you have to obey its rules. There's no area there for negotiation.'

'This whole business was your idea, Minos.'

'It's a good idea, too. But let's look at your odometer again. Sometimes you've had a way of doing things on your own.'

'Maybe that's a matter of perception.'

'You remember that guy you busted with a pool cue in Breaux Bridge? They had to use a mop to clean up the blood. And the guy you cut in half through an attic floor in New Orleans? I won't mention a couple of other incidents.'

'I never dealt the play. You know that.'

'I can see you've had a lot of regret about it, too.'

'I'm just not interested in the past anymore.'

'There are some people who aren't as confident in you as I am.'

'Then let them do it.'

He smiled again.

'That happens to be what I told them,' he said. 'It didn't light up the room with goodwill. But seriously, Dave, we can't have Wyatt Earp on the payroll.'

'You're the skipper. If I do something that causes problems for your office, you cut me loose. What's the big deal?'

'You know, I think you have another potential. Maybe in scholarship. Like reducing the encyclopedia to a simple declarative sentence.'

I set my empty glass on a table. The wafer of sun was low in the sky now, the air cooler, the leaves in the goldfish pond dark and sodden. A neighbor was barbecuing, and smoke drifted over the garden wall into the yard. I leaned forward in the chair, one hand pinched around my wrist.

'I think your concern is misplaced,' I said. 'When I got hurt the second time in Vietnam, it was a million-dollar wound. I was out of it. I didn't have to prove anything, because there was no place to prove it. This one's different. It's ongoing, and I don't know if I'll measure up. I don't know if you have the right man.'

I saw his eyes move over my face.

'You're going to do fine,' he said.

I didn't answer.

'Like I said, it's not much more complicated than a simple sting,' he continued. 'We take it a step at a time and see where it leads. If it starts to get nasty, we pull you out. That has nothing to do with you. We don't want any of our people hurt. It's not worth it. We figure the shitbags all take a fall sooner or later.

'Look, this is the way it's going to work. We've got an apartment for you on Ursulines in the Quarter, and the word's going to be out on the street that you're fired and dirty. There are five or six dealers around there you can approach to make a buy. Nothing real big right now, four or five keys, maybe a fifty-thousand-dollar buy. They're not going to trust you. They'll jerk you around, give you a lot of bullshit probably, maybe test you in some way. But these are low-level, greedy guys who are also dumb, and they get a hard-on when they see money. You set up the score, we let it go through, then we move up to bigger things.'

'Where's all this money coming from?'

'It's confiscated from drug deals. Don't worry, we'll get it back. Anyway, once these guys are convinced you're the real article, you tell them you want to reinvest your profits. Then we offer them some serious gelt. They don't want the action, you tell them you can make the score in Houston. Tony Cardo hates the guy who runs the action out of Houston. The word is he screwed Tony's wife in a bathroom stall at the Castaways in Miami. We're talking about a real class bunch here. The goal, though, is to get Cardo involved in the deal. He's a weird fucking guy.'

I had to laugh.

'What's your idea of normal?' I asked.

'No, this guy's special. He not only looks weird, he's deeply fucked up in the head. Maybe it's his background. His mother used to shampoo corpses for funeral homes.'

'What?'

'That's how she made her money. She washed the hair of corpses for a mortician. Finally she bought her own funeral parlor in Algiers. Tony C. must not have liked it, though, because he put it up for sale two days after he inherited it.'

'What if I run across Jimmie Lee Boggs?'

'You let us handle him. We'll figure out a way to have him picked up without compromising you.'

'There's one other thing. Tee Beau Latiolais, the black kid who escaped with Boggs, he's in New Orleans. He told his girlfriend he's going to try to find Boggs for me.'

'Why does he want to do that?'

'I sent word to him that I'd help him if he'd help me. I didn't mean for him to go looking for Boggs, though.'

'You worry too much. It's just a sting. Hey, you're going back to New Orleans.'

4

I took Alafair to stay at the home of my cousin Tutta, a retired school-teacher in New Iberia. It wasn't easy. I carried her suitcase and her paper bag of Curious George and Baby Squanto books and coloring materials up onto the gingerbread porch and sat down with her in the swing. The sun was bright on the lawn. Bumblebees hummed over the hibiscus and the pale blue hydrangeas in the flower beds.

'It's not going to be for long, little guy,' I said. 'I'm going to call you almost every night, and Tutta will take you out to feed your horse. If I can, I'll come back on a weekend.'

She looked out blankly at the dew shining on the grass.

'It's a business trip, Alafair. It's just something I have to do.'

'You said we wouldn't leave New Iberia again. You said you didn't like New Orleans anymore, that it was full of dope and bad people.'

'That doesn't mean we have to be afraid of those things, does it? Come on, we're not going to let a short trip get us down, are we? Guys like us are too tough for that.'

Her face was sullen. I took off her Astros cap and set it sideways on her head, then looked down into her face.

'Trust me on this one, Alf,' I said. My cousin came out on the porch. I squeezed Alafair against me. Her body felt hard and unyielding. 'Okay, little guy?'

Her eyes were blinking, and I touched her face with my hand.

'Hey, you remember what my father used to do when he had a problem?' I asked. 'He'd grin right in its face, then give the old thumbs-up sign. He'd say, "You mess with us coonass, we gonna spit right in yo' mouth."'

She looked up at me and smiled faintly. My cousin held the screen for her.

'Dave?' Alafair said.

'Yes?'

'When you come back, it's gonna be like it was?'

'What do you mean?'

'Playing and joking, like we always did. You always coming home full of fun.'

'You bet. I just have to clear up some problems, that's all.'

'I can go with you. I can cook meals, I can wash clothes in the machine.'

'Not this time, Alf.'

Tutta took Alafair's hand in her own.

'Dave, those bad people, they're not gonna hurt you again, are they?' Alafair said.

'You remember what Batist did when that gator got inside his fishnet and tore it up?' I said.

She thought, then grinned broadly.

'That's right,' I said. 'He grabbed the gator by its tail, swung it around in the air, and threw it all the way over the levee. Well, that's the way we handle the bad guys when they give us trouble.'

I hugged her again and kissed her forehead.

'Good-bye, little guy,' I said.

''Bye, Dave.'

Her eyes were starting to film, and I walked down to the picket gate before I turned and glanced back at her. She stood in the open screen door, one of her hands in Tutta's, her ball cap low on her ears. She looked back at me from under the bill of her cap and raised her thumb in the air.

I left Batist to manage the bait shop and boat dock, and on Halloween I moved into my apartment on Ursulines in the Quarter. Most people identify the Quarter with the antiques stores on Royal, the sidewalk artists around Jackson Square, and the strip joints and T-shirt shops on Bourbon Street, but it has a residential and community life of its own: a Catholic elementary school, a city park, small grocery stores with screen doors, wood floors, ceiling fans, display coolers loaded with cheeses, sausages, and skinned catfish, and bins of plums and bananas set out on the sidewalk under the colonnade.

My apartment was inside a walled courtyard that you entered through an iron gate and a domed brick walkway. The flower beds were thick with blooming azalea and camellia and untrimmed banana trees, and the people who lived in the second-story apartments had placed coffee cans of begonias and hung baskets of impatiens along the balcony.

My place was on the first floor, and it had a bedroom, a small kitchen, a bath with a shower, and a living room. Like those of most residences in the Quarter, its walls were marked with all the historical attempts of its owners to adapt to technological change. The gas lamps had been removed and plastered over at the turn of the century; bricks had been torn out of the walls to replumb and rewire the kitchen and the bath; big hand-twist electric switches stuck out of the plaster but turned on no light.

I opened the windows and began to hang my clothes in the closet.

Maybe I should have felt good to be back in New Orleans, where I had been a policeman for fourteen years in the First District, but it felt strange to be alone in a rented apartment, with the late-afternoon light cold and yellow on the banana trees outside. Or maybe it was simply a matter of age. Solitude and the years did not go well with me, and even though I had lived over a half century, I had concluded that I was one of those people who would never know with any certainty who they were, that my thoughts about myself would always be question marks; my only identity would remain the reflection that I saw in the eyes of others.

I could feel myself slipping inside that dark alcoholic envelope of depression and regret that for long periods had been characteristic of my adult life. I finished putting my shirts, underwear, and socks in the dresser drawers, stripped down to my skivvies, and did ten one-arm chins on an iron pipe in the kitchen, forty leg lifts, and fifty stomach crunches, and got into the shower and turned the water on so hot that my skin turned red and grainy through my suntan.

I dried off and combed my hair in the mirror. I had lost fifteen pounds since Boggs had shot me; my stomach was flat, the love handles around my waist had almost disappeared, the scar tissue where a bouncing Betty had gotten me in Vietnam looked like a spray of small gray arrow points that had been slipped under the skin on my right thigh and side. I still had my father's thick black hair and mustache, except for the white patch above my ear, and if I didn't pay attention to the lines in my neck and around my eyes and the black-peppery flecks of skin cancer on my arms, I could still pretend it was only the bottom of the fifth.

Question: Where do you score a few grams of coke in New Orleans?

Answer: Almost anywhere you want to.

But where do you score a thousand grams, a kilo? The question becomes more complicated. Minos had accused me of being simplistic. Later I would wonder when he had last been on the street with his own clientele.

It was dusk when I got to the address on Esplanade on the edge of the Quarter; the air was crisp, the dry palm fronds on the neutral ground clattered in the breeze, and costumed Negro children with jack-o'-lanterns ran in groups from one high, lighted gallery to the next. The man I was looking for lived in a garage apartment behind a columned one-story wood house on the corner, which like many New Orleans antebellum homes was built up high above the lawn because of floods. But the wood doors on the drive were padlocked, and the iron gate that gave on to the side yard wouldn't open either. I could see a man working under an automobile in the drive, with a mechanic's lamp attached to an extension cord.

I shook the gate against the iron fastenings in the brick wall. The man slid out from under the car on a creeper. A lighted cigar lay on the cement by his head. One eye squinted at me like a fist.

'What do you want?' he said.

'I'm looking for Lionel Comeaux.'

'What do you want?'

'Are you Lionel Comeaux?'

'Yeah, what do you want?'

'Can I come in?'

'The latch is inside, at the top of the gate,' he said, and picked up a crescent wrench off the cement to begin working under the car again.

I entered the yard and walked through flower beds filled with elephant ears and caladium and waited for him to slide back from under the car again. He didn't, so I had to squat down to talk to him. 'I want to make a buy.'

'Buy what?' he said, blinking at the rust that fell out of the car frame into his eyes. He wore jeans and a purple and gold LSU jersey with the sleeves cut off at the shoulders. His arms were big and covered with tan, and he had a deep red US Navy tattoo on one bicep. His head was square, his dark hair crew cut. He chewed gum, and there were lumps of cartilage behind his ears.

'I want some pure stuff, no cut, a good price,' I said. 'I hear you're the guy who can help me.'

'Pure what? What are you talking about, buddy?'

'What the fuck do you think I'm talking about?'

He stopped working, removed a piece of grit from his eyelashes with his thumb, and looked at me. The backs of his hands were shiny with grease.

'Who sent you here?' he said.

'Some people in Lafayette.'

'Who?'

'People I do business with. What do you care?'

'I care, man. What's your name?'

'Dave Robicheaux.'

He pushed the creeper out from under the car and raised himself up on one elbow. He was maybe twenty-five and had the neck and shoulder tendons of a weight lifter.

'You're talking about dope, right? Skag, reefer, stuff like that?' he said. He picked up his cigar off the cement and puffed it alight.

'I'm talking about cocaine, podna. Ten thou a key. I can take five keys off you.'

'Cocaine?' he said.

'That's right.'

'That's interesting. But number one, I'm not your podna, because I don't know who you are. Number two, I don't know where you got my name or this address, but you've got the wrong information, wrong person, wrong house.'

'You see Tony Cardo?'

'Who?'

'Look, I don't mean to offend you, but the bozo routine is wearing thin. You tell Cardo there's some oil people in Lafayette with a lot of money to invest. He doesn't want the business, that's fine. You don't want to pass on the information, that's fine. We can get what we need in Houston. You know where Clete's Club is?'

'No.'

'You know where Joe Burda's Golden Star is on Decatur?'

'Yeah.'

'It's two doors up from there. If you want to do some business, leave word at the bar.'

'Make sure the gate latches on your way out,' he said.

The next two people whose names and addresses Minos had given me were equally unproductive. One was a bar owner who was in jail in Baton Rouge, and the other, a wrestling promoter, had died of AIDS.

At eleven that night I walked down Bourbon in the roar of noise from the bars and strip joints, amid the Halloween revelers, the midwestern conventioneers, breathless, red-faced college kids who spilled beer from their paper cups down the front of their clothes, and the Negro street dancers whose clip-on taps rang like horse-shoes on the cement. Bourbon is closed to automobile traffic, so that the street itself is like an open-air zoo, but by and large it's a harmless one. The girls still take off their clothes on the runways and hookers work out of taxicabs in the early morning hours. Occasionally a cop will cool out a drunk with a baton in a side-street bar, and the burlesque spielers in candy-striped vests and straw boaters can conjure up visions right out of adolescent masturbation; but ultimately Bourbon offers the appearance of sleaze to the tourists with the implicit understanding that it contains no real threat of injury to them.

In fact, the man I wanted to find ran a T-shirt and souvenir shop, and he was as innocuous in dress and manner as an ice cream salesman. He walked out from behind a curtain in back after his clerk told him I wanted to talk to him, and his oval face was pink and shining, his thin red hair combed back with water, his mouth wide with a grin, his neck powdered with talcum. He wore a white suit and a silver silk shirt, and his appearance gave every indication of a harmless, happy fat man – except that on second glance you noticed that his chest was as broad as his stomach, that he wore gold chains around his neck, that his eyes took your inventory and did not smile with his mouth.

'I know you,' he said, and shook his finger playfully at me. 'You're a police officer. No, you used to be one, right here in the Quarter.'

'That's right.'

'You were a lieutenant.'

'That's right.'

'You probably don't remember me, but I used to see you and your partner over at the Acme. You used to come in at lunch for oysters. What's his name? He's got a club here now.'

'Cletus Purcel.'

'Yeah. I was in his place the other day. Real nice. I think he's going to make it.'

'Could I talk to you in private?'

He looked at the ruby-studded gold watch on his wrist.

'Sure thing,' he said, and held back the curtain for me.

His office was a small, cluttered room in the back, with a desk, three chairs, and old jazz posters on the brick walls. He sat in the swivel chair behind the desk and tapped the bottom of a poster with his finger.

'See that name there?' he said. 'You got to look close, but that's me, Uncle Ray Fontenot. I played trombone right down the street at Sharky Bonnano's Dream Room. You remember him?'

'Sure.'

'You remember those two colored guys used to tap-dance on the stage there, Pork Chops and Kidney Beans?'

'I want to score five kilos of uncut coke. You deliver good stuff at the right price, we'll be doing more business later.'

He peeled the cellophane off a package of Picayune cigarettes.

'Not too many ex-cops come in here with that kind of statement,' he said. He had never stopped smiling.

'Forget the ex-cop business. It all spends.'

'Oh, don't misunderstand me. I'm not knocking a man trying to make a little money. But your information's dated. That's what I'm trying to say.'

'How's that?'

He tilted back in the swivel chair, his silver shirt tight across his broad chest and stomach, his eyes bright and squinted with goodwill.

'I always had problems with weight and high blood pressure,' he said. 'I smoked reefer every night to keep my blood pressure down, then I'd go out and eat a whole pizza by myself. I got on prescription diet pills, then I started using some stuff that was a little more serious. Finally I was in the business myself, you know what I mean? So whoever gave you my name wasn't all wrong. But I bottomed out and went into treatment a year ago. The only problem I've got now is I eat all the time.'

'You're in a twelve-step program?'

'What?'

'You're out of the business?'

'That's about it.'

'Tell me, when you give a guy like Tony C. the deep six, what do you do? Just drop around one day and say, "I bottomed out, Tony. I'm out of the business, see you around, you don't like it, fuck you"?'

This time the words bit into some nerve endings behind that pink and smiling face. He lit his cigarette and blew smoke at an upward angle into the air.

'I've never met the gentleman,' he said, his eyes crinkling again.

'I see. Sorry to have wasted your time. I'll run along now, Mr Fontenot. Say, the next time you give somebody that treatment shuck, you might find out what a twelve-step program is.'

He tipped his ashes into an ashtray and looked pleasantly into his cigarette smoke without seeing anything.

'Tell Tony C. his distribution in southwestern Louisiana is lousy,' I said. 'I can double or triple it. But I've got nothing to prove. There's some guys in Texas who want to branch out.'

'Then maybe that's who you should deal with.'

'They've got a bad reputation. But maybe you're right. If I meet Tony C., I'll tell him what you said.'

'Now, wait a minute . . .'

'I don't blame you for bullshitting me, Mr Fontenot, but if you get serious, leave a message for me at Clete's Club. I'll be back in touch.'

I walked back through the T-shirt shop and out into the neon lights and cacophony of jazz and rock bands on Bourbon Street.

I was tired, unshaved, weary of the people I had been with, my ears thick with the sound of trumpets and trombones and electric guitars, yet I did not want to return to the apartment and be alone. I walked to the Café du Monde for coffee and *beignets*, but it had already closed. So I sat on an iron bench in front of the cathedral in Jackson Square and watched the moon rise in the sky. The air was heavy with the smell of camellias, and the magnolia and banana trees that grew along the piked fence behind me made shifting patterns of shadow and light on the cement. A wind came up off the river, and it started to mist; then a shower clattered across the banana leaves in the square and blew in a spray under the lighted colonnades. I walked home on a quiet street, away from the noise of the tourists, keeping close under the scrolled iron balconies to avoid the rain.

It was warm and muggy the next morning, as it can be in southern Louisiana well into the Christmas season, and I had breakfast and read the *Times-Picayune* at the Café du Monde before the crowds of tourists came in, then walked across the square past the sidewalk artists and went inside the cathedral briefly because it was All Saints' Day. Later, I found two more of the contacts Minos had given me. One was a bail bondsman who told me to get out of his office, and the other was a woman who ran an occult bookstore that smelled of soiled cat litter. Her face was white with makeup, her eyes stenciled with purple eyeliner, her cigarette breath devastating. For fifteen minutes I pretended to examine her racks of books while she carried on a conversation with her customers about telepathic communication with UFOs and a hole in the dimension that exists in the middle of the Bermuda Triangle and operates like a drain in an enormous sink. Finally I bought a book on cats and left.

I called New Iberia that night to check on Alafair, and the next morning I walked over to Clete's Club on Decatur, across from the French Market. For years Clete had been my partner in the First District. He'd learned his law enforcement methods from an uncle who had walked a beat in the Irish Channel – 'Bust 'em or smoke 'em,' Clete always said – and had literally terrorized the lowlifes in the First. All you had to do was mention to a pimp or house creep or jackroller that Cletus Purcel would like to interview him, and he would be on the next bus or plane to Miami. Then Clete got into debt to the shylocks, ruined his marriage with whores and his stomach with booze and aspirin, and finally went on a pad and took ten thousand dollars from some drug dealers and right-wing crazies to get rid of a federal witness.

Later he would run house security at a casino in Nevada and become the bodyguard for a midlevel Mafia character and ex-con by the name of Sally Dio. But eventually what I thought of as Clete's most essential characteristics – his courage and his loyalty to an old friend – had their way, and he managed to walk away reasonably intact from all the wreckage in his life.

He was at the back of the bar, loading the stainless steel cooler with bottles of long-necked Jax. He looked up and smiled when he saw me. His body always looked too big for his clothes. He loved pizza, poor-boy sandwiches, deep-fried shrimp and oysters, dirty rice, *beignets*, ice cream, which he would eat with a tablespoon by the half gallon. He was convinced that he could control his weight by pumping iron every other night in his garage, and limit his ulcer damage by smoking Lucky Strikes through a cigarette filter and drinking his scotch with milk.

'What's happening, Streak?' he said. 'I had a feeling, you'd be by.'

'How's that?'

'I'm hearing weird stuff about you, mon.'

'Did somebody leave a message for me?'

'Nope.'

'Then what did you hear?'

He stood erect from his work, flexed the stiffness out of his back, and grinned at me. His skin was ruddy, his hair sandy and combed straight back on his head, his green eyes intelligent and full of humor. A scar that was the color and texture of a bicycle tire patch ran down through one eyebrow and across the bridge of his nose.

'How about you spring for some oysters and I'll fix you a drink?' he said.

'I don't have time.'

'Yeah, you do.' Then he turned to a Negro who was sweeping between the tables by the dance floor. 'Emory, go down to Joe Burda's and get us a couple of dozen on the half shell.'

The Negro went out, and Clete fixed me a tall glass of shaved ice, 7-Up, Collins mix, candied cherries, and orange slices. He poured a cup of coffee for himself behind the bar, then came around and sat down beside me. The club was empty, the front door open; the light outside was bright under the colonnade.

'What the fuck are you up to, Streak?' he said.

'I've got an apartment over on Ursulines. I haven't bounced back too well since that guy put a hole in me.'

'You like listening to drunks break bottles out in the street all night?'

'It's not bad.'

'I bet. How many queers are in your building?'

'Lay off it, Clete.'

'Then tell me why I'm hearing these weird stories.'

'I don't know what you've heard.'

'That an ex-Homicide reach is trying to score five keys of coke. That he got canned from the Iberia Parish Sheriff's Department because he was taking juice. That he's floating Tony C.'s name around town.'

'Word spreads.'

'Among some people I'd stay away from, the kind we used to mash into the cement.'

'The kind you used to mash.'

'I'm not kidding you, partner. I heard this bullshit from three different guys.'

'Who?'

'I can't control who drinks at my bar. There're some connected guys come in here. They know I used to work for the Dio family out in Vegas and Tahoe, so they're always inviting me back to their booth. You've got to see it, Dave, to appreciate it. About six of them, all guys, cram into the vinyl booth back there on Saturday night. They always sit so all of them can look out at the dance floor and flash their bucks and shake hands with everybody like they're celebrities. I'm talking about guys who couldn't put spaghetti on a plate without a diagram.'

'Those are Cardo's people?'

'One way or another. He pieces off a lot of his action so all the greaseballs stay happy. You ever meet him?'

'No.'

'One of his broads lives in the Pontabla. He brings her in sometimes for a drink. He looks like somebody slammed a door on his head.'

'When does he come in?'

'He's not a regular.'

'What's the woman's name?'

'Who knows? I got a proposition for you, though.'

Emory, the black barman, brought in a tin tray loaded with oysters on the half shell, slice of lemon, and a bottle of Tabasco sauce. I gave him six dollars for the restaurant bill and a dollar for himself. He went into the back of the club and began stacking cartons of empty beer bottles in a storage room.

'Let me in on it,' Clete said. There was a bead of light in his green eyes.

'On what?'

'The sting, mon.' He seasoned one of the oysters, squeezed lemon on it, cupped the shell in his hand, and let the muscle slide down his throat. He smiled and the juice ran down the corner of his mouth. 'I figure it's probably a DEA gig. They've got the gelt, they can afford another player.'

I didn't say anything.

'Here's what you tell them,' he said. 'I can cover your back, I know most of the dealers on a first-name basis. I can open doors. Right now you've probably got a couple of street snitches doing your p.r.'

'You don't buy my cover?'

'Are you kidding?' He started laughing.

'I thought it was pretty good.'

'It is, for anybody who doesn't know you. But you're talking to ole Cletus here, so save the shuck for the lowlifes and the melt-downs. I ain't putting you on, mon, I'd love to get back in it. I'm thinking of opening up a PI office in the Quarter. A lot of it is running down bond jumpers and doing bullshit for attorneys, but so what? I can keep my hand in, carry a piece again, make life more interesting for some of the shitbags.'

'Call up the DEA in Lafayette. Tell them what you told me.'

'Wouldn't that be something, me and you working together again? You remember when we blew up Julio Segura's shit in the back of his Caddy?'

I looked out at the sunlight under the colonnade.

'Hey, I don't feel bad about smoking a pimp and drug dealer,' he said. 'I think it's a mainline perk of the business. There's nothing like the smell of cordite to clear up your sinuses.'

'You almost got us killed.'

'Who's perfect? But let's be serious a minute, mon.' He pushed at an oyster with his fork. There were deep acne scars on the back of his red neck. His big shoulders were bent, and this shirt was stretched tight across the wide expanse of his back. 'I don't know what kind of info you're operating on, but this is what I hear. Cardo's out for the big score.

Florida's already locked up, so is Texas. So he wants to control the Louisiana coast. He's got some nasty types working for him, too, guys who paint the ceiling when they do a job on somebody. You don't want him to think you're a competitor. Look, Dave, they say he's different from the other greaseballs. He's not predictable, he does strange stuff that nobody can figure out.

'The last time he brought his broad in here, a Marine gunnery sergeant sat on the stool next to him. Cardo says, "Give me and the lady another Collins and give the gunny what he wants." Then they start talking about Vietnam and Cherry Alley in Tokyo. This is in front of his broad, can you dig it? All the time I'm washing glasses about two feet away, so Cardo stops talking and says to me, "You got a question about something?"

' "What" I say.

' "You look like you're getting an earful. You got a question?" he says.

' "You're only in the crotch one," I say.

' "You cracking wise or something?" he says.

' "I'm not doing anything. It's a Marine Corps expression. I was in the corps myself," I say.

'He starts grinning and points both fingers to his chest and says, "You think you got to tell me what it means?" and his broad starts making these clicking, no-no sounds with her mouth. "Come on, you explaining to me what the fuck that means?" he says. "Somebody appointed you to explain these things to other people?"

'So I said, "No, I'm just telling you to enjoy your drink," and I walked back to my office. It was about that time I started thinking about changing my line of work.'

'Have you heard of a guy named Jimmie Lee Boggs?'

'A contract man, out of Florida?'

'That's the one.'

'What about him?'

'He's the guy who put a hole in me. Somebody told me he might be back in New Orleans.'

Clete smiled.

'That's the bait they used to get you into the sting, huh?' he said. 'They saw you coming, Streak. That guy's long gone now.'

'Maybe.'

'Get me in on it, mon.'

'I don't call the shots on this one, Cletus. Here's my telephone number and address. But don't give them to anyone, okay? Just keep any messages I get and I'll check back with you.'

'You need somebody to watch your back. Don't trust the feds to do it. You heard it first from ole Clete.'

'I don't know if any of this is going anywhere, anyway,' I said. 'A few more days of this and I might be back in New Iberia.'

He put a matchstick in his mouth. His hands were big and square and callused around the edges, the nails chewed back to the quick.

'Don't underestimate their potential,' he said. 'Most of them wouldn't make good bars of soap. But turn your back on them and they'll take your eyes out.'

That afternoon I talked to another of Minos's contacts, a Negro bartender on Magazine. His head was bald and waxed, and he wore gray muttonchop sideburns that looked as though they were artificially affixed to his face. He was as passive, docile, and uncurious about me as if I had been selling burial insurance. His eyelids were leaded, and his head kept nodding up and down while I talked. He told me: 'See, I ain't in the bidness no more myself. I had a bunch of trouble 'cause of it, had to go out of town for a little while, know what I mean? But somebody came in want the action, I'll tell them you in town. You want another 7-Up?'

'No, this is fine.'

'How about some hard-boiled eggs?'

'No, I'm fine.'

'I got to go in the kitchen and start my stove now.'

'Thanks for your time. You were up at Angola?'

'Where's that at?' he said. His eyes looked speculatively out into space.

The next morning I walked over to the Café du Monde again and had coffee at one of the outside tables. Across the street the spires of the cathedral looked brilliant in the sunlight, and the wind off the river ruffled the banana trees and palm fronds along the black iron piked fence that bordered the park inside Jackson Square. I finished reading the paper, then walked back to the apartment and called Clete's bar for messages. There were none. I called Minos's office in Lafayette.

'Don't be discouraged,' he said.

'I think maybe I'm not cut out for this.'

'Why?'

'I was a Homicide cop. I never worked Vice or Narcotics.'

'It's a different kind of gig, isn't it?'

'Look, busting them is one thing. Pretending to be like them is another.'

'Have a few laughs with it.'

'It's not funny, Minos. You got me into this stuff, and it's not paying off. I've got another problem, too – the reliability of your information.'

'Oh?'

'I find out that people are either dead, or in jail, or they're crazy and run bookstores that smell like cat shit.'

'If our information was perfect, these guys wouldn't be on the street. We get it from snitches and cons cutting deals and wiretaps on pathological liars. You know that.'

'I struck out.'

'You don't think any of these people are dealing now?'

'Maybe a couple of them. But they didn't buy my act.'

'It's like throwing chum overboard to a school of barracuda. They just have to smell the blood.'

'How about another metaphor?'

'Just hang in there. It takes time.'

'I'm ready to pull the plug.'

'Give it two more days.'

'All right. Then that's it, Minos.'

'Now, I want to pick a bone with you about this guy Purcel.'

I had to wince a little on that one.

'He called you?' I asked.

'He called the office. The call finally got referred to me. He said he was calling at your suggestion.'

'He figured out the scam. I didn't tell him anything he didn't already know.'

'He's got some idea he should go undercover for the DEA.'

'Maybe it's not a bad idea,' I said.

'Are you serious? He's got a rap sheet that's longer than some cons'. He was charged with a murder, he worked for the mob, the National Transportation Safety Board thinks maybe he caused a plane crash that killed a bunch of greaseballs.'

'Clete's had a checkered career.'

'It's not going to include working for the DEA.'

'What do you hear on Boggs?'

'Nothing. Look, I'm coming over to New Orleans for the next three weeks. After today call me at the office there. I'll be staying at the Orleans Guest House on St Charles.'

'Think about putting Purcel on the payroll. He knows more about the lowlifes than any cop in New Orleans.'

'Yeah, not many ex-cops can produce letters of reference from the Mafia. You really come up with some good ones, Dave.'

That afternoon a message *was* left for me at Clete's bar. But it was not what I was expecting. It was written in ballpoint in a careful hand on a flattened paper napkin, and it read:

Dear Dave,

I was surprised to learn that you were back in New Orleans. I had heard that you had returned to New Iberia to live. I was surprised to hear some other things, too. But maybe life has changed a lot for both of us. I'd love to see you again. I've thought about you many times over

the years. Call or come by if you feel like it. I live in the Garden District.
It's a long way from Bayou Teche, huh, cher?

> *Your old friend,*
> *Bootsie Mouton Giacano*

Her telephone number and street address were written at the bottom.
Sometimes the heart can sink with a sense of mortality and loss as
abrupt as opening a door to a shop filled with whirring clocks.

5

If her name is Bootsie Mouton and it sends you back to 1957 and the best summer of your life. It was after my sophomore year at Southwestern Louisiana Institute, and my brother and I worked all summer on an offshore seismograph rig to buy a 1946 canary-yellow Ford convertible that we waxed and rubbed with rags until it had a glow like soft butter. One night at a dance out on Spanish Lake I saw her standing by herself under the oak trees by the water's edge, the light from Japanese lanterns flickering on her honey-colored hair, her moist brow and olive skin, the lavender dress she wore with a spray of white flowers pinned above the breast. She kept lifting her hair off her neck in the warm breeze that blew across the water, and pulling at the straps of her dress with her thumb.

'Would you like to dance?' I said.

'I can't. I have a fresh sunburn. We went crabbing at Cypremort Point today.'

'Do you want a drink or a beer or a Coke or something?'

'Somebody went to get one for me.'

'Who?'

'The boy I came with.'

'Who's that?'

She looked at me quizzically. Her eyes were dark, her mouth parted and red in the shadows.

'A boy from Lake Charles,' she said.

'I don't see anybody from Lake Charles here. What kind of drink do you like?'

'A vodka Collins.'

'Don't move. I'll be right back,' I said.

She lived on the lake, out by the little town of Burke, which was composed mostly of Negro tenant farmers. I told her that I wanted to come out to her house, that night, after her date dropped her off. I was insistent, aggressive, rude, I suppose, but I didn't care. She was the most beautiful girl I had ever met. Finally her date got angry and petulant and left with a group headed for Slick's Club in St Martinville, and I drove her home down the blacktop highway between the sugarcane fields, the breeze drowsy with the scent of jasmine and magnolia and blooming four-o'-clocks, the moss-hung oaks and cypress etched against the moon out on the lake.

Two weeks later we lost our virginity together. A man always remembers several details about that initial experience, if he has it with someone he loves. I recall the warmness of the evening, the washed-out lilac color of the sky, the rainwater dripping out of the cypress trees on to the motionless surface of the lake, the banks of scarlet clouds in the west that glowed like fire through the cracks in the boathouse wall. But the image that will always remain in my mind was her face in that final heart-twisting moment. Her eyes closed, her lips parted silently, and then she looked up at me like an opening flower and cupped my face in her hands as she would a child's.

It should never have ended. But it did, and for no reason that I could ever explain to her. Nor could I explain it to my father, a priest in whom I trusted, or myself. Even though I was only twenty years old I began to experience bone-grinding periods of depression and guilt that seemed to have no legitimate cause or origin. When they came upon me it was as though the sun had suddenly become a black cinder, and had gone over the rim of the earth for the last time. I hurt her, pushed her away from me, wouldn't return her telephone calls or answer a poignant and self-blaming note she left on our front screen. Even today I'm hard put to explain my behavior. But I felt somehow that it was intrinsically bad, that anyone who could love me didn't know who I really was, and that eventually I would make that person bad, too.

It was not a rational state of mind. A psychologist would probably say that my problem was related to my mother's running off with a *bourré* dealer from Morgan City when I was a child, or the fact that my father sometimes brawled in bars and got locked up in the parish jail. I don't know if theories like that would be correct or not. But at the time there was no way I could think myself out of my own dark thoughts, and I became convinced that the happy times with Bootsie had simply been part of the summer's rain-spangled illusion, as transient and mutable as the season had been warm and fleeting.

When she would not be dissuaded, I took out another girl, a carhop from up north who wore hair rollers in public and always seemed to have sweat rings under her arms. I took her to a lawn party given by Bootsie's aunt and uncle on Bayou Teche, where she got drunk and called the waiter a nigger.

Later that night I got into a fistfight at Slick's, tore the fenders off my car on the drawbridge over the Teche, and woke up in the morning handcuffed to the bottom of the iron ladder on the Breaux Bridge water tower, because it was during Crawfish Festival and the small city jail was already full. As I looked up at the white sun, smelled the hot weeds around me, and swallowed the bile in my throat, I didn't realize that I had just made the initial departure on a long alcoholic odyssey.

Then the years passed and I would not see her again until I came home from the war. In the meantime I committed myself totally to charcoal-filtered bourbon in a four-inch glass, with a sweating Jax on the side, and finally I didn't care about anything.

Now she lived on Camp Street in the Garden District. Her married name was Giacano, the same as that of the most notorious Mafia family in New Orleans. I told myself that I should put her note away and save it for another time, when I could afford a futile pursuit of the past. But I seldom listen to my own advice, and that evening I rode the old iron streetcar down St Charles under the long canopy of spreading oaks, past yards filled with camellias and magnolia trees, sidewalks cracked by oak roots, without having called first, and found myself on Camp in front of a narrow two-story white-painted brick home with twin chimneys, a gallery, and garden walls that enclosed huge clumps of banana trees and dripped with purple bugle vine.

She answered the door in a one-piece orange bathing suit and an open terry cloth robe, and explained with a flush that she had been dipping leaves out of the pool in back. Her Cajun accent had been softened by the years in New Orleans, and she was heavier now, wider in the hips, larger in the breasts, thicker across the thighs. She brushed the gray straight up in her honey-colored hair, so that it looked as though it had been powdered there. But Bootsie was still good to look at. Her skin was smooth and still tanned from the summer, her hair cut short like a girl's and etched on the neck with a razor. Her smile was as genuine and happy as it had been thirty years before.

We walked through her house and onto the patio and sat at a glass-topped table by the pool. She brought out a tray of coffee and milk and pecan pie. The water in the pool was dark and glazed with the evening light, and small islands of oak leaves floated against the tile sides. She had been widowed twice, she told me. Her first husband, an oil-field helicopter pilot, had flown a crew out to a rig south of Morgan City, then hit a guy wire and crashed right on top of the quarter boat. Five years later she had met her second husband, Ralph Giacano, in Biloxi.

'Have you heard of him?' she asked.

'Yes,' I said, and tried to keep my eyes veiled.

'He told me he had a degree in accounting and owned half of a vending machine company. He didn't have a degree, but he did own part of a company,' she said.

I tried to look pleasant and show no recognition.

'I found out some of the other things he was involved in after we were married,' she said. 'Last year somebody killed him and his girl-friend in the parking lot of the Hialeah racetrack. Poor Ralph. He always said the Colombians wouldn't bother him, he was just a small-business man.'

'I'm sorry, Bootsie.'

'Don't be. I spent two years feeling sorry for Ralph while he mortgaged this house, which was mine from my first marriage, and spent the money in Miami and Las Vegas. So now I own his half of the vending machine business. You know who owns the other half?'

'The Giacanos were always a tight family.'

'I guess I can't surprise you with very much.'

'Ralph's uncle was a guy named Didi Gee. He's dead now, but three years ago he hired a contract killer to shoot my brother. Jimmie's doing okay now, but for a while I thought I was going to lose him.'

'I didn't know.'

'Maybe it's time to get away from your in-laws.'

'When you sell to the Giacanos, it's twenty cents on the dollar, Dave. Nobody else is lining up to buy into their business, either.'

'Get away from them, Bootsie.'

Her eyes glanced into mine. There was a curious bead of light in them.

'I don't understand this,' she said.

'What?'

'You're telling me to get away from them. Then I'm hearing this strange story about you.'

I looked away from her.

'You hear a lot of bullshit in the streets,' I said.

'This is from my in-laws, Dave. They work for Tony Cardo.'

I didn't answer and tried to grin good-naturedly. Her eyes peeled the skin off my face.

'They say you're dirty. Don't they have a wonderful vocabulary?' she said.

I pushed at a piece of piecrust on my plate with my fork.

'They say you want to deal,' she said.

'You have to make up your own mind about people.'

'I *know* you, Dave Robicheaux. I don't care what you've done in your life, this stuff isn't you.'

'Then ignore what they say, Bootsie, and stay out of it.'

'I'm worried about you. I work with these people. You can't believe how they think, what they're capable of doing.'

'Oh yes I can.'

'Then what are you doing?'

'Be my friend on this. Don't mix in it, and don't worry too much about what you hear.'

Her face was lighted with the late sun's glow over the garden wall. She raised her chin slightly, the way she always did when she was angry.

'Dave, you left me. Do you think you should be telling me what to do now?'

'I guess not.'

'I survive among these animals because I have to. It isn't fun. I'm on my own, and that isn't fun, either. But I handle it.'

'I guess you do.'

'Why didn't you marry me?' she said. Her eyes were hot and bright.

'You'd have married a drunk. It wouldn't have been a good life, believe me.'

'You don't know that. You don't know that at all.'

'Yes, I do. I became a full-blown lush. I tried to kill my first wife's lover at a lawn party out by Lake Pontchartrain.'

'Maybe that's what he deserved.'

'I tried to kill him because I had become morally insane.'

'I don't care what you did later in your life. Why'd you close me out, Dave?'

I let my hands hang between my knees.

'Because I was dumb,' I said.

'It's that simple?'

'No, it's not. But how about suffice it to say that I made a terrible mistake, that I've had regret about it all these years.'

Her legs were crossed, her arms motionless on the sides of the cushioned iron chair, her face composed now in the tea-colored light. The top of her terry cloth robe was loose, and I could see her breasts rise and fall quietly with her breathing.

'I do have to go,' I said.

'Are you coming back?'

'If you'd like to see me again, I'd surely like to see you.'

'I'm not moving out of town, *cher*.' Then her face became soft and she said, 'But, Dave, I've learned one thing with middle age. I don't try to correct yesterday's mistakes in the present. I mark them off. I truly mark them off. A person hurts me only once.'

'No one could ever say they were unsure where you stood on an issue, Boots.'

She smiled without answering, then walked me to the front door, put her palms on my shoulders, and kissed me on the cheek. It was an appropriate and kind gesture and would not have meant much in itself, but then she looked into my face and touched my cheek with her fingertips, as though she were saying good-bye to someone forever, and I felt my loins thicken and my heart turn to water.

It was almost dark when I got off the streetcar at the corner of St Charles and Canal and went into the Pearl and had a poor-boy sandwich filled with oysters, shrimp, sliced tomatoes, shredded lettuce, and *sauce piquante*. Then I walked to my apartment and paused momentarily outside my door while I found my key. The people upstairs were partying out on the balcony, and one of them accidentally kicked a coffee can of geraniums into the courtyard. But in spite of the noise I thought I heard someone inside my apartment. I put my hand on the .25-caliber Beretta in my coat pocket, unlocked the door, and let it swing all the way back against the wall on its hinges.

Lionel Comeaux, the man I'd found working under his car on the creeper, was in the kitchen, pulling the pots and pans out of the cabinet and placing them on the table. The jolly fat man who called himself Uncle Ray Fontenot and said he used to play trombone at Sharky's Dream Room had emptied the drawers in the bedroom and had laid all my hangered clothes across the bed. My .45 lay on top of a neatly folded shirt. Both of them looked at me with flat, empty expressions, as though I were the intruder.

The fat man, Fontenot, wore a beige suit and a cream turtleneck shirt. I saw his eyes study my face and my right hand; then he smiled and opened his palms in front of him.

'It's just business, Mr Robicheaux,' he said. 'Don't take it personal. We've treated your things with respect.'

'How'd you get in?'

'It's a simple lock,' he said.

'You've got some damn nerve,' I said.

'Close the door. There's people out there,' Lionel, the man in the kitchen, said. He wore Adidas running shoes, blue jeans with no belt, a gold pullover sweater with the sleeves pushed up over his thick, sun-browned arms.

I could hear my own breathing in the silence.

'Lionel's right,' Fontenot said. 'We don't need an audience here, do we? Getting mad isn't going to make us any money, either, is it?'

I took my hand out of my coat pocket and opened and closed it at my side.

'Come in, come in,' Fontenot said. 'Look, we're putting your things back. There's no harm done.'

'You toss my place and call it no harm?' I said. I pushed the door shut behind me.

'You knew somebody would check you out. Don't make it a big deal,' the younger man said in the kitchen. He lit a dead cigar in his mouth and squatted down and started replacing the pots and pans in the cabinets next to the stove.

'I don't like people smoking in my apartment,' I said.

He turned his head at me and paused in his work. The red Navy tattoo on his flexed bicep was ringed with blue stars. He was balanced on the ball of one foot, the cigar between his fingers, a tooth working on a bloodless spot on his lower lip. Fontenot walked out of the other room.

'Put out the smoke, Lionel,' he said quietly. His eyes crinkled at the corners. 'Go on, put it out. We're in the man's home.'

'I don't think it's smart dealing with him. I said it then, I'll say it in front of him,' Lionel said. He wet the cigar under the tap and dropped it in a garbage bag.

'The man's money is as good as the next person's,' Fontenot said.

'You were a cop,' Lionel said to me. 'That's a problem for me. No insult meant.'

'You creeped my apartment. That's a problem for me.'

'Lionel had a bad experience a few years back,' Fontenot said. 'His name doesn't make campus bells ring for you?'

'No.'

'Second-string quarterback for LSU,' Fontenot said. 'Until he sold some whites on the half shell to the wrong people. I think if Lionel had been first-string, he wouldn't have had to spend a year in Angola. It's made him distrustful.'

'Get off it, Ray.'

'The man needs to understand,' Fontenot said. 'Look, Mr Robicheaux, we're short on protocol, but we don't rip each other off. We establish some rules, some trust, then we all make money. Get his bank, Lionel.'

Lionel opened a cabinet next to the stove, squatted down, and reached his hand deep inside. I heard the adhesive tape tear loose from the top of the cabinet behind the drawer. He threw the brown envelope, with tape hanging off each end, for me to catch.

'We want you to understand something else, too,' Fontenot said. 'We're not here because of some fifty-thou deal. That's toilet paper in this town. But the gentleman we work for is interested in you. You're a lucky man.'

'Tony C is interested?'

'Who?' He smiled.

'Five keys, ten thou a key, no laxative, no vitamin B twelve,' I said.

'Twelve thou, my friend,' Fontenot said.

'Bullshit. New Orleans is white with it.'

'Ten thou is the discount price. You get that down the line,' Fontenot said.

'Then go fuck yourself.'

'Who do you think you are, man?' Lionel said.

'The guy whose place you just creeped.'

'Let's split,' he said.

I looked at Fontenot.

'What I can't seem to convey is that you guys are not the only market around. Ask Cardo who he wants running the action in Southwest Louisiana. Ask him who punched his wife in a bathroom stall in the Castaways in Miami.'

'There're some people I wouldn't try to turn dials on, Mr Robicheaux,' Fontenot said.

'You're the one holding up the deal. Give me what I want and we're in business.'

'You can come in at eleven thou,' he said.

'It's got to be ten.'

'Listen to this guy,' Lionel said.

'The money's not mine. I've got to give an accounting to other people.'

'I can relate to that. We'll call you,' Fontenot said.

'When?'

'About this time tomorrow. Do you have a car?'

'I have a pickup truck.'

He nodded reflectively; then his mouth split in a grin and I could see each of his teeth like worn, wide-set pearls in his gums.

'How big a grudge can a man like you carry?' he asked.

'What?'

'Nothing,' he said, and shook all over when he laughed, his narrowed eyes twinkling with a liquid glee.

The next morning I was walking down Chartres towards the French Market for breakfast when a black man on a white pizza-delivery scooter went roaring past me. I didn't pay attention to him, but then he came roaring by again. He wore an oversized white uniform, splattered with pizza sauce, sunglasses that were as dark as a welder's, and a white paper hat mashed down to his ears. He turned his scooter at the end of the block and disappeared, and I headed through Jackson Square toward the Café du Monde. I waited for the green light at Decatur; then I heard the scooter come rattling and coughing around the corner. The driver braked to the curb and grinned at me, his thin body jiggling from the engine's vibration.

'Tee Beau!' I said.

'Wait for me on the bench. I gotta park my machine, me.'

He pulled out into the traffic again, drove past the line of horse-and-carriages in front of the square, and disappeared past the old Jax brewery. Five minutes later I saw him coming on foot back down Decatur, his hat hammered down to the level of his sunglasses. He sat beside me on a sunlit bench next to the pike fence that bordered the park area inside the square.

'You ain't gonna turn me in, are you, Mr Dave?' he said.

'What are you doing?'

'Working at the pizza place. Looking out for Jimmie Lee Boggs, too. You ain't gonna turn me in, now, are you?'

'You're putting me in a rough spot, Tee Beau.'

'I got your promise. Dorothea and Gran'maman done tole me, Mr Dave.'

'I didn't see you. Get out of New Orleans.'

'Ain't got no place else to go. Except back to New Iberia. Except to the Red Hat. I got a lot to tell you 'bout Jimmie Lee Boggs. He here.'

'In New Orleans?'

'He left but he come back. I seen him. Two nights ago. Right over yonder.' He pointed diagonally across the square. 'I been watching.'

'Wait a minute. You saw him by the Pontabla Apartments?'

'Listen, this what happen, Mr Dave. After he killed that policeman and that white boy, he drove us all the way to Algiers, with lightning jumping all over the sky. He made me sit in back, with chains on, like he a po-liceman and I his prisoner, in case anybody stops us. He had the radio on, and I was 'fraid he gonna find out I didn't shoot you, drive out in that marsh, kill me like he done them poor people in the filling station. All the time he was talking, telling me 'bout what he gonna do, how he got a place in the Glades in Florida, where he say – now this is what he say, I don't use them kind of words – where he say the hoot owls fucks the jackrabbits, where he gonna hole up, then come back to New Orleans and make them dagos give him a lot of money.

'Just befo' we got to town he called somebody from a filling station. I could hear him talking, and he said something 'bout the Pontabla. I heard him say it. He don't be paying me no mind, no, 'cause he say I just a stupid nigger. That's the way he talk all the time I chained up there in the backseat.'

'Tee Beau, are you sure it was Boggs? It's hard to believe you found him when half the cops in Louisiana can't.'

'I found you, ain't I? He don't look the same now, Mr Dave. But it's him. His hair short and black now, he puts glasses, too. But it's Jimmie Lee Boggs. I followed him in my car to make sure.'

'Where'd you get a car?'

'I borrowed it.'

'You borrowed it?'

'Then I put it back.'

'I see.'

'I followed him out to the Airline Highway. To a boxing place. No, it ain't that. They put on gloves, but they kick with the feet, too. What they call that?'

'Full-contact karate.'

'I looked inside, me. Phew, it stink in there. Jimmie Lee Boggs in long sweatpants kicking at some man in the ring. His skin white and hard, shining with sweat. I got to swallow when I look at him, Mr Dave. That man make me that afraid.'

'You did fine, Tee Beau. But I want to ask something of you. You leave

Jimmie Lee Boggs for other people. Don't have anything more to do with this.'

'You gonna get me a new trial?'

'I'll try. But we have to do it a step at a time, partner.'

His hands were folded in his lap, and he was bent forward on the bench. His small face looked like a squirrel's with sunglasses on it. Wiry rings of hair grew across the back of his neck.

'I got bad dreams at night. 'Bout the Red Hat, 'bout they be strapping me down in that chair with that black hood on my face,' he said.

'You killed Hipolyte Broussard, though, didn't you, Tee Beau?'

His breath clicked in his throat.

'I done part of it. But the part I done was an accident. I swear it, 'fore God, Mr Dave. Hipolyte kept cussing me, tole me all the bad things he gonna do to me, do to Dorothea, tole me I got jelly in my ears, me, that I cain't do nothing right, that I better stomp on the brake when he say, take my foot off when he say. He under there clanking and banging and calling me mo' names, saying "Stomp now, stomp now."

'So that what I done. I close my eyes and hit on that brake, and I hit on it and hit on it and pretend it be Hipolyte's face, that I smashing it like a big eggshell, me. Then I feel the bus rock and that jack break like a stick, and I know Hipolyte under the wheel now, I hear him screaming and flopping around in the mud. But I scared, Mr Dave, I be running, run past the shed, down the road past Hipolyte's house, down past the cane field. When I turn round he look like a turtle on its back, caught under that big iron wheel. But I keep on going, I run plumb back to Gran'maman's house, she be shucking crawfish, say, "You go wash, Tee Beau, put on your clean clothes, you, sit down with your *gran'maman* and don't tell them policemens nothing, you."'

'Why was Hipolyte always deviling you?' I said.

He didn't answer.

'Was it because he wanted you to pimp for him? Or make Dorothea get on the bus when he drove the girls out to the camp?'

'Yes suh.'

'But Dorothea said Gros Mama Goula wouldn't let men bother her.'

'Yes suh, that's right.'

'That Hipolyte was afraid of Gros Mama, that she could put a *gris-gris* on him.'

'Yes suh.'

'Then Dorothea was safe, really?'

'What you saying, Mr Dave?'

'Dorothea wasn't your main problem with Hipolyte.'

He looked out at the shadows of the palm fronds on the pavement.

'It was something else,' I said. 'Maybe not just the pimping. Maybe something even worse than that, Tee Beau.'

I could not see his eyes behind the dark glasses, but I saw him swallow.
'What was it?' I said.

'For why you want to study on that?' he said. 'It gonna get me a new trial? It gonna make all them white people believe I ain't knock that bus on Hipolyte, I ain't stuff a dirty rag down his mouth? I ain't talking about it no mo', Mr Dave.'

'You'll need to at some point.'

He looked small inside his white delivery uniform. The sleeves almost covered his folded hands.

'Hipolyte was selling dope for Jimmie Lee Boggs. That ain't all they was doing, either. They send some of them girls to Florida, to Arizona, anywhere Hipolyte take the bus. Them girls never come back. They families ain't ever find out where they at. All I ever done was taken Mr Dore car, taken an old junk fan out his yard, but people be wanting to kill me. I tired of it, Mr Dave. I tired of feeling bad about myself all the time, too.'

I took a piece of paper from my wallet and wrote on it.

'Here's my address and phone number, Tee Beau,' I said. 'Here's the address and number of a bar where you can leave messages, too. Call me if I can help you with anything. Do you have enough money?'

'Yes suh.'

'Don't look for Boggs anymore. You've done enough. Okay?'

'Yes suh. You want to know where I'm staying at?'

'I don't want to know. Give me your word you won't borrow any more cars.'

He didn't bother to reply. He looked down between his knees and tapped the soles of his shoes on the pavement. Then he said, 'You think I ever gonna get out of this?'

'I don't know.'

'Gros Mama tell Dorothea that Jimmie Lee Boggs gonna die in a black box full of sparks. She say you go in there with him, you gonna die, too.'

'Gros Mama's a juju con woman.'

'She put the *gris-gris* on Hipolyte. When he in the coffin, his mouth snap open and a black worm thick as my thumb crawl out on his chin. It ain't no lie, Mr Dave.'

I had breakfast at the Café du Monde, then walked back to the apartment to call Minos at the DEA office. Before I could, the phone rang. It was Ray Fontenot.

'Your offer's accepted,' he said.

'Ten thou a key, not cut?'

'What I just said, Mr Robicheaux.' Then he told me to meet him that afternoon in the parking lot of a bar just the other side of the Huey Long Bridge.

'You want me to make the buy in the parking lot of a bar?' I asked.

'We start it from there. Quit sweating it. You're gonna be rich,' he said, and hung up.

I called Minos.

'It's on at five today,' I said.

'Where?'

I told him about the bar.

'We'll have somebody inside, somebody outside taking pictures with a telephoto lens,' he said. 'But you won't know who they are, so you won't need to look at them. This is what's going to happen, Dave. They'll take you somewhere in their car, or you'll follow them in your truck. At some point they'll probably check you for a wire. We'll have a loose tail on you, but we're not going to get too close and blow it. So when you make the buy, you're pretty much on your own. Are you nervous?'

'A little.'

'Carry your piece. They'll expect that. Look, you've handled it fine so far. The deal's not going to sour. They want you in.'

'This morning I heard that Jimmie Lee Boggs is in town.'

'Where?'

'Somebody saw him around the Pontabla Apartments two nights ago. It makes sense. Tony Cardo's girlfriend lives there. The same night, he was at a full-contact karate place out on the Airline.'

'Who told you all this?'

'A guy I know.'

'Which guy?'

'Just a guy in the street.'

'What are you hiding here, Dave?'

'Are you going to check out the karate club, or do you want me to do it?'

'We'll handle it.'

'His hair's dyed black and cut short now, and he may be wearing glasses.'

'Who's the guy in the street?'

'Forget it, Minos.'

'You never change.'

'What if the deal goes sour today?'

'Then get the fuck out of there.'

'You don't want me to bust them?'

'You walk out of it. We don't borrow people from other agencies to get them hurt.'

'One other thing I didn't mention to you. This guy Fontenot knows I've got a grudge against Boggs. I get the feeling he'd like to see me go up against him.'

'You know what a yard bitch is in the joint? That's Uncle Ray Fontenot, a fat dipshit who gets off watching the swinging dicks carve on each other. Call me after the score and we'll take the dope off you.'

I *was* nervous. My palms were moist. I walked about aimlessly in the apartment, I burned a pan on the stove. Finally I put on my gym shorts, running shoes, and a sweatshirt, jogged along the levee by the river, and circled back on Esplanade. I showered, changed into a fresh pair of khakis and a long-sleeved denim shirt. Then I fastened the holster of the Beretta to my ankle, dropped the .45 automatic in the right-hand pocket of my army field jacket, slipped the brown envelope with the fifty one-thousand bills in it into the left pocket, buttoned the flap, and backed my pickup out of the garage. The sky had turned a solid gray from horizon to horizon, the wind was blowing hard off the Gulf, and I could smell rain in the air. My palms left damp prints on the steering wheel.

Rain began to tumble out of the dome of sky through the girders when I crossed the Mississippi on the Huey Long. The river was wide and yellow far below, and froth was blowing off the bows of the oil barges. The willows along the banks were bent in the wind. As my tires whirred down the long metal-grid incline on the far side, I saw the low, flat-topped brick nightclub set back among oak trees on the left-hand side of old Highway 90. Jax and Dixie neon signs glowed in the rain-streaked windows, and when I crunched on to the oyster shells in the parking lot I saw Ray Fontenot, Lionel Comeaux, and a redheaded woman in a new blue Buick.

The woman was in back, and Fontenot was in the passenger seat and had the door partly open and one leg extended out on the shells in the light rain.

'Park your truck and get in,' he said.

'Where we going?'

'Not far. You'll see. Get in.'

I turned off the ignition, locked my truck, and got into the backseat next to the woman. She wore Levi's, an open leather jacket, and a yellow T-shirt without a bra, so that you could see her nipples against the cloth. The air inside the car was heavy and close with the drowsy smell of reefer.

'Great place to be toking up,' I said.

'What do you care?' Lionel said.

'I care when I'm in your car,' I said.

'Don't worry about it. You won't be long,' he said.

'What?'

He started the engine, drove the Buick behind the nightclub, and parked it under a spreading oak.

'What's the game?' I said.

'Show-and-tell,' he said, got out of the car, walked around, and opened my door. 'Step outside, please.'

'We do the same thing with everybody. Then everybody's comfortable, everybody's relaxed with everybody else,' Fontenot said.

'I'm not relaxed. Who's the girl?' I asked.

'Do I look like a girl to you?' she said. Her eyes were green, the whites tinged red from the reefer hits.

'Who is she?' I said to Fontenot.

'This is Kim. She's a friend, a nice person,' he said.

'I'm not fond of standing out here in the rain. You want to step outside, please,' Lionel said. He spoke with his face turned at an angle from me, as though he were addressing a lamppost.

'What's she doing here?' I said.

'Certain people like her. She goes where she wants. Let's get on with the business at hand, sir,' Fontenot said.

'Boy, talk about a personality problem. Who's he been doing business with?' Kim said. Her red hair was looped over one ear. When she saw me looking at her, she pointed her chin up in the air and lifted her hair off the back of her neck.

'He's just a careful man. He doesn't mean anything by it,' Fontenot said. 'But let's not delay any longer, Mr Robicheaux.'

I stepped outside and let Lionel work his hands up and down my body. He pulled my shirt out of my trousers, patted under my arms, slipped his hands down my spine, felt my pockets and along my legs.

'You think you're going to need all that fire-power?' he asked.

'It's an old habit,' I said.

Fontenot was looking at Lionel's face.

'He's cool,' Lionel said.

'Time to open the candy store,' Fontenot said.

Lionel got back in the Buick and backed it up to where my truck was parked. I glanced again at the girl. She wore no makeup, and her face was hard and shiny. Pretty but hard. She looked like she had a hard body. Her hands were big and knuckled like those on a cannery worker.

'You got something on your mind?' she said.

'Not a thing,' I said.

'Good, because I'm not into eye fucking,' she said.

'Eye fucking?' I said.

Fontenot was grinning from the front seat. He was always grinning, his teeth set like pieces of corn in his gums.

'I have to end your fun now,' he said. 'I'll hop in your truck with you, Mr Robicheaux, and we'll be on our way.'

We headed south of the city into St Charles Parish. Gray clouds tumbled across the sky in the fading light, and white streaks of lightning trembled on the horizon beyond Lake Salvador. The Buick was a quarter mile ahead of us on the tar-surfaced road.

'I need to take a leak,' Fontenot said.

I stopped next to an irrigation ditch between two dry rice fields, and he got out and urinated into the weeds. I could hear him passing gas softly. His beige sports jacket, with brown suede pockets, was spotted with rain. He smiled at me in the wind as he zipped up his pants, then got back in the truck, took a woman's compact from his coat pocket, and gingerly scraped some white powder from it with the blade of his penknife. He lifted the knife to one nostril, then the other, snorting as though he were clearing his nasal passages, widening his eyes, crimping his lips as though they were chapped. Then he licked the flat of the blade with his tongue.

'You want a taste?' he said.

'I never took it up.'

'You think you could take up Kim?'

'I just wonder what she's doing here, that's all.'

'She works in one of Tony's clubs. I suspect he probes her recesses. I know that's what Lionel would like to do.'

'You know Tony now?'

'You're in the business now, my friend. It's a nice one to be in. Lots of good things to be had. You want to meet him?'

'It doesn't matter to me, as long as I get what I want.'

'What is it you want?' There were tiny saliva bubbles between his teeth when he grinned.

'One big score, then maybe I piece off the action and buy a couple of businesses in Lafayette and Lake Charles.'

'Ah, you're a Rotary man at heart. But in the meantime, how about all the broads you want, your own plane to fly down to the islands in, lobster and steak every night at the track? You don't think about those things?'

'I have simple tastes.'

'How about squaring a debt?' he asked.

'With who?'

'Everybody's got a debt to square. Winning's a lot more fun when you get to watch somebody else lose.'

'I never gave it much thought.'

'Oh, I bet.'

'Fontenot, that's the second time you've given me the impression you know something about me that I don't.'

'You used to be a cop. That's not the best recommendation. We had to do some homework, stick our finger into a nasty place or two.'

'Okay . . .'

'I'd be mad at somebody who put a hole in me and left me to die in a ditch.'

'You're right. Do you know where he is?'

'I stay away from some people.'

'Then you don't need to be worrying about it anymore.'

'Of course.'

We crossed a bayou on a wooden bridge and drove across a flooded area of saw grass and dead cypress. Blue herons stood in the shallows, and mud hens were nesting up against the reeds out of the wind. In the distance I could see the hard tin outline of a sugar mill. Fontenot opened the compact, balanced some coke on the tip of his knife blade, and took another hit. His face was an oval pie of satisfaction.

'Are you interested in politics?' he asked.

'Not particularly.'

'Tony is. He writes letters to newspapers. He's a patriot.' He smiled to himself, and his eyes were bright as he looked out at the rain through the front window.

'I thought the mustaches stayed out of politics,' I said.

'Bad word for our friends.'

'Why does he write letters?'

'He was a Marine in Vietnam. He likes to take about "nape." '

Then Fontenot changed his voice, his eyes glittering happily. ' "Five acres of fucking nape climbing up a hill. They smelled like cats burned up in an incinerator. Fucking nape, man." ' He started giggling.

'I think you'd better not put any more shit up your nose.'

'Indeed you are a Rotary man.'

We passed a gray, paintless general store under a spreading oak tree at a four-corners, then drove through a harvested sugarcane field that was covered with stubble and followed a bayou through a wooded area. The bayou was dented with rain, and I could see lights in fishing shacks set back on stilts in the trees. We came out into open fields, and it began to rain harder. It was almost completely dark now.

'There.' Fontenot pointed at a small wood house with a gallery at the end of a dirt road in the middle of a field.

'This is it?'

'This is it.'

'You guys can really pick them.'

'You should be impressed. It's a historic place. You remember when a union man from up north tried to organize the plantation workers around here back in the fifties? He was crucified on the barn wall behind that little house. The barn's not there anymore, but that's where it happened. For some reason the state chamber of commerce hasn't put that on any of its brochures.'

'Look, I want to get my moods and get out of here. How much longer is this going to take?'

'Kim'll fix some sandwiches. We'll have some supper.'

'Forget the supper, Fontenot. I'm tired.'

'You're an intense man.'

'You're making things too complicated.'

'It's your first time out. We make the rules.'

'Fuck your rules. On any kind of score, you get in and out of it as fast as you can. The more people in on it, the more chance you take a fall. You went out on a score holding. That's affected my confidence level here.'

'If you'll look around you, you'll notice that you can see for a mile in any direction. You can hear a car or a plane long before they get here. I think we'll keep doing things our way. Kim's sandwiches are a treat. Kim's a treat. Think about it. You didn't see her flex her stuff when you looked at her? Maybe she'd like you to probe her recesses.'

His lips were purple and moist in the glow of the dashboard.

I followed the Buick down the dirt road to the house. We all went inside, and Lionel turned on the lights. Kim carried a grocery bag into the kitchen, and Lionel started a fire of sticks and wadded-up newspaper in the fireplace.

'Where are my goods?' I said.

'They're being delivered. Be patient,' Fontenot said.

'Delivered? What is this?' I said.

'A guy can always find another store if he doesn't like the way we do it,' Lionel said. He was squatted down in front of the fireplace, and he waved a newspaper back and forth on the flames.

'You've got too many people involved in this,' I said.

'He's an expert all right,' Lionel said without turning his head.

'When's the delivery going to be here?' I said.

'In minutes, in minutes,' Fontenot said.

I sat by myself at the window while the three of them ate ham and cheese sandwiches at a table in the center of the room. The house had no insulation, except the water-streaked and cracked wallpaper, and the yellow flames crawling up the stone chimney did little to break the chill in the room. The sky was black outside, and the rain slanted across the window. When they finished eating, Kim cleaned up the table and Lionel went into the back of the house. Fontenot opened the compact and took another hit on the blade of his penknife.

'I have to use the bathroom,' I said.

He wet his lips and smiled at me.

I walked down a short hallway, opened a closet door, passed a bedroom that was stacked with hay bales, and opened the last door in the hall. Lionel sat on the side of a brass bed, his left arm tied off with his belt, the syringe mounted on a thick purple vein. A lighted candle and a cook spoon with a curdled handle lay on a nightstand next to the bed. He had just taken the hit, and his head was tilted back, his mouth open, his jaws slack as though he were in the midst of orgasm. The flame from the candle flickered on the muscular contours of his body. His breath went in and out with the crush, his eyes trying to focus on me and gain control of his situation again.

He set the syringe down, popped loose the belt on his arm, and straightened his back.

'What the fuck do you want, man?' he said hoarsely.

'I was looking for the bathroom.'

'It's a privy. Out back, where a privy is.'

I closed the door on him, went out into the rain, then walked back through the kitchen. Kim was leaning against the drainboard, looking down at the floor. She had taken off her leather jacket to make the sandwiches, and her breasts were stiff against her T-shirt.

'Is it always this much fun?' I said.

'Always,' she said.

Fifteen minutes later came in the form of a Latin man with a black bandanna tied down on his head, beige zoot pants, a canary-yellow shirt unbuttoned to his navel, a soft pad of chest hair on which a gold St Christopher's medal rested, a leather sports coat that folded and creased as smoothly as warm tallow. He carried a cardboard box wrapped in a black plastic garbage bag. He set the box on the table and removed five individual packages wrapped in butcher paper, opened a single-bladed knife, and handed it to me. I cut through the butcher paper on one of the packages and punched through the clear plastic bag inside. I rubbed the white granules between my fingers, then wiped my fingers clean on the paper.

'You don't want a taste?' he said.

'I trust you.'

'You trust me?' he said.

'Yeah.'

He looked at Fontenot.

'Mr Robicheaux doesn't have certain vices,' Fontenot said.

'It's good shit, man. Like Ray ordered, no cut,' the Latin man said. The hollows of both his cheeks were sprayed with tiny acne scars like needle marks. 'Where's Lionel at?'

'He's a little noddy right now. Must be the weather,' Fontenot said.

I took the brown envelope with the money out of my left pocket and put it in Fontenot's hand. He counted the bills out on his thigh.

'All the stiff and green. It can make the ashes in an old man's furnace glow anew,' he said.

The Latin man looked furtively toward the kitchen, where Kim sat at the table, a cup of coffee balanced on her fingers, her eyes staring listlessly out the window into the darkness.

'Jennifer and Carmen are at the bar on the blacktop,' he said.

'I don't see why they should be left alone,' Fontenot said.

The Latin nodded his head at the kitchen, his face a question mark.

'She's an extraordinary girl. Maybe she can ride back with Mr Robicheaux,' Fontenot said.

I put the five kilos of cocaine back in the cardboard box and wrapped the black garbage bag tightly around it. I lifted it on to my shoulder.

'The next time you guys cut a deal, why not do it in the Greyhound bus depot?' I said.

'Oh, that's good,' Fontenot said.

I walked outside to my truck, set the box on the floor, and started the engine. The Latin man came out the front door, got in a TransAm, turned around in a circle, his headlights bouncing up into my face, and headed down the dirt road in the rain. Through the living room window I could see the girl speaking heatedly to Fontenot.

I went back up on the gallery and opened the door.

'You want to go with me, Red?' I said.

'Red?' she said.

'Kim.'

'Why not?' she said.

She was quiet for a long time in the truck. The rain slackened, and the moon rose among the strips of black cloud. When we crossed the flooded section of saw grass and dead cypress the light reflected off the canals and small bays like quicksilver. I cracked my window, and the wind smelled of rain and moss and wet leaves.

'You were really a cop?' she said.

'Off and on.'

'Why'd you give it up?'

'It gave me up.'

'They say you were taking juice.'

'Sometimes you get some bad press.'

'What do you think about that back there?' she said.

'I think they're going to do time.'

'Have you?'

'What?'

'Done time.'

'I was in the bag a little while in Lafayette,' I said.

'What for?'

'Murder.'

She turned her head and looked at me directly for the first time since she had gotten in the truck.

'I was cleared. I didn't have anything to do with it,' I said.

'You don't add up.'

'Why's that?'

'They could have taken you off tonight. You should have known that.'

'I don't figure them for it.'

'What a laugh. You sure you were a cop?'

'They work for Tony Cardo, right? They're not going to burn his customers. Are they?'

I could feel her eyes roving on the side of my face.

'The raghead who brought your kilos . . .'

'Yes?'

'He and Lionel did a guy with a piece of piano wire. Stop up there at the filling station. I have to pee.'

I parked under a dripping oak tree while she went inside. She came back out and got in the truck, and I drove back on to the blacktop. It had stopped raining completely now; the moon was bright in the sky, and when the wind blew through the flooded saw grass and cypress, the light clicked on the water like silvery dimes.

'Why does everything down here smell like mold and leaking sewage?' she said.

'Maybe because there's a lot of mold and leaking sewage here.'

For the first time she smiled.

'Who'd they do?' I said.

'Did I say that? I talk funny when my bladder's full.'

She tied up her hair with a bandanna and looked out the window.

'You know Jimmie Lee Boggs?' I asked.

'The television minister in Baton Rouge?'

'A guy like Lionel doesn't bother me, but Boggs is special.'

'What's it to me?'

'Nothing. I gave you a ride.'

'Expensive ride.'

'You're a tough lady.'

'You look like a nice guy. I don't know what the fuck you're doing dealing dope, but you're an amateur. Do you know where South Carrollton runs into the levee?'

'Yes.'

'That's where I live. If that's out of your way, I can take the streetcar.'

'I'll drive you home. Do you live with someone?'

'You mean do I live with a guy. Sure, Tony C. is interested in broads who live with guys. You're something else.'

She closed her eyes and went to sleep with the nape of her neck against the back of the seat, her calves resting across the box of cocaine. Her nose had a bump on the bridge like a Roman's. Her face shone with the luminescence of bone in the moon glow.

Later, I drove down South Carrollton to the river and woke her up at the end of the street.

'You're home,' I said.

She rubbed her face with her hand and opened and closed her mouth.

'I'd invite you in for a drink, but I have to be at the club at seven in the morning. The liquor man comes tomorrow. He screws Tony on the bottle count if I'm not there.'

'It's all right.'

She popped open the door and put one leg out on the street. She was poised against the streetlight, her bandanna tied across the crown of her head as in a photograph of a 1940s aircraft worker.

'Watch your buns, hotshot. Or go back on the bayou where you belong,' she said.

Then she was gone.

When I got back to the apartment I called Minos at the guesthouse on St Charles. I told him the buy had gone all right.

'We were only about a mile away. You didn't see us?' he said.

'No.'

'You stopped at a filling station on the way back. You had a girl with you.'

'You guys are pretty good. You know anything about the girl? Her first name is Kim.'

'No. What about her?'

'She seems too smart for the company she keeps.'

'If she's with Tony C.'s crowd, she's somebody's punch.'

'I don't read her like that.'

'A broad's a broad to those guys. They don't keep them around because they have Phi Beta Kappa keys.'

'She said Lionel and the Latin guy who made the delivery killed somebody with a piece of piano wire.'

'I haven't heard that one. But Lionel's got the potential. He was on the boxing team in Angola. They say he did some real damage to a couple of guys.'

'Thanks for telling me, Minos.'

'An agent'll pick up the coke about eight-thirty in the morning. He'll look like a geek, but he's one of ours.'

'I don't want to make this a permanent job. Let's up the ante now.'

'It went well tonight. Be patient. Let things take their own course.'

'Those guys are dipshits and addicts. The mule talked like a pimp. We're not going to get anywhere dealing with them. Let me take a deal straight to Cardo, something that'll make him hungry.'

'Like what?'

'Can you shake loose five hundred thou?'

'Maybe. But you may still end up dealing with the dipshits.'

'No, I'm going to offer him something he doesn't have. But you've got to give me some more help. Get Purcel in on the sting.'

'No.'

'He's a good man.'

'It's out of the question.'

'Minos, I'm by myself in this thing. I want somebody covering my back.'

'What are you going to offer Cardo besides the buy?'

'Deal Purcel in and we'll talk about it.'

'We don't negotiate at this phase of the operation, Dave.'

'We do.'

'I think you're beat,' he said. 'I think you need to get some sleep. We'll talk in the morning.'

'It's not going to change. Clete backs my play or it's up the spout.'

'Good night,' he said. His voice was tired. I didn't answer, and he hung up.

Sleep. It was the most natural and inevitable condition of the human metabolism, I thought, as I sat on the edge of my bed in the dark that night. We can abstain from sex and thrive on the thorns of our desire, deny ourselves water in the desert, keep silent on the torturer's rack, and fast unto the death; but eventually sleep has its way with us.

But if you are a drunk, or a recovering drunk, or what some people innocently call a recovered drunk, that most natural of human state seldom comes to you on your terms. And you cannot explain why one night you will sleep until morning without dreaming while the next you will sit alone in a square of moonlight, your palms damp on your thighs, your breath loud in your chest. No more than you can explain why one day you're anointed with magic. You get high on the weather, you have a lock on the perfecta in the ninth race; then the next morning you're on a dry drunk that fills the day with monstrous shapes prized out of memory with a dung fork.

I could hear revelers out in the street, glass breaking, a beer can rolling across the cement. What was my real fear, or theirs? I suspected mortality more than anything else. You do not wish to go gently into that good night. You rage against it, leave your shining bits of anger for a street sweeper to find in the early morning light, kneel by your bed in the moon glow, the scarlet beads of your rosary twisted around your fist.

But as always, just before dawn, the tiger goes back in his cage and sleeps, and something hot and awful rises from your body and blows away like ash in the wind. And maybe the next day is not so bad after all.

6

The next morning was Saturday. I got up early and, after the DEA agent picked up the coke, invited Bootsie for breakfast at a restaurant on St Charles. When I picked her up at her house on Camp, she had on dark slacks, gray pumps, a white silk blouse that hung over her waist, and a pearl necklace. Her face was fresh and cheerful with the morning, and the dark and light swirls and streaks of gray in her thick hair, which she'd had cut since I had visited her, gave her an elegance that you seldom see in maturing Acadian women.

I opened the door of the pickup and helped her in. The air was balmy, the street full of blowing leaves, the trees in the yards filled with the sounds of blue jays and mockingbirds.

'I hope you don't mind riding down St Charles in a pickup,' I said.

'Darlin', I don't mind riding anywhere with you,' she said, with the innocent flirtatious gaiety that's characteristic of New Orleans, and that allows you to never feel awkward or embarrassed with a woman.

'Bootsie, you look absolutely great.'

'Thank you,' she said, moving her lips without sound, a smile in her eyes.

The restaurant had a domed, glassed-in porch, but it was warm enough to eat at the tables outside. The sunlight looked like bright smoke in the oak trees overhead; the air smelled of green bamboo, gardenias, the camellias that bloomed in yards all along the street, the occasional hot scorch of the old green streetcar that rattled down the esplanade, or what the people in New Orleans call the neutral ground. We ate hot, fresh-baked bread with honey and marmalade, and the Negro waiter poured the coffee and milk from two long-spouted copper pots.

I touched Bootsie on the top of her hand.

'I'm going back to New Iberia for the weekend,' I said. 'I have an adopted daughter there.'

'Yes?'

'Do you ever go home?'

'Not really. My parents are passed away. Sometimes I feel strange back there. New Iberia never changes. But I have, and it hasn't all been for the good.'

'Hey, not beating up on ourselves today, Boots.'

'It's funny looking back at the past, isn't it? That night you asked me to dance under the trees on Spanish Lake, I remember it like a photograph. My back was on fire with sunburn. You brought me a vodka Collins, then a handful of aspirin. I thought how kind you were, but then you wouldn't go away.'

'I see. I was the one who put everything in motion.'

'What are you talking about?' Her eyes were smiling again.

'You remember what you did with that vodka Collins? You took the cherry out and bit it between your teeth and kept chewing it while you looked into my eyes. You knew I wasn't going to leave you alone after that.'

'I did that? It must have been your imagination.'

'Come back with me today. I still live in my father's old house,' I said. Then I added, 'We have a guest room.'

'What are you trying to start, hon?'

'I'm in the one-day-at-a-time club. Tomorrow takes care of itself. I've got three tickets to the LSU-Ole Miss game tonight. We'll take Alafair with us and have crawfish at Mulate's, then go on up to Baton Rouge.'

She didn't answer for a moment; then she said, 'I'm flattered you want me to meet your daughter, but do you think maybe you're trying to fix yesterday's mistakes?'

'No,' I said, and felt my throat color.

'Because if your conscience bothers you, or if you feel that somehow you need to make amends to me, I want you to stop now.'

'It's not that way.'

'Which way is it, then?'

'It's a beautiful day. It's going to be a fine weekend. Why not take a chance on it?'

'You made a choice for both of us thirty years ago, Dave. I didn't have a chance to participate in it. Since then, most of my choices have turned out to be bad ones.'

'Boots, I'll never intentionally hurt you again.'

'We get hurt worse by the people whom we care about. And they seldom mean to do it. That's what makes it so painful, kiddo.'

'At any point you wish, you just say, "Let's go home, Dave. Let's not try to be kids again." It'll end right there.'

'People make lots of promises in the daylight.'

This time I simply looked back across the table at her. Her hair was so thick and lovely. I wanted to reach over and touch it.

'Are you sure this is what you want?' she said finally.

'I can't think of anything better in the whole world,' I said.

I dropped her off at her house, went back to the apartment and packed, left a message for Minos on his answering machine; then two hours later she and I were on our way across the Atchafalaya Basin, on a perfect blue and gold fall day, the wind blowing across the bays and saw grass and dead cypress, the elevated highway like a long white conduit into the past.

You never forget an LSU-Ole Miss game: the tiers upon tiers of seats filled with people, the haze around the banks of lights in the sky, the thunder of marching bands on the field, cheerleaders tumbling like acrobats, Confederate flags waving wildly in the crowd, Mike the Tiger in his cage riding stiff-legged around the track, the coeds with mums pinned on their sweaters, their breath sweet with bourbon and Coca-Cola – then, suddenly, one hundred thousand people rising to their feet in one deafening roar as LSU's team pours on to the field in their gold and purple and white uniforms that shine with light and seem tighter on their bodies than their very muscles.

Alafair fell asleep between us on the way back home, and I carried her into her bedroom and tucked her in. Then I heated some *boudin*, and Bootsie and I ate it at the kitchen table. Her face was sleepy with the long day, and she smiled and tried to stay attentive while I talked, but her eyes kept shutting lazily and finally her hand slipped off the side of the table.

'I think it's time you went to sleep,' I said.

'I'm sorry. I'm so tired. It's been a wonderful day, Dave.'

'It'll be an even better one tomorrow.'

'I know,' she said.

'Good night.'

'Good night. I'm sorry to be so tired.'

'It's all right. You're supposed to be tired. I'll see you tomorrow.'

She went into the back bedroom, and I could see the light for a few minutes under her door. I turned on the television set in the living room and lay down on the couch. Her light went off, and I stared at a late show starring a famous actor who had been deferred from service during the Vietnam War because he had been the sole support of his mother. I didn't blame the actor for his deferment, but I didn't have to watch him, either. I turned off the set and lay back down on the couch with my arm over my eyes. I heard the scream of nutria out in the marsh, the sound of night birds out in the bare sugarcane fields behind my property, the occasional thump of pecans falling to the ground in the front yard.

It *had* been a fine day. Why did I always expect more out of the day than perhaps I had earned?

A few minutes later I heard her click on the bedside lamp; then she opened the door and stood framed against the light. She didn't speak. Her face was dark with shadow, her body outlined against her white nightgown, her short-cropped hair diffused with light.

I went into the room with her, and she closed the door as though it were her house rather than mine. She clicked off the lamp, smoothed the pillows, pulled back the covers, then touched my face with her hand, kissing me on the mouth, lightly at first, then her mouth opening and wet, her face changing the angle, her tongue inside me, her eyes opening and shutting but always focusing on mine as though I might somehow elude the moment she was creating for both of us.

She worked her nightgown over her head and lay down partially on her side with her knees close together, her palm behind her head, and waited for me. When I lay down beside her, she stretched out against me, breathing on my neck and chest, rubbing her hair against my face as though she were a cat. I kissed her eyes and mouth and breasts, and felt the smoothness of her stomach and thighs and the contours of her lips. I brushed her hair with my palm, stroked the stiffness of it where it was tapered at the back of her head, smelled the expensive and delicate perfume behind her ears.

Then she took me in her hand, her thighs widening, and placed me inside her. Her lips parted, her eyes closed and opened, and she slipped her arms low on my back and tucked her face under my chin. She didn't speak while she made love. Her concentration and body heat were so intense, the movement of her hands and thighs and stomach so directed and encompassing, the hoarse, regular sounds in my ear so natural and heart-swelling, that I knew she too was back thirty years before on the float cushions in my father's boathouse, the lavender sky streaked with fire through the cracks, the shrimp boat knocking against the pilings, the raindrops dripping like lead shot out of the cypress into the bay.

But on Monday Alafair was back with my cousin Tutta, Bootsie was at work at her vending machine company, and I was talking with Minos in his room at the guesthouse on St. Charles about New Orleans flake and people who gave you reason to think twice that toxic waste had been dumped in the human gene pool.

He stood at the ceiling-high window with a coffee cup in his hand, looking down on the courtyard behind the guesthouse. Banana trees and bamboo grew along the back brick wall, and on the other side of the wall there were garbage cans in the alley. Minos had on tan slacks and a yellow golf shirt with an alligator on it. As always, his scalp gleamed through his close-cropped hair and his jaws looked as though he had just shaved.

'I understand, they're dangerous. You don't have to convince me of that,' he said. 'But it comes with the territory. I don't think the situation will improve because we make Purcel a player.'

'You don't have anybody inside. So we bring him in with me. Give the guy a break. He has a lot of qualities.'

'He worked for the mob, for Christ's sake.'

'I think he took some of them off the board, too.'

'That's the last kind of cowboy bullshit we want in this operation.'

'What's it going to be, partner?'

'We did some homework over the weekend. Purcel has some bad debts around town. One of them is to a loan company owned by the grease-balls. He's also got a reputation for parking his swizzle stick in anything that looks vaguely female.'

'In or out?' I asked.

He bit a corner of his lip and continued to look down into the courtyard. He seemed almost as tall as the window.

'The money comes out of the snitch fund,' he said. 'You can tell him whatever you want to. But he's not an employee of the DEA. Nor its representative.'

'How much?'

'Two hundred a week.'

'That's an insult.'

'Too bad.'

'Listen, Minos, let's stop messing around. You give the guy five hundred a week, treat him with some respect, or I'm going to walk out of this.'

'I'll talk to somebody about it later.'

'No, make the call now.'

I saw him take a breath, his finger tap on his thigh.

'All right, you've got my word,' he said.

'He was a good cop till he had marital trouble and got on the sauce. He'll do fine. You'll see.'

'I hope so. Because if he doesn't, somebody's going to feed your butt through the paper shredder an inch at a time.'

'You really know how to say it, Minos.'

He picked up a towel from the bathroom floor and started buffing one of his loafers on top of a wood chair.

'Where'd this broad, Kim, the one at the score, tell you she was from?'

'She didn't.'

'Hmmm.'

'What is it?'

'We checked her out. Her last name's Dollinger. She's an assistant manager at one of Cardo's clubs on the Airline Highway. She hit town about six months ago. She tells people she worked at a lounge in North Houston, some dump on Jensen Drive. We made a couple of calls. They never heard of her.'

'She said something. About everything down here smelling like mold and leaking sewage. I don't think she's from Houston.'

'Those kinds of broads make up their own dossiers. I've got something else on my mind that's giving me the start of a migraine, Dave.'

I waited for him to go on.

'Bootsie Giacano,' he said.

'I had a feeling you'd say that. Do you have a tail on me?'

'It wouldn't be a bad idea, but we don't.'

'A tap on her phone?'

'What do you think? She was married to Ralph Giacano. Her business partners are mainline greaseballs.'

'She can't get out from under them.'

'Always the humanist. Look, Dave, what you do with your private life is your business. But if you compromise the operation, it's ours.' He sat on the wood chair and threw the towel back on to the bathroom floor. 'Look, I'm your friend. I got you into this stuff. You think I want to see you hurt?'

'I won't get hurt because of her.'

'You don't know that. Are you sleeping with her?'

'I'm going to be on my way now.'

'She'll know you're running a sting. She tips the greaseballs, it doesn't matter how, in some innocent way, we're going to pull you out of Lake Pontchartrain.'

'It's not going to happen.'

His eyes were level, unblinking, and they stared straight into mine.

'It did two years ago,' he said. 'To a local narc NOPD got inside. They threw his body off the causeway. A .22 Magnum through the mouth, one under the chin, one through the temple. They didn't weight him down either. They wanted to send a floating telegram.'

'You can get the five hundred thou?'

'Yep.'

'I'm going to try to set up a meet with Cardo. I'll call you.'

'Let some time go by, Dave. Let them feel more confident about you.'

'You said it yourself, these guys love money. How do they put it, "Money talks and bullshit walks"? I'm going to play out the hand. If they buy it, fine. If not, I'm going back home.'

He pulled on his ear and made a snuffing sound in his nose.

'What I'm saying is we don't know everything we'd like to know about Cardo. He messes around in politics, sends money to right-wing crazies, stuff like that. He was shooting off his mouth around town about bringing Oliver North to New Orleans. He thinks he's a big intellectual because he's got a degree from a junior college in Miami.'

'So?'

'So he's hard to read. We know there're some guys in Miami and Chicago who think maybe he shouldn't be running things here, that maybe he's crazy or he keeps his brains in that schlong he's so proud of. Figure it out, Dave. What kind of guy would keep Jimmie Lee Boggs around?'

'You're worrying too much, Minos.'

'Because I've been doing this stuff a long time. I told you it was a simple sting. That's what it should be. But you don't hear me when I say things to you, and I'm bothered by that.'

I left by the back entrance and walked down the alley to the side street where my truck was parked. I could hear the streetcar clattering down the tracks on St Charles. The sky was a hard blue, the noon sun bright overhead, and gray squirrels raced each other around the trunks of the oak trees on the street. Now all I had to do was find a way inside the insular and peculiar world of Anthony Cardo.

'You just fucking do it, mon,' Clete said that same day as we ate lunch at the bar in the Golden Star on Decatur. 'The guy lives in a house, right, not the Vatican. We're talking about a bucket of shit, mon, not the pope. You don't get a number and wait when you deal with a bucket of shit, do you?'

He took an enormous bite of his oyster loaf sandwich. His face was ruddy and cheerful, his crushed porkpie hat down low over his eyes, his sports coat as tight as a sausage skin on his broad back. His cigarette burned in an ashtray, and by his elbow was a Bloody Mary with a celery stalk in it.

'Call up the cocksucker and tell him we're coming out,' he said.

'It's not that easy, Cletus.'

'I don't see the problem.' His cheek was as big as a baseball with unchewed food. We were alone at the bar. The walls were covered with the framed and autographed photos of movie stars.

'He has an unlisted number. Minos gave it to me, but I don't have a way to explain to Cardo how I got it. I asked Fontenot for it, and he wouldn't give it to me. He said he had to clear it with Cardo first.'

'Fontenot's the tub, the one with the T-shirt shop on Bourbon?'

'That's the man.'

'He wants to control access to the piggy bank, huh?'

'Something like that.'

'Stay here.'

'Where are you going?'

'Remain cool and copacetic, my mellow man. I'll be back before you finish your gumbo.'

'Wait a minute, Clete.'

But he was out the door. Fifteen minutes later he was back, his green eyes smiling under the short brim of his hat. He dropped a slip of paper with Cardo's phone number on it next to my plate.

'What did you do to him?' I asked.

'Hey, come on, Fontenot's a reasonable guy. I just explained that you and I are in partnership now. He liked the idea. That's right, I ain't putting you on.'

'Clete, if we get into Cardo's, you've got to take your transmission out of overdrive.'

'Trust me, mon.' The fingers of his big hands were spread out like banana peels on top of the bar. He grinned at me, squinted his eyes, and clicked his teeth together. 'You're looking at a model of restraint, I worked Vice, remember. I know these fuckers. They'll love having me on board.'

It was easier than I thought. I called Cardo's house, a maid answered, then Cardo was on the line. He was polite, even expansive. The accent was typical New Orleans Italian, which sounded like both Flatbush and the Irish Channel.

'I've heard a lot about you,' he said. 'I've been looking forward to meeting you. You play tennis?'

'I'm afraid not.'

'You like to watch tennis?'

'Sure.'

'Where are you now?'

'At the Golden Star, across from the French Market.'

'Can you come out in an hour? We'll have some drinks, I'll hit the ball a little bit, we'll talk.'

'Sure. I'd like that. Can you give me your address?'

He gave me directions to a neighborhood out by Lake Pontchartrain.

'How'd you get this number?' he asked.

'It came from Ray.'

'That's strange. Ray usually doesn't give it out.'

The receiver was quiet a moment.

'You haven't been bouncing my help around, have you?' he said; then he laughed. 'Don't worry about it. Ray needs a little excitement. Cleans the fat out of his veins. You didn't hurt him, though, did you?'

'I didn't do anything to him. I'd like to bring along a friend of mine. He's going into business with me.'

'That's fine with me. We'll be expecting you. Say, you know that newsstand a few doors down from you? Pick me up a copy of the *Atlantic*, will you? My subscription didn't come.'

'Sure thing, Mr Cardo.'

'Hey, it's Tony or Tony C. or Tony some-other-things, but nobody calls me Mr Cardo. Do I sound like a Mr Cardo to you?'

'I'm looking forward to it. We'll see you in an hour,' I said.

I hung up the phone and looked at Clete at the bar.

'The *Atlantic*?' I said.

'What?'

'This guy's a beaut.'

His home was a short distance from the lake. The immense, sloping lawn was shaded by live oaks, and the one-story house was long and white with a wide marble porch, a three-car garage, and a gingerbread gazebo in a side yard that was planted with blooming citrus trees and camellias. The swimming pool had a colonnade built on to one side, like a Roman porch, and behind the pool was a screened-in clay tennis court, and I could see a trim, sun-tanned man in white shorts and a polo shirt *whocking* balls at a machine that fired them automatically over the net.

'The mustaches know how to live, don't they?' Clete said, his tie askew, one arm back on the seat, flipping ashes out the window of the truck.

'Play it cool on the remarks.'

'Ease up. There're only two rules when you deal with these guys. Don't mess with their broads and don't steal from them. These guys just aren't complicated. What would a guy like Tony Cardo do if he couldn't deal dope? He'd probably be running a fruit stand. You think a greaseball like that could honestly earn a joint like this?'

'I'll do most of the talking today, all right, Clete?'

'You've got a lot of anxiety over nothing, mon. But it's your gig. What do I know?' He flipped his cigarette in an arc into a flower bed.

A negro man in a white jacket and black pants walked out the side door of the house and stood on the edge of the drive while we got out of the truck.

'Mr Cardo want y'all come out by the pool,' he said. 'He be with y'all in a minute.' He couldn't keep his eyes from glancing sideways at the truck.

'You like it? Dave might part with it for the right price,' Clete said.

'Mr Cardo ax you gentlemens if you want a drink,' the Negro said.

'Give me a double black Jack on ice,' Clete said. 'What do you want, Dave?'

'Nothing.'

'You got a bathroom?' Clete said to the Negro.

'Yes suh, follow me inside.'

I sat in a beach chair under the colonnade by the side of the pool. The bottom of the pool was inset with a mosaic mermaid that glittered with chips of light. The suntanned man on the court was hitting the ball with his back to me, but I felt that he was aware I was watching him through the myrtle trees that grew along the screens. He stayed on the balls of his feet, the muscles in his brown calves and thighs taut and glazed with perspiration, his forehand shot a white blur across the net.

Clete came out of the side of the house with a highball glass in his hand and sat down heavily in a beach chair next to me.

'You ought to see the can,' he said. 'It looks like a pink whorehouse. Erotic art all over the wallpaper, a toilet seat inlaid with silver dollars. The colored guy went in after me and started cleaning the toilet with a brush. Should I take that personally?'

'Probably.'

'Thanks.'

The man on the tennis court turned off the ball machine and walked across the close-clipped lawn towards us, zipping up the case on his racket. He was truly a strange-looking man. His head was long and narrow, his ears tiny and pressed tightly against the scalp as though part of them had been surgically pared away. His hair grew in gray and black ringlets that were tapered on the back of his neck like the flange of a helmet. His smile exposed his long white teeth, and his chest hair was black and slick with perspiration.

'Tony Cardo,' he said, his hand outstretched like a greeter's in a restaurant.

'It's nice to see you, Tony,' I said. 'This is a friend of mine, Clete Purcel.'

'What's happening, Tony?' Clete said, rising up enough from the beach chair to shake hands.

'I remember you from somewhere,' Cardo said to him.

'You drink vodka Collins,' Clete said.

Cardo pursed his lips together in the shape of a tiny butterfly.

'You're a bartender in the Quarter,' he said.

'I own the bar.'

'You were in the corps.'

'That's right.'

'We had some words or something.'

'No, I don't have words with people.'

'Yeah, we did. Something about the corps. No, something about "the crotch", right?'

'You got me. I don't argue with people.'

'Who's arguing? But you said something, almost like getting in a guy's face. Then you walked away. I was buying a drink for the gunny.'

Clete shrugged his shoulders.

'It must be somebody else. I just remember you drink vodka Collins, that's all,' he said.

'Hey, don't sweat it. You're a diplomat. That's good. It means you're a good businessman.'

'I got no beef with anybody, Tony.'

'I like that,' Cardo said.

'Clete was my Homicide partner a few years ago,' I said. I watched Cardo's face.

'What made you change careers?' His eyes smiled as though he were looking at a private conclusion inside himself. The black houseman brought out a tray with a Collins and bowl of chilled shrimp on it and set it on a circular redwood table next to Cardo's chair.

'A little trouble in the department, nothing big,' Clete said. 'I went down to the tropics for a while to get my priorities straight. Then I got into casino security out in Vegas and Tahoe for Sally Dio.'

'Yeah, Sally Dee out of Galveston,' Cardo said. 'His plane smacked into a mountain out in Montana or somewhere.'

'Yeah, it was too bad. He was a great guy to work for,' Clete said.

'I always heard he was a prick,' Cardo said.

'Well, some people had that opinion, too,' Clete said.

'You're not drinking anything, Dave?'

'No thanks. Can we talk some business, Tony?'

'Put on some swimsuits. Let's take a dip,' he said.

'It's a little cool, isn't it?' I said.

'I keep the water at eighty-two degrees. You'll love it. There're some suits over there in the cottage,' he insisted.

He went into his own house to change, and Clete and I walked across the lawn to a small white stucco cottage that was surrounded with palm and banana trees.

'He's one slick motherfucker. You won't get a wire into this place, partner,' Clete said.

Inside the cottage we found a cardboard box full of men's and women's bathing suits on top of the bar. Clete started rooting through them and found only one pair that wasn't too small for him, an enormous pair of red boxer trunks with a white elastic band.

'I bet these belong to that blimp who runs the T-shirt shop,' he said. He looked at my face. 'It's not funny, Dave. These guys pass around VD like a family heirloom.' He went into the bedroom, found a safety pin in a drawer, and began undressing by the bar.

'He really put you under the microscope,' I said.

'They're all the same, mon. They love to peel back your skin.'

'What do you think all that Marine Corps stuff is about?'

'Who cares? Figuring out the greaseballs is like putting your hand in an unflushed toilet.'

I laid my clothes across the back of a couch and slipped on a pair of trunks. Clete poured a glass of Jack Daniel's at the bar and looked at my chest.

'That's where Boggs popped you, huh?' he said. 'Does it give you much trouble?'

'I'm still weak on the left side. Sometimes it throbs a little in the morning.'

'What else?'

'What do you mean "what else"?'

'Don't try to put on your old partner. You remember when that kid planted a couple of .22 rounds in me? I had the nightly sweats for a long time, mon.'

'It comes and goes.'

'Like hell it does.' Then he took a drink and smiled at me. His face looked as big and hard-ribbed as a grinning pumpkin under his porkpie hat. 'But don't worry. Before this is over, we're going to cook Jimmie Lee Boggs's hash, I mean sling some serious shit on the walls. You wait and see, ole Streak.'

He winked at me and walked duck-footed to the door, with his drink in his hand, his red trunks askew on his hips, lighting a cigarette.

'You think he's got any broads around?' he said.

I took the copy of the *Atlantic* out of my pocket and followed him to the pool.

Tony Cardo hit the water in a long, flat dive and swam with deep strokes to the diving board, blowing water out his nose, then made an underwater turn and pushed off the tiled side and swam into the shallow end. He raked the water out of his eyes and curly hair and spit into the trough that surrounded the pool.

'That's a nasty scar on your chest, Dave,' he said.

'A nasty guy put it there.'

'Yeah, I heard about that.'

'He works for you.'

'That's not exactly true, Dave. He used to work for some people I do business with. He doesn't now. I don't know where he is. I heard Florida.'

'I wouldn't want a guy like that to blindside me, Tony.'

'You're an up-front guy. But you got no worries on that. Not in this town.'

'The people I represent like the quality of your product, they like the way you do business. They've given me a half million to work with. I want the same quality goods, same price on the key. Can we do some business today?'

'You cut right to it, don't you?'

'You're a serious man, you have a serious reputation.'

'You're talking a big score.'

'That's why I'm dealing with you. The word is that the Houston people are undependable.'

'The problem I got sometimes is access, Dave. Or what you might call transportation. The product's out there, but there're a lot of nautical factors involved here, you know what I mean? Something happens to the product out on the salt, a lot of people lose money, a lot of people get real mad.'

'That's the other thing I want to talk to you about. I grew up in the wetlands. I know every bayou and channel from Sabine Pass over to Barataria. I can get it through for you, and on a regular basis.'

'I bet you can,' he said.

But his attention was no longer on me. His arms were folded on top of the trough, and he was looking across the blue-green expanse of lawn and trees at the front porch of his house, where a blond woman in a red dress and a hat was counting the suitcases the houseman was bringing inside. A moment later one of the gatemen walked up the drive and backed a restored 1940s Lincoln Convertible out of the garage. It had wire wheels, a deep maroon finish, and an immaculate white top. The gateman and the Negro put the woman's luggage in the trunk. She never glanced in our direction.

'What do you think of my car?' he said finally.

'It looks great.'

'Yeah. That's what I think.' But his eyes were still concentrated on the woman. 'You married?'

'Not now.'

He continued to stare as she got into the Lincoln and the gateman drove her down the long driveway towards the street. Then his eyes clicked back to mine.

'Hey, let me ask you something else. Because I like you. I like the way you talk,' he said. 'What's your attitude about dealing in the product?'

'I don't understand.'

'You're an educated man. I want to know what an educated man thinks about dealing in the product.'

'I never saw anybody chop up lines because somebody forced him to.'

'I think that's an intelligent attitude. But I want you to understand something else, Dave. I got lots of businesses. Vending and video machines, a restaurant, nightclubs, half of a trucking company, real estate development out by Chalmette, some investments in Miami. This other stuff comes and goes. Five years from now the in thing might be huffing used cat litter. There's always a bunch of bozos around with money. Why fight the fashion?'

His eyes looked at the empty drive and the front gate that was closed once again.

'Excuse me,' he said, and raised himself out of the pool, walked dripping to the redwood table, and punched one button on the phone. He put his little finger in one of his tiny ears and shook water out of it. At the end of the drive I saw the other gateman walk to a box that was inset in the stucco wall.

'Tommy, get some people over here, call up the catering service,' he said. 'I got some guests here, I want to entertain them right . . . Don't ask me who, I don't give a shit, get them over here.'

He hung up the phone and looked at me.

'I live in a place that costs a million bucks, and half the time it's like being the only guy in the fucking Superdome,' he said.

'Before your friends get here, can we agree on a deal of some kind, Tony?' I said.

'There's some people I bring out here like I order lawn furniture. There's other people I invite because I respect their experience and what's in their heads. Don't hurt my feelings,' he said.

His guests arrived like actors who played only one role, their smiles welded in place, their eyes aglitter with the moment. They were people without accents or origins, as though they had lived on the edge of a party all their lives. But besides their good looks and their late-season suntans, their most singular common denominator was their carefree trust in the walled-in tropical opulence that surrounded them. They smoked dope by the pool, snorted lines off a mirror in the guest cottage, ate chicken and mayonnaise sandwiches from the caterer's tray, with never a sideways glance at gatemen who wore shoulder holsters or a thick-bodied, silent man in cutoffs who waxed an Oldsmobile in the driveway with such a mean energy that his jailhouse tattoos danced like snakes on his naked back.

Even Clete quickly fell into the ambience, his arms spread out on the tile trough in the deep end, his pale blue canvas hat low on his brow, a twenty-year-old girl hovering within the crook of his arm. Her mouth was red and cold from the whiskey sour she sipped from a glass in one hand, and she laughed at everything he said and balanced herself by cupping his shoulder whenever she started to float away from the pool's edge. I could see her knee rake against his thigh.

The air was becoming cooler now, and I treaded water to stay warm. It was impossible to get Cardo alone. He sat at the redwood table in a white terry cloth robe, one leg crossed on his knee, smoking a Pall Mall in a gold cigarette holder, while four of his guests sat around him and smiled brightly into his words. I hung from the diving board by one arm and began to think it was better to mark the day off.

'How do you like being in the life?' a voice said behind me.

She sat on the diving board mat in a light green dress covered with tiny pink flowers. She had tucked her red hair up into a green beret, but one side of it had fallen down on her neck. Her lipstick was bright red, and she wore too much of it, but when she parted her mouth and looked directly at me, she disturbed me and made me keenly aware that there is no safety for the male in either age or pride.

'What's happening, Kim?' I said.

'What's happening with you, hotshot?'

'Like you say, enjoying the life. You don't want to swim?'

'I think I'll pass. Two nights ago they were screwing in here.'

'I beg your pardon?'

'You heard me. On a rubber raft, with the lights on. What a bunch.'

I lifted myself out of the pool and walked to the guest cottage to shower and dress. I heard her laugh behind me. When I came back out she was sitting on a cushioned, scrolled iron chair with her legs crossed. I sat down on the dry mat on the back edge of the diving board.

'You're a case,' she said.

'How's that?' I said, looking toward the shallow end, where Tony was tapping a beach bail back and forth with two girls.

'You make me think of a cat that's trying to like sitting on a hot stove,' she said.

'Where did you say you're from?'

'I didn't.'

'I need to talk to Tony alone. It's hard to do.'

'You're still out for the big score, huh, hotshot?'

'How about cutting me a little slack?'

'All you want, babe.'

'Are you his girl?'

She looked away from me at the trees in the yard, her face cool and sculpted, her hair thick and dark red where it was pinned up on the back of her neck. She touched at an area between her teeth with her little fingernail, then glanced back into my face. Her eyes looked directly into mine, but they were impossible to read.

'What?' I asked her.

Still she didn't answer, and instead continued to stare into my face. I took a breath.

'I think I need to get something to eat,' I said.

'If you want to see Tony alone, he'll be going up to the house soon to check on his little boy. He always does.'

'His little boy?'

'It's the reason his wife's always taking off. She can't handle it.'

'What are you talking about?'

'Do yourself a favor and go home, Robicheaux.'

She stood up, tucked her hair under her beret, and walked off alone toward the tennis court. A moment later I saw her leaning on her arms against the wire mesh, looking at nothing, her face wan and empty in the shadow of the myrtle bushes.

She was right about Tony Cardo, though. Ten minutes later, when I was about to signal Clete that it was time to hang it up, Cardo excused himself from his guests and walked across his lawn to a glassed-in sun porch at the back of his house. I went to the side door of the house and knocked. The Negro houseman answered, a polishing cloth in his hand.

'I'd like to see Mr Cardo,' I said.

'He be out directly.'

'I'd like to see him inside, please.'

'Just a moment, suh,' he said, and walked into the back of the house. Then he returned and unlatched the screen. 'Mr Cardo want you to wait in the library.'

I followed the houseman through a huge, gleaming kitchen, a living room furnished with French antiques and hung with a chandelier the size of a beach umbrella, into a pine-paneled study whose shelves were filled with encyclopedias, sets of science and popular history books, novels from book clubs, and plastic-bound collections of classics, the kind that are printed on low-grade paper and advertised on cable TV stations. The chairs and couch were red leather, the big glass-topped mahogany desk one that would perhaps befit Leo Tolstoy.

Tony slid open the far door and stepped inside in his terry cloth robe and sandals. Before he closed the door again, I looked out on the sun porch and saw the back of a wheelchair framed against a lighted television screen. The floor around the chair was strewn with toys and stuffed animals.

'I didn't give you your magazine,' I said, and took the copy of the *Atlantic* out of my pocket and handed it to him.

'Hey, thanks, Dave. I appreciate it.'

'I have to go, too. I just wanted to tell you I'd like to do business with you, but I have to have something firm. Like this afternoon, Tony.'

'I want you to understand something, and I don't want you to take offense. The house is a family place, I don't do business in it. Call Ray Fontenot tomorrow. We'll work something out. You got my word on it.'

'All right.'

'Your face looks a little cloudy.'

'I don't trust Fontenot. I don't know that you should, either.'

'Serious charge. What'd he do?'

'He's an addict and he looks after his own butt.'

'They all do.'

'Thanks for having us out.'

'Wait a minute, don't run off. I heard you were in 'Nam.'

'Ten months, before it got real hot.'

'Those scars on your thigh, you got hit?'

'A bouncing Betty on a trail. It was a dumb place to be at night.'

'Sit down a second. Come on, you're not in that big a hurry. Then you got to go back to the States?'

'Sure. A million-dollar wound.'

'In the corps, unless you get the big one, you got to earn two Hearts before you skate.'

'You were hit?'

'Right in the butt. A zip up in a tree, maybe three hundred yards out.'

I looked at my watch. I didn't want to talk more about the war, but it was obvious that he did. His eyes wandered over my face, as though he were searching for a piece of knowledge there that had eluded him in his own life. Then because I had to say something, I asked him a question that produced a strange consequence.

'What was your outfit?'

'Third Battalion, Seventh Regiment, First Marine Division,' he said, and smiled.

'Oh yeah, you guys were around Chu Lai.'

The skin of his face tightened.

'How do you know that?' he said.

'I was there,' I said, confused.

'You were in Chu Lai?' The skin around his eyes and nostrils was white.

'No, I mean I was in Vietnam. I knew some Marines who were around Chu Lai, that's all.'

'Who were these guys?'

'I don't even remember their names, Tony.'

'I just wondered.'

'Are you all right, partner?'

He widened his eyes and breathed air up through his nose.

'It was a fucking meat grinder, man,' he said.

'Maybe it's time to give it the deep six.'

'What?'

'We didn't ask to get sent over there. A time comes when we stop dragging the monsters around.'

'You saying I did something over there?'

'If you didn't, you saw it done.'

He looked at me for a long moment, his mouth a tight line.

'You're an unusual man,' he said.

'I don't think so.'

'One day just kick the door shut on Shitsville?'

'You already lived it. Why watch the replay the rest of your life?'

'Some guys say the war's never over.'

'It is for me.'

'No dreams?'

I didn't answer.

'That's what I thought,' he said. His body was deep in a leather chair. He smiled crookedly at me.

But my strange afternoon at Tony C.'s was not over. When Clete and I waked out to my truck, I noticed that my wallet was gone. I looked into the guest cottage and out by the pool, then realized that it had probably fallen out of my pocket when I was sitting in the library. The black man let me in the side of the house again. This time the sliding door of the library that gave on to the sun porch was open, and I saw Tony dressing a little boy in the wheelchair surrounded by a litter of toys. He did not see me, not at first. The little boy might have been seven or eight. His face was handsome and bright, but his head rested on his shoulders as though he had no neck, his legs were too short for his truncated body, and his back was deformed terribly. His hair was brown and wet, and Tony Cardo parted and combed it and leaned over and kissed him on the brow. Then his eyes glanced up into my face.

'I'm sorry. I dropped my wallet in the chair,' I said.

He walked to the door and slid it shut.

That night it rained. It ran off the roof, the gutters, the balconies, clattered on the palm fronds and banana trees, spun like a vortex of wet light inside the courtyard. Lightning cracked across the sky and rattled the windows, and I slept with a pillow crimped across my head. I did not hear the lock pick in the door nor the handle turn when the bolt clicked free of the jamb. Instead, I felt a drop in the room's temperature, and smelled leaves and rain. I raised up on one elbow and looked into the face of Tony Cardo, who leaned forward on a straight-backed chair by the side of my bed. One of his gatemen stood behind him, dripping water on the floor.

'How scared you ever been?' he said. His narrow, elongated face looked white in the glow of the electric light that shone through the window from the courtyard.

'What?' My hand went toward the drawer of the nightstand.

'No,' he said, took my wrist, and pushed my arm back on the bed.

'What are you—'

'How scared you ever been?' he repeated. His eyes were absolutely black and glazed with light, as though they had no pupils.

I was sitting straight up now. The front door was halfway open, and leaves and mist were blowing inside the living room.

'Listen, Tony—'

'It was after you got hit, wasn't it? When you had to lie in the dark by yourself and think about it.'

I couldn't smell alcohol on him. Then I looked again at his eyes, the lidless intensity, the heat that was like a match burning inside of black glass.

'Admit it,' he said.

'I was scared every minute I was over there. Who cares? You're speeding, Tony.'

Then I saw him raise the revolver from between his thighs.

'You know how to overcome it?' he said.

I looked at the gateman. His face was empty of expression, beaded with raindrops.

'You confront the dragon,' Tony said.

'Ease up, partner. This isn't your style.'

'What the fuck you know about my style?'

'I didn't do it to you. I don't have anything to do with your life. You're talking to the wrong guy.'

'You're the right guy. You know you're the right guy.'

'Everybody was afraid over there. It's just human. What's the matter with you?'

'You buy that? I say fuck you. You stare it in the face. Can you stare it in the face?'

His mouth looked purple in the glow from the window. His ears were like tiny white cauliflowers pressed against his scalp.

'I think you're loaded Tony. I think we're talking black beauties here. I'm not going to help you with this bullshit. Go fuck yourself.'

I could see his thin nostrils quiver as he breathed. He rested the revolver on the top of his right thigh. Then he said, 'This is how you do it, my man.'

He flipped out the cylinder from the frame and ejected six .38 cartridges into his palm. He clinked them all into his coat pocket except one. He fitted it into a chamber and snapped the cylinder back into place.

'Tony, pull the plug on this before it goes any further. It's not worth it,' I said.

He set the hammer on half cock, spun the cylinder twice, then brought the hammer all the way back with his thumb and fitted the barrel's opening under his chin. The skin of his face became as stiff and gray as cardboard, his eyes focused on a distant thought somewhere behind my ear. Then he pulled the trigger.

'Jesus Christ, Tony,' I heard the gateman say, his breath rushing out of his chest.

Tony put an unlit cigarette in his mouth, opened the cylinder again, and fitted the five rounds from his pocket back into the chambers.

'It wasn't even close, two chambers away from the firing pin,' he said. 'Don't ever let me see pity in your face when you look at me and my little boy again.'

A solitary drop of water fell out of his hair and spotted the unlit cigarette in his mouth.

7

The next morning the streets in the Quarter were thick with mist, and I could hear the foghorns of tugs and oil barges out on the river. I had coffee and *beignets* at a table inside the Café du Monde; then the sun broke out of the clouds and Jackson Square looked bright and wet and green after the night's rain. I walked over to Ray Fontenot's T-shirt shop on Bourbon and found him practicing his trombone in a small weed-grown, rubble-strewn courtyard in back. He wore a purple turtle-neck sweater, gray slacks, and shades, even though there was little sunlight in the enclosure. He was not a gelatinous man. The rings of fat across his stomach looked hard, the kind your fist would do little harm to.

My conversation with him did not go well.

'So we're agreed on everything,' he said. 'You'll bring your boat over from Morgan City, and we'll take a little tarpon-fishing trip out on the salt. By the way, what's your boat doing in Morgan City if you live in New Iberia?'

'I just had the engine overhauled.'

'That's good. And you'll have all the money?'

'That's right.'

'Because we want lots of product for all the little boys and girls. It's what keeps everybody's genitalia humming. Like little nests of bees.'

'Day after tomorrow, two A.M. at Cocodrie. Dress warm. It'll be cold out there,' I said, and started to leave.

'Thank you, kind sir. But there's one change.'

He drained the spittle out of his trombone slide on to the weeds at his feet.

'What's that?' I said.

'Your friend Purcel is not going with us.'

'He's my business partner. He's in.'

'Not on this trip.'

'Why not?'

'He hasn't quite learned how to behave. Besides, we don't need him.'

'Listen, Fontenot, if Clete gave you a bad time over Tony's phone number, that's a personal beef you work out on your own. This is business.'

'He no play-a, he no go-a.'

'What does Tony say?'

'I make the deals for Tony, I make the terms. When you talk to me, it's just like you're talking to Tony.'

'You mind if I make a call?'

'I wouldn't have it any other way, good sir.' He took off his sunglasses and smiled. His eyes were flat and dead and looked as if they belonged in another face.

I used the telephone in Fontenot's office. I could hear him blowing into his trombone.

'Hey, good morning. How you doing today?' Tony Cardo said.

'I'm fine.'

'Sure?'

'I'm just fine, Tony.'

'You don't have a hard-on about last night?'

'You've got your own point of view about things. I don't want to intrude upon it.'

'I got strong emotions. About family stuff. I get a little weird sometimes. You got to bear with me.'

'I respect your feelings, Tony.'

'You don't rattle, do you?'

'Morning and night, podna. I've got a problem here. Ray doesn't want my friend along on the tarpon trip.'

'That's too bad.'

'I think my friend should be able to go.'

'I can't interfere, Dave. It's Ray's call.'

'He's got his nose bent out of joint over a personal affront. It's not the way a pro does things.'

'Indulge the man.'

'He's a fat shit, Tony.'

'Hey, catch a big fish for me. And I want you out to dinner this weekend. Bring your buddy, too. I like him.'

He hung up the phone. Ray Fontenot stood in the doorway to the courtyard, his eyes filled with merriment, his tongue thick and pink on his teeth.

At noon I went to Clete's to pick him up for lunch. We drove in his car to a Fat Albert's off St Charles and ordered paper plates of red beans and dirty rice with lengths of sausage. It was warm enough to eat outside, and we sat at a green-painted picnic table under a live oak whose roots had lifted up the slabs of sidewalk and cracked the edge of the parking lot.

Out on St Charles I saw the old iron streetcar rattle past the palm trees on the esplanade.

I told Clete about my conversation that morning with Fontenot. He chewed quietly without speaking, his green eyes thoughtful. I waited for him to say something. He didn't.

'Anyway, he says you're out, and Cardo backed him up.'

He wiped the juice from his sausage off his mouth with a paper napkin, then sucked on the corner of his lip.

'I'd be careful,' he said.

'What are you thinking?'

'He's up to something.'

'I think he just doesn't like you. What did you do to him to get Cardo's phone number?'

'Nothing.'

'Clete?'

'I told him I wasn't leaving till I got the number. I made a little noise in front of his customers. I didn't touch him.'

'It surprises you he doesn't want to see you again?'

'What if I have another talk with him?'

'That's out. The deal has to go through.'

'I'm worried about you, mon. You're not seeing things straight. You're doing the grunt work for the DEA, they take the glory. There's something else to think about, too. How's a drug buy out on the salt going to put Cardo away?'

'I've got to get next to him with a wire.'

'Why not get a Pap smear while you're at it?' He lit a cigarette and blew smoke off into the dappled sunlight. 'We used to call the FBI "Fart, Barf, and Itch", remember? Why do you think these DEA cocksuckers are any different? If you ask me, this deal down at Cocodrie stinks.'

There was no point in arguing. I also felt that he was more disappointed in being cut out of the sting than anything else. But his eyes continued to wander over my face while he smoked.

'For God's sakes, what is it?' I said.

'I don't know if you need this right now, but a colored kid was in the bar looking for you this morning. He wouldn't give his name, but I have an idea who he is.'

'Oh?'

'That kid from New Iberia you were taking up to Angola with Jimmie Lee Boggs.'

'What did he say?'

'"Tell Mr Dave I seen Jimmie Lee yesterday on Bourbon."' Clete continued to look at my face. 'I'm right, that's the kid who got loose from you?'

'Yes.'

'You're in contact with him?'

'More or less.'

'Are you out of your mind?'

'Does he look like a dangerous and violent man to you? You think I ought to send him to the chair?'

'I think you ought to watch out for your own butt once in a while.'

'What else did he say?'

'Nothing. A weird kid. If a black ant wore a pizza uniform, that's what it'd look like. You really think he saw Boggs?'

'I don't know.'

'Why would Boggs be walking around on Bourbon?'

'I don't know, Clete.'

'Come on, don't look so disturbed. The kid's probably imaginative.' Then he pressed his lips together in a tight line. 'Listen, Dave, keep your attitudes simple about this guy. You see him, you smoke him. No warning, no talk, you just blow his fucking head off. Case closed.'

I didn't finish my plate. I rolled it up, dropped it in a trash barrel, then sat back down at the wood table under the tree. Clete kept pushing a ring around on his index finger while his eyes studied me.

'You think you lost your guts?' he said.

'No.'

'Like Boggs has got the Indian sign on you or something?'

'I'm cool. Don't worry about it.'

'You bothered because you want to do this guy?'

'No.'

'You listen to me. It's a perk when you get a chance to grease a guy like that. You take him off at the neck and the world applauds.' But he saw his words were having no effect. 'What happened in that coulee?'

'I thought my clock had run out. I don't think I behaved very well. I always thought I would do better.'

'Nobody handles it well. They cry, they call out for their mother. It's a bad moment. It's supposed to be.'

'You don't feel the same about yourself later.'

He picked at the calluses on his hands, his eyes downcast.

'My noble, grieving mon,' he said.

'Look, Clete, I appreciate—'

'You know what I think all this is about? You want to drink. Whenever I went out on the edge of the envelope, I'd mellow out with some skull-fuck *muta* and JD on the rocks. You can't drink anymore, so you walk around with this ongoing horror show inside you.'

'How about we put the cork in the five-and-dime psychology? Look, I think Cardo's heavy into crank.'

'He's a speed freak?'

'He came into my apartment in the middle of the night and snapped a revolver under his chin.'

Clete grinned, shook his head, and rolled a matchstick across his teeth.

'What's funny?' I said.

'This is the guy you're going to get next to with a wire? And you worry about Boggs or whether you still got your guts? Streak, you're a pistol.'

I talked with Minos Dautrieve that afternoon and made arrangements to have my converted jugboat moved from Morgan City to a commercial dock at Cocodrie, near Terrebonne Bay. Over the phone I sensed a fine wire of anxiety in Minos's voice.

'What is it?' I said.

'It bothers me they don't want Purcel with you.'

'He got in Fontenot's face. Clete has a way of scaring the hell out of people he doesn't like.'

'Maybe.'

'Are you worried about the half a million?'

'I'm worried about you. But some other people are having misgivings about the operation. It's a big expenditure. Cardo's not getting brought into things the way he should.'

'I can't help that.'

'They're thinking about their own butts. They don't want to get burned. But that's not your problem. The Coast Guard's going to track the mother boat and nail it after you're gone. So the government'll get its money back. I don't know why these guys are sweating. They piss me off.'

'Run Cardo's military record for me.'

'What for?'

'Something about Vietnam is eating his lunch.'

'What's new about that?'

'I think he's a complex man. You didn't tell me about his son.'

'Yeah, that's a sad case.'

'Evidently he really looks after him.'

The phone was silent a moment.

'Cardo's a drug dealer, and his hired shitheads kill people. Anything else is irrelevant. It's important to understand that, Dave.'

'I'm just saying you can't dismiss the guy as a geek.'

'Right. He hires them instead. Like Jimmie Lee Boggs. Get your head on straight. I'll be back with you later. Carry your piece out there on the salt. I want your ass back home safe on this one.'

He hung up the phone.

That night I wanted to take Bootsie out for supper, but she had to work late at her office, and when she finally finished it was after ten o'clock. So

I read a book in bed and went to sleep sometime after midnight with the light on and a pillow over my head.

The twilight is purple and the willow trees along the banks of the Mississippi are filled with fireflies when they take the black kid out of the van and walk him inside the Red Hat House in a waist chain. His hair has been shaved down to the scalp and his ears look abnormally large on the sides of his head. The wind is blowing off the river, ruffling the corn and stalks of sugarcane in the fields, but his face is dripping with sweat as though he's been locked inside an iron box. He smokes an unfiltered cigarette without being able to take it from his lips, because his hands are manacled at his sides. Before they go inside the squat, off-white concrete building, a gun-bull takes the cigarette out of the boy's mouth and flips it into a pool of rainwater, where it is suddenly extinguished.

Inside, I sit on one of the wood benches with the other witnesses – television and newspaper reporters, a medical examiner, a Negro preacher, and the parents of the girl the convict shot to death in a filling station robbery. They're Cajuns from New Iberia. They sit rigidly and without expression, their eyes never quite focusing on the boy while he is being strapped arm and leg to the electric chair. The woman keeps twisting a handkerchief in her fingers; finally her husband wipes his hand across his mouth and puts a cigarette between his lips, but he looks at the gun-bull and doesn't light it. Through the barred window the tip of the setting sun is crimson above the green line of willow trees on the river.

Then suddenly the boy begins fighting. It's the moment that no one wants, that embarrasses and shames. His terror has eaten through the Thorazine he's been fed all day, and he gets a foot loose and kicks wildly at a guard. But the guard is a professional and knows how to grab the ankle and calf and use his weight to press the leg firmly back against the oak chair and buckle the leather strap quickly across the shinbone.

The heat and humidity inside the room are almost unbearable. I can smell my own odor and the sweat in the clothes of the people around me. The mother of the murdered girl is looking at the floor now with one white knuckle pressed against her teeth. No one speaks, and I hear the boy's breath sucking in and out of his throat. His eyes are bloodshot and wide, his mouth quivering, and his neck so swollen with fear and blood that it looks as rigid as a fire hydrant. Before the cloth hood and metal skullcap go down over his head he stares straight into my face. An unanswered expectation bulges from his eyes.

I nailed him in New Orleans, busted him in a Negro hot-pillow joint off Magazine, took a .32 automatic and a straight razor off him and dropped them in a toilet bowl while a half dozen of his friends watched, threatened, and finally did nothing. Later I escorted him back to Iberia Parish for trial. For some reason he has asked me to be here in the Red Hat House. I think he is a borderline psychotic or retarded, or perhaps he has simply melted down his head with cocaine. But I'm convinced that in these last few moments he believes I can wave a wand over his circle of torment, pop the straps and buckles loose from his body, and lead him back outside into the wind, the ruffling sugarcane, the smell of distant rain.

When the voltage hits him his body leaps against the straps, stiffens, trembles violently with a life of its own, like that of a man having a seizure. A curl of smoke rises from under the facecloth. They hit him again, and we can hear the leather straining against the oak arms and legs of the chair. The smell is like the electric scorch of a streetcar, like the smell of hair burning in a barbershop trash barrel. A newsman next to me puts his handkerchief in his mouth and begins gagging.

Later I'm in a bar one mile down the road from Angola Penitentiary. The bar is in a remote and thickly wooded area, and the few people who drink in there either work at the penitentiary or in a piney-woods sawmill nearby. It's a joyless place where personal and economic failure and institutional cruelty are not made embarrassing by comparisons with the outside world. The light in the bar is hard and yellow, the wood floor scorched with cigarette and cigar burns.

Dry lightning leaps outside the window and turns the oak trees white. I order a schooner of Jax and a shot of Jim Beam. I lower the jigger into the schooner, release it, and watch it slide down the side of the glass to the bottom. The sour mash rises in a cloud and turns the beer from gold to amber, and I cup the schooner with my fingers and drink it empty with one long swallow.

'You were up at the Red Hat tonight?' the bartender asks. He's a barrel-chested man, with gray hair curling over his shirt lapels. A blue chain is tattooed around his thick neck.

'Yes.'

'What's a guy think in those last few seconds?'

'He begs.'

'I wouldn't do that. Would you?'

I don't answer.

'Would you?' he says again.

I tell him to hit me again. He refills my schooner and pours another shot of Beam on the side.

I empty the jigger into the beer and raise the schooner to my mouth. In the bar mirror the cloud of whiskey floating in beer is the color of blood that has dried in the sun, that has been burned with an electric arc. I can feel the glass begin to boil in my hands. Lightning explodes in the shell parking lot outside, illuminating the battered cars and pickup trucks and racist bumper stickers. The air is filled with a wet sulfurous smell; my ears ring with a sound that is like a scream muffled under a black cloth.

It was two in the morning when I awoke from the dream and sat listlessly on the side of the bed. What did the dream mean? Was it simply a replay of the electrocution that I had in fact witnessed when I was a newly promoted detective with the New Orleans Police Department? Old-timers at AA would probably say it had to do with fear, which they believe is the cause of all the problems of alcoholics. Fear of mortality, fear that we'll drink again, fear of the self's dark potential. And for an alcoholic, *fear* is the acronym for Fuck Everything And Run. Clete had had his hand on it. I had loved bars and bust-head whiskey with the adoration and simple trust of a man kneeling before a votive shrine. That kind of emotional faith and addiction dies no less easily than one's religion.

The phone rang at one the next afternoon. It was Kim Dollinger.

'I want to talk to you,' she said.

'Go ahead.'

'No, come down to your buddy's place. I'll buy you a drink.'

'What is it you want to tell me?'

'What's the matter, your social calendar all full?'

'No, I just—'

'Then come on over, hotshot.'

'I'm not up to nicknames today. My name is Dave. To tell you the truth, Kim, you sound like you got started a little early today.'

'Then buy me a cup of coffee. You have that paternal quality. Are you coming or not?'

Ten minutes later I was at Clete's Club. Clete and his black helper were filling the beer coolers, and she was at the far end of the bar. She wore black stockings, a denim skirt, and a sleeveless orange sweater, and she had had her hair cut so that it was short and thick on her pale neck.

'I want to tell you something before you leave,' Clete said to me as I passed him.

'What is it?'

'Later, noble mon.'

I sat on the stool next to Kim. She had a gin gimlet wrapped in a napkin in front of her.

'You want one?' she asked.

'No, thanks.'

'You don't go to a whorehouse to play the jukebox, do you?'

'I joined the Dr Pepper crowd a few years ago.'

'Too much. You want to be in the candy business, but you don't touch the juice?'

'How about holding it down?'

'You sure you're not just a big put-on?'

'What do you mean?'

'I think somebody shook up your puzzle box, that's what I mean.'

'How about I buy you some gumbo?'

'I think you're weird. Do people in the bayou country grow up weird and think they can make big money in the city dealing with somebody like Ray Fontenot? Are you that dumb?'

'What is it you want to tell me, Kim?'

'I don't know what I want to tell you.' She looked away into space. The green and purple neon tubing on the bar mirror glowed on her face. 'You don't listen to people. Back there where you come from, don't you have something better going than this stuff in New Orleans? You want to risk it for a score with a bunch of dipshits who wouldn't take a leak on you if you were burning?'

'Why all this concern for me?'

'Because you didn't try to put moves on me. Because there're things about you that are nice. Also, because I think you're a fish.'

'I look like a fish?'

'I *know* you're a fish, hon.'

She finished her gimlet and signaled the black barman for another. He took her glass away and filled a fresh one from the blender. The color in her green eyes deepened when she sipped from the glass.

'Is there something I should know, Kim?' I asked.

'You're a big boy. Make up your own mind. Look at the flamingos.'

'What?'

'Painted on the edge of the mirror. The pink flamingos. When I was a little girl we lived in Miami. My father was the guy who took care of the flamingos at the Hialeah racetrack. Before the seventh race he'd chase them with a broom in the center ground and make them fly high above the stands. That was his job. He thought it was a real important job.'

She drank again from her glass and closed and opened her eyes slowly. Her mouth was bright red.

'I see,' I said.

'One morning he took me to work with him and told me to sit on this wood bench by the finish line while he picked up paper from the track with a stick that had a nail in it. But I wandered out in the center ground and started feeding the flamingos. There was a bucket of ground-up shrimp by the lake, and I was throwing handfuls of it at these big, beautiful pink birds. I didn't see or hear him come up behind me. My hair was long then, and he twisted it in his hand and jerked it against my scalp like you'd snap a rope. He pulled me back to the bench and told me if I cried any more I'd get it again when I got home.

'Then this horse trainer walked up and shook his finger at my father and said, "Don't hurt that little girl, Bill. She didn't mean no harm." He picked me up in his arms like my father wasn't there and carried me to his car. "She don't belong out here. I'm going to take her to the zoo. You go on about your work," he said. "I'll bring her back to your trailer later. Don't be giving me any trouble about it, either, Bill."

'He drove me down to Crandon Park to see the flamingos. He said my father wouldn't hurt me anymore, not as long as he was around. Then he bought me some ice cream and parked the car in some palmettos and sat me in his lap. Then he unbuttoned my blouse. I've always thought of it as my morning for flamingos.'

'That's a bad story, Kim.'

'You learn early or you learn late. What difference does it make?'

'Are you really that hard?'

'No, I just like hanging around people like Ray and Lionel and the raghead for kicks. You'll see. It's a great life.'

She finished her drink, went to the women's room, and came back. I could smell mints on her breath. The Negro barman started to pour her another gimlet from the blender but she shook her head negatively. Somebody had put an old recording of 'Please Don't Leave Me' by Fats Domino on the jukebox.

'Dance with me,' she said.

It was dark and the vinyl booths were empty at the back of the dance floor. She felt light and small in my arms, and her head rested against my chest. I felt her hair touch my cheek.

'Look, Kim, let me buy you some gumbo at the Golden Star,' I said.

She didn't answer. I could feel her stomach and breasts against me, and I was becoming increasingly uncomfortable.

'Hey,' I said, and looked at her and smiled. 'I'm an over-the-hill guy who doesn't deserve the kindness of a pretty young woman.'

'Tony lets me use his beach house in Biloxi. Come with me there today.'

'It sounds like a good way to end up in an oil barrel.'

'He won't hurt you. He likes you. I don't think Tony's going to be around much longer, anyway.'

'Why not?'

'People in Miami and Houston want him out of the way. He keeps breaking all their rules. Sometimes I feel sorry for him. Will you come with me?'

'I'm involved, Kim. You're sure a big temptation, though.'

Her feet stopped moving and her hand rested on my arm. She looked out at the light from the opened front door. A lock of her hair hung down on one eyebrow. Her face had the same wan expression on it that I had seen when she had been staring out at Tony Cardo's empty tennis court. Then she touched my throat with her fingers.'

'So long, hotcakes. Don't think too bad of me,' she said.

She left me on the dance floor, picked up her purse from the bar, and walked through the brilliant square of light at the front on to Decatur Street. Clete parted the window blinds with his fingers and squinted out on to the street.

'Yep, there he goes,' he said.

'Who?'

'Nate Baxter, my man.'

'Nate Baxter?'

'Yeah, I didn't think you'd forget him. The one genuine sonofabitch from the First District. I saw him watching her from under the colonnade across the street when she came in. A car just picked him up when she left.'

'Why's a guy from Internal Affairs interested in Kim Dollinger?'

'He's not in Internal Affairs anymore. He's Vice. The perfect guy for it, too. A prick from the crown of his head to the soles of his feet. What's going on, Dave?'

'I don't know.'

'Some sting. Half the city of New Orleans seems to be in on it. Listen, get out of that gig at Cocodrie. I've got a real bad feeling on this one.'

'Those are the ones you skate through. You buy it when you've got your pot off and you're reading a newspaper. You know that.' I winked at him.

'Save the Little Orphan Annie routine for somebody else, Streak. When my ovaries start tingling, I listen to them. Anytime you see that buttwipe Baxter, it's bad news. You can count on it.'

Back at the apartment I called the commercial dock at Cocodrie to check on my jugboat, then called Minos at his office to confirm the pickup of the half million.

'Our special-delivery man will be there with your bus locker key in about two hours,' he said. 'Did you know a half-million dollars in hundred-dollar bills weighs exactly eleven pounds?'

'No, I didn't know that.'

'Don't drop it overboard. As I mentioned before, some of my colleagues are a little anxious about this one.'

'I'm tired of hearing about your colleagues' problems.'

'Your voice sounds funny.'

'I've been doing push-ups. I'm still out of breath.'

'Yeah?'

'Sure. I'm all right.'

'When I was undercover I'd wake up with my heart racing. I'd smoke a pack of cigarettes before noon sometimes.'

'My ears keep popping, like I've been on an airplane.'

'Dave, you can throw it in anytime you want, and nobody will think less of you for it.'

'I'm copacetic. Don't sweat it.'

'Remember, we're never going to be too far away.'

Then I told him about Nate Baxter's surveillance of Kim Dollinger.

'They're interested in Cardo, too,' he said. 'They're probably keeping some strings on his entourage.'

'Why her? She's no dealer.'

'I'll check. They're supposed to coordinate with us, anyway. Have you got some kind of personal involvement with this guy Baxter?'

'He tried to get me fired from the department when he was in Internal Affairs.'

'So?'

'It didn't end there. I split his lip in the squad room, in front of about twenty-five cops.'

'Dave, you never disappoint me,' he said.

I rode the streetcar down St Charles to Bootsie's house that evening, and the wind through the open window was cool and smelled of old brick, wet moss, and moldy pecan husks. But I couldn't concentrate on anything except my anxieties about the buy out on the salt and my questions, which I could not successfully bury, about Bootsie's involvement with the mob. How did an intelligent and educated woman from a small Bayou Teche town like New Iberia marry a member of the Giacano family? I tried to imagine what he must have looked like. Most of the Giacanos were built like piano movers, notorious for their animal energies, their enormous appetites and bovine behavior in restaurants, their emotional-ism and violence. Their weddings and funerals were covered by local television stations with the same sense of mirth and expectation that people might have when visiting an amusement park.

The image just wouldn't fit.

But the image of her first husband sure did. He was a helicopter and pontoon plane pilot for Sinclair Oil Company, and I remembered him most for his suntanned, blond good looks and the confident, unblinking light in his blue eyes. In fact, I could never quite forget the night I met him, at a dance at the Frederic Hotel in New Iberia, right after I had been released from an army hospital. I was on a cane then. It was 1965, when the war was just heating up for other people, and it felt funny to go to a dance by myself and to discover that I was alone in more ways than one, that I was already used up and discarded by a war that waited in a vague piece of neocolonial geography for other boys whose French names could have belonged to Legionnaires.

Then through the potted palm fronds and marble columns, I saw her in a pink organdy dress, dancing with him in her stocking feet. Her face was flushed from the champagne punch, and strands of her hair stuck damply to her skin like wisps of honey. They walked toward the punch table, where I was standing, and I saw her gaze focusing on me as though I had stepped unexpectedly off a bus into the middle of her life. Then I realized she was drunk.

She started blowing air up into her face to get her hair out of her eyes.

'Well!' she said.

'Hello, Boots,' I said.

'Well!' she repeated, and blew a web of hair out of her eyes again. 'John, this is Dave Robicheaux. It looks like Dave has come back to visit New Iberia. What a wonderful event. Maybe he can come to our wedding.'

He smiled with his white teeth when he shook hands. His eyes went back and forth between us, and I could see the recognition grow in them.

'It's nice to meet you, Dave. The wedding is Saturday at St Peter's,' he said. 'Please come if you feel like it.'

'Thank you,' I said. And I cleared my throat so they wouldn't see me swallow.

Bootsie blew more gusts of air up into her face and her eyes became brighter, as though a generator were gaining momentum inside her.

'I could have told you I was pregnant. That would have blown your mind, wouldn't it?' she said.

'What?' I felt my mouth hang open, because in New Iberia at that time it was unthinkable to talk like that in a public place.

'But that would have seriously screwed you up,' she said. 'You would have ended up a family guy with kiddies and you couldn't go off to war, then come home and stand around on a cane like an F. Scott Fitzgerald character. The pose is perfect, Dave. You look so absolutely sad and wounded. We wouldn't rob you of it for anything.'

'I think you're being pretty rotten,' I said.

'Hold on, now,' her fiancé said.

'No, rotten is when you put it in without a rubber because you're really promising that person you're going to marry her, then you leave her like she's yesterday's backseat hand job.'

The band had stopped playing, and her words carried out to the edge of the dance floor. People stared at us with their smiles suddenly frozen on their faces. Bootsie's eyes were watery and shining, and there were beads of perspiration on her upper lip. In the silence I could feel the skin of my face tighten and flex against the bone.

When I woke in the morning a note folded inside an envelope was stuck in my screen door. It read:

I'm sick and trembling with a hangover this morning, and I guess I deserve it. I'm sorry for what I said to you last night. I shouldn't apologize to you, but I do anyway. But tell me this, Dave, please please please tell me this, why did you push me away, why did you destroy it for both of us, why did you ruin everything we'd shared together that summer, tell me in the name of suffering God why you did it, Dave.

Love,
Bootsie

P.S. On second thought it's probably better that you don't answer this note. I'm going to be married to John, and the past is past, right? If I say that enough it'll finally be true. I hope you have a good life. I really mean that even though I think you were a bastard.

But as she said, the past was the past, and after we had dinner, we washed the dishes, put them away, and went upstairs to her bedroom. It was misting outside, and the sky was a soft gray, the sun a low red ball on the western horizon. The long strips of pink cloud above the trees reminded me of flamingo wings.

I took off my shirt, then sat on the side of the bed to remove my shoes. She sat next to me in only her bra and a half-slip and put her hand on my back.

'Your skin's hot,' she said.

'It happens when I'm with a certain lady,' I said, and tried to smile.

'No, your muscles are tight as iron. What is it, Dave?'

'I just have a couple of things on my mind right now.'

'There's a big buy going down, isn't there?'

'Why do you think that?'

'I always know. I hear people talking on the phone, a lot of money gets transferred around. Dave, are you still a cop?'

'No questions tonight, Boots.'

'They'll catch on to you eventually. What you don't understand is that the narcs who get inside the organization are like them. You're not. It's a matter of time before they'll see that.'

'Let's not talk about it anymore.'

'All right, if that's what you want. But at some point you'll have to confide in me. If not now, later. You know that, Dave.'

I touched her lips with my fingers.

'It's going to rain,' I said. 'Remember when we used to go to my father's boathouse in the rain?'

She laid her cheek against my bare shoulder and rested her hand lightly on my arm. I finished undressing, and she pulled her slip up over her thighs and sat on top of me. I felt myself go deeply inside her, felt her heat and wetness spread across my loins. Her face became round and pale in concentration. She made love with the confidence and knowledge of an older woman, and when she came she pressed my palm hard against her breast as though she were forcing me to share the whirrings of her heart.

It was dark outside, and the rain was slanting against the French windows. An oak tree raked wetly against the side of the house. She lay inside my arm, with her hand on my stomach, and I could smell the rose-scented shampoo in her hair and taste the thin film of perspiration on her forehead.

Then, as though determined to pass on all my anxieties and fears to someone else, as though I had to hurt her again as I had many years before, I asked her the question that had bothered me since I'd first gone to her house on Camp Street.

'Why don't you get out from under them?'

'I told you why.'

'You said you didn't know your husband was in the mob when you married him. I never knew one of them who wasn't obvious, Boots.'

'I wasn't very careful, I guess.'

'Bootsie, you *had* to know.'

'He was good-looking and well-mannered. He said he had a degree from Tulane. He smiled all the time. He was fun to be around, Dave.'

'All those game-room machines you distribute are made by a Mafia front in Chicago. You're into it big-time, old pal.'

Her hand left my stomach, and she sat up on the side of the bed and looked out at the wet treetops. Then she walked barefoot in her bra and half-slip to a cabinet above a small desk, her hips creasing softly. I could see the dark outline of her sex through her slip.

'I'm going to have a glass of cream sherry,' she said. 'You don't mind, do you? It helps me to sleep sometimes. I always have trouble sleeping when it thunders. It's a silly way to be.'

She kept her face turned toward the French windows, but I could see the wet shine on her cheeks.

8

It was black and raining hard when I guided the jugboat from the dock down the canal toward open water. The boat was built to float high up in the water, but the tide was out, the canal was shallow, and yellow mud and tangles of dead hyacinths boiled up under the propeller. The long expanses of saw grass on each side of us were bent in the rain.

Ray Fontenot and Lionel Comeaux both wore yellow raincoats with hoods and sat hunched forward in their chairs by my small butane stove, which held a pot of coffee. The weather had turned cold, and their faces were morose and irritable. When we hit open water I pushed the throttle forward and felt the engine surge and the bow lift into the waves. The coastline became gray and indistinct and then dropped behind us altogether. In the distance I could see a gas flare burning on an offshore oil well.

'Turn off your running lights,' Lionel said.

'There's a fogbank up there.'

'I don't care. Turn off your lights.'

'Look, if you're worried about the Coast Guard, it monitors the traffic by radar. You don't become invisible by turning off your lights.'

He got up from his chair, walked to my instrument board, and clicked off the two toggle switches that controlled the red and green running lights on the stern and bow. I pulled the throttle back to idle and cut the ignition. Suddenly it was quiet except for the rain against the roof and the glass. The jugboat pitched in one trough and then slid over the top of a black wave into another; the coffeepot crashed on the floor.

'These are the rules, partner. There's one skipper on a boat,' I said. 'You're looking at him. If that doesn't sit right with you, we'll turn it around here.'

'We've made this run a dozen times. You don't advertise,' Lionel said.

'What's the matter with you?' I said. 'The best way to attract attention is to do something stupid like run without lights.'

'It's your first time out. I'm trying to be helpful.'

'What's it going to be, Fontenot?'

112

'Much ado about nothing,' he said from his chair. 'Let him have his lights, Lionel.'

I hit the starter and pushed the throttle open again. We hit a cresting wave in a shower of foam and then flattened out in a long trough. The water was black and rolling and hammered with raindrops. Then the fogbank slipped over the bow and the pilothouse, as cold and damp on the skin as a gray, wet glove.

'What's Tony going to get out of the score?' I asked Ray Fontenot.

'What do you mean?'

'It's my buy, my stash. What's the profit for him?'

'He gets a cut from the Colombians. The action gets pieced off all the way back to Bogotá.'

'Where's your piece come in?'

'We're doing it as a favor.'

'No kidding?' I said.

'We like you.' He smiled from under his yellow rain hood.

Lionel rubbed the moisture off the window glass with his palm.

'There it is,' he said.

A shrimp boat with its wheelhouse lighted rose in the swell, then slipped down below a long, sliding wave.

'How do we make the exchange?' I said.

'I'll take the money on board and come back with the stash,' Lionel said.

'They're shy?' I said.

'You don't want to meet them,' Fontenot said. 'They're not a nice group, our garlic-scented friends. They seem to like Lionel, though. The colored woman who cooks for them likes him very much. Lionel had a big change of luck at the track after he met her.'

'You ought to get laid more, Ray. You wouldn't have all these cute things to say,' Lionel said.

I saw the shrimp boat drift to the top of the swell again. Its white paint was peeling, its scuppers dripping with rust. Lionel had taken off his raincoat and was putting on a life jacket.

'You should appreciate Lionel's efforts on your behalf,' Fontenot said.

'Forget the appreciation. Just put it hard against the tires and keep it there till I'm on the ladder,' Lionel said.

He laced the life jacket under his chin, then slipped a rope through the aluminum suitcase that contained the money and tied it crossways on his chest.

'I go between the hulls and you're out a half mil,' he said.

'We can make the exchange without you getting on their boat,' I said. 'There's a thirty-foot coil of rope in that forward gear box. Tie it on to the suitcase, throw the other end on the shrimper, and we'll get the stash back the same way.'

'I gotta check it.'

'We'll check it when it's on board.'

'You don't inspect the goods after the fact when you deal with spics,' he said.

'Let's not have discord on the Melody Ranch, boys and girls,' Fontenot said. 'Lionel's an old pro at this, Mr Robicheaux. He's not going to drop your money.'

'I'm going in on the swell,' I said. 'Get ready.'

Two deckhands came out of the wheelhouse and stood by the gunwales in the rain and wind. They were unshaved, and their black hair and beards dripped with water. I came in on the lee side of the shrimper, gunning the engine in the trough, and bumped against the row of tires that were hung along the hull. Lionel grabbed the rope ladder, pushed himself with one foot off the handrail of the jugboat, and scampered on board the shrimper, the aluminum suitcase banging across the gunwale with him.

'What are you going to do with all your money, Mr Robicheaux?' Fontenot said. He had a lit cigarette cupped on his knee, and he was looking out indifferently at the glaze of light from the shrimp boat on the water.

'Why is it I get the feeling you're not interested in the questions you ask other people?' I said.

'Oh, forgive me, good sir, if I ever convey that impression. That would be a terrible sense to give someone, wouldn't it?'

'I'm going back through Atchafalaya Bay, not to Cocodrie. I can put you guys ashore at several places. You tell me where.'

'Not to Cocodrie? But our car is there,' he said. And he said it in a whimsical manner, his eyes still fascinated with the patches of yellow light on the waves.

'I think it's smart to off-load in a different spot. I told Tony I've got the access he needs, a couple of bayous nobody uses except in a pirogue.'

'I'm sure he'll be intrigued.'

I looked at the side of his face in the glow of the instrument lights. Then I saw the color in his eyes brighten and the corner of his mouth twitch in a grin when he realized that I was staring at him.

'Excuse me if I don't bubble up at the perfection of it all,' he said. 'I'm afraid it's my fate to simply be an old mule. But Tony will love a tour through the bayous. You two can talk about "nape."'

I continued to stare at him.

'What are you wondering, kind sir?' he said.

'Why he keeps you guys around.'

'We don't measure up, do we? Listen, you lovely boy, we take the risks but Tony gets the big end of the candy cane. Some might think he's done very well by us. Would you like to jump between boats like Lionel just did? I don't think Tony would.'

'My impression is the guy can handle the action.'

'Oh, you must tell him that. He loves that kind of big-dick talk.'

'I don't know what's bugging you, Fontenot, but I think this is our last run together,' I said.

'You can never tell,' he said, and grinned again and puffed on his cigarette in the luminescence of the instrument panel.

Ten minutes passed, and I kept the jugboat steady in the trough so it wouldn't slam up against the hull of the shrimper. Through the rain I could see the silhouettes of several people in the wheelhouse. Then I saw Lionel talking, but his face was turned toward the front glass, not toward the people around him. I squinted hard through the rain.

'He's talking on the shortwave,' I said.

'Who?'

'Lionel. What's going on, Fontenot?'

'Nothing.'

'Don't tell me that. Why's the man on the radio?'

'I don't know. You think he's calling the Coast Guard? Use your judgment, sir.'

'Fontenot, if you guys—'

'I'm not up to any more words of assurance tonight, Mr Robicheaux. I don't believe you belong in our business, to tell you the truth. It isn't the Rotary Club. It isn't made up of nice people. I've grown a bit weary of you wrinkling your nose at us.'

The two deckhands carried two wooden crates out of the forward hatch and set them inside a cargo net that was slung from a boom. Lionel stepped out of the wheelhouse and waved for me to bring the jugboat alongside again. I waited until the shrimper dipped into the trough, then bumped up against the row of tires. When both boats rose with the swell, Lionel sprang from the shrimper on to my deck. His jeans and denim shirt and canvas life preserver were dark with rain.

One of the deckhands operated the motor on the boom and swung the cargo net out over the jugboat, letting the net collapse in a tangle, with the two crates inside, on the deck. Lionel pulled the crates free, and I put the engine in reverse and backed away from the side of the shrimper. The empty cargo net swung out in open space and cut through the tops of the waves.

I shifted the engine forward again and turned the bow toward the southern horizon.

'I'm going to help him stow it,' I said. 'Hold the wheel and keep it pointed into the waves. The throttle's set, so you don't need to touch it.'

'Really, now?' Fontenot said.

Outside, the rain was cold and stung my face and hands, and the waves broke hard on the bow and blew back across the deck in a salty spray. I unlocked the forward gear box and lifted one of the wooden crates inside. It was heavy, and the sides were stamped with the name of a South American cannery. Lionel swung the second crate up on the edge of the gear box.

'What were you doing on the radio?' I said.

'What?' He wore long underwear buttoned at the throat under his denim shirt, but he was shivering with the cold.

'You heard me.'

'I wasn't on the radio.'

'You had the mike in your hand, partner.'

He wiped the water out of his eyes, then focused on my face again.

'Maybe I got a weather report. Maybe I moved it to pick up my coffee cup. Maybe you need glasses.' He dropped the crate on top of the first one. 'It doesn't matter. Tony C. cut you in as a favor. If you want to know, the weight and quality are right. You got a sweet deal, man. I don't think you deserve it.'

He flipped the top of the gear box shut and walked away toward the pilothouse, balancing himself against the roll of the deck.

It had stopped raining, but the fog was thick and white on the water and I could hardly see the bow of the jugboat.

'This stuff will probably start to lift with first light,' I said. 'When we come out of it, I'm going to turn northwest for Atchafalaya Bay. Where do you guys want to go ashore?'

Lionel was looking out into the fog through the front glass. His eyes were narrowed and red-rimmed with fatigue.

'Where do y'all want me to put you off?' I repeated.

We passed a shut-down oil platform. The waves were black and streaked with oil as they slid through the steel pilings.

Still neither Lionel nor Fontenot answered me. Then I heard a boat engine out in the fog before I saw its running lights. Fontenot looked up from his cup of coffee. I turned to port, away from the sound of the engine, just as the hull of a thirty-foot white cabin cruiser came out of the fogbank. I could see the silhouette of a solitary figure at the wheel. I turned to look again at Lionel and Fontenot, as though all the frames in a strip of film negatives had suddenly made sense, and I guess my right hand was already moving toward the .25-caliber Beretta strapped to my ankle, but it was too late. Lionel had taken a nine-millimeter automatic from the canvas carry-on bag at his foot, and he placed the iron sight hard behind my ear. His free hand went down my right leg and pulled the Beretta from its holster.

'Cut the engine,' he said.

I didn't move.

'It's not a time for thought,' he said.

I heard his thumb cock the hammer. I turned off the ignition switch, and we drifted sideways with the waves and dipped down breathlessly into a trough.

'Oops,' Fontenot said, and his mouth made an O inside the yellow hood of his raincoat.

'Go forward and throw out the anchor, Ray,' Lionel said. 'We'll swing tight against the rope, and he can come around and tie on the stern.'

'I think we're doing it the hard way,' Fontenot said.

'It's the way he wants it. I ain't arguing with him.'

'The tropics beckon, Lionel. We don't want to waste time out here.'

'Tell him that. The guy's got a hard-on about our man here. It's like talking to a vacant lot.'

Fontenot got up from his chair and made his way along the deck, holding on to the rail. His yellow raincoat glistened in the turning fog. I heard the clank of the chain and the X-shaped welded pieces of railroad track that I used for an anchor as he pitched them off the bow. The jugboat swung with the incoming tide toward the coast and straightened against the anchor rope. The cabin cruiser idled past us, then turned in a circle and came up astern. It was a Larson, built for speed and comfort, its paint as white and flawless as enamel.

'I want you to know something before all this goes down,' Lionel said.

I started to turn my head towards him. He nudged the automatic against my ear.

'No, keep your eyes straight ahead,' he said. 'I want you to know it's not personal. I don't like ex-cops, I don't think they should have ever let you in on a buy, but that's got nothing to do with this. We've been somebody's fuck for too long, it's time we got what's ours. You just came along at a real bad time.'

I heard the engine of the cabin cruiser die; then somebody threw a knotted rope from the bow on to the roof of the jugboat's pilothouse.

'That other thing,' he said, 'that other thing I didn't have anything to do with.'

From the direction of his voice I could tell that he was now looking toward the stern.

'What other thing?' I said.

Then his voice came back toward the side of my face: 'Are you kidding, man? You were taking the guy up to Angola to fry. What do you think a guy like that feels about you? I'm sorry for you, man, but I got nothing to do with it.'

I didn't care about the pistol behind my ear now. I turned woodenly in the pilot's seat and looked up at the bobbing, moored bow of the cabin cruiser. As Tee Beau had said, Jimmie Lee Boggs had cut his hair short and dyed it black, but every other detail about him was as though he had walked out of a familiar dream: the mannequinlike head, the pallid skin, the lips that looked like they were rouged, the spearmint-green eyes with a strange light in them.

He wore rubber-soled canvas shoes, dungarees, a heavy blue wool shirt with wide gray suspenders, and when he stepped from the cabin cruiser on to the back rail of the jugboat and grabbed Ray Fontenot's hand, his forearm corded with muscle and his stomach looked as flat and hard as boiler plate.

He put one hand on the edge of the pilothouse's roof and leaned over me. Salt spray dripped from his face, and I could smell snuff on his breath.

'Been thinking of me?' he asked.

'I thought maybe you couldn't find us,' Fontenot said. 'It's thick out there.'

'Lionel told me on the radio y'all would be coming past an oil platform,' Boggs said. 'I just lay south of the rig and listened for your engine. This thing sounds like a garbage truck.'

Then Boggs looked down at me again. I still sat in the pilot's seat. His wrists looked as thick as sticks of firewood.

'This guy give you any trouble?' he said.

'Not really,' Fontenot said. He had removed his raincoat and was putting on a life jacket.

'You guys get the stuff on board. I'll take care of it here,' Boggs said. He took the nine-millimeter from Lionel's hand.

Fontenot cleared his throat. 'We wonder if you . . . if we really need to do that, Jimmie Lee,' he said.

'You got a problem with it?' Boggs said.

'The man isn't likely to call the law,' Fontenot said.

'You got that right,' Boggs said.

'I don't see the percentage,' Fontenot said. 'Right now we're simply transferring some product. Why complicate it?'

'I ain't telling you what to think, Jimmie Lee,' Lionel said, 'but the guy's not going to do anything. He's a fired cop, a drunk. He tries to make any trouble later, you can have him hit for five hundred bucks.'

'I don't pay to clip a guy. Besides, you did a guy with a piano wire, Lionel. Why you giving me this bullshit?'

'I got out of it, too. I don't want to go that route anymore,' Lionel said. 'Look, he's an amateur. You let the amateurs slide, Jimmie Lee. You whack out an amateur, their families make a lot of trouble.'

Lionel blew out his breath. The fog was white and so thick you could lose your hand in it as it rolled off the water and across the deck.

'I don't want to have to lose my piece. I just bought it,' he said.

'Get the coke on board and bring me the shotgun. It's clipped under the forward hatch,' Boggs said.

'You guys got to deal with Tony,' I said to Lionel and Fontenot.

'Good try, prick, but Tony's history. He just don't know it yet,' Boggs said.

'Sorry, Mr Robicheaux,' Fontenot said. Then he looked at Lionel and said, 'See no evil.'

The two of them started up the deck toward the forward gear box, where the two crates of cocaine were stowed. I was sweating heavily inside my clothes, and my breath was coming irregularly in my chest. The jugboat dipped in the ground swell, and the barrel of the automatic touched the side of my head like a kiss.

'I'll say it once, and you guys can believe it or not,' I said. The front glass of the pilothouse was pushed ajar, and they could hear me out on the deck. 'I'm still a cop. I'm undercover for the DEA. We're on Coast Guard radar right now.'

I saw Lionel and Fontenot stop and turn around. The fog drifted across their bodies like strips of torn cotton. They started back toward the pilothouse.

'It's all a sting,' I said. 'Minos Dautrieve's been running it from the start. You know who Minos Dautrieve is, right?'

Boggs's fingers laced in my hair; then he slammed my head forward on the instrument panel. I felt the skin split above my right eye, and the blood and the salt water leaked down across my eyelid.

'Hold on, listen to him,' Fontenot said.

'You guys rattle too easy,' Boggs said.

'Dautrieve's a narc out of Lafayette,' Lionel said.

'So he knows that,' Boggs said.

'Clete Purcel is DEA undercover, too,' I said. 'You clip me, he'll even the score. Ask anybody in New Orleans. Check out what he did to Julio Segura.'

Boggs held the automatic by the barrel and raked it across my mouth as though he were wielding a hammer. My bottom lip burst against my teeth, and a socket of pain raced deep into my throat and up into my nose. I leaned forward on the wheel with my mouth open, as though my jaws had become unhinged, while a long string of blood and saliva dripped between my legs.

'This deal's going sour,' Lionel said.

'There's nothing wrong with the deal. Stop acting like a cunt,' Boggs said.

'I ain't going back to Angola,' Lionel said. 'I ain't going down for snuffing a cop, either.'

'This guy's shark food. Count on it. He don't have to be the only one to go over the gunwale, either. You getting my drift?' Boggs said.

'You got nothing to lose, Jimmie Lee. We do,' Lionel said.

'You got a lot to lose, man. It's important you understand that,' Boggs said. He had shifted the barrel of the automatic so that it now hovered between me and Lionel.

'We just wanted to hear a little more of what Mr Robicheaux had to say,' Fontenot said.

'I'll show you what he's going to say,' Boggs said, and he knotted my shirt in his fist at the back of my neck, pulled me erect, and pushed the barrel of the automatic hard into my spine. 'He's gonna say "please," and he's gonna say, "I'll pay you money," and he's gonna say, "Mr Boggs, I'll do anything you want if you don't hurt me." '

He pushed me ahead of him on the deck, his clenched hand trembling with energy, then stomped on my leg just above the calf, as though he were breaking a slat, and knocked me to my knees. He let the automatic swing loosely over the back of my neck. In the reflection of the running lights the blood from my mouth looked purple on the backs of my hands. My ears were filled with sound: the waves bursting against the bow and hissing back along the hull, Jimmie Lee Boggs's heated breathing, a buoy clanging somewhere beyond the oil platform, a thick, obscene noise like wet cellophane crackling when I tried to swallow.

'Lionel, you got two minutes to load the stash and come back with my shotgun,' Boggs said. 'Don't fuck up my morning.'

'We'll transfer the goods. There's no problem, Jimmie Lee,' Fontenot said.

'I didn't think there was,' Boggs said.

Out of the corner of my vision I could see Fontenot and Lionel carrying the crates back to Boggs's boat. Their rubber-soled shoes squeaked on the deck.

'I'll hand it up to you,' I heard Fontenot say.

'Why don't you take swimming lessons, go to the Y?' Lionel said.

'You know why I like a shotgun?' Boggs asked me. His dungarees were bell-bottomed and dark with water above his white socks.

'No hands, no face,' he said. 'Think of a broken cherry pie.'

The jugboat dropped off the edge of a big wave and slapped hard against the water. Then I heard someone behind me.

'Here it is,' Lionel said.

'Thank you, my man,' Boggs said.

'What do you want to do with his boat?' Lionel said.

'I'll open the cocks and down she goes.'

'Hurry all this up, it's gonna be light.'

'Just get the fat man on board and let me worry about the rest of it.'

Lionel walked away toward the stern, and I saw Boggs's feet and legs move in front of me. I heard him rack a shell into the chamber of a shotgun.

'Would you look up here so I could have your attention a minute?' he said.

I raised my head slowly, my eyes traveling over his thighs, which were tensed against the roll of the deck, his flat stomach under his gray suspenders, his sawed-off pump shotgun with a stock that had been wood-rasped into a pistol grip, his red mouth crimped in expectation, as though he had just sucked on a salted lime. My split eye throbbed, blood and saliva ran off my lip, my pulse roared in my ears.

'Boggs . . . ,' I said.

He didn't answer.

'Boggs . . .'

I opened my mouth to let it drain. I spit on myself.

'Boggs . . .'

'What?' he said.

'You'd fuck up a wet dream. Shoot and be done with it.'

I saw his eyes narrow. They were liquid and rheumy, like a lizard's, the whites flecked almost entirely red with broken blood veins. His right hand, wrapped around the trigger guard, was white and ridged with bone. The edges of his eyes trembled with anger. His tongue tasted his lip, and he looked like a man whose sexual satisfaction was about to be denied him.

'We gotta go, Jimmie Lee,' Lionel said from the stern.

But Boggs's attention had shifted. He stared out into the fog, the shotgun at port arms, his dyed, threadlike hair wet and stuck against his scalp like a duck's feathers. Then I saw and heard it, too: the glow of running lights in the fog, the drone of a big engine, of boat screws that cut a deep trough in the water.

Suddenly no one was interested in me. I raised up slowly from all fours and sat back on my heels. Lionel had been trying to push Fontenot's huge weight up on to the bow of the cabin cruiser, but they were both frozen now on the stern of the jugboat. Fontenot's neck looked like a turtle's inside his life jacket.

The electric arc of a searchlight burst through the fog. It was hot and white and blinding to the eyes, and now the jugboat and the green, white-capping waves had the strange luminescence of objects lighted by a pistol flare.

A man's voice boomed through a bullhorn across the water: 'This is the New Orleans Police Department. You're under arrest. Put down your weapons and place your hands on your head.'

Lionel's arm went up, and he aimed the nine-millimeter across the roof of the pilothouse.

'No!' Fontenot shouted. Then he shouted it again, 'No!' His face was round and soft and full of disbelief.

But it was too late. Lionel and Boggs were both shooting now, the muzzle flashes from their guns almost lost in the searchlight's hot glare. I could hear the brass hulls from Lionel's pistol clinking on the pilothouse roof. Then the searchlight glass shattered and almost simultaneously two kneeling figures on the bow of the police boat, bill caps turned backwards on their heads, began firing M-16 rifles on full automatic.

They blew wood divots out of the deck and pilothouse, exploded my instrument panel, rang metal-jacketed bullets off the deck rails, gear boxes, pots and pans and stove in the galley, scissored through the tin side of a bait well, and trapped Ray Fontenot helplessly against the back rail of the jugboat.

He tried to crouch down behind the corner of the pilothouse, his mouth wide and pink with words that no one could hear. His fists were balled, his wrists crossed in an X in front of his eyes; then the bullets danced across his life jacket, split the canvas like dry blisters popping, and his throat and great heaving chest erupted with red flowers. His mouth hung open as though he had swallowed a chicken bone.

I lay flat on the deck, my arms folded across the crown of my skull. Boggs was hunkered down behind the iron gear box that had held the crates of cocaine, and the M-16 rounds whanged off the top and the sides and sparked in the darkness. But he didn't wince. He kept firing, pumping the empty shell casings out on the deck, his body small and constricted with muscle like a rifleman's. His shotgun must have been loaded with double-aughts or deer slugs, because I could hear the damage to the police boat, the glass breaking, the hard slap of heavy shot across wood surfaces.

Then the police boat veered back into the fog, turning into its own wake, but not before one of the kneeling figures on the bow emptied his clip and bit into the auxiliary gasoline drum welded against the jugboat's deck rail. The gasoline gushed across the deck and drained into the engine well. I don't know what ignited it – a spark jumping off a metal surface, shorted wiring, or an exploded starter battery – but suddenly the deck was flaming, the gas drum was ringed with fire; then it blew with a *whoompth*, like a large furnace kicking on deep in the bowels of a tenement building.

I crawled across the deck, squeezed under the bottom rail, and rolled over the side. I could not see the police boat now, but before I dropped into the water I saw Jimmie Lee Boggs running for the stern, his hard, lean body silhouetted among the flames. Lionel was on his knees by the pilothouse, his hand pressed against a hemorrhaging wound in the center of his throat. His shoulders shook and convulsed as though he were trying to expel a piece of angle iron from his chest. He tried to catch Boggs's dungarees with his fingers as Boggs went past him. The back of Lionel's hand was scarlet and shining in the fire's light. But Boggs pulled the mooring line free, jumped from the stern rail on to the bow of his boat, and in seconds started the engine, opened the throttle full-out, and spun on the back of a breaking wave into the fog.

I treaded water and drifted away from the jugboat. It was burning brightly now, from bow to stern, and when the anchor rope burned through, it floated sideways in the swell, and a big wave broke against the pilothouse and turned to steam. The water was cold and smelled of oil and gas. In the distance I could hear the thinning sound of Boggs's cabin cruiser and the police boat in pursuit. I tried to save my strength and float on my back, but each time I rose with a wave, the water broke across my mouth and nose, and I had to right my head and churn with my hands and feet again.

The tide was coming in, and I couldn't swim against it to the oil platform. The Coast Guard was out there somewhere, but it had probably become occupied with the shrimper. The jugboat was only a red glow in the fog now. I heard another *whoompth*, a sound like boiling water, a rush of air bubbles, the hiss of steam rising from heated metal; then the glow died, and the fogbank was absolutely white.

A few minutes later it began to rain again. The rain danced on the water, drummed on my head, beat in my ears. So this is how your death comes, I thought. You don't buy it with the enemies of your dreams – the black-clad toy men whose breath, even in your sleep, stunk of fish; a psychotic killer of children who tried to push an ice pick behind your ear; the Vegas hit man who handcuffed you to a drainpipe, taped your mouth, and spoke compassionately to you about the means of your execution while you stared helplessly at the white threads of light in his vacuous blue yes. Instead, you slip down into a cold green envelope beneath the roll and pitch of the waves; you drift and bump across the sandy Gulf floor, your clothes stringing bubbles to the surface, your eyes a feast for crabs and eels.

Then the fog began to flatten the water and break up into turning wisps and wraiths that hovered just above the waves, and the eastern sky went gray. A soft rose-colored light broke on the horizon, and I saw the quarter moon for the first time that night. Fifty yards away a round shape, like the back of an enormous seagoing turtle, floated in the swell. I swam to it, one long stroke at a time, breathing sideways, blowing water out of my nose, until finally my hand struck the life jacket that was wrapped around the chest of Ray Fontenot.

I had to roll him over to get to the laces. His body was strung with kelp, his skin blistered with burns and streaked with oil, his sightless eyes poached in his head. I jerked the jacket free and put my arms through the openings and felt the tension and ball of pain go out of my lower back as I was suddenly made weightless, bobbing along in a cresting wave that swept me toward the Louisiana shore.

For a short time I fell asleep, then awoke to the sound of sea gulls, the shadows of pelicans gliding by overhead, the heavy, fecund smell that speckled trout make when they school up, the early sun like a red wafer over the long green roll of the Gulf.

Five minutes later I heard an outboard engine, and I tried to wave my arms above the waves. Then he saw me and turned his engine so that he made a wide circle and approached me with the waves at his stern. It was a bass boat, a long, aluminum, flat-bottomed boat designed for fresh-water fishing, not for weather or being any distance from land. The man sitting at an angle in the stern, with the throttle of the Evinrude in his hand, wore Marine Corps utility pants, a gold and purple LSU jersey with Mike the Tiger on the front, a pale blue porkpie hat mashed down on his big head.

He cut the engine, drifted into me, then reached down and grabbed me by the back of the lifejacket. His face was round and flushed red with windburn and the strain of lifting me.

'What's happening, Streak?' Cletus said.

I lay in the bottom of his boat, my skin numb and dead to the touch and wrinkled with water-soak. I could see the coastline, the tide breaking across a sandbar, and white cranes rising from a cypress swamp.

You went out after me in this? I wanted to say. But I was breathless with cold and the words wouldn't come.

'How you like civil service with the DEA?' he said above the engine's roar. 'Those babies really know how to take care of you, don't they? Yes, indeedy, they do.'

9

Through my hospital room windows I could see the tops of oak trees, a pink two-story house with iron grillwork across the street, palm fronds on the esplanade, and, where the side street fed into St Charles, the big green iron streetcar when it passed. My room was white, and the sunlight was bright above the oak trees outside.

My right eye was crimped partly shut by the tape that covered the stitches in my eyebrow. There were four stitches in my lip, and they felt like a large plastic insect when I moved my tongue across them. I slept through most of the morning, and at noon I ate a lunch of mashed potatoes, baked chicken, early peas, and Jell-O, and fell asleep again. Two hours later I was awakened by Minos's phone call.

'What happened out there?' he said.

I told him.

'How'd you know which hospital I was in?' I asked.

'Your buddy Clete called me. Look, I'm sorry about this, Dave. I really am. There's always a risk in undercover work, but we usually do a better job of protecting our people.'

'How did New Orleans Vice get in on it?'

'I don't know. I talked to this character Nate Baxter. He's a nasty sonofabitch, isn't he?'

'You got it.'

'He stonewalled me, said he couldn't talk to me without clearance, said he wasn't even sure who I was.'

'Did you mention my name?'

'Of course not.'

'Don't tell him anything about our operation. He'll divulge it or use it in some way for his own ends. In the meantime call his superiors.'

'I already have a call in. But I appreciate you telling me how to do these things.'

'You sound a little irritable this afternoon.'

'Your busted head and the loss of your boat weren't the only problems that developed out there.'

'Wait a minute. They got Boggs, didn't they?'

'No.'

'What?'

'Boggs got away. With fifty keys of pure flake.'

'I can't believe it.'

'Evidently he went between two sandbars and they went over the top of one. At least that's what the Coast Guards says. Our man Baxter has no comment.'

'You got the shrimper, didn't you?'

'We got the shrimper. But no dope. No money, either. They dumped it all overboard.' I could almost hear him swallow when he said it.

'It all went for nothing?'

'That's what a few people have been telling me today.'

'What about my boat?'

'We'll see what we can do.'

'Listen, Minos, it'll take me thirty thousand dollars to replace it.'

'People down here are not sympathetic to my point of view right now. A half-million dollars of DEA money is at this moment bouncing along the bottom of the Gulf.'

'Your friends have an interesting attitude about personal responsibility.'

'Nobody here wants to spend the rest of his career in western Nebraska. But it happens. Give me a little time.'

'I mean it, Minos. That's a big part of my livelihood that went down out there. I want it back.'

'You made your point.'

'One other thing. Boggs said something about Cardo's being history. Is there a whack out on him or something?'

'It's funny you say that. We heard rumours like that from both Houston and Miami in just the last two days.'

A nurse came in to take my temperature, and I started to say good-bye to Minos.

'How close did it get out there, Dave?' he said.

'Down to the wire.'

'Are you all right?'

'It's just a few stitches. They're keeping me a day or so because I got some water in my lungs. Sometimes that can cause pneumonia.'

'No. I mean are you all right?'

'I'm fine.' And I looked out at the sunlight on the trees and realized that I meant it.

'I think we're going to pull you out of the sting. It went out of control. It wasn't anybody's fault, it just happens. But you've done enough. I'll be back with you tonight.'

After he hung up and the nurse had taken my temperature, I used the bathroom, then walked to the window and looked down the side street towards St Charles. The streetcar rattled down the esplanade under the massive canopy of oak trees, the wood seats filled with Negroes and working-class white people. Down below, the gutters were full of pink and blue camellias from the previous night's rain, and the wet stone was streaked with color like dye washed out of paper flowers.

Ten minutes later Clete walked through the door with a pizza in a flat box, a can of Jax in one coat pocket, and a Dr Pepper in the other. His porkpie hat was tilted down on his forehead. He sat on the side of my bed and flipped open the top of the box, his intelligent green eyes smiling at me.

'Hospital food usually tastes like a cross between spit and baby pabulum,' he said. 'So I brought you a dynamite combo of anchovies, sausage, pepperoni, and double cheese. How do you like it, my noble mon?'

'How about some peanut brittle? It goes great with stitches in the mouth, too.'

He ate a huge wedge and popped open the can of Jax, drank it half-empty, then picked up another wedge and started chewing, smiling all the time. There were flecks of pizza sauce on his mouth and shirt.

'The next time, I cover your butt from Jump Street,' he said.

'All right.'

'The feds don't send out my old partner on any more Lone Ranger jobs.'

'Okay, Clete.'

'Because you can't depend on these white-collar dickheads.'

'I got your drift.'

'Did that pencil pusher call you yet?'

'Minos?'

'Yeah.'

'About ten minutes ago.'

'His sting has turned to shit. He's not too happy. I told him they took a hell of a risk with a guy they recruited from outside their agency. He didn't seem to like that.'

'Minos is all right. How do you think New Orleans got in on it?'

'Maybe a wiretap, maybe a snitch. Who cares? They saved your tokus, didn't they?'

'Not intentionally. You remember what it was like when somebody opened up on you with an M-16?'

'Maybe we ought to 'front Nate Baxter about it. Sometimes he comes into my club after work. I've always thought his head would make a good toilet brush.'

He continued to study my face.

'What are you thinking about?' he asked.

'It wasn't a tap. The DEA would know about a tap. Somebody dropped the dime on the buy.'

'Who knew about it?'

'Cardo . . . Fontenot . . . Lionel . . . obviously Boggs . . .'

'Why you got that big wrinkle between your eyes, Streak?'

'I'm involved with somebody. She knew about it, too.'

'That's great. Why don't you run an ad in the *Times-Picayune* the next time out?'

'I didn't tell her. She picked up on it somewhere else.'

'What's her name?'

'Bootsie Giacano.'

'Oh, man, I don't believe it. You're in the sack with one of the Giacanos?'

'She's an old friend from New Iberia. She married into the family.'

'Probably like one of Charlie Manson's people, just a casual member of the family.'

'Knock it off, Clete.'

He grinned and squinted at me.

'The other one that bothers me is Kim Dollinger,' I said. 'She was trying to tell me something in your club. I thought she was just bombed.'

'She is one tough badass broad, isn't she? I'd like to get to know her a lot better.'

'I get the feeling you're not too serious about any of this.'

'Why should I be? The whole sting was put together by clowns, if you ask me. They almost got you killed out there. I don't like federal farts doing that to my podjo.'

'I think you need to broaden your attitudes, Clete.'

He opened my can of Dr Pepper, poured it in a glass with ice, set a glass straw in it, and put it in my hand.

'Drink your pop,' he said. 'Hey, you know who I got the pizza from?'

'Don't tell me.'

'You got it, mon. That strange, buglike colored kid. He works in that pizza joint right around the corner from the Pearl. Hey, mon, it's time to get out of this G-man bullshit. Let them clean up their own mess for a while. If you still want to square the beef with Boggs, you and I'll do it together. With no forms to fill out, either. You know what I mean?'

'I'll let you know.'

'Something happened out there, didn't it?' he said.

'What do you mean?'

'The dragon went away.'

'Something like that.'

'It's a rush, isn't it?'

I nodded and looked out the window at the tops of the trees moving in the sunlight.

'Yeah, a real high,' he said. 'Maybe one a guy doesn't always want to turn loose of. Almost as good as a glass of black Jack on ice with a Tuborg to chase it home. Think about it, Dave. The time to go is right after you hit the daily double.'

He folded the pizza box shut and looked directly into my face. His weight made a big dent on the side of the bed. His face was as flat and round as a cake pan.

Later, I phoned New Iberia to check on Alafair, then I called Bootsie to apologize for the things that I had said to her. I hadn't changed my mind about her – if she was involved with the mob in New Orleans, she had become a willing victim – but what right did I have to judge her and wound her again after all these years? It was a difficult conversation because I knew her phone was tapped and I did not want her to compromise herself. But I did apologize.

'It's all right, *cher*,' she said. 'I haven't told you everything. Sometime I will.'

I was silent.

'You came to some conclusions that most people would,' she said.

'Can you come up here?'

'Anytime for you, darlin'.'

'Not today, though. Tomorrow morning. I've got the bed spins now. I guess I had a big drop in body temperature out there. I don't look too good, either.'

'I'll drop by around nine.'

'Boots?' I said.

'What?'

'Boots?' And I wanted to ask her if she knew how it had gone sour on the salt.

'Yes?'

'I always loved you. All these years. I never forgot that summer of 1957.'

'I didn't either, Dave. Who could? You get one like that in a lifetime.'

That evening I ate supper from the tray on my bed and watched the light fade above the trees and the roofs of houses. Then it was dark, and when people turned on their porch lights I could see the black outlines of the palms and philodendron and stands of bamboo in their front yards, and then the iron streetcar clattering by on the St Charles esplanade, the closed windows filled with the purple and green neon glow from the Katz and Bezthof drugstore on the corner.

I fell asleep and dreamed that I was sliding down a wave into a great slate-green trough; the horizon was tilted, the sky a dirty veil of gray like incinerator smoke. My ears were filled with the hiss of water and wind humming in a seashell. My legs were atrophied, bloodless with cold, but I knew there were makos and hammerheads turning below me in the depths, and they could find feeling and extract a torrent of color from skin that had puckered as white as a fish's belly.

I *felt* him at the side of my bed and opened my eyes on the pillow as though someone had clapped his hands close to my face.

'Hey, it's just me,' Tony Cardo said, smiling. 'I don't want to give you a coronary, too.'

I pushed myself up on my arms and licked the dry welt of stitches on my lip.

'You must have some mean dreams,' he said.

He wore a striped brown suit, a pale yellow shirt with French cuffs and a dark brown knit necktie, a fedora tilted on his head, wing-tip shoes that were spit-shined to the soft gleam of melted plastic. The man with jailhouse tattoos I had seen waxing Tony's Oldsmobile stood behind Tony, his hand folded patiently in front of him, his expressionless eyes never quite meeting mine, his bristle-flecked cannonball head motionless as though he were listening for something.

'I feel bad about what happened to you out there, Dave,' Tony said. 'You saw it coming, didn't you, and I didn't listen to you. You're a smart man.'

'Not smart enough, Tony. I walked into it. I lost my boat out there, too.'

'I know all about it.'

'How?'

'The people on the other end. They had to dump a lot of inventory overboard. Your money with it. It was a bad night for business.'

'It was a bad night in a lot of ways, Tony.'

'You mean Lionel and Ray buying it? I never thought those two would try to rip me off. But you have to deal with a lot of untrustworthy types in this business, Dave.'

'You know all about the rip-off, then? You know about Jimmie Lee Boggs?'

'A guy like Boggs has one talent. You probably met one or two like him in 'Nam. He'd take out a water buffalo or spook a farmer out of a rice field so he could drop him. Anything to stay busy. But he's not too bright about anything else. The word's already out, he wants to lay off fifty keys of pure product.'

'Where is he?'

'Here, Miami, Houston. It's all Motel Eight to a guy like that.'

'Do you know why they tried to take you off?' I said.

He sucked in his cheeks, and his mouth became small and button-shaped. The man behind him flexed his shoulders as though he had a neck ache.

'You're telling me something?' Tony said. His eyes were bright, amused.

'Like you said, you didn't think Lionel or Fontenot had it in them.'

'I didn't put it that way, but all right . . .'

'Boggs is a psychopath, but he's a pro. He doesn't make moves without somebody's permission,' I said.

Tony's eyes were dark and friendly, his lashes as long as a girl's.

'Go on, Dave,' he said.

'I'm saying these guys are piranhas. They don't attack until they smell blood in the water.'

'I look like I'm bleeding?' he said, and smiled with the corner of his mouth.

'I'd watch my back.'

'Listen to this guy. He gets beat up, he almost drowns, he loses his boat and money, and he worries about somebody else.'

'Take it for what it's worth, Tony. I think they've got a whack out on you.'

'What do you think, Jess?' he said to the man with the cannonball head.

'I think they'd better not fucking try,' the man said.

'See,' Tony said. 'This is New Orleans. We don't worry about some gumballs in Miami or Houston. They want to get ugly, we take it into their backyard.'

'Lionel used the shortwave on the shrimper to call Boggs. Did they tell you that?'

I saw the pause come into his eyes.

'No, I didn't know that,' he said.

'Maybe they didn't speak English. Or maybe they didn't have any way of knowing he was setting up a rip-off.'

'What you're saying, Davie, is they probably didn't care.'

'Maybe.'

'You're a good guy, Dave, but you're still a newbie. There's two ways you run the business – you don't get greedy, you piece off the action, you treat people fair. Then your conscience is clear, you got respect in your community, people trust you. Then when somebody else breaks the rules, gets greedy, tries to put a lock on your action, you blow up their shit. You don't fuck around when you do it, either. It's like a free-fire zone. Nobody likes it, but the only thing that counts is who walks out of the smoke.'

I got up to go to the bathroom. The floor felt as though it were receding under my feet.

'You still got the deck pitching under you, huh?' Tony said.

'Yeah.'

'Well, you're coming home with us, anyway. You'll sleep better there. I got a good cook, too, fix you some gumbo and dirty rice. How's that, podna?'

'What?'

'You're staying at my place. I already signed you out and paid your bill.'

'You can't sign me out.'

'You know how much I donate to this place each year? What's the matter, you like the smell of bedpans?'

Just then one of his gatemen came through the door with two ambulance attendants pushing a gurney.

'Now wait a minute, Tony,' I said.

'I got a nice room waiting for you. With cable TV, books, magazines, you want a broad to turn the pages for you, you got that, too. Like I told you before, I'm a sensitive man about friendship. Don't be hurting my feelings.'

Then the two attendants and his hired hoods went about packaging me up as though I were a piece of damaged china. I started to protest again as they placed their hands gently on my arms, and gray worms danced before my eyes. But Tony put a finger to his pursed lips and said, almost in a private whisper, 'Hey, guys like us already got our tickets punched. It's all a free lunch now. You're in the magic kingdom, Dave.'

So that's how to the dark tower I came.

Early the next morning Tony, his little boy, and I had breakfast in the glass-enclosed breakfast room, which had a wonderful view of Tony's myrtle-lined tennis court, oak and lemon and lime trees, and blue lawn wet with mist. The back door gave on to a wheelchair ramp that led down to the driveway.

'The bus picks up Paul right here at the door,' Tony said. 'They're going on a field trip today, to an ice factory, to learn how ice is made.'

'It's the gifted class. We get to go on a field trip every Friday,' Paul said. He smiled when he talked. He wore a purple sweater and gray corduroy pants and sat on top of cushions in his wheelchair so he could reach the table adequately. His brown hair had been cut recently, and it was combed with a part that was as exact as a ruler's edge. 'My daddy says you were in the war, too.'

'That's right.'

'You think a war's ever going to come here?' he said.

'No, this is a good place, Paul,' I said. 'We don't worry about things like that. I bet you're going to have a good time at the ice factory.'

'Do you have any little boys or girls?' Paul said.

'A little girl, about your age. Her name's Alafair.'

'What's she like to do?'

'She has a horse. She likes to feed him apples and ride him when she comes home from school.'

'A horse?' he said.

'Yeah, we call him Tex because we bought him over in Texas.'

'Boy.'

He had a genuinely sweet face, with no recognition in it of his own limitations.

'Maybe we'll go riding with Dave and his daughter one day,' Tony said.

'That'd be fine,' I said.

'There's a couple of bridle paths here, or sometimes I take Paul on trips over by Iberia Parish,' Tony said. 'Maybe we'll drive over, take you guys out to eat, go out for a boat ride, something like that,' he said.

'Yeah, that's a good idea, Tony.'

'I hear the bus,' Paul said.

His father hooked his canvas book bag, which had a lunch kit strapped on to it, on the back of the chair and wheeled him down the ramp to the waiting bus. The driver lowered a special platform from the back of the bus, and he and Tony fixed the wheels of Paul's chair to it. Before the driver raised the platform, Tony leaned down and hugged his son, pressed his head against his chest, and kissed his hair.

He came back in and sat down at the table. He wore white tennis slacks and a thick white sweater with blue piping on it.

'You have a fine little podna there,' I said.

'You'd better believe it. How'd you sleep last night?'

'Good.'

'You like my home?'

'It's beautiful.'

'I wish my mom had lived to see it. We lived in Algiers and the Irish Channel. We had colored people living next door and across the street from us. You know what my mom used to do for a living?'

I shook my head no.

'She washed the hair of corpses. She'd come home, and I could smell it on her. Not just the chemicals. That same smell when you pop a body bag. Not as strong, but that same smell. Man, I used to hate it. I think that's why she always talked about lemon and lime trees back in Sicily. She said on her father's farm there was this old Norman tower made out of rocks, and lemon and lime trees grew all around it. When it was real hot she and her sisters would play inside the rocks where it was cool, and they could smell the lemons and limes on the wind.'

Two men walked into the kitchen, their faces full of sleep, and began clattering around in the cabinets.

'Where's the cereal bowls at?' one of them said.

He was dark and thin; he wore slippers and his print shirt was unbuttoned and hung half out of his slacks, but he hadn't forgotten to put on his shoulder holster.

'Right-hand side,' Tony said. 'Look, you guys, there's eggs and bacon in the warmer out in the dining room. There's extra coffee there, too.'

They shuffled around in the kitchen and didn't reply. Then they went out into the dining room. These were only two of eight hired men I had seen in the house since the night before. They had slept on couches, in the attic, the television den, and guest cottage, and had taken turns walking around on the grounds and driveway during the night.

'They're good boys, just not too sophisticated,' Tony said. 'Do they make you uncomfortable?'

'No.'

'A couple of them made you.'

I looked at him blankly.

'They can spot a cop,' he said. 'I told them you're all right, though. You're all right, aren't you, Dave?'

His eyes took on that strange, self-amused light again.

'You have to be the judge of that, Tony.'

'I think you're a solid guy. You know what a solid con is?'

'Yes.'

'You're that kind of guy. You've got character.'

'Maybe you don't know everything about me.'

'Maybe I know more than you think,' he said, and winked.

I didn't know his game, or even if he was playing one, but I didn't like meeting his eyes. I took a bite of my soft-boiled eggs and looked out at the mist in the citrus trees.

'Where's the contract coming from?' I said.

'There's one guy in Houston that wants me out bad. Two or three in Miami. Maybe they got permission from Chicago, maybe they're acting on their own, I don't know. You heard stories about me, Dave, about some stuff I do, waving the flag around, bullshit like that?'

'I guess I have.'

'That I been breaking one of the big rules, getting mixed up in politics, focusing attention on the organization?'

'That's what you hear sometimes.'

'Let me tell you about a guy used to live in Plantation, Florida. You remember the name Johnny—? This guy went back to the days of Bugsy Siegel, I mean he survived gang wars for forty years. But Johnny and a couple of other guys thought they could jerk the CIA around. They told some CIA people they could whack out Castro for the government, like do a patriotic act and maybe get the casinos open in Havana again. So the CIA buys it, and the word is out that our guys are going to clip Castro. Maybe they even sent a couple of kamikaze gumballs to do it, but the bottom line is that Castro looks pretty healthy today. In other words, it looks like it was a scam to pump juice and influence out of the government. So the commission in Chicago tells these guys that what they're doing is stupid and they'd fucking better knock it off. But Johnny doesn't listen. So one day a couple of guys invite him fishing out in Biscayne Bay, except they put one in his ear, cut his legs off, and stuff him inside an oil barrel.

'They weighted the barrel down with chains, and shoved an ice pick in Johnny's stomach to break the gas bag. Nobody would have ever seen him again, but they screwed it up. They missed the wall of his stomach, and he floated the barrel up.

'It makes a good story, doesn't it, about what happens when a guy decides to get political?'

'I've heard it before.'

'Then maybe you also know it's bullshit. Johnny got clipped because of money. It's always money, Dave. Those guys in Miami and Houston want to take over the action on the Louisiana coast. There's four or five other guys in New Orleans they'll have to cut in, guys who are anybody's cornhorn, but the word is I'm definitely not going to be a player.' He smiled and put a dripping spoonful of cereal in his mouth. 'There's supposed to be some real talent in town right now. I hear it's a twenty-five-thou contract.'

'Maybe it's a good time to take the family on a vacation to the islands,' I said.

'They don't hurt families. We don't do that to each other. Not even these guys, Dave.' But I saw the cloud slide across his face. He looked out at the lawn and rubbed his finger against his temple.

'I need to use your phone,' I said. 'A lady was coming up to see me at the hospital this morning.'

'Who is she?' he asked, and smiled again.

'Bootsie Giacano.'

'No kidding? You got good taste. She's a class broad, I mean lady. You gotta excuse my vocabulary. I went to college, but most of the time you wouldn't know it.'

'You know her?'

'Sure. I own part of her business. She's nice. I like her.'

I used the phone in the kitchen and told Bootsie where I was and that I would see her later.

'You're where?' she said.

I cleared my throat and told her again I was at Tony's. I could hear her breathing into the mouth-piece of the receiver.

'I won't ask you any more questions,' she said. 'I'm sure you know what you're doing, Dave. You know what you're doing, don't you?'

'Sure,' I said, then, 'I'll call you tonight. Everything's fine, kiddo.'

'Yeah, sure it is,' she said, and hung up.

I sat back down with Tony just as his wife came into the kitchen in a blue house robe and slippers, her face dull with sleep, her hair in pink foam-rubber curlers. She didn't speak. She filled a coffee cup from the electric pot on the Formica counter, shook two aspirins from a bottle and set them by the side of her saucer, and sat at the kitchen table with her back to us, smoking silently while she drank her coffee. The backs of her hands were coarse and heavily veined, and her nails, long and bright red, made clicking sounds when she picked up her coffee cup.

'Clara, this is Dave Robicheaux. He stayed with us last night,' Tony said.

Again she didn't speak. Her blond hair was dark close to her scalp. I could see nicotine stains on her fingers, dried makeup around the corners of her mouth, her thin whitened nostrils when she breathed.

'Dave and I were talking about taking Paul for a horse ride,' Tony said.

She blew smoke up against the window glass and flicked her ashes in her saucer.

'I think maybe everybody was making a little too much noise last night,' Tony said.

'May I speak to you alone, please?' she said.

'Uh-oh,' he said.

'I'd like to see your tennis court. I'll be outside,' I said.

'Yeah, we'll hit some balls. Tell Jess to load up the ball machine,' he said, but he didn't hide the embarrassment in his face well.

I walked down the wheelchair ramp and across the damp, spongy Saint Augustine grass toward the court. The sun was pale and yellow above the myrtle trees, the canvas windscreens were streaked with water, and the fog blew off the lake in wisps and glistened on the waxy green surface of the citrus leaves. I could hear her voice behind me: 'They can stay in the cottage . . . I don't want them all over my house . . . Did you see the bathroom this morning . . . You wouldn't have this trouble if you were reasonable, if you didn't have to be the big war hero . . . Everyone's tired of it, Tony, they've made allowances for a long time, they're not going to go on doing it forever . . . Maybe you're not going to like this, but I think they've been fair, I think you're acting crazy . . . Go ahead, eat some more of that stuff. It's only eight o'clock in the morning. That'll fix 'em in Miami.'

They went at it for ten minutes. I didn't find Jess, so I began to load the automatic ball machine myself. When Tony came out of the house with an oversized tennis racket across his shoulder, he was grinning as though he were serenely in charge of the morning, but his eyes had a black, electrical gaze in them, the skin of his face was stretched tight against the bone, and I could see the pulse jumping in his neck as though he had been running wind sprints.

'I love Indian summer in Louisiana. I love the morning,' he said.

'It's been a pretty fall.'

'Fucking A,' he said, clicked on the ball machine with a remote control button, and stationed himself like a gladiator behind the baseline.

I sat on a bench and watched while the machine hummed, then

thropped balls across the net, and Tony slammed them back with a fierce energy that left skid marks in the soft green clay.

'It's funny how many people can want a piece out of your ass,' he said. 'Wives, broads, cops, lawyers, these guys I pay to keep me alive. You rent their loyalty by the day. I can name two hundred people in this city I've made rich. Even a psychotic piece of shit like Jimmie Lee Boggs. Can you dig it, when I first met that guy he was doing five-hundred-dollar hits for a couple of Jews out of Miami. Even after he escaped from you, his big score was going to be to blackmail some colored woman in New Iberia. Now he's got a half-million bucks of product.'

'What colored woman?' I said.

'I don't know, he was going to move in on a hot-pillow joint or something. That's Jimmie Lee's idea of the big score.'

'Wait a minute, Tony. This is important. Do you remember the name of the woman?'

'It was French. It was Mama something.' He hit the ball long, into the canvas windscreen. 'To tell you the truth, I'm not real interested in talking about colored whorehouses.'

'I have to ask you anyway. What'd he have on her?'

'Maybe we're not communicating too well here,' he said, and slapped one ball hard against the tape and whanged another off the ball machine itself.

'Maybe he knows something that might keep a kid out of the electric chair.'

'It's got something to do with snuffing a redbone. What the fuck do I know about redbones? I got a problem here, I hear you talking about some colored woman, about keeping a kid out of the electric chair, about a cathouse in New Iberia, but I don't hear you talking about the half million your people put up. That bothers me a little bit, Dave.'

'There's nothing I can do about what happened out on the salt.'

'Yeah? How about the guys who lost their money? Are they cool?'

'They're oil people. They're not in the business. They're not going to do anything about it.'

'You must know a different class of people than me, then. Because the people I've known will do anything because of money. But you're telling me these guys are different?'

'It's just something I'll have to handle myself, Tony.'

'Yeah, if I was you, I'd handle it. I'd really handle it.' He lowered his racket and looked at me, a dark light in his eyes. A ball whizzed past him and bounced off the windscreen behind him. He removed his sweater, wiped the sweat off his face with it, and threw it to the side of the court.

Then a strange transformation took place in him. The tautness of his face, the hard, black shine in his eyes the rigidity of the muscles in his body, suddenly left him like air rushing out of a balloon. His skin grew ashen, sweat ran out of his hair, he began swallowing deep in his throat, and his lungs labored for air.

'What is it, partner?' I said.

'Nothing.'

I took him by the arm and walked him to the bench. His arm felt flaccid and weak in my hand. He propped the racket on the clay and leaned his head down on it. Sweat dripped off the lobes of his tiny ears.

'You want me to take you to a doctor?' I said.

'No.'

'You want me to get your wife?'

'No. It's going to pass.'

I picked up the sweater and blotted his hair and the back of his neck with it, then draped it over his shoulders. He began to breathe more regularly; then he pinched the bridge of his nose and held his head back in the cool air as though he had a nose-bleed.

'I think you need to talk to somebody,' I said. 'I think you're dealing with something that's going to eat your lunch.'

He folded his arm on top of his perpendicular racket and rested his head on his arm.

'What are you gonna do, a kid needs a mother. It's all a pile of shit, man,' he said. 'All of it.'

When I went back to my room, which gave on to a side yard that contained a swing set and a solitary moss-hung oak tree, my clothes from my apartment were laid out neatly on the tester bed. Even my .45, with the spare clip and box of shells, lay on top of a folded flannel shirt. I went to look for Tony, but he was in the shower. I walked out the front door and down the long, tree-lined drive to the front gate, where Jess sat in a chair, wearing a blue jumpsuit. It was zippered only halfway up his chest, and I could see the leather straps of his shoulder holster against his T-shirt.

'Where's the closest drugstore?' I said.

'What do you need?'

'Some razor blades.'

'It's five blocks, down by the lake. We'll send a car.'

'I need the walk. I still feel like I've got rapture of the deep.'

'What?'

'How about opening up?' I said.

He unlocked the chain and slid back the gate wide enough so that I could step out on the street. I walked past the rows of banked lawns and oleander-lined piked fences to a thoroughfare and a tan stucco and red-tiled shopping center that looked as if it had been torn out of the ground in southern California and dropped in the middle of New Orleans. I used a pay phone outside a drugstore to call Minos.

'You pulled it off, Dave. You're across the moat and inside the castle,' he said before I explained.

'How'd you know where I was?'

'Everybody who goes in that gate is on videotape. How do you like it with the spaghetti-and-meatball crowd?'

'I'm not sure.'

'I told you, didn't I, Cardo's head was in the blender too long.'

'Minos, you guys are all turning the screws on this guy, and, to tell you the truth, I'm not sure why.'

'What are you talking about?'

'He's just one guy. What about these guys in Miami and Houston who've got a contract out on him? The odds are Tony's going to lose.'

'Let us worry about Houston and Miami. You want in or out, Dave?'

'I haven't made up my mind.'

'You'd damn well better.'

'I want Boggs.'

'You're in the right place, then. He'll be back. He's not a guy who leaves loose ends. Besides, we hear it's an open contract. It's the perfect opportunity for him.'

'Did you find out who dropped the dime on the buy?'

'Baxter said he couldn't compromise his informant.'

'He's not going to share a bust with a federal agency.'

'Forget about that guy. Look, Washington called yesterday with some information about Cardo's military record. He got a Silver Star for going after a point man who stepped on a mine.'

'He didn't tell me that.'

'After he was wounded, he got moved back to Chu Lai for the last four months of his tour.'

'Why was he moved back to Chu Lai?'

'How should I know?'

'There's something not right. The Marines were real hard-nosed about keeping a guy in his platoon until he had a million-dollar wound or two Purple Hearts.'

'Maybe he had some pull. Listen, Dave, don't get involved with the guy's psychology. Eventually we're going to punch his ticket. You'll probably be there when it happens. Or you'll be in court testifying against him. All this *semper fi* bullshit won't have anything to do with it. You want a lesson from Vietnam? Don't think about the guy who's in your sights.'

'You always cut right to the bone, Minos.'

'I didn't invent the rules. By the way, we have that house under twenty-four-hour surveillance. If it turns to shit inside, throw a lamp or a chair through a window. In the meantime, think about how far you want to take it. Nobody'll blame you if you decide to go back to New Iberia.'

It was cool under the stucco colonnade, and red leaves were blowing out of a heavily wooded lot across the street.

'Dave, are you still there?' he asked.

'Yeah . . . I'll try to call you back tonight or tomorrow. Talk to you later, Minos.'

I hung up the phone and wondered if Minos would tell the lion tamer that he could put down his whip and chair and walk out of the lions' cage whenever he wished. I went inside the drugstore, bought a package of razor blades, and came out just as Tony and Jess pulled to the curb in the maroon Lincoln convertible.

10

Tony was in the passenger's seat. He reached over the backseat and popped open the back door for me. He had changed into loafers, a rust-colored sports shirt, pleated tan slacks, a cardigan, and a yellow Panama hat.

'You could have taken the car, Dave. You didn't have to walk,' he said.

'It's a good day for it.'

'How do you like my hat?'

'It looks sharp.'

'I got a collection of them. Hey, Jess, go inside and get me a copy of *Harper's*,' he said.

'What?' Jess said.

'Get me a copy of *Life*.'

'Sure, Tony,' Jess said, cut the engine, and went inside the drugstore.

Tony smiled at me across the back of the seat. The Lincoln had a rolled leather interior, a fold-out bar, a wooden dashboard with black instrument panels.

'Jess has an IQ of minus eight, but he'd eat thumbtacks with a spoon if I told him to,' he said. Then the smile went out of his face. 'I'm sorry you had to hear that stuff between me and Clara. In particular I'm sorry you had to hear that about me being a war hero. Because I never told anybody I was a hero. I knew some guys who were, but I wasn't one of them.'

'Who was, Tony? Did you ever read a story by Ernest Hemingway called "A Soldier's Home"? It's about a World War I Marine who comes back home and discovers that people only want to hear stories about German women chained to machine guns. The truth is that he was afraid all the time he was over there and it took everything in him just to get by. However, he learns that's not a story anyone is interested in.'

'Yeah. Ernest Hemingway. I like his books. I read a bunch of them in college.'

'Look, on another subject, Tony. I'm not sure your wife is ready for houseguests right now.'

He puffed out his cheeks.

'I invite people to my home. I tell them if they should leave,' he said. 'You're my guest. You don't want to stay, that's your business.'

'I appreciate your hospitality, Tony.'

'So we're going back home now and get you changed, then we're taking Kim out to the yacht club for a little lunch and some golf. How's that grab you?'

'Fine.'

'You like Kim?'

'Sure.'

'How much?'

'She's a pretty girl.'

'She ain't pretty, man. She's fucking beautiful.' His eyes were dancing with light. 'She told me she got drunk and came on to you.'

'She told you that?'

'What's the big deal? She's human. You're a good-looking guy. But you don't look too comfortable right now.' He laughed out loud.

'What can I say?'

'Nothing. You're too serious. It's all comedy, man. The bottom line is we all get to be dead for a real long time. It's a cluster fuck no matter how you cut it.'

We drove back to his house, and I changed into a pair of gray slacks, a charcoal shirt, and a candy-striped necktie, loaded two bags of golf clubs into the Lincoln, and with a white stretch Caddy limousine full of Tony's hoods behind us, we picked up Kim Dollinger and headed for the country club out by the lake.

We filled two tables in the dining room. I couldn't tell if the attention we drew was because of my bandaged head, Tony's hoods, whose dead eyes and toneless voices made the waiters' heads nod rapidly, or the way Kim filled out her gray knit dress. But each time I took a bite from my shrimp cocktail and tried to chew on the side of my mouth that wasn't injured, I saw the furtive glances from the other tables, the curiosity, the titillation of being next to people who suddenly step off a movie screen.

And Tony must have read my thoughts.

'Watch this,' he said, and motioned the maître d' over. 'Give everybody in the bar and dining room a glass of Champagne, Michel.'

'It's not necessary, Mr Cardo.'

'Yeah, it is.'

'Some of our members don't drink, Mr Cardo.'

'Then give them a dessert. Put it on my bill.'

Tony wiped his small mouth with a napkin. The maître d' was a tall, pale man who looked as if he were about to be pushed out an airplane door.

'Hey, they don't want it, that's okay,' Tony said. 'Lighten up, Michel.'

'Very good, sir.' The maître d' assembled his waiters and sent them to the bar for trays of glasses and towel-wrapped bottles of champagne.

'That was mean,' Kim said.

'I didn't come here to be treated like a bug,' Tony said.

We finished lunch and walked outside into the cool afternoon sunlight and the rattle of the palms in the wind off the lake. The lake was murky green and capping, and the few sailboats that were out were tacking hard in the wind, the canvas popping, their glistening bows slapping into the water. Tony and most of his entourage loaded themselves into golf carts for nine holes, and Kim and I sat on a wood bench by the practice green while Jess made long putts back and forth across the clipped grass without ever hitting the cup.

She wore a gray pillbox hat with a net veil folded back on top of it. She didn't look at me and instead gazed off at the rolling fairways, the sand traps and greens, the moss-hung oaks by the tees. The wind was strong enough to make her eyes tear, but in profile she looked as cool and regal and unperturbed as a sculptor's model. Behind her, the long, rambling club building, with its glass-domed porches, was achingly white against the blue of the sky.

'Maybe we should go inside,' I said.

'It's fine, thanks.'

'Do you think it's smart to jerk a guy like Tony around?'

She crossed her legs and raised her chin.

'He's got a burner turned on in his head. I wouldn't mess with his male pride,' I said.

'Is there something wrong with the way I look? I wish you'd stop staring at me.'

'I think you've got a guilty conscience, Kim.'

'Oh you do?'

'Did you drop the dime on us?'

She watched Jess putt across the green. The red flag on the pin flapped above his head in the distance. Finally the bail clunked into the cup. My eyes never left the side of her face. She pulled her dress tight over her knee. Her hips and stomach looked as smooth as water going over stone.

'Somebody told the Man. It wasn't Lionel or Fontenot,' I said.

'Do you think Tony would be taking me out for lunch if he thought I was a snitch?'

'I think only Tony knows what goes on in Tony's head. I think he likes to live on the outer edge of his envelope. Eating black speed is like sliding down the edge of a barber's razor.'

'Why do you keep saying these things to me? I have nothing to tell you.'

'Do you know a Vice cop named Nate Baxter?'

I could see the color in her cheeks.

'Why should I know—,' she began.

'He was following you the day you were in Clete's place. This guy's a lieutenant. Why's he interested in you, Kim?'

Her eyes were wet, and her lip began to tremble.

'All right, come on now,' I said.

'You're a shit.'

Jess had stopped putting and was looking at us. The gray hair on his chest grew like wire out of his golf shirt.

'Maybe I'm just a little worried about you,' I said.

'Leave me alone. Please do that for me.'

'I'll buy you a drink instead.'

'No, you stay away from me.'

'Listen to me, Kim—'

She picked up her purse and walked in her high heels across the lawn toward the club. Her calves looked hard and waxed below the hem of her knit dress. Jess walked off the green with the putter hanging loosely at his side.

'What's wrong with her?' he said.

'I guess I don't know how to talk to younger women very well.'

'She's a weird broad. I don't trust her.'

'Why not?'

'She don't ask for anything. A broad who don't ask you for anything has got a different kind of hustle going. Tony don't see it.' He twirled the putter like a baton in his fingers.

I found her sitting on a tall chair-backed stool in the bar. The bar was done in mahogany and teakwood, with brass-framed round mirrors and barometers on the walls and copper kettles full of ferns hung in the windows that looked out over the yacht basin. Her eyes were clear now, and her hands lay quietly on the polished black surface of the bar, her fingers touching the sides of a Manhattan glass. She nibbled at the orange slice; then her face tightened when she saw me walk into the periphery of her vision.

I ordered a cup of coffee from the bartender.

'What do I have to say? Don't you know how to let someone alone?' she said.

'I think you need a friend.'

'And you're it. What a laugh.'

'I know Baxter. If you've got a deal going with him, he'll burn you.'

I saw her swallow, either with anger or fear.

'What is the matter with you? Are you trying to get me killed?' she said.

'Get on a plane, Kim. LA's great this time of year. I'll get some money for you.'

She looked straight ahead and breathed hard, way down in her chest.

'You're a cop,' she said.

'Ex.'

'Now.'

'You'd better check out my record. Cops with my kind of mileage are the kind they shove out the side door.'

'I can't afford you. I'm going to ask you one more time, get away from me.'

'You're a nice girl. You don't deserve the fall you're headed for.'

She started to speak again, but her words caught in her throat as though she had swallowed a large bubble of air. Then she sipped from her Manhattan, straightened her back, and signaled the bartender.

'This man is annoying me,' she said.

He was young, and his eyes glanced nervously at me and then back at her.

'Did you hear me?' she said.

'Yes.'

'Would you tell him to leave, please?' she said.

'Sir, this lady is making a request,' the bartender said. He wore a long-sleeved white shirt and a black bow tie, and his hair was blond and oiled.

'Yeah, I heard, podna. I don't know where else I should go, though.'

'Would you tell him to get the fuck out of the bar?' she said.

'Miss, please don't use that language.'

'I ordered a drink. I didn't ask to have a dildo sit next to me while I drank it. Tell him to get out.'

'Miss, please.'

'What does it take to get through to you?' she said.

Other people had stopped eating and drinking and were looking at us.

'Sir, would you mind—,' the bartender said.

'No. I don't mind,' I said. 'Where should I go?'

'Try Bumfuck, Kansas,' she said.

'Miss, I'll have to ask you to leave, too.'

'Is that right?' she said. 'Would you page Mr Cardo out on the golf course and tell him that? I would appreciate it if you would tell him that.'

'You're Mr Cardo's guest?' the bartender said. His face was bloodless.

'Don't sweat it, partner. We're leaving,' I said.

'Is that what we're doing? Is that what you think we're doing? I don't think we're doing that at all,' she said, and shattered her highball glass on the liquor bottles behind the bar.

The bar area and dining room were silent. Her gray pillbox hat was askew on top of her forehead, and a lock of red hair hung down in one eye. The bartender stood on the duckboards and stared wide-eyed at Jess, who had just thrust open the outer glass doors to the bar, the putter still in his hand, his face pushed out of shape like white rubber.

*

145

We were driving away from the lakefront, on Orleans Avenue, past City Park. Tony had the window down and was turned in his seat, looking back at me and Kim, and his black and gray hair blew like tiny springs in the wind.

'What were you guys doing?' he said. He tried to hold a grin on his face.

'I was trying to have a drink,' Kim said.

'Some fucking way to get the bartender's attention,' Jess said.

'I'm sorry about that back there,' I said to Tony.

'I can't believe it, eighty-sixed out of my own club,' he said. 'You know what it took for me to get a membership in that place?'

'You want me to go back and talk with somebody about it later?' Jess said.

'What's the matter with you? It's a country club. You can't come crashing into the bar with a golf club in your hand,' Tony said.

'I thought they were in trouble,' Jess said.

'So you had to knock a waiter down?'

'I didn't see him. What the fuck, Tony. Why you reaming me? I didn't start that stuff.'

'I think you ought to consider who you invite out to lunch,' Kim said.

'I think I ought to get a new life. Am I the only person that's sane in this car?' Tony said.

'It's my fault. I'm sorry about it,' I said.

'How gallant,' Kim said.

'All right, all right. I'll try to square it. It's just a club, anyway, right? Jesus Christ,' Tony said, and blew out his breath.

We could see golfers out on the fairways in City Park and children on horseback beyond a grove of oak trees. Jess looked in the rearview mirror and changed lanes. Then he looked in the rearview mirror again, accelerated, and passed two cars. I saw his eyes go back into the mirror.

'We've got some guys behind us,' he said.

'What guys?' Tony said.

'Two guys in a Plymouth. Behind the limo.'

'Can you make 'em?' Tony said.

'No.'

'They look like talent?'

'I don't know. What d'you want to do, Tony?'

'Pull into the park and stop.'

'You want to do that?' Jess said, looking sideways at him.

'They'll cut and run. Watch. Come on, the day's starting to improve.'

'Bad place if it goes down, Tony. Everybody gets pissed when it goes down in a public place,' Jess said.

'Hey, is it our fault? Now, turn in here. Let's have some fun with these guys.'

Kim was looking backward out the window. Tony reached over the seat and touched her on the knee, then winked at her and grinned.

'Tony, I don't need this shit,' she said.

'Will you guys mellow out? Why is everybody trying to drive me nuts today?' he said. Then he slapped open the glove box and took out a chrome-plated .45 automatic.

The white limo followed us into the park. We drove along the side of a grassy lake and stopped under a spreading oak tree. The dry leaves under it blew in the wind and clicked and tumbled across the grass. Jess reached under the seat and took out a double-barrel .410 shotgun pistol wrapped inside a paper bag. He rolled down his window and held the shotgun pistol below the level of the window jamb.

When the Plymouth turned in after us, Tony put the .45 in his right-hand coat pocket and stepped out on the cement, smiling across the top of the car as though he were welcoming guests.

'What a day,' Kim said.

'Hey, give it a break,' Jess said, without turning his head.

The Plymouth followed along the grassy lake, passed the limo, and stopped abreast of us. The man in the passenger's seat hung his badge out the window, then stepped out in the sunlight.

Nate Baxter had changed little since I had last seen him. He still wore two-tone shoes and sports clothes, but as his styled blond hair had receded he had grown a narrow line of reddish beard along his jawbones and chin. He had worked for CID in the army, and as an investigator for Internal Affairs in the New Orleans Police Department he had combined a love of military stupidity with a talent for dismembering the wounded and the vulnerable.

Jess looked straight ahead, lowered the shotgun pistol between his legs, and pushed it back under the seat.

'Put your hands on top of the car, Tony,' Baxter said.

'You're kidding?' Tony said.

'You see me smiling?' Baxter said.

'I don't think this is cool, Lieutenant,' Tony said, his hands now resting casually on the waxed maroon hood of the Lincoln. 'We've been out for some golf. We're not looking to complicate anybody's day.'

'Go tell that limo full of meatballs to get out of here,' Baxter said to his partner, who was now standing behind him. Then he turned back towards Jess and said, 'Get out of the car, Ornella.'

'Why the roust, Lieutenant?' Tony said.

'Close your mouth, Tony. Did you hear what I said, Ornella?'

Jess got out of the car with his palms turned outward, his brow furrowed above his close-set eyes. He set his hands on the convertible roof.

The white limo made a U-turn behind us and drove slowly out of the park, its black-tinted windows hot with sunlight. Baxter's partner came back and stood next to him. He was a muscular, crew-cut man, with a grained, red complexion, who wore shades and a pale blond mustache. Like Baxter, he carried a revolver under his tweed sports jacket in a clip-on belt holster. But in his face, even with his shades on, I could see a question mark about what Baxter was doing.

'Shake them down,' Baxter said.

'Come on, Lieutenant, give it a rest. This is bullshit,' Tony said.

'I look like bullshit to you?' Baxter said.

'We don't make trouble for you guys. It's a chickenshit roust. You know it is.'

Baxter nodded impatiently to his partner.

'I got a piece in my coat pocket. You want the sonofabitch, take it. What the fuck's with you, Baxter?' Tony said.

'Easy, Tony. We don't have a big problem here,' Baxter's partner said, his hands gentle on Tony's back and sides. 'No, no, look straight ahead. Come on, man, you're a pro.'

Then, like a dentist who had just pulled a tooth, he held up Tony's chrome-plated automatic in the sunlight.

'I got a permit for it,' Tony said.

'You want to produce it?' Baxter said.

'It's at home. But I got one. You know I got one.'

'Good. Your lawyer can bring it down to your arraignment,' Baxter said.

His partner pulled Tony's arms behind him, cuffed his wrists, and sat him down on the curb. Then he ran his hands down Jess's sides, back, stomach, and legs. He rose up and shook his head at Baxter.

'Under the seat,' Baxter said.

His partner leaned into the car, worked his hand around under the seat, and pulled out the shotgun pistol. He snapped open the breech and removed the two slender .410 shells and dropped them in his pocket.

'You're under arrest for possession of an illegal firearm, Ornella,' Baxter said.

'You got to have cause to get in the car, Lieutenant,' Jess said.

'You took some law courses up at Angola?' Baxter said.

'You got to have cause,' Jess said.

Baxter's partner cuffed him and led him over to the curb. Two squad cars, the backup that Baxter had probably called for, turned into the park. Baxter opened the back door of the convertible and told me to step out.

'It looks like you finally found your element,' he said.

'It must be a dull day, Nate.'

'How do you like working for the greaseballs?'

'You ought to brush up on your procedure. Probably talk a little bit with your partner. He seems to know what he's doing.'

'No kidding?'

'Nobody here was serious. Otherwise you might have gotten your hash cooked, Nate.'

'I'm probably just lucky you were along to cool things out,' he said, put a filter-tipped cigarette between his teeth at an upward angle, and lit it with a Zippo lighter. He snapped the lighter shut and blew smoke out into the sunlight. Then he said, 'I like your threads. They're elegant.'

'Get to it, Nate. You're wasting a lot of people's time.'

'No, I mean it. You're stylish. I remember you when you smelled like an unflushed toilet with booze poured in it.' He rubbed his fingers up and down the edge of my coat lapel. Then he touched my tie, put one finger under it, drew it slowly from my chest and let it drop.

I looked away at the grassy lake and the way the wind made the light break on the water. The golfers on the other side of the lake had stopped their game and were watching us.

'You like the pockets in that shirt?' And his two fingers slid down inside the cloth, so that I could feel them against the nipple.

'Don't do that, Nate.'

'It's got a nice feel to it. It pays to buy a quality shirt.'

I could see the peppery grain of his skin along the edge of his beard, a piece of yellow mucus in the corner of his eye, the pucker in his mouth that almost made me smile. His fingers felt as thick and obscene as sausages inside my pocket.

I raised my hand and pushed his arm slowly away from me.

'That's not smart,' he said quietly, and reached his hand toward me again.

I put the flat of my hand against his forearm and moved it away from me as you would press back a slowly yielding spring. He smiled and took a puff of the filter tip of his cigarette, his lips making a soft popping sound.

'Bust him. Interference with an officer in the performance of his duty,' he said to his partner. Then to me, 'I'll ask them to process you right into the population so you can eat mainline tonight.'

'Fuck you, Baxter. We'll make bail in two hours,' Tony said as a uniformed cop raised him to his feet.

'It's Friday afternoon, Tony,' Baxter said. 'Next arraignment is Monday morning.'

'What about the broad?' his partner said.

'Tell her to take a cab. Tow his car and tear it apart.'

'Nate, we might be on shaky ground here,' the partner said.

'Not with this bunch,' Baxter said.

A few minutes later I sat handcuffed next to Tony behind the wire-mesh screen of a squad car. Through the window I could see Kim walking hurriedly out of the park toward the avenue, her face as white as bone.

Tony, Jess and I were put in a holding cell a short distance from the drunk tank. Because it was a holding cell, it had no toilet or running water and contained only an iron bench that was bolted to one wall. The bars of the door had been repainted so many times the layers of white paint formed a shell around the metal. The walls were grimed with handprints and scuff marks from people's shoes, covered with scratched drawings of genitalia and names that had been scorched into the paint with butane cigarette lighters. The heat was turned up and the cell was hot. Someone in the drunk tank began screaming and was taken out by two uniformed cops.

Tony paced up and down, took off his rust-colored sports shirt, then worked his T-shirt over his head and used it to wipe his skin.

'What's the drill with this guy? Somebody tell me what the fucking drill is,' he said.

'It's Baxter. He's a bad cop. He can't make his case, so he finds something he can do,' I said.

'We ain't sitting in this shithole three days. That's out,' he said.

'Your lawyer had better know a judge, then.'

'You got it,' Tony said.

'I got to use the toilet,' Jess said.

'Hey, you hear that?' Tony shouted through the bars. 'We got a man in here needs to use the toilet.'

His olive skin glistened with perspiration, and he kept biting his lower lip. By the time we were booked and moved up to the general population, on the second floor, his hands trembled and he couldn't drink enough water. I sat next to him on the edge of an iron bunk that hung from wall chains. His back was running with sweat now. He leaned forward on his thighs and ran his hand through his wet hair.

'Lockup is at eight o'clock,' I said. 'Let's go down to the shower.'

'I'm cool,' he answered.

'You'll feel better after a shower.'

'Don't worry about me. I'm solid, man.' He gripped the edge of the bunk and shuddered as though he had malaria. 'Did anybody make you?'

'I don't think so. I've been out of New Orleans too long now.'

'Anybody make you, get in your face, tell them we're tight.'

'All right, Tony.'

'There's guys in here who'll do an ex-cop, Dave. That's not a shuck.'

'I think you just figured out Nate Baxter.'

'Yeah, well, I'm going to square it with that cat. The word is he's getting freebies from French Quarter street whores. I know one who's got AIDS. I'm going to fix it so she gets in the sack with him.'

Then he bent over and squeezed his palm across the back of his neck and said, 'Oh man, the tiger's got me.'

I stood him up and walked him by the arm down to the shower. Inmates lounging in the open doors of their cells or sitting on the big water pipe against the corridor wall looked at him with the curiosity and reverence of their kind – prisoners in a parish or city jail – when they were in the actual proximity of a mainline con or Mafia don. Some rose to their feet, offered to help, made an extravagant show of sympathy.

'He just got hold of some bad food,' I said.

'Yeah, it's rotten, Tony,' one man said.

'A roach crawled out of the grist one time, man. That's no shit,' another said.

'We got a stinger and some canned goods. You're welcome to it, Tony,' a third said.

Tony stood naked under the shower with his hands propped against the tiles. The water boiled his scalp white and sluiced over his olive skin and the knotted muscles in his back. In one pale buttock was a puckered red scar just above the colon. He held his face into the rush of hot water and opened and closed his small mouth like a guppy. When he turned off the faucets he breathed deeply through his nose, as though he were inhaling the morning air, and wiped his face slick with his palm.

'That's a little better,' he said.

Two men farther down the shower were staring at his phallus.

'You guys got a problem with your gender or something?' he said.

'Sorry, Tony. We don't mean anything,' one man said.

'Then act decent,' he said.

'Sure, Tony. Everybody's glad to have you here. No, I mean, we're sorry you're busted—'

'Get out of here,' Tony said.

'Sure, anything you want. We—' then the man lost his words, and he and his friends walked quickly out of the shower with their towels wrapped around their hips.

'That's what nobody understands about a jail. It's full of degenerates,' Tony said.

I walked with him back to our cell. Through the corridor window I could see downtown New Orleans and the glow of the city against the clouds. He put on his slacks and shirt and lay down barefoot on the bunk across from me. He folded his arm behind his head. Water dripped out of his hair on to the striped mattress.

'I'm supposed to take Paul to a soccer game tomorrow afternoon,' he said.

'He'll understand,' I said.

'That's not the way it works with kids. You're either there for them or you're not there.'

He let out a long breath and stared at the ceiling. Somebody down the corridor shouted, 'Lockup, five minutes.'

'How do I get out of it, man?' he said.

'What?'

'I'm addicted. Big-time. On the spike. I got blood pressure you could cook an egg with.'

'Maybe you should think about a treatment program.'

'One of those thirty-day hospital jobs? What about Paul? What about my fucking wife?'

'What about her?'

'She never dresses him or plays with him. She won't take him shopping with her or to a show. But I kick her out, she'll sue for custody. That's her big edge. And, man, does she work it. I should have used that psycho Boggs to whack her out. Her and that prick over in Houston.'

'Who?'

'She makes it with one of the Dio crowd from Houston. They meet in Miami. That's why she's always flying over there. Come on, man. You read a lot of books. What would you do?'

'You're trying to deal with all the monsters at the same time. Start with the addiction.'

'I tried. Out at the VA I think I'm in it for the whole ride.'

'There're ways out, Tony.'

'Yeah, and you can scrub the stink out of shit, too. You came home okay, Dave. I blew it.'

He turned on his side and faced the wall. When I spoke to him again, he did not answer.

The daytime noise level in any jail is grinding and ceaseless, particularly on a Saturday morning. I woke to the clanging of cell doors, shoes thudding on spiral metal stairs, cleaning crews scraping buckets across the cement floors, shower water drumming on the tile walls, radios tuned to a dozen different stations, someone cracking wind into a toilet bowl or roaring out a belch from the bottom of his bowels, inmates shouting from the windows to friends on the other side of the razor wire that bordered the street – a dirty, iron-tinged, cacophonous mix that echoed down the long concrete corridor with such an ear-numbing intensity that the individual voice was lost in it.

We lined up when the trusties wheeled in the steam carts loaded with grits, sausage, black coffee, and white bread, and later Tony and I played checkers on a homemade board in our cell. Then, because we had nothing else to do, we followed Jess down to the weight room at the end of the corridor. The weather was warm and sunny, so the solitary barred window high up on the wall was open, but the room reeked of the men clanking barbells up and down on the cement. They were stripped to the waist, or wore only their Jockey undershorts or cutoff sweatpants, their bodies laced with rivulets of sweat. They had bulging scrotums, necks like tree stumps, shoulders you could break a two-by-four across. Some of the Negroes were as black as paint, the Caucasians so white their skin had a shine to it. And they all seemed to contain a reservoir of rut and power and ruthless energy that made you shudder when you considered the fact that soon they would be back on the street.

Their tattoos were a marvel: spiders in purple webs stretched across the shoulder blades, serpents twined around biceps and forearms, beret-capped skulls, hearts impaled on knives, swastikas clutched in eagle claws, green dragons blowing fire across loins, Confederate flags, lily-wrapped crucifixes, and the face of Christ with beads of blood upon his tortured brow.

For a moment we almost had trouble. A tall white man with a black goatee, wearing only a jockstrap and tennis shoes, sat against the wall and wiped his chest and stomach with a tattered gray towel. His eyes focused on my face and stayed there; then he said, 'I know that guy. He's a cop.'

The clanking of the barbells stopped. The room was absolutely quiet.

Then a big black man, with a nylon stocking crimped on his head, set down his weights and said to me, 'What about it, Home?'

'I look like heat? Take a look at my charge sheet,' I said.

'No, we don't look at nothing. This guy came in with me,' Tony said. He looked down at the tall white man sitting on the floor with his knees splayed open. 'You saying I brought a cop in with me?'

The man's eyes met Tony's, then became close-set and focused on nothing.

'He looked like a guy I used to see around,' he said. 'Some other guy.'

The room remained quiet. I could hear traffic out on the street. Everyone was watching Tony.

'So don't worry about it,' he said. He laughed, pulled the towel from the man's hand, and rubbed the man's head with it. 'Hey, what's with this crazy guy? Y'all made him weird or is that the way they come in from Jump Street these days?'

The man grinned sheepishly; then everyone was laughing, clanging the barbells again, grabbing themselves, nodding to one another in admiration of Tony's intelligence and wit or whatever quality it was that allowed him to charm a snake back into a basket.

Tony walked past me out the door, his smile welded on his face, and nudged me in the side with his thumb. We walked side by side back toward our cell. He kept his face straight. He whistled a disjointed tune and then said, 'Do you know who that guy was?'

'No, I don't remember him.'

'He did a snitch with an ice pick in Angola for twenty bucks. Let's play a lot of checkers today, hang around the cell, talk about books, you get my drift?'

'You're a piece of work, Tony.'

'What I am is too old for this shit.'

But our worries about the group in the weight room were unnecessary. Tony's lawyer had us sprung by noon, all charges dropped. Nate Baxter had not had probable cause to stop and search us, Tony's lawyer had produced the permit for Tony's pistol, and the charge against me – interfering with an officer in the performance of his duty – was a manufactured one that the prosecutor's office wouldn't waste time on. The only loser was Jess, who had his .410 shotgun pistol confiscated.

We picked up the Lincoln at the car pound and Tony treated us to lunch at an outdoor café on St Charles. It was a lovely fall day, seventy-five degrees, perhaps, with a soft wind out of the south that lifted the moss in the oak trees along the avenue. A Negro was selling snow cones, which people in New Orleans call snowballs, out of a white cart, with a canvas umbrella over it, on the esplanade. The dry fronds of a thick-trunked palm tree covered his white uniform with shifting patterns of etched lines. I heard the streetcar tracks begin to hum, then farther up the avenue I saw the streetcar wobbling down the esplanade in a smoky cone of light and shadow created by the canopy of oaks.

'When we were kids we used to put pennies on the tracks and flatten them out to the size of half dollars,' Tony said, wiping the tomato sauce from his shrimp off his mouth with a napkin. 'They'd still be hot in your hand when you picked them up.'

'That's not all you done when you were a kid,' Jess said. 'You remember when you and your cousins found them arms behind the Tulane medical school?' Jess looked at me. 'That's right. They got this whole pile of arms that was supposed to be burned in the incinerator. Except Tony and his cousins put them on crushed ice in a beer cooler and got on the streetcar with them when all the coloreds were just getting off work. They waited until it was wall-to-wall people, then they hung a half dozen of these arms from the hand straps. People were screaming all over the car, trampling each other to get out the door, climbing out the windows at thirty miles an hour. One big fat guy crashed right on top of the snowball stand.'

'Hey, don't tell Dave that stuff. He's going to think I'm a ghoul or something,' Tony said.

'Tony used to flush M-80s down the commode at the Catholic school,' Jess said. 'See, the fire would burn down through the center of the fuse. They'd get way back in the plumbing before they'd explode, then anybody taking a dump would get douched with pot water.'

People at the other tables turned and stared at us, openmouthed.

'You finished eating, Jess?' Tony said.

'I'm going to get some pecan pie,' Jess said.

'How about bringing the car around? I've got to get home,' Tony said.

'What'd I do this time?'

'Nothing, Jess. You're fine.'

'You make me feel like I ought to be in a plastic bubble or something. I was just telling a story.'

'It's okay, Jess. Just get the car,' Tony said. Then after Jess was gone, he said to me. 'What am I going to do? He's the one loyal guy I got. When it comes to protecting me, you could bust a chair across his face and he wouldn't blink.'

A few minutes later Jess came around the corner in the convertible and waited for us in front of the restaurant. Leaves blew under the wire wheels.

'You guys drop me by my apartment so I can get my truck,' I said. 'I'll be back out to your house a little later.'

Tony grinned, 'I bet you're off to see Bootsie. Tell her hello for me,' he said.

His presumption that Bootsie should have been uppermost in my mind was right – but she wasn't. After they left me at my apartment on Ursulines I called Minos at the guesthouse.

'I'm sorry you had to spend a night in the bag. How was it?' he said.

'What do you think?' Through the window I could see my neighbor's bluetick dog urinating against a banana tree in the flower bed.

'Look, I've got some news about Boggs, some of which I don't understand. An informant told our Lafayette office that Boggs was in New Iberia two days ago. What would he be doing in New Iberia?'

'Where'd your snitch see him?'

'In a black neighborhood, out in the parish. Why would Boggs be in a black neighborhood?'

'Tony said Boggs told him he was going to blackmail a Negro woman who owned a hot-pillow joint. It had something to do with the murder of a redbone. I think the redbone was a migrant-labor contractor named Hipolyte Broussard. But Boggs told all this to Cardo before he ripped off the coke out on the salt. I don't know why he'd be interested in some minor-league blackmail when he's holding a half-million dollars' worth of cocaine.'

'I don't either. Anyway, we have some other information, too. We've got some taps on the greaseballs over in Houston. It's not an open contract on Cardo anymore. Boggs has got the hit. It's fifty grand, a big-money whack even for these guys. But they want it to go down in the next week.'

'Why the hurry?'

'They're afraid of him. Tony C. isn't one to take prisoners. One guy on the tape says it might have to be a slop shot. Have you heard that one before?'

'Yes.'

'There're no innocent bystanders. His wife, his kid, anybody around him, they're all targets if necessary. Dave, if Boggs *was* in New Iberia, do you think it has something to do with you?'

'Why?'

'Who has more reason to want you off the board? It's turned around on him. I bet he gets up thinking about you in the morning.'

'Maybe.'

'Look, I want to push this stuff to a head. Can you get a wire into Cardo's house?'

'I think so.'

'Either you can or you can't, Dave.'

'I can try, Minos.'

'Once again I'm getting a strong impression here of a lack of enthusiasm.'

'What do you expect? I'm a hired Judas goat. You want me to tell you I like it?'

He paused a moment; then he said in an even voice, 'We hear a big load of coke is going to hit town in three or four days. A lot of it is going to end up as crack in the welfare projects.'

I looked out the window into the courtyard, where my neighbor was trying to leash his dog in the flower bed.

'Are you there?'

'Yeah,' I said.

'You know the scene. A human life isn't worth a stick of chewing gum in those places. All thanks to Tony C. and his friends.'

'How do you want to work it?'

'Find out his connections with the shipment. Then we'll wire you. All we need is a statement that he's in on the buy or the distribution.'

'All right.'

'You sound like you've got something else on your mind.'

'It's Kim Dollinger. I think somebody's got her out there twisting in the wind.'

'Why?'

'She was terrified when we got busted yesterday.'

'Who's she afraid of?'

'Tony, Nate Baxter, you guys. How should I know?'

'It's not us. You want us to pick her up?'

'She's a hard-nosed girl. She won't cooperate. Baxter let her walk. Why would he let *her* walk when he rousted the rest of us? It was a good opportunity to squeeze her.'

'From what I hear about this guy, he's about as complicated as an empty closet. Save yourself a lot of grief and don't make a mystery out of morons.'

'If I only had that clarity of line, Minos.'

'Work on it. It'll come with time.'

After I hung up, I shaved, showered, and changed into a pair of clean gray slacks, a maroon shirt, combed my hair in the mirror, put a touch of Vaseline on the hard knot of stitches in my lip and head, and buffed my loafers.

I tried to keep my mind blank and not think about the care I was putting into my appearance.

Then I drove down St Charles to South Carrollton and parked my pickup truck in front of the nineteenth-century building by the levee where Kim Dollinger lived.

Her apartment was on the second floor, and there was a hand-twist bell on the door. I had to ring it twice before she answered, a tower in her hand, her neck spotted with water. She wore jeans, tan sandals, and a white peasant blouse with a pink ribbon threaded through the top. The front of her blouse hung straight down from her breasts.

'Oh boy,' she said.

'May I come in?'

She blotted the water on her neck and looked into my face.

'I'm getting ready to go to work,' she said.

Her back window was open, and I smelled the draft that blew out into the hall.

'That's not all you've been doing,' I said.

'Look—'

'Come on, I just got out of the bag. You can't offer me a cup of coffee?'

She stood back from the door for me to enter. I heard her close it behind me. Through the open window I could see the green of the levee and the wide, flat expanse of the Mississippi and the sandy bank and willow trees on the far side. The living room looked furnished from a secondhand store. Off to the side was a small kitchen with bright yellow linoleum. She sat down at a breakfast table that was located between the kitchen and living room. The legs of the table and chairs were chrome and had rusty scratches on them that looked like dismembered parts of insects.

'Kim, I'm not telling you what to do, but if you've already got the dragons after you, reefer just makes the problem a lot worse,' I said.

She crumpled the towel on the tabletop. Her eyes looked out into space.

'What is it that you want?' she said.

'To talk with you on the square, with no bullshit.'

'That's it? Nothing else?'

'That's right.'

'You wouldn't like to ball me while you're at it, would you?'

'Cut the badass act, Kim. It's a drag.'

'I tried to talk with you. You wouldn't hear me.'

'I can get you out of this.'

'You?'

'That's right.'

'A guy with a mouthful of stitches.'

'I'm tired of being your dartboard. You'd better listen when a friend is talking to you.'

She put the heel of her hand against her forehead. Her skin reddened from the pressure. She crossed her legs and breathed through her mouth. There were patches of color in her throat and cheeks. She made me think of someone who might have been wrapped in invisible rope.

'Have you ever been down?' I said.

'Have I what?' Her mouth hung open.

'Have you ever done time?'

'No.'

'Are you sure?'

'I said no.'

'Have you been in custody?'

'You stop talking to me like this. Why are you saying these things to me?' Her voice started to break.

'Because somebody is turning the screws on you. I suspect it's Nate Baxter. He's a sonofabitch, Kim, and I know what he's capable of.'

She pushed the heel of her hand along her hairline.

'What does Tony know?' she said.

'I couldn't guess. Do you sleep with him?' My eyes shifted away from her face, and I didn't want to hear her answer.

'I used to. When he wanted me to, anyway. He doesn't want to anymore. It's the speed. It's messed him up.'

I glanced back at her face again. Her eyes met mine, then they looked away. There was a tingling in my throat, like a heated wire trembling against a nerve.

'Did somebody make you sleep with him?' I said.

'You don't have the right to ask me these things.'

'If Nate Baxter is behind this, he's going to have the worst experience of his life.'

'There's nothing you can do. It involves somebody else. Oh God, where's my stash?' she said.

She got up from the table, took a clear, sealed plastic bag of reefer from a kitchen drawer, sat back down, and began to roll a joint from a sheaf of ZigZag cigarette papers. Her eyes were narrowed with concentration, but her fingers began to shake and strands of reefer fell from both sides of the paper. Then she gave it up, rested her elbows on the table, and pressed a knuckle from each hand against her temples.

I picked up the plastic bag, splayed it open, dropped the papers inside, raked the loose strands of reefer into it, and walked down a short hallway to the bathroom.

'What are you doing?' she said.

I emptied the bag into the toilet and flushed it. Then I dropped the bag into a kitchen garbage sack. When I turned around she was standing a foot from me. Her hair hung on her forehead, and she had accidentally smeared her lipstick.

'Why did you do that?' she said.

'You don't need it.'

'I don't need it?'

'No.'

'Tony says it's all a cluster fuck.'

'He's wrong.'

Her eyes were green and moist and they looked directly into mine. I could hear the wetness in her throat when she swallowed. The top of her pink-ribboned peasant blouse was crooked on her shoulders.

'There's always a way out of trouble,' I said. 'You just have to trust your friends once in a while.'

I touched her on the upper arm with my palm. I meant it in a protective and friendly way. Yes, I know that was the way I meant it. I could see the freckles on her shoulders, feel her breath on my face. She stepped close to me, and my arms were on her back, my hands lightly touching the coolness of her skin, the thickness of her hair. She rubbed her face under my chin, and I felt a shudder go through her body like tension leaving a metal spring.

Then she remained motionless in my arms, her breath small and regular against my chest. In the distance, I could see the hard, stiff outline of the Huey Long Bridge against a bank of purple rain clouds.

11

After I left Kim's, I drove into the French Quarter and tried to find a place to park close by Clete's nightclub. But it was Saturday afternoon, the Quarter was crowded with tourists, and I had to park off Elysian Fields and walk back down Decatur to the club. A noisy crowd was at the bar, and a five-piece band was blaring out 'Rampart Street Parade' by the dance floor.

'Take a walk with me,' I said to Clete, who was behind the bar in a pair of gray slacks and a green Tulane sweatshirt.

'It's a little busy right now, Streak.'

'It's important.'

We crossed the street and walked down to the Café du Monde, where I ordered *beignets* through the takeout window.

'Beautiful day,' I said.

'I'm not kidding, Dave, I've got a bar to run. What is it?'

'Come on,' I said. We walked over the top of the levee and out on to the gentle green slope that led down to the river. On the far side of the river was the shabby outline of Algiers. 'I need a cover story.'

His eyes went up and down my shirt.

'What are you talking about?' he said.

'Minos is going to put a wire on me. I need to make Tony talk about a big drug delivery that's about to go down. I have to have some way of bringing it up.'

'You might need a cover story about something else,' he said, and reached out and removed a long strand of red hair from my shirtfront. 'Brush up against somebody in the streetcar, did you?'

'Let's keep to the subject.'

'Have you lost your mind?'

'Lay off it, Clete.'

'I told you one of the cardinal rules when you get involved with the greaseballs: Don't mess with their broads.'

'Have you heard anything about a big delivery?'

'I bet she's one hot item, though, isn't she?'

'I need your help. Will you cut out the bullshit.'

He took a *beignet* out of the napkin in my hand and bit off half of it. His green eyes were thoughtful as he looked out at the river.

'I hear crack prices are up in the Iberville welfare project, which means the supply is down,' he said. 'But next week everybody is going to have all the rock they can smoke. That's the word, anyway. What's the DEA say?'

'Same thing.'

'That crack is some mean shit. You ever watch them huff that stuff? They remind me of somebody having a seizure.'

'You know I'm staying out at Cardo's?'

'I called Dautrieve. He told me. Why is it that guy makes me feel like anthrax?'

'Boggs has been given a contract on Cardo.'

'And you're living with him? That's great, Streak. Maybe you ought to look into some real estate buys on the San Andreas fault.'

'I'm going to play it one more week, then I'm out.'

'I think you're *in*. The operative word there, mon, is *in*. Bootsie Giacano wasn't dangerous enough. You had to get in the sack with Cardo's main punch.'

'That's not the way it is. Don't talk about her that way, either, Clete.'

'Excuse me. It's my lack of couth. We're talking the parochial school sodality here. Dave, you'd better get your head on straight. You live among these people, you start to believe they're like us. They're not, mon. When it comes down to saving their own ass, they'd sell their mothers to a puppy farm.'

'Boggs has been in New Iberia. I think he's got me on his dance card. I'd rather deal with him in New Orleans than around Alafair.'

'I think you're being used. I think you should forget Cardo and these DEA jerk-offs and you and I should go after Boggs and blow out his candle. What do you care if Cardo sells dope? You shut him down, the price on the street goes up. The dealers come out ahead any way you cut it. Look, most of the dope has gone back to the slums, anyway. That's where it started, that's where it's going to stay. Then one day the poor dumb bastards will get tired of watching their own kind get hauled away in body bags.'

'I was in jail last night. Nate Baxter rousted Tony and me and his driver. Can you get to somebody in the First District, find out what Baxter's doing?'

'In jail?'

'That's right.'

'You remind me of these kids with their crack pipes. It takes a guy like me twenty years to go to hell. They can do it in six months. But, Streak, you've got a talent for fucking up your life in weeks.'

'Will you see what you can find out about Baxter?'

'A cop who blew the country with a murder warrant on him? I'm your liaison person?'

He put the rest of the *beignet* in his mouth and laughed while he rubbed his palm clean with his napkin.

I walked back to my truck in the cooling shadows and drove down Canal to the corner of St Charles, where Clete had seen Tee Beau Latiolais working in a pizza place. Young black men lounged in front of the liquor stores and arcades, their bodies striped with the purple and pink neon glow from the windows. I found Tee Beau in the back of a long, narrow café, his white paper hat pulled down to his eyebrows, so that he seemed to be staring at me from under a visor.

'Take a break. I need to talk to you, Tee Beau,' I said.

His eyes were peculiar, melancholy, as though he were witnessing a bad fate for a friend that the friend was not aware of.

'What is it?' I said.

He didn't answer. He wiped his hands on his apron and put on a pair of sunglasses. We walked around the corner to the Pearl and sat at the bar. A white man farther down the bar was shucking oysters with a fierce energy on a sideboard. Tee Beau ordered a Falstaff and kept looking at me out of the side of his eye.

'You know, Tee Beau, I don't think sunglasses in the evening are the best kind of disguise.'

'Why you want to see me, Mr Dave?'

'I heard Jimmie Lee Boggs has been in New Iberia. I'd like to find out why. Can you talk to Dorothea?'

'I ain't got to. Talked to her last night. She didn't say nothing about seeing Jimmie Lee. But she tole me what Gros Mama Goula say about you, Mr Dave.'

'Oh?'

'You got the *gris-gris.* she say you been messin' where you ain't suppose to be messin'. You ain't listen to nobody.'

'Listen, Tee Beau, Gros Mama is a big black gasbag. She jerks your people around with a lot of superstition that goes back to the islands, back to the slave days.'

But my words meant nothing to him.

'I made you this, Mr Dave. I was gonna come find you.'

'I appreciate it, but—'

'You put it on your ankle, you.'

I made no offer to take the perforated dime and the piece of red string looped through it from his hand. He dropped them in my shirt pocket.

'You white, you been to colletch, you don't believe,' he said. 'But I seen things. A man that had snakes crawl all over his grave. They was fat as my wrist. Couldn't keep them off the grave with poison or a shotgun. You stick a hayfork in them, shake them off in a fire, they be back the next morning, smelling like they been lying in hot ash.

'A woman name Miz Gold, 'cause her skin was gold, she taken a man away from Gros Mama, then come in Gros Mama's juke with him, wearing a pink silk dress, carrying a pink umbrella, laughing about Gros Mama's tattoos and saying she ain't nothing but a nigger *putain* that does what white mens tells her. The next day Miz Gold woke up with hair all over her face. Just like a monkey. She do everything to get rid of it, Mr Dave, pull it out of her skin with pliers till blood run down her neck. But it didn't do no good. That woman so ugly nobody go near her, no white peoples hire her. She used to go up and down the alley, picking rags out of my *gran'maman*'s trash can.'

'Okay, Tee Beau, I'll keep it all in mind.'

'No, you ain't. In one way you like most white folks, Mr Dave. You don't hear what a black man saying to you.'

He upended his bottle of Falstaff and looked at me over the top of his glasses.

The evening air was cool and moist, purple with shadow, when I walked back to my truck. I saw a car parked overtime at a meter. I broke the red string off the perforated dime that Tee Beau had given me, slipped the dime into the meter, and twisted the handle. In front of the liquor store two Negro men in bright print shirts and lacquered porkpie hats were snapping their fingers to the music on a boom box. One of them smiled at me for no reason, his teeth a brilliant flash of gold.

I didn't go back to Tony's right away. Instead, I parked by Jackson Square and sat on a stone bench in front of St Louis Cathedral and watched people leaving Saturday evening Mass. My head was filled with confused thoughts, like a clatter of birds' wings inside a cage. I used a pay phone on the corner to call Bootsie, but she wasn't home. The square was dark now, the myrtle and banana trees etched in the light from the Café du Monde, and there was a chill in the wind off the river. After the cathedral had emptied, I went inside and knelt in a back pew. A tiny red light, like a drop of electrified blood, glowed at the top of a confessional box, which meant that a priest was inside.

Many people are currently enamored with Cajun culture, but they know little of its darker side: organized dogfights and cockfights, the casual attitude toward the sexual exploitation of Negro women, the environmental ignorance that has allowed the draining and industrial poisoning of the wetlands. Also, few outsiders understand the violent feelings that Cajun people have about the nature of fidelity, and human possession.

When I was twenty I worked as a welder's helper with my father on a pipeline outside of a little town north of the Atchafalaya Basin. Someone discovered that a married woman in the town was having an affair with the priest. A mob came for her at night, in a caravan of cars, and took her from her home and drove her to an empty field next to the church. They formed a circle around her, and while she cried and begged they beat her black and blue with hairbrushes. Simultaneously someone phoned her husband at his job in Baton Rouge and told him of his wife's infidelity. He was killed driving home that night in a rainstorm.

Some might simply explain it as redneck bigotry, but I think it is much more complex than that. In the minds of rural Acadian people the priest is the representative of God, and they will not share him or Him. Their violence seldom has to do with money. Instead, it can reach a murderous intensity within minutes over a betrayed trust, a lie, a wrong against a family member. Their sense of loyalty is atavistic and irrational, their sense of loss at its compromise as painful and unexpected, no matter how many times it happens, as a lesion across the heart.

I went inside the confessional. The priest slid back the small wooden door behind the screen, and I could see the gray outline of his head. His voice was that of an elderly man, and I also discovered that he was hard of hearing. I tried to explain to him the nature of my problem, but he only became more confused.

'I'm an undercover police officer, Father. My work requires that I betray some people. These are bad people, I suppose, or what they do is bad, but I don't feel good about it.'

'I don't understand.'

'I'm lying to people. I pretend to be something I'm not. I feel I'm making an enormous deception out of my life.'

'Because you want to arrest these people?'

'I'm a drunk. I belong to AA. Honesty is supposed to be everything in our program.'

'You're drunk? Now?'

I tried again.

'I've become romantically involved with a woman. She's an old friend from my hometown. I hurt her many years ago. I think I'm going to hurt her again.'

He was quiet. He had a cold and he sniffed into a handkerchief.

'I don't understand what you're telling me,' he said.

'I was shot last summer, Father. I almost died. As a result I developed great fears about myself. To overcome them I became involved in an undercover sting. Now I think maybe other people might have to pay the price for my problem – the woman from my hometown, a man with a crippled child, a young woman I was with today, one I feel an attraction to when I shouldn't.'

His head was bent forward. His handkerchief was crumpled in his hand.

'Can you just tell me the number of the commandments you've broken and the number of times?' he asked. 'That's all we really need to do right now.'

He waited, and it was obvious that his need for understanding, at least in that moment, was as great as mine.

Sunday morning Tony and I took Paul horseback riding on the farm of one of Tony's mobster friends down in Plaquemines Parish. Tony had dressed Paul in a brown corduroy coat and trousers, with a tan suede bill cap, and he balanced Paul in front of him on the saddle while we walked our horses along the edge of a barbed-wire-fenced hardpan field a hundred yards from the Gulf. The grass in the field was pale green, and white egrets picked in the dry cow flop. The few palm trees along the narrow stretch of beach were yellowed with blight, and they clattered and straightened in the wind that was blowing hard off the water. Behind us, parked by a tight grove of oak trees, were the Lincoln and the white Cadillac limousine. Jess and Tony's other bodyguards and gunmen were drinking canned beer and eating fried chicken out of paper buckets in the sunshine and entertaining themselves by popping their pistols at sea gulls out on a sandspit. Tony wore a white cashmere jacket, a safari hat, and riding breeches tucked inside his knee-high leather boots.

He kept wetting his lips in the wind. His skin was stretched tight around his eyes.

'How do I look?' he said.

'Good.'

'I mean how do *I* look?' He turned his face toward me and looked into my eyes.

'You look fine, Tony.'

'It's been two days since I put anything in the tank. It's got butterflies fluttering around in my head.'

'What tank, Daddy?' Paul said.

'I'm trying to get on a diet and get my blood pressure down. That's all, son,' Tony said.

'What butterflies?' Paul said.

'When I don't eat what I want, the butterflies start flitting around me. Big purple and yellow ones. Boy, do I got 'em today. Listen to those guys shooting back there. You go out to a quiet spot in the country, they turn it into a war zone.'

'Who's trying to hurt us, Daddy?' Paul asked.

'Nobody. Who told you that?'

'Jess. He said some bad man wants to hurt us.'

'Jess isn't too bright sometimes, son. He imagines things. Don't pay attention to him.' Tony looked back over his shoulder at the grove of oak trees, where his hired men lounged around the automobile fenders in sport clothes and shoulder holsters. His eyes were dark, and he rubbed his tongue hard against the back of his teeth. Then he took a deep breath through his nose.

'Paul and me have got a place down in Mexico, don't we, Paul?' he said. 'It's not much, thirty acres outside of Guadalajara, but it's got a fishing pond, a bunch of goats and chickens and stuff like that, doesn't it, Paul? It's quiet, too. Nobody bothers us there, either.'

'My mother says it's full of snakes. She won't go there anymore.'

'Which means there's no shopping mall where she can spend three or four hundred bucks a day. You ever been down there, Dave?'

'No.'

'If I could ever get some things straightened out here in the right way, I might want to move down there. If you're a gringo, you've got to pay off a few of the local greasers, but after that, they treat you okay.'

'Can we go eat now, Dad?'

'Sure,' Tony said. 'You want to eat, Dave?'

'That's a good idea.'

We could heard the flat popping sound of the pistols in the wind. We would see the smoke first, then hear the report carried to us across the flattened grass.

'Those guys and their guns. What a pain in the ass,' Tony said.

'You said not to use bad words, Daddy,' Paul said.

Tony smiled and popped up the bill of his little boy's cap.

'You got me there. But what do you do with a bunch like that? Not one of them could rub two thoughts together on his best day.' Then Tony twisted in the saddle and lifted his finger at me. In the chill sunlight his face looked as though it had been boiled empty of all heat and coherence. 'I've got to talk with you, man,' he said.

We tethered our horses in the oak grove, and Tony put Paul in his wheelchair and fixed him a paper plate of fried chicken and potato salad. Then he picked up a half-filled bucket of chicken, tossed it at me, and climbed over the barbed-wire fence out on to the beach. I followed him out on to the damp gray sand.

'I got something bugging the fuck out of me,' he said. 'I got to get rid of it, or I'm gonna shoot up again. I get back on the spike, I'm gonna end. I've got no illusions about that.'

'Maybe it's time to unload, Tony.'

'I already did. It didn't do any good. It just made it worse.'

'Then you're holding on to it for some reason.'

'That's what you think, huh?' He had a half-eaten drumstick in his hand. He flung it hard at a sea gull that was hovering above the waves. The water was dark green and full of kelp. 'Try this. I went to a psychiatrist, a ninety-buck-an-hour Tulane fruit, in a peppermint-stripe shirt with one of these round white collars. You dig the type I'm talking about? A guy about six and a half feet long, except he's made out of marshmallows. So I told him finally about some stuff back there in Vietnam, and he starts to make fun of me. With this simpering voice, like psychiatrists use when they got no answers for the problem. He says, "Ah, I see, you're the big brave warrior who can't have weaknesses like everybody else. Tony's the superstud, the macho man from Mother Green's killing machine. Tony's not going to let anyone know he's human, too. Why, that'd be a disappointment to the whole human race."

'Then he stretches his legs out and looks me in the eye like he's just taken my soul out of my chest with a pair of tweezers. So I say, "Doc, you're one clever guy. But there're certain things you don't say to certain guys unless you've gotten your own ticket punched a couple of times. I've got the feeling you're short on dues. And when you're short on dues and you run off at the mouth with the wrong people, you ought to expect certain consequences. What that means is you get the shit stomped out of you." '

Tony sat down on a beached cypress tree that was white with rot. The sand was littered with jellyfish that had been left behind by the tide. Their air sacs were pink and blue and translucent, their stingers coated with grit.

'So he stops smiling,' Tony said. 'In fact, his mouth is looking a little rubbery, like he just stopped sucking on a doorknob. I say, "But don't sweat it, Doc, because I don't beat up on fruits. But if you ever talk to me like that again, or you talk to other shrinks about me, or you put any of this dog shit in your files, somebody's gonna pull you out of Lake Pontchartrain with some of your parts missing." '

Tony breathed the salt wind through his nose, then popped the air sac of a jellyfish with the tip of his boot.

'Yeah, I guess that really solved your problem,' I said.

'You cracking wise with me, Dave?'

'I just don't know what I can tell you. Or what you want from me.'

'Tell me how come I don't get any relief.'

'I never figured out all my own problems. I'm probably the wrong guy to talk to, Tony.'

'You're the right guy.'

'I think you want forgiveness. From somebody who counts. The psychiatrist didn't count because he hadn't paid any dues.'

'Who's gonna hand out this forgiveness?'

'It'll have to come from somebody who's important to you. God, a priest, somebody whose experience you respect. Finally yourself, Tony. A psychiatrist with any brains would have told you that.'

'A guy like me is going to a priest?' He grinned and scraped out long divots in the sand with his boot heel. In the quiet I could hear the hiss of the waves as they receded from the beach. Then he cocked his eye and looked up at me from under the brim of his safari hat. 'Hey, don't be offended. You know stuff. You know more than any shrink.'

'You inflate my value, Tony.'

'No, I don't. You're one all-together, copacetic motherfucker, Robicheaux.'

His head nodded up and down, one eye squinting at me as though he were fixing me inside telescopic sights.

'You've got the wrong man,' I said.

That evening Tony and Paul and I ate supper by candlelight in his dining room. We had boiled early potatoes, string beans cooked with mushrooms, and lamb glazed with a sauce made from orange marmalade; the burgundy that Tony drank must have cost fifty dollars a bottle. The tablecloth was Irish linen; in the center was a crystal bowl of water filled with floating camellias. The dessert was a choice of chocolate mousse or French vanilla ice cream or both.

Later, while Tony and his son watched television, I strolled through the grounds behind the house in the twilight. The Saint Augustine grass was thick and stiff under my feet, the flower beds absolutely weedless, the dead banana leaves and palm fronds trimmed back daily so that everything in Tony's yard looked green and full of bloom, regardless of the season.

But what was life like for most people in New Orleans that year? I asked myself. Or what had become of the city itself in the last five years?

Even a tourist could answer those questions. The bottom had dropped out of the oil market and the economy was worse than it had been anytime since the Depression. Cardboard boxes and sacks of raw garbage sat on the sidewalks for days, humming with flies; derelicts and bag ladies rooted in trash cans on Canal for food. The homicide rate had reached an average of one murder a day. If your automobile was burglarized, or all its windows smashed out with bricks, you probably would not be able to get a policeman at the scene for an hour and a half. The St Louis Cemetery off Basin, which had always been one of the city's most interesting tourist attractions, was now so dangerous that you could enter it only on a group tour conducted by an off-duty police officer. The welfare projects – the St Bernard, the St Thomas, the Iberville off Canal, or, the worst of them all, the Desire – were spread throughout the city, and within them was everything bad that human society could produce: rats, cockroaches, incest, rape, child molestation, narcotics, and sadistic street gangs. Black teenagers armed with nine-millimeter pistols and semi-automatic assault rifles made large profits trafficking in crack, and they would kill absolutely anyone who tried to stop them. A black leader in the Desire project announced publicly that he was going to run the drug dealers out of the neighborhood. Two days later he was gunned down by a pair of fifteen-year-old kids, and while he lay bleeding on the sidewalk they broke his ribs with a baseball bat.

I sat on a stone bench by Tony's clay tennis court and watched the twilight fade in the stillness. The western sky was the dull gray color of scraped bone. One of the gatemen turned on the flood lamps that were anchored in the oak trees along the outer walls, and the fish ponds, the birdbaths, the alabaster statues on the lawn, seemed to glow with a humid, electric aura as though the coming of the night had no application to Tony's world.

I could see him through the glassed-in sun porch, watching television with Paul, his face laughing at a joke told by a comedian. I wondered if Tony ever thought about life in New Orleans's welfare projects or that army of teenage crack addicts who cooked their brains for breakfast. I thought he probably did not.

I called Bootsie twice that evening. She wasn't home either time, but the next morning I was up early and caught her at six. Her voice was warm and full of sleep.

'I've been trying to get hold of you,' I said.

'I've been out of town.'

'Where?'

'Over at Houston. At Baylor.'

'At the hospital?'

'Yes.'

'What were you doing at Baylor?'

'Oh, it's nothing.'

'Boots?'

'Yes?'

'What are you holding out on me?'

'Don't worry about it, hon. When am I going to see you?'

'Can I come by now?' I said.

'Mmmm, what'd you have in mind?'

I suddenly realized that I didn't have an honest answer to her question.

'Because I have to go to work, hon,' she said.

'I just wanted to see you, to talk to you.'

'Is something wrong?'

'No, not really,' I said. 'Look, Boots, I have to go over to the apartment in a little bit and pick up some things. Your office is only a few blocks away. Can you come by for a few minutes? I'll fix breakfast for us.'

'I'll try,' she said. 'Dave, what is it?'

I took a breath.

'People just need to talk sometimes. This is one of them,' I said.

'Yes, I think it is,' she said.

I gave her my address on Ursulines.

'Dave?' she said.

'Yes.'

'I don't get hurt easily anymore. If that's what we're talking about.'

'We're not talking about that at all,' I said.

After I hung up the phone I looked out the window at the early sun shining through the trees in Tony's yard, the wind ruffling on his fish ponds, the flapping of the dew-soaked canvas screens on his tennis court. But I took no joy in the new morning.

I drove into the center of the city and parked my truck in the garage on Ursulines, then went through the domed brick archway into the court-yard. The flagstones were streaked with water, and I could smell coffee and bacon from someone's apartment. Upstairs on the balcony a fat woman in a print dress was sweeping dust out through the grillwork into the sunlight.

I had my keys in my hand before I noticed the soft white gashes, in the shape of a screwdriver head, between the door and jamb of my apart-ment. I slipped my .45 out of the back of my trousers, let it hang loosely at my side, pushed the sprung door back on its hinges with my foot, and stepped inside.

My eyes would not encompass or accept the interior of the apartment all at once, in the way that your mind rejects the appearance of your car after a street gang has worked it over with curbstones. A large bullfrog was nailed to the back of the door. Its puffed white belly was split by the force of the nail, its legs hung down limply, and its wide flat mouth stretched open as though it were waiting for a fly.

The ceiling, the walls, the cheap furniture, were dotted with blood as though it had been slung there in patterns. Above the kitchen doorway, painted redly into the plaster, were the words YOU ARE DED. The blood had run in strings down the plaster and dripped into the linoleum.

But my bedroom was untouched, and I thought I had seen the worst of it until I looked into the bathroom. The toilet lid was closed, but blood and water had swelled over the lip and streamed down the white porcelain, too thick and dark for the dilution that should have taken place. Written with a ballpoint pen on a damp sheet of lined paper that lay on the toilet lid were the words DONT FLUSH. MY BABY IS INSIDE.

I stuck the .45 through the back of my belt and started to raise the lid, then withdrew my hand. Don't rattle, I thought. They didn't do it, they didn't do *that*.

I went into the kitchen, tore off a section of paper towel, folded it in a neat square, and went back into the bathroom to lift the toilet lid. My neighbor's bluetick dog floated in the purple water, one eye of his severed head staring up at me, his entrails bulging out of the slit that ran from his testicles to a flap of skin on his neck.

I dropped the bloody piece of paper towel in the wastebasket, turned around, and saw Bootsie frozen in the doorway, her hand pinched to her mouth, her cheeks discolored, her pulse leaping in her neck.

12

She sat alone in the bedroom while I talked to two uniformed cops who had been called by the apartment owner. A black man from the city health department dipped the dog's remains out of the toilet with a fishnet, while my neighbors stared through the open front door of the apartment. I told the cops a second time that I had no idea who had done it.

One of them wrote on his clipboard. There were red marks on his nose where he had taken off his sunglasses, and his sky-blue shirt was stretched tightly across his muscular chest.

'You think maybe somebody just doesn't like you?' he asked.

'Could be,' I said.

'You're not in a cult, are you?' He grinned at the corner of his mouth.

'No, I don't know much about cults.'

He put his ballpoint pen in his shirt pocket.

'Well, there're a lot of spaced-out dopers around these days. Maybe that's all there was to it,' he said. 'I'd get some better locks, though.'

'Thank y'all for coming out.'

'Mr Robicheaux, you say you used to be a police officer?'

'That's right.'

'You never heard about a nailed-up frog before?'

I cleared my throat and looked away from his eyes.

'Maybe I heard something. It's a little vague.'

He smiled to himself, then wrote out a number on a piece of paper and handed it to me.

'Here's the report number in case you or the owner needs it for an insurance claim. Call us if we can help you in any way,' he said.

They left and closed the door behind them. There's a cop who won't have to write traffic tickets too long, I thought.

Back in the bedroom Bootsie sat on the side of my bed, her hands folded in her lap. Her cotton dress was covered with gray and pink flowers.

'I'm sorry you had to arrive in the middle of all this,' I said.

'Dave, that officer was talking about a cult. Do you know people like that?'

'It wasn't done by cultists. He knew it, too.'

'What?'

'I'm supposed to think I've got a *gris-gris* on me. You remember a Negro woman called Gros Mama Goula in New Iberia?'

'She ran a brothel?'

'That's the one. She'd like to shake up my cookie bag. She either sent some of her people over here to do this, or it was done by a guy named Jimmie Lee Boggs. But my guess is that the two of them are working together.'

'I just don't understand.'

'These are people who for one reason or another would like me to disappear. So they put on this *gris-gris* show. But whoever did this has probably spent some time in a southern prison. A frog with a nail through it means a guy had better jump or he's going to have a bad fate.'

I saw her face becoming more and more clouded.

'Bootsie, these guys are dimwits. They're always looking for something new or clever to dress up their act. When they do some bullshit like this, it's because they're running scared.'

'I've heard that name Boggs,' she said. 'I get the feeling he's taken very seriously.'

'All right, he's got the contract on Tony C. He's also the guy who shot me last summer. But I think Jimmie Lee's scared. It's turned around on him.'

'Dave, what in God's name are you doing? Why did you bring me here this morning?'

'I'm not sure, Boots.'

'God, you're incredible.'

'Maybe I don't think I'm doing right by you.'

This time her eyes saw meaning in my face.

'I hurt you real bad a long time ago. I don't want to do it again,' I said.

Her eyes kept looking up at me. I pulled up a chair and sat across from her.

'Maybe you have some regrets?' she said softly.

'I didn't say that.'

'You love the past, Dave. You love Louisiana the way it used to be. It's changed. Forever. We are, too. Maybe you're discovering that.' She smiled.

'I don't know. I don't learn anything very easily.'

Her eyes went down in her lap, and she brushed her fingers over the fine hair on the back of her wrist.

'Dave, did you do something that bothers you?' she said.

'No.'

'Are we talking about another woman?'

'I'm mixed up with a bunch of people I can't think straight about right now.'

She was quiet for a moment; then she said, 'Who is she?'

'I haven't been untrue to you.' The words sounded hollow, marital, the banal end of something.

'Is she one of Tony's crowd?'

'I'm in a situation where I'm going to have to hurt some people. I don't feel good about it. I got mixed up in it because I was shot by Jimmie Lee Boggs. Now I'm at a place where I don't understand my own feelings.'

'You're an undercover cop, aren't you?'

'I've gotten involved with people whom cops sometimes call lowlifes or geeks or greaseballs. Except I don't feel that way about all of them now, and I should. That's what it amounts to, Bootsie.'

'Do you want it over between us?'

'I don't think it can ever be over between us.'

'You shouldn't count on that,' she said, and I felt my heart drop.

'Can you tell me why you were over at Baylor?' I said.

'Not today. No more today.'

'You're going to close me out? You're not going to let me be your friend when you need one?'

'Do you love me or the past, Dave? Do you think I'm the past? Do I look like the past? Am I the summer of 'fifty-seven?'

Her eyes and her voice were kind, but I had no answer for her or myself, and the room was so quiet that I could hear the rustle of banana leaves outside the window.

Three hours later I was sitting at a redwood table by the side of Tony's tennis court while he hit balls at Jess Ornella on the opposite side of the net. Jess wore a red sweatsuit and blue boat shoes and clubbed at the balls as though he were under attack. Three dozen balls must have littered the clay court, most of them on his side.

'I tell you what, why don't you get us some iced tea?' Tony said.

'I told you I ain't any good at games,' Jess said.

'You're doing good. Keep working at it. Your stroke's getting better all the time,' Tony said. He sat down at the table with me, patting his neck and face with a towel, and watched Jess walk toward the house. 'He looks like a hog on ice, but you ought to see him fly an airplane.'

'Jess?'

'His old man was a crop duster during the Depression. Jess can thread a needle with anything that has wings on it. One time he flew us upside down under a power line.'

Unconsciously I touched the stitches on my lip. They felt as tight and hard as wire.

'When are you getting them out?' he said.

'Tomorrow.'

'Something on your mind, Dave?'

'I guess I was still thinking about my apartment.'

'Don't go back there. Stay with me as long as you're in New Orleans. You don't need an apartment.'

'I'm still trying to figure out Boggs, too.'

'Why? You like trying to put yourself inside the head of a moron? Look, why do you think a guy like me is successful in this business? I'll tell you. A guy who can walk down the street and chew gum at the same time is king of the block. Take Jess there, and remember he's one of the few I trust, he thinks Peter Pan is the washbasin in a whorehouse.'

'Boggs is smarter than you think.'

'He's a psychopath. Look, the real badasses are in prison or the graveyard. If the're not there yet, they will be. About every two or three months I hear a rumor somebody's going to whack me out. And once in a while somebody tries. But I'm still hitting tennis balls. And a couple of other guys, guys who somebody wound up in Houston or Miami, Jess has driven down into Lafourche Parish and no telling what happened. So if you want into the life, Dave, you don't worry over it. Hey, come on, man, most people grow old and sit on the porch and listen to their livers rot.'

'I've got another problem, too, Tony. My people back in Lafayette want a chance to get their money back. A half million is a lot to lose.'

He picked up his racket cover and began pulling it over the head of his racket.

'They're not looking for a major buy,' I said. 'They just want to recover what they lost.'

He zipped up the leather cover and rested the racket across his thighs.

'Clete says there's a major score about to go down in the projects. I'd like to get in on it,' I said.

He nodded attentively, his eyes looking off into the trees.

'I hear you talking, Dave, but like I once said to you, I don't do business at my house.' Then he glanced into my face.

'I respect that, Tony, but these guys back in Lafayette are turning some dials on me.'

'Fuck 'em.'

'I've got to live around there.'

'Hey, give me a break. Do I take care of you or not?' His small mouth made that strange butterfly shape.

'I'm just telling you about my situation.'

'All right, for God's sakes. We'll take a drive. You're worse than my wife.'

A few minutes later we were in the Lincoln, driving across the twenty-four-mile causeway that spans Lake Pontchartrain, with Jess and the other bodyguards behind us in the Cadillac. The sun was high in the hard, blue sky, and the waves were green and capping in the wind. Tony drove with his arm on the window, a Marine Corps utility cap pulled down snugly to the level of his sunglasses. His gray and black ringlets whipped on his neck. He looked out at a long barge whose deck was loaded with industrial metal drums of some kind.

'We used to fish and swim in the lake when I was a kid,' he said. 'Now the lake's so polluted it's against the law to get in the water.'

'New Orleans has changed a lot.'

'All for the bad, all for the bad,' he said.

'Can you tell me where we're going now?'

'A place I bet you've never seen. Maybe I'll show you my plane, too.'

'Can we talk now?'

'You can talk, I'll listen,' he said, and smiled at me from behind his glasses.

'These guys want to give me another fifty or sixty thou if I can buy into some quick action.'

'So?'

'Can I get in on the score?'

'Dave, the score you're talking about is all going right into the projects. It involves a lot of colored dealers and some guys out in Metairie I don't like to mess with too much.'

'You don't do business with the projects?'

'It's hot right now. Everybody's pissed because these kids are killing each other all over town and scaring off the tourists. Another thing, I never deliberately sold product to kids. I know they get hold of it, but I didn't sell it to them. Big fucking deal. But if you want me to connect you, I can do it.'

'I'd appreciate it, Tony. I figure this is my last score, though. I'm not cut out for it.'

'Like I am?' he said. His face was flat and expressionless when he looked at me.

'I didn't mean anything by that.'

'Yeah, nobody does. I tell you what, Dave, go into Copeland's up on St Charles some Wednesday night. Wednesday is yuppie night in New Orleans. These are people who wouldn't spit on an Italian who grew up in a funeral home. But they got crystal bowls full of flake on their coffee tables. They carry it in their compacts, they chop up lines when they ball each other. In my opinion a lot of them are degenerates. But what the fuck do I know? These are people with law degrees and MBAs. I went to a fucking juco in Miami. You know why? Because it had the best mortuary school in the United States. Except I studied English and journalism. I was on the fucking college newspaper, man. Just before I joined the crotch.'

'I'm not judging you, Tony.'

'The fuck you're not,' he said.

I didn't try to answer him again. He drove for almost a mile without speaking, his tan face as flat as a shingle, the wind puffing his flannel shirt, the sunlight clicking on his dark glasses. Then I saw him take a breath through his nose.

'I'm sorry,' he said. 'When you try to get off crank, it puts boards in your head.'

'It's all right.'

'Let's stop up here and buy some crabs. If I don't feed those guys behind us, they'll eat the leather out of the seats. You're not pissed?'

'No, of course not.'

'You really want me to connect you?'

'It's what my people need.'

'Maybe you should let those white-collar cocksuckers make their own score.'

I had a feeling Clete would agree with him.

We ate outside Covington, then took a two-lane road toward Mississippi and the Pearl River country. Finally we turned on to a dirt road, crossed the river on a narrow bridge, and snaked along the river's edge through a thick woods. The water in the river was low, and the sides were steep and covered with brush and dried river trash.

'It's weird-looking country, isn't it?' Tony said. 'Have you ever been around here before?'

'No, not really. Just on the main highway,' I said. But I could never hear the name of the Pearl River without remembering the lynchings that took place in Mississippi in the 1950s and 1960s and the bodies that had been dredged out of the Pearl with steel grappling hooks. 'Why do you keep your plane over here?'

'A beaver's always got a back door,' he said. 'Besides, nobody over here pays any attention to me.'

We wound our way down toward the coast, splashing yellow water out of the puddles in the road. Then the pines thinned and I could see the river again. It was wider here, and the water was higher, and sunk at an angle on the near bank was an old seismographic drill barge. It was orange with rust, and its deck and rails and four hydraulic pilings were strung with gray webs of dried algae.

'What are you looking at?' Tony said.

'I used to work on a drill barge like that. Back in the fifties,' I said. 'They were called doodlebug rigs because they moved from drill hole to drill hole.'

'Huh,' he said, not really interested.

I turned and looked at the drill barge again. All the glass was broken out of the iron pilothouse, and leaves drifted from the tree branches through the windows.

'You want to stop and take a look?' Tony said.

'No.'

'We got plenty of time.'

'No, that's all right.'

'It makes you remember your youth or something?'

'Yeah, I guess,' I said.

But that wasn't it. The drill barge disturbed me, as though I were looking at something from my future rather than my past.

'You see that hangar and airstrip?' Tony said.

The woods ended, and up ahead was a cow pasture with a mowed area through the center of it, and a solitary tin hangar with closed doors and a wind sock on the roof.

'That's where you keep your plane?' I said.

'No, I keep my plane a mile down the road. Just remember this place.'

'What for?'

'Just remember it, that's all.'

'All right.'

We drove past the pasture and clumps of cows grazing among the egrets, then entered a pine and hackberry woods again. At the end of the shaded road I could see more sunny pastureland.

'I want to tell you something, something I haven't been honest about. Then I want to ask you a question,' Tony said.

'Go ahead.'

'I got a bad feeling, the kind you used to get sometimes in 'Nam. You know what I mean? Like maybe it was really going to happen this time, you were riding back on the dustoff in a body bag. I got that feeling now.'

'It's the withdrawal from the speed.'

'No, this is different. I feel like it's five minutes to twelve and my clock's ticking.'

'They didn't get you over there, did they? Blow it off. Guys like us have a long way to run.'

'Look, like I told you, the only guy working for me I can trust is Jess. But Jess couldn't think his way through wet Kleenex. So I'm going to ask you, if I get clipped, will you look after Paul, make sure that bitch takes care of him, keeps him in good schools, buys him everything he needs?'

'I appreciate the compliment, but—'

'Fuck the compliment. I want an answer.'

'Start thinking about a divorce, Tony, and get these other thoughts out of your head.'

'Yes or no?'

He looked at me, one hand tight on the steering wheel, and we bounced through a deep puddle that splashed water across the windshield.

'I'd do my best for him,' I said.

'I know you will. You're my main man. Right?' And he pointed one finger at me and coked his thumb, as though he were aiming a pistol, and popped his mouth with his tongue. Then he laughed loudly.

Late that afternoon I told Tony I was going to have the oil in my truck changed. I drove to a filling station by the shopping center and used the outside pay phone while the attendant put my truck on the rack. I caught Minos at his office and told him of the trip over to Mississippi.

'When do you think this shipment's coming in?' he said.

'Any day.'

'All right, we'll get the money in the bus locker for you. Now, let's talk about you getting wired.'

'Minos, I think there might be a problem here with entrapment. This isn't Tony's deal. I'm leading him into it.'

'Anywhere there's dope in Orleans or Jefferson Parish, he's getting a cut out of it.'

'I don't think that's true. He talked about some guys in Metairie running this deal.'

'I don't care what he says. Cardo's dirty when he gets up in the morning. Stop pretending otherwise. Look, if somebody hollers later about entrapment, that's our problem, not yours.'

'I think we're shaving the dice.'

'It's not entrapment if this guy has foreknowledge of a narcotics buy and he takes you into it.' He paused to let the exasperation go out of his voice. 'You've only got one thing to worry about, Dave – getting close to him with a wire. Now, we can do it two ways, with a microphone or a miniaturized tape recorder.'

'He's not going to do business in the house.'

'Which do you want to use?'

'How far can the microphone send?'

'Under the best conditions, without electric interference or buildings in the way, maybe up to a quarter of a mile.'

'I think I'll be better off with the recorder. That way we won't have to worry about reception problems with the tail.'

'How do you want to pick it up?' he said.

'I have to go to the doctor's at ten tomorrow morning to get my stitches out. Have somebody at his office.' I gave him the address.

'Then that's about it for right now,' he said.

'Minos, there's one other thing that bothers me. Maybe I imagine it.'

'What?'

'Sometimes it's like he knows I'm still a cop. Like maybe he wants to take a fall.'

'Who knows? A guy who shoots speed up into his arm made a contract to destroy himself a long time ago. They all flame out one way or another. Who cares how they do it? Hang loose,' he said, and hung up.

That night I was watching television on the sun porch with Tony and Paul when the phone rang in the kitchen and the Negro houseman told me that I had a call. I picked the receiver up off the Formica counter, sat down on a stool, and put it to my ear. The counter gave on to the porch, and I could see Tony's and Paul's faces in the illumination of the television screen.

'Hello,' I said.

'Dave, it's Clete. Are you where you can talk?'

'We're watching television.'

'I dig you. Just listen, then. That redhead broad just called me at the club. From what I get, somebody beat the shit out of her. She wants to see you, but she doesn't want Cardo to know about it.'

'Uh-huh,' I said.

'She wouldn't tell me much. She sounds like one scared broad. She's staying at a friend's place out in Metairie. I've got the address.'

'I see.'

'Cardo's right there.'

'That's right.'

'Look, pick me up at the bar, and we'll drive out there tonight. Tell Tony you're lending me some money, I'm having trouble meeting the vig with one of his shylocks. He'll buy that. I owe those fuckers five large.'

'All right, Cletus. I'll see what I can do.'

I hung up the receiver and sat back down in front of the television set. I brushed at my pants leg distractedly.

'What's the trouble?' Tony said.

'Oh, nothing, really. Clete's having some money problems. He gets a little strung out sometimes. I guess I'd better go see him. Would it bother you if I came in late?'

'No, here's the house key. Just tell the guys at the gate you'll be back late so they won't think it's somebody else, you know what I mean?'

'I'll be quiet coming in.'

'Sure, don't worry about it. Somebody's squeezing your friend?'

'A little problem with the vigorish.'

'Tell him to come see me about it. Maybe I can work it out.'

'That's good of you, Tony.'

It took me a half hour to drive to the bar on Decatur. Clete was waiting for me under the colonnade. It had started to mist, and he wore a brown raincoat over his sports jacket. I pulled to the curb, and he jumped in the truck. He read me the address in Metairie off a folded piece of paper, and I headed out of the Quarter toward Interstate 10.

'Who beat her up?' I said.

'She wouldn't say.'

'Why didn't she want Tony to know about it?'

'I didn't ask her. Dave, are you making it with her?'

'No.'

'Are you sure?'

'I told you no.'

'You didn't have just one flop in the hay with her?'

'You heard what I said, Clete.'

'Yeah, well, usually broads like that get remodeled after they let the wrong guy in the bread box. She called for you, not Cardo. What should I conclude on that, Streak? Or am I just full of shit?'

'I didn't talk to her. I don't know what happened. And you're pissing me off.'

We were silent in the cab of the truck. It started to rain harder, and I turned on the windshield wipers.

'I'm just trying to help, believe it or not,' he said.

'I know that, Clete.'

'I'm backing your play, and I don't care if I get paid for it or not.'

'What do you mean?' I looked over at him. Rainy patterns of light ran down his face.

'I didn't get any bucks from the DEA this week. I called Dautrieve, and he said I was terminated.'

'Are you kidding?'

'Wait a minute, don't get heated up. He said some other guys made the decision. He didn't have any control over it.'

'He should have told me.'

'Maybe he didn't have a chance to. Fuck it. Look, there's our exit up there. Welcome to Metairie, the only town in the United States to elect a Klu Klux Klansman and American Nazi as its state representative. What a depressing shithole. This place makes you think maybe the white race ought to be picking the cotton.'

'I've got to have a talk with Minos.'

'Talk all you want to. When you deal with the feds, you're dealing with people whose thought patterns are printed on computer chips. Besides, they all smell like mouthwash. Did you ever trust a guy who smells like mouthwash?'

She opened the apartment door on the night chain. She had on a short-sleeved terry cloth robe. Her right eye was a purple knot, and there was still a crust of dried blood in one nostril. She slipped the chain loose and opened the door wide. Her arms were streaked with yellow and purple bruises, the kind that a man's clenched hand leaves. I could smell the Mentholatum that she had smeared on her skin. She closed the door and locked it again as soon as we were inside.

'I thought maybe you wouldn't come,' she said.

'Why?' I said.

'I don't know, it was just what I thought.' She talked carefully, as though the inside of her mouth were hurt. 'There's some beer and pop in the refrigerator if you want some.'

'Who did it, Kim?' I said.

'Jimmie Lee Boggs.'

'When?'

'This morning. Just after I got up. I opened the door to get the newspaper and he hit me in the face and knocked me back inside the room. I never had anybody hit me like that. I didn't believe anyone could hit that hard.'

I could hear the humiliation in her voice, see the shame in her face. I had seen the same look of debasement in victims of violence many times, and it was almost impossible to convince them that they were not deserving of their fate. I could feel Clete's awkwardness next to me.

'I think I'll take that beer,' he said, walking to the refrigerator. 'Then I'll just step out here on the balcony and have a cigarette.'

He slid open the glass doors that gave on to a small balcony with a barbecue grill on it, then closed them behind him and looked out over a lighted, weed-filled lake that was dented with rain.

She sat on the couch with her hands in her lap and her head bowed.

'Why didn't you think I'd come?' I asked again.

'Because you know I'm a snitch.'

'What else?'

Her eyes were averted. She looked small sitting on the couch. I sat down next to her. She turned her face up, then looked away again.

'What else, Kim?'

'Because you know I betrayed you. I told Lieutenant Baxter about the buy down at Cocodrie. That's why Jimmie Lee Boggs came after me. He said he figured it was either you or me who dropped the dime on him. He beat me all over the apartment. Then he twisted a towel in my mouth and filled the sink and held my head under the water until I almost passed out. He kept saying, "Gargle time, beautiful. Rinse out your mouth, now. Think about the canary I'm gonna stuff in it." He would have killed me if the landlady hadn't started banging on the door for the rent.'

She glanced sideways at my face.

'Why were you snitching for Nate Baxter?'

'My brother's a groom at the Fairgrounds. Lieutenant Baxter has him in jail for possession. He says he can upgrade the charge to conspiracy to distribute, and Albert – that's my brother – will get fifteen years in Angola.'

'Baxter put you inside Tony's crowd?'

'I already had the job at the club. All I had to do was become available.'

'Available?' I said.

'I said to Baxter, "What do you mean, exactly?" He says. "You've got a piece of equipment that'll get you anything you want." He looks across his desk, then he goes, "That's big-picture clear, isn't it? Talk it over with your brother. Let me know what you decide. It doesn't matter to me, hon, one way or another." '

'You should have reported him, Kim.'

'Great. I work in a skin joint run by the Mafia, my brother's a druggie in custody, and I'm going to report a Vice lieutenant? Look, it doesn't matter what he said. I did what he wanted. I told him everything Tony was doing, I told him about you, I'm to blame for what happened down at Cocodrie.'

'You tried to warn me. Give yourself a little credit.'

'Are you going to tell Tony?'

'No. But as of tonight, you're out of the life, Kim. You don't go back to that job, or back to your apartment, or out to Tony's. I also advise you to stay away from Nate Baxter. He's a liar and a coward and a bully. Also, he doesn't have the power to upgrade your brother's charges. That comes out of the prosecutor's office. Believe me, your brother will be better off taking his own chances.'

She took a Kleenex out of her robe and touched one nostril with it. Her face had no makeup on it, and it looked shiny and white where it wasn't bruised.

'I don't know what to do,' she said. 'I only have a little money. I have to have a job.'

'Somebody's going to take care of you. I guarantee it.'

She put the Kleenex away and played with her fingernails.

'I have to ask you something,' she said.

'Yes?'

'It's not a very appropriate question, I guess, but there's no chance, is there? Not now.'

'Of what?' I said, although I already knew the answer.

'What I mean is, it's like when people do something to one another, or maybe to themselves, something shameful, it kills what might have been between them, doesn't it?'

'I don't know, Kim.'

'Yes, you do. It's why my brother Albert is the way he is. Years ago he had a wife and a little girl. Then one night he got drunk at a party and slept with another woman. So he had all this Catholic guilt about what he'd done, and rather than blow it off, he got his wife drunk and talked her into getting into the sack with another guy. All he got out of it was the knowledge that he couldn't love himself anymore, and so he doesn't think anybody else can, either.'

'I wouldn't try to figure it all out now, Kim.'

'Tony's right. We're the cluster fuck. The human race is.'

'Cynics and nihilists are two bits a bagful,' I said. 'Don't let them sell you that same old tired shuck. Listen, a man named Minos Dautrieve is going to contact you. He's an old friend with the DEA, so trust him. We're going to take care of you.'

'I was right, then. You're still a cop.'

'Who cares? The only thing that matters here is that you're out of the life. We're clear on that, aren't we?'

'Yes.'

I put my hand on her forearm.

'Kim, you stood up for your brother,' I said. 'Everything you did took courage. Most people aren't that brave. I think you're one special lady.'

She looked up at me. Her unswollen eye glimmered softly.

'Really?' she said.

'You bet. I've had some good people cover my back, like Cletus out there, but I'd put my money on you anytime.'

She smiled, and her free hand touched the backs of my fingers.

It was still raining when we left the apartment building and got back inside my truck.

'Your face looks like a thunderstorm,' Clete said.

'Nate Baxter,' I said.

'She was working for him?'

'Yep.'

'He's the guy mommies warned them about. I always had the feeling that if we ever had a Third Reich here, you might see Nate manning the ovens.'

'There's a bar up here on the corner. I want to stop and use the phone.'

'You're not going after Baxter?'

'Not now. But he's not going to get away with this.'

'Hmm,' Clete said, grinning in the dashboard light, his eyebrows flipping up and down like Groucho Marx's.

We went inside the corner bar, and Clete ordered a drink while I called Minos at his guesthouse from a phone booth next to a pinball machine. I told him about Kim, the beating she had taken from Jimmie Lee Boggs, the fact that she was an informant for Nate Baxter.

'Can you get her into a safe house?' I said.

'If she wants it.'

'Tomorrow morning.'

'No problem.'

'But I've got one. Why did you guys cut Cletus from the payroll?'

'I was going to tell you about it. It just happened today. I didn't have any say in it.'

'We had a deal.'

'I don't control everything here.'

'He saved my life out on the salt. I didn't see any DEA guys out there.'

'I'm sorry about it, Dave. I'm a federal employee. I'm one guy among several in this office. You need to understand that.'

'I think it's a rotten fucking way to treat somebody.'

'Maybe it is.'

'I think that's a facile answer, too.'

'I can't do anything about it.'

'Tell your office mates Clete has more integrity in the parings of his fingernails than a lot of federal agents have in their whole careers.'

'Drop by and tell them yourself. I'm not up to a harangue tonight. It's always easy to throw baboon shit through the fan when somebody else has to clean it up. We'll pick up the girl in the morning, and we'll get the tape recorder to you at your doctor's office. Good night, Dave.'

He hung up the receiver, and I could hear the pinball machine pinging through the plywood wall of the phone booth. Outside the window, the mist and blowing rain looked like cotton candy in the pink glow of the neon bar sign.

13

The next morning was bright and clear, and I went to the doctor's office off Jefferson Avenue and had the stitches snipped out of my head and mouth. When I touched the scar tissue above my right eyebrow, the skin around my eye twitched involuntarily. I opened my mouth and worked my jaw several times, touching the rubbery stiffness where the stitches had been removed.

'How does it feel?' the doctor asked. He was a thick-bodied, good-natured man who wore his sleeves rolled up on his big arms.

'Good.'

'You heal beautifully, Mr Robicheaux. But it looks like you've acquired quite a bit of scar tissue over the years. Maybe you should consider giving it up for Lent.'

'That's a good idea, Doctor.'

'You were lucky on this one. I think if you'd spent another hour or so in the water, we wouldn't be having this conversation.'

'I think you're right. Well, thank you for your time.'

'You bet. Stay out of hospitals.'

I went outside into the sunlight and walked toward my truck, which was parked under an oak tree. A man in khaki clothes with a land surveyor's plumb bob on his belt was leaning against my fender, eating a sandwich out of a paper bag.

'How about a lift up to the park?' he asked.

'Who are you?'

'I have a little item here for you. Are you going to give me a ride?'

'Hop in,' I said, and we drove up a side street toward Audubon Park and stopped in front of an enormous Victorian house with a wraparound gallery. Out in the park, under the heavy drift of leaves from the oaks, college kids from Tulane and Loyola were playing touch football. The man reached down into the bottom of his lunch sack and removed a miniaturized tape recorder inside a sealed plastic bag. He was thin and wore rimless glasses and work boots, and he had a deep tan and liver spots on his hands.

'It's light and it's flat,' he said. He reached back in the sack and took out a roll of adhesive tape. 'You can carry it in a coat pocket, or you can tape it anywhere on your body where it feels comfortable. It's quiet and dependable, and it activates with this little button here. Actually, it's a very nice little piece of engineering. When you wear it, try to be natural, try to forget it's on your person. Trust it. It'll pick up whatever it needs to. Don't feel that you have to "point" it at somebody. That's when a guy invites problems.'

'Okay.'

'Each cassette has sixty minutes' recording time on it. If you run out of tape and your situation doesn't allow you to change cassettes, don't worry about it. Never overextend yourself, never feel that you have to record more than the situation will allow you. If they don't get dirty on the tape one time, it'll happen the next time. Don't think of yourself as a controller.'

'You seem pretty good at this.'

'It beats being a shoe salesman, I guess. You have any questions?'

'How many undercover people have been caught with one of these?'

'Believe it or not, it doesn't happen very often. We put taps on telephone lines, bugs in homes and offices, we wire up informants inside the mob, and they still hang themselves. They're not very smart people.'

'Tony C. is.'

'Yeah, but he's crazy, too.'

'That's where you're wrong, partner. The only reason guys like us think he's crazy is because he doesn't behave like the others. Mistake.'

'Maybe so. But you'd better talk to Minos. He got some stuff on Cardo from the VA this morning. Our man was locked up with the wet brains for a while.'

'He's a speed freak.'

'Yeah, maybe because of his last few months' service in Vietnam.'

'What about it?'

'Talk to Minos,' he said, got out of the truck, and looked back at me through the window. 'Good luck on this. Remember what I said. Get what you can and let the devil take the rest.'

Then he crossed the street and walked through the park toward St Charles, his attention already focused on the college kids playing football by the lake. The streetcar clattered loudly down the tracks in front of the Tulane campus across the avenue. I went to a small grocery store a few blocks down St Charles, where the owner provided tables inside for working people to eat their lunch at, and called Minos at his office to see if he had relocated Kim in a safe house. I also wanted to know what he had learned about Tony's history in Vietnam, besides the fact that as an addict Tony had been locked up in a psychiatric unit rather than treated for addiction.

Minos wasn't in. But in a few hours I was to learn Tony's story on my own, almost as though he had saved a piece of forgotten memory out of my own experience and thrust it into my unwilling hands.

I took Bootsie to lunch at an expensive Mexican restaurant on Dauphine before I drove back out to Tony's. She looked wonderful in her white suit, black heels, and lavender blouse, and I think perhaps she had the best posture I had ever seen in a woman. She sat perfectly straight in her chair while she sipped from her wineglass or ate small bites of her seafood enchilada, her chin tilted slightly upward, her face composed and soft.

But it was too crowded for us to talk well, and I was beset with questions that I did not know how to frame or ask. I guess my biggest concern about Bootsie was a selfish one. I wanted her to be just as she had been in the summer of 1957. I didn't want to accept the fact that she had married into the Mafia, that she was business partners with the Giacano family, that financial concern was of such great importance in her life that she would not extricate herself from the Giacanos.

For some reason it was as though she had betrayed me, or betrayed the youth and innocence I'd unfairly demanded she be the vessel of. What an irony, I thought: I'd killed off a large portion of my adult life with alcohol, driven away my first wife, delivered my second wife, Annie, into a nightmare world of drugs and psychotic killers, and had become a professional Judas who was no longer sure himself to whom he owed his loyalties. But I was still willing to tie Bootsie to the moralist's rack.

'What's bothering you?' she asked.

'What if we just give it all up? Your vending machine business, your connection with those clowns, my fooling around with the lowlifes and crazoids. We just eighty-six it all and go back to New Iberia.'

'It's a thought, isn't it?'

'I mean it, Boots. You only get one time on the planet. Why spend any more of it confirming yesterday's mistakes?'

'I have to tell you something.'

'What?'

'Not here. Can we be together later tonight?'

'Yeah, sure, but tell me what, Boots?'

'Later,' she said. 'Can you come for supper at the house?'

'I think I can.'

'You *think*.'

'I'm trying to tie some things up.'

'Would you rather another night?' She looked at a distant spot in the restaurant.

'No, I'll do everything I can to be there.'

'You'll do *everything*?'

'What time? I'll be there. I promise.'

'They're not easy people to deal with, are they? You don't always get to set your own schedule, do you? You don't have control over everything when you lock into Tony Cardo's world, do you?'

'All right, Bootsie, I was hard on you.'

'No, you were hard on both of us. When you love somebody, you give up making decisions just for yourself. I loved you so much that summer I thought we had one skin wrapped around us.'

I looked back at her helplessly.

'Six-thirty,' she said.

'All right,' I said. Then I said it again. 'And if anything goes wrong, I'll call. That's the best I can do. But I know I'll be there.'

And I was the one who'd just suggested we eighty-six it all and go back to Bayou Teche.

Her dark eyes were unreadable in the light of the candle burning inside the little red chimney on the table.

When I got back to Tony's house, I hid the tape recorder in my closet. The house was empty, so quiet that I could hear clocks ticking. I put on my gym shorts and running shoes, jogged for thirty minutes through the neighborhood and along Lakeshore Drive, then tried to do ten push-ups out on the lawn. But the network of muscles in my left shoulder was still weak from the gunshot wound, and after three push-ups I collapsed on my elbow.

I showered, put on a pair of jeans and a long-sleeved sports shirt, and walked out by the pool with a magazine just as Tony and Jess came through the front gate in the Lincoln, with the white limo behind them.

Tony slammed the car door and walked toward me, pulling off his coat and tie.

'Come inside with me. I got to get a drink,' he said. He kept pulling off his clothes as we went deeper into the house, kicking his shoes through a bedroom door, flinging his shirt and trousers into a bathroom, until he stood at the bar in his Jockey undershorts. His body was hard, knotted with muscle, and beaded with pinpoints of perspiration. He poured four inches of bourbon into a tumbler with ice and took a big swallow. Then he took another one, his eyes widening above the upended glass.

'I think I'm heading into the screaming meemies,' he said. 'I feel like somebody's pulling my skin off with pliers.'

'What is it?'

'I'm a fucking junkie, that's what it is.' He poured from the decanter into his glass again.

'Better ease up on the fluids.'

'This stuff's like Kool-Aid compared to what my system's used to. What you're looking at, Dave, is a piece of cracked ceramic. Those guys are weirding me out, too. We're in my real estate office out by Chalmette, and I'm talking to my salespeople at a meet while the guys are milling around out there by the front desks. These salespeople are mostly middle-class broads who pretend they don't know what other kinds of businesses I'm in. So we end the meet and walk out to the front door and everybody is bouncy and laughing until they see the guys comparing different kinds of rubbers they bought at some sex shop. It's like my life is part of a Marx Brothers comedy. Except it ain't funny.'

He put his head down on the bar. 'Oh man, I ain't fucking gonna make it.'

'Yeah, you will.'

'Have you ever seen a wet-brain ward at the VA? They wear Pampers, they drool on themselves, they eat mush with their hands. I've been there, man, and this is worse.'

'I've had dead people call me up long-distance. Do you think it gets any worse than that?' I said.

'You think that's a big deal? I'll tell you about a smell—' He stopped and drank out of his glass. The ice clinked against the sides. His eyes were dilated. 'Come outside, I want to show you something.'

He picked up the decanter and walked out the side door on to the lawn. Jess looked up from dipping leaves out of the pool.

'Hey, Tony, you forgot your pants,' he said, then he saw the expression on Tony's face and said, 'So it's a good day to get some sun.'

I followed Tony across the lawn, through the trees, and past the goldfish ponds and birdbaths and tennis court to the back wall of his property. A hooded air vent protruded from the ground close to the base of the wall.

'Find it,' he said.

'What?'

'The trapdoor.'

'I don't see one.'

He bent over and pulled an iron ring set next to a sprinkler head, and a door covered with grass sod raised up out of the lawn and exposed a short, subterranean stairwell.

'It's an atom bomb shelter,' he said. 'But I heard the guy who built it used to pump the maid down here.'

We went down inside, and he clicked on a light and pulled the door shut with a hanging rope. The walls and floor were concrete, the roof steel plate. There were two bunk beds inside the room, a pile of moldy K rations in one corner, and a stack of paperback novels and a disassembled AR-15 rifle on top of a bridge table.

'I come down here when things are bugging me,' he said. 'Sometimes I make up a picnic basket and Paul and me spend the night down here, like we're camping. It's got a chemical toilet, I can hook up a portable TV, nobody knows where I am unless I want them to know.'

He sat down on the bunk bed and leaned back against the concrete wall. A dark line of hair grew up the center of his stomach from the elastic band of his underwear. He stirred the ice in his drink with his finger. Then he was quiet for what seemed a long time.

'After I got hit they didn't send me back to my old platoon,' he said. 'Instead I got reassigned to a bunch of losers. Or maybe they'd just been out too long. One guy had a scalp lock from a woman on his rifle, another guy gave a little boy a heat tab and told him it was candy. Anyway, I didn't like any of them. Which was all right, because they didn't like me, either, and they kept treating me like a newbie.

'So one night the lieutenant tells us to set up an ambush about four klicks up this trail, so we pass a real small ville by a stream after one klick and we go on another klick and finally everybody says, "Fuck it, we sandbag it, let the loot set his own ambush."

'But while we're sitting out there in the dark it's like everybody's got something else on his mind. It's hot and quiet, and water's dripping out of the trees and we're slapping mosquitoes and smelling ourselves and looking at our watches and thinking we got six more hours out here. Then the guy with the scalp lock on his rifle – his name was Elvis Doolittle, that's right, I'm not making it up – Elvis rubs his whiskers with his hand and keeps looking back down the trail and finally he puts a cigarette in his mouth. The doc says, "What the fuck you doing, Elvis?"

'He says, "I'm going back to the ville."

'Then nobody says anything. But everybody had seen these two teenage sisters with their mama-san in front of the hooch. And they know what Elvis is thinking. Then he says, "We'll leave Mouse and the new guy. Nobody'll know. That ville's got something coming anyway. That booby trap that got Brown. They set it."

' "You don't know that," Mouse says.

' "If they didn't set it, they know who did," Elvis says.

'Then they all talked it over and my heart started beating. Not because of what they were going to do, either, but because I was afraid to be left out on the trail with just one guy.

'Elvis turns to me and says, "You ever say anything about this, you ain't getting back home, man." Then they were gone. The trees were so thick all those guys just melted away into the blackness. You could hear monkeys clattering around in the canopy and night birds and sounds like sticks breaking out there in the jungle. Sweat was running out of my pot and my breath started catching in my throat. Then we hear something clank.

'Mouse whispers, "It's up the trail. It's up the fucking trail."

'I tell him to be quiet and listen, and he says, "It's NVA, man."

'I tell him to shut up again, but he says, "They dideed out on us, man. It ain't right. I ain't staying."

'His eyes look big as half-dollars under his pot, and I'm trying to act cool, like I got it under control, but the sweat keeps burning my eyes and my hands are shaking so bad it's like I got malaria. Then I hear something up the trail again.

' "That's it," Mouse says, "Let's get out of here."

'I put my hand on his arm. "All right, man, we go back to the ville," I say. "But what are you gonna do with what you see back there?"

' "I ain't gonna see nothing," he says. "It ain't my business. I got eighteen more days, then it's back to the world. I ain't gonna get pulled into no court-martial, either. You do what you want to, Cardo."

'He takes off, and a minute later I follow him, tagging along like a punk to something I don't even want to know about, all because I'm scared.

'When we get back to the ville, Elvis has put all the zips in their hooches and has sent the doc with a flashlight into the hooch that's got the two teenage sisters. The doc comes out and says, "They're clean," and then Elvis and this big black dude go in. About ten minutes later Elvis comes out fixing his fly and sees me and Mouse squatting by the trail.

' "You dumb shits," he says. "You get the fuck back up that trail."

' "I ain't gonna do it, Elvis," Mouse says.

'He grabs Mouse by the back of his shirt and pulls him up out of the dirt, just like you pick up a dirty clothes bag.

' "Fuck you, man. We're not going back up there by ourselves," I say. "We heard something clank up there. You dideed out on us. They get through, your ass is in a sling."

'He's frozen there, with Mouse hanging from his fist. He says, "What d'you mean, something clanked?"

'Before I can answer an old man runs across the clearing out of nowhere and tries to get in the hooch, where a couple of other guys are taking their turn inside. He's yelling in gook, and the big black dude his holding him by the wrists, and everybody's laughing. Then one of the sisters starts screaming inside, and more zips are coming out of their hooches, and it's all starting to deteriorate in a hurry. Elvis lets loose of Mouse and walks fast across the clearing just as the two guys come back out of the hooch.

'One of them is the guy who gave the kid a heat tab. He and Elvis look at each other, then the guy says, "The shit's already in the fire, man."

'The old man goes in the hooch, and there's more yelling inside, and Elvis says, "What'd you do to her?"

'The guy, the heat-tab guy, says, "Nothing you didn't."

'But the guy who was in there with him says, "He told her he'd kill her baby if she didn't blow him."

'By that time I just wanted to get out of there, so I don't know who threw the grenade. I was already headed down the trail when I heard it go off. But somebody threw it right in the door of the hooch, with the two sisters and the old man and maybe a baby inside. Then I started running. When I looked back I could see the sparks above the trees from the burning hooch. I don't know if they killed anybody else there or not. I never asked, and I never told anybody about it. The next day I volunteered to work in the mortuary at Chu Lai.'

'The mortuary?' I said.

'That's right, man. I peeled them out of the body bags, cleaned the jelly out of their mouths and ears, washed them down, embalmed them, and boxed them. Because I'd had it with the war. And I'd lost my guts, too. I just wasn't going out again. I didn't care if I was a public coward or not.'

He drank from the bourbon, then leaned forward on his thighs. He rubbed the sweat off the back of his neck and looked at his hand.

'Maybe it took courage to do that, Tony,' I said.

'No, I was afraid. There's no way around that fact.' His voice was tired.

'You could have gotten out of the bush in other ways. You could have given yourself a minor wound. A second Heart would have put you in a safe area. You think maybe it's possible you volunteered for the mortuary to punish yourself?'

He looked up at my face. The skin around his left eye was puckered with thought.

'You can beat up on yourself the rest of your life if you want to. But no matter how you cut it, you're no coward. I'll give you something else to think about, too. On your worst day over there, you probably proved yourself in ways that an average person couldn't even imagine. It was *our* war, Tony. People who weren't there don't understand it. Most of them never wanted to understand it. But you ask yourself this question: would any grunt who was in the meat grinder judge you harshly? In fact, is there anyone at all who can say you didn't do your share?'

He widened his eyes and looked between his legs at the concrete floor. He pinched the bridge of his nose and made a snuffling sound. He started to speak, then cleared his throat and looked at the floor again.

'Better get some clothes on,' I said. 'You'll catch cold down here.'

'Yeah, I'll do that.'

'I guess I'll see you at the house,' I said.

'I lied about something. I don't use this place for Paul and me to camp. You see that AR-15? I used to come down here and sit in the dark with it and think about doing myself. When you turn off the light it's just like a black box, like the inside of a grave. I'd put the front sight under my teeth and let it touch the roof of my mouth and my mind would go completely empty. It felt good.'

I pushed on the trapdoor, which was made of steel and overlaid with concrete and swung up and down on thick black springs, and walked up the steps into the balmy November afternoon. The moss-hung oaks by the back wall were loud with blue jays and mockingbirds. I looked back down into the shelter and saw Tony still seated on the side of the bunk, his face pointed downward, the skin of his back as tight as a lampshade, bright with sweat.

I went up to the shopping center and called Minos at his office to find out about Kim, but he still hadn't returned. When I got back to Tony's house, the school bus had just dropped off Paul, and Jess was wheeling him inside.

'How you doing, Paul?' I said.

'Great. Special class got to go on the Amtrak train today.' He wore a striped trainman's hat, a checkered shirt, and blue jeans with a cowboy belt.

'I bet that was fun, wasn't it? Where's your old man?'

'Getting dressed.' He grinned broadly. 'Dad was exercising on the lawn in his underwear.'

'Why not? It's good weather for it,' I said, and winked at him.

'You got a phone message,' Jess said. 'From that friend of yours that runs the bar, what's his name?'

'Clete?'

'Yeah, he says to call him at the bar.'

'Thank you.'

'Dad said we all might go to a movie tonight,' Paul said.

'Well, I'm supposed to have dinner with a friend tonight.'

'Oh.'

'How about tomorrow night, maybe?' I said.

'Sure,' he said, but I could see the disappointment in his face.

Jess wheeled him up the ramp into the house, and I used the phone in the kitchen to call Clete.

'Where are you?' Clete said.

'At Tony's.'

'Can you talk, or do you want to call me back from somewhere else?'

'What is it?'

'Nate Baxter's in the bar.'

'I see.'

'He says he's here if you want to talk to him.'

'What's that supposed to mean?'

'You know Nate. Always looking inside his pants to make sure of his gender.'

'If it makes him happy, tell him I'll be looking him up one of these days.'

'He said one thing, though, that's a little bothersome. He said, "Tell Robicheaux I know he's got the broad stashed."'

The house was quiet except for the sound of shower water in the bathroom that adjoined Tony's bedroom.

'You there, Dave?' Clete said.

'Yes.'

'It sounds like our man knows a little more than he should.'

'What's he doing now?'

'Drinking at the bar.'

'I'll be there in a half hour.'

I told Tony that I had to run a couple of errands downtown, then I was going to Bootsie's for supper.

'Was that Bootsie on the phone?' he asked. He stood in his bedroom door, with a towel wrapped around his waist, raking the water out of his hair with a comb.

'No, it was Clete. He knows a guy who might give me a good deal on a boat.'

'I feel a lot better after a shower.' He stopped combing his hair. 'Hey, tell me straight about something. Down there in the shelter, you weren't just playing with my head? I mean . . . we're not talking about a loss of respect here?'

'No.'

'Because I don't push myself on people.'

'You didn't push yourself on me.'

'You wanted to know what happened, I told you.'

I nodded without replying.

'But if a guy thinks less of me because of it, I don't hold it against him. We're clear on this?' he said.

'You're not the only guy who brought back a problem from there, Tony. I've got my own. Maybe they're worse than yours.'

'Yeah?'

'I got four of my men killed on a trail because I did something reckless and stupid. Everybody has his own basket of snakes to deal with.'

'Your voice has a little edge to it, Dave.'

'I think pride's a pile of shit.'

He laughed. 'You sure don't hide your thoughts, do you?' he said. 'How about bringing Bootsie out here for supper, then we'll all go to a movie.'

'It's kind of a private evening, Tony.'

'Paul was looking forward to it.'

'Then you should have told me earlier, podna.'

He nodded silently, then began dressing in front of a full-length mirror as though I were not there.

I didn't have time to worry any more about Tony's mood changes and his addict's propensity for trying to control everyone and everything in his environment. In fact, maybe we were too much alike in that regard, and for that reason I not only got along better with him than I should have as a policeman, I also saw my own menagerie of snapping dogs at work inside him. When I got to Clete's Club, Nate Baxter was by himself at the far end of the bar, one shined brown loafer propped on the brass footrail. He wore sharply creased tan slacks, an open-necked yellow shirt, and a herringbone sports coat. His gold watch and gold identification bracelet gleamed softly in the light.

'You're looking sharp, Nate,' I said.

He tipped his cigarette ashes neatly into an ashtray and took a sip from his highball glass, his eyes looking at me in the bar mirror.

'You know a DEA agent by the name of Minos Dautrieve?' he asked.

'He's out of Lafayette. Yeah, I know him.'

'He's in New Orleans now. He's running a sting.'

'Why tell the family secrets to me?'

'I underestimated you,' he said.

'I have to be somewhere in a few minutes. What did you want to say to me, Nate?'

'She's my snitch. You shouldn't have messed with her.'

'What are we talking about here?'

'You know what I'm talking about. You were in her place out in Metairie. You got her stashed. But it's not going to do you any good. She's our witness, and she's going to testify for us. You can tell that to Dautrieve for me if you want to.'

'You're going a little fast for me.'

'The girl she was staying with works in the same club out on the Airline Highway. She told us you and Purcel were in her place. She said later some feds picked up the Dollinger broad. So I underestimated you. You've still got your badge, haven't you? But that doesn't mean you get to screw up our operation.'

'This is what you had to tell me?'

He tipped his cigarette ashes into the ashtray again. He still had not looked directly at me. He took a puff off his cigarette, then scratched his beard with one fingernail.

'You can tell Kim Dollinger she either comes in or we send her brother up the road,' he said. 'Don't let that broad jerk you around, Robicheaux. I could have charged her when we busted her brother. She was as dirty as he was.'

'Do you know that Jimmie Lee Boggs almost killed her?'

'You got a vested interest or something? We're talking about a snitch who was setting Tony C. up for a fall while she was banging him cross-eyed over in a beach house in Biloxi.'

'Listen—'

'No, you've got it wrong. You listen. We've worked on this case eight months. You guys come along and think you're going to wrap up Tony C. in a few weeks. In the meantime you don't inform us that you're working undercover, and then you've got the balls to grab my snitch.'

'You coerced her into prostituting herself.'

He turned his head and looked at me. The neon bar lights made the neatly trimmed edge of his beard glow with a reddish tinge.

'She was working at Tony C.'s club before she ever came to our attention,' he said. 'He probably had to tie a board across his ass to keep from falling inside.'

I saw Clete walk out of his office in back and begin changing a light bulb over the bandstand. The back of the club was empty.

'You're a bad cop, Baxter. But worse, you don't have any feelings about people,' I said. 'There's a word for that – pathological.'

'Take somebody else's inventory, Robicheaux. I'm not interested. Here's what it comes down to. You fuck up this investigation, you keep getting in my face, causing me problems, I wouldn't count on the department protecting your cover. Anyway, I've had my say. Just stay away from me.'

He turned back to his drink and ran his tongue along his gums. I opened and closed my hands at my sides.

'You gonna have something, suh?' the black barman said.

'No, thank you,' I said.

I continued to stare at the side of Baxter's face, the grained skin on the back of his neck. I could hear my breath in my nostrils. Then I turned and walked toward the open front door. My body felt wooden, my arms and legs disjointed. The sun reflecting off a windshield outside was like a sliver of glass in the eye. I stopped, looked back, and saw Baxter go into the rest room by the bandstand.

When I pushed open the rest room door he was combing his hair in front of the mirror.

'If you do anything to hurt that girl again, or if you compromise my situation here in New Orleans, I'm going down to your office, in front of people, and give you the worst day in your insignificant life,' I said.

He turned from the mirror, slipped his leather comb case out of his shirt pocket, blew in it before he replaced the comb; his breath reflected into my face. He used the back of his left hand to push me aside.

I heard a sound like a Popsicle stick snapping behind my eyes and saw a rush of color in my mind, like amorphous red and black clouds turning in dark water, and as though it had a life of its own my right fist hooked into his face and caught him squarely in the eye socket. His head snapped sideways, and I saw the white imprints of my knuckles on his skin and the watery electric shock in his eye.

But I had stepped into it. His right hand came out of his coat pocket with a leather-covered blackjack, an old-fashioned one that was shaped like a darning egg, with a spring built into the braided grip. I tried to raise my forearm in front of me, but the blackjack *whopped* across the top of my left shoulder and I felt the blow sink deep into the bone. The muscles in my chest and side quivered and then seemed to collapse, as if someone had run a heated metal rod through the trajectory of Jimmie Lee Boggs's bullet.

I was bent forward, my palm pressed hard against the throbbing pain below my collarbone, my eyes watering uncontrollably, the lip of the washbasin a wet presence across my buttocks. The expression in Baxter's eyes was unmistakable.

'Just one more for the road,' he said softly.

But Clete pushed the door back on its springs and stepped into the room like an elephant entering a phone booth. His unblinking eyes went from me to the blackjack; then his huge fist crashed against the side of Baxter's head. Baxter's face went out of round, his automatic flew from his shoulder holster, and he tripped sideways over the toilet bowl and fell on top of the trash can in a litter of crumpled paper towels.

Clete grimaced and shook his hand in the air, then rubbed his knuckles.

'Are you all right?' he said.

'I don't know.'

'What happened?'

'He threatened to blow my cover.'

Clete looked down at Baxter in the corner. Baxter's eyes were half-closed, his mouth hung open, and one hand twitched on his stomach.

'You hit him first?' Clete said.

'Yep.'

Clete chewed his lip.

'He'll use it, then. That's not good, not good,' he said, and began making clicking sounds with his tongue. He reached down and patted Baxter on the cheek. 'Wake-up time, Nate.'

Baxter widened his eyes, then started to sit up among the wet towels and fell back down again. Clete lifted him by the back of his herringbone jacket and folded him over the rim of the toilet bowl.

'What are you doing?' I said.

'Freshen up, Nate. That's it, my man. Splash a little on your face and it's a brand-new day,' Clete said.

He flushed the toilet and pushed Baxter's head farther down into the bowl.

'That's enough, Clete,' I said.

Someone tried to open the door.

'This toilet is occupied right now,' Clete said. He lifted Baxter off the bowl and propped him against the wall, then squatted down and blotted his face with paper towels. 'Hey, you're looking all right, Nate. How many fingers am I holding up? Three. Look, three fingers. That's it, take a deep breath. You're going to be fine. Look, I'm putting your piece back in your holster. Here's your sap. Come on, look up at me, now.'

Clete patted Baxter's cheek again. The back of Clete's thick neck was red from the effort of squatting down. His stomach and love handles hung over his belt.

'Here's the way I see this deal,' he said. 'We write the whole thing off. It was just a bad day at Black Rock, not even worth talking about later. You had a beef, Dave had a beef, it's over now. Right?'

Baxter blinked his eyes and flexed his jaw as though he had a tooth-ache. Water dripped out of his beard.

'Or you could go back to the First District and get into a lot of paperwork,' Clete said. 'Or you might want to cause Dave some grief with Tony C. But I don't think you're that kind of guy. Because if you were, it'd create some nasty problems for everybody. See, here's the serious part in all this. There's a hooker who comes into the bar. I usually don't let them in because they're bad for business. But I've known this broad since I was in Vice myself, and she's basically a nice girl and she respects my place and doesn't come on to the johns while she's in here. Anyway, she tells a funny story. She says you're getting freebies in the Quarter, and you made her ex-room-o cop your joint. I don't know, maybe she made it up. But you know how those broads are, they carry a grudge a long time. I don't think it'd take a lot to get one of them to drop the dime on you, Nate.'

Clete crimped his lips together and looked Baxter steadily in the eyes. Baxter's face looked as though he were experiencing the first stages of recognition after an earthquake. Clete closed the lid on the toilet and sat Baxter on top of it. His head hung forward. Clete touched him gently on the shoulder with two fingers.

'It ends here, Nate,' he said quietly. 'We're understood on that, aren't we?'

Baxter moved his lips but no sound came out.

'You don't have to say anything, as long as we have an understanding,' Clete said. 'Get yourself a couple of free doubles at the bar, if you want. I'm going to walk Dave outside now. It's a nice day. We're all going back outside into a nice day.'

Clete looked over the top of Baxter's head at me and made a motion toward the door with his thumb. I walked back out through the bar into the sidewalk under the colonnade. Clete followed me. The French Market and the tables in the Café du Monde were crowded with tourists now, and the street was heavy with afternoon traffic. Clete adjusted his tie, lit a cigarette with the lighter cupped in his big hands, and looked up the street as though he had nothing in his mind except a pleasant expectation of the next event in his life.

I rubbed my collarbone and the puckered scar of the .38 wound and straightened my back.

'How's it feel?'

'Like it's packed in dry ice.'

He felt along my shoulder with his thumb and forefinger. He saw me flinch.

'That's where he got you?'

'Yes.'

'There's no break. When your collarbone's broken there's a knot like a basketball.'

'Who's the hooker?'

'You got me. The ones I knew five years ago are probably hags now. Actually, they were hags then.'

'You're pretty slick, Clete.'

'What can I say?' He grinned at me. 'But one word of advice, noble mon. Think about going back to Bayou Teche and let New Orleans go down the drain by itself. For some reason, Dave, having you in town makes me think of a man walking into a clock shop with a baseball bat.'

She had always loved roses and four-o'clocks. The flower beds in her lawn and the shaded areas around the coulee at her home on Spanish Lake had been bursting with them. Now she grew purple and gold four-o'clocks along the wall of her patio on Camp Street. They had already dropped their winter seeds like big black pepper grains on the worn bricks, but her yellow and hybrid blue roses still bloomed as big as fists. The western sky was streaked with magenta through the oak trees, and leaves floated across the tunnels of underwater light in the swimming pool. The air was heavy with the smoky taste of the meat fire in the hibachi, cool and bittersweet with the smell of fall, like the odor of burning sugarcane stubble, of pecans when they mold inside their husks under the tree.

She turned the steaks on the grill with a fork, her eyes watering in the smoke, and smiled at me. She wore leather sandals, faded designer jeans, and a black shirt with red flowers sewn into it. Her honey-colored hair was full of lights, and where it was trimmed on her neck it looked thick and stiff and soft and lovely to the touch, all at the same time.

She saw me press my hand to my shoulder again.

'Is there something wrong, Dave?' she said.

'No, I just have a little flare-up when the weather is about to change. I think it's going to rain. You know how it is this time of year. The leaves turn, then we have a real hard rain and we sort of click into winter.'

'It's too early for that,' she said. 'Besides, winter is never that bad here, anyway.'

'No, it's not. Boots, can I use your phone to call New Iberia? I need to check on Alafair.'

'Sure, hon.'

Alafair's voice made me want to leave New Orleans that night. Or maybe it made me want to escape even more the brooding premonition that seemed to hang between me and Bootsie like a secret both of us knew, but neither of us would broach.

She didn't have to tell me about the Baylor medical center in Houston: I had seen it in her eyes. It's a detached look, as if the person has stepped briefly around a corner and seen to the end of a long, gray street on which there are no other people, I'd flown in a dustoff loaded with wounded grunts, their foreheads painted with Mercurochrome *M*'s to indicate morphine injections, and the two who died before we reached battalion aid had had that look in their eyes, as though the hot wind through the doors, the steely *blat-blat* of the propeller blades, the racing green landscape below, were now all part of somebody else's filmstrip.

'It's bad, isn't it, Boots?' I said. I sat in the scrolled-iron patio chair by the pool and looked at the tops of my hands when I said it.

'Yes,' she said quietly.

'What's the name for it?'

'Lupus,' she said. 'Then she said, 'Systemic lupus. The full Latin name means "red wolf." Sometimes people get a butterfly mask on their face. I don't have that kind, though. It just lives inside me.'

I felt myself swallow, and I looked away from her eyes.

'You know what it is, then?' she said. She pushed the meat to the side of the grill and sat down across from me. Her hair was wreathed in smoke and the lighted turquoise shimmer off the pool.

'I've heard about it. I don't know a lot,' I said.

'It attacks the connective tissues. It starts in the hand sometimes and spreads through the joints. In the worst cases, when it's untreated, people look like they're wrapped in strips of plastic.'

I started to speak, but I couldn't.

'I didn't have medical insurance, no savings, nothing but the vending machine business,' she said. 'I couldn't just walk out on the business at twenty cents on the dollar.'

I saw a flicker of anger in her eyes, a spark, a recrimination that wanted to have its way. But it was only momentary.

Then she reached forward and touched me on the knee as though it were I who should be consoled.

'Dave, there're probably a hundred different degrees of lupus. Today it can be controlled. This new doctor I have in Houston has started me on a different kind of medication, with steroids and some other things. My problem is I ignored some warning signs, some swelling in my fingers in cold weather and stiffness in the joints, and I have some kidney damage. But I'm going to pull it off.'

'How long have you known?' I said. My voice sounded weak, as though I had borrowed it from someone else.

'For the last year.'

Her eyes moved over my face. She took my hand and held it on her knee.

'You shouldn't look like that,' she said.

'I've been getting on your case, Bootsie, criticizing you, telling you that you're mixed up with the greaseballs—'

'You didn't have any way of knowing, *cher.*'

'Boots—'

'Yes?'

'Bootsie, I don't know what to say to you.' I pressed my thumb and forefinger against my eyelids, but it didn't do any good. The wilted four-o'clocks, the black silhouettes of floating leaves, the flames in the grill, all became watery and bright like splinters of light shot through crystal. 'I majored in being a dumb shit. It's the one constant in my life.'

'I know you better than anybody else on earth, Dave. And no matter what you say, or what you believe, you never deliberately hurt anybody in your life.'

Then she stood up, her face smiling down at me, and sat in my lap. She held my head against her breast and kissed my hair and stroked her fingers along my cheek.

'You remember when we used to go to Deer's Drive-In and do this?' she said. 'I think yesterday is always only a minute away.'

I could feel the softness of her breast against my ear and hear the beating of her heart like a clock that told time for both of us.

14

In the hot darkness I smell the village before I see it – the wet reek of duck
and hog shit, dead fish, moldy straw, boiled dog, stagnant pools of water
coated with algae and mosquitoes. The air is breathless, so humid and still
and devoid of movement that every line of sweat running down inside my
fatigues is like the path of an insect across the skin. There is no light in the
hooches, nor sound, and Marines sit listlessly on the ground, smoking,
waiting for something, their weapons propped against their packs. They
chew Red Man and unlit cigars, eat candy bars, and spit constantly between
their legs.

Then for no reason that will ever make sense, somebody pulls the pin on a
fragmentation grenade, releases the spoon, and rolls it inside a hooch. The
explosion blows straw out of the bottom of the walls, lights the doorway in a
rectangle of flame, sends a solitary kettle toppling end over end through the
clearing. For a moment we can see the shapes of people inside, large ones and
small ones, but they've given up, resigned themselves to this chance ending at
the hands of an angry or fearful or bored boy from South Carolina or Texas,
and their silhouettes settle on to the burning straw pallet like shadows
flattening into the earth.

But the flames that crack through the sides of the hooch and lick up to
the roof do not burn naturally. Instead, it is as though a high wind has
struck the fire, fanned it into a vortex that burns with the clean, pure
intensity of white gas. Then it becomes as bright and shattering to the eyes as
a phosphorus shell exploding, and we wilt back from the heat into the
wavering shadows at the edge of the clearing.

Behind me I hear thin-rimmed wire wheels rolling across the dirt, and I
turn and watch Tony push Paul in his wheelchair toward the white
brilliance of the fire. Tony's green utilities are sun-faded, caked with salt,
streaked with sweat and mud and fecal matter from a rice paddy. He wheels
Paul into the burning doorway, and I try to stop them but my feet feel
as though they're wired together, and my hand looks like a meaningless,
outstretched claw.

Tony's utilities steam in the heat; then he and Paul both burst into flame
like huge candles. The fire has sound now, the roar of wind in a tunnel, the

whistle of superheated air cracking through wood, the resinous popping of
everything that we are – skin and organ and bone.

But I am wrong about Tony and Paul. They have not found their
denouement in a Vietnamese village. They emerge from the back of the fire
and walk side by side into the jungle. Their bodies glow with a cool white
brilliance, like a pistol's flare's, that is interrupted intermittently by the
trunks of trees and tangles of vine as they go deeper into the jungle. The
tripping of my heart is the only sound in the clearing.

Tony leaned forward in the chair next to my bed, his head silhouetted
against the early orange sun outside the window. He poked my shoulder
with two stiff fingers.

'Hey, wake up,' he said.

'What?'

'You're having a real mean one.'

'What?' I was raised up on my elbows now.

'Do you always wake up with a chain saw in your head? Come on, get
out of the rack. We got a lot to do today.'

I sat on the side of the bed in my underwear, my forearms propped
on my thighs. I rubbed my face and looked again at Tony, trying to
disconnect him from the dream.

'Did you get crocked last night or something?' he said.

'No.'

'All right, get dressed and let's eat breakfast.'

'What's going on, Tony?'

'You're going with me and Paul over to our fishing camp in Mississippi.'

'It's a school day, isn't it?'

'His school's closed for a couple of days. They've got to tear some
asbestos out of the ceilings or something. You want to go or not?'

'I was going to do some things with Bootsie.'

'Today you put her on hold.'

'I don't think I want to do that.'

'Yeah?'

'I'm meeting her for lunch, Tony.'

'I owe you, I pay my debts. Are you interested or not?'

'What are you saying, partner?'

'Do you have fifty K in place?'

'Yes.'

'Where?'

'Don't worry, I can have it in an hour.'

'So we eat breakfast, then you get it. At ten o'clock we're heading over
for my camp. You're going to follow in your truck.'

'This is all a little vague.'

'You wanted the score. I'm giving you the score. It's a onetime offer. Are you in or out? Tell me now.'

'I'm in. When's it going down?'

'You don't need to know that.'

'Tony, I'm not sure I like being treated like a fish.'

'I don't know when it's going down. That's something I'll find out later. I told you I don't deal with these guys as a rule. But you want the action, so I'm making an exception.'

'Are you mad about something?'

'No, why?'

'You sound like you've got a beef.'

'I'd already promised Paul to take him to the camp today. Then last night I got a message at one of my clubs about your deal. So I'm kind of mixing business with a family trip. Which means I'm breaking one of my own rules, and I don't like that. But I don't go back on my word, either.'

'I'll get dressed and pick up my money.'

'Jess'll drive you.'

'You think I'm going to leave town?' I tried to smile.

'No offense, Dave, but anyone who does business with me does it in a controlled environment. *Anyone.*' He raised his eyebrows. They looked like grease-pencil lines drawn on his olive skin.

We ate cereal and toast and drank coffee in the glass-enclosed breakfast room while the Negro houseman helped Paul get dressed. The early sun had grown pale and wispy in the east, and clouds that were as black as oil smoke were forming in a bank over the Gulf.

'It might be a rough day for a fishing trip,' I said.

'It'll blow over,' he said.

He fiddled with his watchband, *tinked* his coffee spoon nervously against his saucer, looked out at the darkening line across the southern horizon. Then he said, 'You know where Kim might be?'

'No.'

'The manager at my club said she didn't come into work yesterday and she doesn't answer her phone. She didn't call you?'

'Why would she call me?'

'Because she digs you.'

He fluttered his fingers on the tablecloth. 'I'd better send a car out to her place,' he said. His eyes were narrowed, and they looked out through the glass and roved around the backyard. 'Maybe she split. Eventually most of them do. I thought she might be different.'

'Don't worry about her. She's probably all right,' I said.

One of Tony's bodyguards, a black-haired man of about twenty-five, came into the kitchen for coffee. He was barefoot and bare-chested, and his beltless brown slacks hung down low on his flat stomach. He looked at us without speaking, then filled his cup.

'Put a shirt on when you walk around the house,' Tony said.

The man walked back into the dining room without answering.

'It's a frigging zoo,' Tony said. 'I treat people with respect, I pay them decent wages, and they try to wipe their frigging feet on me. You know, I got a cousin runs a lot of action in Panama City. His wife tells him one day he's a drag, he's overweight, he's got bad breath, he's got a putz the size of a Vienna sausage, that the only thing he ever did for her was crush her two feet into the mattress every night. So she dumps him and starts making it with this county judge who's on the pad with the — family in Tampa. Except she and the judge both get juiced out of their minds one night, and both of them get busted while she's blowing the judge in her Porsche behind this nightclub. She gets out of jail in the morning, hung over and trembling and her picture on the front page of the Panama City newspaper, and then she goes home and finds out my cousin had her Porsche towed back to her house, and she thinks maybe something's going right after all, my cousin's going to forgive her and square the sodomy charge with the city. Except she sees the Porsche is sitting flat on its springs because my cousin had a cement truck fill it up with concrete. I ought to take lessons from him.'

He looked again at the sky and at the trees blowing in the yard. He opened his mouth and scratched the tautness of his cheek with his fingernail.

'What's eating you, Tony?' I said.

'Nothing.'

'You haven't gotten back into pharmaceuticals, have you?' I smiled at him.

'I'm cool,' he said.

'You don't have to go into this deal. Let it slide if it doesn't feel right,' I said.

I watched his face. His eyes still roved the backyard. Back out, partner, I thought.

'I already committed you for fifty large,' he said. 'If you don't take it, I have to.'

'I have to call Bootsie.'

'I'll do it for you. While you go for your money with Jess. Nobody needs to know where we're going today, Dave.'

'All right,' I said. And there went my opportunity to tip Minos through the phone tap. Then I began to realize what was really on Tony's mind.

'I guess your little girl misses you,' he said.

'Yes.'

'After today it looks like you'll have everything you need to make your investors happy.'

'I guess I will.'

'To tell you the truth, Dave, I don't think I want to get into distribution over in Southwest Louisiana. There're too many potential problems there, conflicts with the Houston crowd. I don't need it.'

'Suit yourself.'

He didn't answer.

'I'll brush my teeth, then I'll be ready to go with Jess,' I said.

He nodded and made lines on the tablecloth with his cereal spoon. Through the glass the southern sky was as dark as gunmetal, and white veins of lightning pulsated and trembled in the clouds.

I brushed my teeth, rinsed my mouth, and spit into the lavatory. Too bad, Tony, I thought. I didn't know you were a closet Rotarian.

I had seen his kind before. They come into AA and unload some terrible moral guilt, or perhaps the whole travesty of their lives: then they begin to feel better. The ego begins to reassert itself, the tongue licks across the lips for maybe another try at the dirty boogie, and they decide to deep-six the people who've witnessed their moment of weakness and need.

So I had become Tony's disposable confessor. Wrong way to think, Tony, I thought. You commit the crime, you do the time. One way or another, you do the time.

Jess drove me to the bus depot, where I picked up the fifty thousand dollars the DEA had put in a locker for me. For a moment I thought I was going to lose Jess so I could phone Minos.

'I've had a knot in my bowels for two days,' he said, gripping his belt buckle with his fist and frowning with his whole face.

'Go use the men's room and I'll get a cup of coffee. We've got time.'

He thought about it and bent his knees slightly as though he were breaking wind.

'No, there's piss all over the toilet seats. I'll wait,' he said. 'Besides, Tony's acting weird again. When Tony gets weird, he needs somebody around him.'

'Weird about what?'

'Late last night he says to me, "It's all ending, it's all ending." I say, "What the fuck does that mean, Tony?"' Two Catholic nuns in black habits walked past us. 'He wouldn't answer me. He just walks off and stands in the middle of the dark tennis court like a statue. He stood out there half an hour.'

Back at the house Jess and one of the gatemen began loading fishing rods, food, and camping gear into the Lincoln and the Cadillac. A soft rain clicked on the trees in the yard. I told Tony I was going into my bedroom to pack an overnight bag; then I locked my bathroom door, took down my khakis, and taped the miniaturized recorder inside my thigh. I could activate it by simply dropping my hand and appearing to scratch my leg.

What an absurdity, I thought: I had invested all this energy and effort in nailing a man who had nothing to do with my life, who had never harmed me, who lived on the raw edges of narcotic madness. The story about Tony that Jess had told me in the bus depot was no mystery. Psychologists sometimes called it a world destruction fantasy. The recovering addict and drunk are suddenly cut off from their source: they have no fire escape, and the building is burning down. They wake in the middle of the night with a nameless terror and drag it with them like a gargoyle on a chain into their waking hours. Sometimes they can't breathe; their hearts race, blood veins dilate in the brain, a pressure band forms on one side of the head as though someone were tightening a machinist's vise into the bone. The only image that will adequately describe the fear is right out of the Revelation of Saint John the Divine: The beast is climbing up out of the sea, and the edges of the sky are blackening like an enormous sheet of dry paper held against a flame.

Psychologists will say that this is a reenactment of the birth experience. But the words bring no solace, no more than they can to the infant who, just delivered from the womb, waits for the slap of life.

In the meantime, while I was planning to weld the cell door shut on a driven creature like Tony Cardo, I had done little to keep my promise to Tante Lemon and Dorothea to prevent Tee Beau Latiolais from eventually being electrocuted at Angola. And while Tee Beau was twisting in the wind, trying to hide behind a pair of dark glasses in a pizza joint on the corner of St Charles and Canal, the center of downtown New Orleans, a psychopath like Jimmie Lee Boggs was able to run around painting brain matter on walls in three states.

I tucked in my flannel shirt, buttoned my khakis, buckled my belt, and looked into the mirror. One way or another, it's show time, I thought, and carried my overnight bag and the briefcase with the fifty thousand out to the driveway just as Tony was latching the safety belt across Paul in the front seat of the Lincoln. Paul grinned happily at me from under a blue fishing cap with a white anchor stitched on it.

'Dad's going to take us out in the boat after it stops raining,' he said.

'Yeah, they school up in this weather. They'll be in close to shore, too,' Tony said. 'Dave, keep between us and the Caddy.'

'I won't get lost.'

'You might. We're going to take Interstate Ten instead of the back road. Stay in my rearview mirror, okay?'

'You got it,' I said.

So I lost all hope of contacting Minos, and I was on my own. We bounced out the front gate in a caravan. The rain was moving across Lake

Pontchartrain in a gray sheet, and the yellowed palm fronds on the esplanade clattered and stiffened in the wind.

The fishing camp was on the lower portion of the Pearl River basin, not far from the Gulf. It was built of unpainted cypress, with a rusty tin roof, and was set back on a sandy bluff above the river, so that the screened-in gallery had to be supported by stilts. The camp was surrounded by live oaks, and the tops of the willows on the bank grew to eye level on the gallery. It was still raining, and the wind off the Gulf blew a fine mist out of the trees into the screens.

But it was snug and warm inside the cabin, paneled with knotty pine, the floors covered with bright yellow linoleum, the kitchen outfitted with a butane stove, a microwave, and a double-door refrigerator. On the back porch, which gave on to the access road, was a freezer filled with frozen ducks, rib-eye steaks, and gallons of ice cream.

Tony and Paul sat at the kitchen table, tying leaders and huge lead weights and balsa wood bobbers to the saltwater rods and reels. In the front room, Jess and the four bodyguards who had followed in the Cadillac played *bourré* and drank canned beer at a plank table. They were a strange lot to watch, a juxtaposed contrast of the generational changes that had taken place inside the mob.

Jess Ornella was what mob people used to call a soldier. He was built like a hod carrier and looked dumb as dirt and probably was. Tony said that Jess had been in trouble all his life – with the nuns and brothers, truant officers, cops, social workers, probation officers, landlords, jailers, the draft board, bill collectors, wives, and prison psychiatrists (one had recommended that he be lobotomized). He had done time in the Orleans Parish jail for writing bad checks, committing bigamy, and setting fire to a restaurant for refusing him service. In Angola he had been a 'big stripe', a name given to those who were considered dangerous or incorrigible, and who usually stayed in lockdown in the Block. He always gave me the feeling that he could destroy a house simply by running back and forth through its walls.

But the others came from a different mold: young and lithe, tanned year-round, they wore gold chains and religious medallions and thick identification bracelets, and had a hungry look in their eyes. You knew they wanted something, but you weren't sure what it was, in the same way that you stare into a zoo animal's eyes and see an atavistic instinct there that makes you step back involuntarily. They constantly touched the flatness of their stomach, the boxed hairline on their neck, the gold watchband on their wrist; they made cigarette smoking a stylized art form. They seldom smiled, except with women who were new to them, and they talked incessantly about money, either about the amount they had made, or were about to make, or that someone else had made. Like women, they dressed for their own sex, but usually their loyalties went no further than a sentimental attitude towards their parents, whom in reality they seldom saw.

Jess accepted me because Tony had moved me into his house, perhaps just as he would not question Tony's choice of lawn furniture. But the others did not speak to me, other than to reply to a direct question. Jess saw me watching the game with a cup of coffee in my hand.

'You want to play?' he said, and started to move his chair aside.

But the men sitting on each side of him remained stationary. One of them had the deck of cards in his upturned palm and a matchstick in his mouth.

'Cecil just *bourréd* the pot. Wait till we play it out,' he said. His eyes never left the game.

'That's all right. I lose too much at the track, anyway,' I said.

No one looked up or acknowledged my statement, and I went back into the kitchen and began making a sandwich on the sideboard. Rain dripped out of the oak trees in back, and the dirt yard was flooded with a wet green light.

'Dad says we're going out on the salt even if it doesn't stop raining,' Paul said. 'We can put the rods in the sockets and stay in the cabin.'

'Sure, this is good tarpon weather,' I said. 'On a day like this you bounce the bait through the wake and the tarps will hit it so hard the rod will end all the way to the gunwale.'

'Are you glad you came, even though it's raining?' Paul said.

'Sure.'

'Dad says you're probably going to move back home with your little girl.'

I looked at Tony. He had one eye closed and was threading a nylon leader through the eye of a hook.

'Yes, I guess that's true, Paul,' I said.

'Can we come see you? And ride your horse?'

'Anytime you want to.'

Tony tied a blood knot with the leader and snipped off the loose end close to the hook's eye with a pair of fingernail clippers. He held the hook by the shank and pulled on the leader to test the strength of the knot. 'There,' he said to Paul. 'They won't bust that one.'

He wore bell-bottomed denims, a long-sleeved candy-striped shirt, and his Marine Corps utility cap with the brim propped up. His eyes avoided mine, and like his hired help who rode in the Cadillac he did not speak to me unless to answer a question, or to indicate to me that I could entertain myself with whatever was available in the camp.

I walked out under the dripping trees, then down under the screened gallery supported on stilts. The riverbanks were thick with wet brush and wild morning glory vines, and because the river emptied into the Gulf and its level was affected by the tides, trotlines were strung at crazy angles between tree trunks and logs and stakes driven into the mud. The tide was out now, and the highest water level of the river was marked by a gray line of dead hyacinths along the banks. Thunder boomed and rolled out over the Gulf, and the air was charged with the electric smell of ozone. The tree trunks glistened blackly, the canopy overhead and the scrub brush and canebrakes and layers of rotting leaves literally creaked with moisture. I thought of Alafair and Bootsie and realized that I had never felt more alone in my life.

Later, inside, the phone on the kitchen wall rang. Tony answered it, and after he said hello, he listened without speaking, and looked at me over the top of Paul's head. Then he hung up the receiver and said, 'Let's take a ride, Dave. Paul, I have to take care of a little business with Dave. You stay here with Jess, and I'll be back in an hour.'

'What about Dave?' Paul asked.

'He's got to do some stuff. We'll see him later.'

'Aren't you going fishing, Dave?' Paul said.

'We'll see how it works out. I might have to take off for a while,' I said.

'I thought you were going with us.' He was turned sideways in his wheelchair to talk to me. His blue jeans looked brand-new and stiff and too big for him.

'I might have to go back home,' I said. 'I've been gone a long time.'

'Your little girl wants you to come home?'

'Yes, she does.'

He nodded, picked up a piece of leader, and began poking it in a crack on the table.

'Are you coming back to visit at all?' he said.

'I'd like to take you fishing to some places I know around New Iberia. The bass are so big there we have to knock them back into the water with tennis rackets.'

His whole face lighted with his smile.

Tony and I rode in my pickup truck, and the white Cadillac full of his hoods followed us up the dirt road that bordered the river. The chuck-holes were deep and full of rainwater, and we bounced so hard on the springs that Tony had to prop one hand against the dashboard. I rubbed my thigh with my palm and used my thumb to hit the small button on the side of the tape recorder. Before we had left the camp, Tony had put on a raincoat and dropped his chrome-plated .45 automatic in the pocket. I banged through another chuckhole, and the .45 clanked against the door handle. Tony pulled his raincoat straight and kept the weight of the gun on his thigh.

'You think you might need that?' I asked.

'I carry it so I *won't* need it.'

'Did you ever have trouble with these guys?'

'These are guys who operate on the bottom of the food chain. They're not a bold bunch.'

'You don't think highly of them.'

'I don't think about them at all.'

'I appreciate what you're doing for me.'

'You've already told me that, so forget it. Look, my son likes you. You know why? It's because children recognize integrity in adults. I've got some advice for you, Dave. After this score, get out of the business. It's not worth it. There's not a morning I don't get up thinking about the IRS, the DEA, city dicks like Nate Baxter, cowboys who'll clip you just to get invited over to a certain guy's table at the Jockey Club in Miami. It's like they say about marriage: You do it for money and you'll earn every nickel of it.'

'I guess a guy makes his choices, Tony,' I said, and looked at the side of his face.

He turned his head slowly and looked back at me.

'That's right,' he said, 'and I'm making one now. When I got put in with the wet brains at the VA, there was a lot of talk in the therapy sessions about character defects. I've got lots of those, but lying's not one of them. I choose to honor my word, and I don't like righteousness in people, particularly when they're talking about my life.'

He rubbed the moisture off the front glass with his sleeve. Beyond the tunnel of trees we could see pasture and sky up ahead.

'There's my airstrip. We only have another mile to go,' he said. 'Dave, after you get your goods, I think we say good-bye.'

'All right, Tony.'

'You think I'm a hypocrite, don't you?'

'I've got too many problems of my own to be taking other people's inventory.'

'Before you write me off, I want you to understand something. You helped me a lot, man. But right now I've got some heavy shit to work through – with my habit, my douche-bag wife, these fuckheads in Houston and Miami – and I've got to simplify my life and concentrate on Paul and nobody else. That's the way it is.'

He waited for me to reply.

'You're not going to say anything?' he asked.

'It all works out one way or another.'

'Yeah, that's the way I figure it. *Semper fi*, Mac, and fuck it.' He rolled down the window, let the mist blow inside, and took a deep breath. A bolt of lightning splintered into the tree line at the south end of the pasture where Tony kept his plane. The air smelled as metallic and cold as brass.

*

A mile farther on we drove out of the hackberry and pine trees into the pasture with the mowed airstrip and tin hangar that Tony had told me to remember on our first trip to the Pearl River country. Two cars and a van were parked in front of the hangar, and the hangar's main door was slid open about three feet. The surrounding fields were pale green and sopping wet, and from horizon to horizon steel-gray clouds roiled across the sky.

'The plane's not in yet, or these guys wouldn't still be hanging around,' Tony said. 'I'll stay with you through the buy, then I'll ride back in the Caddy and you're on your own.'

'All right, Tony.'

'Make sure you're satisfied with the quality of everything before you leave. Don't think you can go back to these guys with a complaint. They're basically punks, and they won't make it right. In fact, they usually try to cannibalize each other whenever they have a chance.'

'Where's the plane coming in from?'

'They make out like it's a direct connection from Colombia. But I think it's coming out of Florida. There're a lot of abandoned housing developments in the Everglades. So they use these paved roads out in the saw grass for airstrips. What the Miami crowd doesn't need or doesn't want, because maybe the prices are going down too fast, they lay it off on these guys.'

I drove along a two-cart dirt road through the pasture to the front of the hangar. Through the opening door I could see the canary-yellow wings of a crop-duster biplane and rows of industrial metal drums and bright silver liquid propane tanks. I cut the ignition. In the rearview mirror I saw the white limo stop behind me. No one got out.

'What is this place?' I said.

'The guy who owns it is a local peckerwood who runs a farm-supply business or something. Look, Dave, when we go in there, I talk and you just hand them the money.'

'What about them back there?' I nodded toward the limo.

'They're paid to watch my back, not my business dealings. Come on, let's go.'

We walked through the wet grass and drizzling rain and stepped inside the dryness of the hangar. It was immaculately clean; there was another biplane, a red one, at the far end, and a small green John Deere tractor next to it, but there was not a spot of oil or a tread mark from a tire on the concrete floor slab. By a windowed side office were a picnic table and benches that had probably been moved in from outside, because there were pieces of grass on the bottoms of the legs. A fat man in rumpled brown slacks and a T-shirt was turning and flattening hamburger patties on a hibachi with a spatula. The smoke drifted off in the draft created by an opening in the far door that gave on to the mowed landing strip.

Three men sat at the table. Two of them had their backs to us, and the third man was telling them a story, gesturing with his hands, and he did not look at us. On one end of the table was a washtub filled with crushed ice and green bottles of Heineken.

We walked a few feet forward and then stopped. To my right, stacked in a row along the front sliding door, were more metal drums, each of them containing dry chemical fertilizers, and at the end of the drums was a fingernail-polish-red Coca-Cola machine, the old kind with a big, thick lead-colored handle. Tony's eyes were riveted on the picnic table.

I looked at him.

'It's the wrong guys,' he whispered.

'What?'

'The black guys aren't there. The black guys are always in on the score.'

Then I heard the Cadillac's transmission in reverse, backing across the wet ground.

'It's a hit. It's a fucking hit. Get out of here,' Tony said, and he shoved me with one arm toward the opening in the door just as Jimmie Lee Boggs stepped out from behind the Coca-Cola machine and threw a pump ventilated-rib shotgun to his shoulder and let off the round in the chamber.

It was a deer slug, a solid, round piece of lead as thick as the ball of your thumb, and it whanged off a metal barrel just in front of us and ricocheted into the tin wall of the hangar. Tony and I both dove between the barrels at the same time. I heard Boggs eject the spent shell on to the cement and ratchet another into the chamber. Tony was squatted down, breathing hard, his chrome-plated .45 held at an upward angle. I was standing, pressed back against the wall, and I got my .45 out of my fatigue jacket pocket, slid back the receiver, and eased a hollow-point round into the chamber. The men who had been drinking beer and cooking hamburgers at the picnic table had fallen to the floor or piled inside the office below the level of the windows.

Tony tried to look around the side of the barrel, and Boggs fired again, this time a round that was loaded with buckshot. It scoured off the side of the barrel behind us and ripped a pattern of five holes that I could cover with my fingers in the tin wall. Then somebody inside the office started firing with a pistol, probably a revolver, for he let off five rounds that danced all over the concrete; then he stopped to reload. When he did I aimed my .45 with both hands over Tony's head and fired at the office until my palms were numb from the recoil. My ears roared with a sound like the sea, and the breech locked open on the empty clip. The hollow-points blew holes as big as baseballs out of the toppled picnic table and sent triangular panes of glass crashing into the office's interior, but the lower half of the office wall was built of cinderblock, and the hollow-points splintered apart inside the concrete and did no harm to the men on the floor.

My hands were shaking as I pulled out the empty clip and shoved a full one into the .45's magazine. Tony raked his springlike curls back with his fingers.

'We're seriously fucked,' he whispered.

'We wait them out,' I said.

'Are you kidding? If Jimmie Lee or one of those other guys gets outside, he can come around behind us and put it to us through the wall. It's a matter of time. I only got this clip. What have you got?'

'You're looking at it.'

The skin of his face was dry and tight, his eyes as darkly bright as when he'd been loaded on black speed. He began breathing deeply in his chest, as though he were trying to oxygenate his blood. He looked at the big, round silver tanks of liquid propane that were lined against the adjacent wall.

'No,' I said.

'You heard stories about it. But I lived through it, man. The captain called it right in on top of us.'

'Don't do it, Tony.'

'Bullshit. You got to go out there on the screaming edge. That's the only place you win. You don't know that, you don't know anything.'

I wanted to put out my hand, push his gun down toward the floor, somehow in that last terrible moment exorcise the insanity that lived in his soul. Instead, I stared down at him numbly while he pivoted on one knee, aimed at a propane tank, and fired. The automatic leapt upward in his hand, and the round clanged off the top of the tank and hit an iron spar in the wall. He rested one buttock on his heel, propped his wrist across his knee, lowered his sights, and pulled the trigger again.

This time the round hit the tank dead center and cored a hole in it as cleanly as a machinist's punch. The propane gushed out on the cement, its bright, instant reek like a slap across the face.

His .45 lay on the floor now, and his hands were trembling as he tore a match from a matchbook and folded the cover back from the striker. I could hear the men inside the office moving around on top of the broken glass.

'Tony—,' I said. I was pressed back against the wall, between the barrels. The air was thick and wet with the smell of the propane.

'What?' he said.

'Tony—'

'It's the only way, man. You know it.'

I touched my religious medal and closed my eyes and opened them again. My heart was thundering against my rib cage.

'Do it,' I said.

'Listen, you get out of this and I don't, you keep your fucking promise. You look after my son.'

'All right, Tony.'

Boggs stepped out wide from behind the Coca-Cola machine and fired a pattern of buckshot that *thropped* past my ear and blew the top off a metal barrel. It rolled in a circle on the cement. Tony struck the loose match in his hand, touched the other matches with the flame, and flipped the burning folder out into the pool of propane.

The pool burst into white and blue flames; then the fire crawled up the silvery jet of propane squirting from the tank. I heard a window crash on the far side of the Coca-Cola machine, and I heard the men inside the office fighting with one another to get out the office door; but now Tony and I were out from behind the barrels, unprotected, and running for the opening in the hangar door.

The ignition of the propane tanks, the fertilizers, the air itself, was like a bolt of lightning striking inside the building. Through the hangar door I saw the rain falling outside, the sodden fields, the wind ruffling the tree line, then Tony hit me hard on the back and knocked me through the door just as the whole building exploded.

His body was framed against the flash, like a tin effigy silhouetted against a forge. He tumbled across the ground, his clothes smoking, his hair singed and stinking like a burnt cat's. The heat was so intense I couldn't feel the rain on my skin. We stumbled forward, past my pickup, into the field, as Jimmie Lee Boggs floored his van down the two-track road. Behind us, for only a moment, I heard screams inside the fire.

But Tony was not finished yet. He sat down in a puddle of water, his knees pulled up before him, aimed the .45 with both hands, and let off two quick rounds. One tore through the van's back panel, but the second spiderwebbed the window in the driver's door and blew out the front windshield. It hung down like a crumpled glass apron, and the van careered off the road, whipping the grass under its bumper, spinning divots of mud from under the tires.

'Suck on that one, Jimmie Lee,' Tony said.

The van seemed to slow as it made a wide arc through the field; then it lurched on its back springs as the driver shifted down, righted the wheel, and hit the gas again. The tin sides of the buildings were white with heat, as though phosphorus were burning inside; then they folded softly in upon themselves, like cellophane being consumed, and the roof crashed on to the cement slab. Boggs's van hit the main dirt road and disappeared into the corridor of trees.

Tony tried to get to his feet, but gave it up and sat back down in the water. His face was drawn and empty and dotted with mud.

'I'm going to leave you and come back for you, Tony. I'm borrowing your piece, too.' I took the .45 gingerly from his hand and eased the hammer back down.

He wiped his eyes clear with the back of his wrist and looked up and down my trouser legs. Then his hand felt inside my thigh, almost as though he were molesting me. His mouth shaped itself into a small butterfly, and his eyes roved casually over my face.

'Where's your backup people?' he said.

'I don't know. My guess is, though, they've got the road sealed on each end.'

'Yeah, that'd make sense.'

'Will you wait for me here?'

'I'm going to start walking back.'

'I don't think it'd be good for you to meet the guys in the limo.'

'My limo's in the bottom of a pond by now, and those guys are halfway across Lake Pontchartrain.' Then he said, 'Was Kim in on it?'

'No. I never saw her before I got involved with your people.'

'That's good. She's a good kid. Do me a favor, will you?'

'What?'

'Get the fuck away from me.'

I didn't answer him. I got in my pickup and followed Jimmie Lee Boggs's sharply etched tire tracks down the dirt road bordered on each side by pine and hackberry trees, and cows that poked through the underbush and lowed fearfully each time lightning snapped across the sky.

I didn't have to go far. His van was in a ditch opposite the old seismograph drill barge that was sunk at an angle on the other side of the river. I stopped my truck, stuck Tony's .45 inside my belt, and walked up on the driver's side of the van. The light was gray through the trees, and the air had the cold smell of a refrigerator that has been closed up too long with produce inside. The driver's door was partly open, and the dashboard and steering column were littered with chips of broken glass, and painted with blood.

I pulled the door wide open and pointed the .45 inside, but the van was empty. Twelve-gauge shot-gun shells, their yellow casings red with bloody finger smears, were scattered on the passenger's seat and on the floor. A paintless, narrow, wooden footbridge, with a broken handrail and boards hanging out the bottom, spanned the river just downstream from the drill barge. Deep foot tracks led from the opposite side of the bridge along the mudbank through the morning glory vines and cypress roots to the starboard side of the barge, which rested at an upward angle against the incline.

The slats on the bridge were soft with rot, and three of them burst under my weight as loud as rifle shots. The river's surface was dented with water dripping from the trees, and the incoming tide on the coast had raised the river's level, so that the line of dried flotsam along the bank waved on the edge of the current like gray cobweb.

I walked along the bank through the underbrush to the bow of the barge, where the drill tower sat. The hull was rusted out at the waterline, and there were tears in the cast-iron plates like broken teeth. I grabbed hold of the forward handrail and stepped over it on to the deck. The deck was slippery with moldy leaves and pine needles, and somebody's boots had bruised a gray path from the gunwale to the door of the pilothouse.

I put my .45 in my left hand, slipped Tony's out of my belt with my right hand, and pulled the hammer back on full cock with my thumb. The inside of the pilothouse was strewn with leaves and empty wood crates that once held canned dynamite, primers, and spools of cap wire. In one corner were the shriveled remains of a used condom, and somebody had spray-painted on the bulkhead the initials KKK and the words JOE BOB AND CLAUDINE inside a big heart. At the rear of the pilothouse were the door and the steel steps that led down into the engine room.

I put my back against the bulkhead and looked around the corner and down the steps into the half-flooded room below. The water was black and stagnant and streaked with oil, and somebody had tried to retrieve the huge engine on a hoist, then abandoned his task and left it suspended on chains and pulleys inches above the water.

Then I heard something move in the water, something scrape against the hull.

'You're under arrest, Boggs,' I said. 'Throw your shotgun out where I can see it, then come up the steps with your hands on your head.'

It was silent down below now.

'If you're hurt and can't move, tell me so,' I said. 'We'll have you in a hospital in Slidell in a half hour. But first you've got to throw out the shotgun.'

The only sounds were the rain dripping in the water and the tree limbs creaking overhead. Sweat ran out of my hair, and the wind blowing through the windows was cold on my face.

'Look, Boggs, you're in an iron box. It all ends right here. If I open up on you, there's no place you can hide. Use your head. You don't have to die here.'

Then I heard him moving fast through the water, from out of a corner that was tilted at an upward angle against the bank, into full view at the bottom of the steps, his neck and shoulder scarlet with blood, his face and threadlike hair and drenched T-shirt strung with algae and spiderwebs. But he was hurt badly, and the tip of the shotgun barrel caught on the handrail of the steps just as I began firing down into the hold with both pistols.

The bullets ricocheted off the steps and the hull, sparking and whanging from one surface to the next. He dropped the shotgun into the water and tried to cover his face with his arms. But he lost his balance on the sloping floor and toppled forward into the machinist's hoist and suspended engine block. The chains roared loose from the pulleys, and Jimmie Lee Boggs crashed against the flooded bottom of the hull with the engine block and the tangle of chains squarely on top of his loins and lower chest. The blood drained from his face, and he reared back his head and opened his mouth in an enormous O like a man who couldn't find words for his pain.

I set both pistols on the floor of the pilothouse and walked down the steps into the water. The water was cold inside my socks and against my shins, and from the corner I smelled the sweet, fetid odor of a dead nutria whose webbed feet bobbed against the hull. The waterline was up to Boggs's neck, his grease-streaked hands rested on top of the block like claws, and he breathed as though his lungs were filled with some terrible obstruction.

I reached down under the water and caught the end of the crankshaft with both hands and tried to lift it. I strained until my shirt split along my back, and I slipped on the layer of moss and algae that covered the floor and stumbled sideways against the hull. My knee hit the side of his head.

'I'm sorry,' I said.

He cleared his throat and rubbed one eye hard with his palm, but he did not speak.

'Can you move at all?'

'He shook his head.

'I've got a jack in the truck,' I said. 'I'll go get it and come back. But you're going to have to do something for me, Jimmie Lee.'

His elongated spearmint-green eyes looked up into mine. The pupils were like tiny burnt cinders.

'Can you talk to me?' I said.

'Yeah, I can talk.' His voice was thick with phlegm.

'When I come back I want you to tell me what happened to Hipolyte Broussard. I want you to tell me who stuffed that oil rag down his mouth. Are we agreed on that?'

'Why do you give a fuck?'

'Because Tee Beau Latiolais is a friend of mine. Because I'm a police officer.'

His eyes looked away at the rust-eaten line of holes in the hull. Where there had been light from the outside, the river current was now eddying inside the barge. His face was bright with sweat.

'Get me out of here, man. The tide's coming in,' he said.

I climbed hurriedly up the steps, got the jack and a three-battery flashlight out of the equipment box in the bed of my truck, made my way across the footbridge, and climbed back down into the engine room. I clicked on the flashlight and balanced it on a step so that the beam struck the hull above where Boggs was pinned. His skin looked bone-white against the blackness of the water.

I wedged the base of the jack between the tilted floor and the side of the hull and fitted the handle into the ratchet socket. I snugged the top of the jack against the engine block and started pumping the handle.

'Come on, Boggs, talk to me. It's not a time to hold back,' I said.

He strained his chin upward to keep it out of the water.

'The colored kid didn't kill the redbone. Fuck, man, get the sonofabitch off me,' he said.

'Who did?'

'The woman did.'

'Which woman?'

'Mama Goula. Who do you think, man?'

'How do you know this, Jimmie Lee?'

'I was out there. The redbone was under the bus, banging on the brake drums, yelling at the kid. The bus fell on him and the kid took off running. Come on, man, I'm busted up inside.'

'Keep talking to me, Jimmie Lee.'

'Mama Goula had brought some chippies out to the camp. She found the redbone and poked the rag down his throat with her thumb.'

I felt the engine block move slightly; then the jack handle slipped out of the socket and my knuckles raked against the hull. Boggs pushed with both hands against the block, his neck cording with the strain.

'Hang on,' I said, and reset the jack flush against the hull with the other end inserted against the engine's crankshaft. I jacked the handle slowly with both hands, a notch at a time, to try to move the engine's weight on Boggs's legs so he could sit up higher out of the water.

'Why did she want to kill Hipolyte?' I asked.

'She didn't want to split the action. It was a perfect chance to clip the redbone. She knew everybody would blame the kid. Fuck, hurry up, man.'

'Why would they blame Tee Beau?'

'The redbone was queer for him. He wanted to make the kid his punk.'

I eased the jack up another notch, saw it shift the block perhaps a half inch, and then I clicked it up another notch. It popped loose from the crankshaft with such force that it broke through the water's surface like a spring. Boggs's mouth opened breathlessly.

'You sonofabitch, you're gonna tear my insides out,' he said.

'Listen, I've got to find a piece of hose or some pipe.'

'What?' His eyes were filled with fright.

'I've got to get you something to breathe through.'

'No! You get that jack under the block.'

I held it up in my hand.

'It's stripped, Boggs,' I said.

'Oh man, don't tell me that.'

'Come on, we're not finished yet. I'll be right back.'

I hunted through the pilothouse and fore and aft on the deck, but anything of value that could be removed from the barge had long ago been taken by scavengers. Then I recrossed the bridge and tore the radiator hose out of my truck. When I climbed back down into the engine room, Boggs's head was tilted all the way back, so that his ears were underwater and only his face was clear of the surface.

I knelt by him and put my hand under the back of his head.

'Take a breath and lift up your head so you can hear me,' I said.

Then I said it again and nudged the back of his head. He straightened his neck and looked at me wide-eyed, his mouth crimped tight, his nostrils shuddering at the waterline.

'We're going to hold this hose as tight as we can around your mouth,' I said. 'I'll stay with you until the tide goes out. Then I'll get help and we'll pull this block off you. You've got my word, Jimmie Lee. I'm not going anywhere. But we've got to keep the hose sealed against your mouth. Do you understand that?'

He blinked his eyes, then laid his head back in the water again, and I pressed the hard rubber edges of the radiator hose around his mouth.

We held it there together for fifteen minutes while the water climbed higher and covered his face entirely. His hair floated in a dirty aura about his head, and his eyes stared at me like watery green marbles. Then I felt the rubber slip against his skin, heard him choke down inside the hose, and saw a fine bead of air bubbles rise from the side of his mouth.

I tried to screw the hose tighter into his mouth, but he had swallowed water and was fighting now. At first his hands locked on my wrists, as though I were the source of his suffering; then his fists burst through the surface and flailed in the air, and finally caught my shirt and tore it down the front of my chest. I pushed the hose down at him again, but there was no way now he could blow the water out of it and regain his breath.

Then one hand came up from the shirt, and felt my face like a blind man reaching out to discover some fragile and tender human mystery, and a last solitary air bubble floated from his throat to the surface and popped in the dead air.

15

Tony had walked almost all the way back to his fishing camp when I slowed the truck abreast of him under a row of moss-hung oaks. It had stopped raining now, and out in the pasture the cows had broken out of their clumps and were grazing in the grass. The hair on the back of Tony's head was singed the color of burnt copper. He glanced sideways at me, indifferently, and kept walking.

'Get in,' I said.

He jumped over a puddle in front of him and brushed a wet branch out of his face. I let the truck idle slowly forward in first gear.

'Come on, Tony. Get in,' I said.

'Is this a bust? If it is, do it by the numbers. I've got lawyers that'll eat your lunch.'

I braked the truck at an angle in front of him and popped open the passenger door.

'Don't act like a sprout, Tony,' I said. 'I want to tell you something.'

He paused, looked over the fields, pinched his nose, then got in the truck and closed the door. His clothes smelled like smoke and ashes. A volunteer fire truck passed us and splashed a curtain of yellow water across my windshield. Tony watched the fire truck disappear down the road through the back window. Finally, he said, 'Jimmie Lee got away from you?'

'No.'

'You popped him?'

'He drowned.'

'Drowned?'

I told him what happened down in the engine room of the drill barge.

'Then I guess it's a red-letter day for you, Dave. You got to watch Jimmie Lee shuffle off with the hallelujah chorus, and you get to be the narc who made the case on Tony C.'

'Is that the way you read it?'

'I told you once, everybody cuts a piece out of your ass one way or another. Except don't bank your promotion or your pay raise yet, Dave. What you've got here is entrapment. Also, I don't think you've got

222

enough on that tape to get them real excited at the US Attorney's office. You're the DEA, right?'

'Indirectly.'

'I'll put in a word for you. I'll tell them you really did your job well.'

The road bent close to the river again, and up ahead I could see Tony's fish camp and the Lincoln convertible parked in the back under the trees. Smoke rose from the chimney and flattened in the salt breeze off the Gulf. I pulled the truck on to the shoulder of the road and cut the engine.

I took Tony's .45 from the pocket of my fatigue jacket and handed it to him. He looked back at me strangely.

'Here's the lay of the land, Tony,' I said. 'I think you've got a big Purple Heart nailed up in the middle of your forehead. Everybody is supposed to feel you're the only guy who did bad time in Vietnam. You also give me the impression that somebody else is responsible for your addiction and getting you out of it. But the bottom line is you sell dope to people and they fuck up their lives with it.'

'I think maybe it's you who's got the problem with conscience, Dave.'

'You're wrong. As of now you're on your own. As far as I know, you died in that fire back there. I don't think a county medical examiner, particularly in a place like this, will ever sort out the bones and teeth in that hangar. If you disappear into Mexico with Paul and stay out of the business, I think the DEA will write you off. I doubt if your wife will be a problem, either, since she'll acquire almost everything you own.'

He chewed on his lip and looked up the incline at the camp.

'You've got your plane, you've got Jess to fly it, you've got that fine little boy to take with you,' I said. 'I think if you make the right choice, Tony, you might be home free.'

'They won't believe you.'

'Maybe you inflate your importance. Twenty-four hours after you're off the board, somebody else will take your place. In a year nobody will be able to find your file.'

He made pockets of air in his cheeks and switched them back and forth as though he were swishing water around in his mouth.

'It's a possibility, isn't it?' he said. He bit a hangnail off his thumb and removed it from his tongue. 'Just pop through a hole in the dimension and leave a big question mark behind. That's not bad.'

'Like you said to me the other day, it's always about money. Stay away from the money, and the Houston and Miami crowd will probably stay away from you.'

'Maybe.'

'But any way you cut it, it's *adiós*, Tony.'

'My ranch is outside a little village called Zapopan. Maybe you'll get a postcard from there.'

'No, I think your story ends here.'

He pulled the clip from the handle of his .45, slid back the receiver, removed the round from the chamber, and inserted it in the top of the clip. He tapped the clip idly against the chrome-plated finish of the pistol, then put his hand on the door handle.

'I don't guess you're big on shaking hands,' he said.

I rested my palm on the bottom of the steering wheel and looked straight ahead at the yellow road winding through the trees.

'Say good-bye to Paul for me,' I said.

I heard him get out of the truck and close the door.

'Tony?' I said.

He looked back through the window.

'If I ever hear your dealing dope again, we'll pick it up where we left off.'

'No, I don't think so, Dave. I have a feeling your cop days are about over.'

'Oh?'

He leaned down on the window jamb.

'Your heart gets in the way of your head,' he said. 'If you don't know that, the pencil pushers you work for will. They'll get rid of you, too. Maybe you won't accept any thanks from me, and maybe I won't even offer you any, but my little boy up there says thank you. You can wear that in your hat or stick it in your ear. So long, Dave.'

He walked up the pine-needle-covered slope toward the back of the camp. He took his Marine Corps utility cap from his back pocket, slapped the soot off it against his trousers, and fitted it at an angle on his head. I drove slowly down the road past the camp, the truck lurching in the flooded potholes, and saw him open the screen door and smile at someone inside.

I came out of the trees and drove through a winter-green field that was filled with snowy egrets and blue herons feeding by a grassy pond. Ahead I could see the coast, the palm fronds whipping in the wind, and the waves cresting and blowing out on Lake Borgne and the Gulf. The air was cool and flecked with sunlight and smelled like salt and distant rain. And I realized that in the west the sun had broken through the gray seal of clouds, and left a rip in the sky like a yellow and purple rose.

Epilogue

Tony was right. Minos didn't believe me, particularly after I gave him a tape recording that contained a long blank space between the fire in the airplane hangar and Jimmie Lee Boggs's watery statement about Tee Beau's innocence in the murder of Hipolyte Broussard. But I didn't care. I had grown weary of federal agents and wiseguys, narcs and stings and brain-fried lowlifes, and all the seriousness and pretense we invest in the province of moral invalids. I had decided it was time to let someone else wander about in that neon-lit moonscape, where we constantly try to define the source of our national discontent, until our unstated addictions target an antithetically mixed, quixotic figure like Tony Cardo, and lead us away from ourselves.

I don't know what happened to him. The DEA found his Lincoln, his only means of transportation, at the camp, but they matched the tire treads to fresh tire tracks at the hangar where he kept his plane. Perhaps he paid somebody to drive the Lincoln back to the camp; however, the DEA also found his plane still in the hangar. One of Minos's fellow workers, one who was enraged at the fact that the additional fifty thousand dollars given me in the sting had been burned up in the hangar fire, theorized that Tony had had someone else fly a plane into the airstrip and pick him up, Paul, and Jess Ornella. But federal agents in Guadalajara who visited Tony's ranch outside Zapopan reported that Tony had not been seen in the area for almost a year. The next time I saw Minos in Lafayette, to plan a fishing trip, I mentioned Tony's name. He yawned, picked up a file folder off his desk, and showed me a photo of a man whose facial features looked back at me with the dirty luminescence and dark clarity characteristic of booking-room photography.

'You know this guy?' he said.

'No.'

'He lives in Metairie. He's a new boy on the block. We'd like very much to get him into our graybar hotel chain. He—'

But now it was I whose eyes began to glaze, and who tried not to yawn at the sound of the rain on the oak trees outside the window.

Two months later I received a creased and dog-eared envelope post-marked in Lake Charles. Inside it was a color photograph of Paul smiling in a fighting chair on the stern of a sport fishing boat. Squatted down next to the chair, with a four-foot tarpon held in both arms, the enormous hook still protruding from its dead mouth, was Jess Ornella, his jailhouse tattoos as blue against his tan as the sea behind him. With his back turned to the camera was a shirtless man in a huge Mexican sombrero who was baiting a mullet on a feathered spoon. His curly hair was cut short and glistened with sweat above his tiny ears. In the background was a biscuit-colored beach with a few hot-looking, wilted palm trees on it and a desiccated wooden dock, strung with drying butterfly nets, that extended out into the surf.

Someone had written in ballpoint on the back of the photograph:

You said around New Iberia you have to knock the bass back into the water with a tennis racket. That's pretty good. But you ought to try this place. The reefs are so crowded with kingfish there's not room for them all. Just yesterday I saw a couple of them walking down the highway carrying their own canteens. We're living on warm breezes and bananas fried in coconut oil. I'm clean and free, Dave. The tiger went away. Maybe you ought to get yourself a Roman collar, or at least by now I hope you've lost the badge and your dipshit colleagues. Face it, you dug being in the life. Even Jess thought you were one of us. That'd worry me.

Stay solid,
Pancho Gonzales

Tee Beau Latiolais was given a new trial, but before trial date Gros Mama Goula cut a subpoena server's face with a razor and fled New Iberia and the zydeco bar and hot-pillow joint she had operated for thirty years, and the prosecutor's office dropped the murder charge against Tee Beau. But some black people out in the parish said Gros Mama had the powers of a *loup-garou*, and had changed herself into ball lightning. They said when the fog was white among the cypress trunks, people would see a tangle of pink light roll across the lily pads and dead water and explode against the levee. The grass on the bank would be scorched black, and snakes would writhe on the baked dirt.

But Tee Beau was not one to stay locked in a bunch of mojo fear, or even worry any longer about the months of sexual humiliation and shame that Hipolyte Broussard had inflicted on him. He and Dorothea were married, and today she works as a waitress in a seafood restaurant out on the St Martinville road. Tee Beau owns his own taxicab. On Sundays he drives Tante Lemon and Dorothea to church in it, and for some reason they look like triplets inside, all three of their heads barely above the bottom level of the windows. Sometimes they make a special trip past my house and leave me a fat jar of cracklins, what we call *graton*, made with ground-up Tabasco peppers, and the first bite is such a shock to my mouth that sweat runs out of my hair. But every time Tante Lemon gives me another quart, she pats my hand confidently and says, 'You eat that, you, and I gonna give you mo'. Just like your daddy give me fish when I didn't have no food, me, I be comin' out and give you mo'.'

Saint Augustine once said we should never use the truth to injure. So the edge of my coulee is lined with spaded-in holes that contain dozens of mason jars which one day an archaeologist will probably dig up and identify as artifacts used by an ancient cult in a corn-god burial.

This started out as a story about my own fear, or rather about a time in my life when, because of an injury, I was not sure who I was, when I had to wait each night for a protean figure of my own creation to define me as something weak and loathsome and undeserving of breath. Instead, it became a story of others, people I discovered to be far more brave in their way than I am. And I suppose that what I have learned is a lesson that the years, or self-concern, had begun to hide from me, namely, that the bravest and most loyal and loving people in the world seldom have heroic physical characteristics or the auras of saints. In fact, their faces are like those of people whom you might randomly pull out of a supermarket line, their physical makeup so nondescript and unremarkable that it's hard to remember what they looked like ten minutes after they walk out of a room.

Kim Dollinger is the manager of Clete's Club on Decatur now, and Clete has a private investigator's license and an office two blocks from the First District headquarters. He's made enough money running down bail jumpers to pay off all his debts to Tony's old shylocks. He still tries to fight his weight problem by clanking iron up and down in the back of his office and jogging through Louis Armstrong Park in his Budweiser shorts and LSU football jersey, which the black kids from the Iberville welfare project treat like the appearance of a dancing hippo in the middle of their day. People in the Quarter say he and Kim have become an item, but probably not as Clete had expected. When we go out for dinner together she mashes out his cigarettes in the ashtray, cancels his drink order from the bar, and orders low-cholesterol food from the menu for him. But he doesn't complain, and his eyes are gentle when he looks at her.

Bootsie cut her losses and sold out her vending machine business to one of her former in-laws, and that December she and I were married in St Peter's Church in New Iberia. We took Alafair with us to Key West, where the water is warm year-round, and the late-afternoon sun boils into the Gulf like a molten red planet. At night light-fish swim among the coral like electrified wisps of green smoke. In screened-in restaurants by the water's edge we ate big dinners of oysters on the half shell, fried shrimp, and conch fritters, and we trolled for bonefish in the flats and dove Seven-Mile Reef south of the island. At fifty feet the water was as clear and green as Jell-O, shimmering with sunlight, the sand as white as ground diamond, and I watched Bootsie swim deep into the canyons of fire coral, indifferent to the spiked nests of sea urchins and the dark, triangular shapes of stingrays. Her tanned body would be beset with bluefish; then she would kick her flippers, clouding the water below her with sand, and dispel them like a sudden shuddering of thin metal blades.

Minos persuaded the DEA to replace the boat I lost south of Cocodrie, and he said that actually the DEA was happy with the work that I had done for them, because Tony was gone and the man who had moved in on his action, one of the Houston crowd, had evidently been having an affair with Tony's wife. They spent a lot of their time quarreling, even throwing drinks at one another on one occasion, in public places.

But my financial debts are paid off, and I've given up law enforcement, at least for the time being. Bootsie and I run our boat-rental and bait business on the bayou. We barbecue chickens and links of sausage for midday fishermen, and we seine for shrimp out on the long green roll of the Gulf. It's still winter, but we treat winter in South Louisiana as a transitory accident. Even when the skies are black with ducks, the oak and cypress limbs along the bayou teeming with robins, the eye focuses on the tightly wrapped pink buds inside the dark green leaves of the camellia bush, the azaleas and the flaming hibiscus that have bloomed right through the season. South Louisiana is a party, and I've grown old enough to put away vain and foolish concerns about mortality, and to stop imposing the false features of calendars and clocks upon my life, or, for that matter, upon eternity.

Sometimes in the evening, when I'm closing up the bait shop and my shoulder twinges from picking up crates of Jax and Pearl beer, when the wind lifts the moss on the dead cypress in the marsh and blows red embers from a burnt cane field into the darkening sky, I think of juju magic and *gris-gris* charms, I think of Tony and Paul, Kim and Clete, Dorothea, Tee Beau, and Tante Lemon, even ole Jess Ornella, and I have to pause, almost fearfully, at the beating of my heart. Then I see Bootsie and Alafair walk down from the lighted gallery to get me for supper, hand in hand through the pecan trees, and I turn keys in locks and Bootsie and I go back up the path, with Alafair swinging from our arms, our mismatched shadows fused into a single playful shape under the rising moon.

A Stained White Radiance

I would like to thank the following people for all the support and help they have given me over the years: Fran Majors of Wichita, Kansas, who typed and copyedited my manuscripts and was always my loyal friend; Patricia Mulcahy, my editor, who put her career on the line for me more than once; Dick and Patricia Karlan, my film agents whose commitment and faithful advocacy I will never be able to repay; and finally my literary agent, Philip G. Spitzer, one of the most honorable and fine men I've ever known, the only agent in New York who would keep my novel *The Lost Get-Back Boogie* under submission for nine years, making the rounds of almost one hundred publishers, until it found a home.

For Farrel and Patty Lemoine
and my old twelve-string partner, Murphy Dowouis

1

I had known the Sonnier family all my life. I had attended the Catholic elementary school in New Iberia with three of them, had served with one of them in Vietnam, and for a short time had dated Drew, the youngest child, before I went away to the war. But, as I learned with Drew, the Sonniers belonged to that group of people whom you like from afar, not because of what they are themselves, but because of what they represent – failure in the way that they're put together, a collapse of some genetic or familial element that should be the glue of humanity.

The background of the Sonnier children was one that you instinctively knew you didn't want to know more about, in the same way that you don't want to hear the story of a desperate and driven soul in an after-hours bar. As a police officer it has been my experience that pedophiles are able to operate and stay functional over long periods of time and victimize scores, even hundreds, of children, because no one wants to believe his or her own intuitions about the symptoms in the perpetrator. We are repelled and sickened by the images that our own minds suggest, and we hope against hope that the problem is in reality simply one of misperception.

Systematic physical cruelty toward children belongs in the same shoe-box. Nobody wants to deal with it. I cannot remember one occasion, in my entire life, when I saw one adult interfere in a public place with the mistreatment of a child at the hands of another adult. Prosecutors often wince when they have to take a child abuser to trial, because usually the only witnesses they can use are children who are terrified at the prospect of testifying against their parents. And ironically a successful prosecution means that the victim will become a legal orphan, to be raised by foster parents or in a state institution that is little more than a warehouse for human beings.

As a child I saw the cigarette burns on the arms and legs of the Sonnier children. They were scabbed over and looked like coiled, gray worms. I came to believe that the Sonniers grew up in a furnace rather than a home.

It was a lovely spring day when the dispatcher at the Iberia Parish sheriff's office, where I worked as a plainclothes detective, called me at home and said that somebody had fired a gun through Weldon Sonnier's dining-room window and I could save time by going there directly rather than reporting to the office first.

I was at my breakfast table, and through the open window I could smell the damp, fecund odor of the hydrangeas in my flower bed and last night's rainwater dripping out of the pecan and oak trees in the yard. It was truly a fine morning, the early sunlight as soft as smoke in the tree limbs.

'Are you there, Dave?' the dispatcher said.

'Ask the sheriff to send someone else on this one,' I said.

'You don't like Weldon?'

'I like Weldon. I just don't like some of the things that probably go on in Weldon's head.'

'Okay, I'll tell the old man.'

'Never mind,' I said. 'I'll head out there in about fifteen minutes. Give me the rest of it.'

'That's all we got. His wife called it in. He didn't. Does that sound like Weldon?' He laughed.

People said Weldon had spent over two hundred thousand dollars restoring his antebellum home out in the parish on Bayou Teche. It was built of weathered white-painted brick, with a wide columned porch, a second-floor verandah that wrapped all the way around the house, ventilated green window shutters, twin brick chimneys at each extreme of the house, and scrolled ironwork that had been taken from historical buildings in the New Orleans French Quarter. The long driveway that led from the road to the house was covered with a canopy of moss-hung live oaks, but Weldon Sonnier was not one to waste land space for the baroque and ornamental. All the property in front of the house, even the area down by the bayou where the slave quarters had once stood, had been leased to tenants who planted sugarcane on it.

It had always struck me as ironic that Weldon would pay out so much of his oil money in order to live in an antebellum home, whereas in fact he had grown up in an Acadian farmhouse that was over one hundred and fifty years old, a beautiful piece of hand-hewn, notched, and pegged cypress architecture that members of the New Iberia historical pre-servation society openly wept over when Weldon hired a group of half-drunk black men out of a ramshackle, back-road nightclub, gave them crowbars and axes, and calmly smoked a cigar and sipped from a glass of Cold Duck on top of a fence rail while they ripped the old Sonnier house into a pile of boards he later sold for two hundred dollars to a cabinet-maker.

When I drove my pickup truck down the driveway and parked under a spreading oak by the front porch, two uniformed deputies were waiting for me in their car, their front doors open to let in the breeze that blew across the shaded lawn. The driver, an ex-Houston cop named Garrett, a barrel of a man with a thick blond mustache and a face the color of a fresh sunburn, nipped his cigarette into the rose bed and stood up to meet me. He wore pilot's sunglasses, and a green dragon was tattooed around his right forearm. He was still new, and I didn't know him well, but I'd heard that he had resigned from the Houston force after he had been suspended during an Internal Affairs investigation.

'What do you have?' I said.

'Not much,' he said. 'Mr Sonnier says it was probably an accident. Some kids hunting rabbits or something.'

'What does Mrs Sonnier say?'

'She's eating tranquilizers in the breakfast room.'

'What does she *say?*'

'Nothing, detective.'

'Call me Dave. You think it was just some kids?'

'Take a look at the size of the hole in the dining room wall and tell me.'

Then I saw him bite the corner of his lip at the abruptness in his tone. I started toward the front door.

'Dave, wait a minute,' he said, took off his glasses, and pinched the bridge of his nose. 'While you were on vacation, the woman called us twice and reported a prowler. We came out and didn't find anything, so I marked it off. I thought maybe her terminals were a little fried.'

'They are. She's a pill addict.'

'She said she saw a guy with a scarred face looking through her window. She said it looked like red putty or something. The ground was wet, though, and I didn't see any footprints. But maybe she did see something. I probably should have checked it out a little better.'

'Don't worry about it. I'll take it from here. Why don't you guys head up to the café for coffee?'

'She's the sister of that Nazi or Klan politician in New Orleans, isn't she?'

'You got it. Weldon knows how to pick 'em.' Then I couldn't resist. 'You know who Weldon's brother is, don't you?'

'No.'

'Lyle Sonnier.'

'That TV preacher in Baton Rouge? No kidding? I bet that guy could steal the stink off of shit and not get the smell on his hands.'

'Welcome to south Louisiana, podna.'

Weldon shook hands when he answered the door. His hand was big, square, callused along the heel and the index finger. Even when he grinned, Weldon's face was bold, the eyes like buckshot, the jaw rectangular and hard. His brown-gray crewcut was shaved close to the scalp above his large ears, and he always seemed to be biting softly on his molars, flexing the lumps of cartilage behind his jawline. He wore his house slippers, a pair of faded beltless Levi's, and a paint-stained T-shirt that molded his powerful biceps and flat stomach. He hadn't shaved and he had a cup of coffee in his hand. He was polite to me – Weldon was always polite – but he kept looking at his watch.

'I can't tell you anything else, Dave,' he said, as we stood in the doorway of his dining room. 'I was standing there in front of the glass doors, looking out at the sunrise over the bayou, and *pop*, it came right through the glass and hit the wall over yonder.' He grinned.

'It must have scared you,' I said.

'Sure did.'

'Yeah, you look all shaken up, Weldon. Why did your wife call us instead of you?'

'She worries a lot.'

'You don't?'

'Look, Dave, I saw two black kids earlier. They chased a rabbit out of the canebrake, then I saw them shooting at some mockingbirds up in a tree on the bayou. I think they live in one of those old nigger shacks down the road. Why don't you go talk to them?'

He looked at the time on the mahogany grandfather clock at the far end of the dining room, then adjusted the hands on his wristwatch.

'The black kids didn't have a shotgun, did they?' I asked.

'No, I don't think so.'

'Did they have a .22?'

'I don't know, Dave.'

'But that's what they'd probably have if they were shooting rabbits or mockingbirds, wouldn't they? At least if they didn't have a shotgun.'

'Maybe.'

I looked at the hole in the pane of glass toward the top of the French door. I pulled my fountain pen, one almost as thick as my little finger, from my pocket and inserted the end in the hole. Then I crossed the dining room and did the same thing with the hole in the wall. There was a stud behind the wall, and the fountain pen went into the hole three inches before it tapped anything solid.

'Do you believe a .22 round did this?' I asked.

'Maybe it ricocheted and toppled,' he answered.

I walked back to the French doors, opened them on to the flagstone patio, and gazed down the sloping blue-green lawn to the bayou. Among the cypresses and oaks on the bank were a dock and a weathered boat shed. Between the mudbank and the lawn was a low red-brick wall that Weldon had constructed to keep his land from eroding into the Teche.

'I think what you're doing is dumb, Weldon,' I said, still looking at the brick wall and the trees on the bank silhouetted against the glaze of sunlight on the bayou's brown surface.

'Excuse me?' he said.

'Who has reason to hurt you?'

'Not a soul.' He smiled. 'At least not to my knowledge.'

'I don't want to be personal, but your brother-in-law is Bobby Earl.'

'Yes?'

'He's quite a guy. A CBS newsman called him "the Robert Redford of racism."'

'Yeah, Bobby liked that one.'

'I heard you pulled Bobby across a table in Copeland's by his necktie and sawed it off with a steak knife.'

'Actually, it was Mason's over on Magazine.'

'Oh, I see. How did he like being humiliated in a restaurant full of people?'

'He took it all right. Bobby's not a bad guy. You just have to define the situation for him once in a while.'

'How about some of his followers – Klansmen, American Nazis, members of the Aryan Nation? You think they're all-right guys, too?'

'I don't take Bobby seriously.'

'A lot of people do.'

'That's their problem. Bobby has about six inches of dong and two of brain. If the press left him alone, he'd be selling debit insurance.'

'I've heard another story about you, Weldon, maybe a more serious one.'

'Dave, I don't want to offend you. I'm sorry you had to come out here, I'm sorry my wife is wired all the time and sees rubber faces leering in the window. I appreciate the job you have to do, but I don't know who put a hole in my glass. That's the truth, and I have to go to work.'

'I've heard you're broke.'

'What else is new? That's the independent oil business. It's either dusters or gushers.'

'Do you owe somebody money?'

I saw the cartilage work behind his jaws.

'I'm getting a little on edge here, Dave.'

'Yeah?'

'That's right.'

'I'm sorry about that.'

'I drilled my first well with spit and junkyard scrap. I didn't get a goddamn bit of help from anybody, either. No loans, no credit, just me, four nigras, an alcoholic driller from Texas, and a lot of ass-busting work.' He pointed his finger at me. 'I've kept it together for twenty years, too, podna. I don't go begging money from anybody, and I'll tell you something else, too. Somebody leans on me, somebody fires a rifle into my house, I square it personally.'

'I hope you don't. I'd hate to see you in trouble, Weldon. I'd like to talk with your wife now, please.'

He put a cigarette in his mouth, lit it, and dropped the heavy metal lighter indifferently on the gleaming wood surface of his dining-room table.

'Yeah, sure,' he said. 'Just take it a little bit easy. She's having a reaction to her medication or something. It affects her blood pressure.'

His wife was a pale, small-boned, ash-blonde woman, whose milk-white skin was lined with blue veins. She wore a pink silk house robe, and she had brushed her hair back over her neck and had put on fresh makeup. She should have been pretty, but she always had a startled look in her blue eyes, as though she heard invisible doors slamming around her. The breakfast room was domed and glassed-in, filled with sunlight and hanging fern and philodendron plants, and the view of the bayou, the oaks and the bamboo, the trellises erupting with purple wisteria, was a magnificent one. But her face seemed to register none of it. Her eyes were unnaturally wide, the pupils shrunken to small black dots, her skin so tight that you thought perhaps someone was twisting the back of her hair in a knot. I wondered what it must have been like to grow up in the same home that had produced a man like Bobby Earl.

She had been christened Bama. Her accent was soft, pleasant to listen to, more Mississippi than Louisiana, but in it you heard a tremolo, as though a nerve ending were pulled loose and fluttering inside her.

She said she had been in bed when she heard the shot and the glass break. But she hadn't seen anything.

'What about this prowler you reported, Mrs Sonnier? Do you have any idea who he might have been?' I smiled at her.

'Of course not.'

'You never saw him before?'

'No. He was horrible.'

I saw Weldon raise his eyes toward the ceiling, then turn away and look out at the bayou.

'How do you mean?' I asked.

'He must have been in a fire,' she said. 'His ears were little stubs. His face was like red rubber, like a big red inner tube patch.'

Weldon turned back toward me.

'You've got all that on file down at your office, haven't you, Dave?' he said. 'There's not any point in covering the same old territory, is there?'

'Maybe not, Weldon,' I said, closed my small notebook, and replaced it in my pocket. 'Mrs Sonnier, here's one of my cards. Give me a call if you remember anything else or if I can be of any other help to you.'

Weldon rubbed one hand on the back of the other and tried to hold the frown out of his face.

'I'll take a walk down to the back of your property, if you don't mind,' I said.

'Help yourself,' he said.

The Saint Augustine grass was wet with the morning dew and thick as a sponge as I walked between the oaks down to the bayou. In a sunny patch of ground next to an old gray roofless barn, one that still had an ancient tin Hadacol sign nailed to a wall, was a garden planted with strawberries and watermelons. I walked along beside the brick retaining wall, scanning the mudflat that sloped down to the bayou's edge. It was crisscrossed with the tracks of neutrias and raccoons and the delicate impressions of egrets and herons; then, not far from the cypress planks that led to Weldon's dock and boathouse, I saw a clutter of footprints at the base of the brick wall.

I propped my palms on the cool bricks and studied the bank. One set of footprints led from the cypress planks to the wall, then back again, but somebody with a larger shoe size had stepped on top of the original tracks. There was also a smear of mud on top of the brick wall, and on the grass, right by my foot, was a Lucky Strike cigarette butt. I took a plastic Ziploc bag from my pocket and gingerly scooped the cigarette butt inside it.

I was about to turn back toward the house when the breeze blew the oak limbs overhead, and the pattern of sunlight and shade shifted on the ground like the squares in a net, and I saw a brassy glint in a curl of mud. I stepped over the wall, and with the tip of my pen lifted a spent .308 hull out of the mud and dropped it in the plastic bag with the cigarette butt.

I walked through the sideyard, back out to the front drive and my pickup truck. Weldon was waiting for me. I held the plastic bag up briefly for him to look at.

'Here's the size round your rabbit hunter was using,' I said. 'He'd ejected it, too, Weldon. Unless he had a semiautomatic rifle, he was probably going to take a second shot at you.'

'Look, from here on out, how about talking to me and leaving Bama out of it? She's not up to it.'

I took a breath and looked away through the oak trees at the sunlight on the blacktop road.

'I think your wife has a serious problem. Maybe it's time to address it,' I said.

I could see the heat in his neck. He cleared his throat.

'Maybe you're going a little beyond the limits of your job, too,' he said.

'Maybe. But she's a nice lady, and I think she needs help.'

He chewed on his lower lip, put his hands on his hips, looked down at his foot, and stirred a pattern in the pea gravel, like a third-base coach considering his next play.

'There are a bunch of twelve-step groups in New Iberia and St Martinville. They're good people,' I said.

He nodded without looking up.

'Let me ask you something else,' I said. 'You flew an observation plane off a carrier in Vietnam, didn't you? You must have been pretty good.'

'Give me a chimpanzee, three bananas, and thirty minutes of his attention, and I'll give you a pilot.'

'I also heard you flew for Air America.'

'So?'

'Not everybody has that kind of material in his dossier. You're not still involved in some CIA bullshit, are you?'

He tapped his jaw with his finger like a drum.

'CIA . . . yeah, that's Catholic, Irish, and alcoholic, right? No, I'm a coonass, my religion is shaky, and I've never hit the juice. I don't guess I fit the category, Dave.'

'I see. If you get tired of it, call me at the office or at home.'

'Tired of what?'

'Jerking yourself around, being clever with people who're trying to help you. I'll see you around, Weldon.'

I left him standing in his driveway, a faint grin on his mouth, a piece of cartilage as thick as a biscuit in his jaw, his big, square hands open and loose at his sides.

Back at the office I asked the dispatcher where Garrett, the new man, was.

'He went to pick up a prisoner in St Martinville. You want me to call him?' he said.

'Ask him to drop by my office when he has a chance. It's nothing urgent.' I kept my face empty of meaning. 'Tell me, what kind of beef did he have with Internal Affairs in Houston?'

'Actually it was his partner who had the beef. Maybe you read about it. The partner left Garrett in the car and marched a Mexican kid under the bridge on Buffalo Bayou and played Russian roulette with him. Except he miscalculated where the round was in the cylinder and blew the kid's brains all over a concrete piling. Garrett got pissed off because he was under investigation, cussed out a captain, and quit the department. It's too bad, because they cleared him later. So I guess he's starting all over. Did something happen out there at the Sonniers'?'

'No, I just wanted to compare notes with him.'

'Say, you have an interesting phone message in your box.'

I raised my eyebrows and waited.

'Lyle Sonnier,' he said, and grinned broadly.

On my way back to my office cubicle I took the small pile of morning letters, memos, and messages from my mailbox, sat down at my desk, and began turning over each item in the stack one at a time on the desk blotter. I couldn't say exactly why I didn't want to deal with Lyle. Maybe it was a little bit of guilt, a little intellectual dishonesty. Earlier that morning I had been willing to be humorous with Garrett about Lyle, but

I knew in reality that there was nothing funny about him. If you flipped through the late-night cable channels on TV and saw him in his metallic-gray silk suit and gold necktie, his wavy hair conked in the shape of a cake, his voice ranting and his arms flailing in the air before an enrapt audience of blacks and blue-collar whites, you might dismiss him as another religious huckster or fundamentalist fanatic whom the rural South produces with unerring predictability generation after generation.

Except I remembered Lyle when he was an eighteen-year-old tunnel rat in my platoon who would crawl naked to the waist down a hole with a flashlight in one hand, a .45 automatic in the other, and a rope tied around his ankle as his lifeline. I also remembered the day he squeezed into an opening that was so narrow his pants were almost scraped off his buttocks; then, as the rope uncoiled and disappeared into the hillside with him, we heard a *whoomph* under the ground, and a red cloud of cordite-laced dust erupted from the hole. When we pulled him back out by his ankle, his arms were still extended straight out in front of him, his hair and face webbed with blood, and two fingers of his right hand were gone as though they had been lopped off with a barber's razor.

People in New Iberia who knew Lyle usually spoke of him as a flimflam man who preyed on the fear and stupidity of his followers, or they thought of him as an entertaining borderline psychotic who had probably cooked his head with drugs. I didn't know what the truth was about Lyle, but I always suspected that in that one-hundredth of a second between the time he snapped the tripwire with his outstretched flashlight or army .45 and the instant when the inside of his head roared with white light and sound and the skin of his face felt like it was painted with burning tallow, he thought he saw a third eye into all the baseless fears, the vortex of mysteries, the mockery that all his preparation for this moment had become.

I looked at his Baton Rouge phone number on the piece of message paper, then turned the piece of paper over in my fingers. No, Lyle Sonnier wasn't a joke, I thought. I picked up my telephone and started to dial the number, then realized that Garrett, the ex-Houston cop, who was standing in the entrance to my cubicle, his eyes slightly askance when I glanced up at him.

'Oh, hi, thanks for dropping by,' I said.

'Sure. What's up?'

'Not much.' I tapped my fingers idly on the desk blotter, then opened and closed my drawer. 'Say, do you have a smoke?'

'Sure,' he said, and took his package out of his shirt pocket. He shook one loose and offered it to me.

'Lucky Strikes are too strong for me,' I said. 'Thanks, anyway. How about taking a walk with me?'

'Uh, I'm not quite following this. What are we doing, Dave?'

'Come on, I'll buy you a snowball. I just need some feedback from you.' I smiled at him.

It was bright and warm outside, and a rainbow haze drifted across the lawn from the water sprinklers. The palm trees were green and etched against the hard blue sky, and on the corner, by a huge live oak tree whose roots had cracked the curb and folded the sidewalk up in a peak, a Negro in a white coat sold snowballs out of a handcart that was topped with a beach umbrella.

I bought two spearmint snowballs, handed one to Garrett, and we sat down side by side on an iron bench in the shade. His holster and gunbelt creaked like a horse's saddle. He put on his sunglasses, looked away from me, and constantly fiddled with the corner of his mustache.

'The dispatcher was telling me about that IA beef in Houston,' I said. 'It sounds like you got a bad deal.'

'I'm not complaining. I like it over here. I like the food and the French people.'

'But maybe you took two steps back in your career,' I said.

'Like I say, I got no complaint.'

I took a bite out of my snowball and looked straight ahead.

'Let me cut straight to it, podna,' I said. 'You're a new man and you're probably a little ambitious. That's fine. But you tainted the crime scene out at the Sonniers'.'

He cleared his throat and started to speak, then said nothing.

'Right? You climbed over that brick retaining wall and looked around on the mudbank? You dropped a cigarette butt on the grass?'

'Yes, sir.'

'Did you find anything?'

'No, sir.'

'You're sure?' I looked hard at the side of his face. There was a red balloon of color in his throat.

'I'm sure.'

'All right, forget about it. There's no harm done. Next time out, though, you secure the scene and wait on the investigator.'

He nodded, looking straight ahead at some thought hidden inside his sunglasses, then said, 'Does any of this go in my jacket?'

'No, it doesn't. But that's not the point here, podna. We're clear on the real point, aren't we?'

'Yes, sir.'

'Good. I'll see you inside. I have to return a phone call.'

But actually I didn't want to talk with him anymore. I had a feeling that Deputy Garrett was not a good listener.

I called Lyle Sonnier's number in Baton Rouge and was told by a secretary that he was out of town for the day. I gave the spent .308 casing to our fingerprint man, which was by and large a waste of time, since fingerprints seldom do any good unless you have the prints of a definite suspect already on file. Then I read the brief paperwork on the prowler reports made by Bama Sonnier, but it added nothing to my knowledge of what had happened out at the Sonnier place. I wanted to write it all off and leave Weldon to his false pride and private army of demons, whatever they were, and not spend time trying to help somebody who didn't want any interference in his life. But if other people had had the same attitude toward me, I had to remind myself, I would be dead, in a mental institution, or putting together enough change and crumpled one-dollar bills in a sunrise bar to buy a double shot of Beam, with a frosted schooner of Jax on the side, in the vain hope that somehow that shuddering rush of heat and amber light through my body would finally cook into ashes every snake and centipede writhing inside me. Then I would be sure that the red sun burning above the oaks in the parking lot would be less a threat to me, that the day would not be filled with metamorphic shapes and disembodied voices that were like slivers of wood in the mind, and that ten A.M. would not come in the form of shakes so bad that I couldn't hold a glass of whiskey with both hands.

At noon I drove home for lunch. The dirt road along the bayou was lined with oak trees that had been planted by slaves, and the sun flashed through the moss-hung branches overhead like a heliograph. The hyacinths were thick and in full purple flower along the edges of the bayou, their leaves beaded with drops of water, like quicksilver, in the shade. Out in the sunlight, where the water was brown and hot-looking, dragonflies hung motionless in the air and the armored-plated backs of alligator gars turned in the current with the suppleness of snakes.

A dozen cars and pickup trucks were parked around the boat ramp, dock, and bait shop that I owned and that my wife, Bootsie, and an elderly black man named Batist operated when I wasn't there. I waved at Batist, who was serving barbecue lunches on the telephone-spool tables under the canvas awning that shaded the dock. Then I turned in to my dirt drive and parked under the pecan trees in front of the rambling cypress-and-oak house that my father had built by himself during the Depression. The yard was covered with dead leaves and moldy pecan husks, and the pecan trees grew so thick against the sky that my gallery stayed in shadow almost all day, and at night, even in the middle of summer, I only had to turn on the attic fan to make the house so cool that we had to sleep under sheets.

My adopted daughter Alafair had a three-legged pet raccoon named Tripod, and we kept him on a chain attached to a long wire that was stretched between two oaks so he could run up and down in the yard. For some reason whenever someone pulled into the drive Tripod raced back and forth on his wire, wound himself around a tree trunk, tried to clatter up the bark, and usually crashed on top of one of the rabbit hutches, almost garroting himself.

I turned off the truck engine, walked across the soft layer of leaves under my feet, picked him up in my arms, and untangled his chain. He was a beautiful coon, silver-tipped, fat and thick across the stomach and hindquarters, with a big ringed tail, a black mask, and salt-and-pepper whiskers. I opened one of the unused hutches, where I kept his bag of cornbread and dry cracklings, and filled up his food bowl, which was next to the water bowl that he used to wash everything he ate.

When I turned around, Bootsie was watching me from the gallery, smiling. She wore white shorts, wood sandals, a faded pink peasant's blouse, and a red handkerchief tied up in her honey-colored hair. In the shadow of the gallery her legs and arms seemed to glow with her tan. Her figure was still like a girl's, her back firm with muscle, her hips smooth and undulating when she walked. Sometimes when she was asleep I would put my hand against her back just to feel the tone of her muscles, the swell of her lungs against my palm, as though I wanted to assure myself that all the heat, the energy, the whirl of blood and heartbeat under her tanned skin were indeed real and ongoing and not a deception, that she would not awake in the morning stiff with pain, her connective tissue once more a feast for the disease that swam in her veins.

She leaned against the gallery post with one arm, winked at me, and said, '*Comment la vie*, good-lookin'?'

'How you doin' yourself, beautiful?' I said.

'I made *étoufée* for your lunch.'

'Wonderful.'

'Did Lyle Sonnier get hold of you at the office?'

'No. He called here?'

'Yes, he said he had something important to tell you.'

I squeezed her with one arm and kissed her neck as we went inside. Her hair was thick and brushed in swirls, tapered and stiff on her neck and lovely to touch, like the clipped mane on a pony.

'Do you know why he's calling you?' she said.

'Somebody took a shot at Weldon Sonnier this morning.'

'Weldon? Who'd do that?'

'You got me. I think Weldon knows, but he's not saying. The older Weldon gets, the more I'm convinced he has concrete in his head.'

'Has he been in trouble with some people?'

'You know Weldon. He always went right down the middle. I remember once he got caught stealing food out of the back of the poolroom in St Martinville. The bartender pulled him out of the kitchen by his ear and twisted it until he squealed in front of everybody in the room. Ten minutes later Weldon came back through the door with tears in his eyes and grabbed a handful of balls off the pool table and smashed every inch of window glass in the place.'

'That's a sad story,' she said.

'They were sad kids, weren't they?' I sat down at the table in front of my smoking bowl of crawfish *étoufée*. The roux was glazed with butter and sprinkled with chopped green onions. The white window curtains with tiny pink flowers on them rose in the breeze that blew through the oak and pecan trees in the sideyard. 'Well, let's eat and not worry about other people's problems.'

She stood close to me and stroked my hair with her fingers, then caressed my cheek and neck. I put my arm across her soft rump and pulled her against me.

'But you do worry about other people's problems, don't you?' she said.

'Under it all Weldon's a decent guy. I think it's a contract hit of some kind. I think he's going to lose, too, unless he stops acting so prideful.'

'You mean Weldon's mixed up with the mob or something?'

'After he got out of the navy I heard he flew for Air America. It was a CIA front in Vietnam. I think that stuff involves a lifetime membership.' I clicked my spoon on the side of the *étoufée* bowl. 'Or maybe Bobby Earl has something to do with it. A guy like that doesn't forget somebody dragging him through the tossed salad by his necktie.'

'Ah, a big smile on our detective's face.'

'It would have made wonderful footage on the evening news.'

She leaned over me, pressed my head against her breasts, and kissed my hair. Then she sat across from me and started peeling a crawfish.

'Are you busy after lunch?' she asked.

'What'd you have in mind?'

'You can't ever tell.' She looked up and smiled at me with her eyes.

I am one of the few people I have ever known who has been given two second chances in his life. After investing years in being a drunk and sawing myself apart in pieces, I was given back my sobriety and eventually my self-respect by what people in Alcoholics Anonymous call a Higher Power; then after the murder of my wife Annie, Bootsie Mouton came back into my life unexpectedly, as though all the years had not passed and suddenly it was once again the summer of 1957 when we first met at a dance out on Spanish Lake.

I'll never forget the first time I kissed her. It was at twilight under the Evangeline Oaks on Bayou Teche in St Martinville, and the sky was lavender and pink and streaked with fire along the horizon, and she looked up into my face like an opening flower, and when my lips touched hers she came against me and I felt the heat in her suntanned body and suddenly realized that I'd never had any idea of what a kiss could be. She opened and closed her mouth, slowly at first, then wider, changing the angle, her chin lifting, her lips dry and smooth, her face confident and serene and loving. When she let her hands slide down on my chest and rested her head against mine, I could hardly swallow, and the fireflies spun webs of red light in the black-green tangle of oak limbs overhead and the sky from horizon to horizon was filled with the roar of cicadas.

I stopped eating and walked around behind her chair, leaned down and kissed her on the mouth.

'My, what kind of thoughts have you been having this morning?' she said.

'You're the best, Boots,' I said.

She looked up at me, and her eyes were kind and soft, and I touched her hair and cheek with my fingers.

Then she looked out the window toward the front road.

'Who's that?' she said.

A silver Cadillac with television and CB antennas and windows that were tinted almost black turned off the dirt road by the bayou and parked next to my pickup truck under the pecan trees. The driver cut the engine and stepped out into the yard, dressed in a suit that was silver-charcoal, a blue shirt with French cuffs, a striped red-and-blue necktie, and wraparound black sunglasses. He pulled off his sunglasses gingerly with his right hand, which had only a carved, half-moon area where the two bottom fingers should have been, widened his eyes to let them adjust to the light, and walked over the layer of leaves and pecan husks toward the gallery. His black shoes were shined so brightly they could have been patent leather.

'Is that—' Bootsie began.

'Yeah, it's Lyle Sonnier. He shouldn't have come out here.'

'Maybe he tried at the office and they told him you were home.'

'It doesn't matter. He should have arranged to meet me at the office.'

'I didn't know you felt that way about him.'

'He takes advantage of poor and uneducated people, Boots. He used the Ethiopian famine to raise money for that television sideshow of his. Look at the car he drives.'

'Shhhh, he's on the gallery,' she whispered.

'I'll talk to him outside. There's no need to invite him in. Okay, Boots?'

She shrugged and said, 'Whatever you say. I think you're being a little too hard.'

Lyle grinned through the screen when he saw me walking toward the door. He had the same dark Cajun complexion as the other Sonniers, but Lyle had always been the thin one, narrow at the shoulders and hips, a born track runner or poolroom lizard and ultimately one of the most fearless grunts I knew in Vietnam. Except Vietnam and pajama-clad little men who hid in tunnels and spider holes were twenty-five years back down the road.

'What's happenin', Loot?' he said.

'How are you, Lyle?' I said, and shook hands with him out on the gallery. His mutilated hand felt light and thin and unnatural in mine. 'I have to feed the rabbits and my daughter's horse before I go back to work. Do you mind walking with me while we talk?'

'Sure. Bootsie isn't home?' He looked toward the screen. On the right side of his face was a shower of shrapnel scars like a chain of flesh-toned plastic teardrops.

'She'll be out directly. What's up, Lyle?' I walked toward the rabbit hutches under the trees so he would have to follow me.

He didn't speak for a while. Instead he combed his waxed brown conked hair in the shade and looked out toward my dock and the cypress swamp on the far side of the bayou. Then he put his comb in his shirt pocket.

'You don't approve of me, do you?' he said.

I opened the chicken-wire door to one of the hutches and began filling the rabbits' bowl with alfalfa pellets.

'Maybe I don't approve of what you do, Lyle,' I said.

'I don't apologize for it.'

'I didn't ask you to.'

'I can heal, son.'

I looked at my watch, opened up the next hutch, and didn't answer him.

'I don't brag on it,' he said. 'It's a gift. I didn't earn it. But the power comes through my shoulder, through my arm, right through this deformity of a hand, right into their bodies. I can feel the power swell up in my arm just like I was holding a bucket of water by the bail, then it's gone, from me into them, and my arm's so light it's like my sleeve is empty. You can believe it or not, son. But it's God's truth. I tell you another thing. You got a sick woman up in that house.'

I set down the alfalfa bag, latched the hutch door, and turned to look directly into his face.

'I'm going to ask two things of you, Lyle. Don't call me "son" again, and don't pretend you know anything about my family's problems.'

He scratched the back of his deformed hand and looked up toward the house. Then he sucked quietly on the back of his teeth and said, 'It wasn't meant as an offense. That's not my purpose. No, sir.'

'What can I help you with today?'

'You've got it turned around. You went out to Weldon's, but he wouldn't tell you diddly-squat, would he?'

'What about Weldon's?'

'Somebody shot at him. Bama called me right after she called y'all. Look, Dave, Weldon's not going to cooperate with you. He can't. He's afraid.'

'Of what?'

'The same thing most people are afraid of when they're afraid – facing up to the truth about something.'

'Weldon doesn't impress me as a fearful man.'

'You didn't know our old man.'

'What are you talking about, Lyle?'

'The man with the burned-off face that Bama saw through her window. I've seen him, too. He was sitting in the third row at last Sunday's telecast. I almost pulled the mike out of the jack when my eyes got focused on him and I saw the face behind all that scar tissue. It was like holding up a photographic negative to a light until you see the image inside the shadows, you know what I mean? By the end of the sermon sweat was sliding off my face as big as marbles. It was like that old son of a buck reached up with a hot finger and poked it right through my belly button.'

He tried to grin, but it wasn't convincing.

'You're not making any sense, partner,' I said.

'I'm talking about my old man, Verise Sonnier. He was gone when I went down into the audience, but it was him. God didn't make two of his kind.'

'Your father was killed in Port Arthur when you were a kid.'

'That's what they said. That's what we hoped.' He grinned again, then shook the humor out of his face. 'Buried alive under a pile of white-hot boiler-plates when that chemical factory blew. Somebody shoveled up a pillow sack full of ashes and bone chips and said that was him. But my sister Drew got a letter from a man in the San Antonio city jail who said he was our old man and he wanted a hundred dollars to go to Mexico.' He paused and stared at me a moment to emphasize his point, as though he were looking into a television camera. 'She sent it to him.'

'I'm afraid this has the ring of theater to it, Lyle.'

'Yeah?'

'Why would your father want to hurt Weldon?'

He looked away into the trees, his face shadowed, and brushed idly at the chain of scar tissue that seemed to flow out of the corner of his eye.

'He has reason to want to hurt all of us. After we thought he was dead, we did something to somebody who was close to him.' He looked back into my face. 'We hurt this person bad.'

'What did you do?'

'I've made my peace on it. Somebody else will have to tell you that.'

'Then I don't know what I can do for you.'

'I can tell you what Weldon did to him. Or at least what the old man thinks Weldon did to him.' He waited, and when I didn't respond he continued. 'When we were kids the old man had this obsession. He was going to be an independent wildcatter, a kind of legend like Glenn McCarthy over in Houston. He started off as a jug hustler with an

offshore seismographic outfit, roughnecked all over Texas and Okla-
homa, then started contracting board roads in the marsh for the Texaco
Company. After a while he was actually leasing land in the Atchafalaya
basin and buying up a bunch of rusted junk to put his first rig together. A
geologist from Lafayette told him the best place to punch a hole was right
there on our farm.

'Except the old man had a problem with that. He was a *traiture*, you
know, and always claimed he could cure warts, stop bleeding in cut hogs,
blow the fire out of a burn, cause a woman to have a boy or a girl, all
that kind of "white witch" stuff. But he also told us there were Indians
buried in an old Spanish well in the middle of our sugarcane field, and if
he drilled a hole on our property their spirits would be turned loose on
us.

'He was afraid of spirits in the ground, all right, but I think of a
different kind. My uncle got drunk once and told me the old man hired
this black man for thirty cents an hour to plow his field. The black man
ran the plow across a rock and busted it, then just lay down under a tree
and took a nap. The old man found the busted plow and the mule still in
harness in the row, and he walked over to the tree and kicked this fellow
awake and started hollering at him. That black fellow made a big mistake.
He sassed my old man. The old man went into a rage, chased him across
the field, and broke open his skull with a hoe. My uncle said he buried
him somewhere around that Spanish well.'

'What does this have to do with Weldon?'

'Are you sure you're listening to me? As greedy and driven to be a
success as he was, the old man was afraid to drill on his own property.
But not Weldon, podna. That's where he built his first rig, and he cored
right down through the center of that Spanish well, I think just to make a
point. A floorman on that rig told me the drill bit brought up pieces of
bone when they first punched into the ground.'

'I'll keep all this in mind. Thanks for coming out, Lyle.'

'You don't look upon it as the big breakthrough in your case?'

'When people go about trying to kill other people with forethought
and deliberation, it's usually over money. Not always, but most times.'

'Well, a man hears when it's time for him to hear.'

'Is that right?'

'I was never a good listener. At least not till somebody up on high got
my attention. I don't fault you, Dave.'

'Do you know what passive-aggressive behavior is?'

'I never went to college, like you and Weldon. It sounds real deep.'

'It's not a profound concept. A person who has a lot of hostility learns
how to mask it in humility and sometimes even in religiosity. It's very
effective.'

'No kidding? You learn all that in college? It's too bad I missed out.' He grinned with the side of his mouth, his teeth barely showing, like a possum.

'Let me ask you something fair and square, with no bullshit, Lyle,' I said.

'Go ahead.'

'Do you hold your last day against me?'

'What do you mean?'

'In Vietnam. I sent you into that tunnel. I wish we'd blown it and passed it on by.'

'You didn't send me down there. I *liked* it down there. It was my own underground horror show. I made those zips think the scourge of God had crawled down into the bowels of the earth. It wasn't a good way to be, son.' He flinched good-naturedly and raised his hands, palms outward, in front of him. 'Sorry, it's just a manner of speaking.'

I looked at my watch.

'I guess that's my cue to go,' he said. 'Thanks for your time. Say good-bye to Bootsie for me, and don't think too unkindly of me.'

'I don't.'

'That's good.'

Without saying anything further, he turned and walked through the dead leaves toward his Cadillac. Then he stopped, rubbed the back of his neck hard, as though a mosquito had burrowed deep into his skin, then turned around and stared blankly at me, his jaw slack with a sudden and ugly knowledge.

'It's a disease that lives in the blood. It's called lupus. I'm sorry, Dave. God's truth, I am,' he said.

My mouth fell open, and I felt as though a cold wind had blown through my soul.

The next morning was Saturday, and the sun came up as pink as a rose over the willow trees and dead cypress in the marsh and the clouds of mist that rolled out of the bays. Batist and I opened up the bait shop at first light, and the air was so cool and soft, so perfect with blue shadows and the smell of night-blooming jasmine, that I forgot about Lyle's visit and his attempt to appear omniscient about my wife's illness. I had concluded that Lyle was little different from any other televangelist huckster and that somebody close to Bootsie had told him about her problem. But regardless I wasn't going to clutter my weekend with any more thoughts about the Sonnier family.

Some people were born to take a fall, I thought, and Weldon was probably one of them. I also had a feeling that Lyle was one of those theological self-creations whose own neurosis would eventually eat him like an overturned basket of hungry snakes.

After we had rented most of our boats, Batist and I seined the dead shiners out of the aluminum bait tanks, poured crushed ice over the beer and soda pop in the coolers, and started the fire in the barbecue pit I had made by splitting an oil drum with an acetylene torch, hinging it, and welding metal legs on the bottom. By eight o'clock the sun was bright and hot in the sky, burning the mist out of the cypress trees, and on the wind you could smell the faint odor of a dead animal back in the marsh.

'You got somet'ing on your mind, Dave?' Batist asked. He had a head like a cannonball; a pair of surplus navy dungarees hung on his narrow hips, and his wash-torn undershirt looked like strips of white rag on his massive coal-black chest and back.

'No, not really.'

He nodded, put a dry cigar in his mouth, and looked out the window at a tangle of dead trees and hyacinths floating past us in the bayou's current.

'It ain't bad to have somet'ing on your mind, no,' he said. 'It's bad when you don't tell nobody.'

'What do you say we season the chickens?'

'She gonna be all right. You gonna see. That's what they got all them doctors for.'

'I appreciate it, Batist.'

I saw Alafair walk down through the pecan trees from the house with Tripod on his chain. She was in third grade now, a little bit fat across the stomach, so that her old gold-and-purple LSU T-shirt, with a smiling Mike the Tiger on it, exposed her navel and the top of her elastic-waisted jeans. She had shiny black hair cut in bangs, skin that stayed tan year-round, wide-set Indian teeth, and a smile that was so broad it made her dark eyes squint almost completely shut. Nowadays, when I would pick her up, she felt heavy and compact in my arms, full of energy and play and expectation. But three years ago, when I pulled her from a crashed and submerged plane out on the salt, one piloted by a Lafayette priest who was transporting illegal refugees from El Salvador, her lungs had been filled with water, her eyes dilated with terror as we rose in a rush of bubbles toward the Gulf's surface, her little bones as thin and frail as a bird's.

Tripod thumped out on the dock, rattling his chain across the board planks behind him.

'Dave, you left the bag of rabbit food on top of the hutch. Tripod threw it all over the yard,' Alafair said. Her face was beaming.

'You think that's funny, little guy?' I said.

'Yeah,' she said, and grinned again.

'Batist says you brought Tripod down to the bait shop yesterday and he got into the hard-boiled eggs.'

Her face became vague and quizzical.

'Tripod did that?' she said.

'Do you know anyone else who would wash a hard-boiled egg in the bait tank?'

She looked across the bayou speculatively, as though the answer to a profound mystery lay among the branches of the cypress trees. Tripod zigzagged back and forth on his chain, sniffing the smell of fish in the dock.

I rubbed the top of Alafair's head. Her hair was already warm from the sunlight.

'How about a fried pie, little guy?' I said, and winked at her. 'But you and Tripod show some discretion with Batist.'

'Show what?'

'Keep that coon away from Batist.'

I brought a tray of seasoned and oiled chickens out of the shop and began laying them on the barbecue grill. The hickory wood I used for fuel had burned into hot, white coal, and the oil from the chickens dripped into the ash and steamed away in the wind. I could feel Alafair's eyes on the side of my face.

'Dave?'

'What is it, Alf?'

'Bootsie told me not to tell you something.'

'Maybe you'd better not tell me, then.' I turned my head to smile at her, but her dark eyes were veiled and troubled.

'Bootsie dropped a fork on the floor,' she said. 'When she picked it up her face got all white and she sat down real hard in a chair.'

'Was that this morning?'

'Yesterday, when I came home from school. She started to cry, then she saw me looking at her. She made me say I wouldn't tell.'

'It's not bad to tell those kinds of things, Alf.'

'Is Bootsie sick again, Dave?'

'I think maybe we need to change her medicine again. That's all.'

'That's all?'

'It's going to be all right, little guy. Let me finish up here, and we'll get Boots and go to Mulate's for crawfish.'

She nodded her head silently. I hoisted her up on my hip. Tripod ran in circles at our feet, his chain clanking on the wood.

'Hey, let's buy you some new Baby Squanto books today,' I said.

'I'm too old to read Baby Squanto.'

I pressed her against me and looked over the top of her head at the shadowed front of my house and thought I could feel my pulse beating in my throat with the urgency of a damaged watch that was about to run out of time.

I wasn't able to keep our weekend entirely free of the Sonniers after all. That afternoon, after we drove back from Mulate's in a rain shower, the phone was ringing as we ran from the truck through the pecan trees on to the gallery. I picked up the receiver in the kitchen and blotted the rainwater out of my eyes with the back of my wrist.

'I thought I'd check in with you before we left town,' the voice said.

'Weldon?'

'Yeah. Bama and I are going to visit her mother in Baton Rouge. We'll probably be gone a week or so. I thought I should tell you.'

'Why?'

'What do you mean "why"? That's what you're supposed to do when you're part of a case, aren't you? Check in with the authorities, that sort of thing?'

'You weren't cooperative yesterday, Weldon. I think you have information you're not giving me. I have my doubts about our level of sincerity here.'

'I get the feeling I shouldn't have bothered you today.'

'Your brother Lyle paid me a visit. He told me a long story about your father.'

'Lyle's a great entertainer. Did you know he had a zydeco band before he got hit with a bolt of religion?'

'He said the prowler your wife saw was your father. He said he's seen the same man in his TV audience in Baton Rouge.'

'Years ago Lyle put so many chemicals in his head it glows in the dark. He has hallucinations.'

'Was Bama hallucinating?'

'You're poking a stick in the wrong place, Dave.'

Before I spoke again I waited a moment and looked out the screen at the rain falling through the limbs of the mimosa tree in my backyard.

'So there's nothing to Lyle's story, then?' I asked.

'As a matter of fact, there is. But it's not anything you might be interested in. The truth is that Lyle takes money from a lot of pitiful nigras and po' white trash who think heat lightning is a sign out of Revelation. But after the television cameras are off and the audience goes home, my brother has problems with his conscience. Instead of dealing with it, he's developed this obsession that our old man is back from the dead and is trying to thread our souls on a fish stringer.'

'How long will you be gone?'

'A week or so.'

'Give me your mother-in-law's address and phone number.'

I wrote them down on a notepad.

'Did you make plaster casts of those footprints by the bayou?' he asked.

'We're a low-budget department, Weldon. Also, plaster casts usually tell us that the suspect wore shoes. Let me explain something to you. There's not a lot of interest down there about your shooter. Why is that? you ask. Because when the intended victim acts like Little Orphan Annie, with wide, empty eyes, it's hard to get other people to bite their nails over that person's fate. If you want to let a hired gumball cancel your ticket, maybe we figure that's your business.'

In my mind's eye I could almost see his hand squeezing on the receiver.

'What do you mean "hired gumball"?' he said.

'People around here usually kill only their friends and relatives. They usually do it in bars and bedrooms. A long-range shooter, a guy probably using a scope, a guy who got in and out without being seen, I think we're talking about a contract killer, Weldon. There was something else I didn't tell you. Our fingerprint man didn't find even a trace of a print on that shell casing. In all probability that means the shooter wiped each shell clean before he loaded the rifle. It sounds pretty professional to me.'

'You're a smart cop.'

I didn't answer and instead waited for him to speak again. But he remained silent.

'You don't want to tell me anything else?' I said.

'It's a story that involves a lot of players. You couldn't guess at it.'

'When people get into trouble, it's over money, sex, or power. Always. It's not a new script.'

'This one is. It's a real stomach churner.'

I waited again for him to continue, but he didn't.

'How about it?' I said.

'That's all I have to say, except I'm not going to do time and I'm not going to get clipped by some gumball. If that doesn't float with some-body, or if they want more information on that, they might try dialing 1–800–EAT SHIT for assistance. How's that sound?'

'Who said anything about doing time?'

'Nobody.'

'I see. Have a nice trip to Baton Rouge. Tell me, though, before you hang up, how bad did you and Lyle hurt your father's friend?'

'What? What did you say?'

'You heard me.'

'Yeah, I did. You listen to me, Dave. You stay out of my goddamn family's history. It doesn't have anything to do with this. You understand that? Are we clear on that?'

'Call back when you have something of value to tell me, Weldon,' I said, and softly replaced the receiver in the telephone cradle. I suspected that I left him with knives turning in his chest. But Weldon was one of those who became interested in the cathedral only after you barred its entrance to him.

Sunday night it rained again, and Bootsie, Alafair, and I drove to New Iberia and had dinner at Del's on East Main, then went to a movie. Later, it stopped raining, and the moon rose over the freshly plowed sugarcane fields in a sky that looked like black ink wash. I was restless and couldn't concentrate on the book I was reading or the movie that Bootsie was watching on television, and I told Bootsie that I was going back into town to drop off some overdue bills at the post office. Then I drove out to Weldon's place.

Why? I can't say, really – except that I suspected he was involved in something that went way beyond the confines of Iberia Parish. Over the years I had seen all the dark players get to southern Louisiana in one form or another: the oil and chemical companies who drained and polluted the wetlands; the developers who could turn sugarcane acreage and pecan orchards into miles of tract homes and shopping malls that had the aesthetic qualities of a sewer works; and the Mafia, who operated out of New Orleans and brought us prostitution, slot machines, control of at least two big labor unions, and finally narcotics.

They hunted on the game reserve. They came into an area where large numbers of the people were poor and illiterate, where many were unable to speak English and the politicians were traditionally inept or corrupt, and they took everything that was best from the Cajun world in which I had grown up, treated it cynically and with contempt, and left us with oil sludge in the oyster beds, Levittown, and the abiding knowledge that we had done virtually nothing to stop them.

I parked my truck on the blacktop in front of Weldon's house and looked at his flood lamps in the mist, the lighted chandelier that he had left on in the living room, the lawn that sloped away toward Bayou Teche, his boathouse, and the dark line of cypress trees along the bank. The shooter had probably come before dawn, maybe in a boat, and had crouched behind the brick retaining wall until he saw Weldon enter the dining room. So the shooter knew something about the layout of Weldon's house and property, I thought, and maybe about Weldon's habits as well; perhaps he even knew Weldon and had been in his house. If not, the person who hired the shooter was probably on familiar terms with Weldon.

It wasn't a profound theory, nor was it that helpful. I drove back home with the heat lightning flickering whitely over the southern horizon, then lay in the dark beside Bootsie and tried to fall asleep. Why did I preoccupy myself with Weldon's troubles, I asked myself? The answer was not long in coming. I rubbed my hand lightly over the curve of Bootsie's back, kissed the smooth grain of her skin, stroked the short-cropped stiff hair on her neck, and wondered in awe at how the flush of health in her complexion could be so successful a part of nature's masquerade. I had fantasies in which we changed the blood in her whole vascular system and rinsed disease out of her body; saw faith and prayer drive the red wolf from her like an exorcised incubus; or simply awoke one fine morning to discover that a new drug as miraculous as penicillin or the polio vaccine had been invented, and that all our cares and worries about Bootsie had been illusionary and ultimately forgettable.

So when you have a problem that has no solution and you can no longer drink over it, you get psychologically drunk on somebody else's woe, I thought. And maybe I even resented and envied Weldon for what I thought was the simplicity of his problem.

The moon made a square of light on Bootsie's sleeping form. Her white silk gown looked almost phosphorescent, her bare shoulders as cool and bloodless as alabaster. I put my arm across her stomach and drew her against me, hooked one leg inside hers, and buried my face in her hair, as though anger and need were enough to hold both of us aloft, safe from the dark spin and pull of the earth beneath us.

Two days later I would learn that Weldon's problems were not simple ones, either, and my involvement with the Sonnier family would become much more than a dry drunk.

2

After I got home from work the following Tuesday Batist and I closed up the bait shop early because of an electrical storm that blew up out of the south. Three hours later the rain was still pouring down, lightning bolts were popping all over the marsh, and the air was heavy with the wet, sulfurous smell of ozone. The thunder reverberated like echoing cannon across the drenched countryside, and I could barely hear the dispatcher's voice when I answered the telephone in the kitchen.

'Dave, I think I made a mistake,' he said.

'Speak louder. There's a lot of static on the line.'

'I put my foot in something. A little bit ago a black man across the bayou from Weldon Sonnier's called in and said he saw somebody behind Weldon's house with a flashlight. He said he knew Mr Weldon was out of town, so he thought he ought to call us. I was about to send LeBlanc and Thibodeaux, but Garrett was sitting by the cage and said he'd take it. I told him he wasn't on duty yet. He said he'd take it anyway, that he was helping you with the investigation about the shooting. So I let him go out there.'

'Okay . . .'

'Then the old man calls up and wants to know where Garrett is, that he wants to talk with him right now, that there's been another complaint about him. Garrett cuffed a couple of kids and put them in the tank for shooting him the finger. The kids live two houses from the sheriff. That Garrett knows how to do it, doesn't he? Anyway, he doesn't answer his radio now, and I already sent LeBlanc and Thibodeaux somewhere else. You want to help me out?'

'All right, but you shouldn't have sent him out there by himself.'

'You ever try to say "no" to that guy?'

'Send LeBlanc and Thibodeaux for backup as soon as they're loose.'

'You got it, Dave.'

I put on my raincoat and rain hat, took my army .45 automatic from the dresser drawer in the bedroom, inserted the clip loaded with hollow-points into the magazine, and dropped the automatic and a spare clip in the pocket of my coat. Bootsie was reading under a lamp in the living

257

room, and Alafair was working on a coloring book in front of the television set. The rain was loud on the gallery roof.

'I have to go out. I'll be back shortly,' I said.

'What is it?' she said, looking up, her honey-colored hair bright under the lamp.

'It's the prowler report out at Weldon's again.'

'Why do you have to go?'

'The dispatcher messed it up and sent this new fellow from Houston. Now he doesn't answer his radio, and the dispatcher doesn't have a backup.'

'Then let them mess it up on their own. You're off duty.'

'It's my investigation, Boots. I'll be back in a half hour or so. It's probably nothing.'

I saw her eyes become thoughtful.

'Dave, this doesn't sound right. What do you mean he doesn't answer his radio? Isn't he supposed to carry one of those portable radios with him?'

'Garrett's not strong on procedure. Y'all be good. I'll be right back.'

I ran through the rain and the flooded lawn, jumped in the pickup truck, and headed up the dirt road toward town. The oak limbs overhead thrashed in the wind, and a bright web of lightning lit the whole sky over the marsh. The rain on my cab was deafening, the windows swimming with water, the surface of the bayou dancing with a muddy light.

When I pulled into Weldon's drive, the night was so black and rain-whipped I could barely see his house. I hit my bright lights and drove slowly toward the house in second gear. Leaves were shredding out of the oak trees in front of the porch and cascading across the lawn, and I could hear a boat pitching and knocking loudly against its mooring inside the boathouse on the bayou. Then I saw Garrett's patrol car parked at an angle by one corner of the house. I flipped on my spotlight and played it over his car, then across the side of the house, the windows and the hedges along the walls, and finally the telephone box that was fastened into the white brick by the back entrance. There was a line of dull silver-green footprints pressed into the lawn from the patrol car to the telephone box.

Smart man, Garrett, I thought. You know a professional second-story creep always hits the phone box first. But you shouldn't have gone in by yourself.

I left my spotlight burning, took a six-battery flashlight from under the seat, pulled back the receiver on my .45, eased a round into the chamber, and stepped out into the rain.

I stooped in a crouch until I was at the back of the house and past the side windows. The wiring at the bottom of the telephone box had been sliced neatly in half. I looked over my shoulder at the blacktop road, which was empty of cars and glazed with a pool of pink light from a neon bar sign. Where in the hell were LeBlanc and Thibodeaux?

I went up the steps to the back entrance to try the door, but two panes of glass, one by the handle and one by the night chain, had been covered with pipe tape and knocked out of the molding, and the door was open. I eased it back and stepped inside. My flashlight reflected off enamel, brass, and glass surfaces and made rings of yellow-green light all over the kitchen, which was immaculately clean and squared away, but already I could see the disarray that existed deeper in the house.

'Garrett?' I said into the darkness. 'It's Dave Robicheaux.'

But there was no answer. Outside, I could hear the rain pelting the bamboo that grew along the gravel drive. I moved into the dining room, with the .45 extended in my right hand, and swung the flashlight around the room. All the drawers were pulled out of the cabinets and emptied on the floor, the paintings on the walls were knocked down or askew, and the crystalware had been raked off a shelf and ground into the rug.

The front rooms were even worse. The divans and antique upholstered chairs were slashed and gutted, a secretary bookcase overturned on its face and its back smashed in, the marble mantelpiece pried out of the wall, an enormous grandfather's clock shattered into kindling and pieces of glinting brass. A sheet of lightning trembled on the front yard, and in my mind's eye I saw myself silhouetted against the window just as I heard a foot depress a board in the hardwood floor somewhere behind or above me.

I clicked off my flashlight and went back through the dining room to the stairway. There was a closed door at the top of it, but I could see a faint glow at the bottom of the jamb. The stairs were carpeted, and I moved as quietly as I could, a step at a time, toward the door and the rim of light at the bottom, my palm sweating on the grips of the .45, my pulse racing in my neck. I turned the doorknob, pushed it lightly with my fingers, and let the door drift back on its hinges.

The hallway was strewn with sheets, mattress stuffing, clothes, and shoes that had been thrown out of the doorways to the bedrooms. The only light came from behind a partially closed door at the end of the hall. Through the opening I could see a desk, a word processor, a black leather chair whose back had been split in a large X. I moved along the wall with the .45 at an upward angle, past two demolished bedrooms, a linen closet, a darkened bathroom, an overturned dirty-clothes hamper, a dumb-waiter, until I reached the last bedroom, which was only ten feet from the lighted room that Weldon probably used as a home office. I stepped quickly inside the bedroom door and swept my .45 back and forth in the darkness. The room was still intact, except for the fact that the box springs had been shoved halfway off the frame of the canopy bed, a warning that I didn't heed.

I caught my breath, squatted down at the base of the door, wiped the sweat and rainwater out of my eyes with my knuckle, then aimed the .45 along the wall at the lighted opening of the office.

'This is Detective Dave Robicheaux of the Iberia Parish Sheriff's Department. You're under arrest. Throw your weapons out in the hall. Don't think about it. Do it.'

But there was no sound from inside.

'Right now it's breaking and entering,' I said. 'You can be smart and come out on your own. If we have to come in after you, we'll paint the walls with you. I guarantee it.'

Beyond the opening in the door I saw a shadow break across Weldon's desk. I could feel the veins tightening in my head, the sweat dripping out of my hair. It wasn't going to go down right, I thought. When they think about it, they either freeze or become cunning. And my situation was all wrong. I had been forced to take up a position on the right-hand side of the hallway, so that I had to extend my right arm at an awkward angle around the door-jamb. I was getting a charley horse in my leg and a muscle twitch in my back. Where were LeBlanc and Thibodeaux?

'Last chance, partner. We're about to shift up into the dirty boogie,' I said. But it was hard-guy flimflam. All I could do was contain whoever was in there and wait for the backup.

Then the shadow broke across the desk again, a shoe scraped against a piece of furniture, and I straightened my back, stiffened my right arm, and aimed the .45 in the middle of the door, my eyes burning with salt.

But I'd forgotten that old admonition from Vietnam: Don't let them get behind you, Robicheaux.

He came out of the bedroom closet like a spring exploding from a broken clock, a short crowbar raised above his head. His head was huge, his face full of bone, his torso knotted with muscle under his wet T-shirt. I tried to pivot, swing the .45 clear of the doorjamb and aim it at his chest, or simply stand erect and get away from the arch of the crowbar, but my knees popped and burned and seemed to have all the resilience of cobweb. The crowbar thudded into my shoulder and raked down my arm and sent the .45 bouncing across the carpet.

Then he was on me in earnest and I was rolling away from him, toward the canopy bed, my arms wrapped around my head. He hit me once in the back, a blow that felt just like a wild inside pitch that catches you flat and hard in the spine as you try to twist away from it in the batter's box, and I kicked at him with one foot, tripped backward over the box springs, and saw the bone-plated, muddy-eyed resolution in his face as he came toward me again.

'Get away, Eddy! I'm gonna blow up his shit!' a voice behind him said.

A toy of a man stood in the doorway. He looked like a racehorse jockey, except his little body had the rigid lines of a weight lifter's. In his diminutive hand was a blue revolver.

But they had intervened in each other's script and hesitated too long. I saw the .45 on the carpet, next to the hanging box springs, and I grabbed it and tumbled sideways into a half bathroom just as the toy man started firing.

I saw the sparks of gunpowder fly out in the darkness, heard two rounds *whock* into the tile wall and a third *whang* off the toilet bowl and blow the tank apart in a cascade of water and splintered ceramic; then he tried to change his angle of fire, and a fourth round ricocheted off a chrome towel rack and collapsed the shower door in a pile of frosted glass.

I was flat on the floor, in a spreading pool of water, my back and hair covered with bits of glass and tile caulking. But it had turned around on him, and he knew it, because he was already backing fast into the hallway when I raised up and started firing.

The roar of the .45 was deafening, the recoil as powerful and palm-numbing and disconnected as the kick of an air hammer; then the .45 felt suddenly weightless in my hand just before I pulled the trigger again. I fired four times at the bedroom entrance, then stood erect in a tinkle of glass at my feet, opening and closing my mouth to clear my eyes. The bedroom doorway was empty, the layered smoke motionless in the air. Out in the hall, an oil painting lay face down on the carpet, with three holes cored through the back of the canvas.

I could hear them on the stairway, but one of them obviously wanted the game to go into extra innings. He had the high-pitched, metallic voice of a midget.

'Give me your piece! I got that fuck bottled!'

'The boat's leaving, Jewel. Either haul ass or you're on your own,' another man said.

I looked around the edge of the doorjamb and let off the .45 – too quickly, high and wide, scouring a long trench in the wallpaper. But this time I saw three men – the man with the crowbar, the toy man, who wore black, silver-studded cowboy boots and had short-clipped blond hair that looked like duck down, and a third, older man in a brown windbreaker, black trousers like a priest's, black, razor-rimmed hair, and a mouth full of metal fillings that reflected the light from Weldon's office. Or at least that's how the image of the three men froze itself in my mind just before I heard a sound that I thought was the unmistakable ring of opportunity, the cylinder of a revolver being clicked open and ejected brass cartridges rattling on a wood surface.

I gripped the handle of the .45 with both hands and started to step out into the hall and begin firing, but the man in the windbreaker was a pro and had anticipated me. He had gone to one knee, three steps down from the landing, while the other two men had fled past him, and when he squeezed off his automatic I felt my raincoat leap out from my side as though a gust of air had blown through it. I spun back inside the cover of the doorway and heard him running into the darkness of the house below.

They'll drop you coming down the stairs, I thought. *Think, think.* They didn't have a car in front or out on the blacktop. There's no access road in the back. They came on the bayou. They have to go back to it on foot.

I crossed the hallway and went into a bedroom on the opposite side, one with French doors and a verandah that overlooked the driveway, the garage, and the bamboo border of Weldon's backyard. A moment later I heard them running hard on the wet gravel. They were visible for not more than two or three seconds, between the corner of the house and the back of the garage, but I aimed the .45 with both hands across the wood railing and fired until the clip was empty and the breech locked open and a solitary tongue of white smoke rose from the exposed chamber. Just before the three men crashed through the bamboo and disappeared into the rain, just as the man called Eddy was almost home free, the last round in the magazine ripped the corner off the garage and filled his face with a shower of wood splinters. He screamed, and his hand clutched his eye as though he had been scalded.

Then I saw a patrol car turn off the blacktop and head fast up the front drive, the rain spinning in the blue and red kaleidoscopic flashing of emergency lights. I felt in my pocket for my flashlight, but it was gone. I ran down the stairs and out the front door just as LeBlanc and Thibodeaux pulled abreast of the porch, their faces looking at me expectantly through the open passenger window.

'They're headed for the bayou, three of them. They're armed. One guy's hurt. Nail 'em,' I said.

The driver stepped on the accelerator, and the car shot around the side of the house, scouring skid marks in the gravel, gutting a big potted plant by the edge of the rose bed. I pulled the empty clip from the magazine of the .45, inserted a full one, and followed them through the rain toward the back of the property.

But it was all comedy now. They drove through Weldon's bamboo, destroyed his vegetable garden, and spun sideways into the coulee. The back wheels of the car whined and smoked in the mud. Out in the darkness I heard an outboard engine roar away from the dock, up the bayou toward St Martinville.

The driver rolled down his window and looked at me in exasperation.

'Get on the radio,' I said.

'Sorry, Dave. I didn't know that goddamn coulee was there.'

'Forget about it. Call an ambulance, too.'

'Are you all right?'

'Yeah. But I think Garrett's not.'

'What happened in there?' the other deputy said, getting out of the passenger's seat.

But I was already walking back toward the house, the rain cold on my head, the .45 heavy and loose in my coat pocket. I found him at the bottom of the cellar stairs. The green dragon on his right forearm was laced with blood. I didn't even want to look at the rest of it.

An hour later the medical examiner and I stood on the columned marble front porch and watched the two ambulance attendants load the gurney into the ambulance and close the doors on it. The rain had stopped, and the ambulance lights made swinging red patterns in the oaks. I could hear the frogs out on the bayou.

'Have you ever seen one like that before?' the medical examiner said. He was a thin elderly man who wore gold-rimmed glasses and a white shirt and tie and carried a pocket watch on a chain. His sleeves were rolled, and he kept brushing at his wrist with a piece of wet paper towel.

'In New Orleans. When I was at the First District,' I said.

He wadded up the towel and threw it into the flower bed. His face looked disgusted.

'It's a first for me,' he said. 'Maybe that's why I'll stay in New Iberia. Does he have family here?'

'I think he was single. I don't know if he has relatives back in Houston or not.'

'If you have to talk with any of them, you can tell them he was probably out of it with the first shot.'

'Is it true?'

'It's what you can tell them, Dave.'

'I see.'

'His eyes were open when he got the next one. He probably saw it coming. But where's the law say that relatives need to know everything?' A fingerprint man went out the door, and a deputy locked it behind him. They both got in their cars. 'So you figure the shooter's from the mob?' the examiner said.

'Who knows? It's their signature.'

'Why do they do it that way? Just to be thorough?'

'More likely because most of them are degenerates and sadists. But maybe I say that just because I'm tired.' I tried to smile.

'How's your shoulder?'

'All right. I'll put some ice on it.'

'I scraped a blood specimen off the corner of the garage. It might help you later.'

'Thanks, doctor. I'd appreciate it if you'd send me a copy of the autopsy report as soon as it's ready.'

'You're sure you're all right? It got pretty close in there, didn't it?'

'The bottom line is I should have figured someone was in that bedroom. He'd just started to toss it when he heard me in the hallway. I'm lucky I didn't get my eggs scrambled.'

'If it's any consolation, the guy you wounded probably has a sizable slice of wood in his neck or face. He might show up at a hospital. My experience has been that most of these guys are crybabies when it comes to pain.'

'Maybe so. Goodnight, doctor.'

'Goodnight, Dave. Drive carefully.'

The fields were white with mist as I drove back toward New Iberia. My collarbone throbbed and felt swollen and hot when I touched it. The pink neon sign over the roadside bar gleamed softly on the oyster-shell parking lot. In my mind I kept repeating something told me by a platoon sergeant during my first week in Vietnam: don't think about it before it happens, and never think about it afterward. Yes, that was the trick. Just put one logical foot after the other. I yawned and my ears popped like firecrackers.

Back at the office, I called Weldon at his mother-in-law's home in Baton Rouge. I had waked him up, and he kept asking me to repeat myself.

'Look, I think it's better that you drive back to New Iberia in the morning and then we'll have a long talk.'

'About what?'

'I don't think you listen well. The inside of your home is virtually destroyed. Three guys tore it apart because they were looking for something that's obviously important to them. Meanwhile they murdered a sheriff's deputy. Do you want to know how they did it?'

He was silent.

'They shot him through the back, probably when he came down the basement stairs,' I said. 'Then they put one under his chin, one through his temple, and one through the back of his head. Do you know any low-rent wiseguys named Eddy or Jewel?'

I heard him cough in the back of his throat.

'I'm tied up here with some business for the next few days,' he said. 'I'm going to send some repair people out to the house. You've got this number if you need me.'

'Maybe it's about time you plug into reality, Weldon. You don't make the rules in a murder investigation. That means you'll be in this office before noon tomorrow.'

'I don't want to leave Bama by herself, and I don't want to bring her back there, either.'

'That's a problem you're going to have to work out. We're either going to be talking in my office tomorrow morning, or you're going to be in custody as a material witness.'

'Sounds like legalese doodah to me.'

'It's easy to find out.'

'Yeah, well, I'll check my schedule. You want to have lunch?'

'No.'

'You've sure got a dark view of things, Dave. Lighten up.'

'The warrant gets cut one minute after twelve noon,' I said, and hung up.

As was typical of Weldon, which was to do everything possible in a contrary and unpredictable fashion, he came up the front walk of the sheriff's department at eight o'clock sharp, dressed in a pair of khakis, sandals without socks, a green-and-red-flowered shirt hanging outside his trousers, and a yellow panama hat at a jaunty angle on his head. His jaws were clean and red with a fresh shave.

He helped himself to a Styrofoam cup of coffee from the outer office, then sat in a chair across the desk from me, folded one leg over the other, and played with his hat on his knee. My shoulder still throbbed, down in the bone, like a dull toothache.

'What were they after, Weldon?' I asked.

'Search me.'

'You have no idea?'

'Nope.' He put an unlit cigar in his mouth and turned it in circles with his fingers.

'It wasn't money or jewelry. They left that scattered all over the place.'

'There're a lot of weird guys around these days. I think it's got something to do with the times. The country has weirded out on us, Dave.'

'I haven't had to talk with any of Deputy Garrett's family yet. It's something I don't want to do, either. But I hope I have something more to offer them than a statement about the country weirding out on us.'

He looked momentarily shamefaced.

'What do you want me to say?' he asked.

'Who are these guys?'

'You tell me. You saw them. I didn't.'

'Eddy and Jewel. What do those names mean to you? Who's the guy with a mouthful of metal?'

'I'm sorry about your friend in the basement. I wish he hadn't gone in there.'

'It was his job.'

He gazed out the window at a cloud that hung on the edge of the early sun. His face became melancholy.

'Do you believe in karma? I do. Or at least I came to believe in it when I was in the Orient,' he said. His eyes wandered around the room.

'What's the point?'

'I don't know what's the point. You ever hear of a flyer named Earthquake McGoon? His real name was Ed McGovern, from New

Jersey. He was kind of a legend among certain people in the Orient. He was a huge fat guy, and one time he and his copilot, this Chinese kid, got locked up in a Chinese jail. Earthquake kept yelling at the guards, "Goddamn it, you haven't fed me. Give me some goddamn food." They told him he'd already had his rice bowl and to shut his mouth. That night when the guards went home Earthquake bent the bars apart and told his copilot to beat it, then he pushed the bars back into shape. The guards came back in the morning and said, "Where's the other guy?" Earthquake said, "I told you to feed me, and you wouldn't do it, so I ate the sonofabitch."

'He was one of those indestructible guys. Except he was doing a supply drop for the French at Dien Bien Phu and he got hit by some ground fire. He tried to get his parachute on but he was too fat. He told his kickers to jump and he was going to set it down on Highway One going into Hanoi. They said if he was going to ride it down, they would, too. He came in like a powder puff. It looked like they were home free, then his wing tipped a telephone pole, and they flipped and burned.'

He looked at me as though I should find meaning in his face or his story.

'That's what karma is,' he said. 'Highway One outside of Hanoi is waiting for us. It's all part of a piece. I'm sorry about your friend.'

'Have you ever been in jail?' I said.

'No. Why?'

I walked around the side of the desk.

'Let me see your hand,' I said.

'What are you talking about?'

'Let me see your hand.'

'Which hand?'

'It doesn't matter.' I lifted his right hand off the chair arm and snipped one end of my handcuffs around his wrist. Then I locked the other end to the D-ring on the floor.

'What do you think you're doing, Dave?'

'I'm going to have some breakfast. I'm not sure when I'll be back. Do you want me to bring you anything?'

'You listen—'

'You can start yelling or banging around in here if you want and somebody'll move you to the tank. I think today they have spaghetti for lunch. It's not bad.'

He looked simian in the chair, with one shoulder and taut arm stretched down toward the floor, his square face discolored with anger. Before he could speak again I closed the door behind me.

I walked across the street in the sunshine and bought four donuts at a café, then returned to the office. I wasn't gone more than ten minutes. I unlocked the handcuff from his wrist.

'That's what it's like,' I said. 'Except it's twenty-four hours a day. You want to eat now?'

He opened and closed his right hand and rubbed his wrist. His eyes measured me as though he were looking down a gun barrel.

'You want a donut?' I repeated.

'Yeah, why not?'

'You don't trust people, Weldon. And maybe I can understand that. But it's not a private beef anymore.'

'I guess it's not.'

'Who are the three guys?'

'I've heard the name Jewel before. In New Orleans.'

'In connection with what?'

'I flew for some people. Down in the tropics. A lot of different kinds of stuff goes in and out of there, you get my drift?' He closed his eyes and pinched the bridge of his nose. 'I never saw the guy. But you get in bad with the wrong people and guys like that get turned loose on you sometimes.'

'Which people?'

One tooth made a white mark on the corner of his lip.

'I can't tell you any more, Dave. If you want to lock me up, that's the breaks. I'm living in a dark place, and I don't know if I'm ever going to get out of it.'

His face looked as flat and empty as melted tallow.

That same afternoon I drove out to his sister Drew's place on East Main. East Main in New Iberia is probably one of the most beautiful streets in the Old South or perhaps in the whole country. It runs parallel with Bayou Teche and begins at the old brick post office and the Shadows, an 1831 plantation home that you often see on calendars and in motion pictures set in the antebellum South, and runs through a long corridor of spreading live oaks, whose trunks and root systems are so enormous that the city has long given up trying to contain them with cement and brick. The yards are filled with hibiscus and flaming azaleas, hydrangeas, bamboo, blooming myrtle trees, and trellises covered with rose and bugle vine and purple clumps of wisteria. In the twilight, smoke from crab boils and fish fries drifts across the lawns and through the trees, and across the bayou you can hear a band or kids playing baseball in the city park.

Like the other Sonnier children, Drew had never been one to live a predictable life. She had used her share of Weldon's oil strike on her father's farm to buy a rambling one-story white house, surrounded with screened-in gallerys, on a rolling, tree-shaded lot next to the old Burke home. She had been divorced twice, and any number of other men had drifted in and out of her life, usually to be cut loose unexpectedly and sent back to wherever they came from. She never did anything in moderation. Her love affairs were always public knowledge; she took indigent people of color into her home; she was inflexible in matters of principle and never gave an inch in an argument. She was robust and merry and big-shouldered, and sometimes I'd see her at the health club in Lafayette, clanking the weights up and down on the Nautilus machines, her shorts rolled up high on her thighs, her face hot and bright with purpose, a red bandana tied in her wet black hair.

But she did surprise us once, at least until we thought about it. She gave up men for a while and became a lay missionary with the Maryknolls in Guatemala and El Salvador. Then she almost died of dysentery. When she returned home she formed the first chapter of Amnesty International in New Iberia.

I found her behind her house, trimming back the grapevines on the gazebo with two black children. She was barefoot and wore dirty pink shorts and a white T-shirt, and there were twigs and flecks of dead leaves in her hair.

She had a pair of hedge trimmers extended high up on the vine when she turned her head and saw me.

'Hi, Dave,' she said.

'Hello, Drew. How've you been?'

'Pretty good. How's it with you?'

'I've been kind of busy of late.'

'I guess you have.'

I looked down at the two black children, both of whom were about five or six years old. 'I have a six-pack of Dr Pepper on the seat of my truck. Why don't you guys go get it for us?' I said.

They looked at Drew for approval.

'Y'all go ahead,' she said.

'You know a sheriff's deputy was murdered last night at Weldon's house?' I said.

'Yes.'

'Why would some people want to kill your brother, Drew?'

'Isn't he the one to ask?'

'He seems to think that being a standup guy is the same thing as allowing someone to blow his head off. Except now an innocent man is dead.'

She wiped the sweat out of her eyebrows with the back of her hand. The sun winked brightly off the bayou.

'Come inside and I'll give you some iced tea,' she said, wiped both of her hands on her rump, and walked ahead of me into the shade at the rear of her house. She pulled her damp T-shirt off her breasts with her fingers and shook the cloth as she opened the screen door. There was something too cavalier about her attitude, and I had the feeling that she had anticipated my visit and had already made a private decision about the outcome of our conversation.

She took a pitcher of tea out of the icebox, picked up two glasses, and we walked through a dark, cool room that gave on to a side porch. On the wall above her desk were several framed photographs: Weldon in a navy aviator's uniform; Lyle with his zydeco band, the name CATAHOULA RAMBLERS written in white letters at the bottom; and a cracked black-and-white picture of two little boys and a little girl standing in front of a man and woman, with a Ferris wheel in the background. The little girl had a paper windmill in her hand, and the boys were smiling over the tops of their cotton candy. The woman was expressionless and thick-bodied, her shoulders slightly rounded, her straw purse the only orna-ment or bright thing on her person. The man was dark and had a narrow face and wore cowboy boots, a bolo tie, and a cowboy hat at a slant on his head. He was looking at something outside the picture.

Drew had stopped in the doorway to the porch.

'I was just admiring your photographs. Are those your parents?'

She didn't answer.

'I don't remember them very well,' I said.

'What are you asking me, Dave?'

'Lyle says your father's alive.'

'My father was a sonofabitch. I don't concern myself thinking about him.'

'His picture's hanging here, Drew.'

She set down the iced tea and the glasses on the porch and came back in the room.

'I keep it because my brothers and mother are in it,' she said. 'It's the only one I have of her. The day he drove her out of the house her car went through the railing on the Atchafalaya bridge. She drowned in fifty feet of water, down where it was so dark they had to use electric lights to find her.'

'I don't think your father has any connection with this case. But I had to ask anyway. I'm sorry to bring up bad memories.'

'It's the past. Who cares about it?'

'But if you thought your father had anything to do with it, you'd tell me, wouldn't you, Drew?' I looked her directly in the eyes. Her stare remained as intent as mine.

'You should discount most of what Lyle tells you, Dave.'

'And if you knew, you'd also tell me why three guys would tear Weldon's house apart?'

She pushed her tongue into her cheek and let her eyes rove over my face. No matter what the situation, Drew always gave me the feeling that she was about to step two inches from my face.

'Come outside and sit down,' she said.

I followed her out on to the porch, and after I had sat down in a canvas chair, she sat on the corner of a wrought-iron table, with her legs apart, and looked down at me. I looked away through the screening at some bluejays playing in the birdbath on the lawn.

'I'm going to ask you to accept something,' she said. 'I can't help you out about Weldon. If I try to, I may hurt him. That's something I'm not going to do.'

'Maybe it's not yours to decide what degree of involvement you'll have with the law, Drew.'

'You want to put that a little more clearly?'

I raised my eyes to hers.

'Earlier today I cuffed your brother to a D-ring in my office. It was for only a few minutes, but I hope the lesson wasn't lost on him.'

'A what?'

'It's an iron ring, like a tethering ring, inset in the floor. Sometimes we handcuff people in custody to it until we can move them into a holding area.'

'That was supposed to impress Weldon? Are you serious?'

I felt the skin of my face tighten.

'Do you know the kind of life he had growing up?' she said. 'I won't even try to describe it to you. But no matter how bad it was, he'd give whatever he had to me and Lyle. And I mean he'd take the food out of his mouth for us.'

I looked out at the lawn again.

'You've got something to say?' she said.

'I'm at a loss.'

'We perplex you?'

'Your family didn't have the patent on hard times.'

She rubbed the heels of her hands idly on her thighs.

'You'll never get my brother to cooperate with you by pushing him,' she said.

'What's he into, Drew?'

'Forget the D-ring clown act and maybe one day he'll tell you about it.'

'I should revise my methods? That's the problem?'

'Stop acting like a simpleton.'

'You always knew how to say it.'

I could have pressed on with my questions, but Drew was not one to be taken prisoner. Or at least that's what I told myself. I put my iced tea back on the table and stood up.

'See you around,' I said.

'That's it?'

'Why not? You've been straight with me, haven't you?'

I walked across the blue-green lawn through the shade trees and could almost feel her troubled, hot eyes on my neck.

*

I went back to the office and talked with our fingerprint man, who told me that trying to sort out the prints in Weldon's home was a nightmare. There was no single, significant object, such as a murder weapon, for him to work with, and virtually every inch of space inside the house had been touched, handled, or smeared by family members, house guests, servants, meter readers, and a crew of carpenters that Weldon had evidently hired to refurbish several rooms. The fingerprint man asked me if I would present him with an easier job next time, like recovering prints from the Greyhound bus depot.

When I got home I found a note from Bootsie on the kitchen table, saying that she had taken Alafair with her to the grocery store in town. The evening was warm, the western sky maroon with low-hanging strips of cloud, and I put on my gym shorts and running shoes and did three miles along the dirt road by the bayou's edge. Gradually I could feel the fatigue and concerns of the day leave me, and at the drawbridge I turned around and hit it hard all the way home, the blood pounding in my neck, the sweat glazing on my chest. The house was in shadow now, the notched and pegged cypress planks as dark and hard-looking as iron, and I went into the backyard, where I could still see the late sun above the duck pond and the roofless barn at the foot of my property, and began alternating six sets of pushups, leg lifts, and stomach crunches.

I propped my feet on the bench of the redwood picnic table that we kept under the mimosa tree and did each push-up as slowly as I could, my back straight, touching my forehead lightly against the clipped grass, my muscles tightening across my ribs and through my shoulders and biceps. I was old enough to know that most of it was a narcissistic vanity, but at a certain age you're given the luxury of no longer having to be an apologist for yourself. Sometimes it feels good to be over a half-century old and to still be a player, a bit scarred perhaps, but still out there on the mound, messing them up with sliders and spitters when your fastball won't hum anymore. I had a round scar the diameter of a cigar on both sides of my left shoulder, where a psychopath had cored a hole right below my collarbone with a .38 round; a pungi-stick scar on my stomach that looked like a flattened gray worm; and a spray of raised welts across my thigh, like Indian arrowheads wedged under the tissue, a lover's kiss from a bouncing Betty that lighted me on a night trail in Vietnam with such a heated brilliance that I believed my soul left my breast and I could look down and count my bones inside my skin.

But I was all right, I thought. I no longer had dreams about the murder of my wife Annie, and the nocturnal film strips from Vietnam had become less and less distinct, as though the flattening elephant grass under the whirling helicopter blades, the grunts piling out of the Hueys and racing for the cover of the banyan trees, their pots clamped on their heads with one hand, the thump of mortars in a ville across the rice paddy, were all now part of someone else's experience, not really mine anymore or maybe I had finally come to realize that I was only a small part of an army made up of blacks and slum kids and poor-whites from cotton-gin and lumber towns who had a collective cross dropped on them that no one should have to bear. But at least I knew now that it wasn't mine to bear alone anymore, and so maybe I didn't have to bear it at all.

As always in my moments of self-indulgent reverie I had failed to notice an aluminum pot that was sitting in the middle of the redwood table. It was filled with shelled shrimp and an okra and tomato roux, and a red line of ants went from a crack in the table, up one side of the pot and down inside. I picked it up, took a spade from the tool shed, cleaned out the spoiled food in the vegetable garden by the coulee, and buried it.

The doctors at Baylor in Houston and the specialist we used in Lafayette had tried to explain in their best way (and, like most physicians, they were inept with language, even though the compassion was obviously there in their voices) that there was no one answer for lupus. The steroids and medicines that we used to control it, to alleviate its symptoms, to knock it into remission, to protect the connective tissue and the kidneys, were hard to put into perfect balance, and sometimes an imbalance caused moments of hallucination, even temporary periods of psychosis.

I had seen her sway once to music that was not there and had dismissed it; then on a second occasion she told me that perhaps in fact dead people had called me up on the phone when I was having delirium tremens years ago, because just minutes earlier the phone had rung and she had picked up the receiver and had heard the voice of her dead sister.

An hour later she was fine and laughing at her own imagination.

Tomorrow I would call the specialist in Lafayette and make another appointment. It was dusk now, and the purple air was thick with birds. I walked down to the dock to help Batist close up. He wore cutoff Levi's, a tank top, and canvas boat shoes with no socks. His black body looked so hard and muscular you could break barrel slats across it. He was in the back of the bait shop, flinging cases of Jax and Dixie beer into a stack against the wall, an unlit cigar shoved back in his jaw like a stick.

I seined some dead shiners out of the bait tank, then began restocking one of the coolers with long-necked bottles of beer.

'Somet'ing wrong, Dave?' he asked.

'No, not really.'

I could feel his eyes on me.

'Too much work at the office, I suppose,' I said.

'That's funny. It don't usually bother you.'

'It's just one of those days, Batist.'

'When I got some trouble at home, sometimes trouble with my wife, my kids, I don't like to tell nobody about it. So I just study on it. It ain't smart, no.'

'I worry about Bootsie. But there's nothing for it.'

'Don't pretend you be knowing that. You don't know that at all.'

I didn't say anything more. I pushed the bottles of beer deep into the crushed ice. The bare electric bulb overhead glinted dully off the smooth metal caps and filled the inside of the bottles with a trembling gold-brown light. My hands were numb up to my wrists.

'We don't need to ice down no more. We got enough for tomorrow,' Batist said.

'I'll finish closing up. Why don't you go on home?'

'I got to sweep out.'

'I'll do it.'

'I ain't in no hurry, me.'

I took another case of Jax off the walls and laid the bottles flat on the ice, between the necks of the bottles I had already loaded horizontally into the cooler. I slid the aluminum top shut with the heel of my hand.

Batist was still watching me. Then he lit his cigar, flipped the match out the window into the dark, and began sweeping the plank floor. He was a good and kind man, and even though it might be a cliché for a southern white man to talk about the loyalty of a black person, I was convinced that if need be he would open his veins for me.

I said goodnight to him and walked back up to the house. In the kitchen Bootsie and Alafair were taking pieces of pizza out of a box and putting them on plates.

3

The next morning I left early for New Orleans and spent two hours looking through mug books at my former place of employment, First District headquarters just outside the French Quarter, but I did not see any of the three men who had been inside Weldon's house. Most of the men I used to work with were gone – burnt-out, transferred, retired, or dead – and the two detectives I talked with were of no help. One was a new man from Jefferson Parish, and the other was bored and uninterested by a case that had nothing to do with his workload. In fact, he kept yawning and playing with his empty coffee cup while I described the three intruders to him. Finally I said, 'They don't sound like local talent, huh?'

'They don't clang any bells for me.'

I had given him my business card. His cup had already made a half-moon coffee print on it.

'But you'll rack your memory, won't you?' I said.

'What?'

'If I wanted to have somebody whacked out in New Orleans, who would I have to see?'

His face began to grow attentive with the suggestion of the insult.

'What are you getting at?' he asked.

'There are at least four guys in the Quarter who can arrange a contract hit for five hundred dollars. Do you know who they are?'

'I don't care for your tone.'

'Maybe it's just one of those off days. Thanks for the use of your mug books. I'd appreciate your keeping my card in your desk in case you need to call me.'

I drove on over to Decatur by the river and parked my truck down the street from Jackson Square and walked into the French Quarter. The narrow streets were still cool with morning shadow, and I could smell coffee and fresh-baked bread in the cafés, strawberries and plums from the crates set out on the sidewalks in front of small grocery stores, the dank, cool odor of old brick in the courtyards. It had rained just before dawn, and water leaked out of the green window shutters on the pastel sides of the buildings and dripped from the rows of potted plants on the balconies or hanging from the ironworks.

I walked down St Ann in the shadow of the cathedral to a one-story stucco building with a piked gate and a domed brick walkway that led to an office just off a flagstone courtyard. The courtyard was bordered with tight clumps of untrimmed banana trees. Painted on the frosted glass office window were the words CLETUS PURCEL INVESTIGATIVE SERVICES.

He had been my partner in the First District and one of the best cops I ever knew. Among the lowlifes, the wiseguys, the psychopaths, even the contract hit men out of Houston and Miami, he'd had a reputation that was notorious even by the standards of the New Orleans Police Department. Hard-nosed, mainline recidivists who laughed at the threat of ten-year jolts in Angola would swallow with apprehension and reconsider their point of view when they were told that Clete had taken an interest in their situations. Once a recently discharged convict from Parchman, a man who had shot out his wife's eye with a BB gun and whom I busted in a hot-pillow joint on Airline Highway, said he was coming back to New Orleans to cool out the cop who was responsible for his grief. Clete met him at the Greyhound depot, walked him into the restroom, and poured a container of liquid soap down his mouth. We never heard from him again.

But his marriage went bad, and eventually he got into trouble with whiskey, prostitutes, and shylocks, and a teaspoon at a time he began to serve the forces and people he had hated all his life. Finally he took ten thousand dollars to get rid of a witness in a federal investigation and barely made the flight to Guatemala, three minutes before his fellow detectives were racing down the concourse behind him with a murder warrant. Later the murder charge was dropped and he became head of security at two casinos in Las Vegas and Reno and the bodyguard of a Galveston mobster by the name of Sally Dio. I had marked Clete off as a turncoat, a pitiful facsimile of the friend I'd once had, but I came to learn that his loyalty and courage went far deeper into his character than his personal problems. His resignation from the mob came in the form of Sally Dio's private plane exploding all over a mountaintop in western Montana. Sally Dio and his entourage had to be combed out of the ponderosa trees with garden rakes. The National Transportation Safety Board said they suspected that someone had put sand in the fuel tanks.

'How's it hanging, noble mon?' he said from behind his desk when I opened his office door.

He wore a candy-striped shirt that looked like it was about to burst on his huge shoulders, a tie pulled loose at the throat, a blue-black .38 revolver in a nylon shoulder holster, and a powder-blue porkpie hat pushed down low on his forehead. His eyes were green and intelligent, his hair sandy, and his face always had a flush to it because of his weight and high blood pressure. A scar the texture and color of a bicycle patch ran down through one eyebrow and across the bridge of his nose, where he'd been bashed with a length of pipe when he was a kid.

I had already called him and told him about my problems with the Sonnier investigation.

'How'd you make out down at the First?' he said.

'I didn't recognize anyone in the mug books. I didn't get any help from anyone, either. I got the feeling I was a tourist from the provinces.'

'Let's face it, mon. They didn't hold a going-away party when either one of us hung it up.'

'How do you like the PI business?' I sat down across from him in a straw and deer-hide swayback chair. The walls of his office were decorated with bullfight posters, wine bags, and festooned *banderillas*. Through the back window I could see the courtyard and Clete's barbells and weight bench next to a stone well that leaked water at the top.

'It's good,' he said. 'Well, maybe the word's *easy*. You don't get rich at it, but the competition isn't exactly the first team. You know, ex-cops who majored in stupid, redneck jocks from Mississippi who think the big score is working security at Walmart. I'm clearing around five hundred a week after the overhead. It beats running a nightclub for greaseballs, I guess.'

'Sounds all right.'

He took a cigarette out of his package of Camels and held it for a moment in his big hand, then he set it down on the desk blotter and put a stick of gum in his mouth. His eyes smiled at me while he chewed.

'The problem is that a lot of it's a drag,' he said. 'Discovery investigations for lawyers, stuff like that. It's not like the old days in Homicide when we used to really make them wince. You remember when we—'

'No, I don't remember, Clete.'

'Come on, Dave. It was all full-tilt boogie rock'n' roll back then. You loved it, mon. Admit it.' He kept grinning, and his teeth clicked while he chewed his gum.

'Why the piece?'

'It gets interesting once in a while. I run down bail jumpers for a couple of bondsmen. Pimps, street dealers, bullshit like that. What a bunch. I think the Orkin Company ought to get serious in this town. I'm not kidding you, New Orleans is turning to shit. The fucking lowlifes have crawled out of the cracks.'

I looked at my watch.

'You're worried about your parking meter or something?' he said.

'Sorry. I just need to be back in New Iberia this afternoon.'

'How's everything at home?'

'It's okay. Good.'

The smile went out of his eyes. I looked away from him.

He spread his fingers on the desk blotter. His hands looked as big as skillets.

'Bootsie's having trouble again?' he said.

'Yes.'

'How bad?'

'You never know. One day's fine and full of bluebirds. The next day the gargoyles come out of the closet.'

He took the gum out of his mouth and dropped it in the wastebasket. I heard him take a deep breath through his nose.

'Let's walk on over to the Pearl and have some oysters,' he said. 'Then we'll talk about these three buttwipes you're looking for.'

'I'm a little tapped out right now.'

'I've got a tab there. I never pay it, but that's what tabs are for. Let's get out into this beautiful day.'

We walked down Bourbon, which was becoming more crowded with tourists now, past the T-shirt shops, jazz clubs and strip joints that advertised nude dancers and French orgies, to the corner of St Charles and Canal, where we went inside the Pearl and sat at the long counter than ran the length of the restaurant. The tables were covered with checkercloth, wood-bladed fans turned overhead, and three black men in aprons were shucking open raw oysters over the ice bins behind the bar. We ordered two dozen on the half-shell, a glass of iced tea for me and a small pitcher of draft for Clete.

'Run it by me again,' he said.

I went over all the details of Garrett's murder, the shootout, the description of the three intruders, the names I had heard them call each other while my ears had roared like the sea with the sound of my own blood.

Clete was silent, his green eyes thoughtful under his porkpie hat while he squeezed a lemon on his oysters and dotted them with Tabasco sauce.

'I don't know about the guy named Eddy or the guy with the scrap metal in his mouth,' he said. 'But this sawed-off character named Jewel sounds like a local I used to know. I haven't seen him around in a while, but I think we might be talking about Jewel Fluck.'

'What?'

'You heard me. That's his name. His family came from Germany and he grew up in the Channel. He tried to make it as a jockey out at Jefferson Downs, but he was too heavy and so he worked as a hot-walker till they caught him doping a horse. He's a mean little bastard, Dave.'

'*Fluck?*'

'You got it. Maybe his name screwed him up. When you think of Jewel Fluck, think of a hornet somebody just poured hot water on.'

'Why doesn't he have a record?'

'He does. In Mississippi. I think he did four or five years in Parchman.'

'What for?'

'Cutting up a colored guy who was scabbing on a job. Or something like that. Look, the only reason I know about this guy is he hid out a bail jumper I was looking for. The jumper was in the AB. I heard Fluck is, too.'

'The Aryan Brotherhood?'

'Integrated jails breed them like fungus. I used to think it was the Black Muslims we had to worry about. But this is your genuine psychopathic white trash with a political cause up their butts. Hitler would have loved them.'

He signaled the bartender for another pitcher of beer.

'Something wrong with your oysters?' he said.

'I'm just trying to figure this guy's tie-in with Weldon Sonnier,' I said.

'Maybe it was just a robbery gone bad, Dave. Maybe it's not that complicated a deal.'

'You didn't see the inside of the house. They really did a number on it. They were after something specific.'

'Maybe this Sonnier guy is holding some dope. We live in funny times. The coke money's a big temptation. A lot of straights have nosed up to the trough.'

'It could be. When's the last time you saw Fluck?'

'A year or so ago. I don't think he's around town. I'll ask around, though. Look, Dave, from what you've told me, this Sonnier character has invited a pile of shit into his life. He also sounds like one of these white-collar cocksuckers who think cops have about the same status as their yardmen. Maybe it's time he learned the facts of life.'

'Sir, could you watch your language, please?' the bartender said.

'What?' Clete said.

'Your language.'

'What about my language?'

'We're okay here,' I said to the bartender. He nodded and walked farther down the bar and started mixing a drink. Clete continued to stare after him.

'Does Fluck still have relatives in New Orleans?' I asked.

'I don't know,' he answered, his eyes coming back into mine. 'His mother probably wishes she'd thrown him away and raised the afterbirth. Forget about Fluck a minute. I've got a thought, a funny memory about somebody. The guy with the crowbar, the one named Eddy, tell me what he looked like again.'

'His head was real big, his face full of bone. The kind you break your fist on.'

'Did he have a tattoo?'

'I don't remember.'

'A red and yellow tiger on his right arm?'

I tried to see it in my mind's eye, but the only image that came back was the bone-heavy face and the ridges of muscle under the T-shirt.

'Maybe I couldn't even pull him out of a lineup with any certainty,' I said.

'There's one guy around town, he has a head like a pumpkin. His name's Raintree, from Baton Rouge. I don't know his first name, though.'

'Go on.'

'I get a security retainer out at the yacht club. Sometimes I check out backgrounds on potential members, keep out the riffraff supposedly, which means the south-of-the-border crowd. The tomato pickers are very big on clubs these days. But I also do security at dances, receptions, Republican geek shows, that kind of stuff. So one night Bobby Earl has a big gig out there. It's black-tie stuff, respectable, people from the Garden District, no Red Man spitters allowed, get the picture? You couldn't get the word "nigger" out of this bunch at gunpoint.

'Except a guy shows up who Bobby Earl wasn't planning on. Some character from the old States' Rights party, a real oil can, Vitalis running out of his hair, shiny suit, enough cologne to make your nose fall off. He was hooked up with those Klansmen who dynamited that colored church in Birmingham back in the sixties and killed those four children. Anyway, he's shaking hands with Bobby on the steps of the yacht club and this weird-looking kid from a radical newspaper takes their picture.

'That's when this guy Raintree, the guy with the pumpkin head and a red and yellow tiger on his arm, comes down the steps and takes the kid by the arm and walks him through the parking lot down to the lake. When I got there he'd punched the kid in the stomach and thrown his camera in the lake.'

'What did you do?'

'I told Raintree to leave the grounds. I told the kid he ought to go home and leave these guys alone.'

His eyes shifted away from me. He lit a cigarette. When I didn't speak, he turned on the stool and looked at me, a pinched light in his eyes.

'So it's not noble stuff. If I'd had my choices, I'd have clicked off Raintree's switch with a slapjack. But I don't get a city paycheck anymore, Dave.'

'No, that's not what I was thinking about. You just tied the ribbon on the box, partner.'

'You mean the connection between Jewel Fluck, the AB maybe, and this racist politician? But what's Bobby Earl got to do with your man in New Iberia?'

'Weldon Sonnier is his brother-in-law.'

*

Five minutes later we were walking under a colonnade on our way back to Clete's office. The sun had gone behind a cloud, and the air had become close with the smell of rain and the ripe fruit that was stacked in boxes on the sidewalk.

'What are you going to do?' Clete said. His face was heated from our pace.

'Head back to New Iberia and check out this guy Raintree.'

'You think that's the way we ought to do it?'

I looked at him.

'Leave that procedure dogshit to the paper shufflers,' he said.

'Clete, I don't think the word "we" figures into the equation here.'

'Oh yeah?'

'Yeah.'

'You got a lot of help from the guys at the First, did you? You got a lot of backup when those three gumballs were trying to paint the furniture with your brains?'

We turned up Toulouse toward Bourbon. He stopped in front of a cigar and news stand. A black man was shining the shoes of a man who sat in an elevated chair. Clete touched me on the jacket lapel with his finger.

'I won't tell you what to do,' he said. 'But when they try to kill you, it gets personal. Then you play it only one way. You go into the lion's den and you spit in the lion's mouth.'

'I don't have any authority here.'

'That's right. So they won't be expecting us. Fuck, mon, let's give them a daytime nightmare.' He stuck a matchstick in the corner of his mouth and grinned. 'Come on, think about it. Is there anything so fine as making the lowlifes wish they were still a dirty thought in their parents' mind?'

He snapped his fingers and rhythmically clicked his fists and palms together. His green eyes were dancing with light and expectation.

If you grew up in the Deep South, you're probably fond, as I am, of recalling the summertime barbecues and fish fries, the smoke drifting in the oak trees, the high school dances under a pavilion that was strung with Japanese lanterns, the innocent lust we discovered in convertibles by shadowed lakes groaning with bullfrogs, and the sense that the season was eternal, that the world was a quiet and gentle place, that life was a party to be enjoyed with the same pleasure and certainty as the evening breeze that always carried with it the smell of lilac and magnolia and water-melons in a distant field.

But there is another memory, too: the boys who went nigger-knocking in the little black community of Sunset, who shot people of color with BB guns and marbles fired from slingshots, who threw M-80s on to the galleries of their pitiful homes. Usually these boys had burr haircuts, jug ears, half-moons of dirt under their fingernails. They lived in an area of town with unpaved streets, garbage in the backyards, ditches full of mosquitoes and water moccasins from the coulee. Each morning they got up with their loss, their knowledge of who they were, and went to war with the rest of the world.

When we meet the adult bigot, the Klansman, the anti-Semite, we assume that he was bred in that same wretched place. Sometimes that's a correct conclusion. Oftentimes it's not.

'Did this guy grow up in a shithole or something?' Clete said.

We were parked in my truck across from Bobby Earl's home out by Lake Pontchartrain.

'I heard his father owned a candy company in Baton Rouge,' I said.

'Maybe he was an abused fetus.' He blew cigarette smoke out the window and looked at the piked fence, the blue-green lawn and twirling sprinklers, the live oaks that formed a canopy over the long white driveway. 'There must be big bucks in sticking it to the coloreds these days. I bet you could park six cars on his porch.' He looked at his watch. The sky was gray over the lake, and the waves were capping in the wind. 'Let's give it another half hour, then I'll treat you to some rice and red beans at Fat Albert's.'

'I'd better head back pretty soon, Clete.'

He formed a pocket of air in one jaw.

'You always believed in prayer, Streak,' he said.

'Yes?'

'Don't you AA guys call it "turning it over"? Maybe it's time to do that. Worrying about Bootsie and what you can't change is putting boards in your head.'

'It sure is.'

'So?'

'What?'

'Why set yourself up for a lot of grief?' He was looking straight ahead now, his porkpie hat resting on his brow. 'I know you, noble mon. I know the thoughts you're going to have before you have them. Turn the dials on yourself long enough, tamp them down till you got all the gears shearing off against each other, and pretty soon the old life looks pretty good again.'

'That's not the way it is this time.'

'Yeah, probably not. I shouldn't be handing out advice, anyway. When I started drinking my breakfast there for a while, I got sent by the captain to this shrink who was on lend-lease from the psychology department at Tulane. So I told him a few stories, stuff that I thought was pretty ordinary – race beefs when I was growing up in the Irish Channel, a hooker who dosed me while I was married, the time you and I smoked that greaseball dope dealer and his bodyguard in the back of their Cadillac – and I thought the guy was going to throw up in his wastebasket. I always heard these guys could take it. I felt like a freak. I ain't kidding you, the guy was trembling. I offered to buy him a drink and he got mad.'

I couldn't help laughing.

'That's it, mon. Lighten up,' he said. 'Nothing rattles the Bobbsey Twins from Homicide. And my, my, what do we have here?' He adjusted the outside mirror with his hand. 'Yes indeedy, it's the All-American peckerwood. You know this guy's got broads all over New Orleans? That's right, they really dig his rebop. I've got to learn his technique. Come on, fire it up, Streak.'

I turned the ignition and followed the white, chauffeur-driven Chrysler toward the entrance.

'I'm out of my jurisdiction, Clete,' I said. 'No Wyatt Earp stuff. We don't bruise the fruit. Right? Agreed?'

'Sure. We're just out here to visit. Talk some trash, maybe drink some mash. Get some political tips. Step on it, mon.' His arm was pressed flat against the side of the truck door, his face bright, like a man anticipating a carnival ride.

The Chrysler drove through the gate and on up the drive toward the white stucco, blue-tiled home with the sweeping porch and an adjacent swimming pool that was bordered with banana and lime trees and flaring gas torches. A man in pressed black pants and shined shoes, white shirt and black tie, with oiled red hair combed straight back on his head, swung the gate closed and walked away as though we were not there.

Clete got out of the truck and walked to the gate.

'Hey, bubba, does it look like we're from Fuller Brush?' he said.

'What?' the man said.

'We're here to see Bobby Earl. Open up.'

'He's got dinner guests. Who are you?'

'Who am I?' Clete said, smiling, pointing at his chest with his thumb. 'Good question, good question. You see this badge? Dave, do you know who we're talking to here?'

He folded his private investigator's badge and replaced it in his coat pocket when the man reached for it.

'I bet you didn't think I recognized you, did you?' Clete said. 'Gomez, right? You were a middleweight. Lefty Felix Gomez. I saw you fight Irish Jerry Wallace over in Gretna. You knocked his mouthpiece into the third row.'

The gateman nodded, his face unimpressed. 'Mr Earl don't want to be bothered by anybody tonight,' he said. 'That badge you got. Pawnshop windows are full of them.'

'Sharp eye,' Clete said, his mouth still grinning. 'I remember another story about you. You beat up a kid in a filling station. A high school kid. You fractured his skull.'

'I told you what Mr Earl said. You can come back tomorrow, or you can write him care of the state legislature. That's where he works.'

'Nice tie,' Clete said, reached through the gate, knotted the man's necktie in his fist, and jerked his face tightly against the bars. 'You've got a serious problem, Lefty. You're hard of hearing. Now, you get on that box and tell Mr Earl that Clete Purcel and Detective Dave Robicheaux are here to see him. Is my signal getting through to you? Are we big-picture clear on this?'

'Let him go, Clete,' I said.

A tall, good-looking man with angular shoulders in a striped, gray double-breasted suit, his silk shirt unbuttoned on his chest, walked down the drive toward us.

'Sure,' Clete said, and released the gateman, whose face had gone livid with anger except for the two diagonal lines where the flesh had been pressed into the iron bars of the gate.

'What's the trouble, Felix?' the man in the suit said.

'No trouble, Mr Earl. We want a few minutes of your time. I don't think your man here was passing on the information very well,' Clete said.

'I'm Detective Dave Robicheaux of the Iberia Parish sheriff's office,' I said, and opened my badge in my palm. 'I'm sorry for the late hour, but I'm in town only for today. I'd like to talk with you about Mr Raintree.'

'Mr Raintree? Yes. Well, I'm having someone for dinner, but—' His thick brown hair was styled and grew slightly over his collar, giving him a rugged and casual look. His skin was fine-grained, his jaws cleanly shaved, and his smile was easy and good-natured. The only strange characteristic about him was his right eye, whose pupil was larger than the one in his left eye, which gave it a monocular look. 'Well, we can take a minute or two, can't we? Would you like to sit down by the pool? I'm not sure that I can help you, but I'll try.'

'I appreciate your time, sir,' I said, and followed him up the drive.

'Hey, Lefty, I forgot to tell you,' Clete said, winking at the gateman. 'When you were in the ring, I always heard they tried to match you up with cerebral-palsy victims.'

We sat on canvas deck chairs by a swimming pool that was shaped in the form of a cross. The underwater lights were on, and the turquoise surface glistened with a thin sheen of suntan oil. On the flagstone patio a linen-covered table was set with candelabra and service for two. Bobby Earl walked to the side door of his house and spoke to his chauffeur, who had changed into a white butler's jacket. Then a young blonde woman in a pink bathing suit, terry-cloth robe, and high heels came out the door and began arguing with Bobby Earl. His back was to us, but I could see him raise his long, slender hands in a placating gesture. Then she slammed the screen and went back inside.

'I told you he was a gash hound,' Clete said.

'Clete, will you ease up? I mean it.'

'I'm mellow, I'm extremely serene. Don't sweat it. Hey, I didn't mention something else about the gateman back there. He was a coke mule for Joey Gouza and the Giacano family. It's funny he's out here with the white man's hope.'

'We'll run him later. Now stop shaking the screen on the zoo cage.'

'You've got no sense of humour, Streak. The sonofabitch is scared. Watch the corner of his mouth. Now's the time to squeeze his peaches.'

Bobby Earl came back to the pool, with his butler behind him. The butler set a bowl of popcorn crawfish down on a folding table between me and Clete.

'Would you gentlemen like something from the bar?' he said. His face was flat, with a small nose, close-set eyes, and a chin beard.

'Nothing for me, thanks,' I said.

'How about a double Black Jack, no ice, with a 7 on the side?' Clete said.

'I'll have a vodka collins, Ralph,' Bobby Earl said, sat down across from us, and folded one leg across his knee. I studied his handsome face and tried to relate it to the 1970s newspaper photograph I had seen of him in silken Klan robes when he had been imperial wizard of the Louisiana Grand Knights of the Invisible Empire.

'Does Mr Raintree work for you?' I asked. I opened a small notebook in my hand and clicked my ballpoint pen with my thumb.

'No.'

'He doesn't work for you?' I said.

'You mean Eddy?'

'Yes, Eddy Raintree.'

'He did at one time. Not now. I don't know where he is now.'

Then I saw what Clete had meant. The skin at the corner of his mouth wrinkled, like fingernail impressions in putty.

'When's the last time you saw him?' I asked.

'It's been a while. I tried to help him a couple of times when he was out of work. Has Eddy done something wrong? I don't understand.'

'I'm investigating the murder of a police officer. I thought Eddy might be able to help us. Do you know if Eddy has ever been up the road?'

'What?'

'Has he ever done time?'

'I don't know.' Then his peculiar, mismatched eyes focused on me thoughtfully. 'Why do you ask me if he's been in prison? As a police officer, wouldn't *you* know that?'

'I didn't know his first name until you told me,' I said, and smiled at him.

The butler brought the drinks from the poolside bar and served them to Clete and Bobby Earl. Earl took a deep drink from his without his eyes ever leaving my face. When he lowered his glass his mouth looked cold and red, like a girl's.

'When was the last time you talked to him?' I asked.

'It was a while back. I don't remember.'

I nodded and smiled again while I wrote in my notebook. Clete put a handful of popcorn crawfish in his mouth, drank out of his glass of 7 Up and cracked the ice between his molars.

'This is a great place,' he said. 'You own it?'

'I lease it.'

'I hear you're going to run for the US Senate,' Clete said.

'Perhaps.'

'Say, you ever see Jewel Fluck around?' Clete said.

'Who?'

'He's a little sawed-off guy. Hangs around with Eddy. He's in the AB.'

'I'm not sure what you're saying.'

'The Aryan Brotherhood,' Clete said. 'They're jailhouse Nazis.'

'Well . . .' Bobby Earl began.

'You really don't know Fluck, huh?' Clete said.

'No.'

'Streak would really like to talk with him and Eddy. They almost blew out his light. You get Streak mad and he'll throw elephant shit through your window fan.'

Clete held up his glass for the butler to fill it again.

'I think we don't need to talk anymore,' Bobby Earl said. 'I'm not sure why you're here anyway. I have the feeling you'd like to provoke something.'

'Here's my business card, Mr Earl,' I said. 'But I'll be back in touch one way or another. How's Eddy's face?'

'What?'

'He had a lot of splinters in it the last time I saw him. Do you know why he'd want to tear up your brother-in-law's house?'

'Now, you listen—'

'He and two others executed a policeman. They blew his brains all over a basement floor at pointblank range,' I said. 'You'd better think up some better bullshit the next time cops come out to your house.'

The blood had drained out of his cheeks. Then a strange transformation took place in his face. The skin grew taut against the bone, and there was a flat, green-yellow venomous glaze in his eyes, the kind you see only in people who have successfully worked for years to hide the propensity for cruelty that lives inside them.

'You got in here when you shouldn't have. Now you're on your way out,' he said.

'That sounds serious. No JD refills?' Clete said.

The butler rested his hand on the back of Clete's chair. Through the banana trees I saw the gateman walking across the lawn toward us. I stood up to go. Clete lit a cigarette and flipped the match into the swimming pool. It was deep dusk now, and the trees were swimming with fireflies.

'Don't crowd the plate,' he said, his eyes looking straight ahead.

The butler looked at Bobby Earl, who nodded his head negatively and rose from his chair.

'I get it,' Clete said, rising also, his grin back in place. 'You're cutting us some slack. Otherwise the hired help might just stomp the shit out of us. But this ain't niggertown. And it's no time for bad press, right? I've changed my mind about you, Mr Earl. You've got real Kool-Aid. I dig it.' He blew cigarette smoke at an upward angle into the violet air and gazed approvingly about the grounds. 'What a place. I've been in the wrong line of work.'

Then the butler fitted his hand around Clete's biceps to point him toward the driveway.

Clete pivoted and lifted his huge fist into the butler's stomach. It was a deep, unexpected blow, in the soft place right under the sternum, and the butler's face went white with shock. His mouth gasped, and his eyes locked open as big as half dollars.

Then Clete grabbed him by the back of his jacket and threw him spread-eagled across the table that had been set for two.

'Back off, Clete!' I said.

'Yeah? Take a look at the lollipop our man's got in his pocket?' He held up a leather-hided slapjack in one hand, and tossed it over his shoulder in the pool. 'Let's see what other items Bonzo's holding. How about this? A .25-caliber Beretta. What were you going to do with this, fuckhead?'

The side of the butler's face was pressed flat against the table; spittle dripped into his chin beard.

'Answer me. You think this is Beirut?' Clete said, his hand tight on the back of the butler's neck.

Then he straightened his back, released the clip from the pistol's magazine, ejected the round in the chamber, and sailed the pistol over a hedge. He threw the clip and the ejected round into the pool.

The gateman's eyes flicked back and forth between us and Bobby Earl; then he stepped hesitantly out on the flagstones, the skin around his mouth tight with expectation.

'You don't get paid enough money for it, partner,' I said.

'You want me to call the cops, Mr Earl?' he said.

Bobby Earl didn't answer him. Instead he looked at me.

'You've made a grave mistake,' he said. The pupil in his right eye was round and black, like a large, broken drop of India ink.

'I don't think so,' I said. 'I think you're dirty. I think you're involved with the death of a police officer. In Louisiana you don't skate when you kill a cop. Do some research on the Red Hat and find out who they've processed through there.'

'The what?' The rim below his right eye was red and trembling with anger.

'The Red Hat House. You're in the legislature. Call up at Angola and check it out. They used to have a sign on one wall that said, *This is where they knock the fire out of your ass.* I think they meant it.'

Clete and I walked across the lawn toward my truck. I looked back over my shoulder before I opened the door. Bobby Earl was staring after us, his face bathed in the yellow-red light of a flaming gas torch by the pool. The blonde girl in the pink swimsuit and terry-cloth robe clung to his arm like a frightened acolyte, her mouth a silent O. The 1970s photograph of Bobby Earl in silken robes, a cross crawling with fire in the background, no longer seemed out of place and time.

4

The house was dark when I got back home. I looked in on Alafair, who was sleeping with her thumb in her mouth and her stuffed frog on the pillow next to her. Her room was filled with souvenirs from our vacation trips to Houston, Key West, Biloxi, and Disney World: an Astros space helmet, a Donald Duck cap with a quacking bill, conch shells, dried starfish, a huge inflated Goofy figure, rows of sand dollars, a coral-encrusted cannon ball that I had chopped out of Seven-Mile Reef. I took her thumb out of her mouth and stroked her hair when her eyes fluttered temporarily awake. Then I latched her screen window, which had become part of a silent conspiracy three or four nights a week when she forgot to hook it after letting Tripod in her room against house rules.

Then I undressed in the main bedroom and sat on the side of the bed in my skivvies next to Bootsie's sleeping form. The sky had cleared, and the pecan trees clicked with moonlight in the breeze off the bayou; I could smell the fecund odor of bream spawning in the marsh. In the distance I heard a freight train blowing down the line.

I tried to let go of the day's concerns, let all the heat and fatigue and anger drain out of my hands and feet; but I was genuinely wired, wrapped so tight that my skin felt like a prison. I could hear the tiger pacing in his cage, his paws softly scudding on the wire mesh. His eyes were yellow in the darkness, his breath as fetid as meat that had rotted in the sun.

Sometimes I imagined him prowling through trees in William Blake's dark moral forest, his striped body electrified with a hungry light. But I knew that he was not the poet's creation; he was conceived and fed by my own self-destructive alcoholic energies and fears, chiefly my fear of mortality and my inability to affect the destiny of those whom I could not afford to lose.

Then Bootsie rolled against me, and I felt her hand brush my thigh and touch my sex. I took off my shorts and undershirt and lay down next to her, slipped my arms around her back, and put my face in her hair. Her body was warm from sleep, and she spread one leg around my calf, placed me inside her, and pressed her palm in the small of my back. When we made love I always had several images in my mind of Bootsie and I never saw her as one person, maybe because we had both known each other since we were nineteen. I remembered her in an organdy evening dress and the bright redness of her sunburned shoulders under the Japanese lanterns when we first met at a college dance out on Spanish Lake; I saw the fearful innocence in her face when we lost our virginity together in my father's boathouse, the rain dripping out of the cypress trees into the dead water as loudly as the beating of our hearts; and I still saw the pain in her eyes when I rejected her, hurt her deeply, and caused her to marry another man, all because of my own self-loathing and inability to explain to anyone else the dark psychological landscape I had wandered in and out of since I was a child.

But just as Alafair had been given to me in a wobbling bubble of air below the Gulf's surface, I believed my Higher Power had given me back Bootsie when I had lost all claim to her, had undone my youthful mistakes for me, and had made that wonderful summer of 1957 as immediate and tangible and ongoing as the four o'clocks that bloomed nightly under the moon on Bayou Teche.

But how do you cast out the canker from the rose, I thought.

Then she put both her legs in mine, held me tightly inside her, her mouth open and wet against my cheek, and in my mind's eye I saw a wave bursting in a geyser of foam against the hard outline of a distant jetty, a coral boulder ripping loose from the ocean's floor, and a flurry of silver ribbon fish rising from the mouth of an underwater cave.

By the next afternoon I had received the files and photos of Jewel Fluck and Eddy Raintree from the National Crime Information Center in Washington, DC; police departments in New Orleans, Jackson, Biloxi, and Baton Rouge; and Angola and Parchman penitentiaries. Both men belonged to the great body of psychologically misshapen people that I refer to as The Pool. Members of The Pool leave behind warehouses of official paperwork as evidence that they have occupied the planet for a certain period of time. Their names are entered early on in welfare case histories, child-abuse investigations, clinic admissions for rat bites and malnutrition. Later on these same people provide jobs for an army of truant officers, psychologists, public defenders, juvenile probation officers, ambulance attendants, emergency-room personnel, street cops, prosecutors, jailers, prison guards, alcohol- and drug-treatment counselors, bail bondsmen, adult parole authorities, and the county morticians who put the final punctuation mark in their files.

The irony is that without The Pool we would probably have to justify our jobs by refocusing our attention and turning the key on slumlords, industrial polluters, and the coalition of defense contractors and militarists who look upon the national treasury as a personal slush fund.

I looked at the mug shots of Fluck and Raintree and was reasonably sure that these were the same men who had been in Weldon's house (I say 'reasonably sure' because a booking-room photograph is often taken when the subject is tired, angry, drunk, or drugged, and recidivists constantly change their hairstyles, grow and shave mustaches and hillbilly sideburns, and become bloated on jailhouse fare like grits, spaghetti, and mashed potatoes).

But Fluck's file told me little that I didn't already know, or couldn't have guessed at. At seventeen he had pushed another boy down stairs at the Superdome and broken his arm, but the charge had been dropped. He had been banned for life from Louisiana racetracks after he was caught feeding a horse a speedball; he had been in the New Orleans city prison twice, once for beating up a taxicab driver, a second time for distribution of obscene film materials. His mainline fall had been at Parchman, where he did a five-year jolt and went out on what is called 'max-time', which meant he either gave the hacks constant trouble and earned no good-time, or he refused parole because he didn't want to go back on the street under supervision.

But because he had gone out on max-time, Parchman had no address for him, and he hadn't been arrested again in the two years since his discharge. His parents were deceased, and neither the New Orleans phone directory nor any of the utility companies listed anyone by the name of Fluck.

Eddy Raintree's photo stared at me out of his file with a face that had the moral depth and complexity of freshly poured cement. He had a sixth-grade education, a dishonorable discharge from the Marine Corps, and had never had a more skilled job than that of fry cook and hod carrier. He had been in the Calcasieu, West Baton Rouge, and Ascension parish prisons for bigamy, check writing, arson, and sodomy with animals. He went down for three years in Angola for possession of stolen food stamps, and he spent two of those three years in lockdown with the big stripes (the violent and unmanagable) after he was suspected of involvement in a gang rape that left a nineteen-year-old convict dead in a shower stall.

He, like Jewel Fluck, had gone out max-time three years ago, and there was no current address for him. But at the bottom of Raintree's prison sheet was a notation that Captain Delbert Bean had recommended that this man be reclassified as a big stripe, and that no good-time be applied toward his early release from the farm.

Early Monday morning I drove up to Angola, north of Baton Rouge on the Mississippi River, rolled across the cattle guard between the gun towers and the fences topped with rolls of razor wire, and followed the narrow road past the Block, an enormous fenced compound where both the snitches and the big stripes were kept in lockdown, through fields of sweet potatoes and corn and freshly plowed acreage that dipped all the way down to the river basin. I passed the old prison cemetery, where those who die while incarcerated do Angola time for all eternity; the bulldozed and weed-grown foundations of the sweat boxes on Camp A (there had been two of them, upright, narrow cast-iron places of torment, with a hole the diameter of a cigar to breathe through, the space so tight that if a convict collapsed his knees and buttocks would wedge against the walls); the crumbled ruins of the stone buildings left over from the War Between the States (which for years had been used to house Negro inmates, including three of the best twelve-string blues guitarists I know of – Leadbelly, Robert Pete Williams, and Hogman Mathew Maxie); and finally the old Red Hat House down by the river bank, a squat, ugly off-white building that took its name from the red-painted straw hats worn by the big-stripe levee gangs who were locked there before the building became the home of the electric chair, which has since been moved to a more modern environment, one with tile walls that glow with the clean, antiseptic light of a physician's clinic.

The Mississippi was high and churning with mud and uprooted trees, and out on the flat, among the willows, I saw Captain Delbert Bean on horseback, a pearl-gray Stetson hat slanted on his head, working a gang of convicts who were filling sandbags out of a dump truck and laying them along the base of the levee.

That levee is a burial ground for an untold number of convicts who were murdered, some as object lessons, by prison personnel. Ask anyone who ever worked in Angola, or did time there. I will not use their names, but there used to be two old-time gunbulls, brothers, who would get sodden and mean on corn whiskey, sometimes take a nap under a tree, then awake, single out some hapless soul, tell him to start running, and then kill him.

Delbert Bean was a dinosaur left over from that era. He had been a prison guard for forty-seven years, and I don't believe that in his life he had ever traveled farther away from the farm than New Orleans or Shreveport. He had no family or friends that I knew of, no external frame of reference, little knowledge of change in the larger world. His eyes were a washed-out blue, his skin covered with brown spots the size of dimes, his liver eaten away with cirrhosis. His stomach looked like a watermelon under his long-sleeved blue shirt. The accent was north Louisiana hill country, the voice absolutely certain when he spoke, and the face absolutely joyless.

He was not a man whom you either liked or disliked. He had been jailing most of his life, and I suspected that at the center of his existence was a loneliness and perversion so great that if he ever became privy to it he would blow his brains all over the ceiling of the little frame house where he lived with others like himself in the free people's compound.

He handed the reins of his horse to a black inmate and walked with a cane up a path through the willows toward me. The bottom of the cane was seated inside a twelve-inch steel tube. A briar pipe protruded from inside the holster belt of his chrome-plated nine-millimeter automatic. He shook hands with the limpness of a man who was not used to social situations, filled his pipe, and pushed the tobacco down with his thumb while his eyes watched the men filling and hefting sandbags below us. I had known him for fifteen years, and I did not once remember his addressing me by name.

'Eddy Raintree,' he said, acknowledging my question. 'Yeah, he was one of mine. What about him?'

'I think he helped kill a deputy sheriff. I'd like to run him to ground, but I'm not sure where to start.'

He lit his pipe and watched the smoke drift off into the wind.

'His kind used to run their money through their pecker on beer and women. Now they do it with dope. I caught him and another one once cooking down some blues to shoot in an eyedropper. They was using the edge of a dollar bill for an insulator. No more sense than God give a turnip.'

'Was he in any racial beefs?'

'When you got nigger and white boys in the same cage, there ain't any of them wouldn't cut each other's throats.'

'Do you know if he was in the AB?'

'The what?'

'The Aryan Brotherhood.'

'We ain't got that in here.'

'That's funny. It's the fashion everywhere else.' I tried to smile.

But he was not given to humor about his job.

'Let me sit down. My hip's hurting,' he said. He raised his cane in the air and shouted, 'Walnut!' A mulatto convict, his denims streaked with mud and sweat, dropped his shovel, picked up a folding chair, ran it up the incline, and popped it open for the captain.

'Tell Mr Robicheaux what you're in for,' the captain said.

'Suh?'

'You heard me.'

The convict's eyes focused on a tree farther down the levee.

'Murder, two counts,' he said, quietly.

'Whose murder?' the captain said.

'My kids. They say I shot bof' my kids. That's what they say.'

'Get on back to work.'

'Yes, suh.'

The captain waited until the convict was back down the mudflat, then said, pointing with the steel tip of his cane. 'See that big one yonder, the one flinging them bags up on the levee, he raped an eighty-five-year-old woman, then snapped her neck. You tell these white boys they're gonna have to cell with niggers like them two out yonder or they'll lose their good-time, what do you think's gonna happen?'

'I'm not following you.'

He drew in on his pipe, his eyes hazy with a private knowledge. It was overcast, and his lips looked sick and purple against his liver-spotted skin.

'We had two white boys shanked in the Block this year,' he said. 'One a trusty, one a big stripe. We think the same nigger got both of them, but we can't prove it. If you was a white person living up there, what would you do?'

'So maybe there's something *like* the AB in Angola?'

'Call it what you want. They got their ways. The goddamn Supreme Court's caused all this.' He paused, then continued. 'They carve swastikas, crosses, lightning bolts on each other, pour ink in the sores. The black boys don't tend to mess with them, then. Wait a minute, I'll show you something. Shorty! Get it up here!'

'Yow boss!' A coal-black convict, with a neck like a fire hydrant, his face running with sweat, heaved a sandbag against the levee and lumbered up the incline toward us.

'What'd Boss Gilbeau put you in isolation for?' the captain asked.

'Fightin', boss.'

'Who was you fighting with, Shorty?'

'One of them boys back in Ash.' He grinned, his eyes avoiding both of us.

'Was he white or colored, Shorty?'

'He was white, boss.'

'Show Mr Robicheaux how you burned yourself when you got out of isolation.'

'Suh?'

'Pull up your shirt, boy, and don't act ignorant.'

The convict named Shorty unbuttoned his sweat-spotted denim shirt and pulled the tail up over his back. There were four gray, thin, crusted lesions across his spine, like his skin had been branded by heated wires or coat hangers.

'How'd you burn yourself, Shorty?' the captain said.

'Backed into the radiator, boss.'

'What was the radiator doing on in April?'

'I don't know, suh. I wished it ain't been on. It sure did hurt. Yes, suh.'

'Get on back down there. Tell them others to clean it up for lunch.'

'Yes, suh.'

The captain knocked his pipe out on his boot heel and stuck it back in his holster belt. He gazed out on the wide yellow-brown sweep of the river and the heavy green line of trees on the far side. He didn't speak.

'That's the way it is here, huh?' I said.

'Beside dope, Raintree's problem is his prick. He's got rut for brains. It don't matter if it's male or female, if it's warm and moving he'll try to top it. The other thing you might look for is fortunetellers. He had astrology maps all over his cell walls. He give a queer in Magnolia a carton of cigarettes to read his palm. By the way, it ain't the AB you ought to have on your mind. Them with the swastikas I was telling you about, they get mail from some church out in Idaho called Christian Identity. Hayden Lake, Idaho.'

He raised himself up on his cane to indicate that our interview was over. I could almost hear his bones crack.

'I thank you for your time, captain,' I said.

Then as an afterthought he said, 'If you bust that boy, tell him he just as lief hang himself as come back here for killing a policeman.'

His pupils were like black cinders in his washed-out blue eyes.

I arrived back at my office just in time to shuffle some papers around on my desk and sign out at five o'clock. I was tired from the round-trip drive up to Angola; my shoulder still hurt where Eddy Raintree had caught me with the crowbar, and I wanted to go home, eat supper, take a run along the dirt road by the bayou, and maybe go to a movie in Lafayette with Alafair and Bootsie.

But parked next to my pickup truck was a waxed fire-engine-red Cadillac, with the immaculate white canvas top folded back loosely on the body. A man in ice-cream slacks lay almost supine across the leather seats, one purple suede boot propped up on the window jamb, a sequined sunburst guitar hung across his stomach.

'*Allons à Lafayette, pour voir les 'tites françaises,*' he sang, then sat up, pulled off his sunglasses with his mutilated hand, and grinned at me. 'What's happening, lieutenant?'

'Hello, Lyle.'

'Take a ride with me.'

'How many of these do you own?'

'They actually belong to the church.'

'I bet.'

'Take a ride with me.'

'I'm on my way home.'

'You can blow a few minutes. It's important.'

'Do you have anything against talking to me during office hours?'

'Somebody broke into Drew's house last night.'

'I didn't hear anything about it. Did she report it to the city police?'

'No.'

'Why not?'

'Maybe I'll explain that. Take a ride with me.' He lifted his guitar over into the back seat. I opened the door and sat back in the deep flesh-colored leather seat next to him. We clanked across the drawbridge into Bayou Teche and drove out of town on East Main. He picked up a paper cup from the floor and drank out of it. A familiar odor struck my nostrils in the warm air.

'Did you give yourself a dispensation today?' I said.

'I preach against drunkenness, not drinking. There's a big difference.'

'Where are we going, Lyle?'

'Not far. Right there,' he said, and pointed across a sugarcane field to a collapsed barn, a rusted and motionless windmill, and some brick pilings that had once supported a house. The field behind the barn was unplowed, and in it were a half-dozen oil wells.

We pulled off the parish road into a weed-grown dirt lane that led back to the barn. Lyle cut the engine, removed a pint bottle of bourbon from under the seat, and unscrewed the cap with one thumb. His hair, which he wore on-camera in a waved conk that reminded me of a washboard, was windblown and loose and hanging in his eyes.

'I own a third of it, a third of them wells out there, too,' he said. 'But I'm not fond of coming out here. I surely ain't.'

'Why are we here, then?'

'You got to go back where the dragons live if you want to get rid of them.'

'I tried to make myself clear before, Lyle. I sympathize with the problems your family had in the past, but my concern now is with a murdered police officer.'

'Drew came home last night from her Amnesty International meeting and she noticed the light on the back porch was out. She went on into the house, and there was a guy in the kitchen, in the dark, looking at her. He had something in his hand, a screwdriver or a knife. She ran back out the front of the house to the neighbor's and tried to get hold of Weldon, then she called me up in Baton Rouge.'

'Why didn't she call the cops, Lyle?'

'She thinks she's protecting Weldon from something.'

'What?'

'I'm not sure. Neither one of them is real convinced about my religious conversion. They tend to think maybe my brain cells soaked up a little too much purple acid when I came back from Vietnam. So they don't always confide everything in me. But it doesn't matter. I know who that fellow was.'

'Your father?'

'I don't have a doubt.'

'Everybody else seems to, including me.'

He took a sip from his pint bottle and looked away at the red sun over the bayou. The wind was warm, and I could smell the reek of natural gas from the wells.

'What does Drew say? What did this man look like?' I asked.

'She didn't see his face.'

'I'll talk to her tomorrow. Now I'd better get back home.'

'All right, I'm going to tell you all of it. Then you can do any damn thing you want with it, Loot. But by God, first, you're going to listen.'

The scars dripping down the side of his face looked like smooth pieces of red glass in the late sunlight.

5

And this is the way Lyle told it to me, or as I have reconstructed it.

His mother had come home angry from her waitress job in a beer garden on a burning July afternoon, and without changing out of her pink uniform, she had begun butchering chickens on the stump in the backyard, shucking off their feathers in a cauldron of scalding water. The father, Verise, came home later than he should have, parked his pickup by the barn, and walked naked to the waist through the gate with his wadded shirt hanging out the back pocket of his Levi's. His shoulders, chest, and back were streaked with sweat and black hair.

The mother sat on a wood chair, with her knees apart in front of the steaming cauldron, her forearms covered with wet chicken feathers. Headless chickens flopped all over the grass.

'I know you been with her. They were talking at the beer joint. Like you some kind of big ladies' man,' she said.

'I ain't been with nobody,' he said, 'except with them mosquitoes I been slapping out in that marsh.'

'You said you'd leave her alone.'

'You children go inside.'

'That gonna make your conscience right 'cause you send them kids off, you? She gonna cut your throat one day. She been in the crazy house in Mandeville. You gonna see, Verise.'

'I ain't seen her.'

'You sonofabitch, I smell her on you,' the mother said, and swung a headless chicken by its feet and whipped a diagonal line of blood across his chest and Levi's.

'You ain't gonna act like that in front of my children, you,' he said, and started toward her. Then he stopped. 'I said y'all get inside. This is between me and her.'

Weldon and Lyle were used to their parents' quarrels, and they turned sullenly toward the house; but Drew stood mute and fearful under the pecan tree, her cat pressed flat against her chest.

'Come on, Drew. Come see inside. We're gonna play with the

Monopoly game,' Lyle said, and tried to pull her by the arm. But her body was rigid, her bare feet immobile in the dust.

Then Lyle saw his father's large, square hand go up in the air, saw it come down hard against the side of the mother's face, heard the sound of her weeping, as he tried to step into Drew's line of vision and hold her and her cat against his body, hold the three of them tightly together outside the unrelieved sound of his mother's weeping.

Three hours later her car went through the railing on the bridge over the Atchafalaya River. Lyle dreamed that night that an enormous brown bubble arose from the submerged wreck, and when it burst on the surface her drowned breath stuck against his face as wet and rank as gas released from a grave.

The woman called Mattie wore shorts and sleeveless blouses with sweat rings under the arms, and in the daytime she always seemed to have curlers in her hair. When she walked from room to room, she carried an ashtray with her, into which she constantly flicked her lipstick-stained Chesterfields. She had a hard, muscular body, and she didn't close the bathroom door all the way when she bathed; once Lyle saw her kneeling in the tub, scrubbing her big shoulders and chest with a large, flat brush. The area above her head was crisscrossed with improvised clotheslines, from which dripped her wet underthings. Her eyes fastened on his, and he thought she was about to reprimand him for staring at her; but instead her hard-boned, shiny face continued to look back at him with a vacuous indifference that made him feel obscene.

If Verise was out of town on a Friday or Saturday night, she fixed the children's supper, put on her blue suit, and sat by herself in the living room, listening to the *Grand Ole Opry* or the *Louisiana Hayride*, while she drank apricot brandy from a coffee cup. She always dropped cigarette ashes on her suit and had to spot-clean the cloth with dry-cleaning fluid before she drove off for the evening in her old Ford coupe. They didn't know where she went on those Friday or Saturday nights, but a boy down the road told them that Mattie used to work in Broussard's Bar on Railroad Avenue, an infamous area in New Iberia where the women sat on the galleries of the cribs, dipping their beer out of buckets and yelling at the railroad and oil-field workers in the street.

Then one morning when Verise was in Morgan City a man in a new silver Chevrolet sedan came out to see her. It was hot, and he parked his car partly on the grass to keep it in the shade. He wore sideburns, striped brown zoot slacks, two-tone shoes, suspenders, a pink shirt without a coat, and a fedora that shadowed his narrow face. While he talked to her he put one shoe on the car bumper and wiped the dust off with a rag. Then their voices grew louder and he said, 'You like the life. Admit it, you. He ain't given you no wedding ring, has he? You don't buy the cow, no, when you can milk through the fence.'

'I am currently involved with a gentleman. I do not know what you are talking about. I am not interested in anything you are talking about,' she said.

He threw the rag back inside the car and opened the car door.

'It's always trick, trade, or travel, darlin',' he said. 'Same rules here as down on Railroad. He done made you a nigger woman for them children, Mattie.'

'Are you calling me a nigra?' she said quietly.

'No, I'm calling you crazy, just like everybody say you are. No, I take that back, me. I ain't calling you nothing. I ain't got to, 'cause you gonna be back. You in the life, Mattie. You be phoning me to come out here, bring you to the crib, rub your back, put some of that warm stuff in your arm again. Ain't nobody else do that for you, huh?'

When she came back into the house she made the children take all the dishes out of the cabinets, even though they were clean, and wash them over again.

It was the following Friday that the principal at the Catholic element- ary school called about a large welt on Lyle's cheek. Mattie was already dressed to go out. She didn't bother to turn down the radio when she answered the phone, and in order to compete with Red Foley's voice she had to almost shout into the receiver.

'Mr Sonnier is not here,' she said. 'Mr Sonnier is away on business in Port Arthur . . . No, ma'am, I'm not the housekeeper. I'm a friend of the family who is caring for these children . . . There's nothing wrong with that boy that I can see . . . Are you calling to tell me that there's something wrong, that I'm doing something wrong? What is it that I'm doing wrong? I would like to know that. What is your name?'

Lyle stood transfixed with terror in the hall as she bent angrily into the mouthpiece and her knuckles rigid on the receiver. A storm was blowing in from the Gulf, the air smelled of ozone, and the southern horizon was black with thunderclouds that crawled with white electricity. Lyle heard the wind ripping through the trees in the yard and pecans rattling down on the gallery roof like grapeshot.

When Mattie hung up the phone the skin of her face was tight against the bone and one liquid eye was narrowed at him like someone aiming down a rifle barrel.

That winter Verise started working regular hours, what he called 'an indoor job', at a chemical plant in Port Arthur, and the children saw him only on weekends. Mattie cooked only the evening meal and made the children responsible for the care of the house and the other two meals. Weldon started to get into trouble at school. His eighth-grade teacher, a laywoman, called and said he had thumb-tacked a girl's dress to the desk during class, causing her to almost tear it off her body when the bell rang, and he would either pay for the dress or be suspended. Mattie hung up the phone on her, and two days later the girl's father, a sheriff's deputy, came out to the house and made Mattie give him four dollars on the gallery.

She came back inside, slamming the door, her face burning, grabbed Weldon by the neck of his T-shirt, and walked him into the backyard, where she made him stand for two hours on an upended apple crate until he wet his pants.

Later, after she had let him come back inside and he had changed his underwear and blue jeans, he went outside into the dark by himself, without eating supper, and sat on the butcher stump, striking kitchen matches on the side of the box and throwing them at the chickens. Before the children went to sleep he sat for a long time on the side of his bed, next to Lyle's, in a square of moonlight with his hands balled into fists on his thighs. There were knots of muscle in the backs of his arms. Mattie had given him a burr haircut, and his head looked as hard and scalped as a baseball.

'Tomorrow's Saturday. We're gonna listen to the LSU-Rice game,' Lyle said.

'Some colored kids saw me from the road and laughed.'

'I don't care what they did. You're brave, Weldon. You're braver than any of us.'

'I'm gonna fix her.'

His voice made Lyle afraid. The branches of the pecan trees were skeletal, like gnarled fingers against the moon.

'Don't be thinking like that,' Lyle said. 'It'll just make her do worse things. She takes it out on Drew. She made her kneel in the bathroom corner because she didn't flush the toilet.'

'Go to sleep, Lyle,' Weldon said. His eyes were wet. 'She hurts us because we let her. We ax for it. You get hurt when you don't stand up. Just like Momma did.'

Lyle heard him snuffing in the dark. Then Weldon lay down with his face turned toward the opposite wall. His head looked carved out of gray wood in the moonlight.

Three days later the school principal saw the cigarette burn on Drew's leg in the lunchroom and reported it to the social-welfare agency in town. A consumptive rail of a man in a dandruff-flecked blue suit drove out to the house and questioned Mattie on the gallery, then questioned the children in front of Mattie. Drew told him she had been burned by an ember that had popped out of a trash fire in the backyard.

He raised her chin with his knuckle. His black hair was stiff with grease.

'Is that what happened?' he asked.

'Yes, sir.' The burn was scabbed and looked like ringworn on her skin.

He smiled and took his knuckle away from her chin. 'Then you shouldn't play next to the fire,' he said.

'I would like to know who sent you out here,' Mattie said.

'That's confidential.' He coughed on the back of his hand. 'And to tell you the truth, I don't really know. My supervisor didn't tell me.' He coughed again, this time loud and hard, and Lyle could smell his deep-lung nicotine odor. 'But everything here looks all right.'

Weldon's eyes were as hard marbles, but he didn't speak.

The man walked with Mattie to his car, and Lyle felt like doors were slamming all around them. She put her foot on the man's running board and propped one arm on his car roof while she talked, so that her breasts were uplifted against her blouse and her knees were wide-spaced below the hem of her dress.

'Let's tell him,' Lyle said.

'Are you kidding? Look at him. She could make him eat her shit with a spoon,' Weldon said.

It was right after first period the next morning that they heard about the disaster at Port Arthur. A ship loaded with fertilizer had been burning in the harbor, and while people on the docks had watched fire-fighting boats pumping geysers of water on to the ship's decks, the fire had dripped into the hold. The explosion filled the sky with rockets of smoke and rained an umbrella of flame down on the chemical plant. The force of the secondary explosion was so great that it blew out windows in Beaumont, twenty miles away.

Mattie got drunk that night and fell asleep in the living room chair by the radio. When the children returned home from school the next afternoon, Mattie was waiting to tell them that a man from the chemical company had telephoned and said that Verise was listed as missing. Her eyes were pink with either hangover or crying, her face puffy and round like a white balloon.

'Your father may be dead. Do you understand what I'm saying? That was an important man from his company who called. He would not call unless he was gravely concerned. Do you children understand what is being said to you?'

Weldon brushed at the dirt with his tennis shoe, and Lyle looked into a place about six inches in front of his eyes.

'He's worked like a nigra for you, maybe lost his life for you. You have nothing to say?'

'Maybe we ought to start cleaning up our rooms. You wanted us to clean up our rooms,' Lyle said.

'You stay outside. Don't even come into this house,' she said.

'I have to go to the bathroom,' Weldon said.

'Then you can just do it in the dirt like a darky,' she said, and went inside the house and latched the screen behind her.

The next afternoon Verise was still unaccounted for. Mattie had an argument on the phone with somebody, perhaps the man in zoot pants and two-tone shoes; she told him he owed her money and she wouldn't come back and work at Broussard's Bar again until he paid her. After she hung up she breathed hard at the kitchen sink, smoking her cigarette and staring out into the yard. She snapped the cap off a bottle of Jax and drank it half empty, her throat working in one long wet swallow, one eye cocked at Lyle.

'Come here,' she said.

'What?'

'You tracked up the kitchen. You didn't flush the toilet after you used it, either.'

'I did.'

'You did what?'

'I flushed the toilet.'

'Then one of the others didn't flush it. Every one of you come out here. Now!'

'What is it, Mattie? We didn't do anything,' he said.

'I changed my mind. Every one of you outside. All of you outside. Weldon, you too, you get out there right now. Where's Drew?'

'She's playing in the yard. What's wrong, Mattie?' Lyle said.

Outside, the wind was blowing through the trees in the yard, flattening the purple clumps of wisteria that grew against the barn wall.

'Each of you go to the hedge and cut the switch you want me to use on you,' she said.

It was her favorite form of punishment. If they broke off a large switch, she hit them fewer times with it. If they came back with a thin or small switch, they would get whipped until she felt she had struck some kind of balance between size and number.

They remained motionless. Drew had been playing with her cat. She had tied a piece of twine around the cat's neck, and she held the twine in her hand like a leash, her knees and white socks dusty from play.

'I told you not to tie that around the kitten's neck again,' Mattie said.

'It doesn't hurt anything. It's not your cat, anyway,' Weldon said.

'Don't sass me,' she said. 'You will not sass me. None of you will sass me.'

'I ain't cutting no switch,' Weldon said. 'You're crazy. My mama said so. You ought to be in the crazy house.'

She looked hard into Weldon's eyes, and there was a moment of recognition in her colorless face, as though she had seen a growing meanness of spirit in Weldon that was the equal of her own. Then she wet her lips, crimped them together, and rubbed her hands on her thighs.

'We shall see who does what around here,' she said. She broke off a big switch from the myrtle hedge and raked it free of flowers and leaves except for one green sprig on the tip.

Drew looked up into Mattie's shadow, and dropped the piece of twine from her palm.

Mattie jerked her by the wrist and whipped her a half-dozen times across her bare legs. Drew twisted impotently from Mattie's fist, her feet dancing with each blow. The switch raised welts on her skin as thick and red as centipedes.

Then suddenly Weldon ran with all his weight into Mattie's back, stiff-arming her between the shoulder blades, and sent her tripping sideways over a bucket of chicken slops. She righted herself and stared at him open-mouthed, the switch loose in her hand. Then her eyes grew hot and bright with a painful intention, and her jawbone flexed like a roll of dimes.

Weldon burst out the back gate and ran down the dirt road between the sugarcane fields, the soles of his dirty tennis shoes powdering dust in the air.

She waited for him a long time, watching through the screen as the mauve-colored dusk gathered in the trees and the sun's afterglow lit with flame the clouds on the western horizon. Then she took a bottle of apricot brandy into the bathroom and sat in the tub for almost an hour, turning the hot-water tap on and off until the tank was empty. When the children needed to go to the bathroom, she told them to take their problem outside. Finally she emerged in the hall, wearing only her panties and bra, her hair wrapped in a towel, the dark outline of her pubic hair plainly visible.

'I'm going to dress now and go into town with a gentleman friend,' she said. 'Tomorrow we're going to start a new regime around here. Believe me, there will never be a recurrence of what happened here today. You can pass that on to young Mr Weldon for me.'

But she didn't go into town. Instead, she put on her blue suit, a flower-print blouse, her nylon stockings, and walked up and down on the gallery, her cigarette poised in the air like a movie actress.

'Why not just drive your car, Mattie?' Lyle said quietly through the screen.

'It has no gas. Besides, a gentleman caller will be passing for me anytime now,' she answered.

'Oh.'

She blew smoke at an upward angle, her face aloof and flat-sided in the shadows.

303

'Mattie?'

'Yes?'

'Weldon's out back. Can he come in the house?'

'Little mice always return where the cheese is,' she said.

At that moment Lyle wanted something terrible to happen to her.

She turned on one high heel, her palm supporting one elbow, her cigarette an inch from her mouth, her hair wreathed in smoke.

'Do you have a reason for staring through the screen at me?' she asked.

'No,' he said.

'When you're bigger, you'll get to do what's on your mind. In the meantime, don't let your thoughts show on your face. You're a lewd little boy.'

Her suggestion repelled him and made water well up in his eyes. He backed away from the screen, then turned and ran through the rear of the house and out into the backyard, where Weldon and Drew sat against the barn wall, fireflies lighting in the wisteria over their heads.

No one came for Mattie that evening. She sat in the stuffed chair in her room, putting on layers of lipstick until her mouth had the crooked bright-red shape of a clown's. She smoked a whole package of Chesterfields, constantly wiping the ashes off her dark-blue skirt with a hand towel soaked in dry-cleaning fluid; then she drank herself unconscious.

It was hot that night, and dry lightning leaped from the horizon to the top of the blue-black vault of sky over the Gulf. Weldon sat on the side of his bed in the dark, his shoulders hunched, his fists between his white thighs. His chopped haircut looked like feathers on his head in the flicker of lightning through the window. When Lyle was almost asleep Weldon shook him awake and said, 'We've got to get rid of her. You know we got to do it.'

Lyle put his pillow over his head and rolled away from him, as though he could drop away into sleep and rise in the morning into a sun-spangled and different world.

But in the false dawn he woke to Weldon's face close to his. Weldon's eyes were hollow, his breath rank with funk. The mist was heavy and wet in the pecan trees outside the window.

'She's not gonna hurt Drew again. Are you gonna help or not?' he said.

Lyle followed him into the hallway, his heart sinking at the realization of what he was willing to participate in. Mattie slept in the stuffed chair, her hose rolled down over her knees, an overturned jelly glass on the rug next to the can of spot cleaner.

Weldon walked quietly across the rug, unscrewed the cap on the can, laid the can on its side in front of Mattie's feet, then backed away from her. The cleaning fluid spread in a dark circle around her chair, the odor as bright and sharp as white gas.

Weldon slid open a box of kitchen matches, and they each took one, raked it across the striker, and, with the sense that their lives at that moment had changed forever, threw them at Mattie's feet. But the burning matches fell outside of the wet area. Lyle jerked the box from Weldon's hand, clutched a half dozen matches in his fist, dragged them across the striker, and flung them right on Mattie's feet.

The chair was enveloped in a cone of flame, and she burst out of it with her arms extended, as though she were pushing blindly through a curtain, her mouth and eyes wide with terror. They could smell her hair burning as she raced past them and crashed through the screen door out on to the gallery and into the yard. She beat at her flaming clothes and raked at her hair as though it was swarming with yellow jackets.

Lyle and Weldon stood transfixed in mortal dread at what they had done.

A Negro man walking to work came out of the mist on the road and knocked her to the ground, slapping the fire out of her dress, pinning her under his spread knees as though he were assaulting her. Smoke rose from her scorched clothes and hair as in a depiction of a damned figure on a holy card.

The Negro got to his feet and walked toward the gallery, a solitary line of blood running down his black cheek where Mattie had scratched him.

'Yo' mama ain't hurt bad. Go get some butter or some bacon grease. It gonna be fine, you gonna see,' he said. 'Don't be shakin' like that. Where yo' daddy at? It gonna be just fine. You little white children ain't got to worry about nothing.'

He smiled to assure them that everything would be all right.

'They put her in the crazy house at Mandeville,' Lyle said, his face turned into the warm breeze off the bayou. 'She died there about ten years later, I heard.'

'And you've felt guilty about it all this time?' I asked.

'Not really.'

'No?'

'We were kids. Nobody would help us. It was her or us. Besides, I think my sins are forgiven.'

'I don't know what to tell you, Lyle. I just don't believe that your father has reappeared after all these years to do y'all harm. People just don't come back after that long for revenge.'

He sipped from his bottle and shook his head sadly.

'The son of a buck was evil. If ever Satan took a human form, it was my old man,' he said.

'Well, I'll have a talk with Drew about the intruder. But I want to ask you something else while we're out here.'

'Go ahead. I got no secrets.'

'If you really did get religion, was it because of something that happened in Vietnam that I don't know about?'

The oil wells clanked up and down in the unplowed field, which was now pink in the sun's afterglow.

'You think maybe you had something to do with it?' he asked. 'Don't give yourself too much credit, Dave.'

He snuffed dryly and touched at his nostrils with one knuckle.

'I killed a nun,' he said.

'You did what?'

'I never told you about it. I climbed down into what I thought was a spider hole, but one tunnel went off into a room that they must have used as an aid station because there were bloody field dressings all over the floor. I saw something go across the door, and I opened up. It was a nun, a white woman. There were two of them in there. The other one was huddled up against the wall, trembling all over. They must have been from the school in the ville. You remember there were some French nuns in that one ville?'

I nodded silently.

'When I climbed back up, Charlie started firing from the ville and the captain called in the arty,' he said. 'Then we were all hauling butt. You remember? It was short. That's when Martinez got it. So I just never said anything about it. The next day we got into that minefield. I couldn't keep it all straight in my head anymore.'

'It wasn't your fault, Lyle. You were a good soldier.'

'No, I told you before, I dug it down there. The ragin' Cajun, sliding down the tunnel to give Charlie a red-hot enema. What a hand job.'

'I'll give you some advice someone once gave me. Get Vietnam out of your life. We already fought one war. Let the people who made it grieve on it.'

'I don't grieve. I believe I've been reborn. I don't care if you accept that or not. I give those people out there something they ain't found anyplace else. And I couldn't give it to them unless God gave it to me first. And if He gave it to me, that means I've been forgiven.'

'What is it you give them?'

'Power. A chance to be what they're not. They wake up scared every morning of their lives. I show them it doesn't have to be that way anymore. I grew up uneducated, in foster homes, hustled drugs on the street, spent time in a couple of jails, washed dishes for a living with this crippled hand. But the man on high got my attention, and, son, I ain't did bad . . . Sorry, that word's just one I can't seem to get away from.'

'That sounds a little bit vain, Lyle.'

'I never said I was perfect. Look, make me one promise. Watch out for my sister. I suspect you've got personal feelings toward her anyway, don't you?'

'I'm not sure I know what you mean.'

'She said you poked her when y'all were in college.'

I looked at the side of his face, the scars that leaked from one eye, then I gazed at the bayou and a black man fishing in a pirogue and drummed my fingers on the leather seat.

'I'd better get home now,' I said. 'The next time you have information for me, I'd appreciate your bringing it to me at my office.'

'Don't get bent out of shape. Drew made it with a lot of guys. So you were one of them. Why pretend you were born fifty years old?'

'I changed my mind. I really don't need a ride all the way home, Lyle. Just drop me at the four-corners. I'm going to ask Bootsie to come in town for some crawfish.'

'Whatever you want, Loot.' He screwed the cap on his whiskey bottle, dropped it on the seat, and started the engine. 'You might think I have a head full of spiders, but if I do, I don't try to hide them from anybody. You get my meaning?'

'I want you to take this in the right spirit, Lyle. You don't have the franchise on guilt about Vietnam, and you're not the only guy who had his life set back on track by some power outside himself. I think the problem here is peddling it to other people for money.'

'You ever see a bishop drive a Volkswagen?'

'I'll get off right there at the corner. Thanks very much for the evening.'

I stepped out on to the gravel road, closed the car door, and walked toward a clapboard bar that vibrated with the noise from inside. Lyle's fire-engine-red convertible grew small in the distance, then disappeared in the purple shadows between the sugarcane fields.

I had to wait to use the pay phone in the bar, and I drank a 7 Up at a table in the corner and watched a drunk black-haired girl in blue jeans dance by herself in front of the bandstand. Her undulating, slim body was haloed in cigarette smoke.

I hadn't meant to be self-righteous with Lyle. I truly felt for him and his family and what they had endured at the hands of the father and the prostitute named Mattie, but Lyle also made me angry in a way that I couldn't quite describe to myself. It wasn't simply that he pandered to an audience of ignorant and fearful people or that he misused the money they gave him; it went even deeper than that. Maybe it was the fact that Lyle had truly been inside the fire storm, had seen human behavior at its worst and best, had made a mistake down in a tunnel that perhaps beset his conscience with a level of pain that could only be compared to having one's skin ripped off in strips with a pair of pliers. And he sold it all as cheaply as you might market the plastic flowers that adorned the stage of his live TV show.

Yes, that was it, I thought. He had made a meretricious enterprise out of an experience that you share with no one except those who've been there, too. I don't believe that's an elitist attitude, either. There are events you witness, or in which you participate, that forever remain sacrosanct and inviolate in memory, no matter how painful that memory is, because of the cost that you or others paid in order to be there in that moment when the camera lens clicked shut.

How do you tell someone that a drunk blue-collar girl dancing in a low-rent Louisiana bar, her black hair curled around her neck like a rope, makes you remember a dead Vietnamese girl on a trail three klicks from her village? She wore sandals, floppy black shorts, a white blouse, and she lay on her back, with one leg folded under her, her eyes closed as though in sleep, the only disfiguration in her appearance a dried stream of blood that curled from the corner of her mouth like a red snake. Why was she there? I don't know. Was she killed by American or enemy fire? I don't know that either. I only remember that at the time I wanted to see a weapon near her person, to believe that she was one of *them*. But there was no weapon, and in all probability she was simply a schoolgirl returning from visiting someone in another village when she was killed.

That was my third day in-country. That was twenty-six years ago. I had news for Lyle. He might be honest about the spiders crawling around in his head, but he wouldn't get rid of them by trying to sell them through a television tube. You offer them the real thing, Brother Lyle, you tell them the real story about what happened over there, and they'll put you in a cage and take out your brains with an ice cream scoop.

6

The next morning I telephoned Drew to ask her about the intruder in her kitchen, but there was no answer, and later when I went by her house she wasn't home. I stuck my business card in the corner of her screen door.

As I drove back down East Main under the oaks that arched over the street, I saw her jogging along the sidewalk in a T-shirt and a pair of purple shorts, her tan skin glistening with sweat. She raised her arm and waved at me, her breasts big and round against her shirt, but I didn't stop. She could call me if she wanted to, I told myself.

I drove home for lunch and stopped my pickup at the mailbox on the dirt road at the foot of my property. Among the letters and bills was a heavy brown envelope with no postage and my name written across it with no address. I cut the engine, sorted out the junk mail, then sliced open the brown envelope with my pocket knife. Inside were a typed letter and twenty one-hundred dollar bills. The letter read:

> We think this fell out of your pocket in Weldon Sonnier's house. We think you should have it back. The cop in the basement was an accident. Nobody wanted it that way. He could have walked out of it but he wanted to be a hard guy. Sonnier is a welsher and a prick. If you want to be his knothole, that's your choice. But we think you should mark off all this bullshit and stay in New Iberia. What you've got here is two large with more down the road, maybe some business opportunities too, if we get the right signals. Let Sonnier drown in his own shit. If you don't want the money, blow your nose on it. It's all the same to us. We just wanted to offer you an intelligent alternative to being Sonnier's main local fuck.

I replaced the hundred-dollar bills and the letter in the envelope, put the envelope in my back pocket, and walked down to the dock. Batist was squatted down on the boards in the sunlight, scaling a stringer of bluegill with a spoon. The sun was hot off the water, and sweat coursed down between the shoulder blades of his bare back.

'Did you see someone besides the postman up by the mailbox?' I asked.

309

He squinted his eyes in the glare and thought for a moment. The backs of his hands were shiny with fish mucus.

'A man pass by on a motorsickle,' he said.

'Did he stop?'

'Yeah, I t'ink he stopped. Yeah, he sho' did.'

'What did he look like?'

'I ain't real sure. I ain't paid him much mind, Dave. Somet'ing wrong?'

'It's nothing to worry about.'

Batist tapped his spoon on the dock.

'I 'member he was dressed funny,' he said. 'He didn't have no shirt but he wore them t'ings on his pants, what you call them t'ings, you see them in the movies.'

I tried to visualize what he meant, but I was at a loss, as I often was when I tried to talk with Batist in either English or French.

'What movies?' I said.

'The cowboy movies.'

'Chaps? Big leather floppy things that fit over the legs?'

'Yeah, that's it. They was black, and he had tattoos on his back. And he had long hair, too.'

'What kind of tattoos?'

'I don't 'member that.'

'Okay, partner. That's not bad.'

'What ain't bad?'

'Nothing. Don't worry about it.'

'Worry about what?'

'Nothing. I'm going up to the house for lunch now. If you see this guy again, call me. But don't mess with him. Okay?'

'This is a bad guy?'

'Maybe.'

'This is a bad guy, but Batist ain't suppose to worry, no. You somet'ing else, Dave. Lord, if you ain't.'

He went back to scraping the fish with his spoon. I started to speak again, but I had learned long ago to leave Batist alone when I had offended him by underestimating his perception of a situation.

I walked up to the house, and Bootsie and I ate lunch on the redwood table under the mimosa tree in the backyard. She wore a flowered sundress, and had put on lipstick and earrings, which she seldom did in the middle of the day.

'How do you like the sandwich?' she said.

'It's really good.' It was, too. Ham and onion and horseradish, one of my favorites.

'Did something happen today?'

'No, not really.'

'Nothing happened?'

'Somebody put some money in our mailbox. It's a bribery attempt. Batist thinks it was a guy on a motorcycle. Somebody with riding chaps and tattoos on his back. So kind of look out for him, although I doubt he'll be back.'

'Is this about Weldon Sonnier?'

'Yeah, I think Clete and I shook up somebody's cookie bag when we went to Bobby Earl's house.'

'You think Bobby Earl's trying to bribe you?'

'No, he's slicker than that. It's probably coming from somewhere else, maybe somebody who's connected with him. I'm not sure.'

'You got a call from Drew Sonnier.'

'Oh?'

'Why did she call here, Dave?'

'I left my card at her house this morning.'

'At her house. I see.'

'Lyle said somebody broke into her house.'

'Doesn't that involve the city police, not the sheriff's department?'

'She didn't report it to them.'

'I see. So you're investigating?'

I looked at the mallards splashing on the pond at the back of our property.

'I promised Lyle I'd talk to her.'

'Lyle made you promise? Is that right? I had the impression that you had a low opinion of Lyle.'

'Ease up, Boots. This case is a pain in the butt as it is.'

'I'm sure that it is. Why don't we ask Drew over sometime? I haven't seen her in a long time.'

'Because I'm not interested in seeing Drew.'

'I think she's very nice. I've always been fond of her.'

'What should I do, Boots? Pretend she's not part of this case?'

'Why should you do that? I don't think you should do that at all.'

I could see the peculiar cast coming into her eyes, as though inside her head she had seen a thought or a conclusion that should have been as obvious to the rest of the world as it was to her.

'Let's go to the track tonight,' I said.

'Let's do. Will you call her this afternoon? I think you should.'

I tried to read what was in her eyes. The mood swings, the distorted and fearful perception, took place sometimes as quickly as a bird flying in and out of a cage.

'I might talk to her,' I said, and put my hand on top of hers, 'but I don't think she'll be much help in the case. The Sonniers don't trust other people. But I have to try to do what I can.'

'Of course you do, Dave. Nobody said otherwise.' And she looked off at the periwinkles blowing in the shade next to the coulee. The light in her eyes was as private as a solitary candle burning in a church.

'We'll take Alafair to Possum's for *étoufée* before we go to the track,' I said. 'Or maybe we can just come home and rent a movie.'

'That would be wonderful.'

'The sandwiches were really good. It's sure nice to come home and have lunch with you, Boots. Maybe after I close the drawer on this case, I might take leave of the department. We're doing pretty well at the dock.'

'Don't fool yourself. You'll never stop being a cop, Dave.'

I looked into her eyes again, and they were suddenly clear, as though the breeze had blown a dark object away from her line of vision.

I squeezed her hand, rose from the wood bench, and went around behind her and kissed her hair and hugged her against me. I could feel her heart beating under my arms.

At the office I gave the sheriff the envelope containing the two thousand dollars and the unsigned letter.

'It must be a cheap outfit,' he said. 'You'd think they'd pay a little more to get a cop on the pad.'

He had run a dry-cleaning business before he became sheriff. He was also a Boy Scout master and belonged to the Lions Club, not for political reasons but because he thoroughly enjoyed being a Scoutmaster and belonging to the Lions Club. He was a thoughtful and considerate man, and I always hated to correct him or to suggest that his career as an elected police officer would probably always consist of on-the-job training.

'Seduction usually comes a teaspoon at a time,' I said. 'Sometimes a cop who won't take fifty grand will take two. Then one day you find yourself way down the road and you don't remember where you made a hard left turn.'

He wore large rimless glasses, and his stomach swelled over his gunbelt. Through the window behind his desk I could see two black trusties from the parish jail washing petrol cars in the parking lot. He scratched the red and blue veins in his soft cheek with his fingernail.

'Who do you think it came from?' he asked.

'Somebody with long-range plans, somebody who's always looking around to buy a cop. Probably the mob or somebody in it.'

'Not from Bobby Earl?'

'His kind only pay out money when you catch them sodomizing sheep. I'm pretty sure we're dealing with the wiseguys now.'

'What do you think they'll do next?'

'If I stay out of New Orleans, there will probably be another envelope. Then they'll offer me a job providing security in one of their nightclubs or in a counting room at the track.'

He put an unlit cigarette in his mouth and rotated it with his fingers. 'I've got a bad feeling about all this,' he said. 'I surely do.'

'Why?'

'Don't underestimate Bobby Earl's potential. I met him a couple of times ten or twelve years ago, when he was still appearing in Klan robes. This guy could make the ovens sing and grin while he was doing it.'

'Maybe. But I never met one of those guys who wasn't a physical and moral coward.'

'I saw Garrett's body before the autopsy. It was hard to look at, and I was in Korea. Watch your butt, Dave.'

His eyes were unblinking over his rimless glasses.

By two P.M. it was ninety-five degrees outside; the sunlight off the cement was as bright as a white flame; the palm trees looked dry and desiccated in the hot wind; and my own day was just warming up.

I called Drew again and this time she answered. I was ready to argue with her, to lecture her about her and Weldon's lack of cooperation in the case, even blame her for my difficulties with Bootsie at lunch. In fact, my opening statement was 'Who was the guy in your kitchen, Drew, and why didn't you report it?'

I could hear her breathing in the receiver.

'Lyle told you?' she said.

'As well as Lyle can tell me anything, without trying to sell glow-in-the-dark Bibles at the same time. I'll tell you the truth, Drew, I've pretty well had it with your family's attitude. I don't want to be unkind, but the three of you behave like y'all have been shooting up with liquid Drano.'

She was quiet again, then I heard her begin to weep.

'Drew?'

But she continued to cry without answering, the kind of unrelieved and subdued sobbing that comes from deep down in the breast.

'Drew, I apologize. I've had some bad concerns on my mind and I was taking them out on you. I'm truly sorry for what I said. It was thoughtless and stupid.'

I squeezed my temples with my thumb and forefinger.

'Drew?'

I heard her swallow and take a deep breath.

'Sometimes I'm not very smart,' I said. 'You know I've always admired you. You have more political courage than anybody I've ever known.'

'I don't know what to do. I've always had choices before. Now I don't. I can't deal with that.'

'I don't understand.'

'Sometimes you get caught. Sometimes there's no way out. I've never let that happen to me.'

313

'Do you want to come into the office? Do you want me to come out there? Tell me what you want to do.'

'I don't know what I want to do.'

'I'm going to come over there now. Is that all right?'

'I have to take the maid home, and I promised to stop by the market with her. Can you come out about four?'

'Sure.'

'You don't mind?'

'No, of course not.'

'It doesn't make you uncomfortable?'

'No, not at all. That's silly. Don't think that way.'

After I had hung up the phone, I looked wanly at the damp imprint of my hand on the receiver. Were her tears for her brother or herself, I wondered. But then what right had I to be judgmental?

Oh Lord, I thought.

I was almost out the door when the dispatcher caught me in the hallway.

'Pick up your line,' he said. 'A sergeant in the First District in New Orleans has been holding for you.'

'Take a message. I'll call him back.'

'You'd better get it, Dave. He says somebody stomped the shit out of Cletus Purcel.'

After I had finished talking with the sergeant in New Orleans, who had not been the investigative officer and who couldn't tell me much other than Clete's room number in the hospital off St Charles and the fact that Clete wanted to see me, that somebody had worked him over bad with a piece of pipe, I told the dispatcher to send a uniformed deputy out to Drew's house and to call Bootsie and tell her that I would be home late and would call her from New Orleans.

The wind was hot through my truck windows as I drove across the causeway over the Atchafalaya marsh. The air tasted like brass, like it was full of ozone, and I could smell dead fish on the banks of the willow islands and the odor of brine off the Gulf. The willows looked wilted in the heat, and the few fishermen who were out had pulled their boats into the warm shade of the oil platforms that dotted the bays.

I thought of an event, a low moment in my life, that had occurred almost fifteen years ago. I had been sent to Las Vegas to pick up a prisoner at the county jail and escort him back to New Orleans. But the paperwork and the court clearance had taken almost two days, and I walked in disgust from the courthouse down a palm-lined boulevard in 115-degree heat to a casino and cool bar, where I began drinking a series of vodka collinses as though they were soda pop. Then I had a blackout and seven hours disappeared from my day. I woke up in a rented car out on the desert about 10 P.M., my head and body numb and devoid of feeling and connection with the day as if I had been stunned from crown to sole with novocaine, the distant neon city blazing in the purple cup of mountains.

There was blood on my shirt and my knuckles, and a woman's compact was on the floor. My wallet was gone, along with my money, traveler's checks, credit cards, identification, and finally my shield and my .38 special. I remembered nothing except walking from the bar to a twenty-one table with my drink in my hand and sitting among a polite group of players from Ocala, Florida.

I drove trembling back to the hotel and tried to drink myself sober with room-service Jim Beam. By midnight I went into the DTs and believed that the red message light on my phone meant that once again I had received a long-distance call from the dead members of my platoon. When I finally became rational enough to pick up the receiver and talk to the desk clerk, I was told that I had a message from Cletus Purcel.

I had to use both hands to dial his number, while the sweat slid out of my hair and down the sides of my face. Six hours later he was standing in my hotel room in his Budweiser shorts, sandals, porkpie hat, and cutoff LSU T-shirt that looked like a tank top on a hippo.

He sat on the side of the bed and listened to my story again, chewing gum, nodding, looking between his knees at the floor; then he left and didn't come back until three in the afternoon. When he did, he dropped a paper sack on the dresser and said, smiling, 'Time to pick up our prisoner and boogie on down the road. The Chinese broad got away with your traveler's checks, but I got your money, credit cards, your shield, and your piece back. The American guy working with her is heading back to the Coast by Greyhound to make some long-range dental plans. He's looking forward to it, he said. There's no paperwork on this one, mon.'

'What Chinese? What are you talking about?'

'She and her pimp picked you up in a parking lot outside a bar at the end of the Strip. You were too drunk to start your car. They said they'd drive you back to the hotel. You're lucky he didn't put a shank in you. I took a gut ripper off him that must have been eight inches long.'

'I don't remember any of it.' My hands still felt thick and wooden when I tried to open and close them.

'Sometimes you lose. Forget it. Come on, let's eat a steak and blow this shithole. I think they got the architects for this place out of a detox center.'

Then he looked at me quietly, and I saw the pity and concern in his eyes.

'You dropped your brains in a jar of alcohol for a few hours,' he said. 'Big deal. When I worked Vice I got rolled by one of my own snitches.

Plus she gave me the gon. What bothers me is I think I knew she had it when I got in the sack with her.'

He grinned and blew a stream of cigarette smoke into the stale refrigerated air.

That was my old partner before whiskey and uppers and shylocks made him a fugitive from his own police department.

His face whitened when he tried to sit farther up in bed and reach the water glass and the glass straw on the nightstand.

'Don't try to move around with broken ribs, Clete,' I said, and handed him the glass.

His green eyes were red along the rims, and they blinked like a bird's while he sucked on the straw with the corner of his mouth. Divots of hair had been shaved out of his head, and his scalp was sewn with butterfly stitches in a half-dozen places.

'Man, what a drag,' he said. 'They say I'm supposed to be in here two more days. I don't think I can cut it. You ought to see my night nurse. She looks like the Beast of Buchenwald. She tried to shove a thermometer up my butt while I was asleep.'

'They hit you with pipes?'

'No, the little guy had brass knuckles, and Jack Gates, the guy I made for sure, had a baton.'

'The cop I talked to said they beat you up with pipes.'

'Then they got it wrong in the report. They sound like the same incompetent guys we used to work with.'

'How'd they get into your apartment?'

'Picked the lock, I guess. Anyway, Jack Gates was behind the door when I walked in. He caught me right across the ear with the baton. Damn, those things hurt. I crashed right over my new TV set. Then that little fuck was all over me. The last thing I remember I was falling through the furniture, trying to get my piece untangled from my coat, those brass knuckles bouncing off my head, and Gates trying to get a clear swing to take me off at the neck. That's when I grabbed him around the head and tore the stocking off his face. The first thing I saw was all the metal in his teeth. Then it was lights out for Cletus. That sawed-off little fart caught me right at the base of the skull.

'It was just like you said, Gates has a scrap yard for a mouth. I should have made the connection before. He was a button man for Joey Gouza, but I heard he moved to Fort Lauderdale or Hallendale two or three years ago and got ice-picked by a chippy or something. But it was Jack Gates, mon, a real barf bucket. I heard Joey Gouza caught his brother-in-law skimming off his whores, so he told Gates to create an object lesson. The brother-in-law was a big, soft mushy guy who couldn't climb a stairs without pulling himself up the banister with both hands. Gates wined and dined him at Copland's, got him stinking drunk, and kept telling him about these hot-assed Mexican broads over in Galveston. So the tub got his ovaries fired up, and Gates drove them out to a private airport in Kenner, all the time telling the tub what these broads would do for his sex life. Then ole Jack walked him out to the runway, lit a cigar for him, and pushed him into an airplane propeller.'

'You think he's working for Gouza now?'

'He's got to be. You don't resign from Joey Meatballs. It's a lifetime job.'

'Where'd he get that name?'

'His old man ran a spaghetti place on Felicity. In fact, Joey still owns three or four Italian restaurants around town. But the story is when he was a kid in the reformatory a redneck guard made Joey cook him meatballs all the time. Except Joey would always spit in them or mash up dead cockroaches in them. Have you ever seen him? His mother must have been knocked up by a street lamp.'

'The little guy with the brass knuckles is probably Fluck, right?'

'Maybe. But a nylon stocking makes everybody look like Cream of Wheat. All I can tell you is I think he wanted to take my eyes out . . . Why are you looking like that?'

'I got you into this, Clete.'

'No, you didn't. It was my idea to go out to Bobby Earl's and pull on his tallywhacker. But I was right about the connection between Earl and Gouza, wasn't I? I told you that flunky at the gate used to be a mule for Gouza. I think we've got the ultimate daisy chain of Louisiana buttwipes here – Klansmen, Nazis, and wise-guys.'

'You took the beating for me.'

'Bullshit.'

'You haven't heard it all. I received a bribe attempt earlier today. A couple of grand in my mailbox, a letter suggesting I spend a lot of time around New Iberia.'

'Ah,' he said. The streetcar rattled down the tracks on St Charles. 'The carrot and the stick.'

'I think so.'

'And I got the stick.'

'They don't like to beat up cops.'

'They did something else too, Dave, maybe a signal for you about their future potential. After they laid me out, they sprinkled a bagful of rainbows and black beauties all over the room to make it look like a drug deal gone sour. I cleaned them up before I called the First District . . . Dave, I don't like what I'm seeing on your face.'

'What's that?'

'Like you got a piece of barbed wire behind your eyes. You get those thoughts out of your head.'

'You're mistaken.'

'Like hell I am. Ole Streak turns on the Mixmaster and almost drives himself crazy with his own thoughts, then goes out and strikes a match to their balls. You wait till I'm out of here and we'll 'front these guys together. Are we straight on that, podjo?'

I looked at the square of sunlight on his sheets. The palm trees outside the window lifted and straightened in the breeze.

'I'm not supposed to be a player?' he said.

'You want me to bring you anything?'

'Don't go up against Gouza on your own. An Iberia sheriff's badge is puppy shit to these guys.'

'What do you want me to bring you?'

'My piece. It's in a little sock drawer under my bed.' He took his keys off the nightstand and dropped them in my palm. 'There's also a fifth of vodka and a carton of cigarettes on the kitchen counter.'

'I'll be back in a little while.'

'Dave?'

'Yes?'

'Gouza's a weird combo. He's got an ice cube in the center of his head when it comes to business, but he's also a sadistic paranoid. A lot of the greaseballs in this town are scared shitless of him.'

I drove to Clete's apartment on Dumaine in the Quarter, put his .38 revolver and shoulder holster, his vodka and cigarettes in a paper bag and was walking back down the balcony when I saw the apartment manager sweeping dust out his doorway through the railing into the courtyard below. He was a dark-skinned, black-haired man with bad teeth and turquoise eyes. I opened my badge and asked him if he had seen the men who had beaten Clete.

'Yeah, sho' I seen them. I seen them run down the stairs,' he said. He had a heavy Cajun accent.

I asked him what they looked like.

'One man, I didn't see him too good, no, he walked on down Dumaine. I didn't pay him no mind 'cause I didn't know nothing was wrong, me. But there was a little one, a blond-haired fella, he pushed by me on the stair and run out on the street and got on a motorcycle wit' another fella.'

'What did this fellow on the motorcycle look like?'

'Big,' he said. Then he tapped on his biceps with one finger. 'He had a tattoo. A tiger. It was yellow and red. I seen it real good 'cause I didn't like that little fella pushing me on the stair.'

'Who'd you tell this to?'

'I ain't said nothing to nobody.'

'Why not?'

'Ain't nobody ax me.'

After I dropped off the paper sack with Clete's gun, cigarettes, and vodka at the hospital, the sun was low in the sky, red through the oak trees on St Charles Avenue, and swallows were circling in the dusk. I checked into an inexpensive guesthouse on Prytania, just two blocks off St Charles, and called Bootsie and told her that I would have to stay over and that I would be home tomorrow afternoon.

'What is it?' she asked.

'I have to run down a couple of things. It's grunt work mostly. Will you be all right?'

'Yes. Of course.'

'Are you all right, Boots?'

'Yes. Everything's fine this evening. It was hot today, but it's cooling off this evening. It might rain tonight. There's lightning out over the marsh.'

I could feel the day's fatigue in my body. I closed and widened my eyes. The long-distance hum in the telephone receiver was like wet sand in my ear.

'Would you call the dispatcher for me?' I said.

'All right. Don't worry about anything, Dave. We're just fine.'

After I hung up I said a prayer to my Higher Power to watch over my home in my absence, then I called Clarise, an elderly mulatto woman who had worked for my family since I was a child, and asked her to look in on Bootsie that evening and to return in the morning to do house chores.

I showered in a tin stall with water that was so cold it left me breathless, put back on the same clothes I had worn all day, ate a plate of rice, red beans, and sausage at Fat Albert's on St Charles, then began a neon-lit odyssey through the biker bars of Jefferson and Orleans parishes.

It's a strange, atavistic, and tribal world to visit. Individually its members are usually hapless, bumbling creatures who were born out of luck and whose largest successes usually consist of staying out of jail, paying off their bondsmen, and keeping their appointments with their probation officers and welfare workers. It's probably not coincidence that most of them are ugly and stupid. But collectively they are both frightening and a source of fascination for those who wonder what it might be like if they traded off their routine and predictable lives for a real fling out on the ragged edge.

The first bar I hit was one out on Airline Highway. Think of a shale parking lot covered with chopped-down Harleys whose chrome and lacquered-black surfaces seem to glow with a nocturnal iridescence; a leather jackboot stomping down on a starter pedal, the ear-splitting roar of straight exhaust pipes, the tinkle of a beer bottle flung through the limbs of an oak tree, a man urinating loudly on the shale in front of a pickup truck's headlights, his muscular, blue-jean-clad legs spread with the visceral self-satisfaction of a gladiator; the inside of a clapboard building crowded with men in sleeveless Levi jackets, boots sheathed with metal plates, black leather cutouts that etch the genitals and flap on the legs like a gunfighter's chaps; bodies strung with chains and iron crosses, covered with hair and tattoos of swastikas and snakes with human skulls inserted between the fangs; an odor of chewing tobacco, snuff, cigarette smoke rubbed like wet nicotine into the clothes, grease and motor oil, reefer, and a faint hint of testosterone and dried semen.

I was sure that the man with the tiger tattoo who had ridden away from Clete's apartment was Eddy Raintree, but he was not the same biker who had put the bribe money in my mailbox. Which meant that in all probability there was a connection between bikers, the Aryan Brotherhood, ex-convicts, and Bobby Earl or Joey Gouza. It made sense. Most outlaw bikers I had known were sexual fascists, and they were always seeking new and defenseless targets for the anger and dark blood that were trapped in their loins like throbbing birds.

But I got virtually nowhere at the bar on Airline Highway or at any of the other bars I cruised until 3 A.M. No one knew Eddy Raintree, had ever heard of him, or even thought his photograph vaguely familiar. But at the last place I visited, a narrow brick poolroom that used to be run by blacks between two warehouses across the river in Algiers, a drunk woman at the bar let me buy her a bowl of chili, and in her sad way she tried to be helpful.

Her hair was platinum, dark at the scalp, and the number 69 was tattoed on her arm. She wore a sleeveless yellow T-shirt with no bra, and a pair of Clorox-faded Levi's that hung as low as a bikini on her hips. (I had never been able to understand the women who hung with outlaw bikers, because with some regularity they were gang-raped, chain-whipped, and had their hands nailed to trees, but they came back for more, obedient, anesthetized, and bored, like spectators at their own dismemberment.)

She kept lifting spoonfuls of chili to her mouth, then forgetting to eat them, her eyes trying to focus on my face and the photograph of Eddy Raintree I held in my palm.

'What do you want with that dumb shit?' she asked. Her words were phlegmatic, like dialogue in a slow-motion film.

'Could you tell me where he is?'

'In jail, probably. Or out fucking goats or something.'

'When did you see him last?'

She drew in on her cigarette and held the smoke down like she was taking a hit off a reefer.

'You don't want to waste your time with a dumb shit like that,' she said.

'I'd really like to talk with Eddy. I'd really appreciate it if you could help me.'

'He's into astronomy or something. He's weird. I've got enough weirdness in my life without a dumb fuck like that.'

Then her boyfriend came back from the men's room. He was huge, with a wild beard, and he wore striped overalls with no shirt. His massive shoulders were ridged with hair; his odor was incredible.

'What do you think you're doing, man?' he said.

'Just finishing my conversation with this lady.'

'It's finished. Good-bye.'

I left two dollars on the bar for the chili and walked back out into the night. The heat of the day had finally lifted from the streets and the cement buildings, the wind was cool blowing from across the river, and I could see the red and green running lights of the oil barges on the water, and the glow of New Orleans against the clouds.

I slept until nine the next morning, had coffee and *beignets* at a cool table under the pavilion at the Café du Monde, and watched the water from the sprinklers click against the piked fence around the park in Jackson Square and drift in a rainbow haze through the myrtle and banana trees. Then I went over to First District headquarters a few blocks away and read Joey Gouza's file. It was another study in institutional failure, the kind of document that makes you doubt your own convictions and conclude that perhaps the right-wing simpletons are correct when they advocate going at social complexities with a chainsaw.

Since age thirteen, he'd had forty-three arrests. He was in the Louisiana reformatory when he was seventeen, he went up the road twice to Angola, and he did a federal three-bit in Lewisburg. He had been arrested for breaking-and-entering, auto theft, assault and battery, possession of burglar tools, armed robbery, strong-arm robbery, sale of stolen food stamps, possession of counterfeit money, procuring, tax fraud, and murder. He was one of those career criminals who early on had gone about investigating and participating in every kind of illegal activity that a city offered. But, unlike most petty thieves, pimps, smalltime fences, and smash-and-grab artists, Joey had gravitated steadily upward in the New Orleans mob and had developed a skill that was at one time revered in the underworld, that of the safecracker. Evidently he had peeled and cut up safes with burnbars in four states, although he had fallen on only one job, a box in a Baton Rouge pawnshop that netted him eighty-six dollars and a two-year jolt in Angola.

He wasn't hard to find. He owned a small Italian café and delicatessen in an old brick, iron-scrolled building shaded by oak trees on Esplanade. The inside smelled of oregano and meat sauce, crab-boil, sautéed shrimp, cheese and salami, the fried oysters and sliced tomatoes and onions that went into the poor-boy sandwiches on the counter, the steamed coffee from the espresso machines. The café was empty except for a black cook, the counterman, and a couple having breakfast at one of the checkercloth tables.

I asked for Joey Gouza.

'He's back in the office. What's the name?' the counterman said.

'Dave Robicheaux.'

'Just a minute.' He walked to the end of the counter and spoke through a half-opened door.

'Who's the guy?' a peculiar thick voice inside said.

'I don't know. Just a guy.' The counterman looked back at me.

'Then ask him who he is,' the voice said.

The counterman looked back at me again. I opened up my badge.

'He's a cop, Joey,' the counterman said.

'Then tell him to come in, for Christ's sake.'

I walked around the counter and through the door. Joey Gouza looked up at me from behind his desk. He was deeply tanned, tall, his face elongated, almost jug-shaped, his salt-and-pepper hair cut military style and brushed up stiffly on his scalp, his eyes as black as wet paint. He wore pleated gray slacks, a lavender polo shirt, ox-blood loafers; a cream-colored panama hat sat crown down on the corner of his desk. His neck was unnaturally long, like a swan's, hung with gold chains and medallions, and his open shirt exposed the web of veins and tendons in his shoulders and chest, like those in a long-distance runner or javelin thrower.

But it was the eyes that got your attention; they were absolutely black and they never blinked. And the voice: the accent was Irish Channel, but with a knot tied in it, as though the vocal cords were coated with infected membrane.

His smile was easy, as relaxed as the matchstick he rolled on his tongue. A fat dark man in a green visor, who smoked a cigar, sat at a card table in the corner, adding up receipts on a calculator.

'I got some unpaid parking tickets again?' Gouza said.

I held my badge out for him to see. 'No, I'm Dave Robicheaux with the Iberia Parish sheriff's office, Mr Gouza. It's just an informal visit. Do you mind if I sit down?'

If he recognized my name, it didn't show in his eyes or his smile.

'Help yourself, if you don't mind me working. We got to get some stuff ready for the tax man.'

'I'm looking for Jack Gates,' I said.

'Who?'

'Or Eddy Raintree.'

'Who?'

'How about Jewel Fluck?'

'*Fluck?* Is this some kind of put-on?'

'Let's start with Jack Gates again. You never heard of him?'

'Nope.'

'That's funny. I heard he fed your brother-in-law into an airplane propeller.'

He took the matchstick out of the corner of his mouth and laughed.

'It's a great story. I've heard it for years. But it's bullshit,' he said. 'My brother-in-law was killed in a plane accident on his way to Disneyland. A great family tragedy.'

The man at the other table was grinning and nodding his head up and down without interrupting his count of receipts. Then Joey Gouza put the matchstick back in his mouth and leaned his chin on his knuckle. His eyes were filled with an amused light as they moved up and down my person.

'You say Iberia Parish?' he said.

'That's right.'

'You guys gave up shaving or something?'

'We're casual out in the parishes. Let's cut to it, Joey. You're an old-time pete man. Why do you want to give Weldon Sonnier a lot of grief?'

'Weldon Sonnier?'

'You don't know him, either?'

'Everybody in New Orleans knows him. He's a bum and a welsher.'

'Who told you that?'

'That's the word. He borrows big dough, but he doesn't come up with the vig. That'll get you into trouble in this town. You saying I'm connected with him or something?'

'You tell me.'

'I know your name from a long time ago. You were at the First District, weren't you?'

'That's right.'

'So I think maybe you heard stories about me. You probably read my rap sheet before you came here this morning, right? You know I've been up the road a couple of times, you know I burned a box or two. You heard that old bullshit story about how I got this voice, how a yard bitch put a capful of Sani-Flush in my coffee cup. How the yard bitch got his cherry split open in the shower two days later? You heard that one, didn't you?'

'Sure.'

He smiled and said, 'No, you didn't, but I'll give it to you free, anyway. The point is it's not true. I was never a big stripe, I did easy time, I made full trusty in every joint I was in. But the big word there is *did*. Past tense. I did my time. I've been straight seven years. Look—'

He bounced his palm on top of a paper spindle and gazed reflectively out the window at some black children skateboarding by under the oaks.

'I'm a businessman,' he continued. 'I own a bunch of restaurants, a linen service, a movie theater, a plumbing business, and half a vending-machine company. Are we on the same wavelength here?'

He flexed his nostrils as though there were an obstruction in them and rubbed the grained skin of his jaw with one finger.

'I'll try again,' he said. 'You said it a minute ago, I was a pete man. I punched, peeled, and burned 'em. I went down for it twice, too. But safecracking became a historical art a long time ago. Today it's all narcotics.'

'Bad stuff?' I smiled back at him.

He shrugged his shoulders and turned his palms up.

'Who am I to judge?' he said. 'But go out to the welfare projects and see who's running the action. They're all colored kids. They scrape out crack pipes, they call it bazooka or something, and sell it for a buck a hit. Nobody who could think his way out of a wet paper bag is gonna try to compete with that.'

'Maybe my information isn't very good. Or maybe I'm a little bit out of touch. But it's my understanding that you've got connections with Bobby Earl, that Jack Gates is a button man for you.'

He leaned back in his chair and looked out the window again. He took the matchstick out of his mouth and dropped it in the waste can.

'I've tried to be polite,' he said. 'You're from out of town, you had some questions, I tried to answer them. You think maybe you're abusing the situation here?'

'I came here to pass on a couple of observations, Joey. When you try to get a cop on a pad and you don't know anything about him, get somebody to lend him money, don't leave it in his mailbox.'

'What are you talking about?'

'The two thousand is in the Iberia Parish sheriff's desk drawer. At the end of the year it'll probably be donated to the city park program.'

He was grinning again.

'You're saying I tried to bribe you? You drove all the way over here to tell me somebody's two thou is wasted on you? That's the big message?'

'Read it like you want.'

'It's been a lot of fun talking to you. Hey, I didn't tell you I own a couple of goony golf courses. You like goony golf? It's catching on here in New Orleans. Hey, Louis, give him a couple of tickets.'

The man with the cigar and green visor was grinning broadly, nodding his head up and down. He took a thick pack of tickets from his shirt pocket, popped two out from under the rubber band, and placed them on the desk in front of me.

Joey Gouza made a pyramid out of his hands and tapped the ends of his fingers together.

'I heard you were an intelligent man, Joey. But it's my opinion you're a stupid shit,' I said.

His eyes went flat, and his face glazed over.

'You fucked with Cletus Purcel. That's probably the worst mistake you ever made in your insignificant life,' I said. 'If you don't believe me, check out what happened to Julio Garcia and his bodyguard a few years back. I think they wished they had stayed in Managua and taken their chances with the Sandinistas.'

'That's supposed to make me rattle? You come in here like you fell out of a dirty-clothes bag, making noise like you got gas or something, and I'm supposed to rattle?' He pointed into his breastbone with four stiff fingers. 'You think I give a fuck about what some pissant PI's gonna do? Tell me serious, I'm supposed to get on the rag because he whacked out a spick nobody in New Orleans would spit on?'

'Clete didn't kill Garcia. His partner did.'

I saw the recognition grow in his eyes.

'Tell those three clowns they're going down for the murder of a sheriff's deputy,' I said. 'Stay out of Iberia Parish. Stay away from Purcel. If you fall again, Joey, I'm going to make sure you go down for the bitch. Four-time loser, mandatory life.'

I flipped the goony golf passes on his shirt front. The man in the green visor sat absolutely still with his cigar dead in his mouth.

7

When I got back to New Iberia I showered, shaved, put on fresh clothes, and ate lunch with Bootsie in the backyard. I should have felt good about the day; it wasn't hot, like yesterday, the trees were loud with birds, the wind smelled of watermelons, the roses in my garden were as big as fists. But my eye registered all the wrong things: a fire burning in the middle of the marsh, where there should have been none; buzzards humped over a dead rabbit in the field, their beaks hooked and yellow and busy with their work; a little boy with an air rifle on the bank of the bayou, taking careful aim at a robin in an oak tree.

Why? Because we were on our way back to the specialist in Lafayette. The treatment of lupus, in our case, had not been a matter of finding the right medication but the right balance. Bootsie needed dosages of corticosteroid to control the disease that fed at her connective tissue, but the wrong dosage resulted in what is called steroid psychosis. For us her treatment had been like trying to spell a word correctly by repeatedly dipping a spoon into alphabet soup.

There were times I felt angry at her, too. She was supposed to avoid the sun, but I often came home from work and found her weeding the flower beds in shorts and a halter. When we went out on the salt to seine for shrimp, she would break her promise and not only leave the cabin but strip nude, dive off the gunnel, and swim toward a distant sandbar, until she was a small speck and I would have to go after her.

We got back from Lafayette at 4 P.M. with a half-dozen new prescriptions in her purse. I sat listlessly on the front porch and stared at the smoke still rising into the sky from the cypress trees burning in the marsh. Why had no one put it out, I thought.

'What's wrong, Dave?' Alafair said.

'Nothing, little guy. How you doing?' I put my arm around her small waist and pulled her against me. She had been riding her horse, and I could smell the sun in her hair and horse sweat in her clothes.

'Why's there a fire out there?'

'Dry lightning probably hit a tree during the night,' I said. 'It'll burn itself out.'

'Can we go buy some strawberries for dessert?'

'I have to go by the office a few minutes. Maybe we'll go to town for some ice cream after supper. How's that?'

'Dave, did the doctor say something bad about Bootsie?'

'No, she's going to be fine. Why do you think that?'

'Why did she do that with those, what d'you call them, those things the doctor gives her?'

'Her prescriptions?'

'Yeah. I saw her dump her purse all over her bed. Then she wadded up all those 'scriptions. When she saw me she put them all back in her purse and went into the bathroom. She kept running the water a long time. I had to go to the bathroom and she wouldn't let me in.'

'Bootsie's sick, little guy. But she'll get better. You just got to do it a day at a time. Hey, hop on my back and let's check up on Batist, then I have to go.'

She walked up on the steps and then climbed like a frog on to my shoulders, and we galloped like horse and rider down to the dock. But it was hard to feign joy or confidence in the moment or the day.

The wind changed, and I could smell the scorched, hot reek of burnt cypress in the marsh.

I drove to the office, talked briefly with the sheriff about my visit to New Orleans, my search through biker bars for Eddy Raintree, and my conversation with Joey Gouza.

'You think he's pulling strings on this one?' the sheriff said.

'He's involved one way or another. I'm just not sure how. He controls all the action in that part of Orleans Parish. The guys who beat up Clete wouldn't have done it without Gouza's orders or permission.'

'Dave, I don't want you putting a stick in Gouza's cage again. If we nail him, we'll do it with a warrant and we'll work through New Orleans PD. He's a dangerous and unpredictable man.'

'The New Orleans families don't go after cops, sheriff. It's an old tradition.'

'Tell that to Garrett.'

'Garrett stumbled into it. In 1890 the Black Hand murdered the New Orleans police chief. A mob broke eleven of them out of the parish prison, hanged two from street lamps, and clubbed and shot the other nine to death. So cops like me get bribe offers and guys like Clete get brass knuckles.'

'Don't start a new precedent.'

I went to check my mailbox next to the dispatcher's office. It was five-fifteen. All I had to do was glance at my mail and thumb through my telephone messages and make one phone call, and I was sure that when Drew picked up the phone she would be calm, perhaps even apologetic for her distraught behavior of yesterday, and I would be on my way home for dinner.

Wrong.

The dispatcher had written Drew's message in blue ink across the first pink slip on the stack: *Dave, don't you give a damn?*

Her house was only two blocks from the drawbridge that I would cross on my way home, I told myself. I would give myself fifteen minutes there. Friendship and the past required a certain degree of obligation, even if it was only a ritualistic act of assurance or kindness, and it had nothing to do with marital fidelity. Nothing, I told myself.

She was barbecuing in the backyard. She was barefoot, and she wore white tennis shorts and a striped blue cotton shirt. Her face looked hot in the smoke, and the back of her tan neck was beaded with perspiration. The picnic table was covered with a flowered tablecloth, and in the middle of it was a washtub filled with crushed ice and long-neck bottles of Jax. The oaks and myrtle trees in the yard were full of fireflies, and through the gray trunks of the cypresses along the bank I could see some kids waterskiing behind a motorboat on Bayou Teche.

'Maybe I dropped by at the wrong time,' I said.

'No, no, it's fine. I'm glad you're here,' she said, waving the smoke away from her face. 'Weldon and Bama are coming over at eight. Stay for supper if you like.'

'Thanks. I have to be getting on in a minute. I'm sorry I didn't get back to you, but I had to go to New Orleans. Did a uniformed deputy come out yesterday?'

'Yes, he read magazines in my living room for three hours.'

She picked up an opened bottle of beer from the table and drank out of it. The bottle was beaded with moisture, and I watched the foam run down inside the neck into her mouth.

'There's some soda in the refrigerator,' she said.

'That's all right.'

She put the bottle in her mouth again and looked at me. I glanced away from her, then picked up a fork and flipped one of the chickens on the grill. The *sauce piquante* flared in the fire and steamed off in the breeze.

'Why didn't you report the break-in, Drew?'

'I don't know who it was. What good would it do?'

'Was it your father?'

'If he's alive, he'd have no interest in me.'

'Do you think it was one of Joey Gouza's people?'

'That gangster in New Orleans?'

'That's right. I have a feeling he and Weldon are on a first-name basis.'

'If I knew who it was, I'd tell you.'

'Cut it out, Drew. You can't get strung out one day, then the next day go back to the deaf-and-dumb routine.'

'I don't like you talking to me like that, Dave.'

'You made a point of relaying your feelings through the dispatcher. It's a small department, Drew. It's a small town.'

'I don't have those kinds of concerns, thank God. I'm sorry if you do.'

She took a bandana from her pocket and wiped the perspiration off the back of her neck. Her face suddenly looked soft and cool in the mauve-colored light off the bayou.

'I wasn't doing very well yesterday,' she said. 'Maybe I shouldn't have called you. I shouldn't have made it so personal, either.'

'Look, when somebody creeps your house, it's for one of two reasons: either to steal from you or do you bodily harm, or perhaps both. When it happens, it frightens you. You feel violated. You want to take everything out of your closets and dresser drawers and wash them.'

She unsnapped the cap on another bottle of Jax and sat down on the picnic bench. But she didn't drink from the bottle. She just kept drawing a line down through the moisture with her finger.

'I was in northern Nicaragua,' she said. 'When the contras "violated" someone, they cut the person up in pieces.'

'I was just trying to say that your reaction was understandable, Drew.'

'I bought a pistol this morning. The next time someone breaks into my house, I'm going to kill the sonofabitch.'

'That's not going to make the bigger problem go away. You're protecting Weldon from something, and at the same time you know if he doesn't get help, he's going to take a fall. I think you've got another problem, too. Weldon's done something that goes against your conscience, and somehow he's pulled you into it.'

'I wish I could be omniscient. It must be wonderful to have that gift.'

'Has he been mixed up with the contras?'

'No.'

I looked her steadily in the eyes.

'I said no,' she repeated.

'I'm going to say something you probably won't like. Weldon worked for the CIA. Air America flew in and out of the Golden Triangle. Sometimes they ferried around warlords, who were in reality transporting narcotics. The station chiefs knew it, the pilots knew it. Weldon's been involved in some nasty stuff. Maybe it's time he took his own fall. I think he's a chickenshit for hiding behind his sister.'

'Why'd you let everything go between us?'

'Excuse me?'

'You were talking about chickenshit. I thought you were the sun coming up in the morning. That's what I thought you were.'

I felt the skin of my face tighten in the humid air.

'I went to Vietnam. Do you remember what you thought about people who went to Vietnam?' I said.

'That wasn't it at all, and you know it. You blew it with Bootsie, and I was "just passing through." That's what chickenshit means.'

'You're wrong.'

She took a drink from the bottle and looked away toward the bayou so I couldn't see her face.

'I always respected you,' I said. 'You got upset yesterday because under it all you have a tender heart, Drew. Nobody is expected to be a soldier every day of his life. I start every other day with a nervous breakdown.'

Her face was still turned away from me, but I could see her back shaking under my shirt.

I put my hand lightly on her shoulder. Her fingers came up and covered mine, rested there a moment, then she lifted my hand up and released it.

'It's time for you to go, Dave,' she said.

I didn't reply. I walked across the thick Saint Augustine grass, through the shadows and the tracings of fireflies in the trees. When I turned and looked back at her, I didn't see a barefoot woman pushing at her eyes in the smoke but a little Cajun girl of years ago whose bare legs danced in the air while a switch whipped across them.

Early the next morning I sent two uniformed deputies to check the missions and the shelters in Iberia and Lafayette parishes for a man who had been disfigured in a fire. I also told them to check the old hobo jungles along the SP tracks.

'What do we do when we find him?' one deputy said.

'Ask him to ride down with you.'

'What if he don't want to come?'

'Call me and I'll come out.'

'Half the guys in that hobo camp look like their mothers beat on them with a baseball bat.'

'This guy's face looks like red rubber.'

'Can we take him out to lunch?' He was grinning.

'How about getting on it?'

'Yes, sir.'

Then I called Clete's hospital room in New Orleans, but was told by a nurse that he was in X-ray. I asked her to have him call me collect when he got back to his room. Fifteen minutes later I was drinking coffee, eating a donut, and looking out the window at a black man who was selling rattlesnake watermelons and strawberries off the back of his pickup truck, when my phone extension rang. It was Weldon Sonnier.

'What's the idea of leaning on my sister?' he said.

'I think you've got it turned around.'

'What did you say to her?'

I set my doughnut down on a napkin.

'I think that's none of your business,' I said.

'You'd damn well better believe it is.'

'Then why don't you stop dumping your garbage in her life?'

'Listen, Dave—'

'I got a bribe offer from an anonymous letter writer. This guy mentioned your name. He also said you're a prick and a welsher.'

He was silent.

'Then I talked with Joey Gouza. He also called you a welsher.'

'Consider the source.'

'The interesting questions is why I keep seeing or hearing the word "welsher" when your name is mentioned.'

'When did you see Gouza?'

'None of your business.'

'He's a candidate for a lobotomy. I wouldn't mash on his oysters.'

'Why are you mixed up with Gouza?'

'Who says I know him? The guy's notorious. Gouza is to New Orleans what monkey flop is to a zoo.'

'Weldon, the real problem is you've tracked through your own shit and you're laying it off on other people. I think you've put your sister in jeopardy. In my opinion that's a lousy thing to do.'

'Yeah? Is that right? Maybe if you ever get your nose out of the air long enough, I'll clue you in on the facts of life down in the tropics.'

'I think you've sought out the trouble in your life. Nobody forced you to fly for Air America. You were dirty in Indo-China, I think you're dirty now.'

'I wish I had the patent on righteousness. I guess you never called in any 105s on a ville. Stay the fuck away from my sister if you can't handle it any better than you did yesterday.'

He hung up. This time I was the one whose words and anger were caught in my throat like a tangle of fish hooks. Unconsciously I wadded up a sheet of paper on top of my desk and threw it toward the wastebasket, then realized it was my time log for my paycheck.

It was just after one o'clock and it had started to rain again when Clete returned my call. I had opened my windows, and the wind blew a fine spray through the screens.

'Can you come to New Orleans this evening?' he asked.

'I was coming tomorrow.'

'How about today?'

'What's up?'

'I got some information on Bobby Earl that might lead us to those farts who worked me over.'

'Wait a minute, where are you?'

'At home.'

'The hospital cut you loose?'

'I cut myself loose. Somehow the smell of bedpans just doesn't go together with mashed potatoes and boiled carrots. Forget about the hospital. Look, you remember Willie Bimstine and Nig Rosewater?'

'The bondsmen?'

'That's right. I chase down jumpers for them sometimes. So I called them this morning to see if they might have some work for me, since I don't have any medical insurance and my hospital bill is a nightmare. But these guys are also a gold mine of information on the lowlifes of New Orleans. So when I had Nig on the phone I asked him what he knew about the buttwipes who put stitches all over my head. No help there, though. In fact, he said he thought Raintree and Fluck weren't around the city anymore, because when they're in town you hear about it. Fluck in particular. Evidently he likes beating the shit out of people.

'So I asked Nig what kind of action Bobby Earl might be involved in, and he told me this interesting story. Nig went a twenty-five-thousand-dollar bond for this broad over in Algiers. The broad got nailed with four kees of pure Colombian nose candy. But Nig's not worried about her. She's got a high-priced lawyer, it's her first bust, and she knows she can cut a deal and not do any time, so Nig's money is safe. It's her two brothers who are the problem. Nig put up big bucks to get them out on a robbery beef, and they both skipped on him.

'Smart businessman that he is, Nig tells the broad that she either delivers up her brothers or he yanks her bond and she waits for her trial in the parish jail. Which is not what she envisioned for herself, because this broad is one beautiful hot-assed piece of equipment who the bull dykes will cannibalize. So Nig thinks he's got her and she'll have both her brothers in his office in twenty-four hours. But the broad pulls one on Nig that he doesn't expect.

'She says if he messes with her bond, threatens her again, or gets in her face about anything, she'll have a bedtime chat with Bobby Earl, and Willie and Nig's state license is going to be hanging out in the breeze. Nig checked it out. She's Bobby Earl's regular punch across the river. Once a week he's at her pad like clockwork. She brags it around among the lowlifes that she fucks him cross-eyed on the ceiling.'

'I'm not following you, Clete. Who cares? This doesn't get us any closer to Fluck, Gates, or Raintree. Tell Nig to give his story to the *Picayune* about election time.'

'Here's the rest of it. Nig says the broad's brothers are bikers and they were both in the AB in Angola and Huntsville.'

'I don't know if that's a big lead.'

'You got anything else? It's Thursday. Nig says Thursday is poontang night for Bobby in Algiers. We tail him over there and see what happens.

Come on, Bobby Earl's an amateur. We'll make drops of blood pop on his forehead.'

I looked out at the rain denting the trees and thought for a moment. The rain was blowing across the truck awning of the black man selling strawberries and watermelons, and in the south, against a black sky, lightning was striking against the Gulf.

'All right,' I said.

'Why all the thought?'

'No reason. I'll be at your apartment in about three hours.'

Clete had enough problems of his own and didn't need to know everything about a police investigation, I told myself. I called Bootsie and told her that I had to go to New Orleans, but I promised to be back that night, no matter how late it was. I meant it, too.

We used Clete's battered Plymouth for the tail. It was 7:30, and we were parked a block down the street from Bobby Earl's driveway; the sky was still black with clouds and rainwater ran high and dark in the gutters. Out on Lake Pontchartrain I could see the lighted cabins of a yacht rocking in the swell. Clete smoked a cigarette and blew the smoke out his window into the rain-flecked air. He wore his porkpie hat over the scalped divots and stitches in his head, and a purple-and-white-striped shirt and seersucker trousers that rode up high on his ankles. He kept rubbing the back of his thick neck and craning his head.

'Is something wrong?' I asked.

'Yeah, there is. I hurt from head to foot. Man, I must be getting old to let punks like that take me down.'

'Sometimes you lose.'

'You're always quoting Hemingway to me. Do you know what he told his kid when his kid asked something about the importance of being a good loser? He said, "Son, being a good loser requires one thing – practice."'

'Clete, we do it by the numbers tonight.'

'Who said different? But you got to make 'em sweat, mon. When they see you coming, something inside them should try to crawl away and hide.'

'There he goes. Try to stay a block behind him,' I said.

Clete started up the Plymouth's engine. The rusted-out muffler, which was wired to the frame with coat hangers, sounded like a garbage truck's. The white Chrysler headed up the street with its lights on and turned at the corner toward Lakeshore Drive.

'Don't worry, he's not going to make us,' Clete said. 'Our man's got his mind on getting his Johnson serviced. I've got to scope out this broad. Nig says she looks like a movie star. When I was in Vice—'

'He's not going to Algiers. He's turning the wrong way.'

'He's probably picking up some rubbers.'

'Clete—'

'I didn't drag you down here just to fire in the well. Take it easy.'

We watched the Chrysler speed down the wet boulevard along the lakefront, then slow and turn through the iron gates of the yacht club. The taillights disappeared down a palm-lined drive that led to an enormous white glass-domed building by a golf course. Clete pulled to the curb and stared glumly through the windshield. The waves out on the lake were dark green and blowing with strips of froth. He breathed loudly through his nose.

'It's all right,' I said.

'The hell it is. I'm going to take that cocksucker down.'

'We don't need him to talk to the girl.'

'I don't know where she is. He meets her in different bars, then they go to a motel.'

'We'll give it a little while. Maybe he'll head over to Algiers later.'

'Yeah, maybe,' he said. His eyes moved over the rolling fairways and oak trees, the parking lot in front of the main building, the sailboats rising and falling in their slips. 'There're two or three exits to this place. We'd better park inside. I'm going to have a talk with Nig later about credibility. That's the problem with this PI stuff, you've got about the same clout as the lowlifes. I always feel like I'm picking up table scraps.'

We drove through the gate and parked at the back of the lot, where we could see the Chrysler two rows away, under a sodium lamp. Clete reached into the back seat for his Styrofoam cooler, pulled out two fried-oyster poor-boy sandwiches, a can of Jax for himself, and a Dr Pepper for me. He kept brushing crumbs off his shirtfront while he ate. When he finished a beer he crushed the can in his huge hand, threw it out on to the parking lot, and snapped open another one. He squinted one eye at me.

'Dave, have you got something else on the agenda?' he said.

'Not really.'

'You're not going to see Joey Meatballs again and forget to invite your old partner to the party, are you?'

'Gouza doesn't rattle. We're going to have to take down somebody around him.'

'It's been tried before. They're usually a lot more afraid of Joey than they are of us. I heard he busted out a snitch's teeth in Angola with a ballpeen hammer. Every punk and addict and pervert in New Orleans knows that story, too.'

'How heavy do you figure he's into the crack trade?'

'He's not. It's pieced off too many times before it gets to the projects. Gouza's on the other end. Big shipments, pure stuff, out of Florida or South America. I hear his people distribute to maybe four or five guys in Orleans Parish, they make their profit on quantity, then they're out of the chain with minimum risk. Even the greaseballs won't go into the welfare projects. I had to go after a jumper for Nig at the St Thomas. Two kids on the roof filled up a thirty-gallon garbage can with water and dropped it on me, bottom end down. It missed me by a foot and flattened a kid's tricycle like a half-dollar . . . But you didn't really answer my question, noble mon. I think you've got something else on the dance card and you're not cutting ole Cletus in on it.'

'This case has been all dead ends, Clete. When I learn something, I'll tell you. My big problem is the Sonniers. I feel like locking them all up as material witnesses.'

'Maybe it's not a bad idea. Taking showers with child molesters and mainline bone smokers helps get your perspective clear sometimes.'

'I couldn't make it stick. They weren't actually witness to anything.'

'Then let them live with their own shit.'

'I'm still left with a dead cop.'

We sat for a long time in the rain. The band of cobalt light on the horizon gradually faded under the rim of storm clouds, and the lake grew dark and then glazed with the yellow reflection of ballroom lights in the club. I could taste salt in the wind. I pulled my rainhat down over my eyes and fell asleep.

I see Bootsie when she's nineteen, her hair as bright as copper on the pillow, her nude body as pink and soft as a newly opened rose. I put my head between her young breasts.

When I awoke the rain had stopped completely, the moon had broken through a rip in the clouds over the lake, and Clete was not in the car. I could hear orchestra music from the ballroom. Then I saw him, in silhouette, his wide back framed in the opened driver's door of Bobby Earl's Chrysler, his elbows cocked, both his arms pointed down toward his loins. He rotated his head on his neck as though he were standing indifferently at a public urinal. Even at that distance I could see the spray splashing on the dashboard, the steering wheel, the leather seats. Clete shook himself, flexed his knees, and zipped his fly. He cupped his Zippo in his hands, lit a cigarette, and puffed it in the corner of his mouth as he walked back toward the car and squinted up approvingly at the clearing sky overhead.

'I don't believe it.'

'You got to let a guy like Bobby know you're around,' he said, slamming the door behind him. 'Ah, lookie there, our man scored after all. I think he's one of these guys who plans on marrying up and screwing down.'

Bobby Earl walked across the parking lot in a white suit, charcoal shirt, and white-and-black striped tie. A red-headed woman in a sequined evening gown held on to his arm and tried to step across the puddles in her high heels. Both she and Bobby Earl balanced champagne glasses gingerly in their hands. The woman was laughing uncontrollably at something Bobby Earl was telling her.

Earl opened the passenger door for her, then got behind the wheel. The light from the sodium lamp shone through his front window, and I saw his silhouette freeze, then his shoulders stiffen, as though he had just become aware that a geological fissure had opened up below his automobile. Then he got out of the car, staring incredulously at his upturned palms, the wet streaks in his suit, the damp imprints of his shoes.

Clete started the engine, and the rusted-out muffler thundered off the asphalt and reverberated between the rows of cars. He turned out into the aisle and drove slowly past the Chrysler, the engine and frame clanking like broken glass.

'What's happenin', Bob?' he asked, then flipped his cigarette in a high, sparking arc, punched in a rock tape, and gave Bobby Earl the thumbs-up sign.

Bobby Earl's face slipped by the window like an outraged balloon. The woman in the sequined evening gown walked hurriedly back toward the clubhouse, her spiked heels clicking across the puddles.

All men have a religion or totems of some kind. Even the atheist is committed to an enormous act of faith in his belief that the universe created itself and the subsequent creation of intelligent life was simply a biological accident. Eddy Raintree's votive attempt at metaphysics was just a little more eccentric than most. Both the gunbull in Angola and the biker girl in Algiers had said that Raintree was wired into astronomy and weirdness. In New Orleans, if your interest ran to UFOs (called 'ufology' by enthusiasts), Island voodoo, witchcraft, teleportation through the third eye in your forehead, palm reading, the study of ectoplasm, the theory that Atlanteans are living among us in another dimension, and herbal cures for everything from brain cancer to impacted wisdom teeth, you eventually went to Tante Majorie's cult bookstore on Royal Street in the Quarter.

Tante Majorie was big all over and so black that her skin had a purple sheen to it. She streaked her high cheekbones with rouge and wore gold granny glasses, and her hair, which was pulled back tightly in a bun, had grayed so that it looked like dull gunmetal. She lived over her shop with another lesbian, an elderly white woman, and fifteen cats who sat on the furniture, the bookshelves, and the ancient radiator, and tracked soiled cat litter throughout the apartment.

She served tea on a silver service, then studied the photo of Eddy Raintree. Her French doors were open on the balcony, and I could hear the night noise from the street. I had known her almost twenty years and had never been able to teach her my correct name.

'You say he got a tiger on his arm?' she asked.

'Yes.'

'I 'member him. He use to come in every three, four mont's. That's the one. I ain't forgot him. He's 'fraid of black people.'

'Why do you think that?'

'He always want me to read his hand. But when I pick it up in my fingers, it twitch just like a frog. I'd tell him, It ain't shoe polish, darlin'. It ain't gonna rub off on you. Why you looking for him?'

'He helped murder a sheriff's deputy.'

She looked out the French doors at the jungle of potted geraniums, philodendron, and banana trees on her balcony.

'You ain't got to look for him, Mr Streak. That boy ain't got a long way to run,' she said.

'What do you mean?'

'I told him it ain't no accident he got that tiger on his arm. I told him tiger burning bright in the forests of the night. Just like in the Bible, glowing out there in the trees. That tiger gonna eat him.'

'I respect your wisdom and your experience, Tante Majorie, but I need to find this man.'

She twisted a strand of hair between her fingers and gazed thoughtfully at a calico cat nursing a half-dozen kittens in a cardboard box.

'Every mont' I sent out astrology readings for people on my list,' she said. 'He's one of them people. But Raintree ain't the name he give me. I don't 'member the name he give me. Maybe you ain't suppose to find him, Mr Streak.'

'My name's Dave, Tante Majorie. Could I see your list?'

'It ain't gonna he'p. His kind come with a face, what they get called don't matter. They come out of the womb without no name, without no place in the house where they're born, without no place down at a church, a school, a job down at a grocery sto', there ain't a place or a person they belong to in this whole round world. Not till that day they turn and look at somebody at the bus stop, or in the saloon, or sitting next to them in the hot-pillow house, and they see that animal that ain't been fed in that other person's eyes. That's when they know who they always been.'

Then she went into the back of the apartment and returned with several sheets of typing paper in her hand.

'I got maybe over two hundred people here,' she said. 'They're spread all over Lou'sana and Miss'sippi, too.'

'Well, let's take a look,' I said. 'You see, Tante Majorie, the interesting thing about these guys is their ego. So when they use an alias they usually keep their initials. Or maybe their aliases have the same sound value as their real names.'

Her list was in alphabetical order. I sorted the pages to the 'R's.

'How about Elton Rubert?' I asked.

'I don't 'member it, Mr Davis. My clerk must have put it down, and he don't work here anymore.'

'My name is Dave, Tante Majorie. Dave Robicheaux. Where's your clerk now?'

'He moved up to Ohio, or one of them places up North.'

I wrote down the mailing address of Elton Rubert, a tavern in a small settlement out in the Atchafalaya basin west of Baton Rouge.

'Here's my business card,' I said. 'If the man in the photo shows up here again, read his palm or whatever he wants, then call me later. But don't question him or try to find out anything about him for me, Tante Majorie. You've already been a great help.'

'Give me your hand.'

'I beg your pardon?'

She reached out and took my hand, stared into my palm and kneaded it with her fingers. Then she stroked it as though she were smoothing bread dough.

'There's something I ain't told you,' she said. 'The last time that man was in here, I read his hand, just like I'm reading yours. He axed me what his lifeline was like. What I didn't tell him, what he didn't know, was he didn't have no lifeline. It was gone.'

I looked at her.

'You ain't understood me, darlin',' she said. 'When your lifeline's gone, his kind get it back by stealing somebody else's.' She folded my thumb and fingers into a fist, then pressed it into a ball with her palms. I could feel the heat and oil in her skin. 'You hold on to it real hard, Mr Streak. That tiger don't care who it eat.'

I had had trouble finding a parking place earlier and had left my pickup over by Rampart Street, not far from the Iberville welfare project. When I rounded the corner I saw the passenger door agape, the window smashed out on the pavement, the flannel-wrapped brick still in the gutter. The glove box had been rifled and the stereo ripped out of the panel, as well as most of the ignition wires, which hung below the dashboard like broken spaghetti ends.

Because First District headquarters was only two blocks away, it took only an hour to get a uniformed officer there to make out the theft report that my insurance company would require. Then I walked to a drugstore on Canal, called Triple A for a wrecker, and called Bootsie and told her that I wouldn't be home as I had promised, that with any luck I could have the truck repaired by late tomorrow.

'Where will you stay tonight?' she asked.

'At Clete's.'

'Dave, if the truck isn't fixed tomorrow, take the bus back home

and we'll go get the truck later. Tomorrow's Friday. Let's have a nice
weekend.'

'I may have to check out a lead on the way back. It might be a dud, but
I can't let it hang.'

'Does this have to do with Drew?'

'No, not at all.'

'Because I wouldn't want to interfere.'

'This may be the guy who tried to take my head off with a crowbar.'

'Oh God, Dave, give it up, at least for a while.'

'It doesn't work that way. The other side doesn't do pit stops.'

'How clever,' she said. 'I'll leave the answering machine on in case
we're in town.'

'Come on, Boots, don't sign off like that.'

'It's been a long day. I'm just tired. I don't mean what I say.'

'Don't worry, everything's going to be fine. I'll call in the morning. Tell
Alafair we'll go crabbing on the bay Saturday.'

I was ready to say goodnight, then she said, as though she were
speaking out of a mist, 'Remember what they used to teach us in Catholic
School about virginity? They said it was better to remain a virgin until
you married so you wouldn't make comparisons. Do you ever make
comparisons, Dave?'

I closed my eyes and swallowed as a man might if he looked up one
sunny day and felt the cold outer envelope of a glacier sliding unalterably
into his life.

When I was recuperating from the bouncing Betty that sent me home
from Vietnam, and I began my long courtship with insomnia, I used to
muse sometimes on what were the worst images or degrees of fear that
my dreams could present me with. In my innocence, I thought that if I
could face them in the light of the day, imagine them perhaps as friendly
gargoyles sitting at the foot of my bed, even hold a reasonable conversation with them, I wouldn't have to drink and drug myself nightly
into another dimension where the monsters were transformed into pink
zebras and prancing giraffes. But every third or fourth night I was back
with my platoon, outside an empty ville that stunk of duck shit and
unburied water buffalo; then as we lay pressed against a broken dike in
the heated, breathless air, we suddenly realized that somebody back at the
firebase had screwed up bad, and that the 105 rounds were coming in
short.

The dream about an artillery barrage can be as real as the experience.
You want to burrow into the ground like an insect; your knees are pulled
up in a fetal position, your arms squeezed over your pot. Your fear is so
great that you think the marrow in your skull will split, the arteries in
your brain will rupture from their own dilation, blood will fountain from

your nose. You will promise God anything in order to be spared. Right behind you, geysers of mud explode in the air and the bodies of North Vietnamese regulars are blown out of their graves, their bodies luminescent with green slime and dancing with maggots.

I had seen Vietnamese civilians who had survived B-52 raids. They were beyond speech; they trembled all over and made mewing and keening sounds that you did not want to take with you. When I would wake from my dream my hands would shake so badly that I could hardly unscrew the cap on the whiskey bottle that I kept hidden under my mattress.

As I slept on Clete's couch that night, I had to deal with another creation of my unconscious, one that was no less difficult than the old grainy filmstrips from Vietnam. In my dream I would feel Bootsie next to me, her nude body warm and smooth under the sheet. I would put my face in her hair, kiss her nipples, stroke her stomach and thighs, and she would smile in her sleep, take me in her hand, and place me inside her. I would kiss the tops of her breasts and try to touch her all over while we made love, wishing in my lust that she were two instead of one. Then as it built inside of me like a tree cracking loose from a riverbank, rearing upward in the warm current, she would smile with drowsy expectation and close her eyes, and her face would grow small and soft and her mouth become as vulnerable as a flower.

But her eyes would open again and they would be as sightless as milk glass. A scaled deformity like the red wings of a butterfly would mask her face, her body would stiffen and ridge with bone, and her womb would be filled with death.

I sat up in the darkness of Clete's living room, the blood beating in my wrists, and opened and closed my mouth as though I had been pulled from beneath the ocean's surface. I stared through the window and across the courtyard at a lamp on a table behind a curtain that was lifting in the breeze from a fan. I could see someone's shadow moving behind the curtain. I wanted to believe that it was the shadow of a nice person, perhaps a man preparing to go to work or an elderly woman fixing breakfast before going to Mass at St Louis Cathedral. But it was 4 A.M.; the sky overhead was black, with no hint of the false dawn; the night still belonged to the gargoyles, and the person across the courtyard was probably a hooker or somebody on the downside of an all-night drunk.

I put on my shirt and slacks and slipped on my loafers. I could see Clete's massive form in his bed, a pillow over his face, his porkpie hat on the bedpost. I closed the door softly behind me. The air in the courtyard was electric with the smell of magnolia.

The bar was over by Decatur, one of those places that never closes, where there is neither cheer nor anger nor expectation and no external measure of one's own failure and loss.

The bottles of bourbon, vodka, rum, gin, rye, and brandy rang with light along the mirror. The oak-handled beer spigots and frosted mugs in the coolers could have been a poem. The bartender propped his arms impatiently on the dish sink.

'I'll serve you, but you got to tell me what it is you want,' he said. He looked at another customer, raised his eyebrows, then looked back at me. He was smiling now. 'How about it, buddy?'

'I'd like a cup of coffee.'

'You want a cup of coffee?'

'Yes.'

'This looks like a place where you get a cup of coffee? Too much, too much,' he said, then began wiping off the counter with a rag.

I heard somebody laugh as I walked back out on to the street. I sat on the railway tracks behind the French Market and watched the dawn touch the earth's rim and light the river and the docks and scows over in Algiers, turn the sky like the spokes in a wagon wheel. The river looked wide and yellow with silt, and I could see oil and occasionally dead fish floating belly up in the current.

8

My truck was not repaired until six o'clock Friday evening. By the time I hit South Baton Rouge the sun was a red molten ball in the western sky. I crossed the Mississippi and swung off the interstate at Port Allen and continued through the Atchafalaya basin on the old highway. The bar that Eddy Raintree may have been using as his mail drop was on a yellow dirt road that wound through thick stands of dead cypress and copper-colored pools of stagnant water.

It was hammered together from clapboard, plywood, and tarpaper, its screens rusted and gutted, the windows pocked from gravel flung against the building by spinning car tires; it sat up on cinder blocks like an elephant with a broken back. A half-dozen Harleys were parked on the side, and in the back a group of bikers were barbecuing in an oil drum under an oak tree. The yellow dust from the road drifted across their fire.

The Atchafalaya basin is the place you go if you don't fit anywhere else. It encompasses hundreds of square miles of bayous, canals, sandspits, willow islands, huge inland bays, and flooded woods where the mosquitoes will hover around your head like a helmet and you slap your arms until they're slick with a black-red paste. Twenty minutes from Baton Rouge or an hour and a half from New Orleans, you can punch a hole in the dimension and drop back down into the redneck, coonass, peckerwood South that you thought had been eaten up by the developers of Sunbelt suburbs. It's a shrinking place, but there's a group that holds on to it with a desperate and fearful tenacity.

I slipped my .45 in the back of my belt, along with my handcuffs, put on my seersucker coat, and went inside the bar. The jukebox played Waylon and Merle; the men at the pool table rifled balls into side pockets as though they wanted to drive pain into the wood and leather; and a huge Confederate flag billowed out from the tacks holding it to the ceiling.

A metal sign, the size of a bumper sticker, over the men's room door said WHITE POWER. I used the urinal. Above it, neatly written on a piece of cardboard, were the words THIS IS THE ONLY SHIT-HOUSE WE GOT, SO KEEP THE GODDAMN PLACE CLEAN.

The bartender was a small, prematurely balding, suntanned man with thin arms who wore a wash-frayed suit vest with no shirt. On his right forearm was a tattoo of the Marine Corps globe and anchor. He didn't ask me what I wanted; he simply pointed two fingers at me with his cigarette between them.

'I'm looking for Elton Rubert,' I said.

'I don't know him,' he said.

'That's strange. He gets his mail here.'

'That might be. I don't know him. What do you want?'

'How about a 7 Up?'

He took a bottle out of the cooler, snapped off the cap, and set it before me with a glass.

'The ice machine's broken, so there's no ice,' he said.

'That's all right.'

'That's a dollar.'

I put four quarters on the bar. He scraped them up and started to walk away.

'It looks like you have some letters in a box up there. Would you see if Elton's picked up his mail?' I said.

'Like I told you, I don't know the man.'

'You're the regular bartender, you're here most of the time?'

He put out his cigarette in an ashtray, mashing it methodically, then his eyes went out the open front door and across the road as though I were not there. He picked a piece of tobacco off his tongue.

'I'd appreciate your answering my question,' I said.

'Maybe you should ask those guys barbecuing out back. They might know him.'

'You were in the corps?'

'Yeah.'

'You're only in the crotch once.'

'You were in the corps?'

'No, I was in the army. That's not my point. You're only in the AB once, too.'

He lit another cigarette and bit a hangnail on his thumb.

'I don't know what you're saying, buddy, but this is the wrong fucking place to get in somebody's face,' he said.

A barmaid came in the side door, put her handbag in a cabinet, and carried a sack of trash out the back.

'You're saying you don't understand me, my words confuse you?' I asked.

'What's with you, man? Somebody shoved a bumblebee up your ass?'

'What's your name, podna?'

'Harvey.'

'You're treating me like I'm stupid, Harvey. You're starting to piss me off.'

'I don't need this shit, man.' He looked out the back door at the men in jeans, cutoff denim jackets, and motorcycle boots, who were drinking canned beer in the barbecue smoke under the tree.

'It's just you and me, Harvey. Those guys don't have anything to do with it,' I said.

The barmaid came back inside. She looked like she had dressed for work in a dime store. Her blond hair was shaved on one side, punked orange on the tips; she wore black fingernail polish, a pink top, black vinyl shorts, owl glasses with red frames, earrings made from chromed .38 hulls.

'Give this guy a free 7 Up if he wants one. I'm going to the head,' Harvey said to her.

I waited a moment, then followed him into the men's room and shot the bolt on the door. He was in the single stall, urinating loudly into the toilet bowl.

'Zipper it up and come out here, Harvey,' I said.

He opened the stall door and stared at me, his mouth hanging open. I stuck my badge up close to his face.

'This man's real name is Eddy Raintree,' I said. 'Now don't you bullshit me. Where is he?'

'You can bust me, you can kick my ass, it don't matter, I don't know the sonofabitch,' he said. 'Guys get their mail here. They go behind the bar and pick it up. I don't know who they are, I don't ask. Check out those cats behind the building, man. There's one guy drove a pool cue through another guy's lung out there.'

'Where's my man live, Harvey?'

He shook his head back and forth, his mouth a tight line. I rested one hand on his shoulder and looked steadily into his face.

'What are you going to do when you walk out of here?' I said.

'What do you mean going—'

'You think you're going to make some mileage with my butt?'

'Look, man—' He started to shake his head again.

'Maybe ease on over to the phone booth and make a call? Or take a round of beers to the outdoor geek show and mention that the heat is drinking 7 Up inside?'

'I'm neutral. I got no stake in this.'

'That's right. So it's time for you to go. To tell the lady behind the bar you're taking off early tonight. We're understood on this, aren't we?'

'You're the man. I do what you say.'

'But if I find out you talked to somebody you shouldn't, I'll be back. It's called aiding and abetting and obstruction of justice. What that means is I'll take you back with me to the Iberia Parish jail. The guy who runs it is a three-hundred-pound black homosexual with a sense of humor about which cell he puts you guys in.'

He rubbed his mouth. His hand made a dry sound against his whiskers.

'Look, I didn't see you, I didn't talk to you,' he said. 'Okay? I'm going home sick. What you said about the AB, it's true, it's lifetime. If one guy doesn't take you out, another does. I'm a four-buck-an-hour beer bartender. I've got ulcers and a slipped disc. All I want is some peace.'

'You've got it, partner. We'll see you around. Stay away from phones tonight, watch a lot of television, write some letters to the home folks.'

'How about treating me with a little dignity, man? I'm doing what you want. I ain't a criminal, I ain't your problem. I'm just a little guy running around in a frying pan.'

'You've probably got a point, Harvey.'

I unbolted the door and watched him walk to the bar, say something to the barmaid, then leave by the side door and drive up the dirt road in a paintless pickup truck. The dust from the parking lot drifted back through the rusted screens in the late-afternoon sunlight. Once he was out of sight, it would not take Harvey long to decide that his loyalties to the bikers and Eddy Raintree were far more important to his welfare than his temporary fear of me and the Iberia Parish jail.

I returned to the bar and asked the barmaid for a pencil and a piece of paper. She tore a page from a notepad by the telephone and handed it to me. I scribbled two or three sentences on the back and folded it once, then twice.

'Would you give this to Elton for me?' I said.

'Elton Rubert?'

'Yeah.'

'Sure.' She took the note from my hand and dropped it in the letter box behind the bar. 'You probably just missed him. He usually comes in about four o'clock.'

'Yeah, that's what Harvey was saying. Too bad I missed him.'

'Too bad?' She laughed. 'You got stopped-up nostrils or something? Trying to open up your sinuses?'

'What?'

'The guy's got gapo that would make the dead get up and run down the road.'

'He has what?'

'Gorilla armpit odor. You sure you know Elton? He stays in that shack by the levee and doesn't bathe unless he gets rained on. I don't know where he gets off knocking the niggers all the time.'

'I like your earrings.'

'I got them just the other day. You really like them?'

'Sure. I've never seen any made out of .38 shells.'

'My boyfriend made them. He's a gun nut but he's real good at making jewelry and stuff. He's thinking of opening up a mail-order business.'

'Elton doesn't have a phone, does he?'

'He doesn't have any plumbing. I don't know why he'd have a phone.'

I looked at my watch.

'Maybe I have time to stop by his place just a minute. It's not far, is it?' I said.

'Straight down the road to the levee. You can't miss it. Just follow your nose. Hah!'

'By the way, how's Elton's eye?'

'It looks like worms ate it. Are you doing some kind of missionary work or something?'

The violet air was thick with insects as I drove down the yellow road toward the levee and the marsh. The road crossed the Southern Pacific tracks, then followed alongside a green levee that was covered with buttercups. On the other side of the levee were a canal, a chain of willow islands and sandbars, and a bay full of dead cypress. Three hundred yards from the track crossing was a fishing shack, a small box of a place with a collapsed gallery, an outhouse, an overflowing garbage barrel in back. Both a pirogue and a boat with an outboard engine were tied to wood stobs driven into the mudflat. A chopped-down Harley was parked on the far side of the gallery, its chrome glinting with the sun's last red light. The sky was black with birds.

I parked the truck down the levee, took my World War II Japanese field glasses from my locked toolbox, which the kids from the Iberville project hadn't gotten into, and waited. It was going to be a hot night. The air was perfectly still, heated from the long afternoon, stale with the smell of dead water beetles and alligator gars that fishermen had thrown up on the bank. I studied the shack through the field glasses. The garbage barrel boiled with flies, an orange cat was eating a fishhead in a bowl on the shack step, a man walked past a window.

Then he was gone before I could focus on his face.

Finally it was dark, and the man inside the shack lit an oil lamp, opened a tin can at a table, and ate from it with a fork, hunched over with his back toward me. Then he urinated off the back steps with a bottle of beer in one hand, and I saw his big granite head in the light from the door, and the muscles that swelled in his shoulders like lumps of garden hose.

When he was back inside I got out of the truck with my .45 in my hand, crossed the levee, and moved through the darkness toward the shack. The willows were motionless, etched against a yellow moon, and I saw a moccasin as thick as my wrist uncoil off a log, drop into the water, and swim in a silvery V toward a dead neutria who had been hit by a boat propeller. The man moved in silhouette across the window, and I slid back the receiver on the .45, eased a hollow-point into the chamber, and walked quickly up the mudbank to the back steps. I heard train cars jolt together, then a locomotive backing along the tracks on the far side of the levee.

Now, I thought, and I cleared the three steps in one jump, burst into the shack, into a reek of stale sweat that was as close and gray as a damp cotton glove. His head looked up from the comic book that was spread on his knees. I aimed the .45 straight into the face of Eddy Raintree.

'Hands behind your neck, down on the floor! Do it, do it, do it!' I shouted.

The skin around his right eye was puckered with white sores. I shoved him off the chair amid a litter of newspapers, beer cans, and fast-food containers. His weight bowed the floor planks. I put the .45 behind his ear.

'All the way down on your face, Eddy,' I said, and began to pull the handcuffs from the back of my belt.

That should have been the end of it. But I got careless. Maybe my alcoholic dreams and sleeplessness of the previous night were to blame, or the eye-watering body odor that filled the room, or the sudden slamming of freight cars out in the darkness. But in the time it took the handcuffs to drop from my fingers, my vision to slip off the back of his head, he spun around like an animal turning in a box, grabbed the .45 with both hands, and locked his teeth on the knuckle of my right thumb.

His eyes were close-set like a pig's in the lamplight, his jaws knotted with cartilage, trembling with exertion. Blood spurted across the back of my hand; I could feel his teeth biting into the bone. I clubbed desperately at the back of his thick neck. His coarse, oily skin felt like rubber under my knuckles.

I was almost ready to drop the gun when he rammed his shoulder into my chest and dove headlong through the front window curtain.

My right hand quivered uncontrollably. I picked up the .45 with my left and went out the front door after him. He was running along the levee next to a stopped freight that must have been a mile long. The locomotive was haloed with white light and wisps of vapor, and in front of it gandy walkers were repairing track in the red glare of burning flares.

Eddy Raintree must have received his dishonorable discharge from the Marine Corps before a CI could teach him to stay off the crests of hills and embankments and never run in a straight line when someone is making a study of you through iron sights.

It felt strange to fire the .45 with my left hand. It leaped upward in my grasp as though it had a life of its own. Both rounds whanged and sparked off the sides of a gondola, and Eddy Raintree kept running, his head hunched into his shoulders. I knelt in the weeds, sighted low to allow for the recoil, let out my breath slowly, and squeezed off another round. His right leg went out from under him as though it had been struck with a baseball bat, and he toppled down the far side of the levee to the railroad bed.

When I slid down the embankment and got to him he had his palm pressed tightly against his thigh and was trying to pull himself erect on a metal rung at the end of a boxcar. His hand was shining and wet, and his face had already gone white with shock. A sweet, fetid odor came from the car, and then I saw that it was actually built of slats and contained cages.

'Sit down, Eddy,' I said.

He breathed hard through his mouth. His eyes were bright and mean, the whites flecked with blood.

'It's over, partner. Don't have any wrong thoughts about that. Now sit down and give me your wrist,' I said.

He tried not to grimace as he eased himself down on the gravel. I cuffed one wrist, looped the chain through the iron rung on the car, and cuffed the other wrist. Then I patted him down.

'What the fuck's this train carrying?' he said.

I split open his pants legs with my Puma knife. The entry hole in the skin was black and no bigger than the ball of my index finger. But it took my wadded handkerchief to cover the exit wound. I slipped my belt around his thigh and tightened it with a stick.

'What the fuck is in that car?' he said. His long hair hung from his head like string on a pumpkin.

'I'm going to give you the lay of the land, Eddy. You're leaking pretty bad. I'm going to run up ahead and ask those train guys to radio for an ambulance. But if we can't get one out here right away, I think we should dump you into my truck and head into Baton Rouge.'

The side of his face twitched.

'What's the game?' he said.

'No game. You've got a big hole in you. You're going to need some blood.'

'That's it? I'm supposed to get scared now? I had a nigger gunbull sweat me with a cattle prod till he ran out of batteries. Go fuck yourself.'

'Read it like you want. I'm going to the head of the train, then I'll be back and we'll load you in my truck.'

He twisted his head around at a sound inside the railroad car.

'There's fucking lions or tigers in there, man,' he said.

'It's part of a circus. They're in cages. They can't hurt you.'

'What if they back up the fucking train while you're taking a walk?'

'You dealt the play, Eddy. Live with it. Keep that belt tight and don't move your leg around.'

'Hey, man, come here. Cuff me to that light over there.'

'It's too far to move you.'

'What the fuck's with you? You enjoy people's pain or something?'

'I'll be back, Eddy.'

'All right, man, I'll trade. Jewel smoked the cop in the basement. But I didn't have any part in it. We were just there to creep the joint. You saw me, I didn't have a piece.'

'That's not much of a trade.'

He waited a moment, then he said, 'There's a whack out. On Sonnier and the broad, both.'

'Which broad?'

'His sister.' He wet his lips. 'I can't swear it, but I think the whack's out on you, too. You're a hair in the wrong guy's nose.'

'Which guy?'

'That's all you get, motherfucker. I cut a deal, it's in custody, with a lawyer and the prosecutor there.'

'I think you're a gasbag, Eddy, but I don't want to see you die of fright.' I uncuffed one wrist, then locked both of his arms behind him. 'Lie quietly. I'm going to ask a couple of those gandy walkers to help me put you in the truck.'

'Hey, man, those animals smell my blood. Hey, man, come back here!'

He lay on his side in the gravel and weeds, his face sallow and slick with sweat in the humid air. His manacled arms were ropy with muscle, as though he were being hung from a great height, as though his tattoos were about to pop from his skin. A breeze blew across the levee, and I could smell the moist odor of animal dung and almost taste Eddy Raintree's fear of his own kind.

I walked three hundred yards to the head of the train, showed my badge to the engineer, and told him to radio to Baton Rouge for an ambulance. Then I asked two black gandy walkers to help me with Eddy Raintree. They wore dirt-streaked undershirts, and their black skin was beaded with sweat in the red light of the track flares. They looked at their crew foreman, who was white.

'Go ahead boys,' he said.

They walked behind me, back toward where Eddy Raintree lay on his side in the weeds and gravel. I heard the deep-throated sound of a tiger or lion in the wind. I turned to say something light to the black men, when one of them pointed into the distance.

'You got somebody coming yonder on a motorcycle,' he said.

I saw the headlight and the starlit silhouette of the bike and a small rider bounce down the side of the levee and come hard along the line of train cars. I could already see Eddy Raintree trying to rise to one knee, as he realized that he might still have another frolic in the funhouse.

It was very quick after that.

I pulled the .45 from my belt and broke into a run. The motorcycle passed Eddy Raintree, skidded in the gravel, and circled back in the direction it had come from, the headlight beam bouncing off the sides of the train. At first I thought the small rider was trying to swing Eddy up behind him, the way a rodeo pickup man scoops up a thrown cowboy. Then I saw a rigid object about two feet long in his hand, saw him extend it out beside him, and in my naiveté I thought it might be bolt cutters, that Raintree would lift up his manacled wrists, and the small rider would snap him free and I would be left breathless and exhausted while they disappeared over the levee into the darkness.

But I was close enough now to see that it was a shotgun, with the barrel sawed off right in front of the pump. Eddy Raintree had made it to one knee and was frozen in the headlight's radiance, like an armless man trying to genuflect in church, when the shotgun roared upward three inches from his chin.

Then the small rider opened up his bike, one boot skipping along the rocks for balance, and wove the bike up the levee in a shower of dirt and divots of grass and buttercups. My chest was heaving, my arm shaking, when I let off two rounds at his toylike silhouette just before he hit it full-bore, his head bent low, and disappeared in a long roll of diminishing thunder between the levee and the willow islands.

Eddy Raintree's buttocks were collapsed on his heels. His head was turned away from me, as though he were trying to hide his facial expression or a secret that he wished to take with him to another place. The animals in the circus car crashed wildly about in their wire cages. I touched Eddy Raintree lightly on the shoulder, and it rotated downward with gravity on the severed tendons in his neck.

One of the gandy walkers vomited.

'Oh Lord God, look what they done to that po' man,' the other said. 'His face hanging off the wrong side of his head.'

9

It was after midnight before I finished with the paramedics, local sheriff's deputies, an angry detective who accused me of operating in his jurisdiction without first contacting his office, and the parish medical examiner, who, like many of his kind, had aspirations to be a comedian.

'You could can that guy's BO as a chemical weapon and bring the Iranians to their knees,' he said. 'I'd consider rabies shots.'

When I got into my truck I knew I should drive straight back to New Iberia. That would have been the reasonable thing to do. But my late-night hours had never been characterized by reason, neither as a practicing or as a recovering drunk.

Less than an hour later I was on Highland Drive, west of the LSU campus in Baton Rouge, and I turned out of the long corridor of oaks into a brick-paved driveway lined with a rick fence and rosebushes. It led to an enormous white house with antebellum pretensions that might have been built five minutes ago on a Hollywood movie set. The trim on the front door was pink, the brasswork as bright and portentous as gold.

When he opened the front door in his pajamas, the breeze made the chandelier over his head ring with sound and light.

'Bootsie needs your help,' I said. 'No, that's not really true. I need it for her. I'm out there on the rim, Lyle.'

10

The next morning was Saturday, and I should have been off for the day, but the dispatcher called at 9 A.M.

'What do you want to do with these four guys Levy and Guillory brought in?' he asked.

'What four guys?'

'The bums Levy and Guillory brought in from the shelters. Levy said you were looking for guys who'd been in an ugly-man contest. You've got some beats here, Dave.'

I had completely forgotten.

'Where are they now?' I said.

'In the drunk tank.'

'How long have they been there?'

'Since yesterday.'

'Get them out of there. I'll be right down.'

Fifteen minutes later I was at the office. I walked down a corridor to a holding cell, where the four men patiently waited for me on a single wood bench. In the center of the cell floor was a urine-streaked drain hole. The men all had the emaciated characteristics of people whose lives existed on a straight line between the blood bank and the wine store. Like most professional tramps, they had a strange chemical odor about them, as though their glands had long ago stopped functioning properly and now secreted only a synthetic substitute for natural body fluids. I opened up the barrel door.

One man's head was misshapen, broken on one side like a dented walnut; the second's face was eaten with a skin disease that looked like skin cancer; the third had a bad harelip and virtually no cartilage in his nose; but it was the face of the fourth man on the bench that made me wince inside.

'Have you guys eaten?' I said.

They nodded that they had, except the man on the end. His eyes never blinked and never left my face.

'I'm sorry about what happened,' I said. 'I didn't mean for you to be locked up. I had just wanted to talk to you, but I went out of town and my orders got a little confused.'

They made no reply. They shuffled their shoes on the concrete floor and looked at the backs of their hands. Then the man with the skin disease said, 'It ain't bad. They got TV.'

'Anyway, I apologize to you guys,' I said. 'A deputy will drive you back to wherever you want to go. He'll also give you a voucher for a meal at a café in town. Here's my business card. If you ever want to pick up a dollar or two sanding down some boats, call that number.'

They rose as one to go out the open cell door.

'Say, podna, would you stay a minute with me?' I said to the last man on the bench.

He sat back down indifferently and began rolling a cigarette. I took a chair from the corridor and sat opposite him. His whole head looked like it had been put in a furnace. The ears were burnt into stubs; the hairless red scar tissue looked like it had been applied in layers to the bone with a putty knife; part of the lips had been surgically removed so that the teeth and gums were exposed in a permanent sneer.

He rolled the tobacco into a tight cylinder, wet down the glued seam, and crimped the edges. He lifted his eyes up to mine. They looked as lidless, as reptilian and liquid as a chameleon's. He popped a match aflame on his thumbnail. It was as thick and purple as tortoise shell.

'You like my face?' he asked.

'What's your name?'

'Vic'

'Vic what?'

'Vic Who-gives-a-shit? One name's good as another, I figure.'

'How about giving me your last name?'

'Benson.'

'How'd you get hurt, podna?'

He put his cigarette in the hole where his lips were pared away at the corner of his mouth. He blew smoke out towards the bars. 'In a tank,' he said.

'You were in the service?'

'That's right.'

'Where'd you serve?'

'Korea.'

'Your tank got nailed?'

'You got it.'

'Where in Korea?'

'Second day, at Heartbreak Ridge. What's all this stuff about?'

'There're some people who say they've seen a man with your description looking through their windows.'

'Yeah? Must be my twin brother.' He laughed, and saliva welled up on his gum.

'There's a preacher in Baton Rouge who thinks a man who looks like you might be his father.'

'I had a son once. But I didn't raise no preacher.'

'You ever hear of a woman called Mattie?'

He took his cigarette carefully off his lip and tipped the ashes between his knees.

'Did you hear me, podna?' I said.

His eyes regarded me quietly.

'You guys got nothing else to do except this kind of stuff?' he asked.

'Did you know a woman named Mattie?'

'No, I didn't.'

He picked at a scab inside his wasted forearm.

'How often do you go the blood bank?' I asked.

'Once or twice a week. Depends on how many is in town. They keep records.'

'Where do you receive your VA checks?'

'What?'

'Your disability payments.'

'I don't get them no more. I ain't gone in to certify in five or six years.'

'Why not?'

''Cause I don't like them sonsabitches.'

'I see,' I said, then I spoke to him in French.

'I don't speak it,' he said.

'I think you're not telling me the truth, Vic.'

He dropped his cigarette to the cement and mashed it out with his foot.

'You interested in my life story, run my prints,' he said, and turned up his palms. 'We were buttoned down when they put one up our snout. I was the only guy got out. The hatch burned me all the way to the bone when I pushed it open. I don't know no preacher, except at the mission. You saying I look in people's windows, you're a goddamn liar.'

His breath was stale, his eyes like heated marbles inside his red, manikinlike face.

'Where are you staying?' I said.

'At the Sally, in Lafayette.'

'I don't have anything to hold you on, Vic. But I'm going to ask you to stay out of Iberia Parish. If these same people are bothered by a man who looks like you, I want to know that you were somewhere else. Do we have an agreement on that?'

'I go where I want.'

I tapped my fountain pen on the back of my knuckles, then stood up and swung the door wide for him.

'All right, podna. The deputy at the end of the corridor will drive you back to Lafayette,' I said. 'But I'll leave you with a thought. If you're Verise Sonnier, don't blame your children for your unhappiness. They've had their share of it, too. You might even learn to be a bit proud of them.'

'Get out of my way,' he said, and walked past me, tucking in his shirt over his skinny hips.

I went home, turned on the window fan in the bedroom, and slept for four hours. On the edge of my sleep I could hear Alafair and Bootsie weeding the flower beds under the windows, walking through the leaves, scraping ashes out of the barbecue pit. When I awoke, Bootsie was in the shower. Her figure was brown and softly muted through the frosted glass, and I could see her washing her arms and breasts with a rag and a bar of pink soap. I took off my underwear and stepped into the stall with her, rubbed the smooth muscles of her back and shoulders, worked my thumbs up and down her spine, kissed the dampness of her hair along her neck.

Then I dried her off like she was a little girl, although it was I who often had the heart of a child while making love. We lay on top of the sheets, and the fan billowed the curtain and drew its breeze across us. I kissed her thighs and her stomach and put her nipples in my mouth. When I entered her, her body was so hot she felt like she was burning with a high fever.

Later, I took Alafair to Saturday evening Mass at the cathedral, then attended an AA meeting. When it was my turn to talk, I did a partial fifth step before the group, which consists of admitting to ourselves, to another human being, and to God the exact nature of our wrongs.

Why?

Because I had gone to Lyle Sonnier's house in Baton Rouge and compromised my faith in my Higher Power. I had let Him down, and by doing so – seeking out the help of a man whom I had considered a charlatan – I had let Bootsie down, too. Even Lyle had said so.

When he had hit the light switch in his kitchen, the chrome, yellow plastic, white enamel, and flowered wallpaper leaped to life with the brilliance of a flashbulb. He took a bottle of milk and pecan pie from the icebox, set forks, plates, and crystal glasses on the table, then sat across from me, wan-faced, tired, obviously unsure of where he should begin.

'We can talk a long time, Dave, but I guess I ought to tell you straight out I can't give you what you want,' he said.

'Then you *are* a fraud.'

'That's a tough word.'

'You said you can heal, Lyle. I'm calling you on it.' I felt a bubble of saliva break in my throat.

'No, you don't understand. I *was* a fraud. I was strung out on rainbows and purple acid, black speed, you name it, street dealing, breaking into people's cars, hanging in some of those gay places on South Los Angeles Street in LA, you get my drift, when I met this boozehead scam artist named the Reverend Jimmy Bob Clock.

'Jimmy Bob and me went on the tent circuit all over the South. He'd whip up a crowd till they were hysterical, then he'd walk down that sawdust aisle in a white suit with the spotlight dancing on it and grab some poor fellow's forehead in his hands and almost squeeze his brains out his ears. When he'd let go, the guy would be trembling all over and seeing visions through the top of the tent.

'Before the show he'd have me go to the rear of the line and ask some of the old folks if they wouldn't like a wheelchair to sit in, and wouldn't they like to be right down on the front row? I'd wheel them down there, and halfway into his sermon he'd jump off the stage, take them by the hands, and make them rise up and walk. Then he'd shout, "What time you got?" And they'd shout back, "It's time to run the devil around the block with the Reverend Jimmy Bob Clock."

'Jimmy Bob was a pistol, son. On camera he'd grab a handful of somebody's loose flesh and shake it like Jell-O and say he'd just cured it of cancer. He'd lift up somebody's legs from a wheelchair and hold them at an angle so one looked shorter than the other, then he'd straighten them out, praying all the time with his eyes squeezed shut, and holler out that a man born lame could now walk without a limp.

'Except they got Jimmy Bob on a check-writing rap in Hattiesburg, and I had to do the next show in Tupelo by myself. The tent was bursting with people, and I was going to try to get through the night with the wheelchair scam and maybe curing somebody of deafness or back pain or something else that nobody can see, because if that crowd doesn't get a miracle of some kind they're not shelling out the bucks when the baskets go around. But right in the middle of the sermon this old black woman comes up the aisles on two canes and I know I've got a problem.

'She started pulling on my pants leg and looking up at me with these blue cataracts, opening and closing her mouth like a baby bird in its nest. Then everybody in the tent was looking at her, and there wasn't any way out of it, I had to do something.

'I said, "What's brought you here, auntie?" And I held the microphone down to her.

'She said, "My spine's fused. They ain't nothing for the pain. 'Lectric blankets don't do it, chiropractor don't do it, mo'phine don't do it. I wants to die."

'She had on these big thick glasses that were glowing from the spots, and tears were running down her face. I said, "Don't be talking like that, auntie."

'And she said, "*You* can cure this old woman. God done anointed you.

It ain't no different than touching the hem of His garment." And she dropped her canes and set her hands on the tops of my shoes.

'I thought my conscience had been eaten up with dope a long time ago. But I wanted God to take me off the planet, right there. I wanted to tell everybody in that tent they were looking at a man who had gone as low as spit on the sidewalk. I didn't have any words, I didn't know what to do, I couldn't see anything but those spots burning in my eyes. So I got down on my knees and I put my hands on that old woman's head. Her hair was gray and wet with sweat and I could feel the blood beating in her temples. I prayed to God, right up through the top of the canvas, "Punish me, Lord, but let this lady have her way."

'That's when I felt it for the first time. It kicked through both my arms just like I grabbed hold of an electric fence. It made my teeth rattle. She straightened her back, and the pain and misery drained out of her face like somebody had poured cool water through her whole body. I'd never seen anything like it. I was trembling so bad I couldn't get off my knees. Something broke inside me and I started crying. The whole tent went crazy. But I *knew*, even at that moment, the power had come up through that old woman, through the faith in that old, sweaty, tormented black head. Sometimes in my sleep I can still feel her hair on my palms.

'It won't work for you, Dave. You came here for magic. You don't believe in the world I belong to. It's going to make you remorseful later, too.'

I hadn't eaten any of the pie. I pushed it away from me with the back of my wrist and looked through the side window at the headlights of a car clicking whitely along the dark line of oak trees on Highland Drive.

'What I'm saying is, you gave up on your own belief,' he said. 'But don't beat up on yourself about it. You got desperate and you came here to get help for somebody else, not yourself. Just go back to doing what you were before. Sometimes you got to hump it a long way before you get out of Indian country, Loot.'

I looked down between my knees at the linoleum. I didn't think I had ever been so tired.

'I appreciate your time, Lyle,' I said.

He touched the teardrop scar tissue that ran from his right eye.

'Long as you're here, there's something I want to own up to,' he said. 'The last time I saw you, I tried to push buttons on you. I mean, when I mentioned that stuff about you poking my sister.'

'I already forgot it.'

'No, you don't know everything involved, Dave. Drew had the hots for you back in college, and maybe she's still got them. But maybe for a reason you don't understand. You're a lot like Weldon.'

I raised my head and looked at him.

'You're both big, nice-looking guys,' he said. 'You were both officers in the war. Neither one of you likes rules or people telling you what to do. Both of you have electric sparks leaking off your terminals.'

I stared into his eyes.

'Growing up, we didn't have anybody but ourselves,' he said. 'It screws you up. What's sick behavior to one person is love to another. We didn't care what other people said was right or wrong. They were the same people burning us with hot cigarettes or sticking us in foster homes. Weldon and Drew weren't just brother and sister for each other. And I'm not innocent in this, either. But it was always Weldon she loved.'

I looked away from the fine bead of pain in his eyes.

'Why do you think I've had three wives?' he asked. 'Or why's Weldon married to an addict who hangs on him like a child? Or why does Drew get on with anybody who's got hair sticking out the top of his shirt? It's like your feelings and your head are never on the same wavelength. Every time you make love with somebody, you get mad at them and resent them. Figure that one out.

'Dave, you've got a lock on sanity. Don't come to the likes of us for insight.'

He forked a piece of pie into the back of his mouth and chewed it silently, his eyes never leaving my embarrassed averted face.

Sunday morning Bootsie, Alafair, and I went crabbing down by the coast. We tied chicken necks inside the weighted wire traps, whose sides would collapse on the bottom of the bay and then snap back into place with a jerk of the cord that was strung through a ring on the top. In three hours we filled a washtub with bluepoint crabs, washed them later with a garden hose in the backyard, and boiled them in a black iron pot on top of my brick barbecue pit. There was a breeze through the oaks, and the sky had a blue sheen to it, like stretched silk, and white clouds were piled high as a mountain on the western horizon.

It was a wonderful day. I had been to Mass and communion the previous evening. I had done a fifth step on my lapse of faith in my Higher Power, and I had determined once again to stop keeping score in my ongoing contention with the world, time, and mortality, and to simply thank providence for all the good things that had come to me through my plan of my own.

Eddy Raintree, with all the instincts of a mainline con and trapped animal, had tried to trade off information about a hit on Weldon, Drew, and perhaps even me. So far I hadn't talked with either of them about Raintree's possible knowledge of a contract on them, primarily because it was a waste of time; I had already warned them repeatedly about the possible consequence of not cooperating with the investigation, and I was tired of being dismissed as an adverb in their lives.

Also, I didn't take Raintree seriously. Every sociopath or recidivist about to go down for a serious jolt suddenly has access to information about armored-truck scores, judges on the pad for the syndicate, the assassination of John Kennedy, or dope sales to a US vice president.

I would leave Sunday intact, keep it the fine day it was, and let tomorrow and its uncertainties take care of themselves. We drove into New Iberia in the purpling light and ate ice cream under a spreading oak by Bayou Teche and listened to a Cajun band play in the park. I hugged Bootsie and Alafair against me.

'What's that for?' Alafair said, her eyes squinting with her grin.

'I have to make sure you guys don't get away from me,' I said.

At eleven o'clock that night, just as raindrops started to splash on the window fan in our bedroom, the sheriff called and said that Drew Sonnier had been found nailed to the gazebo in her backyard.

11

A neighbor had found her seated on the steps, half conscious, white with shock, her left hand impaled on the gazebo floor with a sixteen-penny nail, a pool of vomit in her lap.

'Hey, are you all right?' the sheriff said.

'Yes.'

'She's at the hospital, she's doing okay. At least under the circumstances.'

'Who did it?'

'I don't know if you're ready for this.'

'The guys from the Garrett killing?'

'Joey Gouza himself. Or at least he gave the orders and watched while two of his goons held her down and drove it through her hand.'

'What?' I said incredulously.

'She said it was Gouza. She can identify him, she'll testify against him. Maybe we just hit the big one . . . What's the matter?'

'She can make Joey Gouza? How does she know him?'

'All I know is what the city cops told me, Dave.'

'What's the motive?'

'Since it's your day off, I was going to send somebody else to take her statement. But I think maybe you'd better do it. Or had you rather somebody else do it?'

He was a good man, but he was basically an administrator and more conscious of the need for professional civility than dealing with realities.

'I'll go on over there in a few minutes,' I said. 'Besides the neighbor, who was the first person at the scene?'

'I think the paramedics got there first, then the city cops.' He paused a moment. The rain was clattering on the tin roof of the gallery now. 'They're cutting a warrant on Gouza now. I don't care if he's in the city jail or ours, but I want that sonofabitch in a cage. Nobody's going to do that to a woman in this parish while I'm sheriff.'

I was surprised. He wasn't given to profanity or anger. I had an idea that Joey Meatballs was about to wish that he had not gotten involved with the Sonnier family and the rural unsophistication of Iberia Parish.

I went to the hospital, but I didn't go up to Drew's room. Instead, I questioned one of the paramedics who had brought her in. I sat next to him on a wood bench by the emergency-room entrance while he drank coffee out of a Styrofoam cup. He told me he had been a navy corpsman before he had gone to work for the parish as a paramedic. His face was young and clean-shaved, and he reminded me of most medics, firemen, or US Forest Service smoke jumpers whom I had known. They were enamored of the adrenalin rush, living on the edge, but they tended to be quiet and self-effacing men, and unlike many cops they didn't have self-destructive obsessions.

'What'd you see at the scene besides Ms Sonnier?' I asked.

'I beg your pardon?'

'Did you see a hammer?'

He looked out the glass door at the rain falling on the bayou.

'No,' he answered. 'I don't think so. But it was getting dark.'

'What do you think they used to nail her hand down?'

'I don't know. But whoever did it drove it all the way down to the skin. It was a son of a gun to pull out of the boards. I had to press her hand down flat while my partner worked the nail out with a pair of vise grips. She passed out while we were doing it, poor lady.'

'Did she look like she had fought with them? Was she bruised or scratched?'

'She could have been, I didn't notice. I was thinking about getting that nail out of her hand.'

'Did she tell you anything?'

'She was in trauma. When something like that happens to them, it's like they've been drug behind a car. Maybe you ought to talk with the city cops. They were up there a little while ago.'

'I will. Thanks for your time. Here's my telephone number in case you think of anything later that might be important.'

'She's a nice lady. She jogs by my house sometimes. She must have got messed up with a bad guy. Maybe they were *both* drunk when he did it to her. I've seen some bad stuff since I came to work here, but not one like this.'

'What do you mean *drunk*?'

'She must have puked up a fifth of gin and vermouth. There's no mistaking the smell.'

I decided not to take a statement from Drew right then. Sometimes trial attorneys use the axiom 'Never ask a question you don't know the answer to.' The same is not absolutely true for a police officer, but you do have to know some of the answers in advance in order to gauge the accuracy or truthfulness of the others.

I drove to the city police station and read the report written up by the investigating officer. It was one paragraph long, ungrammatical, full of misspellings, and described almost nothing about the crime scene or the crime itself except the nature of the injury to the victim and the fact that in the hospital she had identified her assailants as two white males of medium height and build and a third white male by the name of Joey Gouza, who had watched the assault from the driver's window of his automobile.

The only evidence recovered or noted at the crime scene was the sixteen-penny nail.

Drew's house was dark and the rain was slanting through the trees as I walked through her sideyard with a six-battery flashlight. I squatted down on the floor of the gazebo and shined the beam on the planks by the top of the steps. They were smeared with miniature horsetails of dried blood, and one was centered on a blond nail hole. I walked back into the rain and searched in the myrtle bushes around the gazebo. The light flicked across a pop bottle impacted with dirt, two broken bricks, and what looked like a shattered slat from an apple crate that lay propped against some myrtle branches at the base of the gazebo.

But there was no hammer.

I stooped into the wet bushes and examined the bricks by turning them over with my pocket knife and shining the light on all their surfaces. But I saw no chip marks or scratches that would indicate that either had been used to drive a nail into a hardwood surface.

I searched among the oak trees, in the flower beds, and over the lawn, and found no hammer there, either, not that I should, I told myself. But it was something else that I didn't see that bothered me most. According to the report, she had told the city cops that Gouza had watched the assault from the window of his automobile. I returned to the gazebo's steps and shined the flashlight back toward the house. The long driveway and garage were obscured from view by a hedge and two huge clumps of banana trees. If Gouza had had a direct line of vision from his car to the gazebo, he would have had to pull it around the garage and park it on the grass behind the house.

And there were no tire tracks on the lawn. But it had rained, I thought, and maybe the depressed blades of grass had sprung back into place.

What I did find, in the weeded area around a lime tree, was a wet handkerchief spotted with blood. I put it in a Ziploc bag, and I had no idea what it meant, if anything.

The next morning I sat by Drew's hospital bed and put a half dozen mug shots face down on the sheets next to her good hand. Her other hand, her left, was wrapped thickly with bandages and rested on top of a pillow. She wore no makeup, and her hair was unbrushed and her face still puffy with sleep.

'I thought you might wait until after breakfast,' she said. 'Would you excuse me a minute?'

She went into the bath, then came back out a few minutes later, touching at her face with a towel and widening her eyes. She got back in the bed and pulled the sheet up to her stomach.

'Look at the pictures, Drew.'

She turned them over mechanically, one by one. Then she picked up one and dropped it in front of me.

'You have no doubt that's the guy?' I asked.

'Why don't you tell me, Dave? Is that Joey Gouza or not?'

'It's Joey Gouza.'

'So arrest him.'

'Somebody else is taking care of that. Did the city cops show you mug shots last night?'

'No.'

'Then how did you know it was Gouza?'

'He was at a party Weldon gave in New Orleans.'

'When I mentioned his name once before, you seemed a little vague about it, Drew.'

'That's the man who smoked a cigarette while his two pieces of shit tried to crucify me.'

I picked up the photographs and put a rubber band around them. The grass outside the window was bright green, and the sunlight looked hot on the trees, which were still wet from last night's rain.

'Why do you think they did it?' I asked.

'Gouza said, "Tell your brother to pay his debts." '

'What's his voice sound like? Does he have an accent?'

'Why are you asking me things like this?'

'A prosecutor is going to ask you, his defense attorney is. Why do you object to me asking you?'

'He has an accent like any other New Orleans lowlife.'

'I see. That'd make sense, wouldn't it?'

'No, what you're really asking is something else. There's something wrong with his voice. He sounds like he has a strep throat. No, it's worse than that. He sounds like his vocal cords were burnt with acid.'

'Here are some other mug shots, Drew. See if any of these guys look like the two men who hurt you.'

She went through them one at a time, looking carefully at each one. Among the six mug shots were the faces of Jewel Fluck, Eddy Raintree, and Jack Gates. She shook her head.

'I've never seen any of these men,' she said. She touched the tops of my fingers as I gathered up the photographs from the sheet. 'What happened to your thumb?'

'A man bit it the other night.'

'Maybe it's catching.'

'He used to be a bodyguard for Bobby Earl.'

'What did you do with him, put him in the dog pound?'

'No, I didn't get the chance, Drew. I had him cuffed by a railroad track when a guy named Jewel Fluck blew most of his face off with a shotgun. His name was Eddy Raintree. He was one of the guys I just showed you. Would you describe the two men who hurt you?'

'Do you know what victim rape is?' she asked.

'Yes.'

'I'm a little bit used up right now. You said something before about me being a soldier. I'm not. I'm still shaking inside. I don't know if I'll ever stop. If you want to take me over the hurdles, you can. But I think you're acting like a shit.'

'The sheriff told me to come up here last night and take a statement. But I didn't. I figured the city cops had pretty well worn you out. Maybe you ought to consider who your real friends are, Drew.'

She turned her head on the pillow and looked out the window. I could see a tear secrete brightly in the corner of her eye.

'I'll come back later,' I said.

She nodded, her head still turned toward the window. Her skin looked dull in the sunlight.

I paused before I went out the door.

'You're willing to testify against Gouza at a trial, Drew?'

'Yes,' she said quietly.

'You know they'll put Weldon on the stand, too, don't you?'

She twisted her head back toward me on the pillow. I saw that her projections about the future had not yet reached the last probability. She drank from a glass of water and pulled her knees up under the sheet. Her face had the divorced, empty look of a person who might have lived one way all her life only to awake one morning and discover that none of her experience counted, that she was cut loose and voiceless in a place where no other people lived.

On the way out of the hospital I stopped by the gift shop and sent a vase of flowers to her room. I signed the card 'From your many friends in Amnesty International.'

They brought Joey Gouza from New Orleans in leg and waist chains, got him arraigned that afternoon, and amidst a crowd of photographers, news reporters, and onlookers, who behaved like spectators at a cockfight, virtually trundled him from the courtroom to a city jail cell. Bail was set by Judge James Lefleur, an ill-tempered right-wing coonass also known as Whiskey Jim.

When Gouza came out of the court, in pink shirt, cream slacks, and wide black tie with white polkadots, with cops holding him by both arms, he managed to get one hand loose, grab his phallus, and spit into the lens of a television camera.

I checked my .45 with a guard before he worked the levers that slid the barred door on a corridor that led past three holding cells and the drunk tank.

'I'd like to go inside with him,' I said.

'Then you'd better take a stun gun with you,' the guard said.

'What's he done?'

'Look for yourself, look at the floor. The sonofabitch.'

The corridor in front of one cell was splattered with spaghetti, coffee, and cobbler that had obviously been flung with the plastic tray and Styrofoam containers from the iron apron in the cell door.

I walked down the corridor and propped one arm against the bars of Joey Gouza's cell. Tieless and beltless now, he sat on a bunk that was suspended from wall chains; he smoked a cigarette methodically, his fingers pinched on the paper, his furious black eyes staring into the center of the gloom.

Then he saw me. 'It's you.'

'What's happenin', Joey?'

'I should have figured your nose was in this someplace.'

'You're wrong. I'm not a player. It looks like it's between you and other people this time.'

'What people? What the fuck is going on, man?'

'You should have stayed out of Iberia Parish.'

'Are you out of your mind? You think I got an interest in some shithole that counts the mosquitoes in the population? You tell me what the fuck is going on.' His voice rasped and broke wetly in his throat. He breathed deeply to regain his momentum. 'Look, I don't sit still while people ream me. You got that, Jack? You tell me what the fucking game is.'

'I don't think there is one, Joey. I just think you paddled too far up shit creek this time. That's the way it breaks sometime.'

'The way it breaks? What do you got, yesterday's ice cream for brains? That judge, I've never seen him before and he's got a hard-on for me before they unlock me off the chain. He called me a wild animal, in front of all them people. Bail, one-point-seven-million dollars! That's a hundred and seventy thousand large for a bondsman. You telling me these people ain't trying to run a hook through my balls? Those two guys who busted me, they stuck guns in my face in my own restaurant. You've got a real problem here, some people that's totally out of control.'

'You've got good lawyers. They'll get your bail reduced.'

He flipped his cigarette in a shower of sparks off the wall and kneaded his hands together. His long neck and shoulders were webbed with veins.

'What are you down here for, to toss peanut shells at the monkeys?' he said. 'Go tell that screw there's no toilet paper in here.'

'I thought you might want to talk to me.'

He rose from the bunk, breathing hard through his nose, and came toward me.

'That broad's lying,' he said.

'She's been pretty convincing.'

His eyes looked hard into mine and narrowed.

'You know it's a ream. I see it in your face, man,' he said. 'You offering me something?'

'Somebody did it to her. I don't think it was anybody around here. Everybody I talk to thinks you're the number-one candidate, Joey. I think they've got the right person in the cell.'

His hand shot out of the bars, knotting my shirt in his fist. His breath was rife with jailhouse funk. My collar button popped loose on the floor.

'I ain't going down on a phony beef. You tell that broad that,' he said. 'You tell her brother to get her off my back.'

I tore his hand loose.

'You understand me, man?' he said. 'I don't roll over. You push me, I'll leave your hair on the wallpaper.'

'Tell that to everybody at your trial, Joey. It makes good courtroom theater.'

He hit the bars with the heel of his fist. His face was livid, popping with cartilage.

'You're twisting me, man. What's your stake? What's your fucking stake?' he said.

'Why did those guys creep Weldon Sonnier's house?'

He paced back and forth, his nostrils dilating.

'I'll print it out for you in big letters,' he said. 'I'm a businessman, I don't creep houses, I don't drive out to some hole in the road to stoke up a bunch of small-town jackoffs. They're the kind who send you to the electric chair and then go back to watering their plants. Look, you were a New Orleans cop. You know how it gets done. Somebody keeps getting in your face and don't listen to reason, you tell another guy about it, then you forget it. You don't even want to know who does it. If you're a sick guy, with a real bone on for somebody, you get Polaroids, then you burn them.

'That's how it works. You don't drive into some broad's backyard and nail her to a gazebo. You don't end up in a hick court with Elmer Fudd dropping a one-point-seven-million-dollar bond on your head. The point is, when people got dog food between their ears they're dangerous, and I don't fuck with them. Is it starting to clear up for you now?'

He stuck a cigarette in his mouth and hunted in his shirt pockets for a match.

'Gimme a light,' he said.

'How'd you get involved with Bobby Earl?' I said.

He pulled the cigarette out of his mouth and shook it at me.

'You quit trying to jerk my chain, man,' he said. 'You want to know how I got this voice? A swinging dick tried to make me his punk when I was a seventeen-year-old fish. I caught him in the shower with a string knife. Except he was a made guy, and I didn't know the rules about made guys back then, and his friends hung me up in my cell with a coat hanger. They crushed my voice box. But I didn't roll over then, man, and I don't roll over now.

'Explain to the broad I'm a three-time loser. If I go down on the bitch, I got nothing to lose. That means I can cop to anything they want and take Sonnier with me. I'll make sure he gets heavy time, and I'll be inside with him when he does it. Let her think about that.'

'You're a hard man, Joey.'

'Tell that screw down there to get me processed or send up some toilet paper.'

He scratched at the inside of his nostril with his thumbnail and blew air through his nasal passages. He had already lost interest in my presence, but a dark light remained in his face, as though he were breathing bad air, and his heated eyes, the nests of veins in his neck, his unwashed smell, the soft scud of his loafers on the cement, his jug head in silhouette against the cell window, made me think of the circus creatures who pawed the dark while they watched the dénouement of Eddy Raintree from their cages.

Later, I called Weldon at his office and was told that he was with a drilling crew at the old Sonnier farm.

I drove down the dirt road past the rusted windmill and crumbled brick supports where the house had stood before Weldon had hired a gang of drunken blacks to tear it apart with crowbars and sledge-hammers. I parked my truck by a sludge pond and an open-sided shed stacked with pipe and sacks of drilling mud, and walked up the iron steps of a rig that roared with the noise of the drilling engine.

The roughnecks on the floor were slimy with mud, bent into their work at the wellhead with the concentration of men who know the result of a moment's inattention on a rig, when the tongs or a whirling chain can pinch off your fingers or snap your bones like sticks.

A tool pusher put a hard hat on my head.

'Where's Weldon?' I shouted at him.

'What?'

'Where's Weldon Sonnier?' I shouted again over the engine's roar.

He pointed up into the rig.

High up on the tower I saw Weldon in coveralls and hardhat, working with the derrick man on the monkey board. The derrick man was clipped to the tower with a safety belt. I couldn't see one on Weldon. His face was small and round against his yellow hat as he looked down at me.

A moment later he put one foot out on the hoist, grabbed the cable with one hand, and rode it down to the rig floor. There was a single smear of bright grease, like war paint, on one of his cheekbones.

'Coffee time,' he yelled at the floormen.

Somebody killed the drilling engine, and I opened and closed my mouth to clear my ears. Weldon pulled off his bradded gloves, unzipped his coveralls, and stepped out of them. He was wearing slacks and a polo shirt, and his armpits and the center of his chest were dark with sweat.

'Let's go over here in the shade,' he said. 'It must be ninety-five today.'

We walked to the far end of the platform and leaned against the railing under a canvas awning. The air was sour with natural gas.

'I thought you'd pretty well punched out this field,' I said.

'Anyplace there was an ocean, there's oil. You just got to go deep enough to find it.'

I looked out at the wells pumping up and down in the distance and the long spans of silver pipe that sweated coldly from the natural gas running inside.

'With the low price of crude, a lot of outfits are shut down now,' I said.

'That's them, not me. What are you out here for, Dave?'

'To deliver a message.'

'Oh?'

'Actually I'm just passing on an observation. Have you been up to see Drew today?'

'Yeah, a little while ago.'

'You know you're going to end up testifying at Gouza's trial, then?'

'So?'

'I get the feeling you think somebody's going to wave a wand over your situation and you won't ever have to explain your dealings with Gouza. He's not copping a plea. He's facing life in Angola. His defense attorneys are going to use a chain saw when they get you and Drew on the stand.'

'What am I supposed to do about it?'

'Give some thought to what Drew's doing.'

He wiped at the grease on his face with a clean mechanic's cloth.

'Tell Gouza he doesn't want to make bond,' he said. 'Believe me, he doesn't want to see me unless he's got some cops around him.'

'Then you buy it?'

'You think she did it to herself? You've got the right guy in jail. Just make sure he stays there.'

'Here's the problem I have, Weldon. Joey Gouza is what they call a made guy. That's unusual in his case. He wasn't born to it, he didn't have any patrons or political allies greasing the wheels for him. He worked his way up from a reformatory punk. That means that in his world he's a lot smarter than a lot of the people around him. Come on, you know him, Weldon, do you think he'd set himself up for a fall like this?'

He folded the pink mechanic's cloth in a neat square and balanced it on the rail. Then he moved it and balanced it again.

'Stonewall time is over,' I said. 'Your sister just put the tape on fast forward.'

'So you've come out here to tell me she's a liar?'

'No, I've come out here to tell you she's a victim. I'm using the word in a broad sense, too. There's a certain kind of victimization that starts in childhood. Then the person grows older and never learns any other role. Except maybe one other. The word for that one is enabler.'

'You better get to it, Dave.' He turned toward me and rested his hand on the metal rail.

'Lyle understands it and he never finished high school.'

'I'm going to ask you to choose each of your words carefully, Dave.'

I took a deep breath. The air was pungent with gas, acrid with the smell of oil sludge and dead weeds in the sunlight.

'Look, Weldon, if I know about your family history, about some of the complexities in it, do you believe that Gouza's attorneys won't have access to the same information, that they won't use it to tear your sister apart?'

'Say it or shut the fuck up and get out of here.'

'She's not just your sister. In her mind she's your wife, your lover, your mother. She'll do anything for you. It's a way of life for her. You know it, too, you rotten sonofabitch.'

His feet were already set when he swung. He caught me on the chin and my head snapped back and my hard hat rolled across the rig floor.

I straightened up, held the rail with one hand, and looked into his face. It was stretched tight on the bone, and the suntanned skin at the corners of his eyes was filled with white lines.

The roughnecks on the floor stared at us in disbelief.

I pushed at the side of my chin with my thumb.

'They'll melt you into lard in the courtroom, Weldon,' I said. 'Gouza won't even have to take the stand. Instead, you and Drew will be on trial, and those defense attorneys will make you sound like a pornographer's wet dream.'

I saw his hand move, his eyes click again as though he'd been slapped.

'Don't even think about it,' I said. 'The first one was free. You come at me again, and I'll make sure you do time for assaulting a police officer.' I picked up the hard hat from the rig floor and shoved it into his hands, jammed it into his chest. 'Thanks for the tour of the rig. My recommendation is you hire a good lawyer and get some advice about the wisdom of suborning perjury. Or apply for a pilot's job in a country that doesn't have an extradition treaty with the United States. See you around, Weldon.'

I walked down the iron steps to my truck. I could hear the canvas awning flapping in the hot wind, a chain clinking brightly against a piece of pipe, in the embarrassed silence of the roughnecks on the rig floor.

The next morning I drove across the I-10 bridge over the Mississippi to Baton Rouge. The river was high and muddy, almost a mile across, and the oil barges far below looked as tiny as toys. Huge oil refineries and aluminum plants sprawled along the east bank of the river, but what always struck my eye first when I rolled over the apex of the bridge into Baton Rouge was the spire of the capitol building lifting itself out of the flat maze of trees and green parks in the old downtown area. All the state's political actors since Reconstruction had passed through there: populists in suspenders and clip-on bow ties, demagogues, alcoholic buffoons, virulent racists, a hillbilly singer who would be elected governor twice, another governor who broke out of a mental asylum in order to kill his wife, a recent governor who pardoned a convict in Angola, who repaid the favor by murdering the governor's brother, and the most famous and enigmatic player of them all, the Kingfish, who might have given FDR a run for his money had he not died, along with his supposed assassin, in a spray of eighty-one machine-gun bullets in a hallway of the old capitol building.

I parked my truck and sat in the gallery during the morning session of the legislature. I watched the regard with which Bobby Earl was treated by many of his peers, the warm handshakes, the pats on the arm and shoulder, the expression of gentlemanly goodwill by men who should have known better. It reminded me of the deference sometimes shown to a small-town poolroom bully or redneck police chief. The people around him well know his hatred of Jews, intellectuals, news people, Asians, blacks; no one doubts his potential with the leaded baton or the hobnailed boot across the neck. But they make friends with the ape in their midst, no matter how violently the tuning fork vibrates inside them; consequently they absorb his dark powers, and secretly gloat at the fear he inspires in others.

They recessed for lunch, and I followed Bobby Earl and a group of his friends one block to the entrance of an expensive restaurant with an awning that extended out over the sidewalk. The windows were filled with ferns and hanging copper pots. After Earl and his group had entered the restaurant, I put on my seersucker coat, tightened my necktie, and walked inside, too. Most of the tables were filled, the air loud with conversation and scented with the smell of gumbo from the kitchen, bourbon and tropical drinks from the bar.

'I don't think we have a seating for one, sir. Would you like to wait in the bar?' the maître d' said.

'I'm with Mr Earl's party. Ah, there he is right over there,' I said.

'Very well. Please follow me, sir,' he said.

I walked with the maître d' to Bobby Earl's table. The maître d' set a menu down for me at an empty place setting and walked away. Earl turned away from his conversation with another man, then his mouth opened silently as he looked up and realized who was sitting down at his table.

'Hello, Mr Earl. I apologize for bothering you again, but I'm just in town briefly and I didn't want to disturb you at the legislature,' I said. 'How are you gentlemen? I'm Detective Dave Robicheaux, with the Iberia Parish sheriff's office. I just need to ask Mr Earl a question or two. Y'all go right ahead with your lunch.'

They went on talking to each other, as though my presence was perfectly natural, but I could see their eyes, the positions of their bodies, already disassociating themselves from the situation.

Bobby Earl wore a brown pinstripe suit and a yellow silk tie, and his thick hair looked blow-dried and recently cut.

'What are you doing here?' he said.

'Do you know that Joey Gouza's in custody?'

'No.'

I set my notebook on the tablecloth and peeled back several pages. It contained nothing but notes from old investigations and a grocery list I had made out at the office yesterday.

'I interviewed him in his cell yesterday and your name came up,' I said.

'What?'

'Gouza is charged with ordering two men to nail Drew Sonnier's hand to a gazebo. When I questioned him your name came up in the conversation. That fact bothered me, Mr Earl. Is it your statement that you don't know Joey Gouza?'

'I'm not making a statement. What are you trying to do here?'

A man at the end of the table coughed quietly into his fist and went to the restroom.

'You and Joey Gouza seem to have the same friends. Your lines keep crossing in this case, Mr Earl. Originally I questioned you about Eddy Raintree. Now someone has blown Eddy's face off with a shotgun. You knew that, didn't you?'

'No, I don't know anything about this. You listen—'

His voice level rose, and the man next to him excused himself to talk with friends at the bar.

'You're harassing me,' Earl began again. 'I can't prove it, but I suspect you have a political motivation for what you've been doing. It won't work. It just makes my cause stronger. If you doubt me, call the *Morning Advocate* and check the polls.'

'Let me tell you what Gouza said and you can come to your own conclusions. We were talking about *you*, then he begins to tell me that if he goes down for what is called the "bitch", which is a life sentence given to habitual criminals, he's going to take others down with him. What does that seem to suggest to you, Mr Earl?'

'It suggests you're going to have a lawsuit against you for slander.' His monocular right eye, with the enlarged pupil like a spot of India ink, was fixed on my face. The skin along the bottom rim was trembling with anger.

I folded my notebook and put it in my shirt pocket. I picked up a package of crackers from the breadbasket, then dropped it in the basket again.

'You're an intelligent man, and I'll tell you the truth, Mr Earl,' I said. 'I think Joey might be on a bum rap. But unfortunately for him, nobody cares if a guy like Joey is innocent or not. People just want him put away in a cage for a long time, and they don't care how it's done. The prosecutor will probably get a new political career out of it, his lawyers will get rich on his appeals while he's chopping sugarcane at Angola, his wife and mistresses will clean out his bank accounts and sell everything he owns, and his hired stooges will go to work for his competitors and forget they ever heard of him. In the meantime, there are probably some sadistic gunbulls who will ejaculate at the thought of busting Joey's hump on their work gangs.

'Now, if you were Joey Meatballs and facing a prospect like that, wouldn't you be willing to cut a deal, any deal, including maybe putting your mother in harness on a dogsled team?'

The other men at the table had gone quiet now and had given up the pretense of conviviality. They looked at their watches, touched nervously at their mouths with their napkins, stared at a remote part of the restaurant. The cost of their lunch with Bobby Earl was not one they had anticipated.

I rose from the table.

'You like primitive law and vigilante solutions to complex problems, Mr Earl,' I said. 'Maybe you've stumbled into one of your own creations this time. But I wouldn't end up as Joey Gouza's fall partner. He doesn't care about political causes. He had his own brother-in-law fed into an airplane propeller. What do you think his lawyers might have planned for you?'

The tables around Bobby Earl's had now become quiet, too. He turned to speak to the men seated next to him, but their eyes were fixed on the flower arrangement in the center of the table. But I learned then that Bobby Earl was not easily undone in a public situation. He rose from the table, put his napkin neatly by his plate, and walked toward the men's room, pausing to let a black drink waiter pass. His gaze was level, his face handsome, almost pleasant-looking, his thick brown hair tousled by the cool currents from the air-conditioner.

I realized then that Bobby Earl might burn inside with banked fires, and that perhaps I had indeed inserted some broken glass in his head that would saw through brain tissue later; but in front of an audience he was a tragedian actor, a protean figure who could create an emanation of himself out of will power alone and become as benign, photogenic, and seemingly anointed by history as Jefferson Davis in defeat.

I had a feeling this one would go into extra innings.

12

That evening Bootsie, Alafair and I went to a shrimp boil in the park on Bayou Teche. The air smelled of flowers and new-cut grass, the clouds were marbled with pink, the oak trees around the wood pavilion were dark green and thick with birds. School was out for the summer, and Alafair and some other kids played kickball on the baseball diamond with the sense of dusty, knee-grimed joy that's the special province of children during summer. In fact, Alafair's aggressiveness at play made me wonder if she didn't have a bent for adversarial roles. Her cheeks were dirt-streaked and flushed with excitement; she charged without blinking at the kicker and took the volleyball full in the face, and then ran after it again, sometimes knocking another child to the ground.

The last four days with Bootsie had been wonderful. The new balance of medicine seemed to be working. Her eyes smiled at me in the morning, her posture was erect and self-assured, and she helped me and Batist at the dock and in the bait shop with cheerful eagerness. Only an hour ago I had looked up from my work and caught her in a moment when she was unconscious of my glance, just as though I had clicked the camera lens and frozen her in the pose of the healthy and unworried woman that I prayed she would become again for both of us. She had just emptied the bait tanks, her denim shirt stuck wetly to her uplifted breasts, and she was staring abstractedly out the screen window at the bayou, eating a carrot stick, her hair touched by the breeze, one hand set jauntily on her hip, the muscles in her back and neck as strong and firm as a Cajun fishergirl's.

At that moment I realized the error of my thinking about Bootsie. The problem wasn't in her disease, it was in mine. I wanted a lock on the future; I wanted our marriage to be above the governance of mortality and chance; and, most important, in my nightly sleeplessness over her health, and the black fatigue that I would drag behind me into the day like a rattling junkyard, I hadn't bothered to be grateful for the things I had.

She peeled the shell off a shrimp, dipped the shrimp in a horseradish sauce and put it in her mouth. She reached out and touched my chin lightly with two fingers, as though she were examining for a skin blemish.

'Is that where Weldon hit you?' she asked.

'I beg your pardon?'

'Oh my, such innocence.'

I cleared my throat.

'I was in the supermarket this morning,' she said. 'A woman whose husband is a floorman on Weldon's rig couldn't stop herself from asking about your welfare.'

Her eyes crinkled at the corners.

'Weldon's not a rational man,' I said.

'Why didn't you arrest him?'

'He's a tormented man, Boots. He carries a burden nobody should have to carry.'

She stopped chewing. Her eyes looked into mine.

'Lyle told me some things about their childhood, about Weldon's relationship with Drew,' I said.

A crease went across her brow, and she set her half-eaten shrimp back on the paper plate. The children out on the baseball diamond were tumbling in the dust, their happy cries echoing off the backstop.

'They're messed up in the head real bad,' I said. 'Weldon's a pain in the butt, all right, but I suspect he wakes up each morning with the Furies after him.'

'He and Drew?' she said, the meaning clear and sad in her eyes now.

'Probably Lyle, too. I said something pretty rough to Weldon about it. So he had a free one coming.'

'That's an awful story.'

'They'll probably never tell all of it, either.'

She was quiet for a few moments. Her eyes were flat and turned inward; her hair looked like it was touched with smoke in the broken light through the tree.

'When this is over, maybe we can invite them to dinner,' she said.

'That'd be fine.'

'You wouldn't mind?'

'No, of course not.'

'Why didn't anyone—' she began. Then she stopped, coughed in the back of her throat, and said, 'I never guessed. Poor Drew.'

I squeezed her hand; but it felt dry and pliant inside mine. Her mouth had the down-turned expression of someone who might have opened a bedroom door at the wrong moment. Then she stood up and began clearing the table, her face concentrating on her work.

'I'm going to invite her to go shopping with me in Lafayette,' she said. 'You think she'd like that?'

'You bet,' I said.

You'll always be a standup lady, Boots, I thought.

Out on the baseball diamond a shout went up from the children as someone fired the volley ball into the backstop.

It was dusk when we returned home, and the air was heavy and cool, motionless, loud with the croaking of frogs out in the cypress. I parked under the pecan trees in the front yard, and Bootsie and Alafair walked up to the house while I rolled up the truck's windows. The sky had turned blue-black, the color of scorched iron, and I could feel the barometer dropping again, and smell sulfur and distant rain. As I started up the incline toward the gallery, a beat-up flatbed truck bounced through the chuckholes in the dirt road and turned in to my drive. On the back was a huge chrome-plated cross, with the top end propped on the cab's roof and the shaft fastened to the bed with a boomer chain.

Lyle Sonnier cut the ignition and stepped down, grinning, from the running board. He wore a pair of striped overalls without a shirt, and his thin chest and shoulders were red with sunburn.

'I thought I'd take your time just for a minute,' he said. 'What do you think of it?'

'It looks like it's made of car bumpers.'

'It is. Me and this ole boy in Lafayette welded a shell all around the wood beams. What do you think?'

Batist had left on the string of electric bulbs over the dock, and the cross rippled and glowed with a silver and blue light.

'It looks like an artwork. It's beautiful,' I said.

'Thanks, Loot. It's the only thing the Reverend Jimmy Bob Clock left me before they sent him off to Parchman Farm. One time we were outside New Albany, Mississippi, where some Klan uglies had burned a cross in a field, and Jimmy Bob was eating a hamburger in the truck across the road, looking out at that black cross, when he says, "No sense letting good building material go to waste." Then he walks across the road and gives this colored farmer who was out there plowing a dollar for it.

' "What in the world are we gonna do with that?" I say.

'He says, "Son, the most exciting place in a shithole like this is the Dairy Queen on Saturday night. When you run a hallelujah tent show, you gotta give them lights in the sky."

'He went into a supermarket, bought eight rolls of aluminum foil, and wrapped the cross in it, then we drove out to a junkyard and he got a guy to string it with electric bulbs. That night we put it up on a hill, way up the slope from the tent, and hooked it up to the generator, and you could see that cross glowing in the mist for five miles.'

I nodded absently and looked up toward my lighted gallery.

'Well . . . I didn't mean to take up a lot of your evening,' he said. 'I just wanted to tell you I didn't feel good about the other night in Baton Rouge. You came to me for help and I couldn't offer you very much.'

'Maybe you did, Lyle.'

He looked at me curiously, then lifted one of his overall straps off his sunburn with his thumb.

'I'm going to put the cross up on my new bible college,' he said. 'I was going to call it the Lyle Sonnier Bible Institute. Now I'm just going to call it the South Louisiana Bible College. How's that sound?'

'It sounds pretty good.'

'I told you I ain't as bad as you think.'

'I think maybe you're not bad at all, Lyle.'

His eyes looked into the corners of mine, then he brushed at the dirt and leaves in the drive with his shoe.

'I appreciate it, Loot,' he said.

'You want to come in?' I asked.

'No, thanks anyway. I just came into town to see Drew at the hospital and pick up my cross in Lafayette. Weldon told me about him taking a swing on you. I'm sorry that happened. I know you've been as good and fair as you can to both him and Drew. But you really stuck a garden rake in his head.'

'Weldon has to stop jerking everybody around. Maybe it's time he takes his own fall.'

Lyle etched lines in the leaves and dust with the point of his shoe. He rested his mutilated hand, which in the deepening shadows looked almost like part of an amphibian, on the truck's door handle.

'Weldon told me last night what he's been involved in. It's a mess, it surely is,' he said. 'I think he wants to tell you about it. He's pretty well worn-out with it.'

'Do you want to tell me what it is?'

'It's his grief. You'll have to get it from him. No offense meant.' He got up in the cab of his truck and clicked the door shut with his underarm. He smiled. 'I better get out of here before I get in some kind of legal trouble. You know why I keep that burnt cross, why I'm gonna put it up on top of my Bible college? It don't let me forget where I've been and what I'm fixing to be. It's like that ole boy says in the song, "I might be an old chunk of coal but I'm gonna be a diamond someday." Give Weldon a chance. Maybe inside that cinder-block head of his he wants you to like him.'

'What I think is unimportant, Lyle. Your brother's problem is going to be with the court. Anyway, there's something I should tell you before you go. We brought in an old-timer from the Sally in Lafayette, a fellow who'd been in a fire. He might be the same man you saw in your audience.'

'He told you his name was Vic Benson?'

'You know him?'

'Sure. I drove to Lafayette and talked to him the other day. We run a shelter in Baton Rouge and a couple of new guys told me about him.'

'He's not your father, then?'

He smiled again and started his truck.

'It's him, all right. He denied it, said he had only one son and not some diddly-squat TV preacher he wouldn't waste his jizzum on.' He shook his head good-naturedly. 'That old bas— . . . that old son of a buck still knows how to rub a little pain into you. But he's a wet-brain now, been in and out of jails and insane asylums all over Texas, Louisiana, and Mississippi, at least that's what the other wet-brains say. They say maybe he's got cancer in the lungs, too. So what are you gonna do except feel sorry for a guy like that? I gotta deedee, Loot. Hang loose.'

He drove down the dirt road through the dark tunnel of oak trees, the chrome-plated cross vibrating against his cab, just as the first raindrops dimpled the bayou.

I was tired, but I had to drive to Lafayette that night and pick up a new aluminum shiner tank and water pump for the bait shop. On my way back out of town I saw one of Weldon Sonnier's company trucks pull out of the traffic and park under the trees in front of the Catholic home for handicapped children.

Weldon, in a pair of knife-creased brown slacks and a form-fitting T-shirt like a 1950s hood would wear, walked up the sidewalk to the front entrance with a stuffed shopping bag hanging from each hand.

I stopped at the traffic light, clicked my finger-nails on the horn button, turned the radio on and off at least three times, resolved under my breath that I would continue on home and not intrude any more than necessary on Weldon's pride, hard-headedness, and carefully nursed store of private misery.

The light turned green, and I went around the block and parked across the street from Weldon's truck. The moon was up, and the sky in the north, where it hadn't yet started to rain, looked like a lighted ink wash. I headed up the walk toward the entrance.

Why?

Because he needs to know that you don't get the heat off your back by punching out a police officer on an oil rig floor, I told myself.

But that wasn't it. The truth was I wanted to believe in Weldon, in the same way that sometimes you encourage someone you care about to lie to you. Or perhaps I wanted somehow to dispel the fear that one day I would have to make him Joey Gouza's fall partner.

But what would I find in a Catholic children's home that would be of any value in eventually cutting Weldon loose from the investigation or prosecuting the executioners of a deputy sheriff or taking down a racist politician?

Answer: Nothing.

I walked through the front door into a softly lit and immaculately clean oak-floored hallway, with statues of St Anthony, St Theresa, and Jesus resting on pedestals against the walls, and looked through a set of open French doors into a large recreation room.

It was filled with children whom nobody wanted. They were retarded, spastic, mongoloid, born with deformed limbs, locked in metal braces, wired to electronic devices on wheelchairs. Scattered about on the floor was a tangle of torn wrapping paper, colored ribbon and bows, and boxes that had contained all kinds of toys. He must have made several trips back and forth to the truck.

Neither the nuns nor the children looked in my direction. Weldon had taken off his shoes and was walking on his hands in the middle of the room. His face was almost purple with blood, his muscles quivering with tension, while coins and keys from his pockets bounced all over the rug and the children screamed in delight.

When he finally flipped himself over on his back, his mouth grinning crazily, his eyes bright with exertion, the children and nuns clapped as though they had just witnessed the world's greatest aerialist at work.

He sat up and rubbed his knees, still grinning. Then he saw me.

I waved at him with two fingers. His eyes lingered on mine a moment, bemused, faintly embarrassed perhaps, then he turned back to the children and said, 'Hey, you guys, the ice cream man made a big delivery this evening. Sister Agnes says it's time to fang it down.'

I turned and walked back outside into the night and a snap of lightning across the sky and the odor of rain striking warm concrete.

It rained hard during the night, and in the morning the sun came up yellow and hot and wreathed with mist over the marsh. I got up early and went down to the dock to help Batist open up, then had breakfast with Bootsie and Alafair in the kitchen. The backyard was wet and still blue with shadow, and the bloom of the mimosa was as bright as blood where the sun struck the treetop.

'What are you going to do today, little guy?' I said to Alafair.

'Bootsie's taking me to buy a new swimsuit, then we're going have a picnic in the park.'

'Maybe I can join you guys later,' I said.

'Why don't you, Dave? We'll be under the trees by the pool.'

'I'll head over about noon, or a little earlier if I can,' I said. Then I winked at Alafair. 'You keep Boots out of the sun, little guy. She's already got enough tan.'

'It's bad for her?'

Bootsie looked at me and made an impatient face.

'Well, she doesn't listen to us sometimes and we have to take charge of her,' I said.

Bootsie rapped me across the back of the hand with her spoon, and

Alafair's eyes squinted with delight. I grinned back at her, then when Bootsie was putting dishes in the sink I came up behind her and hugged her hard around the middle and kissed her neck.

'Later, later,' she whispered, and patted me quietly on the thigh.

It was going to be a fine day. I kissed Alafair good-bye, then flipped my seersucker coat over my shoulder and was almost out the door when the phone on the counter rang and Bootsie picked it up.

'It's the sheriff,' she said, and handed it to me.

I put my hand over the receiver and touched her shoulder as she walked away. 'The picnic is at noon. I'll be there, I promise, unless he sends me out of town. Okay?' I said.

She smiled without replying and began washing dishes in the sink.

'I just talked to the city chief,' the sheriff said. 'They had to take Joey Gouza to Iberia General at seven last night. He went apeshit in his cell, crashing against the bars, rolling around on the floor, and kicking his feet like he was having a seizure, slurping water out of the toilet.'

'You mean he had a psychotic episode?'

'That's what they thought it was. They got him in a van to take him to the hospital and he puked all over it. The doc at emergency receiving said he acted like he'd been poisoned, so they pumped his stomach out. Except by the time they got the tube down his throat there was hardly anything left inside him except blood from his stomach lining. Evidently the guy's got ulcers on top of his other problems.'

'What do you think happened?'

'A guard found an empty box of ant poison in the food area. Maybe somebody dumped it into his mashed potatoes. But to tell you the truth, Dave, I don't believe the city people are in a hurry to admit they can't provide security for a celebrity prisoner. They're having more fun with Joey Gouza than pigs rolling in slop.'

'What do you want me to do?'

'If he's connected with Garrett's murder, let's nail his butt before they take him out in a body bag. Not that half of New Orleans wouldn't get drunk in the streets.'

I drove over to Iberia General and walked down the hall to Joey Gouza's room. A uniformed cop was reading a magazine outside the door.

'How you doin', Dave?' he said.

'Pretty good. How's our man?'

'I have a fantasy. I see him running down the hall in his nightshirt. I see me parking a big one in his brisket. Does that answer your question?'

'Is he that bad?'

'It probably depends on whether or not you have to clean up his piss.'

'What?'

'He took a piss off the side of the bed, right in the middle of the floor. He said he doesn't use bed-pans.'

I went inside the room and closed the door behind me. Gouza's right wrist was cuffed to the bed rail and one ankle was locked to a leg chain. His elongated face was white on the pillow, his lips caked at the corners with fresh mucus. In the middle of the floor was a freshly mopped damp area. The room smelled bad, and I tried to open the window but it was sealed with locks that could only be turned with an Allen wrench.

He rubbed his nose with his finger. His eyes were black and cavernous in his drawn face.

'You don't like the smell?' he asked. His voice sounded like air wheezing out of sand.

'It's kind of close in here, partner.'

'They told you I took a leak on the floor?'

'Somebody mentioned it.'

'They told you they keep me chained to the bed, they don't even let me walk to the toilet?'

'I'll see what I can do about it.'

'I can't raise my voice. Come closer.'

I moved a chair to his bedside and sat down. His sour breath and the odor from under his sheet made me swallow.

'It's a whack,' he said.

'On who?'

'Who the fuck you think?'

'Maybe it was an accident. It happens. The people who prepare jailhouse food haven't worked in a lot of five-star restaurants.'

'I jailed too long, man. I know when the whack's out. You feel it. It's in people's eyes.'

'You're a superstar, Joey. They're not going to lose you.'

'You listen to me. Yesterday afternoon a trusty, this punk, a kid with mushmelons for buns, is sweeping out the corridor. Then he looks around real careful and walks over to my cell and says, "Hey, Joey, I can get you something."

'I go, "*You* can get me something? What, a case of AIDS?"

'He says, "Stuff you might could use."

'I go, "The only *stuff* I see around here is you, sweetcakes."

'He says, "I can get you a shank."

'I go, "What I need a shank for from a punk like you?"

'He says, "Sometimes there's badasses in the shower, man."

'I go, "You clean the shit out of your mouth when you talk to me."

'He says, "It's just a city jail, but there's a couple of bad guys here. You don't want the shank, you don't want a friend, that's your business. I was only trying to help out."

'I go, "What guys?" But he's already walking off. I go, "Come back, you little bitch,' but he clanks on the door for the screw to open up and shoots me the bone.'

'Like you say, Joey, he's probably just a punk who wants a job when he gets out. What's the big deal?'

'You don't get it. A guy like that don't shoot the bone at a guy like me. Something's happening. There's been some kind of change . . .' His hand motioned vaguely at the air, at the sunlight through the window. 'Out there somewhere. It's a whack. Look, I want a hot plate and canned food brought in.'

Then I saw something in his eye that I hadn't seen before, in the corner, a tremolo, a moist, threadlike yellow light, like a worm feeding.

He and his kind spent a lifetime trying to disguise their self-centered fear. It accounted for their grandiosity, their insatiable sexual appetites, their unpredictable violence and cruelty. But almost always, if you were around them long enough, you saw it leak out of them like a sticky substance from a dead tree.

'I owe you a confession, Joey,' I said.

'You owe me a—' He turned his head on the pillow to look at me.

'Yeah, I haven't been honest with you.'

His brow became netted with lines.

'I cooked the books on you a little bit,' I said. 'You wanted me to tell Weldon you weren't going down by yourself. I did as you asked, but I told the same thing to Bobby Earl.'

His head lifted an inch off the pillow.

'You told Earl—' His breath was rasping. 'You told Earl *what?*'

'That you're going to take other people down with you.'

'Why you trying to tie me with Earl?'

'You seem to know a lot of the same people, Joey.'

His face was gray and dry. His eyes searched in mine.

'I got you figured,' he said. 'You're trying to put out word to the AB I'm gonna roll over. That's it, ain't it? You're gonna keep squeezing me till I cop to some bullshit plea. Do you know what you're doing, man? The AB's not part of the organization. They think somebody's gonna rat-out a member, it's an open contract. They're in every joint in the country. You do time when there's an AB hit on you, you do it in lockup. I mean with a solid iron door, too, man, or they'll get you with a Molotov through the bars. That's what you're trying to bring down on me? That's why you're pulling on Bobby Earl's crank? That's a lousy fucking thing to do, man.'

'Would Jewel Fluck try to whack you, Joey?'

His eyes narrowed and grew wary.

'I saw him take out Eddy Raintree. It was pretty ugly.'

'I got no more to say to you.'

'I can't blame you. I'd feel the same way if all the doors were slamming around me. But think about it this way, Joey. You're a made guy. There're cops who respect that. Are you going to do major time while a guy like Bobby Earl sips Cold Duck and gets his picture on the society page? He's a Nazi, Joey, the honest-to-God real article. Are you going to take a jolt for a guy like that?'

He leaned over the side of the bed and spit in the wastebasket. I looked the other way.

'Drop dead, man. I don't know anything about Bobby Earl.'

I studied his face. His skin was grained, unshaved, filled with twitches.

'What are you staring at?' he said.

'Give him up.'

'You must have some kind of brain tumor or something. Nothing I say seems to get in your head. You guys ain't gonna do this stuff to me. You tell these local bozos I'm walking out of this beef. I'm not doing time, I'm not getting whacked in custody, either. I ain't getting whacked. Can you handle that, Jack?'

'The local bozos aren't taking a lot of interest in your point of view, Joey. Every once in a while a token guy gets dropped in the skillet, and this time it looks like you're it. It might not be fair, but that's the way it works. You never saw a mob run across town to do a good deed, did you?'

He tried to turn away from me, but his wrist clanked the handcuff chain against the bed rail. He hit the mattress with his other fist, then clenched his arm over his eyes.

'I want you to leave me alone,' he said.

I got up from the chair and walked to the door. His chained right foot stuck out from under the sheet. He tried to clear his throat and instead choked on his saliva.

'I'll see about the canned goods and the hot plate,' I said.

He worked the sheet up to his chin, kept his arm pressed tightly across his eyes, and didn't reply.

I arrived in the park before Bootsie and Alafair and walked idly along the bayou's edge under the trees. Desiccated gray leaves were scattered along the mudbank. I squatted down and flipped pebbles at several thin, needle-nosed garfish that were turning in the current.

I was troubled, uncomfortable, but I couldn't wrap my hand around the central concern in my mind.

Joey Gouza was in custody, where he belonged. Why did I worry?

Police often have many personal problems. TV films go to great lengths to depict cops' struggles with alcoholism, bad marriages, mistreatment at the hands of liberals, racial minorities, and bumbling administrators.

But my experience has been that the real enemy is the temptation to misuse power. The weaponry we possess is awesome – leaded batons, slapjacks, Mace, stun guns, M-16s, scoped sniper rifles, 12-gauge assault shotguns, high-powered pistols and steel-jacketed ammunition that can blow the cylinders out of an automobile's engine block.

But the real rush is in the discretionary power we sometimes exercise over individuals. I'm talking about the kind of people no one likes – the lowlifes, the aberrant, the obscene and ugly – about whom no one will complain if you leave them in lockdown the rest of their lives with a good-humored wink at the Constitution, or if you're really in earnest, you create a situation where you simply saw loose their fastenings and throw down a toy gun for someone to find when the smoke clears.

It happens, with some regularity.

I saw Bootsie and Alafair setting out picnic food on a table by the baseball diamond and I walked over to join them. Alafair streaked past me, her face already flushed with expectation.

'Hey, where you going, little guy?' I said.

'To play kickball.'

'Don't blind anyone.'

'What?'

'Never mind.'

Then she turned and plunged into the midst of the game, knocking another child to the ground. I sat down in the shade with Bootsie and ate a piece of fried chicken and two or three bites of dirty rice before my attention wandered.

'Did something happen this morning?' Bootsie asked.

'No, not really. Joey Gouza's probably having his day in the Garden of Gethsemane, but I guess that's the breaks.'

'Do you feel bad about him for some reason?'

'I don't know what I feel. I suppose he deserves anything that happens to him.'

'Then what is it?'

'I think he's in jail for the wrong reasons. I think Drew Sonnier is lying. I also think nobody cares whether Drew is lying or not.'

'That doesn't make sense, Dave. If he didn't do it to her, who did?'

Out on the field the kids had torn loose a base pad from its fastening in the sand, where it served as the home base for one side. Alafair had the volleyball under one arm and was trying to replace the wooden peg in the sand without anyone else taking the ball from her.

'I don't know who did it,' I said. 'Maybe Gouza ordered it done as a warning to Weldon, then Drew lied to put him at the scene. But a guy like Gouza doesn't go out on a job himself.'

'It's the city's case. It's not your responsibility.'

'I twisted him. I made Bobby Earl think Gouza was going to drop the dime on him, then I told Gouza about it. They guy's experiencing some real psychological pain. He thinks a hit's out on him.'

'Is there?'

'Maybe. And if there is, I might be responsible.'

'Dave, a man like that is a human garbage truck. Whatever happens to him is the result of choices he made years ago . . . Are you listening?'

'Sure,' I said. But I was watching Alafair. She couldn't hold the wooden peg with one hand and tamp it down in the sand without releasing the volleyball with the other, so she balanced the peg against her folded knee, then knocked it down with the heel of her free hand.

'What is it?' Bootsie said.

'Nothing,' I said. 'You're right about Joey Gouza. It would be impossible to be more than a footnote in that guy's life.'

'Do you want another piece of chicken?'

'No, I'd better get back to the office.'

'Let the city people handle it, *cher.*'

'Yeah, why not?' I said. 'That's the best idea.'

She squinted one eye at me, and I averted my gaze.

Ten minutes after I was back at the office, my phone rang.

'Dave?' His voice was cautious, almost deferential, as though he were afraid I'd hang up.

'Yeah, what is it, Weldon?'

He waited a moment to reply. In the background I could hear 'La Jolie Blonde' on a jukebox and the rattle of pool balls.

'You want to have a bowl of gumbo down at Tee Neg's?' he asked.

'I've already eaten, thanks.'

'You shoot pool?'

'Once in a while. What's up?'

'Come down and shoot some nine-ball with me.'

'I'm a little busy right now.'

'I'm sorry,' he said.

'About what?'

'For taking a punch at you. I'm sorry I did it. I wanted to tell you that.'

'Okay.'

'That's all . . . "okay"?'

'I pushed you into a hard corner, Weldon.'

'You're not still heated up about it?'

'No, I don't think so.'

'Because I wouldn't want you mad at me.'

'I'm not mad at you.'

'So come down and shoot some nine-ball.'

'No more games, podna. What's on your mind?'

'I've got to get out of this situation. I need some help. I don't know anybody else to ask.'

After I hung up I drove over to Tee Neg's pool hall on Main Street. The interior had changed little since the 1940s. A long mahogany bar with a brass rail and cuspidors ran the length of the room, and on it were gallon jars of cracklings (which are called *graton* in southern Louisiana), hard-boiled eggs, and pickled hogs' feet. Wood-bladed fans hung from the ceiling; green sawdust was scattered on the floor; and the pool tables were lighted by tin-shaded lamps. In the back, under the blackboards that gave ball scores from all around the country, old men played dominoes and *bourée* at the felt tables, and a black man in a porter's apron shined shoes on a scrolled-iron elevated stand. The air was thick and close with the smell of gumbo, boiled crawfish, draft beer, whiskey, dirty-rice dressing, chewing tobacco, cigarette smoke, and talcum from the pool tables. During football season illegal betting cards littered the mahogany bar and the floor, and on Saturday night, after all the scores were in, Tee Neg (which means 'Little Negro' in Cajun French) put oilcloth over the pool tables and served free robin gumbo and dirty rice.

I saw Weldon shooting pool by himself at a table in back. He wore a pair of work boots, clean khakis, and a denim shirt with the sleeves folded in neat cuffs on his tan biceps. He rifled the nine ball into the side pocket.

'You shouldn't ever hit a side-pocket shot hard,' I said.

'Scared money never wins,' he said, sat at a table with his cue balanced against his thigh, knocked back a jigger of neat whiskey, and chased it with draft beer. He wiped at the corner of his mouth with his wrist. 'You want a beer or a cold drink or something?'

'No thanks. What can I do to help you, Weldon?'

He scratched at his brow.

'I want to give it up, but I don't want to do any time,' he said.

'Not many people do.'

'What I mean is, I *can't* do time. I've got a problem with tight places. Like if I get in one, I hear popsickle sticks snapping inside my head.'

He motioned his empty jigger at the bar.

'Maybe your fears are getting ahead of you,' I said.

'You don't understand. I had some trouble over there.'

'Where?'

'In Laos.' He waited until the barman had brought him another shot and in a fresh draft chaser. He tipped the whiskey into the beer and watched it balloon in a brown cloud off the bottom of the glass. 'We operated a kind of flying taxi service for some of the local warlords. We were also transporting some of their home-grown organic. Eventually it got processed into heroin in Hong Kong. For all I know, GIs in Saigon ended up shooting it in their arms. Not too good, huh?'

'Go on.'

'I got sick of it. On one trip I told this colonel, this half-Chinese character named Liu, that I wasn't going to load his dope. I pushed him off the plane and took off down the runway. Big mistake. They shot the shit out of us, killed my copilot and two of my kickers. I got out of the wreck with another guy, and we ran through jungle for two hours. Then the other guy, this Vietnamese kid, said he was going to head for a village on the border. I told him I thought NVA were there, but he took off anyway. I never found out what happened to him, but Liu's lice heads caught me an hour later. They marched me on a rope for three days to a camp in the mountains, and I spent the next eighty-three days in a bamboo cage just big enough to crawl around in.

'I lived in my own stink, I ate rice with worms in it, and I wedged my head through the bamboo to lick rainwater out of the mud. At night the lice heads would get drunk on hot beer and break the bottles against my cage. Then one morning I smelled this funny odor. It was blowing in the smoke from the campfire. It smelled like burned hair or cowhide, then, when the wind flattened out the smoke, I saw a half-dozen human heads on pikes around the fire. I don't want to tell you what their faces looked like.

'Liu's buttholes probably wanted to ransom me, but at the same time they were afraid of our guys because they'd shot up the plane and killed three of my crew. So I figured eventually they'd get tired of busting bottles on my cage and pissing on me through the bars, and my head was going to be curing in the smoke with those others.

'I used to wake with fear in the morning that was unbelievable. I'd pray at night that I would die in my sleep. Then one day some other guys came into the camp, guys who knew I was money on the hoof and who wanted to make some toady points with the CIA. They bought me for a case of Budweiser and six cartons of cigarettes.'

He drank from his boilermaker, his eyes glazed faintly with shame.

'It's a funny experience to have,' he said. 'It makes you wonder about your worth.'

'Cut it loose, Weldon.'

'What?'

'We already paid our dues. Why run the same old tape over and over again?'

'I volunteered for Air America. I can't blame that on somebody else.'

'You didn't volunteer to be a heroin mule.'

He pulled the cellophane off a cigar and rubbed it between his fingers until it was a small ball.

'If you were going to cut a deal with the feds, who would you go to?'

'It depends on what you did.'

'We're talking about guns and dope.'

'You mean you got into it again?'

'Yes and no.'

I looked at him quietly. He made a series of wet rings on the table with his jigger.

'The guns and the dope didn't get delivered, but I burned some guys for one hundred and eighty grand,' he said.

His eyes flicked away from mine.

'This is straight? You actually ripped off some traffickers for that kind of money?' I said.

'Yeah, I guess it was sort of a first for them.'

'One of the guys you burned is right there in the city jail, isn't he?'

'Maybe, maybe not.'

'There's no maybe about it. My advice is you should talk to the DEA or to Alcohol, Tobacco and Firearms. I know a pretty good agent in Lafayette.'

'That's about all you can suggest, huh? No magic answers.'

'You won't confide in me. I'm at a loss to help you.'

'If I did confide in you, I'd probably be under arrest.'

He smiled wanly and started to drink from his glass, then set it back down.

'I'll give what you said some thought, Dave.'

'No, I doubt that, Weldon. You'll go your own way until you beat your head into jelly.'

'I wish I always knew what was going on inside other people. It'd be a great asset in the oil business.'

Before I drove back to the office I walked across the drawbridge over the Teche and watched the current running through the pilings and the backs of the garfish breaking the water in the sunlight. The air was hot, the sky bright with haze, the humidity so intense that my eyes burned with salt and my skin felt like insects were crawling on it. Even under the trees by the old brick firehouse in the park, the air felt close and moist, like steam rising off a stove.

Weldon had his problems, but I had mine, too. This case went far beyond Iberia Parish, and it appeared to involve people and power and politics of a kind that our small law-enforcement agencies were hardly adequate to deal with. Once again, I felt like the outside world was having its way with us, that it had found something vulnerable or weak or perhaps even desirous in us that allowed the venal and the meretricious to leave us with less of ourselves, less of a way of life that had been as sweet in the mouth as peeled sugarcane, as poignant and heartbreaking in its passing as the words to 'La Jolie Blonde' on Tee Neg's jukebox:

> *Jolie blonde, gardez donc c'est t'as fait.*
> *T'a m'as quit-té pour t'en aller,*

Pour t'en aller avec un autre que moi.
Jolie blonde, pretty girl,
Flower of my heart
I'll love you forever,
My jolie blonde.

Still, Joey Gouza was in the city of New Iberia's custody, and if the prosecutor's office had its way he would be hoeing sweet potatoes on Angola Farm the rest of his life.

But something that had bothered me at noon while I had watched Alafair playing in the park was troubling me again, this time because of an idle glance across the bayou at a young man fishing under a cypress tree. I was watching him because he reminded me of so many working-class Cajun boys I had grown up with. He stood while he fished, bare-chested, lean, olive-skinned, his body knotted with muscle, his Marine Corps utilities low on his stomach, smoking a cigarette in the center of his mouth without taking it out. His bobber went under, and he jerked his pole up and pulled a catfish through the lily pads. Then I noticed that his left hand was gone at the wrist and he had to unhook the catfish and string it with one hand. But he was quite good at it. He laid the fish across a rock, pressed the sole of his boot down on its stomach, slipped the hook loose from the corner of its mouth, and worked a shaved willow fork through the gills until the hard white point emerged bloody and coated with membrane from the mouth. Then with his good hand he flopped the fish into the shallows and sank the willow fork deep into the mud.

The sheriff was sitting sideways in his swivel chair, reading a diet book, punching at his stomach with three fingers, when I walked into his office. He looked up at me, then put the book in his drawer and began fiddling with some papers on his blotter. Like many Cajun men, his chin was round and dimpled and his cheeks ruddy and flecked with small veins.

'I was thinking about going on a diet myself,' I said.

'Somebody left that in here. I don't know who it belongs to.'

'Oh.'

'What's up?'

I told him I was going out to Drew Sonnier's again and my suspicions about what had happened at the gazebo.

'All right, Dave, but make sure you get her permission to look around on the property. If she won't give it to you, let's get a warrant. We don't want any tainted evidence.'

He saw me raise my eyebrows.

'What?' he said.

'You're talking about evidence we might use against her?'

'It's not up to us. If she's filed false charges against Joey Gouza, the prosecutor might want to stick it to her. You still want to go out there?'

'Yes.'

'Then do it. By the way, she was discharged from the hospital this morning, so she's back home now.'

'Okeydoke.'

'Dave, a little advice. Try to put the lid on your personal feelings about the Sonniers. They're grown-up people now.'

'All right, sheriff.'

'There're a couple of other things I need to tell you. While you were out the jailer called. It seems one trusty decided to snitch on another one. The night Joey Gouza went apeshit and vomited all over his cell, the trusty preparing the food got swacked on paregoric and accidentally knocked a box of ant poison off the shelf on to a table. It probably got in Gouza's food. Except the trusty didn't tell anybody about it. Instead he wiped off the table and served the trays like nothing had happened.'

'Gouza's convinced there's a hit on him.'

'That might be, but this time it looks like it was an accident.'

'Where's the trusty now?'

'They're moving him over to the parish jail. I'd hate to be that guy when Gouza finds out who fired up his ulcers.'

'There's no chance an AB guy was involved?'

'The guy who spilled the ant poison is a migrant farm worker in for DWI . . . You almost look disappointed.'

'No, I just thought maybe the guys in the black hats were starting to cannibalize each other. Anyway, was there something else?'

'Yeah, I'm afraid there is.' He kept putting one hand on top of the other, which was always his habit when he didn't want to say something offensive to someone. Then he pressed his glasses more tightly against his eyes. 'I got three phone calls, two from state legislators and one from Bobby Earl's attorney. They say you're harassing Earl.'

'I don't read it that way.'

'They say you gave him a pretty bad time in a Baton Rouge restaurant.'

'I had five minutes' conversation with him. I didn't see anything that unusual in it, considering the fact that I think he's involved with a murder.'

'This is another thing that bothers me, Dave. We don't have any evidence that Earl is connected with Garrett's death. But you seem determined to tie Earl to it.'

'Should I leave him alone?' I looked him straight in the face.

'I didn't say that. I'm just asking you to look at your motivations.'

'I want—'

He saw the heat in my face. 'What?' he asked.

'I want to turn the key on the people who killed Garrett. It's that simple, sheriff.'

'Sometimes we have an agenda we don't tell ourselves about. It's just human.'

'Maybe it's time somebody 'fronts a guy like Earl. Maybe he's gotten a free pass too long.'

'You're going to have to ease up, Dave, or it'll be out of my hands.'

'He's got that kind of juice?'

'No, he doesn't. But if you try to shave the dice, you'll give it to him. You got into it at his house, then you created a situation with him in a public place. I don't want a suit filed against this department, I don't want a couple of peckerwood politicians telling me I've got a rogue cop on my hands. It's time to take your foot off the accelerator, Dave.'

My palms were ringing with anger.

'You think I'm being too hard on you?' he asked.

'You have to do what you think is right.'

'You're probably the best cop we ever had in this department. Don't walk out of here thinking my opinion is otherwise, Dave. But you've got a way of kicking it up into overdrive.'

'Then the bottom line is we're cutting Bobby Earl some slack.'

'You once told me the best pitch in baseball is a change of pace. Why not ease up on the batter and see what happens?'

'Ease up on the wrong guy and he'll drill a hole in your sternum with it.'

He turned his hands up on the blotter.

'I tried,' he said, and smiled.

When I left the room, the back of my neck felt as though someone had held a lighted match to it.

Drew answered her door in a print sundress covered with yellow flowers. Her tan shoulders were spotted with freckles the size of pennies. Even though her left hand was swathed in bandages as thick as a boxing glove, she had put on eye shadow, lipstick, and dangling earrings set with scarlet stones, and she looked absolutely stunning as she stood with one plump hip pressed against the doorjamb.

I had called fifteen minutes earlier.

'I don't want to keep you if you're on your way out, Drew,' I said.

'No, it's fine. Let's sit on the porch. I fixed some tea with mint leaves in it.'

'I just need to look around back.'

'What for?'

'I might have missed something when I was out before.'

'I thought you might like some tea.'

'Thanks just the same.'

'I appreciated the flowers.'

'What flowers?'

'The ones you sent up to my hospital room with the Amnesty International card. One of the pink ladies saw you buy them.'

'She must have been mistaken.'

'I wanted to act nice toward you.'

'I need to look around back. If you don't want to give me your permission, I have to get a warrant.'

'Who lit your fuse today?'

'The law's impersonal sometimes.'

'You think I'm trying to get you in the sack?'

'Give it a break, Drew.'

'No, give me an honest answer. You think I'm all heated up for you, that I'm going to walk you into my bedroom and ruin your marriage? Do you think your old girlfriends are lining up to ruin your marriage?'

'Can I go in back?'

She put her good hand on her hip. Her chest swelled with her breathing.

'What do you think you'll find that no one else did?' she asked.

'I'm not sure.'

'Whose side are you on, Dave? Why do you have to spend so much time and effort on me and Weldon? Do you have any doubt at all that an animal like Joey Gouza belongs in jail? Of all the people in the parish, why are you the only one who keeps turning the screws on us? Have you asked yourself that?'

'Should I go after the warrant?'

'No,' she said quietly. 'Look anywhere you want to . . . You're a strange man. You understand principle, but I wonder how well you understand pain in other people.'

'That's a rotten thing to say.'

'Too bad.'

'No, you're not going to get away with that, Drew. If you and Weldon weren't my friends, both of you would have been in jail a long time ago for obstruction of justice.'

'I guess we're very fortunate to have a friend such as you. I'm going to shut the door now. I really wish you had had some tea. I was looking forward to it.'

'Listen, Drew—'

She closed the door softly in my face, then I heard her turn the bolt in the lock.

I went back to my truck, took a screwdriver and three big Ziploc bags off the seat, and walked through the side yard to the gazebo. The lattice-work was thick with bugle and grapevine, and the myrtle bushes planted around the base were in full purple flower. I knelt down in the moist dirt and probed through the bushes until I found the two pieces of brick I had seen previously. I dropped them both in a plastic bag, then found the broken slat from an apple crate and picked it up carefully by the edges. There was a split from the top down to a nail hole in the center of the slat. I turned it over between my fingers. Even in the deep shade I could see a dark smear around the hole on the opposite side. I slipped the slat into another bag and worked my way back out of the myrtle bushes on to the grass.

I glanced behind me and saw her face at a window. Then it disappeared behind a curtain.

Each of the steps on the gazebo had been carpentered with a two-inch gap between the horizontal and perpendicular boards. I tried looking through the openings into the darkness below the gazebo but could see nothing. I used the screwdriver to unfasten a section of latticework at the bottom of the gazebo and lifted it out with my fingers. It was moist and cool inside and smelled of standing water and pack-rat nests. I reached underneath the steps and touched the cold metal head of a ball-peen hammer.

I wondered if she had tried to remove it before I had arrived. I worked it out from under the steps with the screwdriver and carefully fitted it into the third plastic bag, then walked up to the screened-in porch on the side of the house.

When she didn't answer, I banged louder with the side of my fist against the wall.

'What is it?' she said, jerking open the door, her face pinched with both anger and defeat.

I let her take a hard look at the two broken bricks, the split apple-box slat, and the ball-peen hammer.

'I'm going to tell you a speculation or two, Drew, but I don't want you to say anything unless you're willing to have it used against you later. Do you understand that?'

Her mouth was a tight line, and I could see her pulse beating in her neck.

'Do you understand me, Drew? I don't want you to say anything to me unless you're completely aware of the jeopardy it might put you in. Are we perfectly understood on that?'

'Yes,' she said, and her voice almost broke in her throat.

'You punched the nail through the slat, and you laid the slat across the two bricks. Then you put your hand under the nail and drove it all the way through into the step. The pain must have been terrible, but before you passed out, you splintered the slat away from the nail and shoved it and the bricks into the myrtle bushes. Then you pushed the hammer through the gap in the step.'

Her eyes were filming.

'Your prints are probably all over the bricks and the slat, but that won't mean anything in itself,' I said. 'But I have a feeling there won't be any prints on the hammer except yours. That one might be hard to explain, particularly if there are blood traces on the hammer and we know for sure it's the one that was used to drive the nail into the gazebo floor.'

She was breathing hard now, her throat was aflame with color, and her eye shadow had started to run. She licked her lips and started to speak.

'This time listen to me for a minute,' I said. 'I'm going to take this stuff down to the prosecutor's office and they can make of it what they want. In the meantime I recommend you drop the charges against Joey Gouza. Do it without comment or explanation.'

She nodded her head. Her eyes were glistening, and she kept shutting them to clear the tears out of the lashes.

'It happens all the time,' I said. 'People change their minds. If anyone tries to build a case against you, you keep an attorney at your side and you turn to stone. You think you can do that?'

'Yes.'

I wanted to put my arms around her shoulders. I wanted to press her against me and touch her hair.

'Will you be okay?' I asked.

'Yes, I believe I'll be fine.'

'Call Weldon.'

'I will.'

'Drew?'

'Yes.'

'Don't mess with Gouza anymore. You're too good a person to get involved with lowlife people.'

She kept closing and unclosing her good hand. Her knuckles were white and as tight against her skin as a row of nickels.

'You liked me, didn't you?' she said.

'What?'

'Before you went away to Vietnam. You liked me, didn't you?'

'A woman like you makes me wish I could be more than one person and have more than one life, Drew.'

I saw the sunlight bead in her eyes.

A few minutes earlier she had asked me whose side I was on. I felt I knew the answer now. The truth was that I served a vast, insensate legal authority that seemed determined to further impair the lives of the feckless and vulnerable while the long-ball hitters toasted each other safely at home plate.

That night the sheriff called me at home and told me that Joey Gouza was being moved from the hospital back to a jail cell. He also said that in light of the evidence I had found at Drew Sonnier's, the prosecutor's office would probably drop charges against Gouza in the morning.

When I got to the jail on East Main early the next morning, the sun was yellow and hazy through the moss-hung canopy of oak trees over the street, and the sidewalks were streaked with dew. I left my seersucker coat on when I went inside and stopped in the men's room. I took my .45 out of the holster, pulled the clip out of the magazine, ejected the round in the chamber, and slipped the pistol and the clip in the back of my belt under my coat. Then I unclipped the holster from my belt and dropped it in my coat pocket.

I waited for the guard to open the barred door that gave on to the row of cells where Joey Gouza was housed.

'You want to check your weapon, Dave?' he asked.

'They've got it up front.'

'Somebody said he might walk. Is that true?'

'Yep.'

'How the hell'd that happen?'

'Long story.'

'The sonofabitch is eating his soft-boiled eggs now. Can you beat that? Fucking soft-boiled eggs for a piece of shit like that.'

He opened the door, then walked with me down the corridor to Gouza's cell and turned the key in the lock.

'You sure you want inside with this guy?' he asked. 'He won't shower. He thinks somebody's gonna shank him if he leaves his cell.'

'It's all right. I'll yell when I'm ready,' I said.

The guard closed the door behind me and went away. Gouza lay on his bunk in his jockey underwear. A band of dark hair grew in a line from his navel to his sternum. An empty bowl streaked with egg yolk and a wastebasket filled with torn and stained newspaper sat on the floor by his bunk. His face looked as pale as it had been in the hospital. His seemingly lidless black eyes studied me as I pulled up the single chair in the cell and sat on it.

'They're going to kick you loose,' I said.

'Yeah, I owe you one.'

'You really believe that somebody is going to do you in the shower?'

'Put it this way. One guy in this place got poisoned. Me. Your people say it was an accident. Maybe so. But I don't want any more accidents. Does that seem reasonable?'

I leaned forward with my forearms on my thighs. 'I've got a problem,' I said.

'*You've* got a problem?'

'Yeah, a serious one, Joey.'

'What are you talking—'

'You're a made guy. A made guy worries about respect, about what people think of him.'

'So?'

'When you get out of here, you'll probably have a nice dinner some-where, maybe drink a glass of wine, maybe do a few lines with one of your whores. Then after a while all kinds of thoughts will start to turn over in your head. Are you with me?'

'No.'

'You'll think about how you were humiliated, how a woman set you up for a fall, how Elmer Fudd and company turned you into a sideshow. Then you'll remember how you got scared and asked for your own hot plate and canned food and told the screw you wanted to stay in lockup. You'll wake up thinking about it in the middle of the night, then you'll wonder if the people around you are figuring you for a guy who's about to lose it, maybe a guy who's ripe for replacement. That's when you'll decide it's time for an object lesson. So that's what's been on my mind, partner. Sooner or later we'll have a visit from one of your people, a button man from Miami or maybe some AB sex deviate you turn loose on women.'

He leaned over the bunk and spat into the wastebasket, then took a sip from a brown bottle of chalky medicine and screwed the cap back on.

'Think anything you want,' he said. 'I got nothing on my mind except getting treatment for my ulcers before they have to cut out half my stomach. Any beef I got against this shithole I let my lawyers handle with a civil suit. You can thank Fudd and the broad if y'all have to pass a sales tax to pay off the damages.'

'What I'm really trying to do is apologize to you, Joey.'

He raised his elongated head up on his elbow. The skin at the corner of his mouth wrinkled with a smile.

'You're gonna apologize? You're good, man. You ought to get yourself some kind of nightclub act. I can probably book you into a couple of places.'

'Because I was going to pull a cheap ruse on you. I was going to treat you like a punk instead of a made guy. So I'm apologizing.'

'You talk like you got clap in your brain or something. What's with you? You never make sense. Can't you talk to people like you got sense?'

I reached behind me and pulled the .45 from under my coat. I rested it on my thigh.

'You ain't supposed to have that in here, man,' he said.

'You're right. That's what I've been trying to tell you. I want to apologize for what I had in mind.'

He was rigid in the bunk. I stared intently at the floor, then cocked the hammer with my thumb and raised the barrel and fitted it into the hollow of his cheek. His eyes closed, then opened again, and his Adam's apple worked up and down with a dry click in his throat.

I squeezed the trigger, and the hammer snapped on the empty chamber. He gasped, and his face jerked like he'd been slapped.

'I was going to pull a cheap trick like that to scare you,' I said. 'But you're a made guy, Joey, and you deserve more respect than I've shown you. And even if I rattled you a little bit, you'd be back, wouldn't you?' I winked at him. 'You'd really rip some ass, right or wrong?'

A sweat had broken on his ashen face.

'You're a head case, man,' he said. 'You stop this shit. You get the fuck out of my life.'

I pulled the clip from my belt and let it rest against my thigh. The hollow-points were loaded tightly against the spring. I rubbed my thumb casually over the top round in the clip. The fingers of both my hands made tiny, delicate prints in the thin sheen of oil on the steel surfaces of the pistol and the clip. I could hear him breathing loudly through his nose and smell the odor of fear that rose from his armpits.

'You weren't in the service, were you?' I said.

'Who gives a shit?'

'Did you ever kill anybody close up?'

He didn't answer. His eyes went from my hands to my face and back to my hands again. I inserted the clip in the magazine, pulled back the receiver, and slid a hollow-point round into the chamber.

'I'm going to give you your chance,' I said.

'What?'

'To do me. Right in this cell. I lied to the guard and told him I'd already checked my weapon. So everybody will believe you when you tell them I tried to kill you, that you got the weapon away from me and did me instead.'

'I ain't playing this game.'

'Yes, you are.'

'I want the screw.'

'It's just you and me, Joey. Here,' I said, and I laid the .45 on the striped mattress next to him.

His hands were shaking. A drop of sweat fell from the point of his chin.

'I ain't touching it,' he said.

'It's the only chance you'll get at me. If you send anybody back to Iberia Parish to square a beef, I'll be coming through your door two hours after it happens. It'll be under a black flag, too, Joey. No warrant, no rules, just you and me and maybe Clete Purcel as a Lucky Strike extra. Are you going to pick it up?'

He pressed one hand against his naked stomach and grimaced with a spasm that made his eyes close.

'You quit doing this to me. You fucking lay off,' he said hoarsely.

I reached out and took the .45 back and eased the hammer back down. I tried to hide the deep breath that I drew into my lungs.

He leaned his head over the bunk and vomited into the wastebasket. The hair on his bare shoulders was damp with sweat. I wet some paper towels in the washbasin and handed them to him.

'Any vendetta you have against the Sonniers ends here, Joey,' I said. 'Are we understood on this?'

He sat up on the bunk and took the crumpled towels away from his mouth.

'I'll give you what you want,' he said.

'I'm not quite following you.'

'I'll give you the guy you want. You get the guy.'

'Which guy?'

'I'll deliver him up. Packaged. You get the guy.'

' "Packaged"? What do you mean "packaged"?'

'Don't act like a stupid fuck. You know what I mean.'

'You're coming to some wrong conclusions. You don't make terms, you don't do our job.'

'You got a dead cop. You want it squared. So the beef gets squared. Now, you stop pulling my insides out.'

He hung his head over the wastebasket, one hand trembling on his temple. His long neck looked like a bent swan's.

'You can't walk out of here with that kind of misunderstanding, Joey. Do you hear me? This isn't a barter situation. Are you listening to me? Look at me.'

But he continued to stare between his legs, his eyes glazed and dull, focused inward on his own pain.

That evening, eleven hours after Joey Gouza was kicked loose from custody, someone tried to garrote Weldon Sonnier in his boathouse with a strand of piano wire.

13

The AA meeting room upstairs in the Episcopalian church is foul with cigarette smoke. On the walls are framed photographs of our founders, whom we still affectionately call Dr Bob and Bill W., as though their anonymity need be protected even in death. Also on the wall are the twelve steps of AA recovery and the simple two axioms that we attempt to live by: ONE DAY AT A TIME and EASY DOES IT. The meeting is over now, and volunteers are washing coffee cups, emptying ashtrays, and wiping down the tables. I sit by a big floor fan that is blowing the smoke out the windows into the early-morning air. My AA sponsor, Tee Neg, who looks like a mulatto, sits across from me. Before he bought the bar and poolroom that he now owns on East Main, he was a pipeliner and oil-field roughneck, and three fingers on his right hand were snipped off by a drilling chain. He's uneducated, can barely read and write, but he's tough-minded and intelligent and unfailing in his loyalty to me.

'You mad at somet'ing again, Dave. That ain't good,' he says.

'I'm not mad.'

'We get drunk *at* somebody. Or maybe *at* somet'ing. That's the way it works. It's them resentments mess us up. Don't be telling me different, no.'

'I know that, Tee Neg.'

'It ain't worrying about Bootsie this time. It's somet'ing else, ain't it?'

'Maybe.'

'You want to know what I t'ink's on your mind, podna?'

'I have a feeling you're going to tell me, anyway.'

'You're studying on this case all the time. You t'ink that's it, but it ain't. You bothered by the way t'ings are, the way we got trouble with the colored people all the time, you bothered 'cause it ain't like it used to be. You want sout' Lou'sana to be like it was when you and me and yo' daddy went all day and went everywhere and never spoke one word of English. You walk away when you hear white people talking bad about them Negro, like that bad feeling ain't in their hearts. But you keep pretend it's like it used to be, Dave, that these bad t'ings ain't in white people's hearts, then you gonna be walking away the rest of yo' life.'

'That doesn't mean I'm going to get drunk over it.'

'I had seven years sobriety, me. Then I started studying on them fingers I left on that drill pipe. I'd get up with it in the morning, just like you wake up with an ugly, mean woman. I'd drag it around with me all day. I'd look at them pink stumps till they'd start throbbing. Then I went fishing one afternoon, went into a colored man's bait store to buy some shiners, told that man I was gonna catch me a hundred *sac-a-lait* befo' the sun get behind them willow tree. Then I told him I changed my mind, just give me a quart of whiskey and don't bother about no shiners. I got drunk five years. Then I spent one in the penitentiary. Get made about what you can't change and maybe you'll get to do just what Tee Neg done.'

He looks at me reflectively and rubs his palms in a circular motion on his thighs. I twirl my coffee cup on my finger, then one of the cleanup volunteers reaches down and takes it from me.

'That doesn't mean you always have to like what you see around you,' I say.

'It don't mean you got to be miserable about it, neither.'

'I'm not miserable, Tee Neg. Give it a break, will you?'

'It ain't never gonna be the same, Dave. That world we grown up in, it's gone. *Pa'ti avec le vent*, podna.'

I look down from the window at the brick-paved street in the morning's blue light, the colonnades over the sidewalks, a black man pushing a wooden cart laden with strawberries from under the overhang of a dark green oak tree. The scene looks like a postcard mailed from the nineteenth century.

I went out to Weldon's home on Bayou Teche at 9 A.M. the morning after he was attacked in his boathouse. When he opened the door he was dressed in Levi's, a pair of old tennis shoes, and a T-shirt. A folded baseball glove protruded from his back pocket.

'You're headed for a game or something?' I asked.

A red welt ran around his throat, like half of a necklace.

'I've got an apple basket nailed up on the barn wall,' he said. 'I like to see if my fork ball's still got a hop on it.'

'You've been throwing a few?'

'About two hours' worth. It beats smoking cigarettes or fooling around with early-morning booze.'

'How close was it?' I said.

'He came across my throat and I remember I couldn't breathe, that I was trying to get my fingernails under the wire. Then the blood shut off to my brain, and I went down on the deck like I was poleaxed. It all happened real quick. It makes you think about how quick it can happen.'

'Walk me down to your boathouse.'

'I don't know who it was, Dave. I didn't see him, he didn't say any-thing. I just remember that wire popping tight across my windpipe.' He blew out his breath. 'Man, that's a hard feeling to shake. When I was overseas and I thought about buying it, I always figured I'd see it coming somehow, that I'd control it or negotiate with it some way, maybe convince it that I had another season to run. That's a crazy way to think, isn't it?'

'Let's see if we find anything down at your boathouse.'

We strolled across the lawn toward the bayou. When we were abreast of the old barn on the back of his property, he stooped down and picked up a scuffed baseball with split seams.

'Watch this, buddy,' he said.

He wet two of his fingers, took a windup, and whipped the ball like a BB into the apple basket.

'Not bad,' I said.

'I should probably get out of the oil business and start my own base-ball franchise. You remember the old New Iberia Pelicans? Boy, I miss minor-league ball.' He picked up another baseball from the ground.

'The report says some kids scared the assailant off.'

He threw the ball underhanded against the barn door, stuck his hands in his back pockets, and continued walking with me toward the boathouse.

'Yeah, some USL kids ran out of gas on the bayou and paddled in to my dock. Otherwise I would have caught the bus. But they couldn't describe the guy. They said they just saw some fellow take off through the bushes.'

We walked out on to his dock and into the boathouse. Oars and life preservers were hung from hooks on the rafters, and the whole interior rippled with the sunlight that reflected off the water at the bottom of the walls.

'Are you sure he didn't say anything?' I said.

'Nothing.'

'Did you see a ring or a watch?'

'I just saw that wire loop flick down past my nose. But I know it was one of Joey Gouza's people.'

'Why?'

'Because I've got some stuff Joey wants. Joey's been behind all this from the beginning. The guy with the wire was probably Jewel Fluck or Jack Gates. Or any number of mechanics Joey can hire out of Miami or Houston.'

'So you are hooked up with them?'

'Sure, I am. But I've had it. I don't care if I take a fall or not. I can't keep endangering or fucking up other people anymore. Give me a minute and we'll go to the movies.'

'What?'

'You'll see,' he said, moving a pirogue that was upended on sawhorses. Then he knelt on one knee and lifted up a plank in the floor of the boathouse. A videocassette tightly wrapped in a clear plastic bag was stapled to the bottom of the plank. He sliced the cassette out of the bag with his pocketknife. 'Come on up to the house and I'll give you a private screening from Greaseball Productions.'

'What's this about, Weldon?'

'Everything you want is on this tape. I'm going to give it to you.'

'Maybe you should think about calling your lawyer.'

'There's time for that later. Come on.'

I followed him up to his house and into his living room. He turned on his television set and VCR; he plugged in the cassette and paused with the remote control in his palm.

'This is what it amounts to, Dave,' he said. 'I hit two dusters in a row, I was broke, and I was about to lose my business. I borrowed everything I could at the bank, but it wasn't enough to stay afloat. So I started talking with a couple of shylocks in New Orleans. Before I knew it I was dealing with Jack Gates and he made me an offer to do a big arms drop in Colombia.'

'Colombia?'

'That's where it's happening. Bush is sending a lot of arms down there to fight the druglords, but the Colombian government has a way of whacking out some of the peasants with it at the same time. So there are antigovernment people down there who pay big money for weapons, and I figured I could make a couple of runs, twenty thou a drop, and not worry about the political complexities involved. Why not? I dropped everything in Laos from pigs to napalm homemade from gasoline and soap detergent.

'Then Jack Gates offered me the big score, eighty thou for one run. The plan was for me to fly an old C-47 into Honduras, pick up a load of arms, land at this jungle strip in Colombia, where these guys process large amounts of coke, load about eight million dollars worth of flak on board, then do the arms drop up in the mountains and head for the sea.

'But I told Gates I wanted the payoff when I loaded the coke. He said I'd get paid on this end, and I told him it was no deal, then, because I didn't exactly trust the kind of people he represented. So he made a couple of phone calls and finally said all right, since eighty thou is used Kleenex to these guys. Also, Gates and Joey Gouza thought we'd be in business together for a long time. Except I took them over the hurdles. Sit down. You'll enjoy this.'

He pressed the remote button, and for fifteen minutes the screen showed a series of scenes and images that could have been snipped from color footage filmed in Southeast Asia two decades earlier: wind whipping the canvas cargo straps and webbing in the empty bay of a plane; the shadow of the C-47 racing across yellow pastureland, hummocks, earthen dikes, and brown reservoirs, the dark green of coffee plantations, a village of shacks built from discarded lumber and sheets of tin that looked as bright and hot as shards of broken mirror in the sun; then the approach over the crest of a purple mountain and the descent into a long valley that contained a landing strip bulldozed out of the jungle so recently that the broken roots in the soil were still white and pink with life.

The next images looked like they had been taken at an oblique angle from the pilot's compartment: sweat-streaked Indians in cutoff GI fatigues dragging crates of grenades, ammunition, and Belgian automatic rifles into the bay, a man who looked like an American watching in the background, a straw hat shadowing his face; then suddenly an abrupt shift in the location and cast of characters. The second cargo was loaded at twilight, and the bags were pillow-size, wrapped in black vinyl, the ends tucked, folded, and taped, carried on board as lovingly as Christmas packages.

'The next thing you should see is a lot of parachutes popping open in the dark and those crates floating down toward a circle of burning truck flares in the middle of some mountains,' Weldon said. 'That's where I made a change in the script. Watch this.'

The screen showed a moonlit seacoast, the waves sliding up on the beach in a long line of foam, humps of coral reef protruding from the surf like the rose-colored backs of whales. Then the kickers began shoving the cargo out of the C-47.

'I call this part "Weldon pickles the load and says get fucked to the greaseballs," ' Weldon said.

The wind ripped apart the bags of cocaine and covered the black surface of the water with a floating white paste. The crates of arms tumbled out into the darkness like a flying junkyard. Some of the crates sent geysers of foam out of the groundswell; others burst apart on the exposed reef, bejeweling the coral with belts of .50 caliber shells.

The screen went white.

'That's it?' I said.

'Yeah. What do you think of it?'

'This is what Gouza's been after?'

'Yeah, I told both of them I had their whole operation on tape. I told them to get out of my life. I figured they owed me the eighty thou for the earlier runs, anyway. I took thirty-seven holes in the fuselage on one of them. What do you think of it?'

'Not much.'

'What?'

'What else have you got besides this tape?' I said.

'This is the whole show.'

'Have you got something connecting Gouza to arms and dope trafficking?'

'I've just got this tape.'

'Will you make a sworn statement that you were flying for Joey Gouza?'

'I can't.'

'Why not?'

'I made all the arrangements with Jack Gates. Gouza stayed out of it.'

I looked out the ceiling-high window at the live oaks in Weldon's sideyard.

'What's Bobby Earl's part in this?' I said.

'He's got no part.'

'Don't tell me that, Weldon.'

'Bobby doesn't have anything to do with it.'

'Now's not the time to cover for this guy, podna.'

'Bobby's mind is on the US Senate and his putz. Use your head, Dave. Why would he want to get mixed up with dope and guns?'

'Money.'

'He gets all he wants from right-wing simpletons and north Louisiana rednecks. Besides, that's not what he's after. You liberals have never figured him out. Bobby doesn't care about black people one way or another. He's never known any. How could he be upset by them? It's educated and intelligent white people he doesn't like. In his mind you're all just like his parents. I don't think a day went by in his life that they didn't let him know he was a piece of shit. He's got two loves in this world, porking the ladies and provoking the press and people like yourself.'

'That might all be true, but he's hooked up with Joey Gouza and that means he's in this bullshit right up to his kneecaps.'

'You're wrong.'

'I'm weary of you holding out on me, Weldon.'

'I'm not. I've told you everything. What else do you want out of me? A guy tried to take my head off with a piano wire. I can't think about it without shuddering all over. It really got to me, man. I can even smell the guy.'

'What do you mean?'

He stopped, and his eyes looked into space.

'I didn't think about it before,' he said. 'The guy had a smell. It was like embalming fluid or something.'

'Say it again.'

'Embalming fluid. Or chemicals. Hell, I don't know. It was there just a second, then my light switch clicked off.'

'It wasn't one of Gouza's people, Weldon.'

His brow furrowed, and he fingered the red line around his neck.

'I think your brother, Lyle, was right all along,' I said. 'I think your father has made a spectacular reappearance in your life. Take this tape to the DEA or the US Customs office, if you want. It doesn't fall under my jurisdiction.'

'You're not interested in it?'

'We already have a murder warrant out on Jack Gates. You haven't shown or told me anything that will help put any of the other players in jail.'

'You mean I've been holding this evidence and taking all this heat for nothing? And all you can tell me is that my poor demented brother has been right all along, that my own father wants to put my head on a pike?'

'I'm afraid that's about it.'

'No, that's not it, Dave,' he said. 'I think this time I finally read you. You're not interested in Joey Gouza or Jack Gates or any of these Aryan Brotherhood clowns. You want to staple my brother-in-law's butt to the furniture. In fact, if you had your way, you'd blow up his shit big time, wouldn't you? Just like a Gatling gun locking down on Charlie in the middle of a rice field.'

We stared at each other in the silence like a pair of bookends.

I drove to the Salvation Army transient shelter in Lafayette to try and find Vic Benson. A portly, red-cheeked, kindly man with big sideburns who ran the shelter said that Benson had had a fistfight with another man two days ago and had been asked to leave. He had responded by packing his duffel bag quietly and walking out the door without a word; then he stopped, snapped his fingers as though he had forgotten something, and returned to the dormitory long enough to stuff his bed sheets in the toilet bowl.

'Where do you think he went?' I asked.

'Anywhere there's Southern Pacific tracks,' the Salvation Army officer said.

'Can I talk to the other men?'

'I doubt if they know anything. You can try, though. They were a little afraid of Vic. He wasn't like the rest. Most of our men are harmless. Vic always made you feel he was working on a dark thought, like he was grinding sand between his back teeth. One time he was watching television . . .' He stopped, smiled, and shook the memory out of his face.

'Go on,' I said.

'He and some of the other men were watching this minister, then Vic said, "I'd pour lye down that one's throat if his brother didn't deserve it worse."'

'Which minister?'

'That fellow in Baton Rouge, what's-his-name?'

'Lyle Sonnier?'

'Yeah, that's the one. I tried to make a joke out of it, and I said, "Vic, what could you possibly have against that man up there?" He said, "The same thing the rooster's got against the baby chick that thinks the brooder house is his." Talking with Vic could be a little bit like walking through cobwebs. Or accidentally raking your hand across a yellow-jacket nest.'

We talked to a half-dozen men in the dormitory, and they all had the same vacant response and benign, vacuous expressions that they wore and used as habitually as the identities and personal histories that they had created for themselves in hundreds of drunk tanks and trackside jungle camps. They reminded me of figures in a Van Gogh or Munch painting. Palm fronds and the sunlit leaves of banana trees rustled against the screen windows, but in contrast the men inside looked wind-dried, the color of cardboard, weightless in their emaciation, their hollow chests devoid of heartbeat, the skin of their arms wrapped as tight as fish scales around their bones. Their squared-away bunks, which cast no shadows because of the sun's position, looked in their exactitude like a line of coffins.

Why the morbidness over a bunch of drunks? Because they brought back the ever-present knowledge in my life that I was one drink away from their fate – despair, murder of the soul, insanity, or death – and that realization was like someone working my heart muscle with an angry thumb.

The Salvation Army officer and I walked out of the dormitory into the sunlight, into the clean sweep of wind through oak and myrtle trees and a twirling water sprinkler on the grass.

'How would you describe that odor they have?' I asked.

'I beg your pardon?'

'That smell. They all have it. How would you describe it?'

'Oh. It's those short-dogs they drink. It's one step above paint-thinner.'

'It's like they have liquefied mothballs in their blood, isn't it?' I said.

'Yeah, yeah, something like that.'

'Would you say it smelled like embalming fluid?'

He scratched one sideburn with a fingernail.

'I was never a mortician,' he said, 'but, yeah, that seems to come pretty close. Yeah, some of those ole boys are mite near dead and don't know it yet. Poor fellows.'

He didn't understand the direction of my questions, and I didn't explain it to him. I simply gave him my business card and said, 'If Vic comes back here, call me. Don't mess with him. I think your intuitions about him are correct. He's probably a deranged and dangerous man.'

'What's he done?'

'I think only Vic Benson and God could tell you that. I don't think the rest of us would even want to know. He's one of those who make you want to believe that all of us didn't fall out of the same tree.'

'It's got something to do with children, doesn't it?'

'How did you know?'

'One of the old-timers told me Vic flipped a hot cigarette in the face of a little colored boy who was pestering him. I kind of put it out of my mind because I didn't want to believe it.'

His face looked momentarily sad, then he shook hands with me and walked back across the wet, shining lawn into the gloom of the dormitory.

I went back to the office, planning to call Lyle Sonnier in Baton Rouge to ask if he had any idea where his father might have gone. Just as I picked up the phone, I looked through the window and saw Clete Purcel park his automobile in a yellow zone, step out on the street, and stretch his arms like a bear coming out of hibernation. Two fishing rods were sticking out of a back window. I didn't wait for him to come into the office. At best, my colleagues thought of Clete as a happy zoo animal; others had a way of disappearing from a room as soon as he entered it.

I met him outside on the walk.

'What's happening, Dave?' he said. 'Did you eat lunch yet?'

'Nope.'

'Let's eat some red beans and rice, then drown some worms after you get off work.'

He wore a sleeveless tropical shirt. Budweiser shorts that hung off his navel, and his powder-blue porkpie hat slanted over one eye. His huge biceps were glowing with sunburn.

'We're going down to Cypremort Point for crabs tonight. You're welcome to go with us,' I said.

He looked disappointed.

'That's all right,' he said. 'I thought I'd fish a little bit more today, that's all. Anyway, let's get something to eat and I'll fill you in on some stuff I found out about Joey Gouza and the white man's hope.'

We drove down the street to a small café run by a black man. Crushed beer cans littered the floor of Clete's car, and I could smell beer on his breath.

'Are things slow at your office?' I asked.

'I just felt like taking off, that's all. Hey, let's eat.'

We took paper plates loaded with red beans, rice, and links of sausage to a plank table under a live-oak tree. The café owner didn't have a beer license, and Clete went to the trunk of his car and came back with a sweating six-pack of Jax. It was warm in the shade of the trees, and smoke from a barbecue fire floated in a blue haze through the overhead limbs.

'I did some checking on Joey's business connections around town,' Clete said. 'I'm talking about his legitimate businesses – a linen service, a movie house up on Prytania, a bunch of dago restaurants, places where he launders his drug money for the IRS. Anyway, the word is Joey and his people are putting up big gelts for Bobby Earl's US Senate campaign. In other words, the greaseballs are into PACs now.'

I nodded. 'Yeah?'

'That's it.'

'So what's new in that? It's what we thought all along.'

'You're reading it wrong, noble mon.'

'How's that?'

'If Joey Meatballs was piecing off his drug action to Bobby Earl, he wouldn't have to give him money through a bunch of PACs. He'd already own the guy.'

'Maybe that's the way he launders Earl's cut.'

'They don't do it that way, Streak. They give the guy something he can't resist, they bring him in on one of their deals, their shylocks lend him money, they set him up with some hot-ass broad on video tape. But they don't go into the drug business with the guy, then create a lot of public records to show everybody they got the guy's tallywacker tied around their neighborhood fireplug.'

'You drove all the way to New Iberia to tell me Bobby Earl is clean?'

'Oh, they know all the same people, and Joey would like to put a US senator in his pocket, but there's no law against that, mon.'

'Bobby Earl's dirty.'

'Maybe so. I'm just telling you what I found out and what I think. The guy's a sonofabitch but so are half the politicians in Louisiana.'

'I get the feeling something else is bothering you, Clete.'

He ripped open another beer and lit a cigarette, his food unfinished.

'It comes with the territory. It's nothing new,' he said.

'What is it?'

'I might get my PI ticket pulled.'

'What for?'

He bit one of his fingernails and shrugged.

'I've had two or three beefs since I opened my office. It's my own fault,' he said.

'You're always in a beef, Clete. Why is somebody giving you trouble about your ticket now?'

'That's what I asked this bozo who called me up from Baton Rouge.'

'Which bozo?'

'With the state regulatory agency.' His eyes moved around on my face.

'It's Bobby Earl, isn't it?' I said.

'Maybe.'

'There's no "maybe" about it.'

'Anyway, they got these complaints and they're talking about a hearing before their board.'

'What complaints?'

'Well, there was this button man, a real bag of shit out of Miami, a guy who whacked out two Cuban girls who were going to send this greaseball dealer up to Raiford. He jumped a two-hundred-thou bond, and word had it he was hiding out in Ascension or St James Parish. So the bondsman in Miami calls me and tells me he'll pay me a five-grand finder's fee if I can bring in this guy before the bondsman has to come up with the two hundred thou. But the only lead he can give me on the shit bag is that he's somewhere between New Orleans and Baton Rouge, he loves pink Cadillacs, smoking dope, and being a big man around lowlife broads.

'So I spend two weeks cruising these dumps along Airline Highway. Just when I'm about to give up, I see this beautiful, flamingo-pink Cadillac convertible, with Georgia plates, parked in front of this club that's got both white and mulatto broads on stage. I go inside, and the place is filled with smoke and about two hundred geeks that look like somebody beat up on them with an ugly stick. But I don't see my man. So I go back out to the parking lot and pop the door lock on the Caddy with a slim jim. The inside smells like somebody rubbed hash oil into the upholstery. In the glove compartment I find a box of rubbers, a match cover from a Fort Lauderdale bar, an ice pick, and a dozen loose .38 shells. What does that tell me? This has got to be the shit bag's car.

'Except I look all over the bar and I can't find the guy, which means he's probably wearing a disguise. Then it's three in the morning, still no shit bag, and I'm bone-tired. So I kind of hurried things along by setting fire to the pink Caddy.'

'You did what?'

'What was I supposed to do, spend the rest of the week there? I was working on spec. Anyway, the Caddy was burning beautifully in the parking lot, and the geeks came pouring out of the building to watch it, happy as pigs rolling in slop, except of course for the guy who owned the Caddy. Guess what?'

'He wasn't your guy.'

'Right. He was a traveling sporting-goods salesman from Waycross. But guess what again? There, standing in the crowd, is my shit bag. In two minutes I had him in cuffs and locked to a D-ring in the back of my car. So it all worked out all right, except somebody saw me messing around the Caddy and told the cops and the firemen, and I had to come back the next day and answer some questions that made me a little bit uncomfortable. Then Nig got me into a scrape—'

'Nig?' I had finished eating and was glancing at my watch.

'Yeah, Nig Rosewater, the bondsman. I'm sorry to bore you with this stuff, Dave, but I don't get a regular paycheck. I depend upon guys like Nig to keep me afloat.'

I took a breath and let him continue.

'Nig decides to go into the saloon business,' Clete said. 'So he opens a bar on Magazine right next to a black neighborhood. What kind of sign does he put in his window? "HAPPY HOUR 5 TO 7 – HAVE A SWIG WITH NIG." So the first night somebody flings a burning trash can through the plate glass. Then they did it two more nights, even after Nig got rid of the sign. Who did it, you ask. The fucking Crips, not because they're big on civil rights but because it impresses the other punks in the neighborhood. Have you dealt with any of these guys? They knocked off a kid on Calliope, then, to make sure everybody got the message, they walked into the mortuary, in front of his family, and blew his coffin full of holes. They're a real special bunch.

'So I found out the kid who had been remodeling Nig's bar was named Ice Box. They call him that because he pushed a refrigerator on top of his grandmother. I'm not making this up. This kid could blow out your light like he was turning a page in a comic book. Anyway, I had a talk with Ice Box while I held him by his ankles off a fire escape, five stories up from the pavement. I think he's back in California these days. But his grandmother, can you dig it, with dents still in her head, filed charges against me.

'Anyway, somebody in Baton Rouge wants to cut a piece out of my butt. Like I say, I brought it on myself. I learned in the corps you don't mess with the pencil pushers. You stay invisible. You piss off some corporal in personnel and two weeks later you're humping it with an ambush patrol outside Chu Lai.'

'Give me the name of the guy in Baton Rouge who's after you.'

'Leave it alone. It'll probably go away.'

'Bobby Earl won't.'

'That's the point, mon. Earl's got no handles on him. We sent the shit bags up the road because they were born to take a fall. Earl's part of the system. There're people who love him. You think I'm giving you a schuck? Did you see him on *The Geraldo Rivera Show*? Some of those broads were ready to throw their panties at him. It's me and you who've got the problem. We're the geeks, Dave, not this guy. He's a fucking hero.'

His breath was heavy with the smell of beer and cigarettes.

He crushed a beer can in his palm and dropped it on the table, then studied the tops of his big, coarse, red hands. He had tried to comb his sandy hair back over the divots where his stitches had been, but I could still see crusted lesions like thin black worms on his scalp.

'Oh, hell, what do I know?' he said, and looked down the street at the traffic in the hot sunlight, as though it somehow held the answer to his question.

Back in my office, I got hold of Lyle Sonnier at his church.

'Hey, Loot, I'm glad you called,' he said. 'I've been thinking about throwing a big dinner here at the church, actually more like a family reunion, and I wanted to ask you and Bootsie.'

'Thanks, Lyle, but right now I'm looking for Vic Benson, the fellow you think might be your father.'

'What do you want him for?'

'He's part of an investigation.'

'You don't have to look far, then. He's right here.'

'What?'

'We had lunch together just a little while ago. He's out back painting some furniture for our secondhand store right now.'

'How long has he been there?'

'He came in this morning.'

'I think he tried to take your brother's head off last night with a piece of piano wire.'

'Get real, Dave. He's a wino, a bundle of sticks. He has to wear lead shoes on a windy day.'

'Tell that to Weldon.'

'I already talked to Weldon. He says it was a Joey Gouza hit.'

'Believe me, Lyle, Joey has no desire for more trouble in Iberia Parish.'

'So if it wasn't Gouza, it was probably one of the walking brain-dead who follow Bobby Earl around. But no matter how you cut it, it wasn't the old man. Good God, Dave, what's the matter with you? Weldon could beat that poor old drunk to death with his shoe.'

'Why do you think Bobby Earl might be involved in it?'

'He's bad news, that's why. He stirs up grief and hatred among the very people that's sitting out there in my flock – poor white and black folk. I'm tired of that character. Somebody should have stuffed his butt in a garbage can a long time ago.'

'That may be true, Lyle, but that doesn't mean he's trying to whack out your brother.'

I waited for him to say something, to offer me the linkage to Bobby Earl.

'Lyle?'

'Well, anyway, in my opinion the old man's harmless. You gonna arrest him?'

'No, I don't have enough for a warrant.'

'Then what's the big deal?'

'I'll be over there later today or at least by Monday to talk to him. Tell him that for me, too. In the meantime you might ask yourself why he's shown up after all these years? Does he seem like a man of goodwill to you?'

'Maybe he wants to atone but he hasn't learned the words yet. It takes a while sometimes.'

'Like we used to say out in Indian country, don't let them get behind you.'

'That's what somebody said at My Lai, too. Give all that Vietnam stuff to the American Legion, Dave. It's a drag.'

'Whatever you say, Lyle. Hang loose.'

'Hey, I'll get back to you with a date for that dinner. I want your butt there, with no excuses. I'm proud to be your friend, Dave. I look up to you, I always did.'

What do you say to someone who talks to you like that? In order to get a jump-start on the day I used to go on dry drunks that were the equivalent of inserting my head in a microwave for ten minutes. I had come to learn that a conversation with any one of the Sonniers worked just as well.

It was Friday afternoon, and it was too late and I was too tired for a round-trip to Baton Rouge to interview Vic Benson, who was probably Verise Sonnier, particularly in view of the fact that I had no tangible evidence against him and talking to him was like conversing with a vacant lot, anyway.

The heat broke temporarily with a thirty-minute rain shower that evening, then the wind came up cool out of the south, scattering dead pecan leaves up on my gallery, and the late sun broke through the layered clouds as red and molten as if it had been poured flaming from a foundry cup. We had a short-lived crisis at the bait shop. I was filling up the bowls in the rabbit hutches by the side of the house when I heard a loud yell in the shop, then saw Tripod racing out the door, his loose chain slithering across the planks, with Alafair right behind him. Then Batist came through the door with a broom raised over his head.

Alafair caught Tripod up in her arms at the end of the dock, then turned to face down Batist, whose black, thick neck was pulsing with nests of veins.

'I gonna flatten that coon like a bicycle patch, me,' he said. 'I gonna wipe up that bait shop wit' him.'

'You leave him alone!' Alafair shouted back.

'I cain't be runnin' a sto', no, with that nasty coon wreckin' my shelves. You set him down on that dock and I gonna golf him right over them trees.'

'He ain't did anything! Clean up your own mess! Clean up your own nasty cigars!'

In the meantime, Tripod was trying to climb over her shoulder and down her back to get as much geography between him and Batist as possible.

Oh Lord, I thought, and walked down to the dock.

'It's too late, Dave,' Batist said. 'That coon headed for coon heaven.'

'Let's calm down a minute,' I said. 'How'd Tripod get into the bait shop again, Alf?'

'Batist left the screen open,' she said.

'I left the screen open?' he said incredulously.

'You were fishing out back, too, or he wouldn't have gotten up on the shelf,' she said. Her face was flushed and heated, her eyes as bright as brown glass.

'Look his face, look his mouth,' Batist said. 'He eat all the sugar in the can and two boxes them Milky Ways.'

Tripod, whose fur was almost black except for his silver-ringed tail and silver muzzle, didn't make a good witness for the defense. His muzzle and whiskers were slick with chocolate and coated with grains of sugar. I picked up the end of his chain. The clip that we used to fasten him to the clothesline was broken.

'I'm afraid we've got Tripod on a breaking-and-entering rap, Alf,' I said.

'What?' she said.

'It looks like he's going to have to go into lockdown,' I said.

'What?'

'That means let's put him in the rabbit hutch until tomorrow when I can fix his chain. In the meantime, Batist, let's close down the shop and think about going to the drive-in movie.'

'It ain't my sto', it ain't my Milky Way. I just work here all day so I can clean up after some fat no-good coon, me.'

Alafair was about to fire off another shot when I turned her gently by the shoulder and walked her back through the pecan trees in front of the house.

'He was mean, Dave,' she said. 'He was gonna hurt Tripod.'

'No, he's not mean, little guy,' I said. 'To Batist, running the bait shop is an important job. He just doesn't want anything to go wrong while he's in charge.'

'You didn't see what he looked like.' Her eyes were moist in the deep shade of the trees.

'Alafair, Batist grew up poor and uneducated and never learned to read and write. But today he runs a business for a white man. He wants to do everything right, but he has to make an "X" when he signs for a delivery and he can't count the receipts at the end of the day. So he concentrates on things that he can do well, like barbecuing the chickens, repairing the boat engines, and keeping all the inventory squared away. Then Tripod gets loose and makes a big mess of the shelves. So in Batist's mind he's let us down.'

I saw her eyes blinking with thought.

'It's kind of like the teachers at school giving you a job to do, then someone else comes along and messes it up and makes you look bad. Does that make sense?'

She shifted Tripod in her arms, so that he lay on his back with his three paws in the air, his stomach swollen with food.

'I guess so. We going to the show?'

'You bet.'

'Batist is going, too?'

'I don't know, you think he should go?'

She thought about it.

'Yeah, he should go with us,' she said, as though she had just reached a profound metaphysical conclusion.

'You're the best, little guy.'

'You are, too, big guy.'

We popped Tripod into the hutch, then I swung Alafair up on my back and we walked beneath the sparking of fireflies on to the gallery and into the lighted house, where Bootsie was deep-frying *sac-a-lait* and listening to a Cajun song that was playing on the radio propped in the kitchen window. The western sky looked like a blood-streaked ink wash, and I could hear the cicadas in the distant woods, all the way across the waving field of green sugarcane at the back of my property.

The next morning Alafair helped Batist and me open the bait shop. She earned her weekly allowance of five dollars by seining the dead shiners out of the bait tanks, seasoning the chickens that we barbecued on a split oil drum for our midday customers, draining the coolers, and pouring fresh ice over the beer and soda pop. But her favorite Saturday-morning job was sitting on a tall stool behind the cash register, her Astros baseball cap low on her head, ringing up worm and shiner sales with a loud bang on the keys.

It was a wonderful morning to fish. The air was still cool and windless, the early pink light muted in the cypress trees, the moon still visible in one soft blue corner of the sky. After we had rented most of our boats, I started the barbecue fire in the oil drum, then fixed coffee and hot milk and bowls of Grape-Nuts for the three of us, and we ate breakfast on one of the telephone-spool tables under an umbrella out on the dock. I had managed to push the Sonnier case completely out of my mind when the phone rang inside the shop and Alafair got up and answered it.

I could see only the side of her face through the screen window as she held the receiver to her ear, but I had no doubt that she was listening to something that she had never expected to come through our telephone. Her eyes were blinking rapidly and her tan cheeks were filled with white discolorations, and I saw her look at me with her mouth parted as though a childish bad dream had become real in the middle of the day.

I went quickly inside the shop and behind the counter and took the receiver from her hand.

'Dave, he called you real bad names,' Alafair said. She was breathing hard through her mouth.

'Who is this?' I said into the receiver.

'You know who it is. Don't act stupid,' a high, metallic voice, like that of a midget, said. 'You cut a deal with Joey Meatballs, didn't you?'

'You're not shy about frightening a little girl. How about giving me your name?'

'You don't know my name?'

I picked up a pencil and scribbled across the top of a lined notepad: 'Boots, call office, tell them to trace call in shop.' Then I put the pad in Alafair's hands and pushed her toward the door.

'What's the matter, you got nothing wise to say?' the voice asked.

'What do you want, Fluck?'

'I want to know what you're giving Joey Gee so that he puts a whack out on me.'

'There's no deal with Joey.'

'You lying sonofabitch. He's out of the bag one day and everybody in New Orleans hears there's a five-grand open contract on me. You telling me you don't have anything to do with it?'

'That's right.'

'What is it, you guys want to wipe your books clean with my ass? Or is it a personal beef because I almost cooled you out in Sonnier's house?'

'You're going down because you killed a police officer and Eddy Raintree.'

'I'm shaking.'

'To tell you the truth, Fluck, I'm busy right now and you're a boring man to talk to.'

'The only reason somebody from the AB didn't take you out is you're not worth the trouble. But I'm going to give you a deal, one that'll make you big shit in your little town. I get immunity on that dead cop in the Sonnier house, I don't know anything about Eddy Raintree's problems next to a train track, and I give you everything you want on Joey Meatballs. I'm talking about guys he's whacked, the marshmallow Jack Gates shoved into the plane propeller, the crack they're selling to the niggers in the projects, gun deals with spics, you name it, I'll give it to you . . . Are you listening to me, man?'

'I hear you just fine.'

'Then you set it up. I want protective custody, too. Maybe in another state.'

'I think you're overestimating your importance, Fluck. You're not the kind of witness that prosecutors get excited about.'

'Look, I can take you to two graves down by Terrebonne Bay. Two guys that Joey made kneel down on the edge of a trench and suck on a barrel of a .22 mag before he dumped a big one down their throats.'

'It's not a sellers' market these days.'

'What's with you, man? You want to see Joey Gee go down or not?'

'Where are you?'

'Are you kidding?'

'What I mean is, you're probably not too far from a police station of some kind. Turn yourself in. It's the only deal you're going to get from me or probably anyone else. You executed a police officer. You get caught by the wrong guys and you'll never make the jail, Fluck.'

'You're getting off on this, aren't you?'

Through the screen window I saw Bootsie wave at me from the gallery of the house.

'Nope. I'm tired of talking to you,' I said.

'I'm messing up your morning, huh?'

'No, you just made a big mistake today.'

'What mistake, what are you talking—'

'You phoned me at my home. You frightened my little girl. You did it because inside you're a small, scared man, Fluck. That's why you wanted Garrett to see it coming. For just a second you felt you were as big a man as he was.'

'You're talking yourself into something real bad.'

'Call the DEA. They cut deals with snitches all the time.'

I could hear him breathing into the receiver.

'Where you from, outer space? You're fucking with the AB. We're everywhere, man. There ain't anybody we can't clip. Even if I go down, even if I'm in a max unit somewhere, I can have your whole family taken out.'

'For five grand your AB buddies will have you in a soap dish.'

I could almost hear a wet, gastric click in his throat. Then he hesitated a moment, as though he were squeezing his anger back into a small red box down in his chest.

'I want you to remember everything you said to me,' he said. 'Keep running the words over and over in your head. I'm gonna think up something for you, something special, something that you didn't think could ever happen in your life. I was in Parchman, man. You don't know how much pain a wise-ass fuck like you can go through before he dies.'

Then the line went dead. I looked at my watch. I didn't know if there had been enough time for the dispatcher at the office to get a successful trace on the call or not. I dipped a wad of paper towels into the floating ice in the beer cooler and rubbed my face with it, then wiped my skin dry and flung the towels into the trash basket, as though I could somehow rinse and clean the voice of Jewel Fluck out of my day.

I waited ten more minutes, then called the dispatcher.

'They traced it to a pay phone on Decatur in New Orleans,' he said. 'We called First District headquarters, but the guy was gone when they got there. Sorry, Dave. Who was it?'

'The guy who killed Garrett.'

'Fluck? Oh man, if we'd just been a little bit faster—'

'Don't worry about it.'

I walked up through the shade of the pecan trees to the gallery. Bootsie was sitting in the swing with Alafair beside her. Alafair looked up at me from under the brim of her ball cap, her face filled with a pinched light.

'It was just a drunk man, little guy,' I said. 'He thought I was somebody else.'

'His voice, it was—' she began. 'It made me feel bad inside.' She swallowed and looked out into the deep shadows of the trees.

'That's the way drunk people sound sometimes. We just don't pay any attention to them,' I said. 'Anyway, Bootsie had the call traced to New Orleans, and the cops went to pick this guy up. Hey, let's don't waste any more time worrying about this character. I need you to help me get ready for our lunch customers.'

I felt Bootsie's eyes searching my face.

I went inside the house, took my .45 out of the dresser, slipped it down into my khakis, and pulled my shirt over it. At the dock I put Alafair in charge of turning the sausage links and split chickens on the barbecue grill. Her shoulders barely came above the top of the pit, and when the grease and *sauce piquant* dripped on to the coals her head and cap were haloed in smoke.

I put the .45 on a top shelf behind a stand-up display of Mepps spinners. I wouldn't need it, I told myself, not here, anyway. Fluck had too many problems of his own to worry about me. His kind took revenge only when they had nothing at risk, when it came to them as a luxury they could savor. I was sure of that, I told myself.

14

The sheriff learned of Fluck's phone call early Monday from the dispatcher. As soon as I walked into my office, he tapped on the doorjamb and followed me in.

'Jewel Fluck called you at your house?' he said.

'That's right.' I opened the blinds and sat down behind my desk.

'Why do I have to hear that from the dispatcher?'

'I didn't see any point in disturbing you on the weekend.'

'What'd he say?'

'Most of it was douche water. His clock's running out.'

'Come on, Dave, why'd he call you?'

'He wanted to give up Joey Gouza for immunity on Garrett and Eddy Raintree. I told him the store's closed.'

'You did what?'

'I indicated that cop killers don't get any slack, sheriff.'

He sat down in the chair across from me and brushed one hand across the top of the other. He puffed out his cheeks.

'Maybe that's not yours to decide, Dave. There're a half-dozen agencies that want Joey Gouza salted away. The DEA, US Customs, the FBI, Alcohol, Tobacco, and Firearms—'

'Cut a deal with the lowlifes and in the long run you always lose.'

'In law enforcement every man's vote doesn't count the same. Wyatt Earp belongs in the movies, Dave.'

'I tried to keep him on the phone so we could trace the call. You lose the edge on these guys as soon as you let them think they have something you want. That's the way it works, sheriff.'

'What else did he say?'

'He believes Gouza's got a five-grand open contract on him. If you want, you can tell NOPD about it, but I don't think they'll wring their hands over the news.'

'It's still Bobby Earl, isn't it?' he said.

'What?'

He scratched his clean-shaven soft cheek with a fingernail.

'Fluck, Gouza, this button man Jack Gates, I think they're all secondary

418

players for you, Dave. It's Bobby Earl who's always on your front burner, isn't it?'

'Fluck frightened my little girl, sheriff. He also threatened me. You figure who's on my mind.'

'You sound a little sharp, podna.'

'This is the second time you've told me maybe it's me who's got a problem.'

'It wasn't my intention to do so.'

'Look, sheriff, we haven't turned the key on one guy in this case, except Gouza, and that was on a bum charge. When something like that happens, everybody gets impatient. Then a guy like Bobby Earl marshals a little pressure and convinces a few political oil cans that he's a victim, a federal agency decides that it's more interesting to throw a net over a mainline wiseguy like Gouza than a termite like Jewel Fluck, we local guys go along with it, and before you know it, half the cast is on the beach in the Virgin Islands and we're trying to figure out why people think we're schmoes.'

'Maybe after this one's over, you should take a little vacation time.'

'It won't change who's out there.'

He did a *rat-a-tat-tat* on his thighs with his palms, then stood up, smiled, and walked out of my office without saying anything else.

I drove to Baton Rouge that afternoon to question the burned man who called himself Vic Benson. It wasn't to be the kind of interview that I had planned. I parked my truck at the end of Lyle's brick driveway on Highland and walked up on to the columned porch to lift the brass door knocker that rang a set of musical chimes deep in the interior of the house, when Lyle walked out of the sideyard with a garden rake in his hand, wearing a T-shirt and jeans that hung off his hips. There were flecks of dirt and leaves in his mussed hair.

'Hey, Dave, what's happening?' he said. 'You're just in time to fang down some barbecued pork chops. Come on around back.'

'Thanks anyway, Lyle. I just need to ask Vic Benson a few questions. Is he staying over at your mission?'

'No.'

'He took off?'

'No.' He was smiling now.

'He's here?'

'In the backyard. We just put in some pepper plants. It's a little late but I think they'll take.'

'He's living with you?'

'Out in the garage apartment.'

'I think what you're doing isn't smart.'

'I've never done anything smart in my life, Dave. Like Waylon says, "I might be crazy but it's kept me from going insane."'

'I'm not sure you want to hear everything I have to say to this man.'

'The words ain't been made that's gonna upset me, son . . . I mean Loot. Come on around back.'

The sweeping expanse of backyard was dotted with live oaks, lime trees, myrtle bushes, and circular weedless beds of roses and purple hydrangeas. Meat smoke from a stone fire pit drifted across the lawn and hung in the trees, and the Saint Augustine grass was so thick, so deeply blue and green in the evening shadows, that you felt you could dive into it as you would a deep pool of water.

Vic Benson was cutting back a clump of banana trees with a pair of garden shears. The blades of the shears were white and gummy with pulp. Each time he snapped the blades on a dead frond, the muscles in his face and neck flexed like snakes under his red scar tissue.

A thick-bodied black woman in a maid's uniform began setting a table on the flagstone patio.

'Let's sit down to eat, then you can ask the old man whatever you want,' Lyle said.

'This isn't what I had in mind, Lyle.'

'Quit trying to plan everything. What the Man on High plans for you is better than anything you could plan for yourself. Isn't that what y'all learn in AA? Look out yonder.' He pointed across the brick wall and bamboo that bordered his property. 'See it, just above the trees out on Highland, my cross, right up there on top of my Bible college. Look, it's silver and pink in the sunlight. Inside all that chrome is a charred wooden cross that was burned by Klansmen to terrorize black folk. Then the Reverend Jimmy Bob Clock made it his so me and him could run scams on a bunch of north Miss'sippi country people who didn't have two quarters to rub together in their overalls. Now it's on top of a Bible college where kids go to school free and study for the ministry. You think that's all accident? I read a poem once that had a line in it about a white radiance that stains eternity. That's the way I like to think about that cross up there.'

'I don't like to cut into your sense of religiosity, Lyle, but how in the name of God do you justify all this?' I gestured at his house, his manicured lawns.

'I don't own it. I'm mortgaged up to my eyeballs. It all went into the college. That ain't a shuck, either, Loot.'

'What do you pay that black woman with?'

He laughed.

'I don't pay her anything. She works three hours a day for room and board. She just got out of St Gabriel. She did five years for murdering her pimp.'

'What you do is your business, Lyle, but I think you have a dangerous and psychotic man staying at your home.'

'That black gal, Clemmie, might cut my throat, but a good fart would blow ole Vic off the planet like a dandelion. Come on, let's eat. You're too serious about everything, Dave. That's always been your problem. Treat the world seriously and in turn it'll treat you like a clown. You ought to learn that, Loot.'

'How about saving it for a wider audience, Lyle?'

'It's just one guy's opinion,' he said, and shrugged his shoulders. Then he waved at the man who called himself Vic Benson and who was now flinging a pile of dried banana fronds into a trash fire by a brick wall at the back of the property. His body was silhouetted like a figure cut from tin against the puffs of sparks and plumes of black smoke. He walked toward us, out of the shade, his eyes red-rimmed, unblinking, welded on mine, his puckered face as unreal as rubber twisted around a fist.

I didn't look directly at him while the black woman served us plates of black-eyed peas, dirty rice, and barbecued pork chops. But I could smell him, an odor like turpentine, tobacco smoke, winddried sweat.

Because part of his lips had been pared away, you could see everything in his mouth when he chewed his food. He reached across the table for a second pork chop, and a patch of black hair on his arm brushed the rim of my iced-tea glass.

'The way I eat, it bothers you?' he asked.

'No, not at all,' I said.

'I seen them a lot worse than me. In an armed service hospital,' he said. 'They had to eat their food out of toothpaste tubes.'

He drank from his glass. The iced tea gurgled across his teeth. His splayed fingers looked like gnarled and baked tubers.

'Someone used a piano wire on Weldon Sonnier and tried to remodel him into a stump,' I said. 'Do you know anything about that, Vic?'

'About what?'

'You heard me.'

'Piano wire? That's a good one. The last time I seen you, you ax me if I was looking in somebody's windows. Maybe you got a bump on the brain or something.'

The black maid had put on a Walkman headset and was dusting the patio furniture by slapping it with a dish towel, one hand propped on her hip, while she jiggled to music that no one else could hear. Vic pushed a piece of meat back into his mouth with his thumb and studied her undulating curves.

'I talked with the gentleman who runs the Sally in Lafayette,' I said. 'He said you were watching Lyle on TV one time and you mentioned how you'd like to pour lye down his throat.'

Lyle's fork paused over his food a moment, then he continued eating with his eyes askance.

'What a drunk man says don't have no more meaning than horse piss on a rock,' Vic said.

'He says you flipped a hot cigarette into a child's face.'

'Then I say I don't have no recollection of him being there to say what I done and what I ain't done in my life.'

'People sure seem to know when you've been around, though, Vic,' I said.

'How about we ease it down a notch, Dave?' Lyle said.

'It don't bother me none,' Vic said. 'One guy like me gives a job to a hunnerd like him. He knows it, too.'

'You're wrong about that, partner,' I said. 'You become a job for me when I have to cut a warrant on you. But right now I can't prove that you tried to take your son's head off with a piece of piano wire. That means you have another season to run. If I were you, I'd take advantage of my good fortune and change my ways. *Change ta vie, t'connais que je veux dire?*

'I'm tired of this. Where'd you put that tobacco at?' he said, and pushed his plate away with the heel of his hand.

'I think I set it up on the brick wall. Stay where you're at. I'll get it,' Lyle said, rose from his chair, and walked across the lawn.

Vic Benson stared straight into my face. His thin nose was hooked, like a hawk's beak.

'It looks like you drove up here for nothing, don't it?' he said.

I looked back into his face. His puttylike skin was incapable of wearing an expression, and his surgically devastated mouth was cut back into a keyhole over his teeth; but his eyes, which seemed to water as though they were smarting from smoke, contained a malevolent, jittering light that made me want to look away.

'I've got a feeling about you, partner,' I said. 'I think you not only want revenge against your children. I think you want to do something spectacular. A real light show.'

'Go shit in your plate.'

'You might even be thinking about torching Lyle's house, particularly if you could get Weldon and Drew inside with Lyle at the same time. I suspect fire stays on your mind quite a bit.'

His red eyes shifted to the maid, her large breasts, her dress that tightened across her rump as she reached upwards to dust cobwebs off a bug lamp. He took a lucifer match out of his shirt pocket and rolled it across his teeth with his tongue.

'Fire don't know no one place. Fire don't know no one man,' he said.

'Are you threatening me, Vic?'

'I don't waste my time on twerps,' he said.

The moon was down that night, but the pecan trees in the yard seemed to shake with a sudden white-green light when the wind blew out of the south and dry lightning trembled in the marsh. I couldn't sleep. I thought of fire, the vortex of flame that had swirled about Vic Benson (or Verise Sonnier) in a Port Arthur chemical plant, the sheets of hot metal that had buried him alive and branded his soul, the hateful energies that he must have carried with him like a burning chain draped around his neck. He was one of those for whom society had no solution. His life was ashes; he was morally insane and knew it; and his thoughts alone could make a normal person weep. The sight of pity in our eyes made him grind his back teeth. Years ago his kind were lobotomized.

He had nothing to lose. He was a living nightmare to hospital employees; prisons didn't want him; psychiatrists considered him pathological and hence untreatable; and even if he was convicted of a capital crime, judges knew that he could turn his own execution into an electronic carnival of world-class proportions.

Would he take an interest in my home and family? I had no answer. But I was convinced that, like Joey Gouza or Bobby Earl, he was one of those who had gone across a line at some point in his life and had declared war on the rest of us. Whether we elected to recognize that fact or not, Vic would be at work with a penny book of matches or a strand of wire that he would pop musically between his fists. The time of his appearance in our lives would be of his choosing.

I fixed a cup of coffee and walked down the slope of my yard to the dock. The stars looked white and hot in the sky; on the wind I could smell the sour reek of mud and rotted humus in the marsh, and the wet, gray odor of something dead. A white tree of lightning splintered across the southern sky. Sweat ran down my sides. It was going to be a scorching day.

I unlocked the door of the bait shop and went inside and pulled the chain on the electric bulb that hung over the counter. Then I saw the diagonal slash across the back screen window that gave on to the bayou.

But it was too late. He rose up from behind the bait tanks and gently pressed the barrel of a pistol behind my ear.

'No, no, don't turn around, my friend. That'd get both of us in trouble,' he said.

The light threw both of our shadows on the floor. I could see his extended arm, the pistol rounded by his fist, and an object, a sack perhaps, that seemed to dangle from his other hand.

'The till's empty. I've got maybe ten dollars in my wallet,' I said.

'Come on, Mr Robicheaux. Give me a little credit.' The accent was New Orleans, the voice one I had heard before.

'What do you want, partner?'

'To give you something. You just shouldn't have come to work so early . . . No, no, don't turn around—'

He shifted his position so that his face was well behind my range of vision. But when he did I saw his distorted silvery reflection on the aluminum side of a horizontal lunch-meat and cold-drink cooler. Or rather I saw the reflected metal caps and fillings in his mouth.

Then he stooped, set something on the floor, and nudged me toward the counter.

'Lean on it, Mr Robicheaux. You probably don't pack when you come down to your bait shop, but a guy can't take things for granted,' he said, and moved his free hand down my hips and pockets and over my ankles.

'Look, a black man who works for me is going to be here soon. I don't want him to walk in on this. How about telling me what's on your mind and getting out of here?'

'Your ovaries don't get heated up too easy, do they?' He clicked off the light. 'What time's the colored man get here?'

'Anytime now.'

'That sure would change your luck in a bad way, believe me.' Then he said, 'Listen, the man I work for has fixations. Right now you're one of them. Why? Because you keep bugging the shit out of him. It's time you lay off, man. This is an important guy. There's people up in Chicago don't want him puking blood all over New Orleans because of nervous anxiety . . . No, no, eyes forward—'

He rubbed the pistol barrel along my jawbone.

'Is that it?' I said.

'No, that's not it, man. Look, nobody's got a beef with you, Mr Robicheaux. Nobody had a beef with that cop who walked into Sonnier's house, either. That dumb fuck Fluck went out of control. We don't whack cops, you know that, man. So we're making it right.

'But it doesn't have to end here. You're a bright guy and you can have a lot of good things. Nothing illegal, no strings, just good business. Like maybe a nightclub down in Grand Isle. It's yours for the asking. All you got to do is call the right Italian restaurant on Esplanade. You know the place I'm talking about.'

Through the slashed screen I could see the false dawn lighting the gray tops of the cypress trees in the marsh. I heard a fish flop loudly in the lily pads.

'I'll think about it,' I said.

'Good . . . good. Now—'

I felt him shift his weight, felt the dangling object in his hand brush against my pants leg.

'What?' I said.

'I got to figure what to do with you. You keep walking in on me at the wrong time. Nothing personal but you've really fucked up my plans twice now.'

'Like you say, so far it's not personal . . . Don't do the wrong thing, partner.'

I could hear him breathing in the dark. The back of my neck and head felt naked, as though the skin had been peeled away from all the nerve endings.

'What's inside that room, the one with the lock on it?' he said.

'It's just a storage room.'

'Well, that's where you're going.'

From behind, he put his left hand on my shoulder and guided me toward the door. I felt the sacked object bump back and forth below my shoulder blade.

'Unlock it,' he said.

I found the key on my ring and snapped open the long U-shaped shaft on the lock. I wiped the sweat out of my eyes with the back of my wrist.

'Come on, get inside, man,' he said.

'I want to give you something to think about when you leave me.'

'You're gonna give me something to think about? I think you've got it turned around.' He started to push me inside.

'No, I don't. I didn't see your face, so I can't identify you. That means you're home free on this one. But I know who you are, Jack. Don't go near my house. God help you if you get anywhere near my house.'

'You don't know who your friends are. Hey, the man in New Orleans sent you a present. You'll like it. He's not a bad guy. He's got his own problems. How'd you like to have boils all over the lining of your stomach? Why don't you have a little compassion?'

With his knuckles he shoved me into the storage room, then snapped the lock shut. I heard him go out the front door, then moments later a car engine start out on the road.

I braced my back against a stack of beer cases and kicked as hard as I could against the door; but it was sheathed in tin, and the lock and hasp were solid. Then in the dark I tripped over an old twenty-five-horsepower Evinrude engine. I balanced it over my head by the shaft and the housing and hurled it against the slat wall next to the door. Two slats burst from the studs, and I splintered the others loose until I could squeeze through a hole back into the shop. I could hear the diminishing sound of Gates' car on the dirt road that led to the drawbridge over the bayou. I pulled the chain on the light bulb over the counter and started punching the office number on the phone. Both my hands were shaking.

'Sheriff's Department—'

'This is Dave . . . Jack Gates just tore out of my bait shop . . . He's armed and dangerous . . . Call the bridge tender and tell him to lift the bridge . . . I'll meet you guys at the—'

Then I stopped.

'What is it, Dave?'

I looked at the weighted clear plastic bag hanging from a nail on a post in the center of the shop.

'I'll meet you guys at the bayou,' I said.

'What's wrong, Dave? Are you hurt?'

'No, I'm all right. Get hold of the bridge tender and seal the whole area off. Don't let this guy get out of town.'

I put the receiver back in the cradle and stared numbly at the severed head inside the plastic bag. The eyes were rolled, the tongue lolled out of the mouth, the nose was mashed against the folds of plastic, and the blond hair was matted with congealed blood; but even in death the face looked like it belonged on a toy man. And to preclude the possibility that I could ever mistake Jewel Fluck for someone else, one of his fingers had been inserted in the thick, purple residue at the bottom of the bag.

I ran to the house, through the front door and into the bedroom, and grabbed the .45 out of the dresser drawer. Bootsie sat up in bed and clicked on the table lamp.

'What is it?' she said.

'Jack Gates was in the shop. I'm going after him. Don't go in the shop, Boots. Call Batist and tell him not to come to work right now.'

'What is it? What did he—'

'We might have to dust for prints. Let's just keep people out of there for a while.'

I saw her eyes trying to read my expression.

'Everything's all right,' I said. 'Just don't go out of the house, Boots, till we get this guy in custody.'

Then I was out the front door and in the truck, banging over the chuckholes in the dirt road that led to the drawbridge over the bayou, the .45 bouncing on the seat beside me, the early red sun edging the marsh with fire.

I could hear sirens in the distance now. I rounded a corner in second, where the bayou made a wide bend, and through the oak trees which lined the road I could see the drawbridge extended high in the air, a quarter of a mile away.

Jack, I think you're about to be hung out to dry, I thought, and this time Joey the Neck is going down with you. Welcome to Iberia Parish, podjo.

Vanity, vanity, vanity. Jack Gates was an old-time Mafia soldier and thriving button man in a state whose system of capital punishment involved as much charity as you would expect in the deep-frying of pork rinds. Jack was not one you would simply drive into a bottleneck and cork inside the glass and put on display like a light bug.

I heard his car before I saw it: the transmission wound up full-bore, the engine roaring through a defective muffler like a garbage truck, gravel exploding like grapeshot under the fenders. Then the TransAm skidded around the corner in a cloud of yellow dust, low on the springs, streaked and ugly with dried mud, ripping a green gash out of a canebrake.

I looked full into his face through his windshield – into his regret that he didn't take me out when he had the chance, his rage at the cosmic conspiracy that had made him the long-suffering soldier of an ulcer-ridden paranoid like Joey Gee.

I pulled the truck diagonally across the road, leaped from the seat, and aimed the .45 across the hood, straight at Jack Gates's face. He stomped on the brakes, and the TransAm bucked sideways in a chuckhole and fishtailed against the trunk of an oak tree, pinwheeling a hubcap down the center of the road. He stared at me momentarily through the open passenger's window, a blue revolver balanced in one hand on top of the steering wheel, his metal-capped teeth glinting in the sun's hot early light, the engine throttling open and subsiding and then throttling open again under the hood.

'Give it up, Jack,' I said. 'Gouza's a psychotic sack of shit. Let him take his own fall for a change.'

The rooster tail of dust from behind the car drifted across his window, and in the second it took for me to lose eye contact with him, he aimed the revolver quickly out the window and popped off two rounds. The first one was low and kicked up dirt three feet in front of the truck, but the second one whanged off the hood and showered leaves out of the tree behind me.

Then he dropped the transmission into reverse and floored the Trans-Am back down the road, the tires burning into the dirt, spinning with circles of black smoke. He veered from side to side, clipping bark out of the tree trunks, bursting a tail light, ripping loose his bumper. But evidently he had an eye for detail and had remembered passing a collapsed wire gate and a faint trace of a side road that led through a sugarcane field, because he slammed on his brakes, slid in a half circle, then roared over the downed gate – cedar posts, barbed wire, and all.

I ran up the incline by the far side of the road, through a stand of pine trees, splashed across a coulee, and came out on the edge of the field just as the TransAm spun around the corner, rippled back a fender on a parked tractor, and mowed through the short cane toward a flat-topped levee that led back to the main parish road.

He hadn't expected to see me on foot in the field. He started to cut the steering wheel toward me, to drive me back into the trees or the coulee, then he changed his mind, spinning the wheel in the opposite direction with one hand and firing blindly out the window with the other. In the instant that the TransAm flashed by me, his face looked white and round and small through the window, like a spectator's in a theater, as though he had suddenly become aware that he was witnessing his own dénouement.

I went to one knee in the wet grass and began firing. I tried to keep the sights below the level of his window jamb to allow for the elevation caused by the recoil, but in reality it was unnecessary. The eight hollow-point rounds, which flattened to the size of quarters with impact, destroyed his automobile. They pocked silvery holes in the doors, spiderwebbed the windows, blew divots of upholstery into the air, exploded a tire off the rim, gashed a geyser of steam out of the radiator, and whipped a single streak of blood across the front windshield.

His foot must have locked down on the accelerator, because the TransAm was almost airborne when it roared along the lip of an irrigation ditch and sliced through the fence surrounding a Gulf States Power Company substation. The front end crashed right into the transformers, and the tiers of transmission wires and ceramic insulators crumpled in a crackling net on the car's roof.

But he was still alive. He let the revolver drop outside the window, then started to push open the door with the palms of his hands like a man trying to extricate himself from the rubble of a collapsed building.

'Don't get out, Jack! Don't touch the ground!'

He sat back down on the seat, his face bloodless and exhausted, then the sole of one shoe came to rest on the damp earth.

The voltage contorted his face as if he were having an epileptic seizure. His body stiffened, shook, and jerked; spittle flew from his mouth; electricity seemed to leap and dance off his capped teeth. Then his car horn and radio began blaring simultaneously, and a scorched odor, like hair and feces burning in an incinerator, rose from his clothes and head in dirty strings of smoke.

I turned and walked back to the road. The grass was wet against my trouser legs and swarming with insects, the sun hot and yellow above the treeline in the marsh. The drawbridge was down now, and ambulances, firetrucks, and sheriff's cars were careening toward me, emergency lights blazing, under the long canopy of oaks. My saliva tasted like copper pennies; my right ear was a block of wood. The .45, the receiver locked open on the empty clip, felt like a silly appendage hanging from my hand.

Paramedics, cops, and firemen were rushing past me now. I kept walking down the road, by the bayou's edge, toward my house. Bream were feeding close into the lily pads, denting the water in circles like raindrops. The cypress roots along the far bank were gnarled and wet among the shadows and ferns, and I could see the delicate prints of egrets in the damp sand. I pulled the clip from the automatic, stuck it in my back pocket, and let the receiver slam back on the empty chamber. I opened and closed my mouth to clear my right ear, but it felt like it was full of warm water that would not drain.

The sheriff came up behind me and gently put his hand inside my arm.

'When they deal the hand, we shut down their game,' he said. 'If it comes out any different, we did something wrong. You know where I learned that?'

'It sounds familiar.'

'It should.'

'We could have used Gates to get Joey Gee.'

'Yeah, so we'll catch up with Fluck and use *him*. Six of one, half dozen of the other.'

I nodded silently.

'Right?' he said.

'Sure.'

'It's just a matter of time.'

'Yeah, that's all it is,' I agreed, and looked away into the distance, where I could almost feel the sun's heat cooking the tin roof on the bait shop.

15

I locked up the bait shop and let no one in it for the rest of the day. I thought about the events of that morning for a long time. Things had worked out for Joey Gouza in better ways than he could have ever planned. I had been responsible for springing him on the phony assault-and-battery charges filed by Drew Sonnier; Weldon's long-sought-after film evidence had turned out to be worthless; Eddy Raintree, a superstitious dimwit as well as pervert, who would have probably ratted out Joey Gee for an extra roll of toilet paper in his cell, had had his face blown into a bloody mist by Jewel Fluck while he was locked in my handcuffs; then Gates had gotten to Fluck, and I in turn had killed Gates, the only surviving person who could implicate Joey in the Garrett murder.

I wondered if Joey Gee got up this morning and said a prayer of thanks that I had wandered into his life.

In the meantime one of his hired sociopaths had terrified my daughter, then he had ordered his chief button man to deliver a human head and severed finger to our family business.

I suspected that today had proved special for Joey, a day in which he took an extra pleasure in chopping up lines with his whores, sipping iced rum drinks with them by the pool, or maybe inviting them out to the clubhouse at the track for lobster-steak dinners and rolls of six-dollar parimutuel tickets. I suspected at this moment that Joey Gee did not have a care in the world.

After I wrote up my report at the office, I went back home and sat in the shade on the dock by myself, staring at the sun's hot yellow reflection on the bayou, the dragonflies that seemed to hang motionless over the cattails and lily pads. Even in the shade I was sweating heavily inside my clothes. Then I unlocked the bait shop and used the phone inside to call Clete Purcel. The heat was stifling, and the plastic bag that hung from the post in the center of the room had clouded with moisture.

When I had finished talking with Clete, the damp outline of my hand looked like it had been painted on the phone receiver.

I worked in the yard the rest of the afternoon, and when it rained at four o'clock, I sat on the gallery by myself and watched the water drip out of the pecan trees and *tick* in the dead leaves and *ping* on top of Tripod's cage. Then at sunset I went back into the bait shop with a hat box, and five minutes later I was on my way to New Orleans.

'You look tired,' Bootsie said at the breakfast table the next morning.

'Oh, I'm just a little slow this morning,' I said.

'What time did you come in last night?'

'I really didn't notice.'

'How's Clete?'

'About the same.'

'Dave, what are you two doing?'

I kept my eyes on Alafair, who was packing her lunch kit for a church group picnic.

'Be sure to put a piece of cake in there, Alf,' I said.

She turned around and grinned.

'I already did,' she said.

'Do you want to talk about it later?' Bootsie said.

'Yeah, that's a good idea.'

Ten minutes later Alafair raced out the screen door to catch the church bus. Bootsie watched her leave, then came back into the kitchen.

'I just saw Batist carrying some lumber into the shop. What's he doing?' she asked.

'A few repairs.'

'Did that man Gates do something in our shop? Is that why you wouldn't let anybody in it yesterday?'

'It just wasn't a day for business-as-usual.'

'What's Clete's involvement with this?'

'It was Gouza's goons who put him in the hospital. That makes him involved, Boots.'

She took the dishes off the table and put them in the sink. She gazed out the window into the backyard.

'When you go to see Clete, it always means a shortcut,' she said.

'You don't know everything that's happened.'

'I'm not the problem, Dave. What bothers me is I think you're hiding something from the people you work with.'

'Joey Gouza ordered this man Gates to throw Gouza's brother-in-law into an airplane propeller. Then he sent this same man to our house with a—'

'What?'

I caught my breath and pinched my temples with my fingers.

'Gouza has a furnace instead of a brain,' I said. 'He's left his mark on our home, and I can't touch him. Do you think I'm going to abide that?'

She rinsed the plates in the sink and continued to look out the window.

'Two of the men who murdered the deputy are dead,' she said. 'One day it'll be Joey Gouza's turn. Can't you just let events take their course? Or let other people handle things for a while?'

'There's another factor, Boots. Gouza's a paranoid. Maybe today he feels wonderful, he's hit the daily double, the dragons are dead. But next week, or maybe next month, he'll start thinking again about the individuals who've hurt or humiliated him most, and he'll be back in our lives. I'm not going to let that happen.'

She dried her hands on a dish towel, then used it to mop off the counter. She brushed back her hair with her fingers, straightened the periwinkles in a vase. Her eyes never looked at mine. She turned on the radio on the windowsill, then turned it off and took a pair of scissors out of a drawer.

'I'm going to cut some fresh flowers. Are you going to the office now?' she said.

'Yes, I guess so.'

'I'll put your lunch in the icebox. I have to run some errands in town today.'

'Boots, listen a minute—'

She popped open a paper bag to place the cut flowers in and went out the back door.

That afternoon the sheriff came into my office with my report on Gates's shooting in his hands. He sat down in the chair across from me and put on his rimless glasses.

'I'm still trying to puzzle a couple of things out here, Dave. It's like there's a blank space or two in your report,' he said.

'How's that?'

'I'm not criticizing it. You were pretty used up when you wrote this stuff down. But let me see if I understand everything here. You went down a little early to open up your bait shop?'

'That's right.'

'That's when you saw Gates?'

'That's correct.'

'You called the dispatcher, then you went after him in your truck?'

'Yeah, that's about it.'

'So it was already first light when you saw him?'

'It was getting there.'

'It had to be, because the sun was up when you nailed him.'

'I'm not following you, sheriff.'

'Maybe it's just me. But why would a pro like Gates come around your house at sunrise when he could have laid for you at night?'

'Who knows?'

'Unless he didn't mean to hurt you, unless he was there for some other reason—'

'Like Clete once told me, trying to figure out the greaseballs is like putting your hand in an unflushed toilet.'

He looked down at the report again, then folded his glasses and put them in his shirt pocket.

'There's something that really disturbs me about this, Dave. I know there's an answer, but I can't seem to put my hand on it.'

'Sometimes it's better not to think about things too much. Just let events unfold.' I placed my hands behind my neck, yawned, and tried to look casually out the window.

'No, what I mean is, Gouza just got off the hook in Iberia Parish. Is this guy crazy enough to send a hit man after another one of our people, right to his house, right at the break of day? It doesn't fit, does it?'

'I wish Gates were here to tell us. I don't know what else to say, sheriff.'

'Well, I'm just glad you didn't get hurt out there. I'll see you later. Maybe you ought to go home and get some sleep. You look like you haven't slept since World War II.'

He went out the door. I tried to complete the paperwork that was on my desk, but my eyes burned and I couldn't concentrate or keep my thoughts straight in my head. Finally I shoved it all into a bottom drawer and fiddled absently with a chain of paper clips on top of my desk blotter.

Had I lied to the sheriff, I asked myself? Not exactly. But then I hadn't quite told the truth, either.

Was my report dishonest? No, it was worse. It concealed the commission of a homicide.

But some situations involve a trade-off. In this case the fulfillment of a professional obligation would require that my home and family become the center of a morbid story that would live in the community for decades, and Joey Gouza would succeed in inflicting a level of psychological damage on my daughter, in particular, that might never be undone. Saint Augustine once admonished that we should never use the truth to injure. I believe there are dark and uncertain moments in our lives when it's not wrong for each of us to feel that he wrote those words especially for us.

I left the office and drove home on the oak-lined dirt road that followed the bayou past my dock. The first raindrops were starting to fall out of a sunny sky, as they did almost every summer afternoon at three o'clock, and I could feel the air becoming close, suddenly cooler, as the barometric pressure dropped, and the bream and goggle-eyed perch started feeding on the bayou's surface by the edge of the lily pads. I passed the collapsed wire gate that Jack Gates had shredded when he had pointed the TransAm into the sugarcane field, and I avoided looking at the trashed substation and the bullet-pocked car that a wrecker had winched loose from the transformers and left upside down amid a litter of broken cane stalks. But I wasn't going to brood upon the death of Jack Gates; I had already turned over yesterday to my Higher Power, and I was determined not to relive it. My problems with Bootsie as well as the sheriff were sufficient to keep my mind occupied today. And if that was not enough, a man ahead of me in a pickup truck was stapling Bobby Earl posters on the tree trunks along the road.

By the time I turned in to my drive, he had just smoothed one to the contours of a two-hundred-year-old live oak at the edge of my yard and hammered staples into each of the corners. I closed the truck door and walked over to him, my hands in my back pockets. I even tried to smile. He looked like an innocuous individual hired out of a labor office.

'Say, podna, that tree's on my property and I don't want any nail holes in it.'

A foot above my head was Bobby Earl's chiseled face, with stage lights shining up into it so that his features had the messianic cast of a Billy Graham. Below was his most oft-quoted statement, LET ME BE YOUR VOICE, LET ME SPEAK YOUR THOUGHTS. Then farther down was some information about a rally and barbecue with Dixieland bands on Friday night in Baton Rouge.

'Sorry,' the man with the hammer and staples said. 'The guy just said to stick 'em up on all the trees.'

'Which guy?'

'The guy who give me the signs.'

'Well, just don't nail any more up till you get around that next corner, okay?'

'Sure.'

I tried to free the staples from the bark, then I simply tore the poster down the middle, handed it to him, and walked up to the house.

Bootsie was in town and Alafair had not gotten home from her picnic yet. I undressed in the bedroom, turned on the window fan, lay down on top of the sheets with the pillow over my head, and tried to sleep. I could hear the rain hitting the trees in large, flat drops now and *tink*ing on the blades of the fan.

But I couldn't sleep, and I kept trying to sort through my thoughts in the same way that you pick at a scab you know you should leave alone.

No matter how educated a southerner is, or how liberal or intellectual he might consider himself to be, I don't believe you will meet many of my generation who do not still revere, although perhaps in a secret way, all the old southern myths that we've supposedly put aside as members of the New South. You cannot grow up in a place where the tractor's plow can crack minié balls and grapeshot loose from the soil, even rake across a cannon wheel, and remain impervious to the past.

As a child I had access to few books, but I knew all the stories about General Banks's invasion of southwestern Louisiana, the burning of the parish courthouse, the stabling of horses in the Episcopalian church on Main Street, the union gunboats that came up the Teche and shelled the plantation on Nelson's Canal west of town, and Louisiana's boys in butternut brown who lived on dried peas and gave up ground a bloody foot at a time.

Who cared if their cause was just or not? The stories made your blood sing; the grooved minié ball that you picked out of the freshly plowed row and rolled in your palm made you part of a moment that happened over a century ago. You looked away at the stand of trees by the bayou, and rather than the tractor engine idling beside you, you heard the ragged popping of small-arms fire and saw black plumes of smoke exploding out of the brush into the sunlight. And you realized that they died right here in this field, that they bled into this same dirt where the cane would grow eight feet tall by autumn and turn as scarlet as dried blood.

But why did large numbers of people buy into a man like Bobby Earl? Were they that easily deceived? Would any group of reasonable people entrust the conduct of their government to an ex-American Nazi or Ku Klux Klansman? I had no answer.

I wondered if any of them ever asked themselves what Robert Lee or Thomas Jackson might have to say about a man like this.

I finally fell asleep. Then I heard the brakes on the church bus and a moment later the screen door slam. Other sounds followed: a lunch kit clattering on the drainboard, the icebox door opening, the back screen slamming, Tripod racing up and down on the chain that was attached to the clothesline, the screen slamming again, tennis shoes in the hallway outside the bedroom door, then a pause full of portent.

Alafair hit the bed running and bounced up and down on her knees, lost her balance, and fell across my back. I raised my head up from under the pillow.

'Hi, big guy. What you doing home early?' she said.

'Taking a nap.'

'Oh.' She started bouncing again, then looked at my face. 'Maybe you should go back to sleep?'

'Why would I want to do that, Alf?'

'Are you mad about something?'

I put on my trousers, then sat back down on the side of the bed and tried to rub the sleep out of my face.

'Hop up on my back,' I said. 'Let's check out what Batist is doing. It's not a day for lying around in bed.'

She put her arms around my neck and clamped her legs around my ribcage, and we walked down through the wet leaves to the dock. It was raining lightly out of a gray sky now, the lily pads were bright green and beaded with water, and the bayou was covered with rain rings.

Batist had slid the canvas awning out on wires over the dock, and several fishermen sat under it, drinking beer and eating *boudin* out of wax paper. He had also allowed someone to put Bobby Earl posters in the bait-shop windows and on the service counter.

I let Alafair climb down off my back. Batist was taking some *boudin* out of the microwave. He wore canvas boat shoes without socks, a pair of ragged, white cutoffs whose top button had popped off, and a wash-faded denim shirt tied under his chest, which reminded me of black boilerplate. His shirt pocket was bursting with cigars.

'Batist, who put these posters here?'

'Some white man who come ax if he could leave them.'

'Next time send the man up to the house.'

'You was sleepin', you.' He put a dry cigar in his mouth and began slicing the *boudin* on a paper plate and inserting matchsticks into each slice. 'Why you worried about them signs, Dave? People leave them here all the time.'

'Because they're for Bobby Earl, and Bobby Earl's a shit!' Alafair said.

I looked down at her, stunned.

'Put the cork in that language, Alf,' I said.

'I heard Bootsie say it,' she answered. 'He's a shit. He hates black people.'

Two men at the beer cooler were grinning at me.

'Dave, that's right. Them is for that fella Earl?' Batist said.

'Yeah, but you didn't know, Batist,' I said. 'Here, I'll throw them in the trash.'

'I ain't never seen him on TV, me, so I didn't pay his picture no mind.'

'It's all right, podna.'

The men at the cooler were still grinning in our direction.

'Do you gentlemen need something?' I said.

'Not a thing,' one of them said.

'Good,' I said.

I took Alafair by the hand, and we walked back up the slope to the gallery. The wind was cool blowing out of the marsh and smelled of wet leaves and moldy pecan husks and the purple four-o'clocks that were just opening in the shadows. Alafair's hand felt hot and small in mine.

'You mad, Dave?' she said.

'No, I'm real proud of you, little guy. You're what real soldiers are made of.'

Her eyes squinted almost completely shut with her smile.

That evening Alafair went to a baseball game with the neighbors' children, and Bootsie and I were left alone with each other. It had stopped raining, and the windows were open and you could hear the crickets and the cicadas from horizon to horizon. Our conversation, when it occurred, was spiritless and morose. At nine o'clock the phone rang in the kitchen.

'Hello,' I said.

'Hey, Streak, I thought I'd pass on some information in case you're wondering about life down here in the Big Sleazy.'

'Just a minute, Clete,' I said.

I took the telephone on its extension wire out on the back steps and sat down.

'Go ahead,' I said.

'I found the perfect moment to drop the dime on our man. His dork just went into the electric socket big time.'

In the background I could hear people talking loudly and dishes clattering.

'Where are you?'

'I'm scarfing down a few on the half shell and chugging down a few brews at the Acme, noble man. There's also a French lady at my table who's fascinated with my accent. I told her it's Irish-coonass. She's talking about painting me in the nude . . . Hey, trust me, Dave, everything's copacetic. It'll never go down in a manual on police procedure, but when it's time to mash on their scrots, you do it with hobnailed boots. Hang loose, partner, and come on down this weekend and let's catch some green trout.'

I replaced the receiver in the phone cradle and went back inside the house. Bootsie had just put away some dishes in the cabinet and was watching me.

'That was Clete, wasn't it?' she said. She wore a sundress printed with purple and green flowers. She had just brushed her hair, and it was full of small lights.

'Yep.'

'What have you two done, Dave?'

I sat down at the breakfast table and looked at the tops of my hands. I thought about telling her all of it.

'Back at the First District, we used to call it "salting the mine shaft."'

'What?'

'The wiseguys have expensive lawyers. Sometimes cops fix it so two and two add up to five.'

'What did you do?'

I cleared my throat and thought about continuing, then I made my mind go empty.

'Let's talk about something else, Boots.'

I gazed out the back screen at the fireflies lighting in the trees. I could feel her eyes looking at me. Then she walked out of the kitchen and began sorting canned goods in the hallway pantry. I thought about driving into town and reading the newspaper at the bar in Tee Neg's poolroom. In my mind I already saw myself under the wood-bladed fan and smelled the talcum, the green sawdust on the floor, the flat beer, and the residue of ice and whiskey poured into the tin sinks.

But Tee Neg's was not a good place for me to be when I was tired and the bottles behind the bar became as seductive and inviting as a woman's smile.

I heard Bootsie stop stacking the canned goods and shut the pantry door. She walked up behind my chair and paused for a moment, then rested her hand lightly on the back of the chair.

'It was for me and Alafair, wasn't it?' she said.

'What?'

'Whatever you did last night in New Orleans, it wasn't for yourself. It was for me and Alafair, wasn't it?'

I put my arm behind her thigh and drew her hand down on my chest. She pressed her cheek against my hair and hugged me against her breasts.

'Dave, we have such a wonderful family,' she said. 'Let's try to trust each other a little more.'

I started to say something, but whatever it was, it was better forgotten. I could hear her heart beating against my ear. The sun-freckled tops of her breasts were hot, and her skin smelled like milk and flowers.

By nine o'clock the next morning I had heard nothing of particular interest out of New Orleans. But then again the local news often featured stories of such national importance as the following: the drawbridge over the Teche had opened with three cars on it; the school-board meeting had come to an end last night with a fistfight between two high school principals; several professional wrestlers had to be escorted by city police from the National Guard armory after they were spat upon and showered with garbage by the fans; the drawbridge tender had thrown a press photographer's camera into the Teche because he didn't believe anyone had the right to photograph his bridge.

So I kept diddling with my paperwork, looking at my watch, and wondering if perhaps Clete hadn't simply spent too much time at the draft beer spout in the Acme before he had decided to telephone me.

Then, just as I was about to drive home for lunch, I got a call from Lyle Sonnier.

'Sorry to be so late getting back to you, Loot, but it was hard getting everybody together. Anyway, it's on for tomorrow night,' he said.

'What's on?'

'Dinner. Actually, a crab boil. We're gonna cook up a mess of 'em in the backyard.'

'Lyle, that's nice of you but—'

438

'Look, Dave, Drew and Weldon feel the same way I do. You treated our family decent while we sort of stuck thumbtacks in your head.'

'No, you didn't.'

'I know better, Loot. Anyway, can y'all make it or not?'

'Friday night we always take Batist and Alafair to the drive-in movie in Lafayette.'

'Bring them along.'

'I don't know if your father is anxious to see me again.'

'Come on, Dave, he operates on about three brain cells, poor old guy. Have a little compassion.'

'That's the second time this week somebody has said that to me about the wrong person.'

'What?'

'Never mind. I'll ask Boots and Batist and get back to you. Thanks for the invitation, Lyle.'

I drove home, and Bootsie and I fixed a pitcher of iced tea and poor-boy sandwiches of shrimp and fried oysters and took them out on the redwood picnic table under the mimosa tree.

'You sure you don't mind going?' I said.

'No. Why should I mind?'

'Their father may be there. He's terribly disfigured, Boots.'

She smiled. The wind in the mimosa tree made drifting, lacy patterns of shadow on her skin.

'What you mean is, Drew will be there,' she said.

'Well, she will be.'

'I think I can survive the knowledge of your college romances, Dave.' Her brown eyes crinkled at the corners.

I was late getting back to the department. When I walked through my office door the sheriff was sitting in my chair, one of his half-topped boots propped on the corner of my desk. A videotape cassette rested on his belt buckle. He looked at his watch, then his eyes glanced at my damp hair and shirt.

'You look like you just got out of the shower,' he said.

'I did.'

'You go home to take a shower in the middle of the day?'

'I had to change a tire.'

'I'll be,' he said, clicking his nails on the plastic cassette case.

'What's up, sheriff?'

'An FBI agent dropped this tape by about an hour ago. It was shot last night in front of a house that's under surveillance out by Lake Pontchartrain. The home is owned by one of the Giacanos, the head greaseballs in New Orleans.'

'Yeah?'

'They had a big party there last night. The Vitalis crowd from three states was milling around on the lawn, including Joey the Neck and a couple of his whores. Did you know that he makes his whores carry validated health certificates because he's terrified of catching AIDS from them? That's what this FBI agent said.'

'I didn't know that.'

'Anyway, this FBI agent knew we had a vested interest in Joey's career, and that's why he dropped off this tape.' The sheriff removed his foot from my desk and swiveled the chair around to face me. 'So I watched the tape. It's quite a show. You don't want to get up and go for popcorn on this one. And while I was watching it, I kept remembering something you said to me the other day.'

He sucked on his bottom lip and stared into my face, his rimless glasses low on his nose.

'Okay, I'll bite, sheriff. What did I say to you?'

'You mentioned something about letting events unfold. So when I finished watching the tape, I got to thinking. Is Dave omniscient? Does he have insight into the future that none of the rest of us have? Or does he know about things that I don't?'

'I'm not good at being a straight man, sheriff. You want to cut to it?'

'Let's take a walk down to my office and stick this in the VCR. These guys do quite a job. It's even got sound. I sure wish we had their equipment.'

As we went down the hallway I kept looking into the faces of other people. But there was nothing unusual in their expressions that I could see.

'I think there should be some screen credits on this,' he said, clicking on his television set and fitting the cassette into the VCR. 'Maybe something like "Directed by Cletus Purcel and Unnamed Friend."'

'What about Purcel?'

He sucked in his cheeks, and his eyes looked into the corners of mine.

'You don't know?'

'I'm truly lost.'

'Gouza pulled up to the house and parked. A few minutes later Purcel cruised by. It looked like he'd been following Gouza.'

'How do they know it was Purcel?'

'A fed made him. Also they ran his tag. Then about twenty minutes later NOPD gets this anonymous phone call that Joey Gouza has got a body in the trunk of his car and his car can be found at this address out on the lake. That's where our film starts, Dave. Sit down and watch, then tell me what you think.'

The sheriff closed the blinds, sat on the corner of his desk, and activated the VCR with a remote control in his palm. In the first black-and-white frames the screen showed an enormous Tudor house with lines of Cadillacs, Lincolns, Mercedes, and Porsches parked in the circular driveway and at the curbs. The oak trees in the sideyard were strung with Japanese lanterns, and through the piked fence and myrtle bushes you could see perhaps a hundred people milling around the food and drink tables.

Then a solitary city patrol car cruised down the street, its emergency lights off, slowed, and stopped. The driver got out with a clipboard and flashlight and walked up and down the line of cars at the curb, shining his light on the tags. He paused by a white Cadillac limo with black-tinted windows just as a dog unit pulled into the camera lens from the opposite end of the block.

The action was very quick after that. A uniformed cop, with a German shepherd straining at its leash, approached the back of the limo. Then the dog took one sniff and went crazy, leaping against its leash, clacking its nails on the bumper and trunk.

One of the cops used his radio, and moments later city police cars, with emergency lights flashing, poured into the block. They parked sideways in the street and blocked both driveway entrances; then uniformed cops swarmed across lawns and through hedges, shined their flashlights into cars, wrote down the numbers on every license tag in the neighborhood, arrived with more leashed dogs, and turned a quiet residential lakefront street into a carnival.

Two plainclothes detectives walked up to the rear of the limo and inserted a crowbar in the jamb of the truck. By now the guests at the lawn party had started drifting out toward the curb, led by Joey Gouza and, behind him, a bald-headed barrel of a man in a white sports coat with a carnation, dark trousers, and white shoes.

'How you enjoying it so far?' the sheriff said.

'It's great stuff.'

He paused the VCR.

'You recognize the guy in the sports coat?' he said.

'No.'

'That's Dominic the Pipe Gabelli. He got his name from bashing a fellow inmate in Lewisburg. He's also a member of the Chicago commission. What do you think those cops are going to find in the trunk?'

I didn't answer.

'It's not a body,' he said.

'You asked me down here to watch this, sheriff. If you want to make an implication about my involvement in the events in a surveillance film, then you should go ahead and do that. But you're going to have to get somebody else to listen to it.'

'That's a little strong, don't you think?'

'No, I don't.'

'Well, let's see what happens.'

He started the tape again and increased the volume. The two

plainclothes cops leaned their weight down on the crowbar, and you could hear the tip biting into metal, peeling back the lip of the trunk from the latch, snapping bolts loose from a welded surface. Gouza tried to grab one of the plainclothes cops and was shoved backward by a patrolman.

The audio wasn't the best; the voices of the crowd, the cops, the squawk of radios, the beating of helicopter blades overhead, a peal of thunder out on the lake, sounded like apples rolling around in a deep barrel. But Joey Gouza's furious, arm-waving outrage came through the television set with the painful clarity of a rupturing ulcer. 'What the fuck you guys think you're doing?' he said. 'You got to have a warrant to do that. You got to have probable cause. You get that fucking dog away from me. Hey, I said get him away!'

The trunk sprang open, and the faces of the two plainclothes cops blanched and snapped back as though they had been slapped. A woman in an evening dress vomited on the grass.

'Jesus Christ, I don't believe it,' somebody said.

'Get a shovel or a broom or something. I ain't picking that up with my hands.'

'What the fuck you guys talking about?' the man in the white sports coat said, pushing his way, along with Gouza, to get a better view of the trunk. Then he pressed his hand over his mouth and nose.

'Put in a call for the ME,' one of the plainclothes cops said.

A uniformed sergeant, his hands inside a vinyl evidence bag, reached into the truck of the car, took out Jewel Fluck's head, and laid it on the grass. Joey Gouza's face was stunned; his mouth dropped open; he stared speechless at the man in the white sports coat. He gestured emptily with both hands at the air.

'I don't know what it's doing there, Dom,' he said. 'It's a setup. These fuckheads are working with some pisspot cops over in Iberia Parish. I swear it, Dom. They been trying to put an iron hook through my stomach and tear my insides out.'

'Shut up, Joey. You're under arrest,' one of the plainclothes cops said. 'Put your hands on the car and spread your legs. You know the drill. The rest of you people go back to your lasagne.'

The uniformed sergeant shoved Joey face-forward against the side of the Cadillac and hit him under both arms. Joey's face went livid with rage, and he whirled and drove his elbow into the sergeant's nose.

Then NOPD went to work with the subtlety of method for which they're famous. While the sergeant tried to cup his hands over the blood that fountained from his nose, two other uniformed cops rained their batons down on Joey's back.

'We got a perp on dust,' somebody yelled.

Then as though that one declaration justified any means of restraint, another cop ran from the far side of the street with a Taser gun. The cops flailing with their batons jumped back just as he fired.

But Joey had seen what was coming, too, and he drove sideways and the dart embedded in the thick, fat neck of the man in the white sports coat. He went down as though he had been bludgeoned with an ax, his body convulsing, his arms writhing in the damp grass with electric shock.

Then a cop garroted Joey across the throat with his baton and lifted him, strangling, to his feet while two other cops cuffed his wrists behind him. The last frames in the film showed Joey being stuffed behind the wire screen of a patrol car, one foot kicking wildly at the window glass.

The sheriff put the VCR on rewind.

'The anonymous call was traced to the Acme Oyster Bar on Iberville,' he said. 'When the arresting plainclothes got there, they ran into none other than Cletus Purcel, bombed on boilermakers with seven dozen empty oyster shells piled on his table. The plainclothes don't think it's coincidence that Purcel was sitting in the Acme.'

'But they didn't take him in, did they?'

'No.'

'They won't, either.'

'Why not?'

'Because they don't care, sheriff. Gouza won't go down on a murder beef, but they'll put him away for resisting arrest and assault and battery on a police officer. The court considers him a habitual. That means this time he goes into lockdown with the big stripes at Angola and they weld the door shut on him. Why should they worry about Clete?'

'You misunderstand me, Dave. I don't care about Purcel. I'm bothered by the possibility that one of my men shaved the dice. You know that was Jewel Fluck's head, don't you?'

'Maybe.'

'You want to tell me what really happened with you and Jack Gates?'

I rubbed my palms together between my legs. The sunlight outside was white and hot through the cracks in the blinds.

'The evidence was found on the right person, sheriff. There's no way around that conclusion. You have my word on it.'

He picked at his thumbnail, then raised his eyes to mine.

'That's about all I'm going to get from you, huh?' he said.

'Yeah, I guess that's about it.'

'Well, maybe it's time I talk to Garrett's family again over in Houston.'

I studied his face and waited.

'I think you wrote your signature on this case with a baseball bat, Dave. But anyway we're closing the file on it. The three men who killed Garrett are dead. The man they worked for is in the New Orleans city prison under a two-million-dollar bond. I think the slate's wiped clean.' He gave me a measured look. 'For everybody, you got my drift?'

'That's for other people to decide.'

'I figured you might say that. Pride can be a sonofabitch sometimes, can't it?'

He pulled up the blinds. The hot, white radiance off the cement outside and the violent green of the trees and shrubs and grass made my eyes water. As I walked out of the office, I heard him pull the cassette from the VCR and drop it carelessly into a metal file drawer, then slam the drawer shut.

16

I took a vacation day from work the next day. Alafair and I packed a lunch, iced down some soft drinks, paddled a pirogue deep into the green light of the marsh, and fished with red worms and spinners for bluegill and goggle-eye. The morning air was moist and cool among the flooded trees, and in the shadows and mist rising off the water you could hear big-mouth bass flopping on the edge of the lily pads, hear a heron lift and flap his wings as he flew down a canal through a long corridor of trees and disappeared like a black cipher in a cone of sunlight at the end.

But as I pulled the paddle through dark water, heard it knock against a wet cypress knee, watched the earnestness in Alafair's face as she cast her baited spinner next to the water lilies and slowly retrieved it through a nest of bream, I knew that something else was taking hold of me, too. Age had finally taught me that there was a time to go with the season, to let go of the world's seriousness, to leave the terrible obligation of defining both yourself and the world to others.

Yesterday at the dock I had told Batist that Lyle Sonnier had invited him to the crab boil in Baton Rouge.

'What for he ax a black man?' he said.

'Because he likes you, because he'd like us *all* to come over.'

He cocked one eye at me.

'You sure he want me there, Dave?'

'Yeah, or I wouldn't ask you, Batist.'

He looked at me and reflected a moment.

'All right, that sounds nice. I'd like to go wit' y'all,' he said.

Then, when I turned to go back up to the house, he added, 'Dave, why *you* want to go? I had the feeling for a while you might want to put all them Sonniers in a tote sack with some bricks and t'row it in the bayou.'

I smiled at his joke and didn't reply.

Did I indeed still feel guilt for letting Lyle go down a VC tunnel when we could have blown it and passed it by? Or did I feel obligated to Drew because of our young impetuosity in the back seat of my convertible on a summer night years ago? Was I so self-destructively flawed that I had taken on Weldon's problems only because I saw myself mirrored in him?

No, that wasn't it.

A therapist once told me that we're born alone and we die alone.

It's not true.

We all have an extended family, people whom we recognize as our own as soon as we see them. The people closest to me have always been marked by a peculiar difference in their makeup. They're the walking wounded, the ones to whom a psychological injury was done that they will never be able to define, the ones with the messianic glaze in their eyes, or the oblique glance, as though an M-1 tank is about to burst through their mental fortifications. They drive their convertibles into automatic carwashes with the tops down, cause psychiatrists and priests to sigh helplessly, leave IRS auditors speechless, turn town meetings into free-fire zones, and even frighten themselves when they wake up in the middle of the night and think they've left the light on, and then realize that perhaps their heads simply glow in the dark.

But they save us from ourselves. Whenever I hear and see a politician or a military leader, a bank of American flags at his back, trying to convince us of the rightness of a policy or a deed that will cause harm to others; when I am almost convinced myself that setting humanitarian concern in abeyance can be justified in the interest of a greater good, I pause and ask myself what my brain-smoked friends would have to say. Then I realize that the rhetoric would have no effect on them, because for those who were most deeply injured as children, words of moral purpose too often masked acts of cruelty.

So that's when you let go of reason and slip deep into the wobbling, refracted green light of a marsh, with a child as your guide, and let the season have its way with your heart.

Alafair decided to go to a movie with the neighbor's children that evening and spend the night at their house. So Bootsie fixed her an early supper, and just as the heat began to go out of the day, Bootsie, Batist, and I got in her car and, in the lengthening shadows, took the back road along the Teche, through St Martinville, to the interstate and Baton Rouge.

We went over the wide sweep of the Mississippi at Port Allen, looked out over the crimson-yellow wash of sunlight on the capitol building and the parks and green trees in the center of Baton Rouge, and passed the old brick warehouses on the river that had been refurbished into restaurants and shops and named Catfish Town by the Chamber of Commerce (one block away from a black neighborhood of paintless cypress shacks, with sagging galleries and dirt yards, where emancipated slaves had lived during Reconstruction). Then we turned out on to Highland, toward the LSU campus, and began to see more and more posters advertising Bobby Earl's barbecue and political rally.

I slowed the car at a congested intersection where directional signs had been nailed to telephone posts pointing to the site of the rally at a public park two blocks away. Many of the cars around us had yellow ribbons tied on their radio aerials and Bobby Earl stickers plastered on their bumpers.

I felt Bootsie's eyes on my face.

'What?' I said.

'Don't be bothered by them,' she said. 'It's just Louisiana. Think about the Longs.'

'It's not the same thing, Boots. The Longs weren't racists. They didn't sponsor legislation that would make it a twenty-five-dollar fine to beat up flag burners.'

'Well, I'm just not going to let a person like that affect me.'

'Yeah, I guess that's why you told Alafair that Bobby Earl was a shit.'

My window was down. So was the window of the pickup truck next to me. The man in the passenger seat, whose chewing tobacco in his jaw looked as stiff as a biscuit, glanced directly into my face.

'You got a problem, partner?' I asked.

He rolled up his window and looked directly ahead.

'Dave . . .' Bootsie said.

'All right, I'm sorry. Sometimes I'm just not sure that democracy is the right idea.'

'Talk about narrow attitudes,' she said.

'Hey, Dave, that man Bobby Earl ain't been all bad,' Batist said from the back seat.

'What?' I said.

'*Mais* black folk wasn't votin' for a long time. Now they is. I bet you ain't t'ought about that, no.'

Bootsie smiled and punched me in one of my love handles, then reached across the seat and brushed a strand of hair out of my eyes. How do you argue with that kind of company?

Lyle had tried to do it right. He had strung bunting in the trees, laid out a wonderful hors d'oeuvre and salad table, hired a professional bartender, piped music out on to the patio, and hung baskets of petunias from the ironwork on the upstairs veranda. The lawn had just been mowed, and the air was heavy with the smell of freshly cut grass and the wood smoke curling around the iron caldron on the brick barbecue pit.

He wore a pair of cream-colored pleated slacks, shined brown loafers, and a Hawaiian shirt outside his belt; his hair was wet and combed back on his collar, his cheeks still glowing from a fresh shave. His smile was electric when he greeted us in the sideyard and shook hands and walked us to the patio, where Weldon, his wife Bama, Drew, and several people whom I didn't know stood around the drink table. The deference, the unrelenting smile, the nervous light in Lyle's eyes made me feel almost as though he were trying to rearrange all the elements in his life in front of a camera so he could freeze-frame the moment and correct the inadequacies of a past, a childhood, that would never be acceptable to him or finally to anyone who had had a similar one imposed upon him.

But I didn't see Vic Benson, and while we fixed paper plates of chilled shrimp and popcorn crawfish and tried to be convivial, as though we had not all been brought together by a violent event, my eyes kept wandering to the garage apartment where he lived. Clemmie, the black maid who had done time in St Gabriel, picked up a washtub filled with live bluepoint crabs and poured them skittering into the caldron on the fire pit.

'My, that surely smells good,' Bama said. Her ash-blond hair was brushed out thick on her shoulders, and she wore a yellow sundress, gold earrings, and a tiny gold cross and chain around her neck. I never saw anyone with skin so white. You could see her blue veins as though they had been painted on her with the fine point of a watercolor brush.

'I'm real glad y'all could make it,' Weldon said. He had already put out a cigarette in his plate and was drinking a beer out of the bottle, his eyes, like mine, glancing sideways unconsciously at the garage apartment. 'I'm glad you brought Batist, too. It looks like he's making friends with Clemmie. I hope she doesn't pull a razor on him.'

'Lyle is very good to people of color,' Bama said.

'Lyle's known Batist since he was knee-high to a tree frog,' Weldon said.

'I was speaking of Lyle's kindness to the woman, Weldon.'

'Oh.'

She turned toward me. Her face was as small as a child's. Her mouth made a red button before she spoke. There was a steady, serene blue light in her eyes, and I wondered how many downers she had dropped before her first highball.

'Weldon is overly conscious about who my brother is,' she said.

'Dave gets a little upset on the subject of Bobby's politics,' Weldon said.

'I don't subscribe to everything my brother stands for, but I don't deny that he's my brother, either,' she said.

'I see,' I said.

'He has many fine qualities of which the press is not aware or which they seem to have no interest in writing about.'

Weldon idly twirled a shrimp on a toothpick between his fingers.

'Actually, today is Bobby's birthday,' she continued. 'We have to leave a bit early and drop off his presents at the rally.'

'Bama—' Weldon began.

'It'll take a few minutes. You can stay in the car,' she said to him.

He made a face and looked away into the shadows. A moment later Clemmie passed our table.

'Go up and ask Vic to join us, would you, Clemmie?' Lyle said.

She began clearing paper plates off the glass-topped table as though she hadn't heard him. Her breasts looked like watermelons inside her gray-and-white uniform.

'Clemmie, would you please tell Vic all our guests are here?' Lyle said.

'I got to live on the other side of the wall from that nasty old man. That don't mean I got to talk to him,' she said.

Lyle's face reddened with embarrassment.

'Maybe he doesn't want to come down. Leave him alone,' Weldon said.

'No, he's going to come down here and eat with us,' Lyle said. 'He's paid for whatever he did to us, Weldon.'

'You don't even know that it's him,' Weldon said.

'Do you want me to go up there?' Drew said.

Good ole Drew, I thought. Always letter-high and right down the middle. She stood by the bar, her weight resting on one foot, her thick round arms covered with tan and freckles.

'No, I'll do it,' Lyle said.

'Why do you keep stirring up the past all the time?' Weldon said. 'If it's not moving, don't poke it. Why don't you learn that?'

'Have another beer, Weldon,' Lyle said.

'Lyle, this is your craziness. Don't act like somebody else is responsible,' Weldon said.

Lyle got up from his chair and walked across the lawn toward the garage apartment.

'Lord h'ep me Jesus,' he said to no one in particular.

Later, he came back down the stairs. Then, a few minutes later, the man who called himself Vic Benson stepped out the door and walked slowly down the stairs, a shaft of late sunlight breaking across his destroyed face.

He wore a frayed white shirt that was gray with washing and creaseless shiny black trousers that were hitched tightly around his bony hips. People glanced once at his face, then focused intensely on their conversations with the people next to them. He was smoking a hand-rolled cigarette without removing it from the corner of his mouth, and the paper was wet with saliva all the way down to the glowing ash. His eyes made you think he was being entertained by a private joke. He stopped by the edge of the patio, threw his cigarette into a flower bed, and picked up an empty glass off the bar. Then he knotted up a handful of mint from a silver bowl and bruised it around the inside of the glass.

'What you having, suh?' the black bartender asked.

Vic Benson didn't reply. He simply reached over the bar, picked up a bottle of Jack Daniel's and poured four fingers straight up.

Lyle rose from his chair and stood beside him awkwardly.

'This is Vic,' he said to Bama and his brother and sister.

'Glad to meet you,' Vic said.

Drew's and Weldon's eyes narrowed, and I saw Drew wet her lips. Weldon stuck an unlit cigarette in his mouth, then took it out.

'I'm Weldon Sonnier. Do you know me?' he said.

'I don't know you. But I heard about you,' Vic said.

'What'd you hear?' Weldon asked.

'You're a big oil man here'bouts.'

'I've got a record for dusters,' Weldon said.

'You only got to hit a pay sand one in eight. Ain't that right?'

'You sound like you've been around the oil business, Vic,' Weldon said.

'I roughnecked some. But I ain't ever run acrost you, if that's what you're asking. I seen *her* though.' He lifted a shriveled forefinger at Drew.

I saw the side of her face twitch. Then she recovered herself.

'I'm afraid I don't recall meeting you,' she said.

'I didn't say you'd met me. I seen you jogging on the street. In New Iberia. You was with some other people. But a man don't forget a handsome woman.'

Her eyes looked away. Bama stared down at her hands.

'Lyle says you're our old man, Vic,' Weldon said.

'I ain't. But I don't argue with it. People abide the likes of me for different reasons. Mostly because they feel guilty about something. It don't matter to me. What time we eat? There's a TV show I want to watch.'

'Yeah, those crabs ought to be good and red now,' Lyle said.

'You cook them in slow water, they taste better,' Vic said. 'There's people don't like to do it 'cause of the sound they make in the pot.'

He took a long drink from his whiskey, his eyes roving over us as though he had just made a profound observation.

Batist and Lyle began dipping the crabs out of the boiling water with tongs and dropping them in the empty washtub to cool. Vic filled half of a paper plate with dirty rice, walked to the fire pit ahead of everyone else, picked up two hot crabs from the tub with his bare hand, and began eating by himself on a folding chair under an oak tree.

'Is that the man you saw at your window?' Drew said to Bama.

Bama's pulse was quivering like a severed muscle in her throat.

'I'm not sure what I saw,' she said. 'It was quite dark. Perhaps it was a man in a mask. To be frank, I've tried to put it out of my mind. I prefer not to talk about it, Drew. I don't know why we should be talking about these things at a dinner party.'

Weldon smoked a cigarette and watched Vic Benson with a whimsical look on his face.

'Weldon?' Drew said.

'What?'

'Say something.'

'What do you want me to say?'

'Is it him?'

'Of course it's him. I'd recognize that old sonofabitch if you melted him into glue.'

Bootsie and I got in the serving line, then tried to isolate ourselves from the Sonniers' conversation. But Bama was having her troubles with it, too. She made a mess of shelling the crab on her plate, spraying her dress and face with juice when she squeezed a claw between the nutcrackers, then rushing from the table as though the deck of the *Titanic* had just tilted under her.

When she returned from the bathroom, her face was fresh and composed and her eyes were rekindled with an ethereal blue light.

'My, I didn't realize it had gotten so late,' she said. 'We must be running, Weldon.'

'Give it a minute. Bobby's not going anywhere,' he said. But he wasn't looking at her. His eyes were still on Vic Benson, who was hunkered forward on the folding chair under the oak tree, drinking another glass of whiskey as though it were Kool-Aid.

'I don't want him to think we've forgotten his birthday,' she said.

'Maybe he'd like for you to forget it, Bama. Maybe that's why he has the wrinkles chemically rinsed out of his face,' Weldon said.

'I think that's an unkind remark to make, Weldon,' she said.

But he wasn't listening to her.

'You know, the old fart did a lot of bad things to us,' he said. 'But there's one that always stuck in my mind.' He shook his head back and forth. 'He caught me whanging it when I was about thirteen, and he clipped a clothespin on my penis and made me stand out in the backyard like that for a half hour.'

'Hey, ease up, Weldon,' Lyle said.

'I insist that we not continue this,' Bama said.

Bootsie was already excusing herself from the table, and I was looking at my watch.

'You're right, damn it,' Weldon said. 'Let's drive the nail in this bullshit, give Bobby his present, then come back for some serious drinking.'

Weldon got up from his chair and walked toward the tree under which Vic Benson sat.

'What are you going to do?' Lyle said. Then, 'Weldon?'

But he paid no attention. He was talking to Vic Benson now, his back to us, his big hands gesturing, while Benson looked up at him silently. Then Benson set his glass down and rose to his feet. Clemmie poured the water from the caldron into the fire pit, and steam billowed out of the bricks and drifted across Benson and Weldon's bodies.

We couldn't hear what Weldon said, but the puckered skin of Benson's face was pulled back from his mouth in a leer of teeth and blackened gums, and his thin shoulders were as rectangular and stiff as if they were made of wire. Then Weldon walked back to the bar, pulled a sweating bottle of Jax out of the ice bin, and cracked off the cap.

'Quit staring at me like that, Lyle,' he said.

'I ain't here to judge you,' Lyle said.

'What'd you *think* I was going to tell him?' Weldon said.

'You got a lot of anger. Nobody can blame you for it.'

'I offered him a job,' Weldon said.

'Doing what?'

'Roustabout, driving a truck, whatever he wants to do. I also told him no matter what he decides the past between him and us is quits.'

'What'd he say?' Lyle asked.

Weldon blew little puffs of air out his lips.

'I already forgot it,' he said. 'I tell you what, though. If I were you, I'd either buy that man an airplane ticket to Iraq or put bars over his doors and windows.'

After Bama and Weldon were gone, Vic Benson stared at us for a long time from under the tree, then he turned and mounted the stairs to the garage apartment. The trees were deep in shadow, and down the street, against the lavender sky and amid the flights of swallows, you could see the sun's last red light reflecting on the chrome-plated cross atop Lyle's Bible college.

We were leaving also when we heard someone start a car engine immediately below the garage apartment.

'What's he doing with Clemmie's car?' Lyle said.

We turned and saw Vic Benson backing an ancient, dented gas guzzler, with red cellophane taped over the broken taillights, out the driveway. Smoke poured from under the frame.

'Oh, boy, I got a bad feeling,' Lyle said.

He headed for the garage apartment, and I followed him.

We found Clemmie in her small living room, sitting very still in a lopsided stuffed chair, her right hand balanced carefully in the palm of the other, as though any movement would put her in peril. Her rouge was streaked with tears, and her nostrils and mouth were smeared with blood and mucus. Two fingers of her right hand were as bulbous as balloons at the joints.

'What happened?' Lyle said.

'He say, "Gimme your car keys, you nigger bitch." I say, "You ain't getting them. I work hard for my car. I ain't giving it to no nasty white trash to drive round in." He hit me in the face with his belt, hard as he could. I tried to run and throw my keys out the do', but he twisted them outta my hand, broke my fingers, Rev'end Lyle, just like twigs snapping. Then he spit in my hair.'

Her shoulders were shaking. You could smell smoke, perfume, and dried sweat in her clothes. Lyle wet a towel and blotted her face with it. I lifted her hand and set it gingerly on the arm of the chair. A silver ring with a yellow stone was almost buried in the flesh below one knuckle.

'We'll take you to the hospital, Clemmie, then we'll get your car back,' I said. 'Don't worry about Vic Benson, either. He's going to be in the Baton Rouge city jail tonight. Do you know where he was going with your car?'

'He axed where that park at,' she said.

'Which park?' I said.

'The place where Mr Weldon gonna go see Bobby Earl. He got a pistol, Rev'end Lyle. He gone back in his room and come out with it, a little shiny pistol ain't no bigger than yo' hand. He say, "You go down there and tell them people 'bout this I'll be back and cut off yo' nose." That's what he say to me.'

Lyle stroked her hair and patted her shoulders. I told Lyle to take her to the hospital, and I used the phone to call the Baton Rouge police department.

Outside, I asked Bootsie to wait for me, then I headed for the car. I didn't expect Batist to follow me.

But he did. And in so doing turned the two of us into a historical footnote.

17

I tried to dissuade him, too, as he stood with his huge hand on the door handle, about to get in the passenger's seat.

'It's just not a good idea,' I said.

'You t'ink I scared, Dave? That's what you t'ink after all these years?'

His flower-print tie was knotted wrong; the top button of his white short-sleeved shirt had popped off; his seersucker slacks were stretched as tight as cheesecloth on his muscular thighs and buttocks. I don't think I ever loved a man more.

'Batist, there's some low-rent white people there,' I said.

'There's places I still cain't go, huh? That's what you tellin' me, Dave, and I don't like to hear that, me.'

'I'm asking you to stay with Bootsie, Batist.'

'I ain't stayin' here no mo'. You don't want me wit' you, I'll walk back to Catfish Town. Y'all can pick me up on your way back home.'

I looked at the injury in his face, and I remembered my father admonishing me never to treat a brave man as anything other than a fire walker, and I wondered if I was guilty of that old southern white conceit that we must protect people of color from themselves.

'Well, I think the city cops will probably grab the old man before he does any more harm. But let's check it out, partner,' I said. 'It's really just the roller-derby crowd with a political agenda.'

'What?'

'Never mind.'

We drove back down Highland, through the LSU campus, to the park where Bobby Earl's constituency had come out in force. Amid the pin oaks, the pine and chinaberry trees, against the backdrop of tennis courts and a dusty softball diamond and picnic tables, it looked like a festive and innocent celebration of the coming of summer. A Dixieland band thundered under a pavilion; black cooks in white uniforms turned flank steaks on a huge portable barbecue pit that had been towed in on a truck; the back of the speaker's platform was lined with a thick row of American flags, and under trees that were strung with red, white, and blue bunting children raced breathlessly across the pine needles and queued up for free lemonade and ice cream.

Who were the parents? I asked myself. Their cars came from Bogalusa, Denham Springs, Plaquemine, Bunkie, Port Allen, Vidalia, and mosquito-infested dirt-road communities out in the Atchafalaya basin. But these were not ordinary small-town blue-collar people. This was the permanent underclass, the ones who tried to hold on daily to their shrinking bit of redneck geography with a pickup truck and gun rack and Jones on the jukebox and a cold Coors in the hand.

They were never sure of who they were unless someone was afraid of them. They jealously guarded their jobs from blacks and Vietnamese refugees, whom they saw as a vast and hungry army about to descend upon their women, their neighborhoods, their schools, even their clapboard church houses, where they were assured every Sunday and Wednesday night that the bitterness and fear that characterized their lives had nothing to do with what they had been born to, or what they had chosen for themselves.

But when you looked at them at play in a public park, in almost a tattered facsimile of a Norman Rockwell painting, it was as hard to be angry at them for their ignorance as it would be to condemn someone for the fact that he was born disfigured.

Then on a side street we saw Clemmie's junker car parked in a yellow zone. I found a parking place farther down the street, and Batist walked back to Clemmie's car, raised the hood, disconnected a fistful of spark-plug wires, and locked them in our trunk. I took my holstered .45 out of the glovebox, clipped it on to my belt, and put on my sports coat.

'You're sure you want to go?' I said.

'What else I'm gonna do, me? Stand here and wait for a man that's got a pistol?'

'Well, I don't think anybody is going to give us any trouble,' I said. 'They feel secure when they're in numbers. But if anybody gets in our face, we walk on through it. All right, Batist?'

'Dave, ain't nobody know these people better than a black man. They ain't worried by the likes of me, no. They scared of the young ones. They ain't gonna admit that, but that's what's on they mind. They scared to death of some noisy kids whose mamas should have whupped them upside the head a long time ago.'

'They're scared of anybody who looks them in the eye, partner.'

'We gonna set around here and wait for that man to shoot Mr Sonnier?'

'No, you're right. Let's go see what they're doing at the bottom of the food chain these days.'

Batist peeled the cellophane off a cigar, put it deep into his jaw, and we walked back down the block and into the park, where someone had just turned on the field lights over the softball diamond.

'Hey, Dave, wasn't there s'posed to be a lot of policemens here?' Batist said.

'Yep.'

'Where they at?'

I saw one uniformed cop directing traffic, another one eating a bar-becue sandwich under a chinaberry tree. I saw no one in the crowd who looked like plainclothes. I walked up to the cop under the chinaberry tree and unfolded my badge in my palm.

'I'm Detective Dave Robicheaux, Iberia Parish Sheriff's Department,' I said. 'Did you guys get a report about a man with a pistol?'

His face was round, and his mouth was full of bread and meat. He wiped his lips with the back of his wrist and shook his head.

'*I* didn't,' he said. 'There's a guy around here with a gun?'

'Maybe. Have you seen a man with a burned face? You can't miss him. His skin looks like red putty.'

'No.'

'Where's your supervisor?'

'He was over at the pavilion a while ago. This is no shit, some guy's after Bobby Earl?'

'No, not Earl. His brother-in-law, a man named Weldon Sonnier. Do you know him?'

'I never heard of him. Look, you want me to, we can get on the mike and find this guy.'

'You can do what?'

'We can page him. We can get him out of the crowd.'

I tried to hide the expression that must have been on my face.

'How about finding your supervisor for me, then calling for some more help?' I said.

'Sure.' Then he looked over my shoulder. 'Who's *he*?'

'Find your supervisor, podna. Okay?' I said.

Batist and I walked through the crowd toward the concrete band shell. The western sky was piled with purple clouds that were scorched black and crimson on the edges in the sun's fiery afterglow. In the distance an emergency siren was pealing through the streets. The band in the pavilion stopped playing a moment, then suddenly it struck up 'Dixie' and a second band, inside the concrete shell, in candy-striped vests and straw boaters, joined in as though on cue, and in the deafening exchange of trombones, clarinets, trumpets, and martial drum rolls, the crowd went insane.

Then somebody released the restraining ropes on a huge net filled with red, white, and blue balloons, which rose by the hundreds into the windstream, and I realized what was going on. It was Bobby Earl's moment. Amid a throng of applauding people he was walking from the pavilion, dressed in a double-breasted tropical suit, his dry, wavy hair tousled by the breeze, toward the speaker's stand that had been constructed in front of the concrete shell, where the microphones, American flags, television cameras, and banks of loud-speakers waited for him. His smile had all the ease and confidence of a man who knew that he was loved, that he had truly found his place in this world.

We worked our way through the crowd. The bands were still blaring out 'Dixie' and a drunk fat man in a sweat-stained pink shirt had climbed up on a picnic table and was screaming rebel yells at the speaker's platform. The smell of flat beer, deodorant, chewing tobacco, and talcum powder seemed to rise in a collective sticky layer from the people around us. I tried to push our way through the edge of the crowd into the picnic area behind the band shell. A uniformed police sergeant shouldered his way through a bunch of college kids and stood in front of me. He was a large man, with a ridged brow, sunken green eyes, a fresh sunburn on his face, and sweat rings under his arms. His love handles hung over his gunbelt, and he rested one palm on the butt of his .357 magnum.

'You the sheriff's detective from New Iberia?' he asked.

'That's right. I'm Dave Robicheaux.'

His eyes shifted to Batist, then back to me.

'I just heard about this burned man with a gun,' he said. 'What's going on?'

'His name is Vic Benson. He's deranged, and I think he plans to harm Bobby Earl's brother-in-law.'

'He's got a gun?'

'A chrome-plated revolver, caliber unknown.'

'Hell of a fucking place to have a crazy man running loose with a gun. Every time I have to work one of these things, I have dreams the night before about earthquakes and tornados. My wife says I eat too much before I go to bed. Who's *this* man?'

'He's a friend.'

'All right, I'm going to get some more uniforms into the crowd. In the meantime, you find Earl's brother-in-law, you get him out of here. A bunch like this can take to religion or flattening your town, either one, in about five minutes.'

'Thanks for your help, sergeant.'

'Don't thank me, podna. I worked a riot once at the stadium. The next time I get caught in one, I'm going home, open a beer, and sit in the backyard. Maybe listen to it on the radio.' He smiled.

The crowd began to thin at the edges, and finally Batist and I stepped out into an area of pine trees, barbecue pits, overflowing trash barrels, and a small sandy stretch of playground with seesaws and swing sets.

There, sitting in a child's swing, sipping beer out of a deep paper cup, was Weldon Sonnier.

'I think you aged me about ten years tonight,' I said.

He looked up at me.

'Hey, Dave. Hey, Batist. What's up?'

'Your father is around here somewhere with a pistol. Guess who he's looking for?'

'What?'

'After you left, he beat up the black maid and stole her car. It's parked about a block from here. He's got a revolver.'

He made a clucking sound. 'The old man's always up to new tricks, huh?' he said.

'The Baton Rouge cops want you out of the area. I do, too.'

He sipped his beer and gazed lackadaisically at some kids shagging flies on the softball diamond.

'Where's Bama?' I asked.

'She went to give Bobby his present. You got to get a number and wait. You'd think he was the pope.'

'It's time for you to go back to Lyle's. I'll find Bama and bring her along.'

'What the hell are you talking about, Dave?'

'You're leaving.'

'Are you serious?'

'You're leaving on your own or you're leaving in custody. It's up to you, Weldon.'

'I don't know about legal jurisdiction and that sort of thing, but I doubt you have much authority here, Dave. And I don't see any Baton Rouge cops, and I don't see any old man with a pistol. Take a break and get a soft drink over at the pop stand.'

'You're starting to piss me off again, Weldon.'

'That's your problem.'

'No, it's yours. I think you were born with a two-by-four up your butt.'

'I never said I was perfect.'

'Do you have to prove that you're not afraid of your father? You flew hundreds of combat missions. Didn't you ever learn who you are?'

He raised his face and looked at me in an odd way. For just a moment in the fading light, his big ears, his square face, his close-cropped head made me remember the young boy of years ago, his bare feet gray with dust, his overalls grimed at the knees, swamping out the poolroom for two bits an hour.

Then the light in his eyes changed, and he took a drink of beer and looked down between his knees.

'You've done your job, Dave. Now let it go,' he said.

I felt Batist pull my sleeve, felt the urgency in his hand even before I heard it in his voice.

'Dave, look yonder,' he said.

Bobby Earl and his entourage of bodyguards and political aides had gone into the grassy area between the speaker's platform and the concrete shell. Bama had worked her way through the throng and was giving him an oblong box wrapped with satin-finish white paper and a pink ribbon. But that was not what Batist had seen.

On the other side of the concrete shell, Vic Benson had just exited one of the portable bathrooms that stood in a long row under the trees, a baseball cap on his head, dark glasses on his nose. And as quickly as I saw him, he disappeared behind the far wall of the shell.

Then it hit me.

He knows Bama went to the park with Weldon. Through the crowd he got a glimpse of Bama talking with Bobby Earl. At a distance he's mistaken Bobby Earl for Weldon.

'Good God, he's going to shoot Bobby Earl,' I said.

'What?' Weldon said.

I took my badge from my coat pocket, held it open in front of me, and ran toward the grassy area behind the speaker's platform, the weight of the .45 knocking against my hip. I heard Batist hard on my heels. People paused in midsentence and stared at us, their expressions caught between laughter and alarm. Then Earl's bodyguards were moving toward us, spreading out, their faces heating with expectation and challenge.

Through their bodies I saw Earl's peculiar monocular vision focus on my face.

'Get that man out of here!' he said.

Two men in suits stepped in front of me, and one of them stiff-armed me in the shoulder with the heel of his hand. His coat hung at an odd angle because of a weight in the right-hand pocket.

'Where you think you're going, buddy?' he said. His breath was rife with the smell of cigars.

'Iberia Parish sheriff's office. There's a man in the crowd with—' I began.

'Yeah? Who's that with you? The African paratroopers?' he said.

'He's FBI, you peckerwood shithead,' I said. 'Now, you get the fuck out of my way.'

Mistake, mistake, I thought, even as the words came out of my mouth. Don't humiliate north Louisiana stump-jumpers in front of either their women or the boss man.

'Iberia Parish don't mean horse piss on a rock here,' the second man said. 'You better haul your ass 'fore you get it hauled for you.'

Then more of Earl's bodyguards and aides pressed toward me, as though I were the source of all their problems, the spoiler of a grand moment in which they had been allowed to participate.

I stepped back from them and held my palms outward. Then I pointed one finger at them.

'I'll make it brief,' I said. 'Get your man out of sight before he gets dusted. Second, I'm going to be back later and bust every one of you for interfering with an officer in the performance of his duty.'

I moved out of the crowd and behind the concrete shell to the far side. Lines had formed in front of the portable bathrooms, and large numbers of people were now drifting out of the picnic areas and the pavilion toward the speaker's platform. The wind had suddenly died, and the air had grown close and hot, with a dusty, metallic smell to it, and the field lights were white and haloed with humidity against the darkening sky. I kicked over a trash barrel, rolled it snug against the concrete shell, stood on it, and tried to see Vic Benson's baseball cap among the hundreds of heads in the crowd.

It seemed impossible.

Then I heard a woman scream and I saw people separating themselves from some terrible or frightening presence in their midst, tripping on each others' ankles, falling backward to the ground. Not twenty feet from me, Vic Benson was racing through the crowd, the way a barracuda would slice through a school of bluefish, a small silver pistol in his upraised hand.

Bama saw him before Bobby Earl, whose back was turned as he signed autographs for children. Her face went white, and her mouth opened in a round red O.

I knocked a woman down, felt somebody bounce hard off my shoulder, crashed across a folding wheelchair, and dove headlong into the small of Vic Benson's back.

He hit the ground under me, and I heard the breath go out of his lungs in a gasp, and once again I smelled that odor that was like turpentine or embalming fluid, wind-dried sweat, nicotine, smoke rubbed into the skin and clothes. His baseball cap toppled off his head, his dark glasses were askew on his face, and his eyes stared into mine the way a lizard's might if it were trapped on top of a hot rock in the middle of a burning field.

His lips moved, and I knew he wanted to curse or wound me in some fresh way, but his breath rasped in his throat like a man whose lungs were perforated with holes. I slipped my hand along his arm and removed the unfired pistol from his fingers.

I thought it was over. It should have been.

But Batist, when he had seen what was about to happen, had plunged through the crowd from the other side, his arms outspread, and had flung both Bama and Bobby Earl to the ground and had landed with his huge weight on top of both of them. People were screaming and shoving one another; photographers and TV cameramen were trying to get Bobby Earl's prone body, with Batist's on top of it, into their cameras' lenses;

and three uniformed cops were fighting desperately to get through the rim of the crowd and into the center before a riot spread throughout the park.

Then I realized that most of the people pressed into the center of the grassy area had not seen Vic Benson or understood what he had tried to do. Instead, some of them obviously believed that Batist had attacked Bobby Earl.

As Batist tried to raise himself on his arms, a man on the edge of the crowd swung a doubled-over dog chain at his head, then two of Earl's bodyguards grabbed him by the belt and began tugging him backward.

'Put that fucking nigger in a cage,' someone yelled.

Then the crowd surged forward, toppling over one another, trampling others who had already fallen to the ground. Between their legs I saw the desperation in Batist's face as he tried to shield his eyes from a solitary fist that was flailing at his head. A string of saliva and blood drooled from his lower lip.

I tore into their midst. I drove my fist as hard as I could into the back of a man's thick neck; I ripped my elbow into someone's rib cage and felt it go like a nest of popsicle sticks; I lifted an uppercut into another man's stomach and saw him cave to his knees in front of me, his face gray and his mouth hanging open as if he had been eviscerated.

Then they rolled over both Batist and me.

There are moments in your life when you think the last frames in your film strip have just snapped loose from the reel. When one of those moments occurs, you hear your own blood thundering in your ears, or a sound like waves bursting over a coral reef, or hundreds of feet pounding dully on the earth.

Or perhaps the last frame in the strip simply freezes and you hear nothing at all.

Then as though sound and sight, trees and sky and air had all been given back to me, I saw the sunburned police sergeant with the hard, green eyes, knocking people backward with his baton, gripping it horizontally with both hands, swinging it violently from side to side, pushing the crowd back into a wider and wider circle.

Then other cops were in the circle, and you could feel the energies go out of the crowd the way air leaves a punctured balloon. When I got to my feet, I pulled my shirt out of my trousers and wiped my face on it. It was smeared with spittle and blood.

'I'm taking your piece and cuffing you and your friend together till I can get y'all out of here. Don't argue about it,' the sergeant said.

'No argument, podna,' I said.

He snapped one cuff of a set on my wrist and the other on Batist's. Batist's white shirt hung in strips off his massive shoulders.

Bobby Earl was standing among his bodyguards, his double-breasted tropical suit smudged with grass stains. He held a folded handkerchief to the corner of his mouth and combed back his wavy hair with his fingers. I felt the sergeant's hand tighten under my arm.

'Just a minute,' I said to him. 'Hey, Bobby, a black man just saved your worthless pink ass. You and your constituency might think that over. There's another thought I want to leave you with, too, and I don't want you to take it the wrong way. But if you ever try to hurt my friend Cletus Purcel again, they'll have to scrub you out of your garbage grinder with a toothbrush.'

Batist and I walked to a squad car, surrounded by cops, our wrists chained together, our clothes in rags, just as lightning flickered across the sky and raindrops as heavy as marbles began to strike the leaves of the pin oaks above our heads.

Through the back window of another squad car, his arms manacled behind him, Vic Benson's destroyed face stared out at the cops, the milling crowd, the trees, the park, the slanting rain, the blackened sky, perhaps the earth itself, as though the invisible forces that had driven him all his life had gathered at this place, in this moment, to finally and irrevocably have their way with him.

Epilogue

We took our vacation in Key West in late summer, when the weather is hot and bright, prices are cheap, the streets are empty of tourists, and the Gulf is lime green and streaked with whitecaps as far as the eye can see, and dark patches of water, like clouds of India ink, drift across the coral reefs.

But it was more than simply a respite from police work. I had taken indefinite leave from the sheriff's department. I let other people's problems, the seriousness, all the fury and mire and complexity, pull out of my grasp, in the same way that you finally tire of grief or guilt or a bonegrinding ongoing contention with the world. One morning, perhaps just before sunrise, you turn your eyes in a different direction and notice a blue heron rising from the reeds along the bayou's edge, a gator's walnut-ridged eyes moving silently through a milky skim of algae and floating twigs, a glowing radiance on the earth's rim that suddenly breaks through the black trunks of the cypress trees with such a white brilliance that you want to shield your eyes.

Joey Gouza is back with the big stripes in Angola pen, but not for the murder of Garrett or Jewel Fluck, or even the assault-and-battery beef. Joey's final legal chapter was written in the New Orleans city prison. He set fire to his mattress, plugged up the commode with his clothes, flooded the whole cell block, and urinated through the bars on a gunbull. He tried to tell anyone who would listen that both the Aryan Brotherhood and the Mexican Mafia had put a hit on him. No one was interested, or perhaps, more accurately, no one cared.

Finally he was moved into an isolation cell with a solid iron door, because he was convinced that an AB member, with the consent of the Mafioso who had taken a Taser dart in the neck that had been intended for Joey, was going to turn him into a flaming object lesson by hurling a Molotov cocktail through his bars.

Two days later a new guard walked him down to the shower stalls and the small concrete room that contained barbells and a broken universal gym, where Joey was supposed to shower and exercise by himself. Then the guard let eight other men out of their cells. Joey Gouza broke off a

463

five-inch shank, made from a jagged sliver of window glass, in another inmate's shoulder.

The investigator's report stated that the other inmate had celled with Jewel Fluck in Parchman, that his upper torso was tattooed with swastikas and iron crosses, and that at the time of the attack he had been carrying a razor blade mounted on a toothbrush handle.

But who cared?

Joey Gouza went down for attempted murder.

I'd like to be able to tell you that Bobby Earl's political career ended, that somehow the events in the park revealed him publicly as a fraud or a physical coward, or that his followers turned against him. But it didn't happen. It couldn't.

I had been determined to prove that Bobby Earl was fronting points for Joey Gouza, or that he was connected with arms and dope trafficking in the tropics. I was guilty of that age-old presumption that the origins of social evil can be traced to villainous individuals, that we just need to identify them, lock them in cages, or even march them to the executioner's wall, and this time, yes, this time, we'll catch a fresh breeze in our sails and set ourselves on a true course.

But Bobby Earl is out there by consent. He has his thumb on a dark pulse, and like all confidence men, he knows that his audience wishes to be conned. He learned long ago to listen, and he knows that if he listens carefully they'll tell him what they need to hear. It's a contract of mutual deceit by which they open up their flak vests and take it right through the breastbone.

If it were not he, it would be someone like him – misanthropic, beguiling, educated, someone who, as an ex-president's wife once said, allows the rest of us to feel comfortable with our prejudices.

I think the end for Bobby Earl will come in the same fashion as it does for all his kind. Unlike the members of The Pool and that great army of villainous buffoons trying to sneak through life on side streets, Bobby Earl's ilk want power so badly that at some point in their lives they make a conscious choice to embrace evil. It's not a gradual seduction. They do it without reservation, and that's when they leave the rest of us. You know it when it happens, too. No amount of cosmetic surgery can mask the psychological deformity in their eyes.

Then unbeknown to themselves they set about erecting their own scaffolds; their most loyal adherents become their executioners, just as Mussolini's people hanged him upside down in a filling station and Robespierre's followers trundled him over their heads to the guillotine.

Then the audience moves on and seeks a new magician.

But people like Bobby Earl don't read history books.

As I watched Alafair dive off our rented boat, just the other side of Seven-Mile Reef, her tan body glazed with sunlight and saltwater, I thought of children everywhere, and I thought of the pain that can be inflicted on them like a stone bruise in the soul, like a convoluted, blood-red rose pushed deep into the tissue by a brutal thumb.

She floated above the reef, watching the schools of clown fish and mackerel, blowing saltwater out her snorkel, the small waves lapping across her back and thighs. Thirty feet below, the sand was like ground diamonds; you could see each black spike in the nests of sea urchins, and the fire coral was so bright it looked as if it would scorch your hand with the intensity of a hot stove.

Then I saw a long, tubular shadow ripple across the crown of the reef and flatten out on the ocean floor. It must have been eight feet long. A floating island of kelp obscured my angle of vision, then the shadow changed directions and I saw the glistening brown back of a hammerhead shark. When he turned and flipped his tail fin I could see one round, flat, glassy eye, his gash of a mouth, the jagged row of razor teeth, the obscene pale whiteness of his stomach.

I yelled at Alafair, but her ears were half underwater and she didn't hear me. I kicked off my canvas shoes, stepped up on the gunwale, hit the water in a long, flat dive, and reached her in three strokes. By now she had seen the shark, and her face was terrified when I grabbed her around the waist and began swimming back to the boat. Then a peculiar thing happened. She knew that we were fighting against each other, that our legs were thrashing impotently in a shimmering cone of wet light above the shark's murderous gaze, and I saw a quiet, almost naïve expression of resolution replace the fear in her face. She worked the mask and snorkel off her head, hooked them on her arm, and began to swim with me toward the boat ladder, her body horizontal, her head twisting from side to side so she could breathe above the chop.

I pushed her rump over the gunwale, then toppled over it myself on to the deck. I hugged her against me on the hot boards, and pressed her head tightly under my chin.

She looked up at me, and I saw concern coming back into her face.

'Wow!' I said, and tried to grin.

'What kind of shark was that, Dave?'

'It was a nurse shark. They're big wimps. But who wants to take any chances?'

'His head . . . it was ugly. It looked like he'd eaten a big brick.' Then she smiled at her own joke.

'Those nurse sharks are not only wimps, they're dumb wimps. They're always swimming into the sides of boats and reefs and things,' I said.

Her brown eyes were happy and full of light again.

'Hey, Dave, we gonna put out the lines and troll for mackerel?'

'Sure, little guy,' I said, and squeezed her against my chest again, my eyes tightly shut, hoping that she would not feel the fearful beating of my heart.

In the Electric Mist with Confederate Dead

For Frank and Tina Kastor
and
Jerry and Maureen Hoag

1

The sky had gone black at sunset, and the storm had churned inland from the Gulf and drenched New Iberia and littered East Main with leaves and tree branches from the long canopy of oaks that covered the street from the old brick post office to the drawbridge over Bayou Teche at the edge of town. The air was cool now, laced with light rain, heavy with the fecund smell of wet humus, night-blooming jasmine, roses, and new bamboo. I was about to stop my truck at Del's and pick up three crawfish dinners to go when a lavender Cadillac fishtailed out of a side street, caromed off a curb, bounced a hubcap up on a sidewalk, and left long serpentine lines of tire prints through the glazed pools of yellow light from the street lamps.

I was off duty, tired, used up after a day of searching for a nineteen-year-old girl in the woods, then finding her where she had been left in the bottom of a coulee, her mouth and wrists wrapped with electrician's tape. Already I had tried to stop thinking about the rest of it. The medical examiner was a kind man. He bagged the body before any news people or family members got there.

I don't like to bust drunk drivers. I don't like to listen to their explanations, watch their pitiful attempts to affect sobriety, or see the sheen of fear break out in their eyes when they realize they're headed for the drunk tank with little to look forward to in the morning except the appearance of their names in the newspaper. Or maybe in truth I just don't like to see myself when I look into their faces.

But I didn't believe this particular driver could make it another block without ripping the side off a parked car or plowing the Cadillac deep into someone's shrubbery. I plugged my portable bubble into the cigarette lighter, clamped the magnets on the truck's roof, and pulled him to the curb in front of the Shadows, a huge brick, white-columned antebellum home built on Bayou Teche in 1831.

I had my Iberia Parish Sheriff's Department badge opened in my palm when I walked up to his window.

'Can I see your driver's license, please?'

He had rugged good looks, a Roman profile, square shoulders, and

469

broad hands. When he smiled I saw that his teeth were capped. The woman next to him wore her hair in blond ringlets and her body was as lithe, tanned, and supple-looking as an Olympic swimmer's. Her mouth looked as red and vulnerable as a rose. She also looked like she was seasick.

'You want driver's what?' he said, trying to focus evenly on my face. Inside the car I could smell a drowsy, warm odor, like the smell of smoke rising from a smoldering pile of wet leaves.

'Your driver's license,' I repeated. 'Please take it out of your billfold and hand it to me.'

'Oh, yeah, sure, wow,' he said. 'I was really careless back there. I'm sorry about that. I really am.'

He got his license out of his wallet, dropped it in his lap, found it again, then handed it to me, trying to keep his eyes from drifting off my face. His breath smelled like fermented fruit that had been corked up for a long time in a stone jug.

I looked at the license under the street lamp.

'You're Elrod T. Sykes?' I asked.

'Yes, sir, that's who I am.'

'Would you step out of the car, Mr Sykes?'

'Yes, sir, anything you say.'

He was perhaps forty, but in good shape. He wore a light-blue golf shirt, loafers, and gray slacks that hung loosely on his flat stomach and narrow hips. He swayed slightly and propped one hand on the door to steady himself.

'We have a problem here, Mr Sykes. I think you've been smoking marijuana in your automobile.'

'Marijuana . . . Boy, that'd be bad, wouldn't it?'

'I think your lady friend just ate the roach, too.'

'That wouldn't be good, no, sir, not at all.' He shook his head profoundly.

'Well, we're going to let the reefer business slide for now. But I'm afraid you're under arrest for driving while intoxicated.'

'That's very bad news. This definitely was not on my agenda this evening.' He widened his eyes and opened and closed his mouth as though he were trying to clear an obstruction in his ear canals. 'Say, do you recognize me? What I mean is, there's news people who'd really like to put my ham hocks in the frying pan. Believe me, sir, I don't need this. I cain't say that enough.'

'I'm going to drive you just down the street to the city jail, Mr Sykes. Then I'll send a car to take Ms Drummond to wherever she's staying. But your Cadillac will be towed to the pound.'

He let out his breath in a long sigh. I turned my face away.

'You go to the movies, huh?' he said.

'Yeah, I always enjoyed your films. Ms Drummond's, too. Take your car keys out of the ignition, please.'

'Yeah, sure,' he said, despondently.

He leaned into the window and pulled the keys out of the ignition.

'El, *do* something,' the woman said.

He straightened his back and looked at me.

'I feel real bad about this,' he said. 'Can I make a contribution to Mothers Against Drunk Driving, or something like that?'

In the lights from the city park, I could see the rain denting the surface of Bayou Teche.

'My Sykes, you're under arrest. You can remain silent if you wish, or if you wish to speak, anything you say can be used against you,' I said. 'As a long-time fan of your work, I recommend that you not say anything else. Particularly about contributions.'

'It doesn't look like you mess around. Were you ever a Texas ranger? They don't mess around, either. You talk back to those boys and they'll hit you upside the head.'

'Well, we don't do that here,' I said. I put my hand under his arm and led him to my truck. I opened the door for him and helped him inside. 'You're not going to get sick in my truck, are you?'

'No, sir, I'm just fine.'

'That's good. I'll be right with you.'

I walked back to the Cadillac and tapped on the glass of the passenger's door. The woman, whose name was Kelly Drummond, rolled down the window. Her face was turned up into mine. Her eyes were an intense, deep green. She wet her lips, and I saw a smear of lipstick on her teeth.

'You'll have to wait here about ten minutes, then someone will drive you home,' I said.

'Officer, I'm responsible for this,' she said. 'We were having an argument. Elrod's a good driver. I don't think he should be punished because I got him upset. Can I get out of the car? My neck hurts.'

'I suggest you lock your automobile and stay where you are, Ms Drummond. I also suggest you do some research into the laws governing the possession of narcotics in the state of Louisiana.'

'Wow, I mean, it's not like we hurt anybody. This is going to get Elrod in a lot of trouble with Mikey. Why don't you show a little compassion?'

'Mikey?'

'Our *director*, the guy who's bringing about ten million dollars into your little town. Can I get out of the car now? I really don't want a neck like Quasimodo.'

'You can go anywhere you want. There's a pay phone in the poolroom you can use to call a bondsman. If I were you, I wouldn't go down to the station to help Mr Sykes, not until you shampoo the Mexican laughing grass out of your hair.'

'Boy, talk about wearing your genitalia outside your pants. Where'd they come up with you?'

I walked back to my truck and got in.

'Look maybe I can be a friend of the court,' Elrod Sykes said.

'What?'

'Isn't that what they call it? There's nothing wrong with that, is there? Man, I can really do without this bust.'

'Few people standing before a judge ever expected to be there,' I said, and started the engine.

He was quiet while I made a U-turn and headed for the city police station. He seemed to be thinking hard about something. Then he said: 'Listen, I know where there's a body. I saw it. Nobody'd pay me any mind, but I saw the dadburn thing. That's a fact.'

'You saw what?'

'A colored, I mean a black person, it looked like. Just a big dry web of skin, with bones inside it. Like a big rat's nest.'

'Where was this?'

'Out in the Atchafalaya swamp, about four days ago. We were shooting some scenes by an Indian reservation or something. I wandered back in these willows to take a leak and saw it sticking out of a sandbar.'

'And you didn't bother to report it until now?'

'I told Mikey. He said it was probably bones that had washed out of an Indian burial mound or something. Mikey's kind of hard-nosed. He said the last thing we needed was trouble with either cops or university archaeologists.'

'We'll talk about it tomorrow, Mr Sykes.'

'You don't pay me much mind, either. But that's all right. I told you what I saw. Y'all can do what you want to with it.'

He looked straight ahead through the beads of water on the window. His handsome face was wan, tired, more sober now, resigned perhaps to a booking room, drunk-tank scenario he knew all too well. I remembered two or three wire-service stories about him over the last few years – a brawl with a couple of cops in Dallas or Fort Worth, a violent ejection from a yacht club in Los Angeles, and a plea on a cocaine-possession bust. I had heard that bean sprouts, mineral water, and the sober life had become fashionable in Hollywood. It looked like Elrod Sykes had arrived late at the depot.

'I'm sorry, I didn't get your name,' he said.

'Dave Robicheaux.'

'Well, you see, Mr Robicheaux, a lot of people don't believe me when I tell them I see things. But the truth is, I *see* things all the time, like shadows moving around behind a veil. In my family we call it "touched." When I was a little boy, my grandpa told me, "Son, the Lord done touched you. He give you a third eye to see things that other people cain't. But it's a gift from the Lord, and you mustn't never use it otherwise." I haven't ever misused the gift, either, Mr Robicheaux, even though I've done a lot of other things I'm not proud of. So I don't care if people think I lasered my head with too many recreational chemicals or not.'

'I see.'

He was quiet again. We were almost to the jail now. The wind blew raindrops out of the oak trees, and the moon edged the storm clouds with a metallic silver light. He rolled down his window halfway and breathed in the cool smell of the night.

'But if that was an Indian washed out of a burial mound instead of a colored man, I wonder what he was doing with a chain wrapped around him,' he said.

I slowed the truck and pulled it to the curb.

'Say that again,' I said.

'There was a rusted chain, I mean with links as big as my fist, crisscrossed around his rib cage.'

I studied his face. It was innocuous, devoid of intention, pale in the moonlight, already growing puffy with hangover.

'You want some slack on the DWI for your knowledge about this body, Mr Sykes?'

'No, sir, I just wanted to tell you what I saw. I shouldn't have been driving. Maybe you kept me from having an accident.'

'Some people might call that jailhouse humility. What do you think?'

'I think you might make a tough film director.'

'Can you find that sandbar again?'

'Yes, sir, I believe I can.'

'Where are you and Ms Drummond staying?'

'The studio rented us a house out on Spanish Lake.'

'I'm going to make a confession to you, Mr Sykes. DWIs are a pain in the butt. Also I'm on city turf and doing their work. If I take y'all home, can I have your word you'll remain there until tomorrow morning?'

'Yes, sir, you sure can.'

'But I want you in my office by nine A.M.'

'Nine A.M. You got it. Absolutely. I really appreciate this.'

The transformation in his face was immediate, as though liquified ambrosia had been infused in the veins of a starving man. Then as I turned the truck around in the middle of the street to pick up the actress whose name was Kelly Drummond, he said something that gave me pause about his level of sanity.

'Does anybody around here ever talk about Confederate soldiers out on that Lake?'

'I don't understand.'

'Just what I said. Does anybody ever talk about guys in gray or

473

butternut-brown uniforms out there? A bunch of them, at night, out there in the mist.'

'Aren't y'all making a film about the War Between the States? Are you talking about actors?' I looked sideways at him. His eyes were straight forward, focused on some private thought right outside the windshield.

'No, these guys weren't actors,' he said. 'They'd been shot up real bad. They looked hungry, too. It happened right around here, didn't it?'

'What?'

'The battle.'

'I'm afraid I'm not following you, Mr Sykes.'

Up ahead I saw Kelly Drummond walking in her spiked heels and Levis toward Tee Neg's poolroom.

'Yeah, you do,' he said. 'You *believe* when most people don't, Mr Robicheaux. You surely do. And when I say you *believe*, you know exactly what I'm talking about.'

He looked confidently, serenely, into my face and winked with one blood-flecked eye.

2

My dreams took me many places: sometimes back to a windswept firebase on the top of an orange hill gouged with shell holes; a soft, mist-streaked morning with ducks rising against a pink sun while my father and I crouched in the blind and waited for that heart-beating moment when their shadows would race across the cattails and reeds toward us; a lighted American Legion baseball diamond, where at age seventeen I pitched a perfect game against a team from Abbeville and a beautiful woman I didn't know, perhaps ten years my senior, kissed me so hard on the mouth that my ears rang.

But tonight I was back in the summer of my freshman year in college, July of 1957, deep in the Atchafalaya marsh, right after Hurricane Audrey had swept through southern Louisiana and killed over five hundred people in Cameron Parish alone. I worked offshore seismograph then, and the portable drill barge had just slid its iron pilings into the floor of a long, flat yellow bay, and the jug-boat crew had dropped me off by a chain of willow islands to roll up a long spool of recording cable that was strung through the trees and across the sand spits and sloughs. The sun was white in the sky, and the humidity was like the steam that rises from a pot of boiled vegetables. Once I was inside the shade of the trees, the mosquitoes swarmed around my ears and eyes in a gray fog as dense as a helmet.

The spool and crank hung off my chest by canvas straps, and after I had wound up several feet of cable, I would have to stop and submerge myself in the water to get the mosquitoes off my skin or smear more mud on my face and shoulders. It was our fifth day out on a ten-day hitch, which meant that tonight the party chief would allow a crew boat to take a bunch of us to the levee at Charenton, and from there we'd drive to a movie in some little town down by Morgan City. As I slapped mosquitoes into a bloody paste on my arms and waded across sand bogs that sucked over my knees, I kept thinking about the cold shower that I was going to take back on the quarter-boat, the fried-chicken dinner that I was going to eat in the dining room, the ride to town between the sugarcane fields in the cooling evening. Then I popped out of the woods on the edge of another bay, into the breeze, the sunlight, the hint of rain in the south.

475

I dropped the heavy spool into the sand, knelt in the shallows, and washed the mud off my skin. One hundred yards across the bay, I saw a boat with a cabin moored by the mouth of a narrow bayou. A Negro man stepped off the bow onto the bank, followed by two white men. Then I looked again and realized that something was terribly wrong. One of the white men had a pistol in his hand, and the black man's arms were pinioned at his sides with a thick chain that had been trussed around his upper torso.

I stared in disbelief as the black man started running along a short stretch of beach, his head twisting back over his shoulder, and the man with the pistol took aim and fired. The first round must have hit him in the leg, because it crumpled under him as though the bone had been snapped in two with a hammer. He half rose to his feet, stumbled into the water, and fell sideways. I saw the bullets popping the surface around him as his kinky head went under. The man with the pistol waded after him and kept shooting, now almost straight down into the water, while the other white man watched from the bank.

I didn't see the black man again.

Then the two white men looked across the flat expanse of bay and saw me. I looked back at them, numbly, almost embarrassed, like a person who had opened a bedroom door at the wrong moment. Then they walked calmly back to their boat, with no sign of apprehension or urgency, as though I were not even worthy of notice.

Later, I told the party chief, the sheriff's department, and finally anybody who would listen to me, about what I had seen. But their interest was short-lived; no body was ever found in that area, nor was any black man from around there ever reported as missing. As time passed, I tried to convince myself that the man in chains had eluded his tormentors, had held his breath for an impossibly long time, and had burst to the surface and a new day somewhere downstream. At age nineteen I did not want to accept the possibility that a man's murder could be treated with the social significance of a hangnail that had been snipped off someone's finger.

At nine sharp the morning after I had stopped Elrod T. Sykes for drunk driving, a lawyer, not Elrod Sykes, was in my office. He was tall and had silver hair, and he wore a gray suit with red stones in his cuff links. He told me his name but it wouldn't register. In fact, I wasn't interested in anything he had to say.

'Of course, Mr Sykes is at your disposal,' he said, 'and both he and I appreciate the courtesy which you extended to him last night. He feels very bad about what happened, of course. I don't know if he told you that he was taking a new prescription for his asthma, but evidently his system has a violent reaction to it. The studio also appreciates—'

'What is your name again, sir?'

'Oliver Montrose.'

I hadn't asked him to sit down yet. I picked up several paper clips from a small tin can on my desk and began dropping them one by one on my desk blotter.

'Where's Sykes right now, Mr Montrose?'

He looked at his watch.

'By this time they're out on location,' he said. When I didn't respond, he shifted his feet and added, 'Out by Spanish Lake.'

'On location at Spanish Lake?'

'Yes.'

'Let's see, that's about five miles out of town. It should take no longer than fifteen minutes to drive there from here. So thirty minutes should be enough time for you to find Mr Sykes and have him sitting in that chair right across from me.'

He looked at me a moment, then nodded.

'I'm sure that'll be no problem,' he said.

'Yeah, I bet. That's why he sent you instead of keeping his word. Tell him I said that, too.'

Ten minutes later the sheriff, with a file folder open in his hands, came into my office and sat down across from me. He had owned a dry-cleaning business and been president of the local Lions Club before running for sheriff. He wore rimless glasses, and he had soft cheeks that were flecked with blue and red veins. In his green uniform he always made me think of a nursery manager rather than a law officer, but he was an honest and decent man and humble enough to listen to those who had more experience than he had.

'I got the autopsy and the photographs on that LeBlanc girl,' he said. He took off his glasses and pinched the red mark on the bridge of his nose. 'You know, I've been doing this stuff five years now, but one like this—'

'When it doesn't bother you anymore, that's when you should start to worry, sheriff.'

'Well, anyway, the report says that most of it was probably done to her after she was dead, poor girl.'

'Could I see it?' I said, and reached out my hand for the folder.

I had to swallow when I looked at the photographs, even though I had seen the real thing only yesterday. The killer had not harmed her face. In fact, he had covered it with her blouse, either during the rape or perhaps before he stopped her young heart with an ice pick. But in the fourteen years that I had been with the New Orleans Police Department, or during the three years I had worked on and off for the Iberia Parish sheriff's office, I had seen few cases that involved this degree of violence or rage against a woman's body.

Then I read through the clinical prose describing the autopsy, the nature of the wounds, the sexual penetration of the vagina, the absence of any skin samples under the girl's fingernails, the medical examiner's speculation about the moment and immediate cause of death, and the type of instrument the killer probably used to mutilate the victim.

'Any way you look at it, I guess we're talking about a psychopath or somebody wired to the eyes on crack or acid,' the sheriff said.

'Yeah, maybe,' I said.

'You think somebody *else* would disembowel a nineteen-year-old girl with a scalpel or a barber's razor?'

'Maybe the guy wants us to think he's a meltdown. He was smart enough not to leave anything at the scene except the ice pick, and it was free of prints. There weren't any prints on the tape he used on her wrists or mouth, either. She went out the front door of the jukejoint, by herself, at one in the morning, when the place was still full of people, and some-how he abducted her, or got her to go with him, between the front door and her automobile, which was parked only a hundred feet away.'

His eyes were thoughtful.

'Go on,' he said.

'I think she knew the guy.'

The sheriff put his glasses back on and scratched at the corner of his mouth with one fingernail.

'She left her purse at the table,' I said. 'I think she went outside to get something from her car and ran into somebody she knew. Psycho-paths don't try to strongarm women in front of bars filled with drunk coonasses and oil-field workers.'

'What do we know about the girl?'

I took my notebook out of the desk drawer and thumbed through it on top of the blotter.

'Her mother died when she was twelve. She quit school in the ninth grade and ran away from her father a couple of times in Mamou. She was arrested for prostitution in Lafayette when she was sixteen. For the last year or so she lived here with her grandparents, out at the end of West Main. Her last job was waitressing in a bar about three weeks ago in St Martinville. Few close friends, if any, no current or recent romantic involvement, at least according to the grandparents. She didn't have a chance for much of a life, did she?'

I could hear the sheriff rubbing his thumb along his jawbone.

'No, she didn't,' he said. His eyes went out the window then refocused on my face. 'Do you buy that about no romantic involvement?'

'No.'

'Neither do I. Do you have any other theories except that she probably knew her killer?'

'One.'

'What?'

'That I'm all wrong, that we *are* dealing with a psychopath or a serial killer.'

He stood up to leave. He was overweight, constantly on a diet, and his stomach protruded over his gunbelt, but his erect posture always gave him the appearance of a taller and trimmer man than he actually was.

'I'm glad we operate out of this office with such a sense of certainty, Dave,' he said. 'Look, I want you to use everything available to us on this one. I want to nail this sonofabitch right through the breastbone.'

I nodded, unsure of his intention in stating the obvious.

'That's why we're going to be working with the FBI on this one,' he said.

I kept my eyes flat, my hands open and motionless on the desk blotter.

'You called them?' I said.

'I did, and so did the mayor. It's a kidnapping as well as a rape and murder, Dave.'

'Yeah, that could be the case.'

'You don't like the idea of working with these guys?'

'You don't *work* with the feds, sheriff. You take orders from them. If you're lucky, they won't treat you like an insignificant local douche bag in front of a television camera. It's a great learning exercise in humility.'

'No one can ever accuse you of successfully hiding your feelings, Dave.'

Almost thirty minutes from the moment the attorney, Oliver Montrose, had left my office, I looked out my window and saw Elrod T. Sykes pull his lavender Cadillac into a no-parking zone, scrape his white-walls against the curb, and step out into the bright sunlight. He wore brown striped slacks, shades, and a lemon-yellow short-sleeve shirt. The attorney got out on the passenger's side, but Sykes gestured for him to stay where he was. They argued briefly, then Sykes walked into the building by himself.

He had his shades in his hand when he stepped inside my office door, his hair wet and freshly combed, an uneasy grin at the corner of his mouth.

'Sit down a minute, please,' I said.

The skin around his eyes was pale with hangover. He sat down and touched at his temple as though it were bruised.

'I'm sorry about sending the mercenary. It wasn't my idea,' he said.

'Whose was it?'

'Mikey figures he makes the decisions on anything that affects the picture.'

'How old are you, Mr Sykes?'

He widened his eyes and crimped his lips.

'Forty. Well, actually forty-three,' he said.

'Did you have to ask that man's permission to drive an automobile while you were drunk?'

He blinked as though I'd struck him, then made a wet noise in his throat and wiped his mouth with the backs of his fingers.

'I really don't know what to say to you,' he said. He had a peculiar, north Texas accent, husky, slightly nasal, like he had a dime-sized piece of melting ice in his cheek. 'I broke my word, I'm aware of that. But I'm letting other people down, too, Mr Robicheaux. It costs ten thousand dollars an hour when you have to keep a hundred people standing around while a guy like me gets out of trouble.'

'I hope y'all work it out.'

'I guess this is the wrong place to look for aspirin and sympathy, isn't it?'

'A sheriff's deputy from St Mary Parish is going to meet us with a boat at the Chitimacha Indian reservation, Mr Sykes. I think he's probably waiting on us right now.'

'Well, actually I'm looking forward to it. Did I tell you last night my grandpa was a Texas ranger?'

'No, you didn't.' I looked at my watch.

'Well, it's a fact, he was. He worked with Frank Hammer, the ranger who got Bonnie and Clyde right up there at Arcadia, Louisiana.' He smiled at me. 'You know what he used to tell me when I was a kid? "Son, you got two speeds – wide-open and fuck it." I swear he was a pistol. He—'

'I'd like to explain something to you. I don't want you to take offense at it, either.'

'Yes, sir?'

'Yesterday somebody raped and murdered a nineteen-year-old girl on the south side of the parish. He cut her breasts off, he pulled her entrails out of her stomach, he pushed twigs up her vagina. I don't like waiting in my office for you to show up when it's convenient, I'm not interested in your film company's production problems, and on this particular morning I'd appreciate it if you'd leave your stories about your family history to your publicity people.'

His eyes tried to hold on mine, then they watered and glanced away.

'I'd like to use your bathroom, please,' he said. 'I'm afraid I got up with a case of the purple butterflies.'

'I'll be out front. I'll see you there in two minutes, Mr Sykes.'

The sky was bright and hazy, the wind hot as a flame as we drove toward the Atchafalaya River. I had to stop the truck twice to let Elrod Sykes vomit by the side of the road.

It felt strange to go back into that part of the Atchafalaya Basin after so many years. In July of 1957, after the hurricane had passed through and the rains had finally stopped, the flooded woods and willow islands, the canals whose canopies were so thick that sunlight seldom struck the water, the stretches of beach along the bays had smelled of death for weeks. The odor, which was like the heavy, gray, salty stench from a decaying rat, hung in the heat all day, and at night it blew through the screen windows on the quarter-boat and awaited you in the morning when you walked through the galley into the dining room.

Many of the animals that did not drown starved to death. Coons used to climb up the mooring ropes and scratch on the galley screen for food, and often we'd take rabbits out of the tops of trees that barely extended above the current and carry them on the jugboat to the levee at Charenton. Sometimes at night huge trees with root systems as broad as barn roofs floated by in the dark and scraped the hull with their branches from the bow to the stern. One night when the moon was full and yellow and low over the willow islands, I heard something hit the side of the boat hard, like a big wood fist rolling its knuckles along the planks. I stood on my bunk and looked through the screen window and saw a houseboat, upside down, spinning in the current, a tangle of fishing nets strung out of one window like flotsam from an eye socket.

I thought about the hundreds of people who had either been crushed under a tidal wave or drowned in Cameron Parish, their bodies washed deep into the marshes along the Calcasieu River, and again I smelled that thick, fetid odor on the wind. I could not sleep again until the sun rose like a red molten ball through the mists across the bay.

It didn't take us long to find the willow island where Elrod Sykes said he had seen the skeletal remains of either an Indian or a black person. We crossed the wide sweep of the Atchafalaya in a sheriff's department boat with two outboard engines mounted on the stern, took a channel between a row of sandbars whose sun-dried crests looked like the backs of dolphin jumping in a school, crossed a long bay, and slid the boat onto a narrow strip of beach that bled back into a thick stand of willow trees and chains of flooded sinkholes and sand bogs.

Elrod Sykes stepped off the bow onto the sand and stared into the trees. He had taken off his shirt and he used it to wipe the sweat off his tanned chest and shoulders.

'It's back in yonder,' he said, and pointed. 'You can see my footprints where I went in to take a whiz.'

The St Mary Parish deputy fitted a cloth cap on his head and sprayed his face, neck, and arms with mosquito dope, then handed the can to me.

'If I was you, I'd put my shirt on, Mr Sykes,' he said. 'We used to have a lot of bats down here. Till the mosquitoes ate them all.'

Sykes smiled good-naturedly and waited for his turn to use the can of repellent.

'I bet you won't believe this,' the deputy said, 'but it's been so dry here on occasion that I seen a catfish walking down the levee carrying his own canteen.'

Sykes's eyes crinkled at the corners, then he walked ahead of us into the gloom, his loafers sinking deep into the wet sand.

'That boy's a long way from his Hollywood poontang, ain't he?' the deputy said behind me.

'How about putting the cork in the humor for a while?' I said.

'What?'

'The man grew up down South. You're patronizing him.'

'I'm wha—'

I walked ahead of him and caught up with Sykes just as he stepped out of the willows into a shallow, water-filled depression between the woods and a sandbar. The water was stagnant and hot and smelled of dead garfish.

'There,' he said. 'Right under the roots of that dead tree. I told y'all.'

A barkless, sun-bleached cypress tree lay crossways in a sandbar, the water-smooth trunk eaten by worms, and gathered inside the root system, as though held by a gnarled hand, was a skeleton crimped in an embryonic position, wrapped in a web of dried algae and river trash.

The exposed bone was polished and weathered almost black, but sections of the skin had dried to the color and texture of desiccated leather. Just as Sykes had said, a thick chain encased with rust was wrapped around the arms and rib cage. The end links were fastened with a padlock as wide as my hand.

I tore a willow branch off a tree, shucked off the leaves with my Puma knife, and knelt down in front of the skeleton.

'How do you reckon it got up under those roots?' Sykes said.

'A bad hurricane came through here in '57,' I said. 'Trees like this were torn out of the ground like carrots. My bet is this man's body got caught under some floating trees and was covered up later in this sandbar.'

Sykes knelt beside me.

'I don't understand,' he said. 'How do you know it happened in '57? Hurricanes tear up this part of the country all the time, don't they?'

'Good question, podna,' I said, and I used the willow branch to peel away the dried web of algae from around one shinbone, then the other.

'That left one's clipped in half,' Sykes said.

'Yep. That's where he was shot when he tried to run away from two white men.'

'You clairvoyant or something?' Sykes said.

'No, I saw it happen. About a mile from here.'

'You saw it happen?' Sykes said.

'Yep.'

'What's going on here?' the deputy said behind us. 'You saying some white people lynched somebody or something?'

'Yeah, that's exactly what I'm saying. When we get back we'll need to talk to your sheriff and get your medical examiner out here.'

'I don't know about y'all over in Iberia Parish, but nobody around here's going to be real interested in nigger trouble that's thirty-five years old,' the deputy said.

I worked the willow branch around the base of the bones and peeled back a skein of algae over the legs, the pelvic bones, and the crown of the skull, which still had a section of grizzled black hair attached to the pate. I poked at the corrugated, blackened work boots and the strips of rag that hung off the pelvis.

I put down the branch and chewed on the corner of my thumb-nail.

'What are you looking for, Mr Robicheaux?' Sykes said.

'It's not what's there, it's what isn't,' I said. 'He wasn't wearing a belt on his trousers, and his boots have no laces.'

'Sonofabitch probably did his shopping at the Goodwill. Big fucking deal,' the deputy said, slapped a mosquito on his neck, and looked at the red and black paste on his palm.

Later that afternoon I went back to work on the case of the murdered girl, whose full name was Cherry LeBlanc. No one knew the whereabouts of her father, who had disappeared from Mamou after he was accused of molesting a black child in his neighborhood, but I interviewed her grandparents again, the owner of the bar in St Martinville where she had last worked, the girls she had been with in the clapboard jukejoint the night she died, and a police captain in Lafayette who had recommended probation for her after she had been busted on the prostitution charge. I learned little about her except that she seemed to have been an uneducated, unskilled, hapless, and fatally beautiful girl who thought she could be a viable player in a crap game where the dice for her kind were always shaved.

I learned that about her and the fact that she had loved zydeco music and had gone to the jukejoint to hear Sam 'Hogman' Patin play his harmonica and bottleneck blues twelve-string guitar.

My desk was covered with scribbled notes from my note pad, morgue and crime-scene photos, interview cassettes, and Xeroxes from the LeBlanc family's welfare case history when the sheriff walked into my office. The sky outside was lavender and pink now, and the fronds on the palm trees out by the sidewalk were limp in the heat and silhouetted darkly against the late sun.

'The sheriff over in St Mary Parish just called,' he said.

'Yes?'

'He said thanks a lot. They really appreciate the extra work.' He sat on the corner of my desk.

'Tell him to find another line of work.'

'He said you're welcome to come over on your days off and run the investigation.'

'What's he doing with it?'

483

'Their coroner's got the bones now. But I'll tell you the truth, Dave, I don't think it's going anywhere.'

I leaned back in my swivel chair and drummed my fingers on my desk. My eyes burned and my back hurt.

'It seems to me you've been vindicated,' the sheriff said. 'Let it go for now.'

'We'll see.'

'Look, I know you've got a big workload piled on you right now, but I've got a problem I need you to look into when you have a chance. Like maybe first thing tomorrow morning.'

I looked back at him without speaking.

'Baby Feet Balboni,' he said.

'What about him?'

'He's in New Iberia. At the Holiday Inn, with about six of his fellow greaseballs and their whores. The manager called me from a phone booth down the street he was so afraid one of them would hear him.'

'I don't know what I can do about it,' I said.

'We need to know what he's doing in town.'

'He grew up here.'

'Look, Dave, they can't even handle this guy in New Orleans. He cannibalized half the Giacano and Cardo families to get where he is. He's not coming back here. That's not going to happen.'

I rubbed my face. My whiskers felt stiff against my palm.

'You want me to send somebody else?' the sheriff asked.

'No, that's all right.'

'Y'all were friends in high school for a while, weren't you?'

'We played ball together, that's all.'

I gazed out the window at the lengthening shadows. He studied my face.

'What's the matter, Dave?'

'It's nothing.'

'You bothered because we want to bounce a baseball buddy out of town?'

'No, not really.'

'Did you ever hear that story about what he did to Didi Giacano's cousin? Supposedly he hung him from his colon by a meat hook.'

'I've heard that same story about a half-dozen wiseguys in Orleans and Jefferson parishes. It's an old NOPD heirloom.'

'Probably just bad press, huh?'

'I always tried to think of Julie as nine-tenths thespian,' I said.

'Yeah, and gorilla shit tastes like chocolate ice cream. Dave, you're a laugh a minute.'

3

Julie Balboni looked just like his father, who had owned most of the slot and racehorse machines in Iberia Parish during the 1940s and, with an Assyrian family, had run the gambling and prostitution in the Underpass area of Lafayette. Julie was already huge, six and a half feet tall, when he was in the eleventh grade, thick across the hips and tapered at both ends like a fat banana, with tiny ankles and size-seven feet and a head as big as a buffalo's. A year later he filled out in serious proportions. That was also the year he was arrested for burglarizing a liquor store. His father walked him out into the woods at gunpoint and whipped the skin off his back with the nozzle end of a garden hose.

His hair grew on his head like black snakes, and because a physician had injured a nerve in his face when he was delivered, the corner of his mouth would sometimes droop involuntarily and give him a lewd or leering expression that repelled most girls. He farted in class, belched during the pledge of allegiance, combed his dandruff out on top of the desk, and addressed anyone he didn't like by gathering up his scrotum and telling them to bite. We walked around him in the halls and the locker room. His teachers were secretly relieved when his mother and father did not show up on parents' night.

His other nickname was Julie the Bone, although it wasn't used to his face, because he went regularly to Mabel White's Negro brothel in Crowley and the Negro cribs on Hopkins Avenue in New Iberia.

But Julie had two uncontested talents. He was both a great kick boxer and a great baseball catcher. His ankles twisted too easily for him to play football; he was too fat to run track; but with one flick of a thick thigh he could leave a kick-box opponent heaving blood, and behind the plate he could steal the ball out of the batter's swing or vacuum a wild pitch out of the dust and zip the ball to third base like a BB.

In my last time out as a high school pitcher, I was going into the bottom of the ninth against Abbeville with a shut-out almost in my pocket. It was a soft, pink evening, with the smell of flowers and freshly cut grass in the air. Graduation was only three weeks away, and we all felt that we were painted with magic and that the spring season had been

485

created as a song especially for us. Innocence, a lock on the future, the surge of victory in the loins, the confirmation of a girl's kiss among the dusky oak trees, like a strawberry bursting against the roof of the mouth, were all most assuredly our due.

We even felt an acceptance and camaraderie toward Baby Feet. Imminent graduation and the laurels of a winning season seemed to have melted away the differences in our backgrounds and experience.

Then their pitcher, a beanballer who used his elbows, knees, and spikes in a slide, hit a double and stole third base. Baby Feet called time and jogged out to the mound, sweat leaking out of his inverted cap. He rubbed up a new ball for me.

'Put it in the dirt. I'm gonna let that cocksucker have his chance,' he said.

'I don't know if that's smart, Feet,' I said.

'I've called a shutout for you so far, haven't I? Do what I tell you.'

On the next pitch I glanced at the runner, then fired low and outside, into the dirt. Baby Feet vacuumed it up, then spun around, throwing dust in the air like an elephant, and raced toward the backstop as though the ball had gotten past him.

The runner charged from third. Suddenly Baby Feet reappeared at the plate, the ball never having left his hand, his mask still on his face. The runner realized that he had stepped into it and he tried to bust up Baby Feet in the slide by throwing one spiked shoe up in Feet's face. Baby Feet caught the runner's spikes in his mask, tagged him across the head with the ball, then, when it was completely unnecessary at that point, razored his own spikes into the boy's ankles and twisted.

The players on the field, the coaches, the people in the stands, stared numbly at home plate. Baby Feet calmly scraped his spikes clean in the sand, then knelt and tightened the strap on a shin guard, his face cool and detached as he squinted up at the flag snapping on a metal pole behind the backstop.

It wasn't hard to find him at the Holiday Inn. He and his entourage were the only people in and around the swimming pool. Their tanned bodies glistened as though they had rubbed them with melted butter. They wore wraparound sunglasses that were as black as a blind man's, reclined luxuriously on deck chairs, their genitalia sculpted against the bikinis, or floated on rubber mattresses, tropical drinks in holders at their sides, a glaze of suntan oil emananting from the points of their fingers and toes.

A woman came out the sliding door of a room with her two children, walked them to the wading pool, then obviously realized the nature of the company she was keeping; she looked around distractedly, as though she heard invisible birds cawing at her, and returned quickly to her room with her children's hands firmly in hers.

Julie the Bone hadn't changed a great deal since I had last seen him seven years ago in New Orleans. His eyes, which were like black marbles, were set a little more deeply in his face; his wild tangle of hair was flecked in places with gray; but his barrel chest and his washtub of a stomach still seemed to have the tone and texture of whale hide. When you looked at the ridges of scar tissue under the hair on his shoulders and back where his father had beaten him, at the nests of tendons and veins in his neck, and the white protrusion of knuckles in his huge hands, you had the feeling that nothing short of a wrecking ball, swung by a cable from a great height, could adequately deal with this man if he should choose to destroy everything in his immediate environment.

He raised himself on one elbow from his reclining chair, pushed his sunglasses up on his hair, and squinted through the haze at me as I approached him. Two of his men sat next to him at a glass table under an umbrella, playing cards with a woman with bleached hair and skin that was so tanned it looked like folds of soft leather. Both men put down their cards and got to their feet, and one of them, who looked as though he were hammered together from boilerplate, stepped directly into my path. His hair was orange and gray, flattened in damp curls on his head, and there were pachuco crosses tattooed on the backs of his hands. I opened my seersucker coat so he could see the badge clipped to my belt. But recognition was already working in his face.

'What's happening, Cholo?' I said.

'Hey, lieutenant, how you doin'?' he said, then turned to Baby Feet. 'Hey, Julie, it's Lieutenant Robicheaux. From the First District in New Orleans. You remember him when—'

'Yeah, I know who it is, Cholo,' Baby Feet said, smiling and nodding at me. 'What you up to, Dave? Somebody knock a pop fly over the swimming-pool wall?'

'I was just in the neighborhood. I heard you were back in town for a short visit.'

'No kidding.'

'That's a fact.'

'You were probably in the barbershop and somebody said, "The Bone's in town," and you thought, "Boy, that's great news. I'll just go say hello to ole Feet."'

'You're a famous man, Julie. Word gets around.'

'And I'm just here for a short visit, right?'

'Yeah, that's the word.'

His eyes moved up and down my body. He smiled to himself and took a sip from a tall glass wrapped in a napkin, with shaved ice, fruit, and a tiny paper umbrella in it.

'You're a sheriff's detective now, I hear.'

'On and off.'

He pushed a chair at me with his foot, then picked it up and set it in a shady area across from him. I took off my seersucker coat, folded it on my arm, and sat down.

'Y'all worried about me, Dave?'

'Some people in New Iberia think you're a hard act to follow. How many guys would burn down their own father's nightclub?'

He laughed.

'Yeah, the old man lost his interest in garden hoses after that,' he said.

'Everybody likes to come back to his hometown once in a while. That's a perfectly natural thing to do. No one's worried about that, Julie.' I looked at his eyes. Under his sweaty brows, they were as shiny and full of light as obsidian.

He took a cigarette out of a package on the cement and lit it. He blew smoke out into the sunlight and looked around the swimming-pool area.

'Except I've only got a visa, right?' he said. 'I'm supposed to spread a little money around, stay on the back streets, tell my crew not to spit on the sidewalks or blow their noses on their napkins in the restaurants. Does that kind of cover it for you, Dave?'

'It's a small town with small-town problems.'

'Fuck.' He took a deep breath, then twisted his neck as though there were a crick in it. 'Margot—' he said to the woman playing cards under the umbrella. She got up from her chair and stood behind him, her narrow face expressionless behind her sunglasses, and began kneading his neck with her fingers. He filled his mouth with ice, orange slices, and cherries from his glass and studied my face while he chewed.

'I get a little upset at these kind of attitudes, Dave. You got to forgive me,' he said, and pointed into his breastbone with his fingertips. 'But it don't seem to matter sometimes what a guy does *now*. It's always *yesterday* that's in people's minds. Like Cholo here. He made a mistake fifteen years ago and we're still hearing about it. What the fuck is that? You think that's fair?'

'He threw his brother-in-law off the roof of the Jax's brewery on top of a Mardi Gras float. That was a first even for New Orleans.'

'Hey, lieutenant, there was a lot of other things involved there. The guy beat up my sister. He was a fucking animal.'

'Look, Dave, you been gone from New Orleans for a long time,' Baby Feet said. 'The city ain't anything like it used to be. Black kids with shit for brains are provoking everybody in the fucking town. People get killed in Audubon Park, for God's sake. You try to get on the St Charles streetcar and there's either niggers or Japs hanging out the doors and windows. We used to have understandings with the city. Everybody knew the rules, nobody got hurt. Take a walk past the Desire or St Thomas project and see what happens.'

'What's the point, Julie?'

'The point is who the fuck needs it? I own a recording studio, the same place Jimmy Clanton cut his first record. I'm in the entertainment business. I talk on the phone every day to people in California you read about in *People* magazine. I come home to this shithole, they ought to have "Welcome Back Balboni Day." Instead, I get told maybe I'm like a bad smell in the air. You understand what I'm saying, that hurts me.'

I rubbed one palm against the other.

'I'm just a messenger,' I said.

'That laundry man you work for send you?'

'He has his concerns.'

He waved the woman away and sat up in his chair.

'Give me five minutes to get dressed. Then I want you to drive me somewhere,' he said.

'I'm a little tied up on time right now.'

'I'm asking fifteen minutes of you, max. You think you can give me that much of your day, Dave?' He got up and started past me to his room. There were tufts of black hair like pig bristles on his love handles. He cocked his index finger at me. 'Be here when I get back. You won't regret it.'

The woman with the bleached hair sat back down at the table. She took off her glasses, parted her legs a moment, and looked into my face, her eyes neither flirtatious nor hostile, simply dead. Cholo invited me to play gin rummy with them.

'Thanks. I never took it up,' I said.

'You sure took it up with horses, lieutenant,' he said.

'Yep, horses and Beam. They always made an interesting combination at the Fairgrounds.'

'Hey, you remember that time you lent me twenty bucks to get home from Jefferson Downs? I always remembered that, Loot. That was all right.'

Cholo Manelli had been born of a Mexican washerwoman, who probably wished she had given birth to a bowling ball instead, and fathered by a brain-damaged Sicilian numbers runner, whose head had been caved in by a cop's baton in the Irish Channel. He was raised in the Iberville welfare project across from the old St Louis cemeteries, and at age eleven was busted with his brothers for rolling and beating the winos who slept in the empty crypts. Their weapons of choice had been sand-filled socks.

He had the coarse, square hands of a bricklayer, the facial depth of a pie plate. I always suspected that if he was lobotomized you wouldn't know the difference. The psychiatrists at Mandeville diagnosed him as a sociopath and shot his head full of electricity. Evidently the treatment had as much effect as charging a car battery with three dead cells. On his first jolt at Angola he was put in with the big stripes, the violent and the incorrigible, back in the days when the state used trusty guards, mounted on horses and armed with double-barrel twelve-gauge shotguns, who had to serve the time of any inmate who escaped while under their supervision. Cholo went to the bushes and didn't come back fast enough for the trusty gunbull. The gunbull put four pieces of buckshot in Cholo's back. Two weeks later a Mason jar of prune-o was found in the gunbull's cell. A month after that, when he was back in the main population, somebody dropped the loaded bed of a dump truck on his head.

'Julie told me about the time that boon almost popped you with a .38,' he said.

'What time was that?'

'When you were a patrolman. In the Quarter. Julie said he saved your life.'

'He did, huh?'

Cholo shrugged his shoulders.

'That's what the man said, lieutenant. What do I know?'

'Take the hint, Cholo. Our detective isn't a conversationalist,' the woman said, without removing her eyes from her cards. She clacked her lacquered nails on the glass tabletop, and her lips made a dry, sucking sound when she puffed on her cigarette.

'You working on that murder case? The one about that girl?' he said.

'How'd you know about that?'

His eyes clicked sideways.

'It was in the newspaper,' he said. 'Julie and me was talking about it this morning. Something like that's disgusting. You got a fucking maniac on the loose around here. Somebody ought to take him to a hospital and kill him.'

Baby Feet emerged resplendent from the sliding glass door of his room. He wore a white suit with gray pin stripes, a purple shirt scrolled with gray flowers, a half-dozen gold chains and medallions around his talcumed neck, tasseled loafers that seemed as small on his feet as ballet slippers.

'You look beautiful, Julie,' Cholo said.

'Fucking A,' Baby Feet said, lighting the cigarette in the corner of his mouth with a tiny gold lighter.

'Can I go with y'all?' Cholo asked.

'Keep an eye on things here for me.'

'Hey, you told me last night I could go.'

'I need you to take my calls.'

'Margot don't know how to pick up a phone anymore?' Cholo said.

'My meter's running, Julie,' I said.

'We're going out to dinner tonight with some interesting people,' Baby Feet said to Cholo. 'You'll enjoy it. Be patient.'

'They're quite excited about the possibility of meeting you. They called and said that, Cholo,' the woman said.

'Margot, why is it you got calluses on your back? Somebody been putting starch in your sheets or something?' Cholo said.

I started walking toward my truck. The sunlight off the cement by the poolside was blinding. Baby Feet caught up with me. One of his other women dove off the board and splashed water and the smell of chlorine and suntan oil across my back.

'Hey, I live in a fucking menagerie,' Baby Feet said as we went out onto the street. 'Don't go walking off from me with your nose bent out of joint. Did I ever treat you with a lack of respect?'

I got in the truck.

'Where we going, Feet?' I said.

'Out by Spanish Lake. Look, I want you to take a message back to the man you work for. I'm not the source of any problems you got around here. The coke you got in this parish has been stepped on so many times it's baby powder. If it was coming from some people I've been associated with in New Orleans, and I'm talking about past associations, you understand, it'd go from your nose to your brain like liquid Drano.'

I headed out toward the old two-lane highway that led to the little settlement of Burke and the lake where Spanish colonists had tried to establish plantations in the eighteenth century and had given Iberia Parish its name.

'I don't work narcotics, Julie, and I'm not good at passing on bullshit, either. My main concern right now is the girl we found south of town.'

'Oh, yeah? What girl's that?'

'The murdered girl, Cherry LeBlanc.'

'I don't guess I heard about it.'

I turned and looked at him. He gazed idly out the window at the passing oak trees on the edge of town and a roadside watermelon and strawberry stand.

'You don't read the local papers?' I said.

'I been busy. You saying I talk bullshit, Dave?'

'Put it this way, Feet. If you've got something to tell the sheriff, do it yourself.'

He pinched his nose, then blew air through it.

'We used to be friends, Dave. I even maybe did you a little favor once. So I'm going to line it out for you and any of the locals who want to clean the wax out of their ears. The oil business is still in the toilet and your town's flat-ass broke. Frankly, in my opinion, it deserves anything that happens to it. But me and all those people you see back on that lake—' He pointed out the window. Through a pecan orchard, silhouetted against the light winking off the water, I could see cameras mounted on booms and actors in Confederate uniforms toiling through the shallows in retreat from imaginary federal troops. 'We're going to leave around ten million dollars in Lafayette and Iberia Parish. They don't like the name

Balboni around here, tell them we can move the whole fucking operation over to Mississippi. See how that floats with some of those coonass jackoffs in the Chamber of Commerce.'

'You're telling me you're in the movie business?'

'Coproducer with Michael Goldman. What do you think of that?'

I turned into the dirt road that led through the pecan trees to the lake.

'I'm sure everyone wishes you success, Julie.'

'I'm going to make a baseball movie next. You want a part in it?' He smiled at me.

'I don't think I'd be up to it.'

'Hey, Dave, don't get me wrong.' He was grinning broadly now. 'But my main actor sees dead people out in the mist, his punch is usually ripped by nine A.M. on weed or whites, and Mikey's got peptic ulcers and some kind of obsession with the Holocaust. Dave, I ain't shitting you, I mean this sincerely, with no offense, with your record, you could fit right in.'

I stopped the truck by a small wood-frame security office. A wiry man in a khaki uniform and a bill cap, with a white scar like a chicken's foot on his throat, approached my window.

'We'll see you, Feet,' I said.

'You don't want to look around?'

'Adios, partner,' I said, waited for him to close the door, then turned around in the weeds and drove back through the pecan trees to the highway, the sun's reflection bouncing on my hood like a yellow balloon.

It happened my second year on the New Orleans police force, when I was a patrolman in the French Quarter and somebody called in a prowler report at an address on Dumaine. The lock on the iron gate was rusted and had been bent out of the jamb with a bar and sprung back on the hinges. Down the narrow brick walkway I could see bits of broken glass, like tiny rat's teeth, where someone had broken out the overhead light bulb. But the courtyard ahead was lighted, filled with the waving shadows of banana trees and palm fronds, and I could hear a baseball game playing on a radio or television set.

I slipped my revolver out of its holster and moved along the coolness of the bricks, through a ticking pool of water, to the entrance of the courtyard, where a second scrolled-iron gate yawned back on its hinges. I could smell the damp earth in the flower beds, spearmint growing against a stucco wall, the thick clumps of purple wisteria that hung from a tile roof.

Then I smelled *him*, even before I saw him, an odor that was at once like snuff, synthetic wine, rotting teeth, and stomach bile. He was a huge black man, dressed in a Donald Duck T-shirt, filthy tennis shoes, and a pair of purple slacks that were bursting on his thighs. In his left hand was a drawstring bag filled with goods from the apartment he'd just creeped. He swung the gate with all his weight into my hand, snapped something in it like a Popsicle stick breaking, and sent my revolver skidding across the flagstones.

I tried to get my baton loose, but it was his show now. He came out of his back pocket with a worn one-inch .38, the grips wrapped with black electrician's tape, and screwed the barrel into my ear. There was a dark clot of blood in his right eye, and his breath slid across the side of my face like an unwashed hand.

'Get back in the walkway, motherfucker,' he whispered.

We stumbled backward into the gloom. I could hear revelers out on the street, a beer can tinkling along the cement.

'Don't be a dumb guy,' I said.

'Shut up,' he said. Then, almost as as angry afterthought, he drove my head into the bricks. I fell to my knees in the water, my baton twisted uselessly in my belt.

His eyes were dilated, his hair haloed with sweat, his pulse leaping in his neck. He was a cop's worst possible adversary in that situation – strung-out, frightened, and stupid enough to carry a weapon on a simple B & E.

'Why'd you have to come along, man? Why'd you have to do that?' he said.

His thumb curled around the spur of the pistol's hammer and I heard the cylinder rotate and the chamber lock into place.

'There's cops on both ends of the street,' I said. 'You won't get out of the Quarter.'

'Don't say no more, man. It won't do no good. You messed everything up.'

He wiped the sweat out of his eyes, blew out his breath, and pointed the pistol downward at my chest.

Baby Feet had on only a bathrobe, his jockey underwear, and a pair of loafers without socks when he appeared in the brick walkway behind the black man.

'What the fuck do you think you're doing here?' he said.

The black man stepped back, the revolver drifting to his thigh.

'Mr Julie?' he said.

'Yeah. What the fuck you doing? You creeping an apartment in my building?'

'I didn't know you was living here, Mr Julie.'

Baby Feet took the revolver out of the black man's hand and eased down the hammer.

'Walter, if I want to, I can make you piss blood for six months,' he said.

'Yes, suh, I knows that.'

'I'm glad you've taken that attitude. Now, you get your sorry ass out of here.' He pushed the black man toward the entrance. 'Go on.' He kept nudging the black man along the bricks, then he kicked him hard, as fast as a snake striking, between the buttocks. 'I said go on, now.' He kicked him again, his small pointed shoe biting deep into the man's crotch. Tears welled up in the man's eyes as he looked back over his shoulder. 'Move it, Walter, unless you want balls the size of coconuts.'

The black man limped down Dumaine. Baby Feet stood in front of the sprung gate, dumped the shells from the .38 on the sidewalk, and flung the .38 into the darkness after the black man.

'Come on upstairs and I'll put your hand in some ice,' he said.

I had found my hat and revolver.

'I'm going after that guy,' I said.

'Pick him up in the morning. He shines shoes in a barbershop on Calliope and St Charles. You sure you want to stay in this line of work, Dave?'

He laughed, lit a purple-and-gold cigarette, and put his round, thick arm over my shoulders.

The sheriff was right: Baby Feet might be a movie producer, but he could never be dismissed as a thespian.

4

My brief visit with Julie Balboni should have been a forgettable and minor interlude in my morning. Instead, my conversation with him in the truck had added a disturbing question mark in the murder of Cherry LeBlanc. He said he had heard nothing about it, nor had he read about it in the local newspaper. This was ten minutes after Cholo Manelli had told me that he and Baby Feet had been talking about the girl's death earlier.

Was Baby Feet lying or was he simply not interested in talking about something that wasn't connected with his well-being? Or had the electro-shock therapists in Mandeville overheated Cholo's brain pan?

My experience with members of the Mafia and sociopaths in general had been that they lie as a matter of course. They are convincing because they often lie when there is no need to. To apply some form of forensic psychology in attempting to understand how they think is as productive as placing your head inside a microwave oven in order to study the nature of electricity.

I spent the rest of the day retracing the geography of Cherry LeBlanc's last hours and trying to recreate the marginal world in which she had lived. At three that afternoon I parked my truck in the shade by the old wood-frame church in St Martinville and looked at a color photograph of her that had been given to me by the grandparents. Her hair was black, with a mahogany tint in it, her mouth bright red with too much lipstick, her face soft, slightly plump with baby fat; her dark eyes were bright and masked no hidden thought; she was smiling.

Busted at sixteen for prostitution, dead at nineteen, I thought. And that's what we knew about. God only knew what else had befallen her in her life. But she wasn't born a prostitute or the kind of girl who would be passed from hand to hand until someone opened a car door for her and drove her deep into a woods, where he revealed to her the instruments of her denouement, perhaps even convinced her that this moment was one she had elected for herself.

Others had helped her get there. My first vote would be for the father, the child molester, in Mamou. But our legal system looks at nouns, seldom at adverbs.

I gazed at the spreading oaks in the church's graveyard, where Evangeline and her lover Gabriel were buried. The tombstones were stained with lichen and looked cool and gray in the shade. Beyond the trees, the sun reflected off Bayou Teche like a yellow flame.

Where was the boyfriend in this? I thought. A girl that pretty either has a beau or there is somebody in her life who would like to be one. She hadn't gone far in school, but necessity must have given her a survivor's instinct about people, about men in particular, certainly about the variety who drifted in and out of a south Louisiana jukejoint.

She had to know her killer. I was convinced of that.

I walked to the bar, a ramshackle nineteenth-century wooden building with scaling paint and a sagging upstairs gallery. The inside was dark and cool and almost deserted. A fat black woman was scrubbing the front windows with a brush and a bucket of soap and water. I walked the length of the bar to the small office in back where I had found the owner before. Along the counter in front of the bar's mirror were rows upon rows of bottles – dark green and slender, stoppered with wet corks: obsidian black with arterial-red wax seals; frosted-white, like ice sawed out of a lake; whiskey-brown, singing with heat and light.

The smell of the green sawdust on the floor, the wood-handled beer taps dripping through an aluminum grate, the Collins mix and the bowls of cherries and sliced limes and oranges, they were only the stuff of memory, I told myself, swallowing. They belong to your Higher Power now. Just like an old girlfriend who winks at you on the street one day, I thought. You already gave her up. You just walk on by. It's that easy.

But you don't think about it, you don't think about it, you don't think about it.

The owner was a preoccupied man who combed his black hair straight back on his narrow head and kept his comb clipped inside his shirt pocket. The receipts and whiskey invoices on his desk were a magnet for his eyes. My questions couldn't compete. He kept running his tongue behind his teeth while I talked.

'So you didn't know anything about her friends?' I said.

'No, sir. She was here three weeks. They come and they go. That's the way it is. I don't know what else to tell you.'

'Do you know anything about your bartenders?'

His eyes focused on a spot inside his cigarette smoke.

'I'm not understanding you,' he said.

'Do you hire a bartender who hangs around with ex-cons or who's in a lot of debt? I suspect you probably don't. Those are the kind of guys who set up their friends with free doubles or make change out of an open drawer without ringing up the sale, aren't they?'

'What's your point?'

'Did you know she had been arrested for prostitution?'

'I didn't know that.'

'You hired her because you thought she was an honor student at USL?'

The corner of his mouth wrinkled slightly with the beginnings of a smile. He stirred the ashes in the ashtray with the tip of his cigarette.

'I'll leave you my card and a thought, Mr Trajan. One way or another we're going to nail the guy who killed her. In the meantime, if he kills somebody else and I find out that you held back information on me, I'll be back with a warrant for your arrest.'

'I don't care for the way you're talking to me.'

I left his office without replying and walked back down the length of the bar. The black woman was now outside, washing the front window. She put down her scrub brush, flung the whole bucket of soapy water on the glass, then began rinising it off with a hose. Her skin was the color of burnt brick, her eyes turquoise, her breasts sagging like water-filled balloons inside her cotton-print dress. I opened my badge in my palm.

'Did you know the white girl Cherry LeBlanc?' I asked.

'She worked here, ain't she?' She squinted her eyes against the water spray bouncing off the glass.

'Do you know if she had a boyfriend, *tante*?'

'If that's what you want to call it.'

'What do you mean?' I asked, already knowing the answer that I didn't want to hear.

'She in the bidness.'

'Full time, in a serious way?'

'What you all sellin' out of your pants?'

'Was Mr Trajan involved?'

'Ax him.'

'I don't think he was, otherwise you wouldn't be telling me these things, *tante*.' I smiled at her.

She began refilling the bucket with clear water. She suddenly looked tired.

'She a sad girl,' she said. She wiped the perspiration off her round face with her palm and looked at it. 'I tole her they ain't no amount of money gonna he'p her when some man make her sick, no. I tole her a pretty white girl like her can have anything she want – school, car, a husband wit' a job on them oil rig. When that girl dress up, she look like a movie star. She say, "Jennifer, some people is suppose to have only what people let them have." Lord God, her age and white and believing somet'ing like that.'

'Who was her pimp, Jennifer?'

'They come here for her.'

'Who?'

'The mens. When they want her. They come here and take her home.'

'Do you know who they were, their names?'

'Them kind ain't got no names. They just drive their car up when she get off work and that po' girl get in.'

'I see. All right, Jennifer, this is my card with my telephone number on it. Would you call me if you remember anything else that might help me?'

'I don't be knowin' anything else, me. She wasn't goin' to give the name of some rich white man to an old nigger.'

'What white man?'

'That's what I tellin' you. I don't know, me.'

'I'm sorry, I don't understand what you're saying.'

'You don't understand English, you? Where you from? She say they a rich white man maybe gonna get her out of sellin' jellyroll. She say that the last time I seen her, right befo' somebody do them awful t'ings to that young girl. Mister, when they in the bidness, every man got a sweet word in his mouth, every man got a special way to keep jellyroll in his bed and the dollar in his pocket.'

She threw the bucket of clear water on the glass, splashing both of us, then walked heavily with her brushes, cleaning rags, and empty bucket down the alley next to the bar.

The rain fell through the canopy of oaks as I drove down the dirt road along the bayou toward my house. During the summer it rains almost every afternoon in southern Louisiana. From my gallery, around three o'clock, you could watch the clouds build as high and dark as mountains out on the Gulf, then within minutes the barometer would drop, the air would suddenly turn cool and smell like ozone and gun metal and fish spawning, the wind would begin to blow out of the south and straighten the moss on the dead cypress trees in the marsh, bend the cattails in the bayou, and swell and ruffle the pecan trees in my front yard; then a sheet of gray rain would move out of the marsh, across the floating islands of purple hyacinths in the bayou, my bait shop and the canvas awning over my boat-rental dock, and ring as loud on my gallery as marbles bouncing on corrugated tin.

I parked the truck under the pecan trees and ran up the incline to the front steps. My father, a trapper and oil-field roughneck who worked high up on the derrick, on what they called the monkey board, built the house of cypress and oak back in the Depression. The planks in the walls and floors were notched and joined with wooden pegs. You couldn't shove a playing card in a seam. With age the wood had weathered almost black. I think rifle balls would have bounced off it.

My wife's car was gone, but through the screen door I could smell shrimp on the stove. I looked for Alafair, my adopted daughter, but didn't see her either. Then I saw that the horse lot and shed were empty and Alafair's three-legged coon, Tripod, was not in his cage on top of the rabbit hutches or on the chain that allowed him to run along a clothesline between two tree trunks.

I started to go inside, then I heard her horse paw the leaves around the side of the house.

'Alafair?'

Nothing.

'Alf, I've got a feeling somebody is doing something she isn't supposed to.'

'What's that, Dave?' she said.

'Would you please come out here and bring your friends with you?'

She rode her Appaloosa out from under the eave. Her tennis shoes, pink shorts, and T-shirt were sopping, and her tanned skin glistened with water. She grinned under her straw hat.

'Alf, what happened the last time you took Tripod for a ride?'

She looked off reflectively at the rain falling in the trees. Tripod squirmed in her hands. He was a beautiful coon, silver-tipped, with a black mask and black rings on his thick tail.

'I told him not to do that no more, Dave.'

'It's "anymore." '

'Anymore. He ain't gonna do it anymore, Dave.'

She was grinning again. Tex, her Appaloosa, was steel gray, with white stockings and a spray of black and white spots on his rump. Last week Tripod had spiked his claws into Tex's rump, and Alafair had been thrown end over end into the tomato plants.

'Where's Bootsie?'

'At the store in town.'

'How about putting Tex in the shed and coming in for some ice cream? You think you can handle that, little guy?'

'Yeah, that's a pretty good idea, Dave,' she said, as though both of us had just thought our way through a problem. She continued to look at me, her dark eyes full of light. 'What about Tripod?'

'I think Tripod probably needs some ice cream, too.'

Her face beamed. She set Tripod on top of the hutches, then slid down off her horse into a mud puddle. I watched her hook Tripod to his chain and lead Tex back to the lot. She was eleven years old now. Her body was round and hard and full of energy, her Indian-black hair as shiny as a raven's wing; when she smiled, her eyes squinted almost completely shut. Six years ago I had pulled her from a wobbling envelope of air inside the submerged wreckage of a twin-engine plane out on the salt.

She hooked Tripod's chain on the back porch and went into her bedroom to change clothes. I put a small amount of ice cream in two bowls and set them on the table. Above the counter a telephone number was written on the small blackboard we used for messages. Alafair came back into the kitchen, rubbing her head with a towel. She wore her slippers, her elastic-waisted blue jeans, and an oversized University of Southwestern Louisiana T-shirt. She kept blowing her bangs out of her eyes.

'You promise you're going to eat your supper?' I said.

'Of course. What difference does it make if you eat ice cream before supper instead of after? You're silly sometimes, Dave.'

'Oh, I see.'

'You have funny ideas sometimes.'

'You're growing up on me.'

'What?'

'Never mind.'

She brought Tripod's pan in from the porch and put a scoop of ice cream in it. The rain had slackened, and I could see the late sun breaking through the mist, like a pink wafer, above the sugarcane at the back of my property.

'Oh, I forgot, a man called,' she said. 'That's his number.'

'Who was it?'

'He said he was a friend of yours. I couldn't hear because it was real noisy.'

'Next time have the person spell his name and write it on the blackboard with his number, Alf.'

'He said he wanted to talk with you about some man with one arm and one leg.'

'What?'

'He said a soldier. He was mixing up his words. I couldn't understand him.'

'What kind of soldier? That doesn't make too much sense, Alf.'

'He kept burping while he talked. He said his grandfather was a Texas ranger. What's a Texas ranger?'

Oh, boy, I thought.

'How about Elrod T. Sykes?' I said.

'Yeah, that's it.'

Time for an unlisted number, I thought.

'What was he talking about, Dave?'

'He was probably drunk. Don't pay attention to what drunk people say. If he calls again like that when Bootsie and I aren't here, tell him I'll call him and then hang up.'

'Don't you like him?'

'When a person is drunk, he's sick, Alafair. If you talk to that person while he's drunk, in a funny way you become like him. Don't worry, I'll have a talk with him later.'

'He didn't say anything bad, Dave.'

'But he shouldn't be calling here and bothering little people,' I said, and winked at her. I watched the concern in her face. The corners of her mouth were turned down, and her eyes looked into an empty space above her ice-cream dish. 'You're right, little guy. We shouldn't be mad at people. I think Elrod Sykes is probably an all-right guy. He probably just opens too many bottles in one day sometimes.'

She was smiling again. She had big, wide-set white teeth, and there was a smear of ice cream on her tan cheek. I hugged her shoulders and kissed her on the top of her head.

'I'm going to run now. Watch the shrimp, okay?' I said. 'And no more horseback rides for Tripod. Got it, Alf?'

'Got it, big guy.'

I put on my tennis shoes and running shorts and started down the dirt road toward the drawbridge over the bayou. The rain looked like flecks of spun glass in the air now, and the reflection of the dying sun was blood-red in the water. After a mile I was sweating heavily in the damp air, but I could feel the day's fatigue rise from my body, and I sprang across the puddles and hit it hard all the way to the bridge.

I did leg stretches against the rusted girders and watched the fireflies lighting in the trees and alligator gars turning in the shadows of a flooded canebrake. The sound of the tree frogs and cicadas in the marsh was almost deafening now.

At this time of day, particularly in summer, I always felt a sense of mortality that I could never adequately describe to another person. Sometimes it was like the late sun was about to burn itself into a dead cinder on the earth's rim, never to rise again. It made sweat run down my sides like snakes. Maybe it was because I wanted to believe that summer was an eternal song, that living in your fifty-third year was of no more significance than entering the sixth inning when your sidearm was still like a resilient whip and the prospect of your fork-ball made a batter swallow and step back from the plate.

And if it all ended tomorrow, I should have no complaint, I thought. I could have caught the bus any number of times years ago. To be reminded of that fact I only had to touch the punji-stick scar, coiled like a flattened, gray worm, on my stomach; the shiny, arrow-shaped welts from a bouncing Betty on my thigh; the puckered indentation below my collarbone where a .38 round had cored through my shoulder.

They were not wounds received in a heroic fashion, either. In each case I got them because I did something that was careless or impetuous. I also had tried to destroy myself in increments, a jigger at a time.

Get outside your thoughts, partner, I told myself. I waved to the bridge tender in his tiny house at the far end of the bridge and headed for home.

I poured it on the last half mile, then stopped at the dock and did fifty pushups and stomach crunches on the wood planks that still glowed with the day's heat and smelled of dried fish scales.

I walked up the incline through the trees and the layer of moldy leaves and pecan husks toward the lighted gallery of my house. Then I heard a car behind me on the dirt road and I turned and saw a taxicab stop by my mailbox. A man and woman got out, then the man paid the driver and sent him back toward town.

I rubbed the salt out of my eyes with my forearm and stared through the gloom. The man drained the foam out of a long-necked beer bottle and set the empty behind a tree trunk. Then the woman touched him on the shoulder and pointed toward me.

'Hey, there you are,' Elrod Sykes said. 'How you doin', Mr Robicheaux? You don't mind us coming out, do you? Wow, you've got a great place.'

He swayed slightly. The woman, Kelly Drummond, caught him by the arm. I walked back down the slope.

'I'm afraid I was just going in to take a shower and eat supper,' I said.

'We want to take y'all to dinner,' he said. 'There's this place called Mulate's in Breaux Bridge. They make gumbo you could start a new religion with.'

'Thanks, anyway. My wife's already fixed supper.'

'Bad time of day to knock on doors, El,' Kelly Drummond said, but she looked at me when she said it, her eyes fixed directly on mine. She wore tan slacks, flats, and a yellow blouse with a button open that exposed her bra. When she raised her hand to move a blond ringlet off her forehead, you could see a half-moon sweat stain under her arm.

'We didn't mean to cause a problem,' Elrod said. 'I'm afraid a drunk-front blew through the area this afternoon. Hey, we're all right, though. We took a cab. Did you notice that? How about that? Look, I tell you what, we'll just get us some liquids to go down at that bait shop yonder and call us a cab.'

'Tell him why you came out, El,' Kelly Drummond said.

'That's all right. We stumbled in at a bad time. I'm real sorry, Mr Robicheaux.'

'Call me Dave. Would you mind waiting for me at the bait shop a few minutes, then I'll shower and drive y'all home.'

'You sure know how to avoid the stereotypes, don't you?' the woman said.

'I beg your pardon?' I said.

'Nobody can ever beat up on you for showing off your southern hospitality,' she said.

'Hey, it's okay,' Elrod said, turning her by the arm toward the bait shop.

I had gone only a short distance up the slope when I heard the woman's footsteps behind me.

'Just hold on a minute, Dick Tracy,' she said.

Behind her I could see Elrod walking down the dock to the shop, where Batist, the black man who worked for me, was drawing back the canvas awning over the tables for the night.

'Look, Ms Drummond—'

'You don't have to invite us into your house, you don't have to believe the stuff he says about what he sees and hears, but you ought to know that it took guts for him to come out here. He fucks up with Mikey, he fucks up with this film, maybe he blows it for good this time.'

'You'll have to excuse me, but I'm not sure what that has to do with the Iberia Parish Sheriff's Department.'

She carried a doeskin drawstring bag in her hand. She propped her hand on her hip. She looked up at me and ran her tongue over her bottom lip.

'Are you that dumb?' she asked.

'You're telling me a mob guy, maybe Baby Feet Balboni, is involved with your movie?'

'A mob guy? That's good. I bet y'all really send a lot of them up the road.'

'Where are you from, Ms Drummond?'

'East Kentucky.'

'Have you thought about making your next movie there?'

I started toward the house again.

'Wait a minute, Mr Smart Ass,' she said. 'Elrod respects you. Did you ever hear of the Chicken Ranch in LaGrange, Texas?'

'Yes.'

'Do you know what it was?'

'It was a hot-pillow joint.'

'His mother was a prostitute there. That's why he never talks about anyone in his family except his gran'daddy, the Texas ranger. That's why he likes you, and you'd damn well better be aware of it.'

She turned on her heel, her doeskin bag hitting her rump, and walked erectly down the slope toward the bait shop, where I could see Elrod opening a beer with his pocket knife under the light bulb above the screen door.

Well, you could do a lot worse than have one like her on your side, Elrod, I thought.

I took a shower, dried off, and was buttoning on a fresh shirt in the kitchen when the telephone rang on the counter. Bootsie put down a pan on the stove and answered it.

'It's Batist,' she said, and handed it to me.

'*Qui t'as pr'est faire?*' I said into the receiver.

'Some drunk white man down here done fell in the bayou,' he said.

'What's he doing now?'

'Sittin' in the middle of the shop, drippin' water on my flo'.'

'I'll be there in a minute,' I said.

'Dave, a lady wit' him was smokin' a cigarette out on the dock didn't smell like no tobacco, no.'

'All right, podna. Thanks,' I said, and hung up the phone.

Bootsie was looking at me with a question mark in the middle of her face. Her auburn hair, which she had pinned up in swirls on her head, was full of tiny lights.

'A man fell in the bayou. I have to drive him and his girlfriend home,' I said.

'Where's their car?'

'They came out in a cab.'

'A cab? Who comes fishing in a cab?'

'He's a weird guy.'

'*Dave*—' she said, drawing my name out in exasperation.

'He's one of those actors working out at Spanish Lake. I guess he came out here to tell me about something.'

'Which actor?'

'Elrod Sykes.'

'*Elrod Sykes* is out at the bait shop?'

'Yep.'

'Who's the woman with him?'

'Kelly Drummond.'

'Dave, I don't believe it. You left Kelly Drummond and Elrod Sykes in the bait shop? You didn't invite them in?'

'He's bombed, Boots.'

'I don't care. They came out to see you and you left them in the shop while you took a shower?'

'Bootsie, this guy's head glows in the dark, even when he's not on chemicals.'

She went out the front door and down the slope to the bayou. In the mauve twilight I could see her touching at her hair before she entered the bait shop. Five minutes later Kelly Drummond was sitting at our kitchen table, a cup of coffee balanced in her fingers, a reefer-induced wistfulness on her face, while Elrod Sykes changed into dry clothes in our bedroom. He walked into the kitchen in a pair of my sandals, khaki trousers, and the Ragin' Cajuns T-shirt, with my name ironed on the back, that Alafair had given me for Father's Day.

His face was flushed with gin roses, and his gaze drifted automatically to the icebox.

'Would you like a beer?' Bootsie said.

'Yes, if you wouldn't mind,' he said.

'Boots, I think we're out,' I said.

'Oh, that's all right. I really don't need one,' he said.

Bootsie's eyes were bright with embarrassment. Then I saw her face set.

'I'm sure there's one back in here somewhere,' she said, then slid a long-necked Dixie out of the bottom shelf and opened it for him.

Elrod looked casually out the back door while he sipped from the bottle.

'I have to feed the rabbits. You want to take a walk with me, Elrod?' I said.

'The rice will be ready in a minute,' Bootsie said.

'That's all it'll take,' I said.

Outside, under the pecan trees that were now black-green in the fading light, I could feel Elrod watching the side of my face.

'Boy, I don't know quite what to say, Mr Robicheaux, I mean Dave.'

'Don't worry about it. Just tell me what it is you had on your mind all day.'

'It's these guys out yonder on that lake. I told you before.'

'Which guys? What are you talking about?'

'Confederate infantry. One guy in particular, with gold epaulets on his coat. He's got a bad arm and he's missing a leg. I think maybe he's a general.'

'I'll be straight with you. I think maybe you're delusional.'

'A lot of people do. I just didn't think I'd get the same kind of bullshit from you.'

'I'd appreciate it if you didn't use profanity around my home.'

'I apologize. But that Confederate officer was saying something. It didn't make sense to me, but I thought it might to you.'

I filled one of the rabbit bowls with alfalfa pellets and latched the screen door on the hutch. I looked at Elrod Sykes. His face was absolutely devoid of guile or any apparent attempt at manipulation; in fact, it reminded me of someone who might have just been struck in the head by a bolt of lightning.

'Look, Elrod, years ago, when I was on the grog, I believed dead people called me up on the telephone. Sometimes my dead wife or members of my platoon would talk to me out of the rain. I was convinced that their voices were real and that maybe I was supposed to join them. It wasn't a good way to be.'

He poured the foam out of his bottle, then flicked the remaining drops reflectively at the bark of a pecan tree.

'I wasn't drunk,' he said. 'This guy with the bad arm and one leg, he said to me, "You and your friend, the police officer in town, must repel them." He was standing by the water, in the fog, on a crutch. He looked right in my face when he said it.'

'I see.'

'What do you think he meant?'

'I'm afraid I wouldn't know, partner.'

'I got the notion he thought you would.'

'I don't want to hurt your feelings, but I think you're imagining all this and I'm not going to pursue it any further. Instead, how about your clarifying something Ms Drummond said earlier?'

'What's that?'

'Why is it a problem to your director, this fellow Mikey, if you come out to my place?'

'She told you that?'

'That's what the lady said.'

'Well, the way he put it was, "Stay out of that cop's face, El. Don't give him reason to be out here causing us trouble. We need to remember that a lot of things happened in this part of the country that are none of our business."'

'He's worried about the dead black man you found?' I said. 'That doesn't make too much sense.'

'You got another one of these?' he said, and held up his empty bottle.

'Why is he worried about the black man?'

'When Mikey worries, it's about money, Mr Robicheaux. Or actually about the money he needs to make the kind of pictures he wants. He did a mini-series for television on the Holocaust. It lost ten million dollars for the network. Nobody's lining up to throw money at Mikey's projects right now.'

'Julie Balboni is.'

'You ever heard of a college turning down money from a defense company because it makes napalm?'

He opened and closed his mouth as though he were experiencing cabin pressure in an airplane. The moon was up now, and in the glow of light through the tree branches the skin of his face looked pale and grained, stretched tight against the bone. 'Mr Robicheaux . . . Dave . . . I'm being honest with you, I need a drink.'

'We'd better go inside and get you one, then. I'll make you a deal, though. Maybe you might want to think about going to a meeting with me. I don't necessarily mean that you belong there. But some people think it beats waking up like a chainsaw every morning.'

He looked away at a lighted boat on the bayou.

'It's just a thought. I didn't mean to be intrusive,' I said. 'Let's go inside.'

'You ever see lights out in the cypress trees at night?'

'It's swamp gas. It ignites and rolls across the water's surface like ball lightning.'

'No, sir, that's not what it is,' he said. 'They had lanterns hanging on some of their ambulances. The horses got mired in the bogs. A lot of those soldiers had maggots in their wounds. That's the only reason they lived. The maggots ate out the infection.'

I wasn't going to talk any more about the strange psychological terrain that evidently he had created as a petting zoo for all the protean shapes that lived in his unconscious.

I put the bag of alfalfa pellets on top of the hutches and turned to go back to the house.

'That general said something else,' Elrod said behind me.

I waved my hand negatively and kept walking.

'Well, I cain't blame you for not listening,' he said. 'Maybe I *was* drunk this time. How could your father have his adjutant's pistol?'

I stopped.

'What?' I said.

'The general said, "Your friend's father took the revolver of my adjutant, Major Moss." . . . Hey, Mr Robicheaux, I didn't mean to say the wrong thing, now.'

I chewed on the corner of my lip and waited before I spoke again.

'Elrod, I've got the feeling that maybe I'm dealing with some kind of self-manufactured mojo-drama here,' I said. 'Maybe it's related to the promotion of your film, or it might have something to do with a guy floating his brain in alcohol too long. But no matter how you cut it, I don't want anyone, and I mean *anyone*, to try to use a member of my family to jerk me around.'

He turned his palms up and his long eyelashes fluttered.

'I don't know what to say. I apologize to you, sir,' he said. Then his eyes focused on nothing and he pinched his mouth in his hand as though he were squeezing a dry lemon.

At eleven that night I undressed and lay down on the bed next to Bootsie. The window fan billowed the curtains and drew the breeze across the streets, and I could smell watermelons and night-blooming jasmine out in the moonlight. The closet door was open, and I stared at the wooden footlocker that was set back under my hangered shirts and trousers. Bootsie turned her head on the pillow and brushed her fingers along the side of my face.

'Are you mad at me?' she asked.

'No, of course not.'

'They seem to be truly nice people. It would have been wrong not to invite them in.'

'Yeah, they're not bad.'

'But when you came back inside with Elrod, you looked bothered about something. Did something happen?'

'He says he talks with dead people. Maybe he's crazy. I don't know, Boots, I—'

'What is it, Dave?' She raised herself on her elbow and looked into my face.

'He said this dead Confederate general told him that my father took his adjutant's revolver.'

'He had too much to drink, that's all.'

I continued to stare at the closet. She smiled at me and pressed her body against me.

'You had a long day. You're tired,' she said. 'He didn't mean any harm. He probably won't remember what he said tomorrow.'

'You don't understand, Boots,' I said, and sat up on the edge of the bed.

'Understand what?' She put her hand on my bare back. 'Dave, your muscles are tight as iron. What's the matter?'

'Just a minute.'

I didn't want to fall prey to superstition or my own imaginings or Elrod Sykes's manipulations. But I did. I clicked on the table lamp and pulled my old footlocker out of the closet. Inside a half-dozen shoe boxes at the bottom were the memorabilia of my childhood years with my father back in the 1940s: my collections of baseball cards, Indian banner stones and quartz arrow points, and the minié balls that we used to find in a freshly plowed sugarcane field right after the first rain.

I took out a crushed shoe box that was tied with kite twine and sat back down on the bed with it. I slipped off the twine, removed the top of the box, and set it on the nightstand.

'This was the best gift my father ever gave me,' I said. 'On my brother's and my birthday he'd always fix *cush-cush* and sausage for our breakfast, and we'd always find an unusual present waiting for us by our plate. On my twelfth birthday I got this.'

I lifted the heavy revolver out of the box and unwrapped the blackened oil rag from it.

'He had been laid off in the oil field and he took a job tearing down some old slave quarters on a sugar plantation about ten miles down the bayou. There was one cabin separate from the others, with a brick foundation, and he figured it must have belonged to the overseer. Anyway, when he started tearing the boards out of the walls he found some flattened minié balls in the wood, and he knew there had probably been a skirmish between some federals and Confederates around there. Then he tore out what was left of the floor, and in a crawl space, stuck back in the bricks, was this Remington .44 revolver.'

It had been painted with rust and cobweb when my father had found it, the cylinder and hammer frozen against the frame, the wood grips eaten away by mold and insects, but I had soaked it for a week in gasoline and rubbed the steel smooth with emery paper and rags until it had the dull sheen of an old nickel.

'It's just an antique pistol your father gave you, Dave,' she said. 'Maybe you said something about it to Elrod. Then he got drunk and mixed it up with some kind of fantasy he has.'

'No, he said the officer's name.' I opened the nightstand drawer and took out a small magnifying glass. 'He said it had belonged to a Major Moss.'

'So what?'

'Boots, there's a name cut into the trigger guard. I haven't thought about it in years. I couldn't have mentioned it to him.'

I rested the revolver across my thighs and looked through the magnifying glass at the soft glow of light off the brass housing around the trigger. The steel felt cold and slick with oil against my thighs.

'Take a look,' I said, and handed her the glass and the revolver.

She folded her legs under her and squinted one eye through the glass. 'It says "CSA," ' she said.

'Wrong place. Right at the back of the guard.'

She held the pistol closer to the glass. Then she looked up at me and there were white spots in her cheeks.

'J. Moss.' Her voice was dry when she said it. Then she said the name again. 'It says J. Moss.'

'It sure does.'

She wrapped the blackened oil cloth around the pistol and replaced it in the shoe box. She put her hand in mine and squeezed it.

'Dave?'

'Yes?'

'I think Elrod Sykes is a nice man, but we mustn't have him here again.'

She turned out the light, lay back on the pillow, and looked out at the moonlight in the pecan trees, her face caught with a private, troubled thought like the silent beating of a bird's wings inside a cage.

5

Early the next morning the sheriff stopped me in the corridor as I was on my way to my office.

'Special Agent Gomez is here,' he said. A smile worked at the corner of his mouth.

'Where?'

'In your office.'

'So?'

'I think it's a break the FBI's working with us on this one.'

'You told me that before.'

'Yeah, I did, didn't I?' His eyes grew brighter, then he looked away and laughed out loud.

'What's the big joke?' I asked.

'Nothing.' He rubbed his lips with his knuckle, and his eyes kept crinkling at the corners.

'Let me ask you something between insider jokes,' I said. 'Why is the FBI coming in on this one so early? They don't have enough work to do with the resident wiseguys in New Orleans?'

'That's a good question, Dave. Ask Agent Gomez about that and give me feedback later.' He walked off smiling to himself. Uniformed deputies in the corridor were smiling back at him.

I picked up my mail, walked through my office door, and stared at the woman who was sitting in my chair and talking on my telephone. She was looking out the window at a mockingbird on a tree limb while she talked. She turned her head long enough to point to a chair where I could sit down if I wished.

She was short and dark-skinned, and her thick, black hair was chopped stiffly along her neck. Her white suit coat hung on the back of my chair. There was a huge silk bow on her blouse of the sort that Bugs Bunny might wear.

Her eyes flicked back at me again, and she took the telephone receiver away from her ear and slipped her hand over the mouthpiece.

'Have a seat. I'll be right with you,' she said.

'Thank you,' I said.

I sat down, looked idly through my mail, and a moment later heard her put down the phone receiver.

'Can I help you with something?' she asked.

'Maybe. My name's Dave Robicheaux. This is my office.'

Her face colored.

'I'm sorry,' she said. 'A call came in for me on your extension, and I automatically sat behind your desk.'

'It's all right.'

She stood up and straightened her shoulders. Her breasts looked unnaturally large and heavy for a woman her height. She picked up her purse and walked around the desk.

'I'm Special Agent Rosa Gomez,' she said. Then she stuck her hand out, as though her motor control was out of sync with her words.

'It's nice to know you,' I said.

'I think they're putting a desk in here for me.'

'Oh?'

'Do you mind?'

'No, not at all. It's very nice to have you here.'

She remained standing, both of her hands on her purse, her shoulders as rigid as a coat hanger.

'Why don't you sit down, Ms . . . Agent Gomez?'

'Call me Rosie. Everyone calls me Rosie.'

I sat down behind my desk, then noticed that she was looking at the side of my head. Involuntarily I touched my hair.

'You've been with the Bureau a long time?' I said.

'Not really.'

'So you're fairly new?'

'Well, just to this kind of assignment. I mean, out in the field, that sort of thing.' Her hands looked small on top of her big purse. I think it took everything in her to prevent them from clenching with anxiety. Then her eyes focused again on the side of my head.

'I have a white patch in my hair,' I said.

She closed then opened her eyes with embarrassment.

'Someone once told me I have skunk blood in me,' I said.

'I think I'm doing a lot of wrong things this morning,' she said.

'No, you're not.'

But somebody at Fart, Barf, and Itch is, I thought.

Then she sat erect in her chair and concentrated her vision on something outside the window until her face became composed again.

'The sheriff said you don't believe we're dealing with a serial killer or a random killing,' she said.

'That's not quite how I put it. I told him, I think she knew the killer.'

'Why?'

'Her father appears to have been a child molester. She was streetwise herself. She had one prostitution beef when she was sixteen. Yesterday I found out she was still hooking – out of a club in St Martinville. A girl like that doesn't usually get forced into cars in front of crowded jukejoints.'

'Maybe she went off with a john.'

'Not without her purse. She left it at her table. In it we found some—'

'Rubbers,' she said.

'That's right. So I don't think it was a john. In her car we found a carton of cigarettes, a brand-new hairbrush, and a half-dozen joints in a Baggy in the trunk. I think she went outside to get some cigarettes, a joint, or the hairbrush, she saw somebody she knew, got in his car, and never came back.'

'Maybe it was an old customer, somebody she trusted. Maybe he told her he just wanted to get something up for later.'

'It doesn't fit. A john doesn't pay one time, then come back the next time with a razor blade or scalpel.'

She put her thumbnail between her teeth. Her eyes were brown and had small lights in them.

'Then you think the killer is from this area, she knew him, and she trusted him enough to get in the car with him?'

'I think it's something like that.'

'We think he's a psychopath, possibly a serial killer.'

'*We*?'

'Well, actually *I*. I had a behavioral profile run on him. Everything he did indicates a personality that seeks control and dominance. During the abduction, the rape, the killing itself, he was absolutely in control. He becomes sexually aroused by power, by instilling fear and loathing in a woman, by being able to smother her with his body. In all probability he has ice water in his veins.'

I nodded and moved some paper clips around on my desk blotter.

'You don't seem impressed,' she said.

'What do you make of the fact that he covered her face with her blouse?' I said.

'Blindfolding humiliates the victim and inspires even greater terror in her.'

'Yeah, I guess it does.'

'But you don't buy the profile.'

'I'm not too keen on psychoanalysis. I belong to a twelve-step fellowship that subscribes to the notion that most bad or evil behavior is generated by what we call a self-centered fear. I think our man was afraid of Cherry LeBlanc. I don't think he could look into her eyes while he raped her.'

She reached for a folder she had left on the corner of my desk.

'Do you know how many similar unsolved murders of women have been committed in the state of Louisiana in the last twenty-five years?'

'I sent in an information-search request to Baton Rouge yesterday.'

'We have an unfair advantage on you in terms of resources,' she said. She leafed through the printouts that were clipped together at the top of the folder. Behind her, I saw two uniformed deputies grinning at me through the glass in my office partition.

'Excuse me,' I said, got up, closed the door, and sat back down again.

'Is this place full of comedians?' she said. 'I seem to make a lot of people smile.'

'Some of them don't get a lot of exposure to the outside world.'

'Anyway, narrowing it down to the last ten years, there are at least seventeen unsolved homicides involving females that share some similarity with the murder of Cherry LeBlanc. You want to take a look?' she said, and handed me the folder. 'I have to go down to the sheriff's office and get my building keys. I'll be right back.'

It was grim material to read. There was nothing abstruse about the prose. It was unimaginative, flat, brutally casual in its depiction of the bestial potential among the human family, like a banal rendering of our worst nightmares: slasher cases, usually involving prostitutes; the garroting of housewives who had been abducted in broad daylight in supermarket and bowling-alley parking lots; the roadside murders of women whose cars had broken down at night; prostitutes who had probably been set on fire by their pimps; the drowning of two black women who had been wrapped to an automobile engine block with barbed wire.

In almost all the cases rape, sodomy, or torture of some kind was involved. And what bothered me most was the fact that the perpetrators were probably still out there, unless they were doing time for other crimes; few of them had known their victims, and consequently few of them would ever be caught.

Then I noticed that Rosie Gomez had made check marks in the margins by six cases that shared more common denominators with the death of Cherry LeBlanc than the others: three runaways who had been found buried off highways in a woods; a high school girl who had been raped, tied to a tree in a fish camp at Lake Chicot, and shot at point-blank range; two waitresses who had gone off from their jobs without explanation and a few hours later had been thrown, bludgeoned to death, into irrigation ditches.

Their bodies had all showed marks, in one way or another, of having been bound. They all had been young, working class, and perhaps unsuspecting when a degenerate had come violently and irrevocably into their lives and had departed without leaving a sign of his identity.

My respect for Rosie Gomez's ability was appreciating.

She walked back through the door, clipping two keys onto a ring.

'You want to talk while we take a ride out to Spanish Lake?' I said.

'What's at Spanish Lake?'

'A movie director I'd like to meet.'

'What's that have to do with our case?'

'Probably nothing. But it beats staying indoors.'

'Sure. I have to make a call to the Bureau, then I'll be right with you.'

'Let me ask you an unrelated question,' I said.

'Sure.'

'If you found the remains of a black man, and he had on no belt and there were no laces in his boots, what speculation might you make about him?'

She looked at me with a quizzical smile.

'He was poor?' she said.

'Could be. In fact, someone else told me about the same thing in a less charitable way.'

'No,' she said. She looked thoughtfully into space, puffed out one jaw, then the other, like a chipmunk might. 'No, I'd bet he'd been in jail, in a parish or a city holding unit of some kind, where they were afraid he'd do harm to himself.'

'That's not bad,' I said. Not at all, I thought. 'Well, let's take a ride.'

I waited for her outside in the shade of the building. I was sweating inside my shirt, and the sunlight off the cement parking lot made my eyes film. Two of the uniformed deputies who had been grinning through my glass earlier came out the door with clipboards in their hands, then stopped when they saw me. The taller one, a man named Rufus Arceneaux, took a matchstick out of his mouth and smiled at me from behind his shades.

'Hey, Dave,' he said, 'does that gal wear a Bureau buzzer on each of her boobs or is she just a little top-heavy?'

They were both grinning now. I could hear bottleflies buzzing above an iron grate in the shade of the building.

'You guys can take this for what it's worth,' I said. 'I don't want you to hold it against me, either, just because I outrank you or something like that. Okay?'

'You gotta make plainclothes before you get any federal snatch?' Arceneaux said, and put the matchstick back in the corner of his mouth.

I put on my sunglasses, folded my seersucker coat over my arm, and looked across the street at a black man selling rattlesnake watermelons off the tailgate of a pickup truck.

'If y'all want to act like public clowns, that's your business,' I said. 'But you'd better wipe that stupid expression off your faces when you're around my partner. Also, if I hear you making remarks about her, either to me or somebody else, we're going to take it up in a serious way. You get my drift?'

Arceneaux rotated his head on his neck, then pulled the front of his shirt loose from his damp skin with his fingers.

'Boy, it's hot, ain't it?' he said. 'I think I'm gonna come in this afternoon and take a cold shower. You ought to try it too, Dave. A cold shower might get the wrong thing off your mind.'

They walked into the shimmering haze, their leather holsters and cartridge belts creaking on their hips, the backs of their shirts peppered with sweat.

Rosie Gomez and I turned off the highway in my pickup truck and drove down the dirt lane through the pecan orchard toward Spanish Lake, where we could see elevated camera platforms and camera booms silhouetted against the sun's reflection on the water. A chain was hung across the road between a post and the side of the wood-frame security building. The security guard, the wiry man with the white scar embossed on his throat like a chicken's foot, approached my window. His face looked pinched and heated in the shadow of his bill cap.

I showed him my badge.

'Yeah, y'all go on in,' he said. 'You remember me, Detective Robicheaux?'

His hair was gray, cut close to the scalp, and his skin was browned and as coarse as a lizard's from the sun. His blue eyes seemed to have an optical defect of some kind, a nervous shudder like marbles clicking on a plate.

'It's Doucet, isn't it?' I said.

'Yes, sir, Murphy Doucet. You got a good memory. I used to be with the Jefferson Parish Sheriff's Department when you were with NOPD.'

His stomach was as flat as a shingle. He wore a .357 chromeplated revolver, and also a clip-on radio, a can of Mace, and a rubber baton on his belt.

'It looks like you're in the movie business now,' I said.

'Just for a while. I own half of a security service now and I'm a steward for the Teamsters out of Lafayette, too. So I'm kind of on board both ways here.'

'This is Special Agent Gomez from the FBI. We'd like to talk to Mr Goldman a few minutes if he's not too busy.'

'Is there been some kind of trouble?'

'Is Mr Goldman here?'

'Yes, sir, that's him right up yonder in the trees. I'll tell him y'all on your way.' He started to take his radio off his belt.

'That's all right. We'll find him.'

'Yes, sir, anything you say.'

He dropped the chain and waited for us to pass. In the rearview mirror I saw him hook it to the post again. Rosie Gomez was looking at the side of my face.

'What is it?' she said.

'The Teamsters. Why does a Hollywood production company want to come into a depressed rural area and contract for services from the Teamsters? They can hire labor around here for minimum wage.'

'Maybe they do business with unions as a matter of course.'

'Nope, they usually try to leave their unions back in California. I've got a feeling this has something to do with Julie Balboni being on board the ark.'

I watched her expression. She looked straight ahead.

'You know who Baby Feet Balboni is, don't you?' I said.

'Yes, Mr Balboni is well known to us.'

'You know he's in New Iberia, too, don't you?'

She waited before she spoke again. Her small hands were clenched on her purse.

'What's your implication?' she said.

'I think the Bureau has more than one reason for being in town.'

'You think the girl's murder has secondary importance to me?'

'No, not to you.'

'But probably to the people I work under?'

'You'd know that better than I.'

'You don't think well of us, do you?'

'My experience with the Bureau was never too good. But maybe the problem was mine. As the Bible says, I used to look through a glass darkly. Primarily because there was Jim Beam in it most of the time.'

'The Bureau's changed.'

'Yeah, I guess it has.'

Yes, I thought, they hired racial minorities and women at gunpoint, and they stopped wire-tapping civil-rights leaders and smearing innocent people's reputations after their years of illegal surveillance and character assassination were finally exposed.

I parked the truck in the shade of a moss-hung live-oak tree, and we walked toward the shore of the lake, where a dozen people listened attentively to a man in a canvas chair who waved his arms while he talked, jabbed his finger in the air to make a point, and shrugged his powerful shoulders as though he were desperate in his desire to be understood. His voice, his manner, made me think of a hurricane stuffed inside a pair of white tennis shorts and a dark-blue polo shirt.

'—the best fucking story editor in that fucking town,' he was saying. 'I don't care what those assholes say, they couldn't carry my fucking jock strap. When we come out of the cutting room with that, it's going to be solid fucking gold. Has everybody got that? This is a great picture. Believe it, they're going to spot their pants big time on this one.'

His strained face looked like a white balloon that was about to burst. But even while his histrionics grew to awesome levels and inspired mute reverence in his listeners, his eyes drifted to me and Rosie, and I had a feeling that Murphy Doucet, the security guard, had used his radio after all.

When we introduced ourselves and showed him our identification, he said, 'Do you have telephones where you work?'

'I beg your pardon?' I said.

'Do you have telephones where you work? Do you have people there who know how to make appointments for you?'

'Maybe you don't understand, Mr Goldman. During a criminal investigation we don't make appointments to talk to people.'

His face flexed as though it were made of white rubber.

'You saying you're out here investigating some crime? What crime we talking about here?' he said. 'You see a crime around here?' He swiveled his head around. 'I don't see one.'

'We can talk down at the sheriff's office if you wish,' Rosie said.

He stared at her as though she had stepped through a hole in the dimension.

'Do you have any idea of what it costs to keep one hundred and fifty people standing around while I'm playing pocket pool with somebody's *criminal* investigation?' he said.

'You heard what she said. What's it going to be, partner?' I asked.

'*Partner?*' he said, looking out at the lake with a kind of melancholy disbelief on his face. 'I think I screwed up in an earlier incarnation. I probably had something to do with the sinking of the *Titanic* or the assassination of the Archduke Ferdinand. That's gotta be it.'

Then he rose and faced me with the flat glare of a boxer waiting for the referee to finish with the ring instructions.

'You want to take a walk or go in my trailer?' he said. 'The air conditioner in my trailer is broken. You could fry eggs on the toilet seat. What d'you want to do?'

'This is fine,' I said.

'Fine, huh?' he said, as though he were addressing some cynical store of private knowledge within himself. 'What is it you want to say, Mr Robicheaux?'

He walked along the bank of the lake, his hair curling out of his polo shirt like bronze wire. His white tennis shorts seemed about to rip at the seams on his muscular buttocks and thighs.

'I understand that you've cautioned some of your people to stay away from me. Is that correct?' I said.

'What people? What are you talking about?'

'I believe you know what I'm talking about.'

'Elrod and his voices out in the fog? Elrod and skeletons buried in a sandbar? You think I care about stuff like that? You think that's what's on my mind when I'm making a picture?' He stopped and jabbed a thick finger at me. 'Hey, try to understand something here. I live with my balls in a skillet. It's a way of life. I got no interest, I got no involvement, in people's problems in a certain locale. Is that supposed to be bad? Is it all right for me to tell my actors what I think? Are we all still working on a First Amendment basis here?'

A group of actors in sweat-streaked gray and blue uniforms, eating hamburgers out of foam containers, walked past us. I turned and suddenly realized that Rosie was no longer with us.

'She probably stepped in a hole,' Goldman said.

'I think you *are* worried about something, Mr Goldman. I think we both know what it is, too.'

He took a deep breath. The sunlight shone through the oak branches over his head and made shifting patterns of shadow on his face.

'Let me try to explain something to you,' he said. 'Most everything in the film world is an illusion. An actor is somebody who never liked what he was. So he makes up a person and that's what he becomes. You think John Wayne came out of the womb John Wayne? He and a screenwriter created a character that was a cross between Captain Bly and Saint Francis of Assisi, and the Duke played it till he dropped.

'Elrod's convinced himself he has magic powers. Why? Because he melted his head five years ago and he has days when he can't tie his shoestrings without a diagram. So instead of admitting that maybe he's got baked mush between his ears, he's a mystic, a persecuted clairvoyant.'

'Let's cut the dog shit, Mr Goldman. You're in business with Baby Feet Balboni. *That's* your problem, not Elrod Sykes.'

'Wrong.'

'You know what a "fall partner" is?'

'No.'

'A guy who goes down on the same bust with you.'

'So?'

'Julie doesn't have fall partners. His hookers do parish time for him, his dealers do it for him in Angola, his accountants do it in Atlanta and Lewisburg. I don't think Julie has ever spent a whole day in the bag.'

'Neither have I. Because I don't break the law.'

'I think he'll cannibalize you.'

He looked away from me, and I saw his hands clench and unclench and the veins pulse in his neck.

'You look here,' he said. 'I worked nine years on a mini-series about the murder of six million people. I went to Auschwitz and set up cameras on the same spots the SS used to photograph the people being pulled out of the boxcars and herded with dogs to the ovens. I've had survivors tell me I'm the only person who ever described on film what they actually went through. I don't give a fuck what any critic says, that series will last a thousand years. You get something straight, Mr Robicheaux. People might fuck me over as an individual, but they'll never fuck me over as a director. You can take that to the bank.'

His pale eyes protruded from his head like marbles.

I looked back at him silently.

'There's something else?' he said.

'No, not really.'

'So why the stare? What's going on?'

'Nothing. I think you're probably a sincere man. But as someone once told me, hubris is a character defect better left to the writers of tragedy.'

He pressed his fingers on his chest.

'I got a problem with pride, you're saying?'

'I think Jimmy Hoffa was probably the toughest guy the labor movement ever produced,' I said. 'Then evidently he decided that he and the mob could have a fling at the dirty boogie together. I used to know a button man in New Orleans who told me they cut Hoffa into hundreds of pieces and used him for fish chum. I believe what he said, too.'

'Sounds like your friend ought to take it to a grand jury.'

'He can't. Three years ago one of Julie's hired lowlifes put a crack in his skull with a cold chisel. Just for kicks. He sells snowballs out of a cart in front of the K & B drugstore on St Charles now. We'll see you around, Mr Goldman.'

I walked away through the dead leaves and over a series of rubber-coated power cables that looked like a tangle of black snakes. When I looked back at Mikey Goldman, his eyes were staring disjointedly into space.

6

Rosie was waiting for me by the side of the pickup truck under the live-oak tree. The young sugarcane in the fields was green and bending in the wind. She fanned herself with a manila folder she had picked up off the truck seat.

'Where did you go?' I asked.

'To talk to Hogman Patin.'

'Where is he?'

'Over there, with those other black people, under the trees. He's playing a street musician in the film.'

'How'd you know to talk to him?'

'You put his name in the case file, and I recognized him from his picture on one of his albums.'

'You're quite a cop, Rosie.'

'Oh, I see. You didn't expect that from an agent who's short, Chicana, and a woman?'

'It was meant as a compliment. How about saving that stuff for the right people? What did Hogman have to say?'

Her eyes blinked at the abruptness of my tone.

'I'm sorry,' I said. 'I didn't mean to sound like that. I still have my mind on Goldman. I think he's hiding some serious problems, and I think they're with Julie Balboni. I also think there might be a tie-in between Julie and Cherry LeBlanc.'

She looked off at the group of black people under the trees.

'You didn't bother to tell me that earlier,' she said.

'I wasn't sure about it. I'm still not.'

'Dave, I'll be frank with you. Before I came here I read some of your history. You seem to have a way of doing things on your own. Maybe you've been in situations where you had no other choice. But I can't have a partner who holds out information on me.'

'It's a speculation, Rosie, and I just told you about it.'

'Where do you think there might be a tie-in?' she said, and her face became clear again.

'I'm not sure. But one of his hoods, a character named Cholo Manelli, told me that he and Julie had been talking about the girl's death. Then ten minutes later Julie told me he hadn't heard or read anything about it. So one of them is lying, and I think it's Julie.'

'Why not the hood, what's his name, Cholo?'

'When a guy like Cholo lies or tries to jerk somebody around, he doesn't involve his boss's name. He has no doubt about how dangerous that can be. Anyway, what did you get from Hogman?'

'Not much. He just pointed at you and said, "Tell that other one yonder ain't every person innocent, ain't every person listen when they ought to, either." What do you make of that?'

'Hogman likes to be an enigma.'

'Those scars on his arms—'

'He had a bunch of knife beefs in Angola. Back in the 1940s he murdered a white burial-insurance collector who was sleeping with his wife. Hogman's a piece of work, believe me. The hacks didn't know how to deal with him. They put him in the sweat box on Camp A for eighteen days one time.'

'How'd he kill the white man?'

'With a cane knife on the white man's front gallery. In broad daylight. People around here talked about that one for a long time.'

I could see a thought working in her eyes.

'He's not a viable suspect, Rosie,' I said.

'Why not?'

'Hogman's not a bad guy. He doesn't trust white people much, and he's a little prideful, but he wouldn't hurt a nineteen-year-old girl.'

'That's it? *He's not a bad guy*? Although he seems to have a lifetime history of violence with knives? Good God.'

'Also the nightclub owner says Hogman never left the club that night.'

She got in the truck and closed the door. Her shoulders were almost below the level of the window. I got in on the driver's side and started the engine.

'Well, that clears all that up, then,' she said. 'I guess the owner kept his eyes on our man all night. You all certainly have an interesting way of conducting an investigation.'

'I'll make you a deal. I'll talk with Hogman again if you'll check out this fellow Murphy Doucet.'

'Because he's with the Teamsters?'

'That's right. Let's find out how these guys developed an interest in the War Between the States.'

'You know what "transfer" is in psychology?'

'What's the point?'

'Earlier you suggested that maybe I had a private agenda about Julie Balboni. Do you think that perhaps it's you who's taking the investigation into a secondary area?'

'Could be. But you can't ever tell what'll fly out of the tree until you throw a rock into it.'

It was a flippant thing to say. But at the time it seemed innocent and of little more consequence than the warm breeze blowing across the cane and the plum-colored thunderclouds that were building out over the Gulf.

Sam 'Hogman' Patin lived on the bayou south of town in a paintless wood-frame house overgrown with banana trees and with leaf-clogged rain gutters and screens that were orange with rust. The roof was patched with R. C. Cola signs, the yard a tangle of weeds, automobile and washing-machine parts, morning-glory vines, and pig bones; the gallery and one corner of the house sagged to one side like a broken smile.

I had waited until later in the day to talk to him at his house. I knew that he wouldn't have talked to me in front of other people at the movie set, and actually I wasn't even sure that he would tell me anything of importance now. He had served seventeen years in Angola, the first four of which he had spent on the Red Hat gang. These were the murderers, the psychotics, and the uncontrollable. They wore black-and-white stripes and straw hats that had been dipped in red paint, always ran double-time under the mounted gunbulls, and were punished on anthills, in cast-iron sweatboxes, or with the Black Betty, a leather whip that could flay a man's back to marmalade.

Hogman would probably still be in there, except he got religion and a Baptist preacher in Baton Rouge worked a pardon for him through the state legislature. His backyard was dirt, deep in shadow from the live-oak trees, and sloped away to the bayou, where a rotted-out pirogue webbed with green algae lay half-submerged in the shallows. He sat in a straight-backed wood chair under a tree that was strung with blue Milk of Magnesia bottles and crucifixes fashioned out of sticks and aluminum foil. When the breeze lifted out of the south, the whole tree sang with silver and blue light.

Hogman tightened the key on a new string he had just strung on his guitar. His skin was so black it had a purple sheen to it; and his hair was grizzled, the curls ironed flat against his head. His shoulders were an ax handle wide, the muscles in his upper arms the size of grapefruit. There wasn't a tablespoon of fat on his body. I wondered what it must have been like to face down Hogman Patin back in the days when he carried a barber's razor on a leather cord around his neck.

'What did you want to tell me, Sam?' I asked.

'One or two t'ings that been botherin' me. Get a chair off the po'ch. You want some tea?'

'No, that's fine, thank you.'

I lifted a wicker chair off the back porch and walked back to the oak tree with it. He had slipped three metal picks onto his fingers and was running a blues progression up the neck of the guitar. He mashed the strings into the frets so that the sound continued to reverberate through the dark wood after he had struck the notes with his steel picks. Then he tightened the key again and rested the big curved belly of the twelve-string on his thigh.

'I don't like to have no truck with folks' bidness,' he said. 'But it bother me, what somebody done to that girl. It been botherin' me a whole lot.'

He picked up from the dirt a jelly glass filled with iced tea and drank out of it.

'She was messin' in somet'ing bad, wouldn't listen to me or pay me no mind about it, neither. When they that age, they know what they wanta do.'

'Messing in what?'

'I talked to her maybe two hours befo' she left the juke. I been knowing that girl a long time. She love zydeco and blues music. She tell me, "Hogman, in the next life me and you is gonna get married." That's what she say. I tole her, "Darlin', don't let them mens use you for no chicken."

'She say, "I ain't no chicken, Hogman. I going to New Orleans. I gonna have my own coop. Them others gonna be the chickens. I gonna have me a townhouse on Lake Pontchartrain." '

'Wait a minute, Sam. She told you she was going to have other girls working for her?'

'That's what I just tole you, ain't I?'

'Yes, you did.'

'I say, "Don't be talkin' like that. You get away from them pimps, Cherry. Them white trash ain't gonna give you no townhouse. They'll use you up, t'row you away, then find some other girl just like you, I mean in five minutes, that quick."

'She say, "No, they ain't, 'cause I got the mojo on the Man, Hogman. He know it, too."

'You know, when she say that, she smile up at me and her face look heart shape, like she just a little girl doin' some innocent t'ing 'stead of about to get herself killed.'

'What man did she mean?'

'Probably some pimp tole her she special, she pretty, she just like a daughter to him. I seen the same t'ing in Angola. It ain't no different. A bunch take a young boy down on the flo', then when they get finish with him, he ready, he glad to put on a dress, make-up, be the punk for some wolf gonna take care of him, tell him he ain't just somebody's poke chops in the shower stall.'

'Why'd you wait to tell me this?'

''Cause ain't nothin' like this ever happen 'round here befo'. I don't like it, me. No, suh.'

'I see.'

He splayed his long fingers on the belly of the guitar. The nails were pink against his black skin. His eyes looked off reflectively at the bayou, where fireflies were lighting in the gloom above the flooded cattails.

Finally he said, 'I need to tell you somet'ing else.'

'Go ahead, Sam.'

'You mixed up with that skeleton they found over in the Atchafalaya, ain't you?'

'How'd you know about that?'

'When somebody find a dead black man, black people know about it. That man didn't have on no belt, didn't have no strings in his boots, did he?'

'That wasn't in the newspaper, podna.'

'The preacher they call up to do the burial is my first cousin. He brought a suit of clothes to the mo'tuary to dress the bones in. They was a black man workin' there, and my cousin say, "That fella was lynched, wasn't he?" The black man say, "Yeah, they probably drug him out of bed to do it, too. Didn't even have time to put strings in his boots or run a belt through his britches."'

'What are you telling me, Sam?'

'I remember somet'ing, a long time ago, maybe thirty, thirty-five years back.' He patted one hand on top of the other and his eyes became muddy.

'Just say it, Sam.'

'A bluejay don't set on a mockin'bird's nest. I ain't got no use for that stuff in people, neither. The Lord made people a different color for a reason.'

He shook his head back and forth, as though he were dispelling a troubling thought.

'You're not talking about a rape, are you?'

'White folk call it rape when it fit what they want,' he said. 'They see what they need to see. Black folk cain't be choicy. They see what they gots to see. They was a black man, no, that ain't right, this is a nigger I'm talkin' about, and he was carryin' on with a white woman whose husband he worked for. Black folk knowed it, too. They tole him he better stop what he doin' befo' the cars start comin' down in the quarters and some innocent black man end up on a tree. I t'ink them was the bones you drug up in that sandbar.'

'What was his name?'

'Who care what his name? Maybe he got what he ax for. But them people who done that still out there. I say past is past. I say don't be messin' in it.'

'Are you cautioning me?'

'When I was in the pen, yo' daddy, Mr Aldous, brought my mother food. He care for her when she sick, he pay for her medicine up at the sto'. I ain't forgot that, me.'

'Sam, if you have information about a murder, the law requires that you come forward with it.'

'Whose law? The law that run that pen up there? You want to find bodies, go dig in that levee for some of them boys the gunbulls shot down just for pure meanness. I seen it.' He touched the corner of his eye with one long finger. 'The hack get drunk on corn liquor, single out some boy on the wheelbarrow, hollor out, "Yow! You! Nigger! Run!" Then he'd pop him with his .45, just like bustin' a clay duck.'

'What was the white woman's name?'

'I got to be startin' my supper now.'

'Was the dead man in a jail?'

'Ain't nobody interested back then, ain't nobody interested now. You give it a few mo' years, we all gonna be dead. You ain't goin' change nothin' for a nigger been in the river thirty years. You want to do some good, catch the pimp tore up that young girl. 'Cause sho' as God made little green apples, he gonna do it again.'

He squinted one eye in a shaft of sunlight that fell through the tree branches and lighted one half of his face like an ebony stage mask that was sewn together from mismatched parts.

It was almost dusk when I got home that evening, but the sky was still as blue as a robin's egg in the west and the glow of the late sun looked like pools of pink fire in the clouds. After I ate supper, I walked down to the bait shop to help Batist close up. I was pulling back the canvas awning on the guy wires over the spool tables when I saw the sheriff's car drive down the dirt road and park under the trees.

He walked down the dock toward me. His face looked flushed from the heat, puffy with fatigue.

'I guarantee you, it's been one scorcher of a day,' he said, went inside the shop, and came back with a sweating bottle of orange pop in his hand. He sat down at a table and wiped the sweat off his neck with his handkerchief. Grains of ice slid down the neck of the pop bottle.

'What's up, sheriff?' I said.

'Have you seen Rosie this afternoon?' He took a drink out of the bottle.

I sat down across from him. Waves from a passing boat slapped against the pilings under the dock.

'We went out to the movie location, then she went to Lafayette to check out a couple of things,' I said.

'Yeah, that's why I'm here.'

'What do you mean?'

'I've gotten about a half-dozen phone calls this afternoon. I'm not sure what you guys are doing, Dave.'

'Conducting a murder investigation.'

'Oh, yeah? What does the director of a motion picture have to do with the death of Cherry LeBlanc?'

'Goldman got in your face?'

'*He* didn't. But you seem to have upset a few other people around here. Let's see, I received calls from two members of the Chamber of Commerce; Goldman's lawyer, who says you seem to be taking an undue interest in our visiting film community; and the mayor, who'd like to know what the hell my people think they're doing. If that wasn't enough, I also got a call from a Teamster official in Lafayette and a guy named Twinky Hebert Lemoyne who runs a bottling plant over there. Are you two working on some kind of negative outreach program? What was she doing over in Lafayette Parish?'

'Ask her.'

'I have a feeling she was sent over there.'

'She was checking out the Teamsters' involvement with Goldman and Julie Balboni.'

'What does that have to do with our investigation?'

'I'm not sure. Maybe nothing. What did this guy Twinky Lemoyne call about?'

'He owns half of a security service with a guy named Murphy Doucet. Lemoyne said Rosie came out to his bottling plant, asked him questions that were none of her business, and told him that he should give second thought to doing business with the mob. Do you know who Twinky Lemoyne is?'

'Not really.'

'He's a wealthy and respected man in Lafayette. In fact, he's a decent guy. What are y'all trying to do, Dave?'

'You sent me to invite Julie Balboni out of town. But now we find that Julie has made himself a big part of the local economy. I think that's the problem, sheriff, not me and Rosie.'

He rubbed his whiskers with the backs of his fingers.

'Maybe it is,' he said finally, 'but there's more than one way to do things.'

'What would you suggest that we do differently?'

His eyes studied a turkey buzzard that floated on the hot-air currents above the marsh.

'Concentrate on nailing this psychopath. For the time being forget about Balboni,' he said. His eyes didn't come back to meet mine when he spoke.

'Maybe Julie's involved.'

'He's not. Julie doesn't do anything unless it's for money.'

'I'm getting the strong feeling that the Spanish Lake area is becoming off limits.'

'No, I didn't say that. It's a matter of priorities. That brings up another subject, too – the remains of that black man you found out in the Atchafalaya Basin.'

'Yes?'

'That's St Mary Parish's jurisdiction. Let them work the case. We've got enough on our own plate.'

'They're not going to work it.'

'Then that's their choice.'

I didn't speak for a moment. The twilight was almost gone. The air was heavy and moist and full of insects, and out in the cypress I could hear wood ducks fluttering across the surface of the water.

'Would you like another cold drink?' I asked.

'No, this is fine,' he answered.

'I'd better help Batist lock up, then. We'll see you, sheriff,' I said, and went inside the bait shop. I didn't come back out until I heard his car start and head down the dirt road.

Sam 'Hogman' Patin was wrong. Cherry LeBlanc's killer would not merely find another victim in the future. He already had.

7

I got the call at eleven o'clock that night. A fisherman running a trotline by the levee, way down in the bottom of Vermilion Parish, almost to the salt water, had seen a lidless oil drum half submerged on its side in the cattails. He would have paid little attention to it, except for the fact that he saw the backs of alligator gars arching out of the water in the moonlight as they tore at something inside the barrel.

I drove down the narrow dirt track on top of the levee through the miles of flooded sawgrass that eventually bled into the Gulf. Strips of black cloud floated across the moon, and up ahead I could see an ambulance and a collection of sheriff's cars parked on the levee in a white and red glow of floodlamps, burning flares, and revolving emergency lights.

The girl was already in a body bag inside the ambulance. The coroner was a tired, overweight Jewish man with emphysema and a terrible cigarette odor whom I had known for years. There were deep circles under his eyes, and he kept rubbing mosquito repellent onto his face and fat arms.

Down the bank a Vermilion Parish plainclothes was interviewing the fisherman, whose unshaven face looked bloodless and gray in the glare of the floodlamps.

'You want to see her, Dave?' the coroner asked.

'Should I?'

'Probably.'

We climbed into the back of the ambulance. Even with the air conditioner running, it was hot and stale-smelling inside.

'I figure she was in the water only a couple of days, but she's probably been dead several weeks,' he said. 'The barrel was probably on the side of the levee, then it rolled into the water. Otherwise, the crabs and the gars would have torn her up a lot worse.'

He pulled the zipper from the girl's head all the way down to her ankles.

I took a breath and swallowed.

'I'd say she was in her early twenties, but I'm guessing,' he said. 'And you can see, we won't get much in the way of prints. I don't think an artist will be able to recreate what her face looked like, either. Cause of death doesn't appear to be a mystery – asphyxiation with a plastic bag taped around her neck. The same electrician's tape he used to bind her hands and ankles. Rape, sodomy, sexual degradation, that kind of stuff. When their clothes are gone, you can put it in the bank.'

'No rings, bracelets, tattoos?'

He shook his head.

'Have they found anything out there?'

'Nothing.'

'Tire tracks?'

'Not after all the rain we've had.'

'Do y'all have any missing-persons reports that coincide with—'

'Nope.'

A long strand of her blond hair hung outside the bag. For some reason it bothered me. I picked it up and placed it on her forehead. The coroner looked at me strangely.

'Why would he stuff her in a barrel?' I said.

'Dave, the day you can put yourself inside the head of a cocksucker like that, that's the day you eat your gun.'

I stepped back outside into the humid brilliance of the floodlamps, then walked along the slope of the levee and down by the water's edge. The darkness throbbled with the croaking of frogs, and fireflies were lighting in the tops of the sawgrass. The weeds along the levee had been trampled by cops' feet; fresh cigarette butts floated in the water; a sheriff's deputy was telling two others a racial joke.

The Vermilion Parish plainclothes finished interviewing the fisherman, put his notebook in his shirt pocket, and walked up the slope to his car. The fisherman continued to stand by his pirogue, scratching at the mosquito bites on his arms, evidently unsure of what he was supposed to do next. Sweat leaked out of the band of his cloth cap and glistened on his jawbones. When I introduced myself, his handshake, like most Cajun men's, was effeminate.

'I ain't never seen nothing like that, me,' he said. 'I don't want to never see nothing like that again, neither.'

The bottom of his pirogue was piled with mudcat. They quivered on top of each other, their whiskers pasted back against their yellow sides and bloated white bellies. On the seat of his pirogue was a headlamp with an elastic strap on it.

'When'd you first see that metal barrel?' I said.

'Tonight.'

'Do you come down here often?' I asked.

'Not too often, no, suh.'

'You've got a nice bunch of fish there.'

'Yeah, they feed good when the moon's up.'

I gazed into the bottom of his pirogue, at the wet shine of moonlight on the fish's sides, the tangles of trotlines and corks, and a long object wrapped in a canvas tarp under the seat.

I caught the pirogue by the gunwale and slid it partly up on the mudbank.

'Do you mind if I look at this?' I said, and flipped back the folds of the canvas tarp.

He didn't answer. I took a pen flashlight out of my shirt pocket and shone it on the lever-action .30-.30 rifle. The bluing was worn off and the stock was wrapped with copper wire.

'Walk down here a little ways with me,' I said.

He followed me out to the edge of the lighted area, out of earshot of the Vermilion Parish deputies.

'We want to catch the guy who did this,' I said. 'I think you'd like to help us do that, wouldn't you?'

'Yes, suh, I sho' would.'

'But there's a problem here, isn't there? Something that's preventing you from telling me everying you want to?'

'I ain't real sho' what you—'

'Are you selling fish to restaurants?'

'No, suh, that ain't true.'

'Did you bring that .30-.30 along to shoot frogs?'

He grinned and shook his head. I grinned back at him.

'But you might just poach a 'gator or two?' I said.

'No, suh, I ain't got no 'gator. You can look.'

I let my expression go flat.

'That's right. So you don't have to be afraid,' I said. 'I just want you to tell me the truth. Nobody's going to bother you about that gun, or your headlamp, or what you might be doing with your fish. Do we have a deal?'

'Yes, suh.'

'When'd you first notice that barrel?'

'Maybe t'ree, fo' weeks ago. It was setting up on dry ground. I didn't have no reason to pay it no mind, no, but then I started to smell somet'ing. I t'ought it was a dead nutria, or maybe a big gar rotting up on the bank. It was real strong one night, then t'ree nights later you couldn't smell it 'less the wind blow it right across the water. Then it rained and the next night they wasn't no smell at all. I just never t'ought they might be a dead girl up there.'

'Did you see anyone up there?'

'Maybe about a mont' ago, at evening, I seen a car. I 'member t'inking it was new and why would anybody bring his new car down that dirt road full of holes.'

'What kind of car?'

'I don't remember, suh.'

'You remember the color?'

'No, suh, I'm sorry.'

His face looked fatigued and empty. 'I just wish I ain't been the one to find her,' he said. 'I ain't never gonna forget looking inside that barrel.'

I put my business card in his shirt pocket.

'Call me if you think of anything else. You did just fine, podna,' I said, and patted him on the arm.

I turned my truck around in the middle of the levee and headed back toward New Iberia. Up ahead the glow of the red and blue emergency lights on the ambulance sped across the tops of the sawgrass, cattails, and bleached sandpits where the husks of dead gars boiled with fire ants.

What had I learned from it all?'

Not much.

But maybe in his cynical way my friend the sleepless coroner had cut right to the heart of the problem: How do you go inside the head of a homicidal sadist who prowls the countryside like a tiger turned loose in a schoolyard?

I've seen films that portray detectives who try to absorb the moral insanity of their adversaries in order to trap them inside their own maniacal design. It makes an interesting story. Maybe it's even possible.

But four years ago I had to go to Huntsville, Texas, to interview a man on death row who had confessed to almost three hundred murders throughout the United States. Suddenly, from all over the country, cops with unsolved homicide cases flocked to Huntsville like flies on pig flop. We were no exception. A black woman in New Iberia had been abducted out of her house, strangled to death, and thrown in the Vermilion River. We had no suspects, and the man in Huntsville, Jack Hatfield, had been through Louisiana many times in his red tracings across the map.

He turned out to be neither shrewd nor cunning; there was no malevolent light in his eyes, nothing hostile or driven about his behavior. His accent was peckerwood, his demeanor finally that of a simpleton. He told me about his religious conversion and glowing presences that appeared to him in his cell; it was quickly apparent that he wanted me to like him, that he would tell me anything I wanted to hear. All I had to do was provide him the details of a murder, and he would make the crime his own.

(Later, an unemployed oil-field roughneck would confess to murdering the black woman after being given title to a ten-year-old car by her husband.)

I asked Jack Hatfield if he was trying to trade off his cooperation for a commutation of his sentence. He answered, 'Naw, I got no kick comin' about that, long as it's legal.'

With a benign expression on his face, he chronicled his long list of roadside murders from Maine to southern California. He could have been talking about a set of embossed ceramic plates that he had collected from each state that he had visited. If he had indeed done what he told me, he was completely without remorse.

'My victims didn't suffer none,' he said.

Then he began to talk about his mother and an incredible transformation took place in him. Tears streaked down his homely face, he trembled all over, his fingers left white marks on his arms. Evidently she had been not only a prostitute but perverse as well. When he was a little boy she had made him stand by the bed and watch her copulate with her johns. When he had tried to hide in the woods, she beat him with a quirt, brought him back to the house, and made him watch some more.

He spent fifteen years in the Wisconsin penitentiary for her murder.

Then he paused in his story, wiped his face with his hand, pulled his T-shirt out from his chest with his finger, and smelled himself.

'I killed three more people the day I come out of prison. I told them I was gonna do it, and I done it,' he said, and began cleaning his fingernails with a toothpick as though I were not there.

When I walked back out into the autumn sunshine that afternoon, back into the smell of east Texas piney woods and white-uniformed convicts burning piles of tree stumps on the edge of a cottonfield, I was convinced that Jack Hatfield's story about his mother was true but that almost everything else he had told me would remain as demonstrably elusive as a psychotic dream. Perhaps the answer to Jack Hatfield lay with others, I thought. Perhaps we should ask those who would eventually strap him to the gurney in the execution room, poke the IV needle into the vein, tape it lovingly to the skin, and watch him through the viewing glass as the injection dulled his eyes then hit his heart like a hammer. Would his life, his secret and dark knowledge, be passed on to them?

I'd had little sleep when I set out for the office the next morning. The sun had come up red and hot over the trees, and because I had left the windows down the night before, the inside of my truck was full of mosquitoes and dripping with humidity. I stopped at a traffic light on the east side of town and saw a purple Cadillac limousine, with tinted black windows, pull into a yellow zone by a restaurant and park squarely in front of the fire plug.

Cholo Manelli stepped out of the driver's door, stretched, rotated a crick out of his neck, looked up and down the street a couple of times, then walked around to the other side of the limo and opened the back door for Julie Balboni. Then the rest of Julie's entourage – three men and the woman named Margot – stepped out onto the sidewalk, their faces dour in the heat, their eyes sullen with the morning's early hour.

Cholo went up the sidewalk first, point man and good soldier that he was, his head turning slightly from side to side, his simian shoulders rolling under his flowered shirt. He opened the front door of the restaurant, and Julie walked inside, with the others in single file behind him.

I didn't plan any of the events that followed.

I drove through the light and went almost two blocks before I made a U-turn, drove back to the restaurant, and parked under a live-oak tree across the street from the limo. The early sun's heat was already rising from the cement, and I could smell dead water beetles in the curb gutters.

My eyes burned from lack of sleep, and though I had just shaved, I could feel stubble, like grit, along the edge of my jaw. I got out of the truck, put my seersucker coat over my arm, and walked across the street to the limo. The waxed purple surface had the soft glow of hard candy; the tinted black windows swam with the mirrored images of oak trees and azalea bushes moving in the breeze.

I unfolded the blade of my Puma knife, walked from fender to fender, and sawed the air stems off all four tires. The limo went down on the rims like it had been dropped from a chain. A black kid who had been putting circulars on doors stopped and watched me as he would a fascinating creature inside a zoo cage.

I walked to the filling station on the corner, called the dispatcher, and told him to have a wrecker tow the limo into the pound.

Then I went inside the restaurant, which gleamed with chrome and silverware and Formica surfaces, and walked past the long table where two waitresses were in the process of serving Julie and his group their breakfast. Cholo saw me first and started to speak, but I looked straight ahead and continued on into the men's room as though they were not there.

I washed my face with cold water, dried it with paper towels, and combed my hair in the mirror. There were flecks of white in my mustache now, and lines around my eyes that I hadn't noticed only a week before. I turned on the cold water and washed my face again, as though somehow I could rinse time and age out of my skin. Then I crumpled up the damp paper towel in my hand, flung it into the trash can, fixed my tie, put on my coat and sunglasses, and walked back into the restaurant.

Showtime, Julie, I thought.

Even sitting down, he towered above the others at the head of the table, in a pink short-sleeve shirt, suspenders, and gray striped slacks, his tangled black hair ruffling on his brow in the breeze from the fan, his mouth full of food while he told the waitress to bring more coffee and to reheat Margot's breakfast steak. Cholo kept trying to smile at me, his false teeth as stiff as whale bone in his mouth. Julie's other hoods looked up at me, then at Julie; when they read nothing in his face, they resumed eating.

'Hey, lieutenant, I thought that was you. You here for breakfast?'
Cholo said.

'I was just passing by,' I said.

'What's going on, Dave?' Julie said, his mouth chewing, his eyes fixed
on the flower vase in front of him.

'I had a long night last night,' I said.

'Yeah?' he said.

'We found a girl in a barrel down in south Vermilion Parish.'

He continued to chew, then he took a drink of water. He touched his
mouth with his napkin.

'You want to sit down, or are you on your way out?' he said.

Just then I heard the steel hook of the wrecker clang somewhere on the
limo's frame and the hydraulic cables start to tighten on the winch. Cholo
craned his head to look beyond the angle of the front window that gave
onto the street.

'I always thought you were standup, Feet,' I said.

'I appreciate the compliment, but that's a term they use in a place I've
never been.'

'That's all right, I changed my mind. I don't think you're standup
anymore, Feet.'

He blew up both his cheeks.

'What are you trying to say, Dave?'

'The man I work for got a bunch of phone calls yesterday. It looks like
somebody dropped the dime on me with the Kiwanis Club.'

'It ain't a bunch I got a lot of influence with. Talk with Mikey
Goldman if you got that kind of problem.'

'You use what works, Julie.'

'Hey, get real, Dave. When I want to send a message to somebody, it
don't come through Dagwood Bumstead.'

Outside, the driver of the wrecker gunned his engine, pulled away from
the curb, and dragged the limo past the front window. The limo's two
front tires, which were totally deflated and still on the asphalt, were sliced
into ribbons by the wheel rims.

Cholo's mouth was wide with unchewed scrambled eggs.

'Hey, a guy's got our car! A guy's driving off with the fucking limo,
Julie!' he said.

Julie watched the wrecker and his limo disappear up the street. He
pushed his plate away an inch with his thumb. One corner of his mouth
dropped, and he pressed against it with his napkin.

'Sit down,' he said.

Everyone had stopped eating now. A waitress came to the table with a
pitcher of ice water and started to refill the glasses, then hesitated and
walked back behind the counter. I pulled out a chair and sat at the corner
of the table, a foot from Julie's elbow.

'You're pissed off about something and you have my fucking car towed in?' he said.

'Don't park in front of fire plugs.'

'Fire plugs?'

'Right.'

'I'm getting this kind of dog shit because of a fucking fire plug?'

'No, what I'm wondering, Julie, is why you and Cholo have to hit on a small-town teenage hooker. Don't y'all have enough chippies back in New Orleans?'

'What?'

'Cherry LeBlanc,' I said.

'Who the fuck is Cherry LeBlanc?'

'Give it a break and stop acting like you just popped out of your mama's womb.'

He folded his napkin, placed it carefully by the side of his plate, pulled a carnation out of the flower vase, and pinched off the stem.

'You calling me a pimp?' he said. 'You trying to embarrass me in public. That's what this is about?'

'You didn't listen to what I said. We just found another murdered girl. Cholo knew about the murder of the LeBlanc girl, and he said you did, too. Except you lied about it when I mentioned her to you.'

His eyes drifted lazing to Cholo's face. Cholo squeezed his hands on his wrists.

'I'm all lost here. I'm—' he began.

'You know what the real trouble is, Dave?' Julie said. He flipped the carnation onto the tablecloth. 'You never understood how this town worked. You remember anybody complaining about the cathouses on Railroad and Hopkins? Or the slot machines that were in every bar and restaurant in town? Nobody complained 'cause my old man delivered an envelope to certain people at the end of every month. But those same people treated our family like we were spit on the sidewalk.

'So you and that FBI broad went around town stirring up the Bumstead crowd, shoving a broomstick up their ringus, and your boss man called you in to explain the facts of life. But it's no fun finding out that the guys you work for don't want to scare a few million dollars out of town. So you fuck my car and get in my face in a public place. I think maybe you should go back to work in New Orleans. I think maybe this shithole is starting to rub off on you.'

The manager had come from behind the glass cashier's counter and was now standing three feet from me and Julie, his clip-on bow tie askew, his tongue wetting his lips.

'Sir, could you gentlemen lower your, I mean, could you not use that language in—' he began.

Julie's eyes, which were filled with a black light, flipped up into the manager's face.

'Get the fuck away from my table,' he said.

'Sir—' the manager said.

'It's all right, Mr Meaux. I'm leaving in just a second,' I said.

'Oh, sad to hear it,' the woman, Margot, said. Except Cholo, the other hoods at the table smiled at her humor. She wore a sundress, and her hair, which was bleached the color of ash, was pulled back tightly on her head. She smoked a cigarette and the backs of her arms were covered with freckles.

'You want to come down to the office and look at some morgue pictures? I think that'd be a good idea,' I said. 'Bring your girlfriend along if you like.'

'I'm going to say this just once. I don't know none of these girls, I don't have nothing to do with your problems, you understand what I'm saying? You said some ugly things to me, Dave, but we're old friends and I'm going to let it slide. I'll call a couple of cabs, I'll pay the fine on my car, I'll buy new tires, and I'll forget everything you been saying to me. But don't you never try to get in my face in a public place again.'

One of his hoods was getting up, scraping back his chair, to use the restroom.

I folded my sunglasses, slipped them into my shirt pocket, and rubbed the burning sensation in my eyes with my thumb and forefinger.

'Feet, you're full of more shit than a broken pay toilet,' I said quietly.

The hood rested his hand on my shoulder. He was perhaps twenty-eight or thirty, lithe and olive-skinned, his dark hair boxed on his neck. A long pink scar, as thick as a soda straw, ran down the inside of one arm.

'Everybody's been pretty polite here,' he said.

I looked at his hand and at his feet. I could smell the faint hint of his sweat through his deodorant, the nicotine on the backs of his fingers.

'But you keep offending people,' he said. He raised his palm slightly, then set it on my shoulder again.

'Don't let your day get complicated,' I said.

'It's time to let people alone, Mr Robicheaux,' he said. Then he began to knead my shoulder as a fellow ballplayer might out on the pitcher's mound.

I felt a balloon of red-black color rise out of my chest into my head, heard a sound behind my eyes like wet newspaper tearing, and for some reason saw a kaleidoscopic image of the blond girl in the black body bag, a long strand of algae-streaked hair glued to the gray flesh of her forehead.

I hit him so hard in the stomach that my fist buried itself up to the wrist right under his sternum and spittle flew from his mouth onto the tabletop. Then I came up out of the chair and hooked him in the eye, saw the skin break against the bone and well with blood. He tried to regain his balance and swing a sugar shaker at my face, but I spun him sideways, caught him in the kidney, and drove him to his knees between two counter stools. I didn't remember hitting him in the mouth, but his bottom lip was drooling blood onto his shirt front.

I didn't want to stop. I heard the roar of wind in sea shells, the wheels of rusted engines clanging cog against cog. Then I saw Cholo in front of me, his big square hands raised in placation, his mouth small with sound.

'What?' I said.

'It ain't your style, Loot,' he was whispering hoarsely. 'Ease off, the guy's new, he don't know the rules, Loot. Come on, this ain't good for nobody.'

My knuckles were skinned, my palms ringing. I heard glass crunch under the sole of my shoe in the stunned silence, and looked down numbly at my broken sunglasses on the floor like a man emerging from a blackout.

Julie Balboni scraped back his chair, took his gold money clip from his slacks, and began counting out a series of ten-dollar bills on the table.

He didn't even look up at me when he spoke. But everybody in the restaurant heard what he said. 'I think you're losing it, Dave. Stop being a hired dildo for the local dipshits or get yourself some better tranqs.'

8

It was ten A.M. Batist had gone after a boat with a fouled engine down the bayou, and the bait shop and dock were empty. The tin roof was expanding in the heat, buckling and pinging against the bolts and wood joists. I pulled a can of Dr Pepper out of the crushed ice in the cooler and sat outside in the hot shade by myself and drank it. Green dragonflies hung suspended over the cattails along the bayou's banks; a needle-nose gar that had probably been wounded by a boat propeller turned in circles in the dead current, while a school of minnows fed off a red gash behind its gills; a smell like dead snakes, sour mud, and rotted hyacinth vines blew out of the marsh on the hot wind.

I didn't want to even think about the events of this morning. The scene in the restaurant was like a moment snipped out of a drunk dream, in which I was always out of control, publicly indecent or lewd in the eyes of others.

The soda can grew warm in my palm. The sky in the south had a bright sheen to it like blue silk. I hoped that it would storm that afternoon, that rain would thunder down on the marsh and bayou, roar like grapeshot on the roof of my house, pour in gullies through the dirt and dead leaves under the pecan trees in my yard.

I heard Bootsie behind me. She sat down in a canvas chair by a spool table and crossed her legs. She wore white shorts, sandals, and a denim shirt with the sleeves cut off. There were sweat rings under her arms, and the down on top of her thighs had been burned gold by the sun.

We met at a dance on Spanish Lake during the summer of 1957, and a short time later we lost our virginity together in my father's boathouse, while the rain fell out of the sunlight and dripped off the eaves and the willow trees into the lake and the inside of the boathouse trembled with a wet green-yellow light.

But even at that age I had already started my long commitment to sour mash straight up with a sweating jax on the side. Bootsie and I would go separate ways, far from Bayou Teche and the provincial Cajun world in which we had grown up. I would make the journey to Vietnam as one of our new colonials and return with a junkyard in my hip and thigh and nocturnal memories that neither whiskey nor army hospital dope could kill. She would marry an oil-field pilot who would later tip a guy wire on an offshore rig and crash his helicopter right on top of the quarter-boat; then she would discover that her second husband, an accounting graduate from Tulane, was a bookkeeper for the Mafia, although his career with them became short-lived when they shotgunned him and his mistress to death in the parking lot of the Hialeah racetrack.

She had lupus disease that we had knocked into remission with medication, but it still lived in her blood like a sleeping parasite that waited for its moment to attack her kidneys and sever her connective tissue. She was supposed to avoid hard sunlight, but again and again I came home from work and found her working in the yard in shorts and a halter, her hot skin filmed with sweat and grains of dirt.

'Did something happen at work?' she said.

'I had some trouble at Del's.'

'What?'

'I busted up one of Baby Feet Balboni's lowlifes.'

'In the restaurant?'

'Yeah, that's where I did it.'

'What did he do?'

'He put his hand on me.' I set down my soda can and propped my forearms on my thighs. I looked out at the sun's reflection in the brown water.

'Have you been back to the office?' she said.

'Not yet. I'll probably go in later.'

She was quiet a moment.

'Have you talked to the sheriff?' she asked.

'There's not really much to talk about. The guy could make a beef but he won't. They don't like to get messed up in legal action against cops.'

She uncrossed her legs and brushed idly at her knee with her fingertips.

'Dave, is something else going on, something you're not telling me about?'

'The guy put his hand on my shoulder and I wanted to tear him apart. Maybe I would have done it if this guy named Manelli hadn't stepped in front of me.'

I saw her breasts rise and fall under her shirt. Far down the bayou Batist was towing a second boat behind his outboard and the waves were slapping the floating hyacinths against the banks. She got up from her chair and stood behind me. She worked her fingers into my shoulders. I could feel her thigh touch my back.

'New Iberia is never going to be the same place we grew up in. That's just the way things are,' she said.

'It doesn't mean I have to like it.'

'The Balboni family was here a long time. We survived, didn't we? They'll make their movie and go away.'

'There're too many people willing to sell it down the drain.'

'Sell what?'

'Whatever makes a dollar for them. Redfish and *sac-a-lait* to restaurants, alligators to the Japanese. They let oil companies pollute the oyster beds and cut canals through the marsh so salt water can eat up thousands of square miles of wetlands. They take it on their knees from anybody who's got a checkbook.'

'Let it go, Dave.'

'I think a three-day open season on people would solve a lot of our problems.'

'Tell the sheriff what happened. Don't let it just hang there.'

'He's worried about some guys at the Chamber of Commerce, Bootsie. He's a good guy most of the time, but these are the people he's spent most of his life around.'

'I think you should talk to him.'

'All right, I'm going to take a shower, then I'll call him.'

'You're not going to the office?'

'I'm not sure. Maybe later.'

Batist cut the engine on his boat and floated on the swell into the dock and bumped against the strips of rubber tire we had nailed to the pilings. His shirt was piled on the board seat beside him, and his black shoulders and chest were beaded with sweat. His head looked like a cannonball. He grinned with an unlit cigar in the corner of his mouth.

I was glad for the distraction.

'I was up at the fo'-corners,' he said. 'A man there said you mopped up the restaurant flo' with one of them dagos.'

Thanks, Batist, I thought.

I showered in water that was so cold it left me breathless, changed clothes, and drove to the bottling works down by the Vermilion River in Lafayette. The two-story building was an old one, made of yellow brick, and surrounded by huge live-oak trees. In back was a parking lot, which was filled with delivery trucks, and a loading dock, where a dozen black men were rattling crates of soda pop out of the building's dark interior and stacking them inside the waiting trucks. Their physical strength was incredible. Some of them would pick up a half-dozen full cases at a time and lift them easily to eye level. Their muscles looked like water-streaked black stone.

I asked one of them where I could find Twinky Hebert Lemoyne.

'Mr Twinky in yonder, in the office. Better catch him quick, though. He fixin' to go out on the route,' he said.

'He goes out on the route?'

'Mr Twinky do everyt'ing, suh.'

I walked inside the warehouse to a cluttered, windowed office whose door was already open. The walls and cork boards were papered with invoices, old church calendars, unframed photographs of employees and fishermen with thick-bellied large-mouth bass draped across their hands. Lemoyne's face was pink and well-shaped, his eyebrows sandy, his gray hair still streaked in places with gold. He sat erect in his chair, his eyes behind his rimless glasses concentrated on the papers in his hands. He wore a short-sleeved shirt and a loose burnt-orange tie (a seersucker coat hung on the back of the chair) and a plastic pen holder in his pocket; his brown shoes were shined; his fingernails were trimmed and clean. But he had the large shoulders and hands of a working man, and he radiated the kind of quiet, hard-earned physical power that in some men neither age nor extra weight seems to diminish.

There was no air conditioning in his office, and he had weighted all the papers on his desk to keep them from blowing away in the breeze from the oscillating fan.

After I had introduced myself, he gazed out at the loading dock a moment, then lifted his hands from the desk blotter and put them down again as though somehow we had already reached a point in our conversation where there was nothing left to be said.

'Can I sit down?' I said.

'Go ahead. But I think you're wasting your time here.'

'It's been a slow day.' I smiled at him.

'Mr Robicheaux, I don't have any idea in the world why either you or that Mexican woman is interested in me. Could you be a little bit more forthcoming?'

'Actually, until yesterday I don't believe I ever heard your name.'

'What should I make of that?'

'The problem is you and a few others tried to stick a couple of thumbtacks in my boss's head.' I smiled again.

'Listen, that woman came into my office yesterday and accused me of working with the Mafia.'

'Why would she do that?'

'You tell me, please.'

'You own half of a security service with Murphy Doucet?'

'That's right, I surely do. Can you tell me what y'all are looking for, why y'all are in my place of business?'

'When you do business with a man like Julie Balboni, you create a certain degree of curiosity about yourself.'

'I don't do business with this man, and I don't know anything about him. I bought stock in this motion picture they're making. A lot of business people around here have. I've never met Julie Balboni and I don't plan to. Are we clear on this, sir?'

'My boss says you're a respected man. It looks like you have a good business, too. I'd be careful who I messed with, Mr Lemoyne.'

'I'm not interested in pursuing the subject.' He fixed his glasses, squared his shoulders slightly, and picked up several sheets of paper in his hands.

I drummed my fingers on the arms of my chair. Outside I could hear truck doors slamming and gears grinding.

'I guess I didn't explain myself very well,' I said.

'You don't need to,' he said, and looked up at the clock on the wall.

'You're a solid businessman. There's nothing wrong with buying stock in a movie company. There's nothing wrong with providing a security service for it, either. But a lady who's not much taller than a fireplug asks you a couple of questions and you try to drop the dime on her. That doesn't seem to fit, Mr Lemoyne.'

'There're people out there committing rapes, armed robberies, selling crack to children, God only knows what else, but you and that woman have the nerve to come in here and question me because I have a vague business relationship with a movie production. You don't think that's reason to make someone angry? What's wrong with you people?'

'Are your employees union?'

'No, they're not.'

'But your partner in your security service is a Teamster steward. I think you're involved in some strange contradictions, Mr Lemoyne.'

He rose from his chair and lifted a set of keys out of his desk drawer.

'I'm taking a new boy on his route today. I have to lock up now. Do you want to stay around and talk to somebody else?' he said.

'No, I'll be on my way. Here's my business card in case you might like to contact me later.'

He ignored it when I extended it to him. I placed it on his desk.

'Thank you for your time, sir,' I said, and walked back out onto the loading dock, into the heated liquid air, the blinding glare of light, the chalky smell of crushed oyster shells in the unsurfaced parking lot.

When I was walking out to my pickup truck, I recognized an elderly black man who used to work in the old icehouse in New Iberia years ago. He was picking up litter out by the street with a stick that had a nail in the end of it. He had a rag tied around his forehead to keep the sweat out of his eyes, and the rotted wet undershirt he wore looked like strips of cheesecloth on his body.

'How do you like working here, Dallas?' I said.

'I like it pretty good.'

'How does Mr Twinky treat y'all?'

His eyes glanced back toward the building, then he grinned.

'He know how to make the eagle scream, you know what I mean?'

'He's tight with a dollar?'

'Mr Twinky so tight he got to eat a whole box of Ex-Lax so he don't squeak when he walk.'

'He's that bad?'

He tapped some dried leaves off the nail of his stick against the trunk of an oak tree.

'That's just my little joke,' he said. 'Mr Twinky pay what he say he gonna pay, and he always pay it on time. He good to black folks, Mr Dave. They ain't no way 'round that.'

When I got back to New Iberia I didn't go to the office. Instead, I called from the house. The sheriff wasn't in.

'Where is he?' I said.

'He's probably out looking for you,' the dispatcher said. 'What's going on, Dave?'

'Nothing much.'

'Tell that to the greaseball you bounced off the furniture this morning.'

'Did he file a complaint?'

'No, but I heard the restaurant owner dug the guy's tooth out of the counter with a screwdriver. You sure know how to do it, Dave.'

'Tell the sheriff I'm going to check out some stuff in New Orleans. I'll call him this evening or I'll see him in the office early in the morning.'

'I got the impression it might be good if you came by this afternoon.'

'Is Agent Gomez there?'

'Yeah, hang on.'

A few seconds later Rosie picked up the extension.

'Dave?'

'How you doing?'

'*I'm* doing fine. How are you doing?'

'Everything's copacetic. I just talked with your man Twinky Lemoyne.'

'Oh?'

'It looks like you put your finger in his eye.'

'Why'd you go over there?'

'You never let them think they can make you flinch.'

'Hang on a minute. I want to close the door.' Then a moment later she scraped the receiver back up and said, 'Dave, what happens around here won't affect my job or career to any appreciable degree. But maybe you ought to start thinking about covering your butt for a change.'

'I had a bad night last night and I acted foolishly this morning. It's just one of those things,' I said.

'That's not what I'm talking about, and I think you know it. When you chase money out of a community, people discover new depths in themselves.'

'Have you gotten any feedback on the asphyxiated girl down in Vermilion Parish?'

'I just got back from the coroner's office. She's still Jane Doe.'

'You think we're dealing with the same guy?'

'Bondage, humiliation of the victim, a prolonged death, probable sexual violation, it's the same creep, you'd better believe it.' I could hear an edge in her voice, like a sliver of glass.

'I've got a couple of theories, too,' she said. 'He's left his last two victims where we could find them. Maybe he's becoming more compulsive, more desperate, less in control of his technique. Most psychopaths eventually reach a point where they're like sharks in feeding frenzy. They never satisfy the obsession.'

'Or he wants to stick it in our faces?'

'You got it.'

'Everything you say may be true, Rosie, but I think prostitution is connected with this stuff somewhere. You want to take a ride to New Orleans with me this afternoon?'

'A Vermilion Parish sheriff's detective is taking me out on the levee where you all found the girl last night. Do all these people spit Red Man?'

'A few of the women deputies don't.'

I heard her laugh into the telephone.

'Watch out for yourself, slick,' she said.

'You, too, Rosie.'

Neither Bootsie nor Alafair was home. I left them a note, packed a change of clothes in a canvas bag in case I had to stay overnight, and headed for I-10 and New Orleans as the temperature climbed to one hundred degrees and the willows along the bayou drooped motionlessly in the heat as though all the juices had been baked out of their leaves.

I drove down the elevated interstate and crossed the Atchafalaya Basin and its wind-ruffled bays dotted with the oil platforms and dead cypress, networks of canals and bayous, sand bogs, willow islands, stilt houses, flooded woods, and stretches of dry land where the mosquitoes swarmed in gray clouds out of the tangles of brush and intertwined trees. Then I crossed the wide, yellow sweep of the Mississippi at Baton Rouge, and forty-five minutes later I was rolling through Jefferson Parish, along the shores of Lake Pontchartrain, into New Orleans. The lake was slate green and capping, the sky almost white in the heat, and the fronds on the palm trees were lifting and rattling dryly in the hot breeze. The air smelled of salt and stagnant water and dead vegetation among the sand bogs on the west side of the highway; the asphalt looked like it could fry the palm of your hand.

But there were no rain clouds on the horizon, no hint of relief from the scorching white orb in the sky or the humidity that crawled and ran on the skin like angry insects.

I was on the New Orleans police force for fourteen years, first as a beat cop and finally as a lieutenant in Homicide. I never worked Vice, but there are a few areas in New Orleans law enforcement that don't eventually lead you back into it. Without its pagan and decadent ambiance, its strip shows, hookers, burlesque spielers, taxi pimps, and brain-damaged street dopers, the city would be as attractive to most tourists as an agrarian theme park in western Nebraska.

The French Quarter has two populations, almost two sensory climates. Early in the morning black children in uniforms line up to enter the Catholic elementary school by the park; parishioners from St Louis Cathedral have coffee *au lait* and *beignets* and read the newspaper at the outdoor tables in the Café du Monde; the streets are still cool, the tile roofs and pastel stucco walls of the buildings streaked with moisture, the scrolled ironwork on the balconies bursting with flowers; families have their pictures sketched by the artists who set up their easels along the piked fence in Jackson Square; in the background the breeze off the river blows through the azalea and hibiscus bushes, the magnolia blossoms that are as big as fists, and the clumps of banana trees under the equestrian statue of Andy Jackson; and as soon as you head deeper into the Quarter, under the iron, green-painted colonnades, you can smell the cold, clean odor of fresh fish laid out on ice, of boxed strawberries and plums and rattlesnake watermelons beaded with water from a spray hose.

But by late afternoon another crowd moves into the Quarter. Most of them are innocuous – college kids, service personnel, Midwestern families trying to see past the spielers into the interiors of the strip houses, blue-suited Japanese businessmen hung with cameras, rednecks from dry counties in Mississippi. But there's another kind, too – grifters, Murphy artists, dips and stalls, coke and skag dealers, stables of hookers who work the hotel trade only, and strippers who hook out of taxicabs after 2 A.M.

They have the franchise on the worm's-eye view of the world. They're usually joyless, indifferent to speculations about mortality, bored with almost all forms of experience. Almost all of them either free-base, mainline, do coke, or smoke crack. Often they straighten out the kinks with black speed.

They view ordinary people as carnival workers do rubes; they look upon their victims with contempt, sometimes with loathing. Most of them cannot think their way out of a paper bag; but the accuracy of their knowledge about various bondsmen, the hierarchy of the local mob, the law as it applies to themselves, and cops and judges on a pad, is awesome.

As the streets began to cool and turn purple with shadow, I went from one low-rent club to the next amid the din of Dixieland and rockabilly bands, black kids with clip-on taps dancing on the sidewalk for the tourists, spielers in straw boaters and candy-striped vests hollering at college boys, 'No cover, no minimum, you studs, come on in and get your battery charged.'

Jimmie Ryan's red mustache and florid, good-humored face made you think of a nineteenth-century bartender. But he was also known as Jimmie the Dime, because with a phone call he could connect you, in one way or another, with any form of illegal activity in New Orleans.

Inside the crook of both his arms his veins were laced with scar tissue, like flattened gray garden snakes.

He tilted his straw boater back on his head and drank from his beer. Above him, a topless girl in a sequined G-string danced barefoot on a runway, her hips moving like water to the music from the jukebox, her skin rippled with neon light, her mouth open in feigned ecstasy.

'How you been, Streak?' he said.

'Pretty good, Jimmie. How's the life?' I said.

'I ain't exactly in it anymore. Since I got off the super-fluid, I more or less went to reg'lar employment, you know what I mean? Being a human doorbell for geeks and dipshits has got some serious negative drawbacks, I'm talking about self-esteem here, this town's full of sick people, Streak, who needs it is what I'm trying to say.'

'I see. Look, Jimmie, do you know anybody who might be trying to recruit girls out of the parishes?'

He leaned his elbows back on the bar. His soft stomach swelled out of his striped vest like a water-filled bottom-heavy balloon.

'You mean somebody putting together his own stable?' he asked.

'Maybe.'

'A guy who goes out looking for the country girls, the ones who's waiting for a big sugar daddy or is about to get run out of town, anyway?'

'Possibly.'

'It don't sound right.'

'Why?'

'New Orleans is full of them. Why bring in more and drive the prices down?'

'Maybe this guy does more than jump pimp, Jimmie. Maybe he likes to hurt them. You know a guy like that?'

'We're talking about another type of guy now, somebody who operates way down on the bottom of the food chain. When I was in the business of dimeing for somebody, making various kinds of social arrangements around the city, I made it a point not to know no guys like that, in fact, maybe I'm a little bit taken aback here you think I associate with them kind of people.'

'I respect your knowledge and your judgment, Jimmie. That's why I came to you instead of someone else. My problem is two dead girls in Vermilion and Iberia parishes. The same guy may have killed others.'

He removed something from the back of his teeth with his little finger.

'The city ain't like it used to be,' he said. 'It's turning to shit.'

'Okay—'

'Years ago there were certain understandings with New Orleans cops. A guy got caught doing the wrong stuff, I'm talking about sick stuff, molesting a child, robbing and beating up old people, something like that, it didn't go to the jailhouse. They stomped the shit out of the guy right there, I mean they left him with his brains running out of his nose.

'Today, what'd you got? Try to take a stroll by the projects and see what happens. Look, Streak, I don't know what you're looking for, but there's one special kind of cocksucker that comes to mind here, a new kind of guy in the city, why somebody don't walk him outside, maybe punch his ticket real hard, maybe permanent, you know what I'm saying, I don't know the answer to that one, but when you go down to the bus depot, you might think about it, I mean you're from out of town, right, and there ain't nobody, I mean nobody, gonna be upset if this kind of guy maybe gets ripped from his liver to his lights.'

'The bus depot?'

'You got it. There's three or four of them. One of them stands out like shit in an ice-cream factory. Nothing against colored people.'

I had forgotten what a linguistic experience a conversation with Jimmie the Dime could be.

He suppressed a beer belch and stared up at the girl on the runway.

'Could Baby Feet Balboni be involved in this?' I asked.

He rolled a matchstick on his tongue, looked upward at an oblique angle to a spot on the ceiling.

'Take a walk with me, breathe the night air, this place is like the inside of an ashtray. Some nights I think somebody poured battery acid in my lungs,' he said.

I walked outside with him. The sidewalks were filled with tourists and revelers drinking beer out of deep paper cups. Jimmie looked up and down the street, blew air out his nose, smoothed his mustache with one knuckle.

'You're using the names of local personalities now,' he said.

'It stays with me, Jimmie. Nobody'll know where it came from.'

'Anything I might know about this certain man is already public knowledge, so it probably won't do no good for me to be commenting on the issue here.'

'There's no action around here that doesn't get pieced off to Julie one way or another. Why should procuring be any different?'

'Wrong. There's fifteen-year-old kids in the projects dealing rock, girls, guns, Mexican brown, crank, you name it, the Italians won't fool with it, it's too uncontrollable. You looking for a guy who kills hookers? It ain't Feet, lieutenant. The guy's got sub-zero feelings about people. I saw him wipe up a barroom in Algiers with three guys from the Giacano family who thought they could come on like wise-asses in front of their broads. He didn't even break a sweat. He even stopped stomping on one guy just so he could blow a long fart.'

'Thanks for your time, Jimmie. Get in touch if you hear anything, all right?'

'What do I know? We're living in sick times. You want my opinion? Open up some prison colonies at the North Pole, where those penguins live. Get rid of the dirt bags, bring back some decency, before the whole city becomes a toilet.' He rocked on the balls of his feet. His lips looked purple in the neo glow from the bar, his face an electric red, as though it were flaming from sunburn.

I gave him my business card. When I was down the block, under the marquee of a pornographic theater, and looked back at him, he was picking his teeth with it.

I hit two biker bars across the river in Algiers, where a few of the mamas hooked so their old men would have the money they needed to deal guns or dope. Why they allowed themselves to be used on that level was anybody's guess. But with some regularity they were chain-whipped, gang-raped, nailed through their hands to trees, and they usually came back for more until sometimes they were murdered and dumped in a swamp. One form of their sad, ongoing victimization probably makes about as much sense as another.

The ones who would talk to me all had the same odor, like sweaty leather, the warm female scent of unwashed hair, reefer smoke and nicotine, and engine grease rubbed into denim. But they had little knowledge or interest about anything outside of their tribal and atavistic world.

I found a mulatto pimp off Magazine who also ran a shooting gallery that specialized in black-tar heroin, which was selling at twenty-five dollars a hit and was back in fashion with adult addicts who didn't want to join the army of psychotic meltdowns produced by crack in the projects.

His name was Camel; he had one dead eye, like a colorless marble, and he wore a diamond clipped in one nostril and his hair shaved in ridges and dagger points. He peeled back the shell on a hard-boiled egg with his thumb at the sandwich counter of an old dilapidated grocery and package store with wood-bladed fans on the ceiling. His skin had the bright copper shine of a newly minted penny.

After he had listened to me for a while, he set his egg on a paper napkin and folded his long fingers reflectively.

'This is my neighborhood, place where all my friends live, and don't nobody here hurt my ladies,' he said.

'I didn't say they did, Camel. I just want you to tell me if you've heard about anybody who might be recruiting out in the parishes. Maybe a guy who's seriously out of control.'

'I don't get out of the neighborhood much no mo'. Age creeping up on me, I guess.'

'It's been a hot day, partner. My tolerance for bullshit is way down. You're dealing Mexican skag for Julie Balboni, and you know everything that's going on in this town.'

'What's that name again?'

I looked into his face for a long moment. He scraped at a bit of crust on the corner of his dead eye with his fingernail.

'You're a smart man, Camel. Tell me honestly, do you think you're going to jerk me around and I'm just going to disappear?'

He unscrewed the cap on a Tabasco bottle and began dotting drops of hot sauce on his egg.

'I hears stories about a white guy, they say a strange guy reg'lar peoples in the bidness don't like to fool with,' he said.

'All right—'

'You're looking in the wrong place.'

'What do you mean?'

'The guy don't live around here. He sets the girls up on the Airline Highway, in Jefferson Parish, puts one in charge, then comes back to town once in a while to check everything out.'

'I see, a new kind of honor system. What are you trying to feed me, Camel?'

'You're not hearing me. The reg'lar peoples stay away from him for a reason. His chippies try to short him, they disappear. The word there is *disappear*, gone from the crib, blipped off the screen. Am I getting this acrost to you all right?'

'What's his name?'

'Don't know, don't want to know. Ax yourself something. Why y'all always come to a nigger to solve your problem? We ain't got nothing like that in a black neighborhood.'

'We'll see you around, Camel. Thanks for your help. Say, what's the name of the black guy working the bus depot?'

'I travel by plane, my man. That's what everybody do today,' he said, and licked the top of the peeled egg before he put it in his mouth.

For years the Airline had been the main highway between Baton Rouge and New Orleans. When I-10 was built, the Airline became a secondary road and was absorbed back into that quasi-rural slum culture that has always characterized the peckerwood South: ramshackle nightclubs with oyster-shell parking lots; roach-infested motels that feature water beds and pornographic movies and rent rooms by the day or week; truck stops with banks of rubber machines in the restrooms; all-night glaringly lit cafés where the smell of fried food permeates the counters and stools as tangibly as a film of grease.

I went to three clubs and got nowhere. Each time I walked through the door the bartender's eyes glanced up to meet me as they would somebody who had been expected all evening. As soon as I sat at the bar the girls went to the women's room or out the back door. The electronic noise of the country bands was deafening, the amplified squelch in the microphones like metal raking on a blackboard. When I tried to talk to someone, the person would nod politely in the din as though a man without vocal cords were speaking to him, then go back to his drink or stare in the opposite direction through the layers of cigarette smoke.

I gave up and walked back to my truck, which was parked between the clapboard side of a nightclub and a squat six-room motel with a small yellow lawn and a dead palm tree by the drive-in registration window. The air smelled of creosote and burnt diesel fuel from the railway tracks by the river, dust from the shell parking lot, liquor and beer from a trash barrel filled with empty bottles. The sky out over the Gulf trembled with dry lightning.

I didn't hear her behind me.

'Everyone on the strip knew you were coming two hours ago, cutie,' she said.

I turned and squinted my eyes at her. She drank out of her beer bottle, then puffed off her cigarette. Her face was porcine, her lipstick on crooked, her dyed red hair lacquered like tangled wire on her head. She put one hand on her hip and waited for me to recognize her.

'Charlotte?'

'What a memory. Have I tubbed up on you?'

'No, not really. You're looking good.'

She laughed to herself and blew her cigarette smoke at an upward angle into the dark.

Thirty years ago she had been a stripper and hooker on Bourbon Street, then the mistress of a loanshark who blew his brains out, the wife of an alcoholic ex-police sergeant who ended up in Angola for doping horses at the Fairgrounds, and the last I heard the operator of a massage parlor in Algiers.

'What are you doing out here on the Airline?' I said.

'I run the dump next door,' she said, and nodded toward the motel. 'Hey, I got to sit down. I really got crocked tonight.' She shook a wooden chair loose from the trash pile by the side of the nightclub and sat down in it with her knees splayed and took another drink from her beer bottle. An exhaust fan from a restroom was pinging above her head. 'I already heard what you're looking for, Streak. A guy bringing the chickens in from the country, right?'

'Do you know who he is?'

'They come and they go. I'm too old to keep track of it anymore.'

'I'd sure like to talk to this guy, Charlotte.'

'Yeah, somebody ought to run an iron hook through his balls, all right, but it's probably not going to happen.'

'Why not?'

'You got the right juice, the play pen stays open.'

'He's connected?'

'What do you think?'

'With the Balboni family?'

'Maybe. Maybe he's got juice with the cops or politicians. There's lots of ways to stay in business.'

'But one way or another, most of them go down. Right?'

She raised her beer bottle to her mouth and drank.

'I don't think anybody is going to be talking about this guy a whole lot,' she said. 'You hear stories, you know what I mean? That this guy you're looking for is somebody you don't want mad at you, that he can be real hard on his chippies.'

'Is it true?'

She set her empty bottle down on the shells and placed her hands loosely in her lap. For a moment the alcoholic shine left her eyes and her expression became strangely introverted, as though she were focusing on some forgotten image deep inside herself.

'When you're in the life, you hear a lot of bad stories, cutie. That's because there aren't many good ones,' she said.

'The man I'm looking for may be a serial killer, Charlotte.'

'That kind of guy is a john, not a pimp, Streak.' She leaned on her forearms, puffing on her cigarette, staring at the hundreds of bottle caps pressed into the dirt at her feet. Her lacquered hair was wreathed in smoke. 'Go on back home. You won't change anything here. Everybody out on this road signed up for it one way or another.'

'Nobody signed up to be dead.'

She didn't reply. She scratched a mosquito bite on her kneecap and looked at a car approaching the motel registration window.

'Who's the main man working the bus depot these days?' I said.

'That's Downtown Bobby Brown. He went up on a short-eyes once. Now he's a pro, a real piece of shit. Go back to your family, Streak, before you start to like your work.'

She flipped her cigarette away backhandedly, got to her feet, straightened her dress on her elephantine hips, winked at me as though she might be leaving a burlesque stage, and walked delicately across the oyster shells toward her motel and the couple who waited impatiently for her in the heat and the dust and the snapping of an electric bug killer over the registration window.

You can find the predators at the bus depot almost any time during the twenty-four-hour period. But they operate best during the late hours. That's usually when the adventurers from Vidalia or De Ridder or Wiggins, Mississippi, have run out of money, energy, and hope of finding a place to sleep besides an empty building or an official shelter where they'll be reported as runaways. It's not hard to spot the adventurers, either. The corners of their mouths are downturned, their hair is limp and lies like moist string on their necks; often their hands and thin arms are flecked with home-grown tattoos; they wash under their arms with paper towels and brush their teeth in the depot restroom.

I watched him walk across the waiting room, a leather satchel slung on a strap over his shoulder, his eyes bright, a rain hat at an angle on his head, his tropical white shirt hanging outside his khakis. A gold cross was painted on the side of his satchel.

The two girls were white, both blonde, dressed in shapeless jeans, tennis shoes without socks, blouses that looked salt-faded and stiff with dried perspiration. When he talked with them, his happy face made me think of a mythical goat-footed balloonman whistling far and wee to children in springtime. Then from his satchel he produced candy bars and ham sandwiches, a thermos of coffee, plums and red apples that would dwarf a child's hand.

The girls both bent into their sandwiches, then he was sitting next to them, talking without stop, the smile as wide as an ax blade, the eyes bright as an elf's, the gold cross on his satchel winking with light under his black arm.

I was tired, used up after the long day, wired with too many voices, too many people on the hustle, too many who bought and sold others or ruined themselves for money that you could make with a Fuller-brush route. There was grit in my clothes; my mouth tasted bad; I could smell my own odor. The inside of the depot reeked of cigar butts and the diesel exhaust that blew through the doors to the boarding foyer.

I took the receiver off a pay phone by the men's room and let it hang by its cord.

A minute later the ticket salesman stared down at my badge that I had slid across the counter.

'You want me to do what?' he said.

'Announce that there's a call at the pay phone for Mr Bob Brown.'

'We usually don't do that.'

'Consider it an emergency.'

'Yes, sir.'

'Wait at least one minute before you do it. Okay, podna?'

'Yes, sir.'

I bought a soft drink from a vending machine and looked casually out the glass doors while a bus marked 'Miami' was being loaded underneath with luggage. The ticket salesman picked up his microphone, and Bob Brown's name echoed and resonated off the depot walls.

Downtown Bobby Brown's face became quizzical, impish, in front of the girls, then momentarily apologetic as he explained that he'd be right back, that somebody at his shelter probably needed advice about a situation.

I dropped my soda can into a trash bin and followed him to the pay phone. Downtown Bobby was streetwise, and he turned around and looked into my face. But my eyes never registered his glance, and I passed him and stopped in front of the USA Today machine.

He picked up the telephone receiver, leaning on one arm against the wall, and said, 'This is Bobby. What's happenin'?'

'The end of your career,' I said, and clenched the back of his neck, driving his face into the restroom door. Then I pushed him through the door and flung him inside the room. Blood drained from his nose over his lip; his eyes were wide, yellow-white – like a peeled egg – with shock.

A man at the urinal stood dumbfounded with his fly opened. I held up my badge in front of him.

'This room's in use,' I said.

He zipped his trousers and went quickly out the door. I shot the bolt into the jamb.

'What you want? Why you comin' down on me for? You cain't run a shake on somebody, run somebody's face into a do' just because you—'

I pulled my .45 out of the back of my belt and aimed it into the center of his face.

He lifted his hands in front of him, as though he were holding back an invisible presence, and shook his head from side to side, his eyes averted, his mouth twisted like a broken plum.

'Don't do that, man,' he said. 'I ain't no threat to you. Look, I ain't got a gun. You want to bust me, do it. Come on, I swear it, they ain't no need for that piece, I ain't no trouble.'

He was breathing heavily now. Sweat glistened like oil on his temples. He blotted drops of blood off his nose with the backs of his fingers.

I walked closer to him, staring into his eyes, and cocked the hammer. He backed away from me into a stall, his breath rife with a smell like sardines.

'I want the name of the guy you're delivering the girls to,' I said.

'Nobody. I ain't bringing nobody to nobody.'

I fitted the opening in the barrel to the point of his chin.

'Oh, God,' he said, and fell backward onto the commode. The seat was up, and his butt plummeted deep into the bowl.

'You know the guy I'm talking about. He's just like you. He hunts on the game reserve,' I said.

His chest was bent forward toward his knees. He looked like a round clothespin that had been screwed into a hole.

'Don't do this to me, man,' he said. 'I just had an operation. Take me in. I'll he'p y'all out any way I can. I got a good record wit' y'all.'

'You've been up the road for child molesting, Bobby. Even cons don't like a short-eyes. Did you have to stay in lockdown with the snitches?'

'It was a statutory. I went down for nonconsent. Check it out, man. No shit, don't point that at me no more. I still got stitches inside my groin. They're gonna tear loose.'

'Who's the guy, Bobby?'

He shut his eyes and put his hand over his mouth.

'Just give me his name, and it all ends right here,' I said.

He opened his eyes and looked up at me.

'I messed my pants,' he said.

'This guy hurts people. Give me his name, Bobby.'

'There's a white guy sells dirty pictures or something. He carries a gun. Nobody fucks wit' him. Is that the guy you're talking about?'

'You tell me.'

'That's all I know. Look, I don't have nothin' to do wit' dangerous people. I don't hurt nobody. Why you doin' this to me, man?'

I stepped back from him and eased down the hammer on the .45. He put the heels of his hands on the rim of the commode and pushed himself slowly to his feet. Toilet water dripped off the seat of his khakis. I wadded up a handful of paper towels, soaked them under a faucet, and handed them to him.

'Wipe your face,' I said.

He kept sniffing, as though he had a cold.

'I cain't go back out there.'

'That's right.'

'I went to the bathroom in my pants. That's what you done, man.'

'You're never coming back here, Bobby. You're going to treat this bus depot like it's the center of a nuclear test zone.'

'I got a crib . . . a place . . . two blocks from here, man. What you—'

'Do you know who —— is?' I used the name of a notorious right-wing racist beat cop from the Irish Channel.

His hand stopped mopping at his nose with the towels.

'I got no beef wit' that peckerwood,' he said.

'He broke a pimp's trachea with his baton once. That's right, Bobby. The guy strangled to death in his own spit.'

'What you talkin' 'bout, man? I ain't said nothing 'bout ——. I know what you're doin', man, you're—'

'If I catch you in the depot again, if I hear you're scamming runaways and young girls again, I'm going to tell —— you've been working his neighborhood, maybe hanging around school grounds in the Channel.'

'Who the fuck are you, man? Why you makin' me miserable? I ain't done nothing to you.'

I unlocked the bolt on the door.

'Did you ever read the passage in the Bible about what happens to people who corrupt children?' I said.

He looked at me with a stupefied expression on his face.

'Start thinking about millstones or get into another line of work,' I said.

I had seventeen dollars in my billfold. I gave twelve to the two runaway girls and the address of an AA street priest who ran a shelter and wouldn't report them.

Outside, the air tasted like pennies and felt like it had been superheated in an electric oven. Even the wind blew off the pavement like heat rising from a wood stove. I started my truck, unbuttoned my shirt to my waist, and headed toward I-10 and home.

When I passed Lake Pontchartrain, the moon was up and small waves were breaking against the rim of gray sandy beach by the highway. I wanted to stop the truck, strip to my skivvies, wade out to the drop-off, then dive down through the descending layers of temperature until I struck a cold, dark current at the bottom that would wash the last five hours out of my pores.

But Lake Pontchartrain, like the city of New Orleans, was deceptive. Under its slate-green, capping waves, its moon-glazed surfaces, its twenty-four-mile causeway glowing with electric light, waste of every kind lay trapped in the dark sediment, and the level of toxicity was so high that it was now against the law to swim in the lake.

I kept the truck wide open, the plastic ball on the floor stick shaking under my palm, all the way to the Mississippi bridge at Baton Rouge. Then I rolled down the elevated causeway through the Atchafalaya marsh and the warm night air that smelled of sour mud and hyacinths blooming back in the trees. Out over the pewter-colored bays, the dead cypress trunks were silhouetted against burning gas flares and the vast black-green expanse of sawgrass and flooded willow islands. Huge thunder-clouds tumbled one upon another like curds of black smoke from an old fire, and networks of lightning were bursting silently all over the southern sky. I thought I could smell raindrops on the wind, as cool and clean and bright as the taste of white alcohol on the tip of the tongue.

9

Outside our bedroom window the pecan trees were motionless and gray, soaked with humidity, in the false dawn. Then the early red sun broke above the treeline in the marsh like a Lucifer match being scratched against the sky.

Bootsie slept on her side in her nightgown, the sheet molded against her thigh, her face cool, her auburn hair ruffled on the pillow by the window fan. In the early morning her skin always had a glow to it, like the pale pink light inside a rose. I moved her body against mine and kissed her mouth lightly. Without opening her eyes she smiled sleepily, slipped her arms around my back, widened her thighs, and pressed her stomach against me.

Out on the bayou, I thought I heard a bass leap from the water in a wet arc and then reenter the surface, slapping his tail, as he slid deep into the roots of the floating hyacinths.

Bootsie put her legs in mine, her breath warm against my cheek, one hand in the small of my back, her soft rump rolling against the bed; then I felt that heart-twisting moment begin to grow inside me, past any point of control, like a log dam in a canyon resisting a flooded streambed, then cracking and bursting loose in a rush of white water and uprooted boulders.

I lay beside her and held one of her hands and kissed the thin film of perspiration on her shoulders.

She felt my face with her fingers and touched the white patch in my hair as though she were exploring a physical curiosity in me for the first time.

'Ole Streak,' she said, and smiled.

'Cops get worse names.'

She was quiet a moment, then she said my name with a question mark beside it the way she always did when she was about to broach a difficult subject.

'Yes?' I said.

'Elrod Sykes called while you were in New Orleans. He wanted to apologize for coming to our house drunk.'

'Okay.'

'He wants to go to an AA meeting with you.'

'All right, I'll talk to him about it.'

She looked at the revolving shadows the window fan made on the wall.

'He's rented a big boat,' she said. 'He wants to go fishing out on the salt.'

'When?'

'Day after tomorrow.'

'What'd you tell him?'

'That I'd have to check with you.'

'You don't think we should go?'

'He troubles me, Dave.'

'Maybe the guy *is* psychic. That doesn't mean he's bad news.'

'I have a strange feeling about him. Like he's going to do something to us.'

'He's a practicing alcoholic, Boots. He's a sick man. How's he going to harm us?'

'I don't know. It's just the way I feel. I can't explain it.'

'Do you think he's trying to manipulate me?'

'How do you mean?'

I raised up on one elbow and looked into her face. I tried to smile.

'I have an obligation to help other alcoholics,' I said. 'Maybe it looks like Elrod's trying to pull some strings on me, that maybe instead of helping him I'll end up back on the dirty-boogie again.'

'Let him find his own help, Dave.'

'I think he's harmless.'

'I should have listened to you. I shouldn't have invited them into the house.'

'It's not good to do this, Boots. You're worrying about a problem that doesn't exist.'

'He's too interested in you. There's a reason for it. I know it.'

'I'll invite him to go to a meeting. We'll forget about the fishing trip.'

'Promise me that, Dave.'

'I do.'

'You mean it, no going back on it?'

'You've got my word.'

She cupped my fingers in her hand and put her head under my chin. In the shadowy light I could see her heart tripping against her breast.

I parked in the lot behind the office and walked toward the back door. Two uniformed deputies had just taken a black man in handcuffs into the building, and four others were drinking coffee out of foam cups and smoking cigarettes in the shade against the wall. I heard one of them use my name, then a couple of them laugh when I walked by.

I stopped and walked back to them.

'How y'all doing today?' I said.

'What's going on, Dave?' Rufus Arceneaux said. He had been a tech sergeant in the Marine Corps and he still wore his sunbleached hair in a military crewcut. He took off his shades and rubbed the bridge of his nose.

'I'd better get back on it,' one deputy said, flipped away his cigarette, and walked toward his cruiser.

'What's the joke about, Rufus?' I said.

'It's nothing I said, Dave. I was just quoting the boss man,' Rufus said. His green eyes were full of humor as he looked at the other deputies.

'What did the sheriff have to say?'

'Hey, Dave, fair is fair. Don't lay this off on me,' he said.

'Do you want to take the mashed potatoes out of your mouth and tell me what you're talking about?'

'Hey, come on, man,' he said, chuckling.

'What the fuck, it's no big deal. Tell him,' the deputy next to him said.

'The sheriff said if the governor of Lou'sana invited the whole department to dinner, Dave would be the one guy who'd manage to spit in the punch bowl.'

Then the three of them were silent, suppressing their grins, their eyes roving around the parking lot.

'Drop by my office sometime today, Rufus,' I said. 'Anytime before five o'clock. You think you can work it in?'

'It's just a joke, Dave. I'm not the guy who said it, either.'

'That's right. So it's nothing personal. I'd just like to go through your jacket with you.'

'What for?'

'You've been here eight or nine years, haven't you?'

'That's right.'

'Why is it that I always have the feeling you'd like to be an NCO again, that maybe you have some ambitions you're not quite telling us about?'

His lips became a tight, stitched line, and I saw a slit of yellow light in his eye.

'Think about it and I'll talk to you later, Rufus,' I said, and went inside the building, into the air-conditioned odor of cigar butts and tobacco spittle, and closed the door behind me.

Ten minutes later the sheriff walked into my office and sat down in front of my desk with his arms propped stiffly on his thighs. In his red-faced concentration he reminded me of a football coach sitting on the edge of a bench.

'Where do you think we should begin?' he said.

'You got me.'

'From what I hear about that scene in the restaurant, you tried to tear that fellow apart.'

'Those guys think they're in the provinces and they can do what they want. Sometimes you have to turn them around.'

'It looks like you got your message across. Balboni had to take the guy to the hospital. You broke his tooth off inside his gums.'

'It was a bad morning. I let things get out of control. It won't happen again.'

He didn't answer. I could hear him breathing through his nose.

'You want some coffee?' I said.

'No.'

I got up and filled my cup from my coffee maker in the corner.

'I've had two phone calls already about your trip to New Orleans last night,' he said.

'What about it?'

He took a folded-back notebook out of his shirt pocket and looked at the first page.

'Did you ever hear of a black guy named Robert Brown?' he asked.

'Yep, that's Downtown Bobby Brown.'

'He's trying to file charges against you. He says you smashed his face into a men's-room door at the bus depot.'

'I see.'

'What the hell are you doing, Dave?'

'He's a pimp and a convicted child molester. When I found him, he was scamming two girls who couldn't have been over sixteen years old. I wonder if he passed on that information when he filed his complaint.'

'I don't give a damn what this guy did. I'm worried about a member of my department who might have confused himself with Wyatt Earp.'

'This guy's charges aren't going anywhere and you know it.'

'I wish I had your confidence. It looks like you got some people's attention over in Jefferson Parish, too.'

'I don't understand.'

'The Jefferson Parish Sheriff's Department seems to think we may have a loose cannon crashing around on our deck.'

'What's their problem?'

'You didn't check in with them, you didn't coordinate with anybody, you simply went up and down the Airline Highway on your own, questioning hookers and bartenders about a pimp with no name.'

'So?'

He rubbed the cleft in his round chin, then dropped the flat of his hand on his thigh.

'They say you screwed up a surveillance, that you blew a sting operation of some kind,' he said.

'How?'

'I don't know.'

'It sounds like bullshit to me, sheriff. It sounds like cops on a pad who don't want outsiders walking around on their turf.'

'Maybe that's true, Dave, but I'm worried about you. I think you're overextending yourself and you're not hearing me when I talk to you about it.'

'Did Twinky Lemoyne call?'

'No. Why should he?'

'I went over to Lafayette and questioned him yesterday afternoon.'

He removed his rimless glasses, wiped them with a Kleenex, and put them back on. His eyes came back to meet mine.

'This was after I talked to you about involving people in the investigation who seem to have no central bearing in it?' he asked.

'I'm convinced that somehow Baby Feet was mixed up with Cherry LeBlanc, sheriff. Twinky Lemoyne has business ties to Feet. The way I read it, that makes him fair game.'

'I'm really sorry to hear this, Dave.'

'An investigation clears as well as implicates people. His black employees seem to think well of him. He didn't call in a complaint about my talking to him, either. Maybe he's an all-right guy.'

'You disregarded my instructions, Dave.'

'I saw the bodies of both those girls, sheriff.'

'And?'

'Frankly I'm not real concerned about whose toes I step on.'

He rose from his chair and tucked his shirt tightly into his gunbelt with his thumbs while his eyes seemed to study an unspoken thought in midair.

'I guess at this point I have to tell you something of a personal nature,' he said. 'I don't care for your tone, sir. I don't care for it in the least.'

I picked up my coffee cup and sipped off it and looked at nothing as he walked out of the room.

Rosie Gomez was down in Vermilion Parish almost all day. When she came back into the office late that afternoon her face was flushed from the heat and her dark hair stuck damply to her skin. She dropped her purse on top of her desk and propped her arms on the side of the air-conditioning unit so the windstream blew inside her sleeveless blouse.

'I thought Texas was the hottest place on earth. How did anyone ever live here before air conditioning?' she said.

'How'd you make out today?'

'Wait a minute and I'll tell you. Damn, it was hot out there. What happened to the rain?'

'I don't know. It's unusual.'

'Unusual? I felt like I was being cooked alive inside wet cabbage leaves. I'm going to ask for my next assignment in the Aleutians.'

'I'm afraid you'll never make the state Chamber of Commerce, Rosie.'

She walked back to her desk, blowing her breath up into her face, and opened her purse.

'What'd you do today?' she asked.

'I tried to run down some of those old cases, but they're pretty cold now – people have quit or retired or don't remember, files misplaced, that sort of thing. But there's one interesting thing here—' I spread a dozen National Crime Information Center fax sheets over the top of my desk. 'If one guy committed several of these unsolved murders, it doesn't look like he ever operated outside the state. In other words, there don't seem to be any unsolved female homicides that took place during the same time period in an adjoining area in Texas, Arkansas, or Mississippi.

'So this guy may not only be homegrown but for one reason or another he's confined his murders to the state of Louisiana.'

'That'd be a new one,' she said. 'Serial killers usually travel, unless they prey off a particular local community, like gays or street-walkers. Anyway, look at what jumped up out of the weeds today.'

She held up a plastic Ziploc bag with a wood-handled, brass-tipped pocket knife inside. The single blade was opened and streaked with rust.

'Where'd you find it?'

'A half mile back down the levee from where the girl was found in the barrel. It was about three feet down from the crest.'

'You covered all that ground by yourself?'

'More or less.'

I looked at her a moment before I spoke again. 'Rosie, you're kind of new to the area, but that levee is used by fishermen and hunters all the time. Sometimes they drop stuff.'

'All my work for nothing, huh?' She smiled and lifted a strand of hair off her eyebrow.

'I didn't say that—'

'I didn't tell you something else. I ran into an elderly black man down there who sells catfish and frogs legs off the back of his pickup truck. He said that about a month ago, late at night, he saw a white man in a new blue or black car looking for something on the levee with a flashlight. Just like that alligator poacher you questioned, he wondered why anybody would be down there at night with a new automobile. He said the man with the light wasn't towing a boat trailer and he didn't have a woman with him, either. Evidently he thinks those are the only two reasonable explanations for anyone ever going down there.'

'Could he give you a description of the white man?'

'No, he said he was busy stringing a trotline between some duck blinds. What's a trotline, anyway?'

'You stretch a long piece of twine above the water and tie it to a couple of stumps or flooded trees. Then intermittently you hang twelve-inch pieces of weighted line with baited hooks into the water. Catfish feed by the moon, and when they hook themselves, they usually work the hook all the way through their heads and they're still on the trotline when the fisherman picks it up in the morning.'

I sat on the corner of her desk and picked up the plastic bag and looked at the knife. It was the kind that was made in Pakistan or Taiwan and could be purchased for two dollars on the counter of almost any convenience store.

'If that was our man, what do you think happened?' I said.

'Maybe that's where he bound her with the electrician's tape. He used the knife to slice the tape, then dropped it. He either searched for it that night or came back another night when he discovered it was missing.'

'I don't want to mess up your day, Rosie, but our man doesn't seem to leave fingerprints. At least there were none on the electrician's tape in the two murders that we think he committed. Why should he worry about losing the knife?'

'He needs to orchestrate, to be in control. He can't abide accidents.'

'He left the ice pick in Cherry LeBlanc.'

'Because he meant to. He gave us the murder weapon; it'll never be found on him. But he didn't plan to give us his pocket knife. That bothers him.'

'That's not a bad theory. Our man is all about power, isn't he?'

She stood her purse up straight and started to snap it shut. It clunked on the desk when she moved it. She reached inside and lifted out her .357 magnum revolver, which looked huge in her small hand, and replaced it on top of her billfold. She snapped the catch on the purse.

'I said the obsession is about power, isn't it?'

'Always, always, always,' she said.

The concentration seemed to go out of her eyes, as though the day's fatigue had just caught up with her.

'Rosie?'

'What is it?'

'You feel okay?'

'I probably got dehydrated out there.'

'Drop the knife off with our fingerprint man and I'll buy you a Dr Pepper.'

'Another time. I want to see what's on the knife.'

'This time of day our fingerprint man is usually backed up. He probably won't get to it until tomorrow.'

'Then he's about to put in for some overtime.'

She straightened her shoulders, slung her purse on her shoulder, and walked out the door into the corridor. A deputy with a girth like a hogshead nodded to her deferentially and stepped aside to let her pass.

When I was helping Batist clean up the shop that evening I

remembered that I hadn't called Elrod Sykes about his invitation to go fishing out on the salt. Or maybe I had deliberately pushed it out of my mind. I knew that Bootsie was probably right about Elrod. He was one of the walking wounded, the kind for whom you always felt sympathy, but you knew eventually he'd rake a whole dustpan of broken glass into your head.

I called up to the house and got the telephone number that he had left with Bootsie. While Elrod's phone was ringing, I gazed out the screen window at Alafair and a little black girl playing with Tripod by the edge of a corn garden down the road. Tripod was on his back, rolling in the baked dirt, digging his claws into a deflated football. Even though there was still moisture in the root systems, the corn looked sere and red against the late sun, and when the breeze lifted in the dust the leaves crackled dryly around the scarecrow that was tilted at an angle above the children's heads.

Kelly Drummond answered the phone, then put Elrod on.

'You cain't go?' he said.

'No, I'm afraid not.'

'Tomorrow's Saturday. Why don't you take some time off?'

'Saturday's a big day for us at the dock.'

'Mr Robicheaux . . . Dave . . . is there some other problem here? I guess I was pretty fried when I was at your house.'

'We were glad to have you all. How about I talk with you later? Maybe we'll go to a meeting, if you like.'

'Sure,' he said, his voice flat. 'That sounds okay.'

'I appreciate the invitation. I really do.'

'Sure. Don't mention it. Another time.'

'Yes, that might be fine.'

'So long, Mr Robicheaux.'

The line went dead, and I was left with the peculiar sensation that I had managed both to be dishonest and to injure the feelings of someone I liked.

Batist and I cleaned the ashes out of the barbecue pit, on which we cooked sausage links and split chickens with a *sauce piquante* and sold them at noon to fishermen for three-ninety-five a plate; then we seined the dead shiners out of the bait tanks, wiped down the counters, swept the grained floors clean, refilled the beer and soda-pop coolers, poured fresh crushed ice over the bottles, loaded the candy and cigarette machines, put the fried pies, hard-boiled eggs, and pickled hogs' feet in the icebox in case Tripod got into the shop again, folded up the beach umbrellas on the spool tables, slid back the canvas awning that stretched on wires over the dock, emptied water out of all our rental boats, ran a security chain through a welded ring on the housing of all the outboard engines, and finally latched the board flaps over the windows and turned keys in all the locks.

I walked across the road and stopped by the corn garden where Alafair and the black girl were playing. A pickup truck banged over the ruts in the road and dust drifted across the cornstalks. Out in the marsh, a solitary frog croaked, then the entire vault of sky seemed to ache with the reverberation of thousands of other frogs.

'What's Tripod been into today?' I said.

'Tripod's been good. He hasn't been into anything, Dave,' Alafair said. She picked Tripod up and thumped him down on his back in her lap. His paws pumped wildly at the air.

'What you got there, Poteet?' I said to the little black girl. Her pigtails were wrapped with rubber bands and her elbows and knees were gray with dust.

'Found it right here in the row,' she said, and opened her hand. 'What that is, Mr Dave?'

'I told you. It's a minié ball,' Alafair said.

'It don't look like no ball to me,' Poteet said.

I picked it out of her hand. It was smooth and cool in my palm, oxidized an off-white, cone-shaped at one end, grooved with three rings, and hollowed at the base. The French contribution to the science of killing people at long distances. It looked almost phallic.

'These were the bullets that were used during the War Between the States, Poteet,' I said, and handed it back to her. 'Confederate and federal soldiers fought all up and down this bayou.'

'That's the war Alafair say you was in, Mr Dave?'

'Do I look that old to you guys?'

'How much it worth?' Poteet said.

'You can buy them for a dollar at a store in New Orleans.'

'You give me a dollar for it?' Poteet said.

'Why don't you keep it instead Po'?' I said, and rubbed the top of her head.

'I don't want no nasty minié ball. It probably gone in somebody,' she said, and flung it into the cornstalks.

'Don't do that. You can use it in a slingshot or something,' Alafair said. She crawled on hands and knees up the row and put the minié ball in the pocket of her jeans. Then she came back and lifted Tripod up in her arms.

'Dave, who was that old man?' she said.

'What old man?'

'He got a stump,' Poteet said.

'A stump?'

'That's right, got a stump for a leg, got an arm look like a shriveled-up bird's claw,' Poteet said.

'What are y'all talking about?' I said.

'He was on a crutch, Dave. Standing there in the leaves,' Alafair said.

I knelt down beside them.

'You guys aren't making a lot of sense,' I said.

'He was right up there in the corn leaves. Talking in the wind,' Poteet said. 'His mouth just a big hole in the wind without no sound coming out.'

'I bet y'all saw the scarecrow.'

'If scarecrows got BO,' Poteet said.

'Where'd this old man go?' I said.

'He didn't go anywhere,' Alafair said. 'The wind started blowing real hard in the stalks and he just disappeared.'

'Disappeared? I said.

'That's right,' Poteet said. 'Him and his BO.'

'Did he have a black coat on, like that scarecrow there?' I tried to smile, but my heart had started clicking in my chest.

'No, suh, he didn't have no black coat on,' Poteet said.

'It was gray, Dave,' Alafair said. 'Just like your shirt.'

'Gray?' I said woodenly.

'Except it had some gold on the shoulders,' she said.

She smiled at me as though she had given me a detail that somehow would remove the expression she saw on my face.

My knees popped when I stood up.

'You'd better come home for supper now, Alf,' I said.

'You mad, Dave? We done something wrong?' Alafair said.

'Don't say "we done," little guy. No, of course, I'm not mad. It's just been a long day. We'll see you later, Poteet.'

Alafair swung on my hand as she held on to Tripod's leash, and we walked up the slope through the pecan trees toward the lighted gallery of our house. The thick layer of humus and leaves and moldy pecan husks cracked under our shoes. Behind the house the western horizon was still as blue as a robin's egg and streaked with low-lying pink clouds.

'You're real tired, huh?' she said.

'A little bit.'

'Take a nap.'

'Okay, little guy.'

'Then we can go to Vezey's for ice cream,' she said. She grinned up at me.

'Were they epaulets?' I said.

'What?'

'The gold you saw on his shoulders. Sometimes soldiers wear what they call epaulets on the shoulders of their coats.'

'How could he be a soldier? He was on a crutch. You say funny things sometimes, Dave.'

'I get it from a certain little fellow I know.'

'That man doesn't hurt children, does he?'

'No, I'm sure he's harmless. Let's don't worry about it anymore.'

'Okay, big guy.'

'I'll feed Tripod. Why don't you go inside and wash your hands for supper?'

The screen door slammed after her, and I looked back down the slope under the overhang of the trees at the corn garden in the fading twilight. The wind dented and bent the stalks and straightened the leaves and swirled a column of dust around the blank cheesecloth visage of the scarecrow. The dirt road was empty, the bait shop dark, the gray clouds of insects hovering over the far side of the bayou almost like a metamorphic and tangible shape in the damp heat and failing light. I stared at the cornstalks and the hot sky filled with angry birds, then pinched the moisture and salt out of my eyes and went inside the house.

A tropical storm that had been expected to hit the Alabama coast changed direction and made landfall at Grand Isle, Louisiana. At false dawn the sky had been bone white, then a red glow spread across the eastern horizon as though a distant fire were burning out of control. The barometer dropped; the air became suddenly cooler; the bream began popping the bayou's darkening surface; and in less than an hour a line of roiling, lightning-forked clouds moved out of the south and covered the wetlands from horizon to horizon like an enormous black lid. The rain thundered like hammers on the wood dock and the bait shop's tin roof, filled our unrented boats with water, clattered on the islands of lily pads in the bayou, and dissolved the marsh into a gray and shapeless mist.

Then I saw a sleek white cabin cruiser approaching the dock, its windows beaten with rain, riding in on its own wake as the pilot cut back the throttle. Batist and I were under the awning, carrying the barbecue pit into the lee of the shop. Batist had two inches of a dead cigar in the corner of his mouth; he squinted through the rain at the boat as it bumped against the strips of rubber tire nailed to the dock pilings.

'Who that is?' he said.

'I hate to think.'

'He wavin' at you, Dave. Hey, it's that drunk man done fell in the bayou the ot'er night. That man must surely love water.'

We set the barbecue pit under the eave of the building and got back inside. The rain was whipping off the roof like frothy ropes. Through the screen window I could see Elrod and Kelly Drummond moving around inside the boat's cabin.

'Oh, oh, he trying to get out on the dock, Dave. I ain't goin' out there to pull him out of the bayou this time, me. Somebody ought to give that man swimmin' lessons or a big rock, one, give people some relief.'

Our awning extended on wires all the way to the lip of the dock, and Elrod was trying to climb over the cruiser's gunwale into the protected area under the canvas. He was bare-chested, his white golf slacks soaked and pasted against his skin, his rubber-soled boat shoes sopping with water. His hand slipped off the piling, and he fell backward onto the deck, raked a fishing rod down with him and snapped it in half so that it looked like a broken coat hanger.

I put on my rain hat and went outside.

Elrod shielded his eyes with his hands and looked up at me in the rain. A purple and green rose was tattooed on his upper left chest.

'I guess I haven't got my sea legs yet,' he said.

'Get back inside,' I said, and jumped down into the boat.

'We're going after speckled trout. They always hit in the rain. At least they do on the Texas coast.'

The rain was cold and stung like BBs. From two feet away I could smell the heavy surge of beer on his breath.

'I'm going inside,' I said, and pulled open the cabin door.

'Sure. That's what I was trying to do. Invite you down for a sandwich or a Dr Pepper or a tonic or something,' he said, and closed the cabin door behind us.

Kelly Drummond wore leather sandals, a pair of jeans, and the Ragin' Cajuns T-shirt with my name ironed on the back that Alafair had given to Elrod after he had fallen into the bayou. She picked up a towel and began rubbing Elrod's hair with it. Her green eyes were clear, her face fresh, as though she had recently awakened from a deep sleep.

'You want to go fishing with us?' she said.

'I wouldn't advise going out on the salt today. You'll probably get knocked around pretty hard out there.'

She looked at Elrod.

'The wind'll die pretty soon', he said.

'I wouldn't count on that,' I said.

'The guy who rented us the boat said it can take pretty heavy seas. The weather's not that big a deal, is it?' he said.

On the floor was an open cooler filled with cracked ice, long-necked bottles of Dixie, soda pop, and tonic water.

'I can outfit you with some fly rods and popping bugs,' I said. 'Why not wait until the rain quits and then try for some bass and goggle-eye perch?'

'When's the last time you caught fresh-water fish right after a rain?' He smiled crookedly at me.

'Suit yourself. But I think what you're doing is a bad idea,' I said. I looked at Kelly.

'El, we don't have to go today,' she said. 'Why don't we just drive down to New Orleans and mess around in the French Quarter?'

'I planned this all week.'

'Come on, El. Give it up. It looks like Noah's flood out there.'

'Sorry, we've got to do it. You can understand that, cain't you, Mr Robicheaux?'

'Not really. Anyway, watch the bend in the channel about three miles south. The water's been low and there's some snags on the left.'

'Three miles south? Yeah, I'll watch it,' he said, his eyes refocusing on nothing. His suntanned, taut chest was beaded with water. His feet were wide spread to keep his balance, even though the boat was not moving. 'You sure you don't want a tonic?'

'Thanks, anyway. Good luck to you all,' I said.

Before I went out the cabin door, Kelly made her eyes jump at me, but I closed the door behind me and stepped up on the gunwale and onto the dock.

I began pushing huge balloons of water out of the awning with a broom handle and didn't hear her come up behind me.

'He'll listen to you. Tell him not to go out there,' she said. There was a pinched indentation high up on her right cheek.

'I think you should tell him that yourself.'

'You don't understand. He had a big fight with Mikey yesterday about the script and walked off the set. Then this morning he put the boat on Mikey's credit card. Maybe if we take the boat back now, the man'll tear up the credit slip. You think he might do that?'

'I don't know.'

'El's going to get fired, Mr Robicheaux.'

'Tell Elrod you're staying here. That's about all I can suggest.'

'He'll go anyway.'

'I wish I could help you.'

'That's it? *Au revoir*, fuck you, boat people?'

'In the last two days Elrod told both me and my wife he'd like to go to an AA meeting with me. Now it's ten in the morning and he's already ripped. What do you think the real problem is – the boat, your director, the rain, me, or maybe something else?'

She turned around as though to leave, then turned back and faced me again. There was a bright, painful light in her green eyes, the kind that comes right before tears.

'What do I do?' she said.

'Go inside the shop. I'll try again,' I said.

I climbed back down into the boat and went into the cabin. He had his elbows propped on the instrument panel, while he ate a po'-boy sandwich and stared at the rain dancing in a yellow spray on the bayou.

His face had become wan and indolent, either from fatigue or alcoholic stupor, passive to all insult or intimidation. The more I talked, the more he yawned.

'She's a good lady, El,' I said. 'A lot of men would cut off their fingers with tin snips to have one like her.'

'You got that right.'

'Then why don't you quit this bullshit, at least for one day, and let her have a little serenity?'

Then his eyes focused on the cooler, on an amber, sweating bottle of Dixie nestled in the ice.

'All right,' he said casually. 'Let me borrow your fly rods, Mr Robicheaux. I'll take good care of them.'

'You're not going out on the salt?'

'No, I get seasick anyway.'

'You want to leave the beer box with me?'

'It came with the boat. That fellow might get mad if I left it somewhere. Thanks for your thoughtfulness, though.'

'Yeah, you bet.'

After they were gone, I resolved that Elrod Sykes was on his own with his problems.

'Hey, Dave, that man really a big movie actor?' Batist said.

'He's big stuff out in Hollywood, Batist. Or at least he used to be.'

'He rich?'

'Yeah, I guess he is.'

'That's his reg'lar woman, too, huh?'

'Yep.'

'How come he's so unhappy?'

'I don't know, Batist. Probably because he's a drunk.'

'Then why don't he stop gettin' drunk?'

'I don't know, partner.'

'You mad 'cause I ax a question?'

'Not in the least, Batist,' I said, and headed for the back of the shop and began stacking crates of canned soda pop in the storeroom.

'You got some funny moods, you.' I heard him say behind me.

A half hour later the phone rang.

'Hello,' I said.

'We got a problem down here,' a voice said.

There was static on the line and rain was throbbing on the shop's tin roof.

'Elrod?'

'Yeah. We hit some logs or a sandbar or something.'

'Where are you?'

'At a pay phone in a little store. I waded ashore.'

'Where's the boat?'

'I told you, it's messed up.'

'Wait until the water rises, then you'll probably float free.'

'There's a bunch of junk in the propeller.'

'What are you asking me, Elrod?'

'Can you come down here?'

Batist was eating some chicken and dirty rice at the counter. He looked at my face and laughed to himself.

'How far down the bayou is the boat?' I said.

'About three miles. That bend you were talking about.'

'The bend I was talking about, huh?'

'Yeah, you were right. There's some dead trees or logs in the water there. We ran right into them.'

'We?'

'Yeah.'

'I'll come after you, but I'm also going to give you a bill for my time.'

'Sure thing, absolutely, Dave. This is really good of you. If I can—'

I put the receiver back on the hook.

'Tell Bootsie I'll be back in about an hour,' I said.

Batist had finished his lunch and was peeling the cellophane off a fresh cigar. The humor had gone out of his face.

'Dave, I ain't one to tell you what to do, no,' he said. 'But there's people that's always gonna be axin' for somet'ing. When you deal with them kind, it don't matter how much you give, it ain't never gonna be enough.'

He lit his cigar and fixed his eyes on me as he puffed on the smoke.

I put on my raincoat and hat, hitched a boat and trailer to my truck, and headed down the dirt road under the canopy of oak trees toward the general store where Elrod had made his call. The trailer was bouncing hard in the flooded chuckholes, and through the rearview mirror I could see the outboard engine on the boat's stern wobbling against the engine mounts. I shifted down to second gear, pulled to a wide spot on the road, and let a car behind me pass. The driver, a man wearing a shapeless fedora, looked in the opposite direction of me, out toward the bayou, as he passed.

Elrod was not at the general store, and I drove a quarter mile farther south to the bend where he had managed to put the cabin cruiser right through the limbs of a submerged tree and simultaneously scrape the bow up on a sandbar. The bayou was running high and yellow now, and gray nests of dead morning-glory vines had stuck to the bow and fanned back and forth in the current.

I backed my trailer into the shallows, then unwinched my boat into the water, started the engine, and opened it up in a shuddering whine against the steady clatter of the rain on the bayou's surface.

I came astern of the cabin cruiser and looped the painter on a cleat atop the gunwale so that my boat swung back in the lee of the cruiser. The current was swirling with mud and I couldn't see the propeller, but obviously it was fouled. From under the keel floated a streamer of torn hyacinth vines and lily pads, baited trotline, a divot ripped out of a conical fish net, and even the Clorox marker bottle that went with it.

Elrod came out of the cabin with a newspaper over his head.

'How does it look?' he said.

'I'll cut some of this trash loose, then we'll try to back her into deeper water. How'd you hit a fish net? Didn't you see the Clorox bottle?'

'Is that how they mark those things?'

I opened my Puma knife, reached as deep below the surface as I could, and began pulling and sawing away the flotsam from the propeller.

'I 'spect the truth is I don't have any business out here,' he said.

I flung a handful of twisted hyacinths and tangled fish line toward the bank and looked up into his face. The alcoholic shine had gone out of his eyes. Now they simply looked empty, on the edge of regret.

'You want me to get down in the water and do that?' he asked. Then he glanced away at something on the far bank.

'No, that's all right,' I said. I stepped up on the bow of my boat and over the rail of the cabin cruiser. 'Let's see what happens. If I can't shake her loose, I'll tie my outboard onto the bow and try to pull her sideways into the current.'

We went inside the dryness of the cabin and closed the door. Kelly was sleeping on some cushions, her face nestled into one arm. When she woke, she looked around sleepily, her cheek wrinkled with the imprint of her arm; then she realized that little had changed in her and Elrod's dreary morning and she said, 'Oh,' almost like a child to whom awakenings are not good moments.

I started the engine, put it in reverse, and gave it the gas. The hull vibrated against the sandbar, and through the back windows I could see mud and dead vegetation boiling to the bayou's surface behind the stern. But we didn't move off the sandbar. I tried to go forward and rock it loose, then I finally cut the engine.

'It's set pretty hard, but it might come off if you push against the bow, Elrod,' I said. 'You want to do that?'

'Yeah, sure.'

'It's not deep there. Just stay on the sandbar, close to the hull.'

'Put on a life jacket, El,' Kelly said.

'I swam across the Trinity River once at flood stage when houses were floating down it,' he said.

She took a life jacket out of a top compartment, picked up his wrist, and slipped his arm through one of the loops. He grinned at me. Then his eyes looked out the glass at the far bank.

'What's that guy doing?' he said.

'Which guy?' I said.

'The guy knocking around in the brush out there.'

'How about we get your boat loose and worry about other people later?' I said.

'You got it,' he said, tied one lace on his jacket, and went out into the rain.

He held on to the rail on the cabin roof and worked his way forward toward the bow. Kelly watched him through the glass, biting down on the corner of his lip.

'He waded ashore before,' I said, and smiled at her. 'He's not in any danger there.'

'El has accidents. Always.'

'A psychologist might say there's a reason for that.'

She turned away from the glass, and her green eyes moved over my face.

'You don't know him, Mr Robicheaux. Not the gentle person who gives himself no credit for anything. You're too hard on him.'

'I don't mean to be.'

'You are. You judge him.'

'I'd like to see him get help. But he won't as long as he's on the juice or using.'

'I wish I had those kinds of easy answers.'

'They're not easy. Not at all.'

Elrod eased himself over the gunwale, sinking to his chest, then felt his way through the silt toward the slope on the sandbar.

'Can you stand in the stern? For the weight,' I said to Kelly.

'Where?'

'In the back of the boat.'

'Sure.'

'Take my raincoat.'

'I'm already sopped.'

I restarted the engine.

'Just a minute,' I said, and put my rain hat on her head. Her wet blond curls were flattened against her brow. 'I don't mean to be personal, but I think you're a special lady, Ms Drummond, a real soldier.'

She used both her hands to pull the hat's floppy brim down tightly on her hair. She didn't answer, but for the first time since I had met her, she looked directly into my eyes with no defensiveness or anger or fear and in fact with a measure of respect that I felt in all probability was not easily won.

I waved at Elrod through the front glass, kicked the engine into reverse, and opened the throttle. The exhaust pipes throbbed and blew spray high into the air at the waterline, the windows shook, the boards under my feet hummed with the vibrations from the engine compartment. I looked over my shoulder through the back glass and saw Kelly bent across the gunwale, pushing at the bottom of the bayou with a tarpon gaff; then suddenly the hull scraped backward in the sand, sliding out of a trench in a yellow and brown gush of silt and dead reeds, and popped free in the current.

Elrod was standing up on the sandbar, his balled fists raised over his head in victory.

I cut the gas and started out the cabin door to get the anchor.

Just as the rain struck my bare head and stung my eyes, just as I looked across the bayou and saw the man in the shapeless fedora kneeling hard against an oak tree, his shadowed face aimed along the sights of a bolt-action rifle, the leather sling twisted military style around the forearm, I knew that I was caught in one of those moments that will always remain forever too late, knew this even before I could yell, wave my arms, tell him that the person in the rain hat and Ragin' Cajuns T-shirt with my name on the back was not me. Then the rifle's muzzle flashed in the rain, the report echoing across the water and into the willow islands. The bullet cut a hole like a rose petal in the back of Kelly's shirt and left an exit wound in her throat that made me think of wolves with red mouths running through trees.

10

It was a strange week, for me as well as the town. Kelly's death brought journalists from all over the country to New Iberia. They filled all the motels, rented every available automobile in Lafayette, and dwarfed in both numbers and technical sophistication our small area news services.

Many of them were simply trying to do their jobs. But another kind came among us, too, those who have a voyeuristic glint in their eyes, whose real motivations and potential for callousness are unknown even to themselves.

I got an unlisted phone number for the house.

I began to be bothered by an odor, both in my sleep and during the late afternoon when the sun baked down on the collapsed barn at the back of our property. I noticed it the second day after Kelly's death, the day that Elrod escorted her body back to Kentucky for the burial. It smelled like dead rats. I scattered a bag of lime among the weeds and rotted boards and the smell went away. Then the next afternoon it was back, stronger than before, as invasive as a stranger's soiled palm held to your face.

I put our bedroom fan in the side window so it would draw air from the front of the house, but I would dream of turkey buzzards circling over a corrugated rice field, of sand-flecked winds blowing across the formless and decomposing shape of a large animal, of a woman's hair and fingernails wedging against the sides of a metal box.

On the seventh morning I woke early, walked past the duck pond in the soft blue light, soaked the pile of boards and strips of rusted tin with gasoline, and set it afire. The flames snapped upward in an enormous red-black handkerchief, and a cottonmouth moccasin, with a body as thick as my wrist, slithered out of the boards into the weeds, the hindquarters of an undigested rat protruding from its mouth.

The shooter left nothing behind, no ejected brass, no recoverable prints from the tree trunk where he had fired. The pocket knife Rosie had found on the levee turned out to be free of prints. Almost all of our work had proved worthless. We had no suspects; our theories about motivation were as potentially myriad as the time we were willing to invest in thinking about them. But one heart-sinking and unalterable conclusion remained in front of my eyes all day long, in my conversations with Rosie, the sheriff, and even the deupties who went out of their way to say good morning through my office door – Kelly Drummond was dead, and she was dead because she had been mistaken for me.

I didn't even see Mikey Goldman walk into my office. I looked up and he was standing there, flexing the balls of his feet, his protruding, pale eyes roving about the room, a piece of cartilage working in his jaw like an angry dime.

'Can I sit down?' he said.

'Go ahead.'

'How you doing?'

'I'm fine, thanks. How are you?'

'I'm all right.' His eyes went all over me, as though I were an object he was seeing for the first time.

'Can I help you with something?' I said.

'Who's the fucking guy who did this?'

'When we know that, he'll be in custody.'

'In custody? How about blowing his head off instead?'

'What's up, Mr Goldman?'

'How you handling it?'

'I beg your pardon?'

'How you handling it? I'm talking about you. I've been there, my friend. First Marine Division, Chosin Reservoir. Don't try to bullshit me.'

I put down my fountain pen on the desk blotter, folded my hands, and stared at him.

'I'm afriad we're operating on two different wavelengths here,' I said.

'Yeah? The guy next to you takes a round, and then maybe you start wondering if you aren't secretly glad it was him instead of you. Am I wrong?'

'What do you want?'

He rubbed the curly locks of salt-and-pepper hair on his neck and rolled his eyes around the room. The skin around his mouth was taut, his chin and jaw hooked in a peculiar martial way like a drill instructor's.

'Elrod's going to go crazy on me. I know it, I've seen him there before. He's a good kid, but he traded off some of his frontal lobes for magic mushrooms a long time ago. He likes you, he'll listen to you. Are you following me?'

'No.'

'You keep him at your place, you stay out at his place, I don't care how you do it. I'm going to finish this picture.'

'You're an incredible man, Mr Goldman.'

'What?' He began curling his fingers backward, as though he wanted to pull words from his chest. 'You heard I got no feelings, I don't care about my actors, movie people are callous dipshits?'

'I never heard your name before you came to New Iberia. It seems to me, though, you have only one thing on your mind – getting what you want. Anyway, I'm not interested in taking care of Elrod Sykes.'

'If I get my hands on the fuckhead who shot Kelly, you're going to have to wipe him off the wallpaper.'

'Eventually we're going to get this guy, Mr Goldman. But in the meantime, the vigilante histrionics don't float too well in a sheriff's department. Frankly, they're not too convincing, either.'

'What?'

'Ask yourself a question: How many professional killers, and the guy who did this is a professional killer, could a rural parish like this have? Next question: Who comprises the one well-known group of professional criminals currently with us in New Iberia? Answer: Julie Balboni and his entourage of hired cretins. Next question: Who's in a movie partnership with these characters?'

He leaned back in his chair, bouncing his wrists lightly on the chair's arms, glancing about the room, his eyes mercurial, one moment almost amused, then suddenly focused on some festering inner concern.

'Mr Goldman?' I said.

'Yeah? You got something else to say?'

'No, sir, not a thing.'

'Good. That's good. You're not a bad guy. You've just got your head up your hole with your own problems. It's just human.'

'I see. I'm going down the hall for a cup of coffee now,' I said. 'I suspect you'll be gone when I get back.'

He rose to his feet and flexed a kink out of his back. He unwrapped a short length of peppermint candy and stuck it in his jaw.

'You want one?' he said.

'No, thanks.'

'Don't pretend to be a Rotary man. I checked out your background before I asked you to babysit Elrod. You're as crazy as any of us. You're always just one step away from blowing up somebody's shit.'

He cocked his finger, pointed it at me, and made a hollow popping sound with his mouth.

That night I dreamed that I was trying to save a woman from drowning way out on the Gulf of Mexico. We were sliding down a deep trough, the froth whipping across her blond curls and bloodless face, her eyes sealed against the cobalt sky. Our heads protruded from the water as though they had been severed and placed on a plate. Then her body turned to stone, heavier than a marble statue, and there was no way I could keep her afloat. She sank from my arms, plummeting downward into a vortex of spinning green light, down into a canyon hundreds of feet below, a gush of air bubbles rising from a pale wound in her throat.

Rosie came through the door, clunked her purse loudly on her desk, and began rummaging through the file cabinet. She had to stand on her toes to see down into the top drawer.

'You want to have lunch today?' she asked.

'What?'

'Lunch . . . do you want to have lunch? Come in, Earth.'

'Thanks, I'll probably go home.' Then as an afterthought I said, 'You're welcome to join us.'

'That's all right. Another time.' She sat down behind her desk and began shifting papers around in a couple of file folders. But her eyes kept glancing up into my face.

'Have you got something on your mind?' I asked.

'Yeah, you.'

'You must be having an uneventful day.'

'I worked late last night. The dispatcher and I had a cup of coffee together. He asked me how I was getting along here, and I told him real good, no complaints. Then he asked me if I'd experienced any more smart-aleck behavior from some of the resident clowns in the department. I told him they'd been perfect gentlemen. I bet you can't guess what he said next.'

'You got me.'

She imitated a Cajun accent. ' "Them guys give you any mo' trouble, you just tell Dave, Miz Rosie. He done tole 'em what's gonna happen the next time they bother you." '

'He was probably exaggerating a little bit.'

'You didn't need to do that for me, Dave.'

'I apologize.'

'Don't be a wise-ass, either.'

'Boy, you're a pistol.'

'How should I take that?'

'I don't know. How about easing up?'

She rested one small hand on top of the other. She had the same solid posture behind her desk that I remembered in the nuns at the elementary school I attended.

'You look tired,' she said.

'I have bouts of insomnia.'

'You want to talk about what happened out on the bayou?'

'No.'

'Do you feel guilty about it?'

'What do you think I feel? I feel angry about it.'

'Why?'

'What kind of question is that?'

'Do you feel angry because you couldn't control what happened? Do you think somehow you're to blame for her death?'

'What if I said "yes to all the above"? What difference would it make? She's dead.'

'I think beating up on yourself has about as much merit as masturbation.'

'You're a friend, Rosie, but let it go.'

I busied myself with my paperwork and did not look back up for almost a minute. When I did, her eyes were still fixed on me.

'I just got some interesting information from the Bureau about Julie Balboni,' she said. She waited, then said, 'Are you listening?'

'Yes.'

'This year NOPD Vice has closed up a half-dozen of his dirty movie theaters and two of his escort services. His fishing fleet just went into bankruptcy, too.' When I didn't respond, she continued. 'That's where he laundered a lot of his drug money. He'd declare all kinds of legitimate profits to the IRS that never existed.'

'That's how all the wiseguys do it, Rosie. In every city in the United States.'

'Except the auditors at the IRS say he just made a big mistake. He came up with millions of dollars for this Civil War movie and he's going to have a hard time explaining where he got it.'

'Don't count on it.'

'The IRS nails their butts to the wall when nobody else can.'

I sharpened a pencil over the wastebasket with my pocket knife.

'I have a feeling I'm boring you,' she said.

'No, you're just reviving some of my earlier misgivings.'

'What?'

'I think your agency wants Julie's ass in a sling. I think these murders have secondary status.'

'That's what you think, is it?'

'That's the way it looks from here.'

She rose from her chair, closed the office door, then stood by my desk. She wore a white silk blouse with a necklace of black wooden beads. Her fingers were hooked in front of her stomach like an opera singer's.

'Julie's been a longtime embarrassment to the feds,' I continued. 'He's connected to half the crime in New Orleans and so far he's never spent one day in the bag.'

'When I was sixteen something happened to me I thought I'd never get over.' There was a flush of color in her throat. 'Not just because of what two drunken crew leaders did to me in the back of a migrant farmworkers' bus, either. It was the way the cops treated it. In some ways that was even worse. Have I got your attention, sir?'

'You don't need to do this, Rosie.'

'Like hell I don't. The next day I was sitting with my father in the waiting room outside the sheriff's office. I heard two deputies laughing about it. They not only thought it was funny, one of them said something about pepper-belly poontang. I'll never forget that moment. Not as long as I live.'

I folded up my pocket knife and stared at the tops of my fingers. I brushed the pencil shavings off my fingers into the wastebasket.

'I'm sorry,' I said.

'When I went to work for the Bureau, I swore I'd never see a woman treated the way I was. So I take severe exception to your remarks, Dave. I'd like to bust Julie Balboni, but that has nothing to do with the way I feel about the man who raped and murdered these women.'

'Where'd this happen?'

'In a migrant camp outside of Bakersfield. It's not an unusual story. Ask any woman who's ever been on a crew bus.'

'I think you're a solid cop, Rosie. I think you'll nail any perp you put in your sights.'

'Then change your goddamn attitude.'

'All right.'

She was waiting for me to say something else, but I didn't.

Her shoulders sagged and she started back toward her desk. Then she turned around. Her eyes were wet.

'That's all you've got to say?' she asked.

'No, it's not.'

'What, then?'

'I'm proud to be working with you. I think you're a standup lady.'

She started to take a Kleenex out of her purse, then she snapped the purse shut again and took a breath.

'I'm going down the hall a minute,' she said.

'All right.'

'Are we both clear about the priority in this investigation, Dave?'

'Yeah, I think we are.'

'Good. Because I don't want to have this kind of discussion again.'

'Let me mention just one thing before you go. Several years ago my second wife was murdered by some drug dealers. You know that, don't you?'

'Yes.'

'One way or another, the guys and the woman who killed her went down for it. But sometimes I wake up in the middle of the night and the old anger comes back. Even though these people took a heavy fall, for a couple of them the whole trip, sometimes it still doesn't seem enough. You know the feeling I'm talking about, don't you?'

'Yes.'

'Fair enough.' Then I said, 'You're sure you don't want to come home and have lunch with us today?'

'This isn't the day for it, Dave. Thanks, anyway,' she said, and went out the door with her purse clutched under her arm, her face set as impassively as a soldier's.

Elrod Sykes called the office just after I had returned from lunch. His voice was deep, his accent more pronounced.

'You know where there's some ruins of an old plantation house south of your boat dock?' he asked.

'What about it?'

'Can you meet me there in a half hour?'

'What for?'

'I want to talk to you, that's what for.'

'Talk to me now, Elrod, or come into the office.'

'I get nervous down there. For some reason police uniforms always make me think of a breathalyzer machine. I don't know why that might be.'

'You sound like your boat might have caught the early tide.'

'Who cares? I want to show you something. Can you be there or not?'

'I don't think so.'

'What the fuck is with you? I've got some information about Kelly's death. You want it or not?'

'Maybe you ought to give some thought as to how you talk to people.'

'I left my etiquette in Kelly's family plot up in Kentucky. I'll meet you in thirty minutes. If you're not interested, fuck you, Mr Robicheaux.'

He hung up the phone. I had the feeling I was beginning to see the side of Elrod's personality that had earned him the attention of the tabloids.

Twenty minutes later I drove my pickup truck down a dirt lane through a canebrake to the ruins of a sugar planter's home that had been built on the bayou in the 1830s. In 1863 General Banks's federal troops had dragged the piano outside and smashed it apart in the coulee, then as an afterthought had torched the slave quarters and the second story of the planter's home. The roof and cypress timbers had collapsed inside the brick shell, the cisterns and outbuildings had decayed into humus, the smithy's forge was an orange smear in the damp earth, and vandals had knocked down most of the stone markers in the family cemetery and, looking for gold and silver coins, had pried up the flagstones in the fireplaces.

Why spend time with a rude drunk, particularly on the drunk's terms?

Because it's difficult to be hard-nosed or righteous toward a man who, for the rest of his life, will probably wake sweating in the middle of the night with a recurring nightmare or whose series of gray dawns will offer no promise of light except that first shuddering razor-edged rush that comes out of a whiskey glass.

I leaned against the fender of my truck and watched Elrod's lavender Cadillac come down the dirt lane and into the shade of the oak trees that grew in front of the ruined house. The security guard from the set, Murphy Doucet, was behind the wheel, and Elrod sat in the passenger's seat, his tanned arm balanced on the window ledge, a can of Coca-Cola in his hand.

'How you doing today, Detective Robicheaux?' Doucet said.

'Fine. How are you?'

'Like they say, we all chop cotton for the white man one way or another, you know what I mean?' he said, and winked.

He rubbed the white scar that was embossed like a chicken's foot on his throat and opened a newspaper on the steering wheel. Elrod came around the side of the Cadillac in blue swimming shorts, a beige polo shirt, and brand-new Nike running shoes.

He drank from his Coca-Cola can, set it on the hood of the car, then put a breath mint in his mouth. His eyes wandered around the clearing, then focused wanly on the sunlight winking off the bayou beyond the willow trees.

'Would you like to continue our conversation?' I said.

'You think I was out of line or something?'

'What did you want to tell me, Elrod?'

'Take a walk with me out yonder in those trees and I'll show you something.'

'The old cemetery?'

'That isn't it. Something you probably don't know about.'

We walked through a thicket of stunted oaks and hackberry trees, briars and dead morning-glory vines, to a small cemetery with a rusted and sagging piked iron fence around it. Pines with deep-green needles grew out of the graves. A solitary brick crypt had long ago collapsed in upon itself and become overgrown with wild roses and showers of four o'clocks.

Elrod stood beside me, and I could smell the scent of bourbon and spearmint on his breath. He looked out into the dazzling sunlight but his eyes didn't squint. They had a peculiar look in them, what we used to call in Vietnam the thousand-yard stare.

'There,' he said, 'in the shade, right on the edge of those hackberry trees. You see those depressions?'

'No.'

He squeezed my arm hard and pointed.

'Right where the ground slopes down to the bayou,' he said, and walked ahead of me toward the rear of the property. He pointed down at the ground. 'There's four of them. You stick a shovel in here and you'll bring up bone.'

In a damp area, where rainwater drained off the incline into a narrow coulee, there were a series of indentations that were covered with mushrooms.

'What's the point of all this?' I said.

'They were cooking mush in an iron pot and an artillery shell got all four of them. The general put wood crosses on their graves, but they rotted away a long time ago. He was a hell of an officer, Mr Robicheaux.'

'I'll be going now,' I said. 'I'd like to help you, Elrod, but I think you've marked your own course.'

'I've been with these guys. I know what they went through. They had courage, by God. They made soup out of their shoes and rifle balls out of melted nails and wagon-wheel rims. There was no way in hell they were going to quit.'

I turned and began walking back to my truck. Through the shade I could see the security guard urinating by the open door of the Cadillac. Elrod caught up with me. His hand clenched on my arm again.

'You want to write me off as a wet-brain, that's your business,' he said. 'You don't care about what these guys went through, that's your business, too. I didn't bring you out here for this, anyway.'

'Then why am I here?'

He turned me toward him with his hand.

'Because I don't like somebody carrying my oil can,' he said.

'What?'

'That's a Texas expression. It means I don't want somebody else toting my load. You've convinced yourself the guy who killed Kelly thought he had you in his sights. That's right, isn't it?'

'Maybe.'

'What makes you so goddamn important?'

I continued to walk toward my truck. He caught up with me again.

'You listen to me,' he said. 'Before she was killed I had a blowout with Mikey. I told him the script stinks, the screenwriters he's hired couldn't get jobs writing tampon ads, he's nickel-and-dimeing the whole project to death, and I'm walking off the set unless he gets his head on straight. The greaseballs heard me.'

'Which greaseballs?'

'Balboni's people. They're all over the set. They killed Kelly to keep me in line.'

His facial skin high up on one cheek crinkled and seemed almost to vibrate.

'Take it easy, El.'

'They made her an object lesson, Mr Robicheaux.'

I touched his arm with my hand.

'Maybe Julie's involved, maybe not,' I said. 'But if he is, it's not because of you. You've got to trust me on this one.'

He turned his face away and pushed at one eye with the heel of his hand.

'When Julie and his kind create object lessons, they go right to the source of their problem,' I said. 'They don't select out innocuous people. It causes them too many problems.'

I heard his breath in his throat.

'I made them keep the casket closed,' he said. 'I told the funeral director in Kentucky, if he let her parents see her like that, I'd be back, I'd—'

I put my arm over his shoulder and walked back through the cemetery with him.

'Let's go back to town and have something to eat,' I said. 'Like somebody said to me this morning, it's no good to kick ourselves around the block, is it? What do you think?'

'She's dead. I cain't see her, either. It's not right.'

'I beg your pardon?'

'I see those soldiers but I cain't see her. Why's that? It doesn't make any sense.'

'I'll be honest with you, partner. I think you're floating on the edge of delirium tremens. Put the cork in the jug before you get there, El. Believe me, you don't have to die to go to hell.'

'You figure me for plumb down the road and around the bend, don't you? I don't blame you. I got my doubts about what I see myself.'

'Maybe that's not a bad sign.'

'When we were driving through that canebrake, I said to Murph, the security guy, "Who's that standing behind Mr Robicheaux?" Then I looked again and I knew who it was. Except I've never seen him in daylight before. When I looked again, he was gone. Which isn't the way he does things.'

'I'm going to an AA meeting tonight. You want to come?'

'Yeah, why not? It cain't be worse than having dinner with Mikey and the greaseballs.'

'You might be a little careful about your vocabulary when you're around those guys.'

'Boy, I wonder what my grandpa would say if he saw me working with the likes of that bunch. I told you he was a Texas ranger, didn't I?'

'You surely did.'

'You know what he once told me about Bonnie Parker and Clyde Barrow? He said—'

'I have to get back to the office. How about I pick you up at your place at seven-thirty?'

'Sure. Thanks for coming out, Mr Robicheaux. I'm sorry about my bad manners on the phone. I'm not given to using profanity like that. I don't know what got into me.' He picked up his soda can off the hood of his Cadillac and started to drink out of it. 'It's just Coca-Cola. That's a fact.'

'You'd better drink it then.'

He smiled at me.

'It rots your teeth,' he said, and emptied the can into the dirt.

That night I sat alone in the bait shop, a glass of iced coffee in my hand, and tried to figure the connection between Kelly's death and the pursuit of a serial killer who might also be involved with prostitution. Nothing in the investigation seemed to fit. Was the serial killer also a pimp? Why did his crimes seem to be completely contained within the state of Louisiana? If he had indeed mistaken Kelly for me, what had I discovered in the investigation that would drive him to attempt the murder of a police officer? And what was Baby Feet Balboni's stake in all this?

Equally troubling was the possibility that Kelly's death had nothing to do with our hunt for a serial killer. Maybe the rifleman in the fedora had had another motivation, one that was connected with a rat's nest of bones, strips of dried skin, rotted clothing, and a patch of kinky hair attached to a skull plate. Did someone out there believe that somehow that gaping mouth, impacted with sand, strung with green algae, could whisper the names of two killers who thought they had buried their dark deed in water thirty-five years ago?

We live today in what people elect to call the New South. But racial fear, and certainly white guilt over racial injustice, die hard. Hogman Patin, who probably feared very little in this world, had cautioned me because of my discovery of the lynched black man out in the Atchafalaya. He had also suggested that the dead man had been involved with a white woman. To Hogman, those events of years ago were still alive, still emblematic of an unforgiven and collective shame, to be spoken about as obliquely as possible, in all probability because some of the participants were still alive, too.

Maybe it was time to have another talk with Hogman, I thought.

When I drove out to his house on the bayou, the interior was dark and the white curtains in his open windows were puffing outward in the breeze. In the back I could hear the tinkling of the Milk of Magnesia bottles and the silver crosses that he had hung all over the branches of a live oak.

Where are you, Hogman? I thought. I wedged my business card in the corner of his screen door.

The moon was yellow through the trees. I could smell the unmistakable odor of chitterlings that had been burned in a pot. Out on the blacktop I heard a car engine. The headlights bounced off the tree trunks along the roadside, then the driver slowed and I thought he was about to turn into the grove of trees at the front of Hogman's property. I thought the car was probably Hogman's, and I started to walk toward the blacktop. Then the driver accelerated and his headlights swept past me.

I would have given no more notice to the driver and his vehicle, except that just as I started to turn back toward my truck and leave, he cut his lights and really gave it the gas.

If his purpose had been to conceal his license number, he was successful. But two other details stuck in my mind: the car looked new and it was dark blue, the same characteristics as the automobile that two witnesses had seen on the levee in Vermilion Parish where the asphyxiated girl had been stuffed nude into a metal barrel.

Or maybe the car had simply contained a couple of teenage neckers looking for a little nocturnal privacy. I was too tired to think about it anymore. I started my truck and headed home.

The night was clear, the constellations bursting against the black dome of sky overhead. There was no hint of rain, no sudden drop or variation in temperature to cause fog to roll off the water. But two hundred yards down from Hogman's house the road was suddenly white with mist, so thick my headlights couldn't penetrate it. At first I thought a fire was burning in a field and the wind had blown the smoke across the road. But the air smelled sweet and cool, like freshly turned earth, and was almost wet to the touch. The mist rolled in clouds off the bayou, covered the tree trunks, closed about my truck like a white glove, drifted in wisps through my windows. I don't know whether I deliberately stopped the truck or my engine killed. But for at least thirty seconds my headlights flickered on and off, my starter refused to crank, and my radio screamed with static that was like fingernails on a blackboard.

Then as suddenly as it had come, the mist evaporated from the road and the tree trunks and the bayou's placid surface as though someone had held an invisible flame to it, and the night air was again as empty and pristine as wind trapped under a glass bell.

In the morning I made do with mechanical answers in the sunlight and cleaned the terminals on my truck battery with baking soda, water, and an old toothbrush.

Hogman called the next afternoon from the movie set out on Spanish Lake.

'What you want out at my house?' he said.

'I need to talk with you about the lynched black man.'

'I done already tole you what I know. That nigger went messin' in the wrong place.'

'That's not enough.'

'Is for me.'

'You said my father helped your mother when you were in prison. So now I'm asking you to help me.'

'I already have. You just ain't listen.'

'Are you afraid of somebody, Sam? Maybe some white people?'

'I fear God. Why you talkin' to me like this?'

'What time will you be home today?'

'When I get there. You got your truck?'

'Yes.'

'My car hit a tree last night. It ain't runnin' no mo'. Come out to the set this evenin' and give me a ride home. 'Bout eight or nine o'clock.'

'We'll see you then, partner,' I said, and hung up.

The sun was red and half below the horizon, the cicadas droning in the trees, when I drove down the lane through the pecan orchard to the movie set on Spanish Lake. But I soon discovered that I was not going to easily trap Hogman Patin alone. It was Mikey Goldman's birthday and the cast and crew were throwing him a party. A linen-covered buffet table was piled with catered food, a huge pink cake, and a bowl of champagne punch in the center. The tree trunks along the lake's edge were wrapped with paper bunting, and Goldman's director's chair must have had two dozen floating balloons tied to it.

It was a happy crowd. They sipped punch out of clear plastic glasses and ate boiled shrimp and thin slices of *boudin* off paper plates. Mikey Goldman's face seemed to almost shine in the ambiance of goodwill and affection that surrounded him.

In the crowd I saw Julie Balboni and his entourage, Elrod Sykes, the mayor of New Iberia, the president of the Chamber of Commerce, a couple of Teamster officials, a state legislator, and Twinky Hebert Lemoyne from Lafayette. In the middle of it all sat Hogman Patin on an up-ended crate, his twelve-string guitar resting on his crossed thighs. He was dressed like a nineteenth-century Negro street musician, except he also wore a white straw cowboy hat slanted across his eyes. The silver picks on his right hand rang across the strings as he sang,

> Soon as day break in the mornin'
> I gone take the dirt road home.
> 'Cause these blue Monday blues
> Is goin' kill me sure as you're born.

'You ought to get yourself a plate.'

It was Murphy Doucet, the security guard. He was talking to me but his eyes were looking at a blond girl in shorts and a halter by the punch bowl. He ate a slice of *boudin* off a toothpick, then slipped the toothpick into the corner of his mouth and sucked on it.

'It doesn't look like everybody's broken up about Kelly Drummond's death, does it?' I said.

'I guess they figure life goes on.'

'You're in business with Mr Lemoyne over there, Murph?'

'We own a security service together, if that's what you mean. For me it's a pretty good deal, but for him it's nothing. If there's a business around here making money, Twinky's probably got a piece of it. Lord God, that man knows how to make money.'

Lemoyne sat by the lake in a canvas chair, a julep glass filled with bourbon, shaved ice, and mint leaves in his hand. He looked relaxed and cool in the breeze off the water, his rimless glasses pink with the sun's afterglow. His eyes fixed for a moment on my face, then he took a sip from his glass and watched some kids waterskiing out on the lake.

'Get something to eat, Dave. It's free. Hell, I'm going to take some home,' Murphy Doucet said.

'Thanks, I've already eaten,' I said, and walked over to where Hogman sat next to two local black women who had been hired as extras.

'You want a ride?' I said.

'I ain't ready yet. They's people want me to play.'

'It was your idea for me to come out here, Sam.'

'I'll be comin' directly. That's clear, ain't it? Mr Goldman fixin' to cut his cake.'

Then he began singing,

> *I ax my bossman, Bossman, tell me what's right.*
> *He whupped my left, said, Boy, now you know what's right.*
> *I tole my bossman, Bossman, just give me my time.*
> *He say, Damn yo' time, boy,*
> *Boy, you time behind.*

I waited another half hour as the twilight faded, the party grew louder, and someone turned on a bank of floodlamps that lit the whole area with the bright unnatural radiance of a phosphorus flare. The punch bowl was now empty and had been supplanted by washtubs filled with cracked ice and canned beer, a portable bar, and two white-jacketed black bartenders who were making mint juleps and Martinis as fast as they could.

'I've got to head for the barn, Hogman,' I said.

'This lady axin' me somet'ing. Give me ten minutes,' he said.

A waiter came by with a tray and handed Hogman and the black woman with him paper cups streaming with draft beer. Then he handed me a frosted julep glass packed with shaved ice, mint leaves, orange slices, and candied cherries.

'I didn't order this,' I said.

'Gentlemen over yonder say that's what you drink. Say bring it to you. It's a Dr Pepper, suh.'

'Which gentleman?'

'I don't rightly remember, suh.'

I took the cup off the tray and drank from it. The ice was so cold it made my throat ache.

The lake was black now, and out in the darkness, above the noise of the revelers, I could hear somebody trying to crank an outboard engine.

I finished my drink and set the empty glass on the buffet table.

'That's it for me, Sam,' I said. 'You coming or not?'

'This lady gonna carry me home,' he said. His eyes were red from drinking. They looked out at nothing from under the brim of his straw cowboy hat.

'Hogman—' I said.

'This lady live down the road from my house. Some trashy niggers been givin' her trouble. She don't want to go home by herself. That's the way it is. I be up to yo' office tomorrow mornin'.'

I tried to look into his face, but he occupied himself with twisting the tuning pegs on his guitar. I turned and walked back through the shadows to my pickup truck. When I looked back at the party through my windshield, the blonde girl in shorts and a halter was putting a spoonful of cake into Mikey Goldman's mouth while everyone applauded.

It rained hard as I approached the drawbridge over the bayou south of town. I could see the bridge tender in his lighted window, the wet sheen and streaks of rust on the steel girders, the green and red running lights of a passing boat in the mist. I was only a few minutes from home. I simply had to cross the bridge and follow the dirt road down to my dock.

But that was not what I did or what happened.

A bolt of lightning exploded in a white ball by the side of the road and blew the heart of a tree trunk, black and smoking, out into my headlights. I swallowed to clear my ears, and for just a second, in the back of my throat, I thought I could taste black cherries, bruised mint leaves, and orange rind. Then I felt a spasm go through me just as if someone had scratched a kitchen match inside my skull.

The truck veered off the shoulder, across a collapsed barbed-wire cattle gate, onto the levee that dissected the marsh. I remember the wild butter-cups sweeping toward me out of the headlights, the rocks and mud whipping under the fenders, then the fog rolling out of the dead cypress trees and willow islands, encircling the truck, smothering the windows. I could hear thunder crashing deep in the marsh, echoing out of the bays, like distant artillery.

I knew that I was going off the levee, but I couldn't unlock my hands from the steering wheel or move my right foot onto the brake pedal. I felt myself trembling, my insides constricting, my back teeth grinding, as though all my nerve endings had been severed and painted with iodine. Then I heard lightning pop the levee and blow a spray of muddy water across my windshield.

Get out, I thought. *Knock the door handle down with your elbow and jump.*

But I couldn't move.

The mist was as pink and thick as cotton candy and seemed to snap with electric currents, like a kaleidoscopic flickering of snakes' tongues. I felt the front wheels of the truck dip over the side of the levee, gain momentum with the weight in the rear end, then suddenly I was rumbling down an incline through weeds and broken cane, willow saplings and cattails, until the front wheels were embedded up to the axle in water and sand.

I don't know how long I sat there. I felt a wave of color pass through me, like nausea or the violent shudder that cheap bourbon gives you when you're on the edge of delirium tremens; then it was gone and I could see the reflection of stars on the water, the tips of the dead cypress silhouetted against the moon, and a campfire, where there should have been no fire, burning in a misty grove of trees on high ground thirty yards out from the levee.

And I knew that was where I was supposed to go.

As I waded through the lily pads toward the trees, I could see the shadows of men moving about in the firelight and hear their cracker accents and the muted sound of spoons scraping on tin plates.

I walked up out of the shallows into the edge of the clearing, dripping water, hyacinth vines stringing from my legs. The men around the fire paid me little notice, as though, perhaps, I had been expected. They were cooking tripe in an iron pot, and they had hung their haversacks and wooden canteens in the trees and stacked their rifle-muskets in pyramids of fives. Their gray and butternut-brown uniforms were sun-bleached and stiff with dried salt, and their unshaved faces had the lean and hungry look of a rifle company that had been in the field a long time.

Then from the far side of the fire a bearded man with fierce eyes stared out at me from under a gray hat with gold cord around the crown. His left arm was pinned up in a black sling, and his right trouser leg flopped loosely around a shaved wooden peg.

He moved toward me on a single crutch. I could smell tobacco smoke and sweat in his clothes. Then he smiled stiffly, the skin of his face seeming almost to crack with the effort. His teeth were as yellow as corn.

'*I'm General John Bell Hood. Originally from Kentucky. How you do, suh?*' he said, and extended his hand.

11

'*Do you object to shaking hands?*' he said.

'*No. Not at all. Excuse me.*'

The heel of his hand was half-mooned with calluses, his voice as thick as wet sand. A holstered cap-and-ball revolver hung on his thigh.

'*You look puzzled,*' he said.

'*Is this how it comes? Death, I mean.*'

'*Ask them.*'

Some of his men were marked with open, bloodless wounds I could put my fist in. Beyond the stacked rifles, at the edge of the firelight, was an ambulance wagon. Someone had raked a tangle of crusted bandages off the tailgate onto the ground.

'*Am I dead?*' I said.

'*You don't look it to me.*'

'*You said you're John Bell Hood.*'

'*That's correct.*'

His face was narrow, his cheeks hollow, his skin grained with soot.

'*I've read a great deal about you.*'

'*I hope it met your approval.*'

'*You were at Gettysburg and Atlanta. You commanded the Texas Brigade. They could never make you quit.*'

'*My political enemies among President Davis's cabinet sometimes made note of that fact.*'

'*What's the date?*' I asked.

'*It's April 21, 1865.*'

'*I don't understand.*'

'*Understand what?*'

'*Lee has already surrendered. The war's over. What are you doing here?*'

'*It's never over. I would think you'd know that. You were a lieutenant in the United States Army, weren't you?*'

'*Yes, but I gave my war back to the people who started it. I did that a long time ago.*'

'*No, you didn't. It goes on and on.*'

He eased himself down on an oak stump, his narrow eyes lighting with pain. He straightened his artificial leg in front of him. The hand that hung out of his sling had wasted to the size of a monkey's paw. A corporal threw a log into the campfire, and sparks rose into the tree branches overhead.

'*It's us against them, my friend,*' he said. '*There's insidious men abroad in the land.*' He swept his crutch at the marsh. '*My God, man, use your eyes.*'

'*The federals?*'

'*Are your eyes and ears stopped with dirt?*'

'*I think this conversation is not real. I think all of this will be gone with daylight.*'

'*You're not a fool, Mr Robicheaux. Don't pretend to be one.*'

'*I've seen your grave in New Orleans. No, it's in Metairie. You died of the yellowjack.*'

'*That's not correct. I died when they struck the colors, suh.*' He lifted his crutch and pointed it at me as he would a weapon. The firelight shone on his yellow teeth. '*They'll try your soul, son. But don't give up your cause. Occupy the high ground and make them take it foot by bloody foot.*'

'*I don't know what we're talking about.*'

'*For God's sakes, what's wrong with you? Venal and evil men are destroying the world you were born in. Can't you understand that? Why do I see fear in your face?*'

'*I think maybe I'm drunk again. I used to have psychotic episodes when I went on benders. I thought dead men from my platoon were telephoning me in the rain.*'

'*You're not psychotic, lieutenant. No more than Sykes is.*'

'*Elrod is a wet-brain, general.*'

'*The boy has heart. He's not afraid to be an object of ridicule for his beliefs. You mustn't be either. I'm depending on you.*'

'*I have no understanding of your words.*'

'*Our bones are in this place. Do you think we'll surrender it to criminals, to those who would use our teeth and marrow for landfill?*'

'*I'm going now, general.*'

'*Ah, you'll simply turn your back on madness, will you? The quixotic vision is not for you, is it?*'

'*Something's pulling me back. I can feel it.*'

'*They put poison in your system, son. But you'll get through it. You've survived worse. The mine you stepped on, that sort of thing.*'

'*Poison?*'

He shrugged and put a cigar in his mouth. A corporal lit it with a burning stick from the fire. In the shadows a sergeant was putting together a patrol that was about to move out. Their faces were white and wrinkled like prunes with exhaustion and the tropical heat.

'*Come again,*' he said.

'*I don't think so.*'

'*Then goodnight to you, suh.*'

'*Goodnight to you, general. Goodnight to your men, too.*'

He nodded and puffed on his cigar. There were small round hollows in his cheeks.

'*General?*'

'*Yes, suh?*'

'*It's going to be bad, isn't it?*'

'*What?*'

'*What you were talking about, something that's waiting for me down the road.*'

'*I don't know. For one reason or another I seem to have more insight into the past than the future.*' He laughed to himself. Then his face sobered and he wiped a strand of tobacco off his lip. '*Try to keep this in mind. It's just like when they load with horseshoes and chain. You think the barrage will last forever, then suddenly there's a silence that's almost louder than their cannon. Please don't be alarmed by the severity of my comparison. Goodnight lieutenant.*'

'Goodnight, general.'

I waded through the shallows, into deeper water, back toward the levee. The mist hung on the water in wisps that were as dense as thick-bodied snakes. I saw ball lightning roll through the flooded trees and snap apart against a willow island; it was as bright and yellow as molten metal dipped from a forge. Then rain began twisting out of the sky, glistening like spun glass, and the firelight behind me became a red smudge inside a fog bank that billowed out of the marsh, slid across the water, and once again closed around my truck.

The air was so heavy with ozone I could almost taste it on my tongue; I could hear a downed power line sparking and popping in a pool of water and smell a scorched electrical odor in the air like the metallic, burnt odor the St Charles streetcar makes in the rain. I could hear a nutria crying in the marsh for its mate, a high-pitched shriek like the scream of a hysterical woman. I remember all these things. I remember the mud inside my shoes, the hyacinth vines binding around my knees, the gray-green film of algae that clung to my khaki trousers like cobweb.

When a sheriff's deputy and two paramedics lifted me out of the truck cab in the morning, the sun was as white as an arc welder's flame, the morning as muggy and ordinary as the previous day, and my clothes as dry as if I had recently taken them from my closet. The only physical change the supervising paramedic noted in me was an incised lump the size of a darning sock over my right eye. That and one other cautious, almost humorous observation.

'Dave, you didn't fall off the wagon on your head last night, did you?' he asked. Then, 'Sorry. I was just kidding. Forget I said that.'

Our family physician, Dr Landry, sat on the side of my bed at Iberia General and looked into the corner of my eye with a small flashlight. It was late afternoon now, Bootsie and Alafair had gone home, and the rain was falling in the trees outside the window.

'Does the light hurt your eyes?' he asked.

'A little. Why?'

'Because your pupils are dilated when they shouldn't be. Tell me again what you felt just before you went off the road.'

'I could taste cherries and mint leaves and oranges. Then I felt like I'd bitten into an electric wire with my teeth.'

He put the small flashlight in his shirt pocket, adjusted his glasses, and looked at my face thoughtfully. He was an overweight, balding, deeply tanned golf player, with rings of blond hair on his forearms.

'How do you feel now?' he said.

'Like something's torn in my head. The way wet cardboard feels when you tear it with your hands.'

'Did you eat anything?'

'I threw it up.'

'You want the good news? The tests don't show any booze in your system.'

'How could there be? I didn't drink any alcohol.'

'People have their speculations sometimes, warranted or not.'

'I can't help that.'

'The bad news is I don't know what did this to you. But according to the medics you said some strange things, Dave.'

I looked away from his face.

'You said there were soldiers out there in the marsh. You kept insisting they were hurt.'

The wind began gusting, and rain and green leaves blew against the window.

'The medics thought maybe somebody had been with you. They looked all over the levee,' he said. 'They even sent a boat out into those willow islands.'

'I'm sorry I created so much trouble for them.'

'Dave, they say you were talking about Confederate soldiers.'

'It was an unusual night.'

He took a breath, then made a sucking sound with his lips.

'Well, you weren't drunk and you're not crazy, so I've got a theory,' he said. 'When I was an intern at Charity Hospital in New Orleans back in the sixties, I treated kids who acted like somebody had roasted their brains with a blowtorch. I'm talking about LSD, Dave. You think one of those Hollywood characters might have freshened up your Dr Pepper out there in Spanish Lake?'

'I don't know. Maybe.'

'It didn't show up in the tests, but that's not unusual. To really do a tox screen for LSD, you need a gas chromatograph. Not many hospitals have one. We sure don't, anyway. Has anything like this ever happened to you before?'

'When my wife was killed, I got drunk again and became delusional for a while.'

'Why don't we keep that to ourselves?'

'Is something being said about me, doc?'

He closed his black bag and stood up to go.

'When did you start worrying about what people say?' he said. 'Look, I want you to stay in here a couple of days.'

'Why?'

'Because you didn't feel any gradual effects, it hit you all at once. That indicates to me a troubling possibility. Maybe somebody really loaded you up. I'm a little worried about the possibility of residual consequences, Dave, something like delayed stress syndrome.'

'I need to get back to work.'

'No, you don't.'

'I'll talk with the sheriff. Actually I'm surprised he hasn't been up yet.'

Dr Landry rubbed the thick hair on his forearm and looked at the water pitcher and glass on my nightstand.

'What is it?' I said.

'I saw him a short while ago. He said he talked with you for a half hour this morning.'

I stared out the window at the gray sky and the rain falling in the trees. Thunder boomed and echoed out of the south, shaking the glass in the window, and for some reason in my mind's eye I saw rain-soaked enlisted men slipping in the mud around a cannon emplacement, swabbing out the smoking barrel, ramming home coils of chain and handfuls of twisted horseshoes.

I couldn't sleep that night, and in the morning I checked myself out of the hospital and went home. The doctor had asked me how I felt. My answer had not been quite accurate. I felt empty, washed-out inside, my skin rubbery and dead to the touch, my eyes jittering with refracted light that seemed to have no source. I felt as if I had been drinking sour mash for three days and had suddenly become disconnected from all the internal fires that I had nourished and fanned and depended upon with the religious love of an acolyte. There was no pain, no broken razor blades were twisting inside the conscience; there was just numbness, as though wind and fleecy clouds and rain showers marching across the canefields were a part of a curious summer phenomenon that I observed in a soundless place behind a glass wall.

I drank salt water to make myself throw up, ate handfuls of vitamins, made milkshakes filled with strawberries and bananas, did dozens of pushups and stomach crunches in the back yard, and ran wind sprints in the twilight until my chest was heaving for breath and my gym shorts were pasted to my skin with sweat.

I showered with hot water until there was none left in the tank, then kept my head under the cold water for another five minutes. Then I put on a fresh pair of khakis and a denim shirt and walked outside into the gathering dusk under the pecan trees. The marsh across the road was purple with haze, sparkling with fireflies. A black kid in a pirogue was cane fishing along the edge of the lily pads in the bayou. His dark skin seemed to glow with the sun's vanishing red light. His body and pole were absolutely still, his gaze riveted on his cork bobber. The evening was so quiet and languid, the boy so transfixed in his concentration, that I could have been looking at a painting.

Then I realized, with a twist of the heart, that something was wrong – there was no sound. A car passed on the dirt road, the boy scraped his paddle along the side of the pirogue to move to a different spot. But there was no sound except the dry resonance of my own breathing.

I went into the house, where Bootsie was reading under a lamp in the living room. I was about to speak, with the trepidation a person might have if he were violating the silence of a church, just to see if I could hear the sound of my own voice, when I heard the screen door slam behind me like a slap across the ear. Then suddenly I heard the television, the cicadas in the trees, my neighbor's sprinkler whirling against his myrtle bushes, Batist cranking an outboard down at the dock.

'What is it, Dave?' Bootsie said.

'Nothing.'

'Dave?'

'It's nothing. I guess I got some water in my ears.' I opened and closed my jaws.

'Your dinner is on the table. Do you want it?'

'Yeah, sure,' I said.

Her eyes studied mine.

'Let me heat it up for you,' she said.

'That'd be fine.'

When she walked past me she glanced into my face again.

'What's the deal, Boots? Do I look like I just emerged from a hole in the dimension?' I said, following her into the kitchen.

'You look tired, that's all.'

She kept her back to me while she wrapped my dinner in plastic to put in the microwave.

'What's wrong?' I said.

'Nothing, really. The sheriff called. He wants you to take a week off.'

'Why didn't he tell *me* that?'

'I don't know, Dave.'

'I think you're keeping something from me.'

She put my plate in the microwave and turned around. She wore a gold cross on a chain, and the cross hung at an angle outside her pink blouse. Her fingers came up and touched my cheek and the swelling over my right eye.

'You didn't shave today,' she said.

'What did the sheriff say, Boots?'

'It's what some other people are saying. In the mayor's office. In the department.'

'What?'

'That maybe you're having a breakdown.'

'Do you believe I am?'

'No.'

'Then who cares?'

'The sheriff does.'

'That's his problem.'

'A couple of deputies went out to the movie location and questioned some of the people who were at Mr Goldman's birthday party.'

'What for?'

'They asked people about your behavior, things like that.'

'Was one of those deputies Rufus Arceneaux?'

'Yes, I think so.'

'Boots, this is a guy who would sell his mother to a puppy farm to advance one grade in rank.'

'That's not the point. Some of those actors said you were walking around all evening with a drink in your hand. People believe what they want to hear.'

'I had blood and urine tests the next morning. There was no alcohol in my system. It's a matter of record at the hospital.'

'You beat up one of Julie Balboni's hoods in a public place, Dave. You keep sending local businessmen signals that you just might drive a lot of big money out of town. You tell the paramedics that there're wounded Confederate soldiers in the marsh. What do you think people are going to say about you?'

I sat down at the kitchen table and looked out the back screen at the deepening shadows on the lawn. My eyes burned, as though there were sand under my eyelids.

'I can't control what people say,' I said.

She stood behind me and rested her palms on my shoulders.

'Let's agree on one thing,' she said. 'We just can't allow ourselves to do anything that will help them hurt us. Okay, Dave?'

I put my right hand on top of hers.

'I won't,' I said.

'Don't try to explain what you think you heard or saw in the marsh. Don't talk about the accident. Don't defend yourself. You remember what you used to say? "Just grin and walk through the cannon smoke. It drives them crazy." '

'All right, Boots.'

'You promise?'

'I promise.'

She folded her arms across my chest and rested her chin on the top of my head. Then she said, 'What kind of person would try to do this to us, Dave?'

'Somebody who made a major mistake,' I said.

But it was a grandiose remark. The truth was that I had taken the drink at the party incautiously and that I had walked right into the script someone else had written for me.

Later that night, in bed, I stared at the ceiling and tried to recreate the scene under the oak trees at Spanish Lake. I wanted to believe that I could reach down into my unconscious and retrieve a photographic plate on which my eye had engraved an image of someone passing his hand over the glass of Dr Pepper, black cherries, orange slices, and bruised mint that a waiter was about to serve me.

But the only images in my mind were those of a levee extending out into gray water and an electrically charged fog bank rolling out of the cypress trees.

Bootsie turned on her side and put her arm across my chest. Then she moved her hand down my stomach and touched me.

I stared up into the darkness. The trees were motionless outside the window. I heard a 'gator flop in the marsh.

Then her hand went away from me and I felt her weight turn on the mattress toward the opposite wall.

An hour later I dressed in the darkness of the living room, slipped my pickup truck into neutral, rolled it silently down the dirt lane to the dock, and hooked my boat and trailer to the bumper hitch.

I put my boat into the water at the same place I had driven my truck off the levee. I used the paddle to push out into the deeper water, past the cattails and lily pads that grew along the bank's edge, then I lowered the engine and jerked it alive with the starter rope.

The wake off the stern looked like a long V-shaped trench roiling with yellow mud, bobbing with dead logs. Then the moon broke through the clouds, gilding the moss in the cypress with a silver light, and I could see cottonmouths coiled on the lower limbs of willow trees, the gnarled brown-green head of a 'gator in a floating island of leaves and sticks, the stiffened, partly eaten body of a coon on a sandbar, and a half-dozen wood ducks that skittered across the water in front of the high ground and the grove of trees where I had met the general.

I cut the throttle and let the boat ride on its wake until the bow slid up on the sand. Then I walked into the trees with a six-battery flashlight and a GI entrenching tool.

The ground was soft, oozing with moisture, matted with layers of dead leaves and debris left by receding water. Tangles of abandoned trotlines were strung about the tree trunks; Clorox marker bottles from fish traps lay half-buried in the sand.

In the center of the clearing I found the remains of a campfire.

A dozen blackened beer cans lay among the charred wood. Crushed into the grass at the edge of the fire was a used rubber.

I kicked the wood, ashes, and cans across the ground, propped my flashlight in the weeds, folded the E-tool into the shape of a hoe, screwed down and locked the socket at the base of the blade, and started chopping into the earth.

Eighteen inches down I hit what archaeologists call a 'fireline,' a layer of pure black charcoal sediment from a very old fire. I sifted it off the blade's tip a shovelful at a time. In it was a scorched brass button and the bottom of a hand-blown bottle, one that had tiny air bubbles inside the glass's green thickness.

But what did that prove? I asked myself.

Answer: That perhaps nineteenth-century trappers, cypress loggers, or even army surveyors had built a campfire there.

Then I thought about the scene the other night: the stacked rifle muskets, the haversacks suspended in the trees, the exhaustion in the men who were about to move out on patrol, the dry, bloodless wounds that looked like they had been eaten clean by maggots, the ambulance wagon and the crusted field dressings that had been raked out onto the ground.

The ambulance wagon.

I picked up my flashlight and moved to the far side of the clearing. The water was black under the canopy of flooded trees out in the marsh. I knelt and started digging out a two-by-four-foot trench. The clearing sloped here, and the ground was softer and wetter, wrinkled with small eroded gullies. I scraped the dirt into piles at each end of the hole; a foot down, water began to run from under the shovel blade.

I stopped to reset the blade and begin digging back toward the top of the incline. Then I saw the streaks of rust and bits of metal, like small red teeth, in the wet piles of dirt at each end of the hole. I shined the flashlight into the hole, and protruding from one wall, like a twisted snake, was a rusted metal band that might have been the rim of a wagon wheel.

Five minutes later I hit something hard, and I set the E-tool on the edge of the hole and used my fingers to pry up the hub of a wagon wheel with broken spokes the length of my hand radiating from it. I placed it on the slope, and in the next half hour I created next to it a pile of square nails, rotted wood as light as balsa, metal hinges, links of chain, a rusted wisp of a drinking cup, and a saw. The wood handle and the teeth had been almost totally eaten away by groundwater, but there was no mistaking the stubby, square, almost brutal shape; it was a surgeon's saw.

I carried everything that I had found back to the boat. My clothes were streaked with mud; I stunk of sweat and mosquito repellent. My palms rang with popped water blisters. I wanted to wake up Bootsie, call Elrod or perhaps even the sheriff, to tell anybody who would listen about what I had found.

But then I had to confront the foolishness of my thinking. How sane was any man, at least in the view of others, who would dig for Civil War artifacts in a swamp in the middle of the night in order to prove his sanity?

In fact, that kind of behavior was probably not unlike a self-professed extraterrestrial traveler showing you his validated seat reservations on a UFO as evidence of his rationality.

When I got back home I covered my boat with a tarp, took a shower, ate a ham-and-onion sandwich in the kitchen while night birds called to each other under the full moon, and decided that the general and I would not share our secrets with those whose lives and vision were defined by daylight and a rational point of view.

12

I slept late the next morning, and when I awoke, I found a note from Bootsie on the icebox saying that she had taken Alafair shopping in town. I fixed chicory coffee and hot milk, Grape-Nuts, and strawberries on a tray and carried it out to the redwood table under the mimosa tree in the backyard. The morning was not hot yet, and blue jays flew in and out of the dappled shade and my neighbor's sprinkler drifted in an iridescent haze across my grass.

Then I saw Rosie Gomez's motor-pool government car slow by our mailbox and turn into our drive. Her face was pointed at an upward angle so she could see adequately over the steering wheel. I got up from the table and waved her around back.

She wore a white blouse and white skirt with black pumps, a wide black belt, and black purse.

'How you feeling?' she asked.

'Pretty good. In fact, great.'

'Yeah?'

'Sure.'

'You look okay.'

'I am okay, Rosie. Here, I'll get you some coffee.'

When I came back outside with the pot and another cup and saucer, she was sitting on the redwood bench, looking out over my duck pond and my neighbor's sugarcane fields. Her face looked cool and composed.

'It's beautiful out here,' she said.

'I'm sorry Bootsie and Alafair aren't here. I'd like you to meet them.'

'Next time. I'm sorry I didn't come see you in the hospital. I'd left for New Orleans early that morning. I just got back.'

'What's up?'

'About three weeks ago an old hooker in the Quarter called the Bureau and said she wanted to seriously mess up Julie Balboni for us. Except she was drunk or stoned and the agent who took the call didn't give it a lot of credence.'

'What'd she have to offer?'

600

'Nothing, really. She just kept saying, "He's hurting these girls. Somebody ought to fix that rotten dago. He's got to stop hurting these girls." '

'So what happened?'

'Three days ago there was a power failure at the woman's apartment building on Ursulines. With the air conditioning off it didn't take long for the smell to leak through the windows to the courtyard. The ME says it was suicide.'

I watched her face. 'You don't think it was?' I said.

'How many women shoot themselves through the head with a .38 special?'

'Maybe she was drunk and didn't care how she bought it.'

'Her refrigerator and cupboards were full of food. The apartment was neat, all her dishes were washed. There was a sack of delicatessen items on the table she hadn't put away yet. Does that suggest the behavior of a despondent person to you?'

'What do they say at NOPD?'

'They don't. They yawn. They've got a murder rate as high as Washington, DC's. You think they want to turn the suicide of a hooker into another open homicide case?'

'What are you going to do?'

'I don't know. I think you've been right about a tie with Balboni. The most common denominator that keeps surfacing in this case is prostitution in and around New Orleans. There isn't a pimp or chippy working in Jefferson or Orleans parishes who don't piece off their action to Julie Balboni.'

'That doesn't mean Julie's involved with killing anyone, Rosie.'

'Be honest with me. Do I continue to underwhelm you as a representative of Fart, Barf, and Itch?'

'I'm not quite sure I—'

'Yeah, I bet. What do pimps call the girls in the life? "Cash on the hoof," right?'

'That's right.'

'Do you think anybody kills one of Balboni's hookers and gets away with it without his knowledge and consent?'

'Except there's a bump in the road here. The man who murdered Kelly Drummond probably thought he was shooting at me. The mob doesn't kill cops. Not intentionally, anyway.'

'Maybe he's a cowboy, out of control. We've got rogue cops. The wiseguys have rogue shitheads.'

I laughed. 'You're something else,' I said.

'Cut the patronizing attitude, Dave.'

'Sorry,' I said, still smiling.

Her eyes looked into mine and darkened.

'I'm worried about you. You don't know how to keep your butt down,' she said.

'Everything's copacetic. Believe me.'

'Sure it is.'

'You know something I don't?'

'Yes, human beings and money make a very bad combination,' she said.

'I'd appreciate it if you could stop speaking to me in hieroglyphics.'

'Few people care about the origins of money, Dave. All they see is a president's picture on a bill, not Julie Balboni's.'

'Let's spell it out, okay?'

'A few of the locals have talked to the sheriff about your taking an extended leave. At least that's what I've heard.'

'He's not a professional cop, but he's a decent man. He won't give in to them.'

'He's an elected official. He's president of the Lions Club. He eats lunch once a week with the Chamber of Commerce.'

'He knows I wasn't drinking. The people in my AA group know it, too. So do the personnel at the hospital. Dr Landry thinks somebody zapped me with LSD. What else can I say?'

Her face became melancholy, and she looked out at the sunlight on the field with a distant, unfocused expression in her eyes.

'What's the trouble?' I asked.

'You don't hear what you're saying. Your reputation, maybe your job, are hanging in the balance now, and you think it's acceptable to tell people that somebody loaded your head with acid.'

'I never made strong claims on mental health, anyway.'

I tried to smile when I said it. But the skin around my mouth felt stiff and misshaped.

'It isn't funny,' she said. She stood up to go, and the bottom of her purse, with the .357 magnum inside, sagged against her hip. 'I'm not going to let them do this to you, Dave.'

'Wait a minute, Rosie. I don't send other people out on the firing line.'

She began walking through the sideyard toward her car, her back as square and straight as a small door.

'Rosie, did you hear me?' I said. 'Rosie? Come back here and let's talk. I appreciate what you're trying to—'

She got into her automobile, gave me the thumbs-up sign over the steering wheel, and backed out onto the dirt road by the bayou. She dropped the transmission into low and drove down the long tunnel of oaks without glancing back.

Regardless of Rosie's intentions about my welfare, I still had not resolved the possibility that the racial murder I had witnessed in 1957 and the sack of skin and polished bones Elrod Sykes had discovered in the Atchafalaya Basin were not somehow involved in this case.

However, where do you start in investigating a thirty-five-year-old homicide that was never even reported as such?

Although southern Louisiana, which is largely French Catholic, has a long and depressing record of racial prejudice and injustice, it never compared in intensity and violence to the treatment of black people in the northern portion of the state or in Mississippi, where even the murder of a child, Emmett Till, by two Klansmen in 1955 not only went unpunished but was collectively endorsed after the fact by the town in which it took place. There was no doubt that financial exploitation of black people in general, and sexual exploitation of black women in particular, were historically commonplace in our area, but lynching was rare, and neither I nor anyone I spoke to remembered a violent incident, other than the one I witnessed, or a singularly bad racial situation from the summer of 1957.

The largest newspapers in Louisiana are the Baton Rouge *Morning Advocate* and the New Orleans *Times-Picayune*. They also have the best libraries, or 'morgues,' of old newspapers and cross-referenced clippings. However, I started my strange odyssey into the past on the microfilm in the morgue of the *Daily Iberian*.

Actually I had little hope of finding any information that would be helpful. During that era little was published in Louisiana newspapers about people of color, except in the police report or perhaps on a separate page that was designated for news about black marriages.

But in my mind's eye I kept seeing the dead man's stringless boots and the rotted strips of rag about his pelvis instead of a belt. Had he been in custody? Was he being transported by a couple of cops who had decided to execute him? If that was the case, why wasn't he in handcuffs? Maybe they had locked the chain on him to sink his body, I thought. No, that couldn't be right. If the victim was being transported by cops, they would have kept him in cuffs until they had murdered him, *then* they would have removed the cuffs and weighted down the body. Also, why would cops want to sink the body in the Atchafalaya, anyway? They could have claimed that they stopped the car to let him relieve himself, he had taken off for the woods, and they had been forced to shoot him. That particular explanation about a prisoner's death was one that was seldom challenged.

Then I found it, on the area news page dated July 27, 1957. A twenty-eight-year-old Negro man by the name of DeWitt Prejean had been arrested in St Landry Parish, north of Lafayette, for breaking into the home of a white family and threatening the wife with a butcher knife. There was no mention of motivation or intent. In fact, the story was not about his arrest but about his escape. He had been in custody only eleven hours, had not even been formally charged, when two armed men wearing gloves and Halloween masks entered the parish prison at four in the morning, locked the night jailer in the restroom, and took DeWitt Prejean out of a downstairs holding cell.

The story was no more than four column inches.

I rolled the microfilm through the viewer, looking for a follow-up story. If it was there, I didn't find it, and I went through every issue of the *Daily Iberian* to February 1958.

Every good cop who spends time in a newspaper morgue, particularly in the rural South, knows how certain kinds of news stories were reported or were not reported in the pre-civil-rights era. 'The suspect was subdued' usually meant that somebody had had his light switch clicked off with a baton or blackjack. Cases involving incest and child molestation were usually not treated at all. Stories about prisoners dying in custody were little more than obituaries, with a tag line to the effect that an autopsy was pending.

The rape or attempted rape of a white woman by a black man was a more complicated issue, however. The victim's identity was always protected by cops and prosecutors, even to the extent that sometimes the rapist was charged with another crime, one that the judge, if at all possible, would punish as severely as he would rape. But the level of white fear and injury was so collectively intense, the outrage so great, that the local paper would be compelled to report the story in such a way that no one would doubt what really happened, or what the fate of the rapist would be.

Also, the 1957 story in the *Iberian* had mentioned that DeWitt Prejean had been taken from a holding cell eleven hours after his arrest.

People didn't stay in holding cells eleven hours, particularly in a rural jail where a suspect could be processed into lock-down in twenty minutes.

I left Bootsie a note, then drove to Lafayette and continued on north for another twenty miles into St Landry Parish and the old jailhouse in Opelousas.

The town had once been the home of James Bowie before he became a wealthy cotton merchant and slave trader in New Orleans. But during the 1950s it acquired another kind of notoriety, namely for its political corruption, an infamous bordello named Margaret's that had operated since the War Between the States, and its gambling halls, which were owned or controlled by the sheriff and which were sometimes raided by the state police when a legislative faction in Baton Rouge wanted to force a change in the parish representatives' vote.

I parked my truck at the back of the courthouse square, right next to the brick shell of the old jail, whose roof had caved in on top of the cast-iron tank, perforated with small square holes, that had served as the lock-down area. As I walked under the live oaks toward the courthouse entrance, I looked through the jail's glassless windows at the mounds of soft, crumbled brick on the floor, the litter of moldy paper, and wondered where the two gloved men in Halloween masks had burst inside and what dark design they had planned for the Negro prisoner DeWitt Prejean.

I got nowhere at the courthouse. The man who had been sheriff during the fifties was dead, and no one now in the sheriff's department remembered the case or the escape; in fact, I couldn't even find a record of DeWitt Prejean's arrest.

'It *happened*. I didn't make it up,' I said to the sheriff, who was in his late thirties. 'I found the account in a 1957 issue of the *Daily Iberian*.'

'That might be,' he answered. He wore his hair in a military crewcut and his jaws were freshly shaved. He was trying to be polite, but the light of interest kept fading from his eyes. 'But they didn't always keep good records back then. Maybe some things happened that people don't want to remember, too, you know what I mean?'

'No.'

He twirled a pencil around on his desk blotter.

'Go talk to Mr Ben. That is, if you want to,' he said. 'That's Mr Ben Hebert. He was the jailer here for thirty years.'

'Was he the jailer in 1957?'

'Yeah, he probably was.'

'You don't sound enthusiastic.'

He rubbed the calluses on his hands without looking up at me.

'Put it this way,' he said. 'His only son ended up in Angola, his wife refused to see him on her deathbed, and there's still some black people who cross the street when they see him coming. Does that help form a picture for you?'

I left the courthouse and went to the local newspaper to look for a follow-up story on the jailbreak. There was none. Twenty minutes later I found the old jailer on the gallery of his weathered wood-frame home across from a Popeye's fast-food restaurant. His yard was almost black with shade, carpeted with a wet mat of rotted leaves, his sidewalks inset with tethering rings, cracked and pyramided from the oak roots that twisted under them. The straw chair he sat in seemed about to burst from his huge bulk.

I had to introduce myself twice before he responded. Then he simply said, 'What you want?'

'May I sit down, sir?'

His lips were purple with age, his skin covered with brown spots the size of dimes. He breathed loudly, as though he had emphysema.

'I ax you what you want,' he said.

'I wondered if you remembered a black man by the name of DeWitt Prejean.'

He looked at me carefully. His eyes were clear-blue, liquid, elongated, red along the rims.

'A nigger, you say?' he asked.

'That's right.'

'Yeah, I remember that sonofabitch. What about him?'

'Is it all right if I sit down, Mr Hebert?'

'Why should I give a shit?'

I sat down in the swing. He put a cigarette in his mouth and searched in his pocket for a match while his eyes went up and down my body. Gray hair grew out of his nose and on the back of his thick neck.

'Were you on duty the night somebody broke him out of jail?' I said.

'I was the jailer. A jailer don't work nights. You hire a man for that.'

'Do you remember what that fellow was charged with?'

'He wasn't charged with nothing. It never got to that.'

'I wonder why he was still in a holding cell eleven hours after he was arrested.'

'They busted him out of the tank.'

'Not according to the newspaper.'

'That's why a lot of people use newspaper to wipe their ass with.'

'He went into a white woman's home with a butcher knife, did he?'

'Find the nigger and ax him.'

'That's what puzzles me. Nobody seems to know what happened to this fellow, and nobody seems to care. Does that make sense to you?'

He puffed on his cigarette. It was wet and splayed when he took it out of his mouth. I waited for him to speak but he didn't.

'Did y'all just close the books on a jailbreak, Mr Hebert?' I asked.

'I don't remember what they done.'

'Was DeWitt Prejean a rapist?'

'He didn't know how to keep his prick in his pants, if that's what you mean.'

'You think her husband broke him out?'

'He might have.'

I looked into his face and waited.

'That is, if he could,' he said. 'He was a cripple-man. He got shot up in the war.'

'Could I talk to him?'

He tipped his cigarette into an ashtray and looked out toward the bright glare of sunlight on the edge of his yard. Across the street black people were going in and out of the Popeye's restaurant.

'Talk to him all you want. He's in the cemetery, out by the tracks east of town,' he said.

'What about the woman?'

'She moved away. Up North somewhere. What's your interest in nigger trouble that's thirty-five years old?'

'I think I saw him killed. Where's the man who was on duty the night of the jailbreak?'

'Got drunk, got hisself run over by a train. Wait a minute, what did you say? You saw what?'

'Sometimes rivers give up their dead, Mr Hebert. In this instance it took quite a while. Y'all took his boot strings and his belt, didn't you?'

'You do that with every prisoner.'

'You do it when they're booked and going into the tank. This guy was never booked. He was left in a holding cell for two armed men to find him. You didn't even leave him a way to take his own life.'

He stared at me, his face like a lopsided white cake.

'I think one of the men who killed Prejean tried to kill me,' I said. 'But he murdered a young woman instead. A film actress. Maybe you read about it.'

He stood up and dropped his cigarette over the gallery railing into a dead scrub. He smelled like Vick's VapoRub, nicotine, and an old man's stale sweat. His breath rasped as though his lungs were filled with tiny pinholes.

'You get the fuck off my gallery,' he said, and walked heavily on a cane into the darkness of his house, and let the screen slam behind him.

I stopped at Popeye's on Pinhook Road in Lafayette and ate an order of fried chicken and dirty rice, then I drove down Pinhook through the long corridor of oak trees, which had been planted by slaves, down toward the Vermilion River bridge and old Highway 90, which led through the little sugar town of Broussard to New Iberia.

Just before the river I passed a Victorian home set back in a grove of pecan trees. Between the road and the wide, columned porch a group of workmen were trenching a water or sewer line of some kind. The freshly piled black dirt ran in an even line past a decorative nineteenth-century flatbed wagon that was hung with baskets of blooming impatiens. The bodies and work clothes of the men looked gray and indistinct in the leafy shade, then a hard gust of wind blew off the river through the trees, the dappled light shifted back and forth across the ground like a bright yellow net, and when I looked back at the workmen I saw them dropping their tools, straightening their backs, fitting on their military caps that were embroidered with gold acorns, picking up their stacked muskets, and forming into ranks for muster.

The general sat in the spring seat of the wagon, his artificial leg propped stiffly on the iron rim of a wheel, a cigar in his mouth, the brim of his campaign hat set at a rakish angle over one eye.

607

He screwed his body around in the wagon seat and raised his hat high over his head in salute to me.

Gravel exploded like a fusillade of lead shot under my right fender. I cut the wheel back off the shoulder onto the pavement, then looked back at the wide sweep of leafy lawn under the pecan trees. A group of workmen were lowering a long strip of flexible plastic pipe into the ground like a white worm.

Back in New Iberia I parked behind the sheriff's department and started inside the building. Two deputies were on their way out.

'Hey, Dave, you're supposed to be in sick bay,' one of them said.

'I'm out.'

'Right. You look good.'

'Is the skipper in?'

'Yeah. Sure. Hey, you look great. I mean it.'

He gave me the thumbs-up sign.

His words were obviously well intended, but I remembered how I was treated after I stepped on a bouncing Betty in Vietnam – with a deference and kindness that not only separated me from those who had a lock on life but constantly reminded me that the cone of flame that had illuminated my bones had also given me a permanent nocturnal membership in a club to which I did not want to belong.

The dispatcher stopped me on my way to the sheriff's office. He weighed over three hundred pounds and had a round red face and a heart condition. His left-hand shirt pocket was bursting with cellophane-wrapped cigars. He had just finished writing out a message on a pink memo slip. He folded it and handed it to me.

'Here's another one,' he said. He had lowered his voice, and his eyes were hazy with meaning.

'Another what?'

'Call from this same party that keeps bugging me.'

'Which party?'

His eyebrows went up in half-moons.

'The Spanish broad. Or Mexican. Or whatever she is.'

I opened the memo and looked at it. It read, *Dave, why don't you return my calls? I'm still waiting at the same place. Have I done wrong in some way?* It was signed '*Amber.*'

'*Amber?*' I said.

'You got eight or nine of them in your mailbox,' he said. 'Her last name sounded Spanish.'

'Who is she?'

'How should I know? You're the guy she's calling.'

'All right, thanks, Wally,' I said.

I took all my mail out of my box, then shuffled through the pink memo slips one at a time.

The ones from 'Amber' were truly an enigma. A few examples:

I've done what you asked. Please call.

Dave, leave a message on my answering machine.

It's me again. Am I supposed to drop dead?

You're starting to piss me off. If you don't want me to bother you again, say so. I'm getting tired of this shit.

I'm sorry, Dave. I was hurt when I said those things. But don't close doors on me.

I walked back to the dispatcher's cage.

'There's no telephone number on any of these,' I said.

'She didn't leave one.'

'Did you ask her for one?'

'No, I got the impression y'all were buddies or something. Hey, don't look at me like that. What is she, a snitch or something?'

'I don't have any idea.'

'She sounds like she's ready to bump uglies, though.'

'Why don't you give some thought to your language, Wally?'

'Sorry.'

'If she calls again, get her telephone number. If she doesn't want to give it to you, tell her to stop calling here.'

'Whatever you say.'

I wadded up the memo slips, dropped them into a tobacco-streaked brass cuspidor, and walked into the sheriff's office.

A manila folder was open on his desk. He was reading from it, with both his elbows propped on the desk blotter and his fingertips resting lightly on his temples. His mouth looked small and down-turned at the corners. On his wall was a framed and autographed picture of President Bush.

'How you doing?' I said.

'Oh, hello, Dave,' he said, looking up at me over his glasses. 'It's good to see you. How do you feel today?'

'Just fine, sheriff.'

'You didn't need to come in. I wanted you to take a week or so off. Didn't Bootsie tell you?'

'I went up to Opelousas this morning. I think I found out who those bones out in the Atchafalaya might belong to.'

'What?'

'A couple of armed men broke a black prisoner named DeWitt Prejean out of the St Landry Parish jail in 1957. The guy was in for threatening a white woman with a butcher knife. But it sounds like an attempted rape. Or maybe there's a possibility that something was going on with consent. The old jailer said something about Prejean not being able to keep his equipment in his pants. Maybe the woman and Prejean just got caught and Prejean got busted on a phony charge and set up for a lynching.'

The sheriff's eyes blinked steadily and he worked his teeth along his bottom lip.

'I don't understand you,' he said.

'Excuse me?'

'I've told you repeatedly that case belongs to St Mary Parish. Why is it that you seem to shut your ears to whatever I say?'

'Kelly Drummond's death doesn't belong to St Mary Parish, sheriff. I think the man who killed her was after me because of that lynched black man.'

'You don't know that. You don't know that at all.'

'Maybe not. But what's the harm?'

He rubbed his round cleft chin with his thumb. I could hear his whiskers scraping against the skin.

'An investigation puts the right people in jail,' he said. 'You don't throw a rope around half the people in two or three parishes. And that's what you and that woman are doing.'

'That's the problem, is it?'

'You're damn right it is. Thirty minutes ago Agent Gomez marched into my office with all her findings.' He touched the edge of the manila folder with his finger. 'According to Agent Gomez, New Iberia has somehow managed to become the new Evil Empire.'

I nodded.

'The New Orleans mob is laundering its drug money through Bal-Gold Productions,' he said. 'Julie Balboni is running a statewide prostitution operation from Spanish Lake, he's also having prostitutes killed, and maybe he laced your Dr Pepper with LSD when he wasn't cutting illegal deals with the Teamsters. Did you know we had all those problems right here in our town, Dave?'

'Julie's a walking shit storm. Who knows what his potential is?'

'She also called some of our local business people moral weenies and chicken-hearted buttheads.'

'She has some eloquent moments.'

'Before she left my office she said she wanted me to know that she liked me personally but in all honesty she had to confess that she thought I was full of shit.'

'I see,' I said, and fixed my eyes on a palm tree outside the window.

The room was quiet. I could hear a jail trusty mowing the grass outside. The sheriff turned his Southwestern class ring on his finger.

'I want you to understand something, Dave,' he said. '*I* was the one who wanted that fat sonofabitch Balboni out of town. *You* were the one who thought he was a source of humor. But now we're stuck with him, and that's the way it is.'

'Why?'

'Because he had legitimate business interests here. He's committed no crime here. In fact, there's no outstanding warrant on this man anywhere. He's never spent one day in jail.'

'I think that's the same shuck his lawyers try to sell.'

He exhaled his breath through his nose.

'Go home. You've got the week off,' he said.

'I heard my leave might even be longer.'

He chewed on a fingernail.

'Who told you that?' he said.

'Is it true or not?'

'You want the truth? The truth is your eyes don't look right. They bother me. There's a strange light in them. Go home, Dave.'

'People used to tell me that in bars. It doesn't sound too good to hear it where I work, sheriff.'

'What can I say?' he said, and held his hands up and turned his face into a rhetorical question mark.

When I walked back down the corridor toward the exit, I stuffed my mail back into my mailbox, unopened, and continued on past my own office without even glancing inside.

My clothes were damp with sweat when I got home. I took off my shirt, threw it into the dirty-clothes hamper, put on a fresh T-shirt, and took a glass of iced tea into the backyard where Bootsie was working chemical fertilizer into the roots of the tomato plants by the coulee. She was in the row, on her hands and knees, and the rump of her pink shorts was covered with dirt.

She raised up on her knees and smiled.

'Did you eat yet?' she asked.

'I stopped in Lafayette.'

'What were you doing over there?'

'I went to Opelousas to run down a lead on that '57 lynching.'

'I thought the sheriff had said—'

'He did. He didn't take well to my pursuing it.'

I sat down at the redwood picnic table under the mimosa tree. On the table were a pad of lined notebook paper and three city library books on Texas and southern history.

'What's this?' I said.

'Some books I checked out. I found out some interesting things.'

She got up from the row of tomato plants, brushing her hands, and sat down across from me. Her hair was damp on her forehead and flecked with grains of dirt. She picked up the note pad and began thumbing back pages. Then she set it down and looked at me uncertainly.

'You know how dreams work?' she said. 'I mean, how dates and people and places shift in and out of a mental picture that you wake up with in the morning? The picture seems to have no origin in your experience, but at the same time you're almost sure you lived it, you know what I mean?'

'Yeah, I guess.'

'I looked up some of the things that, well, maybe you believe you saw out there in the mist.'

I drank out of my iced tea and looked down the sloping lawn at the duck pond and the bright, humid haze on my neighbor's sugarcane.

'You see, Dave, according to these books, John Bell Hood never had a command in Louisiana,' she said. 'He fought at Gettysburg and in Tennessee and Georgia.'

'He was all through this country, Boots.'

'He lived here but he didn't fight here. You see, what's interesting, Dave, is that part of your information is correct but the rest you created from associations. Look here—'

She turned the notebook around so I could see the notes she had taken. 'You're right, he commanded the Texas Brigade,' she said. 'It was a famous cavalry outfit. But look here at this date. When you asked the general what the date was, he told you it was April 21, 1865, right?'

'Right.'

'April 21 is Texas Independence Day, the day the battle of San Jacinto was fought between the Mexican army and the Texans in 1836. Don't you see, your mind mixed up two historical periods. Nothing happened out in that mist, Dave.'

'Maybe not,' I said. 'Wait here a minute, will you?'

I walked to the front of the house, where my boat trailer was still parked, pulled back the tarp, which was dented with pools of rainwater, reached down inside the bow of the boat, and returned to the backyard.

'What is it?'

'Nothing.'

'Why'd you go out front?'

'I was going to show you some junk I found out in the marsh.'

'What junk?'

'Probably some stuff left by an old lumber crew. It's not important.'

Her face was puzzled, then her eyes cleared and she put her hand on top of mine.

'You want to go inside?' she said.

'Where's Alf?'

'Playing over at Poteet's house.'

'Sure, let's go inside.'

'I'm kind of dirty.'

She waited for me to say something but I didn't. I stared at my iced-tea glass.

'What is it, babe?' she said.

'Maybe it's time to start letting go of the department.'

'Let go how?'

'Hang it up.'

'Is that what you want?'

'Not really.'

'Then why not wait awhile? Don't make decisions when you're feeling down, *cher*.'

'I think I've already been cut loose, Boots. They look at me like I have lobotomy stitches across my forehead.'

'Maybe you read it wrong, Dave. Maybe they want to help but they just don't know how.'

I didn't answer. Later, after we had made love in the warm afternoon gloom of our bedroom, I rose from the softness of her body and sat listlessly on the side of the bed. A moment later I felt her nails tick lightly on my back.

'Ask the sheriff if he wants your resignation,' she said.

'It won't solve the problem.'

'Why won't it? Let them see how well they'll do without you.'

'You don't understand. I'm convinced Kelly Drummond's killer was after me. It's got something to do with that dead black man. That's the only thing that makes sense.'

'Why?'

'We've gotten virtually nowhere in trying to find this serial killer or psychopath or whatever he is. So why would *he* want to come after me? But the lynched black man is another matter. I'm the only one making noise about it. That's the connection. Why doesn't the sheriff see that?'

I felt her nails trace my vertebrae.

'You want to believe that all people are good, Dave,' she said. 'When your friends don't act the way they should, you feel all this anger and then it turns inward on you.'

'I'm going to take down that guy, Boots. Even if I have to do it outside the department.'

It was quiet for a long time. Then I felt her weight shift on the mattress and I thought she was getting up to get dressed. Instead, she rose to her knees, pressed her body hard against my back, and pulled my head against her breasts.

'I'll always love you, Dave,' she said. 'I don't care if you're a cop or a commercial fisherman or if you hunt down this bastard and kill him, I'll always love you for the man you are.'

How do you respond to a statement like that?

The phone call came at 9:30 that night. I answered it in the kitchen.

'You're a hard man to catch,' she said.

'Who's this?'

'The lady who's been trying to catch you, sugar.'

'How about giving me a name?'

'It's Amber. Who else, darlin'?' Her voice sounded sleepy, indolent, in slow motion.

'Ah, the lady of the mysterious phone messages.'

'You don't remember me? Don't hurt my feelings.'

'No, I'm sorry, I don't recall who you are. What can I do for you?'

'It's me that's going to do you a big favor, darlin'. It's because I like you. It's because I remember you from New Orleans a long time ago.'

'I appreciate all this, but how about we cut to it?'

'I'm gonna give you the guy you want, sweetheart.'

'Which guy are we talking about?'

'He's a nasty ole pimp and he's been doin' some nasty things to his little girls.'

Through the back window I could see my neighbor burning filed stumps in the dark. The sparks spun upward against the black sky.

'What's his name, Amber?'

'I've got a temporary problem, though. I want to go back to Florida for a little while, you know what I mean?'

'What do you need?'

'Just the air ticket and a little pin money. Three or four hundred dollars. That's not a lot to ask, is it?'

'We might be able to arrange that. Would you like to come into my office?'

'Oh, I don't know if I should do that. All those handsome men make me self-conscious. Do you know where Red's Bar is in Lafayette?'

'On the north side?'

'You got it, sugar. How about in an hour? I'll be at the bar, right by the door.'

'You wouldn't try to take me over the hurdles, would you, Amber?'

'Tell me you don't recognize me and break my heart. Ooou, ooou,' she said, and hung up.

Who was she? The rhetoric, the flippant cynicism, the pout in the voice, the feigned little-girlishness, all spelled hooker. And the messages she had left at my office were obviously meant to indicate to others that there was a personal relationship between us. It sounded like the beginning of a good scam. But she had also sounded stoned. Or maybe she was simply crazy, I thought. Or maybe she was both stoned and crazy and simply running a hustle. Why not?

There are always lots of possibilities when you deal with that vast army of psychological mutants for whom police and correctional and parole officers are supposed to be lifetime stewards. I once knew a young psychiatrist from Tulane who wanted to do volunteer counseling in the women's prison at St Gabriel. He lasted a month. The inkblot tests he gave his first subjects not only drove him into clinical depression but eventually caused him to drop his membership in the ACLU and join the National Rifle Association.

I made a call to the home of an AA friend named Lou Girard who was a detective sergeant in Vice at the Lafayette Police Department. He was one of those who drifted in and out of AA and never quite let go of the old way of life, but he was still a good cop and he would have made lieutenant had he not punched out an obnoxious local politician at Democratic headquarters.

'What's her name again?' he said.

I told him.

'Yeah, there's one broad around calls herself Amber, but she's a Mexican,' he said. 'You said this one sounds like she's from around here?'

'Yep.'

'Look, Dave, these broads got about two dozen names they trade around – Ginger, Consuela, Candy, Pepper, there's even a mulatto dancer named Brown Sugar. Anyway, there're three or four hookers that float in and out of Red's. They're low-rent, though. Their johns are oil-field workers and college boys, mostly.'

'I'm going to drive over there in a few minutes. Can you give me some backup?'

'To check out a snitch?'

'What about your own guys?'

'I'm supposed to be on sick leave right now.'

'Is something wrong over there, Dave?'

'Things could be better.'

'All right, I'll meet you behind the bar. I'll stay in my car, though. For some reason my face tends to empty out a place. Or maybe I need a better mouthwash.'

'Thanks for doing this.'

'It beats sitting at home listening to my liver rot.'

Red's Bar was located in a dilapidated, racially mixed neighborhood of unsurfaced streets, stagnant rain ditches coated with mosquitoes, and vacant lots strewn with lawn trash and automobile parts. Railway tracks intersected people's dirt yards at crazy angles, and Southern Pacific freight cars often lumbered by a few feet from clotheslines and privies and bedroom windows.

I parked my truck in the shadows behind the bar. The shell parking lot was covered with hundreds of flattened beer cans, and the bushes that bordered the neighbor's property stank from all the people who urinated into them nightly. The owner of Red's had built his bar by knocking out the front wall of a frame house and attaching a neon-lit house trailer to it perpendicularly. Originally he had probably intended it to be the place it looked like – a low-bottom bar where you didn't have to make comparisons or where you could get laid and not worry about your own inadequacies.

But the bar became a success in ways that the owner didn't anticipate. He hired black musicians because they were cheap, and through no fault of his own he ended up with one of the best new *zydeco* bands in southwestern Louisiana. And on Saturday nights he french-fried potatoes in chicken fat and served them free on newspaper to enormous crowds that spilled out into the parking lots.

But tonight wasn't Saturday, there was no band; little sound except the jukebox's came from the bar, and the dust from my truck tires floated in a cloud across the bushes that were sour with urinated beer.

Lou Girard got out of his car and walked over to my window. He was a huge man, his head as big as a basketball, who wore cowboy boots with his suits and a chrome-plated .357 magnum in a hand-tooled belt holster. He also carried a braided slapjack in his back pocket and handcuffs that he slipped through the back of his belt.

'It's good to see you, Streak,' he said.

'You too, Lou. How's everything at home?'

'My wife finally took off with her beautician. A woman, I'm talking about. I guess I finally figured out why she seemed a little remote in the sack. What are we doing tonight?'

'I'll go inside and look around. I'd like you to be out here to cover my back. It's not a big deal.'

He looked at the clapboard back of the bar, at the broken windows and the overflow of the garbage cans, and hooked his thumb in his belt.

'When'd you start needing backup for bullshit like this?'

'Maybe I'm getting over the hill for it.'

'Be serious, my friend.'

'You know about Kelly Drummond being killed?'

'That actress? Yeah, sure.'

'I think maybe the shooter was after me. I don't want to walk into a setup.'

'This is a weird fucking place for a setup, Dave. Why would a guy want to bring a cop to a public place in Lafayette for a whack?'

'Why do these guys do anything?'

'You have any idea who the shooter might be?'

'Maybe a guy who was in on a lynching thirty-five years ago.'

He nodded and his eyes became veiled.

'That doesn't sound plausible to you?' I asked.

'What's plausible? I try to get off the booze and my liver swells up like a football, my wife turns out to be a dyke, and for kicks I'm standing by a bunch of bushes that stink like somebody with a kidney disease pissed on them.'

I pulled my tropical shirt out of my khakis, stuck my .45 inside the back of my belt, and walked through the rear entrance of the building.

The inside smelled like refrigerated bathroom disinfectant and tobacco smoke. The wood floors were warped and covered with cigarette burns that looked like black insects. Some college boys were playing the jukebox and drinking pitcher beer at the bar, and two or three couples were dancing in the adjacent room. A lone biker, with a lion's mane of blond hair and arms wrapped with jailhouse art, hit the cue ball so hard on the pool table that it caromed off the side of the jukebox. But it was a dead night at Red's, and the only female at the bar was an elderly woman who was telling a long tale of grief and discontent to a yawning bartender.

'What'll you have?' he said to me.

'Has Amber been in?'

He shook his head to indicate either that she had not or he had no idea whom I was talking about.

'She hasn't been here?' I said.

'What do you want to drink?'

'A 7 Up.'

He opened it and poured it into a glass full of ice. But he didn't serve it to me. He walked to the rear of the long bar, which was empty, set it down, and waited for me. When he leaned on the bar, the biceps of his brown arms ridged with muscles like rocks. I walked down the length of the bar and sat on the stool in front of him.

'Which Amber you looking for?' he asked.

'I only know one.'

'She don't come in here reg'lar. But I could call somebody who probably knows where she's at. I mean if we're talking bout the same broad.'

'A Mexican?'

'Yeah, that's right.'

'She talks like a Mexican?'

'Yeah. What's a Mexican supposed to talk like?'

'That's not the one I'm looking for, then.'

'Enjoy your 7 Up,' he said, and walked away from me.

I waited a half hour. The biker went out and I heard him kick-start his motorcycle and peel down the dirt street in a roar of diminishing thunder. Then the college boys left and the bar was almost deserted. The bartender brought me another 7 Up. I reached for my billfold.

'It's on the house,' he said.

'It's my birthday?' I said.

'You're a cop.'

'I'm a cop.'

'It don't matter to me. I like having cops in. It keeps the riffraff out.'

'Why do you think I'm a cop, partner?'

'Because I just went out back for a breath of air and Lou Girard was taking a leak on our banana trees. Tell Lou thanks a lot for me.'

So I gave it up and walked back outside into the humid night, the drift of dust off the dirt road, and the heat lightning that flickered silently over the Gulf.

'I'm afraid it's a dud,' I said to Lou through his car window. 'I'm sorry to get you out for nothing.'

'Forget it. You want to get something to eat?'

'No, I'd better head home.'

'This hooker, Amber, her full name is Amber Martinez. I heard she was getting out of the life. But I can pick her up for you.'

'No, I think somebody was just jerking me around.'

'Let me know if I can do anything, then.'

'All right. Thanks again. Goodnight, Lou.'

'Goodnight, Dave.'

I watched him drive around the side of the building and out onto the dirt street. Raindrops began to ping on the top of my truck.

But maybe I was leaving too early, I thought. If the bartender had made Lou Girard, maybe the woman had, too.

I went back inside. All the bar stools were empty. The bartender was rinsing beer mugs in a tin sink. He looked up at me.

'She still ain't here. I don't know what else to tell you, buddy,' he said.

I put a quarter in the jukebox and played an old Clifton Chenier record, *Hey 'Tite Fille*, then I walked out onto the front steps. The rain was slanting across the neon glow of the Dixie beer sign and pattering in the ditches and on the shell parking lot. Across the street were two small frame houses, and next to them was a vacant lot with a vegetable garden and three dark oaks in it and an old white Buick parked in front. Then somebody turned on a light inside the house next to the lot, and I saw the silhouette of somebody in the passenger seat of the Buick. I saw the silhouette as clearly as if it had been snipped out of tin, and then I saw the light glint on a chrome or nickel-plated surface as brightly as a heliograph.

The shots were muffled in the rain – *pop, pop*, like Chinese firecrackers under a tin can – but I saw the sparks fly out from the pistol barrel through the interior darkness of the Buick. The shooter had fired at an odd angle, across the seat and through the back window, but I didn't wait to wonder why he had chosen an awkward position to take a shot at me.

I pulled the .45 from under my shirt, dropped to my knees behind the bumper of a pickup truck, and began firing with both hands extended in front of me. I let off all eight rounds as fast as I could pull the trigger. The roar was deafening, like someone had slapped both his palms violently against my eardrums. The hollow-points exploded the glass out of the Buick's windows, cored holes like a cold chisel through the doors, *whanged* off the steering wheel and dashboard, and blew the horn button like a tiddly-wink onto the hood.

The slide locked open on the empty magazine, and the last spent casing tinkled on the flattened beer cans at my feet. I stood erect, still in the lee of the pickup truck, slipped the empty magazine out of the .45's butt, inserted a fresh one, and eased a round into the chamber. The street was quiet except for the pattering of the rain in the ditches. Then I heard a siren in the distance and the bar door opening behind me.

'What the fuck's going on?' the bartender said, his whole body framed in the light. 'You fucking crazy or something?'

'Get back inside,' I said.

'We never had trouble here. Where the fuck are you from? People lose licenses because of bullshit like this.'

'Do you want to get shot?'

He slammed the door shut, locked it, and pulled the blinds.

I started across the street just as an electrical short in the Buick caused the horn to begin blowing non-stop. I kept the .45 pointed with both hands at the Buick's windows and moved in a circle around the front of the car. No one was visible above the level of the windows nor was there any movement inside. The hollow-points had cut exit holes the size of half-dollars in the passenger door.

A Lafayette city police car came hard around the corner, its emergency lights whirling in the rain. The police car stopped twenty yards from the Buick and both front doors sprang open. I could see the cop in the passenger's seat pulling his pump shotgun out of its vertical mount on the dashboard. I got my badge holder out of my back pocket and held it high over my head.

'Lay your weapon on the ground and step back from the car,' the driver said, aiming his revolver at me between the door and the jamb.

I held my right arm at a ninety-degree angle, the barrel of the .45 pointing into the sky.

'I'm Detective Dave Robicheaux, Iberia Parish Sheriff's Department,' I said. 'I'm complying with your request.'

I crouched in the beam of their headlights, laid my .45 by the front tire of the Buick, and raised back up again.

'Step away from it,' the driver said.

'You got it,' I said, and almost lost my balance in the rain ditch.

'Walk this way. Now,' the driver said.

People were standing in their front porches and the rain was coming down harder in big drops that stung my eyes. I kept my badge turned outward toward the two Lafayette city cops.

'I've identified myself. Now how about jacking it down a couple of notches?' I said.

The cop with the shotgun pulled my badge holder out of my hand and looked at it. Then he flexed the tension out of his shoulders, made a snuffing sound in his nose, and handed me back my badge.

'What the hell's going on?' he said.

'Somebody took two shots at me. In that Buick. I think maybe he's still inside.'

They both looked at each other.

'You're saying the guy's still in there?' the driver said.

'I didn't see him go anywhere.'

'Fuck, why didn't you say so?'

I didn't get a chance to answer. Just then, Lou Girard pulled abreast of the police car and got out in the rain.

'Damn, Dave, I thought you'd gone home. What happened?'

'Somebody opened up on me,' I said.

'You know this guy?' the cop with the shotgun said.

'Hell, yes, I do. Put your guns away. What's wrong with you guys?' Lou said.

'Lou, the shooter fired at me twice,' I said. 'I put eight rounds into the Buick. I think he's still in there.'

'What?' he said, and ripped his .357 from his belt holster. Then he said to the two uniformed cops. 'What have you fucking guys been doin' out here?'

'Hey, Lou, come on. We didn't know who this—'

'Shut up,' he said, walked up to the Buick, looked inside, then jerked open the passenger door. The interior light went on.

'What is it?' the cop with the shotgun said.

Lou didn't answer. He replaced his revolver in his holster and reached down with his right hand and felt something on the floor of the automobile.

I walked toward him. 'Lou?' I said.

His hands felt around on the seat of the car, then he stepped back and studied the ground and the weeds around his feet as though he were looking for something.

'Lou?'

'She's dead, Dave. It looks like she caught one right through the mouth.'

'*She*?' I said. I felt the blood drain from my heart.

'You popped Amber Martinez,' he said.

I started forward and he caught my arm. The headlights of the city police car were blinding in the rain. He pulled me past the open passenger door, and I saw a diminutive woman in an embryonic position, a white thigh through a slit in a cocktail dress, a mat of brown hair that stuck wetly to the floor carpet.

Our faces were turned in the opposite direction from the city cops'. Lou's mouth was an inch from my ear. I could smell cigarettes, bourbon, and mints on his breath.

'Dave, there's no fucking gun,' he whispered hoarsely.

'I saw the muzzle flashes. I heard the reports.'

'It's not there. I got a throw-down in my glove compartment. Tell me to do it.'

I stared woodenly at the two uniformed cops, who stood in hulking silhouette against their headlights like gargoyles awaiting the breath of life.

13

The sheriff called me personally at 5 A.M. the next morning so there would be no mistake about my status with the department: I was suspended without pay. Indefinitely.

It was 7 A.M. and already hot and muggy when Rosie Gomez and I pulled up in front of Red's Bar in her automobile. The white Buick was still parked across the street. The bar was locked, the blinds closed, the silver sides of the house-trailer entrance creaking with heat.

We walked back and forth in front of the building, feeling dents in the tin, scanning the improvised rain gutters, even studying the woodwork inside the door jamb.

'Could the bullets have struck a car or the pickup truck you took cover behind?' she said.

'Maybe. But I didn't hear them.'

She put her hands on her hips and let her eyes rove over the front of the bar again. Then she lifted her hair off the back of her neck. There was a sheen of sweat above the collar of her blouse.

'Well, let's take a look at the Buick before they tow it out of here,' she said.

'I really appreciate your doing this, Rosie.'

'You'd do the same for me, wouldn't you?'

'Who knows?'

'Yeah, you would.' She punched me on the arm with her little fist.

We walked across the dirt street to the Buick. On the other side of the vacant lot I could hear freight cars knocking together. I opened all four doors of the Buick and began throwing out the floor mats, tearing up the carpet, raking trash out from under the seats while Rosie hunted in the grass along the rain ditch.

Nothing.

I sat on the edge of the backseat and wiped the sweat out of my eyes. I felt tired all over and my hands were stiff and hard to open and close. In fact, I felt just like I had a hangover. I couldn't keep my thoughts straight, and torn pieces of color kept floating behind my eyes.

'Dave, listen to me,' she said. 'What you say happened is what happened. Otherwise you would have taken up your friend on his offer.'

'Maybe I should have.'

'You're not that kind of cop. You never will be, either.'

I didn't answer.

'What'd your friend call it?' she asked.

'A "throw-down." Sometimes cops calls it a "drop." It's usually a .22 or some other piece of junk with the registration numbers filed off.' I got up off the seat and popped the trunk. Inside, I found a jack handle. I drove the tapered end into the inside panel of the back door on the driver's side.

'What are you doing?' Rosie said.

I ripped the paneling away to expose the sliding frame and mechanism on which the window glass had been mounted.

'Let me show you something,' I said, and did the same to the inside panel on the driver's door. 'See, both windows on this side of the car were rolled partially up. That's why my first rounds blew glass all over the place.'

'Yes?'

'Why would the shooter try to fire through a partially opened window?'

'Good question.'

I walked around to the passenger side of the Buick. The carpet had a dried brown stain in it, and a roach as long and thick as my thumb was crawling across the stiffened fibers.

'But *this* window is all the way down,' I said. 'That doesn't make any sense. It had already started to rain. Why would this woman sit by an open window in the rain, particularly in the passenger seat of her own car?'

'It's registered to Amber Martinez?'

'That's right. According to Lou Girard, she was a hooker trying to get out of the life. She also did speedballs and was ninety pounds soaking wet. Does that sound like a hit artist to you?'

'Then why was she in the car? What was she doing here?'

'I don't know.'

'What did the homicide investigator have to say last night?'

'He said, "A .45 sure does leave a hole, don't it?" '

'What else?'

'He said, "Did you have to come over to Lafayette to fall in the shithouse?" '

'Look at me,' she said.

'What?'

'How much sleep did you get last night?'

'Two or three hours.'

I threw the tire iron on the front seat of the Buick.

'What do you feel now?' she said.

'What do you mean?' I was surprised at the level of irritation in my voice.

'You *know* what I mean.'

My eyes burned and filmed in the haze. I saw the three oaks in the vacant lot go out of focus, as though I were looking at them inside a drop of water.

'Everyone thinks I killed an unarmed woman. What do you think I feel?' I said. I had to swallow when I said it.

'It was a setup, Dave. We both know it.'

'If it was, what happened to the gun? Why aren't there any holes in the bar?'

'Because the guy behind this is one smart perp. He got a woman, probably a chippy, to make calls to your dispatcher to give the impression your fly was open, then he got you out of your jurisdiction and involved you in another hooker's death. I think this guy's probably a master at control.'

'Somehow that doesn't make me feel a lot better, Rosie.'

I looked at the stain on the Buick's carpet. The heat was rising from the ground now and I thought I could smell a salty odor like dead fish. I closed the passenger door.

'I really walked into it, didn't I?' I said.

'Don't worry, we're going to bust the guy behind this and lose the key on him.' Her eyes smiled, then she winked at me.

I had brought a garden rake from home. I took it out of Rosie's car and combed a pile of mud and soggy weeds from the bottom of the ditch next to the Buick. Then Rosie said, 'Dave, come over here and look at this.'

She stood next to the vegetable patch that was located on the edge of the vacant lot. She pointed at the ground.

'Look at the footprints,' she said. 'Somebody ran through the garden. He broke down the tomato stakes.'

The footprints were deep and wide-spaced in the soft earth. The person had been moving away from the street toward the three oak trees in the center of the lot. Some of the tomato and eggplant bushes were crushed down flat in the rows.

A wrecker came around the corner with two men in it and stopped behind the Buick. The driver got out and began hooking up the rear end of the Buick. A middle-aged plainclothes detective in short sleeves with his badge on his belt got out with him. His name was Doobie Patout, a wizened and xenophobic man, with faded blue tattoos on his forearms; some people believed he'd once been the official executioner at Angola.

He didn't speak. He simply stared through the heat at me and Rosie.

'What's happening, Doobie?' I said.

'What y'all doin' out here?' he said.

'Looking for a murder weapon,' I said.

'I heard you were suspended.'

'Word gets around.'

'You're not supposed to be messin' 'round the crime scene.'

'I'm really just an observer.'

'Who's she?' He raised one finger in Rosie's direction.

'Special Agent Gomez,' Rosie said. 'This is part of an FBI investigation. Do you have a problem with that?'

'You got to coordinate with the city,' he said.

'No, I don't,' she said.

The driver of the wrecker began winching the Buick's weight off its back wheels.

'I wouldn't hang around here if I was you,' Doobie said to me.

'Why not?' Rosie said.

'Because he don't have legal authority here. Because he made a mistake and nobody here'll probably hold it against him. Why piss people off, Robicheaux?'

'What are you saying, Doobie?'

'So you got to go up against Internal Affairs in your own department. That don't mean you're gonna get indicted in Lafayette Parish. Why put dog shit on a stick and hold it under somebody's nose?'

Behind us, an elderly fat mulatto woman in a print dress came out on her porch and began gesturing at us. Doobie Patout glanced at her, then opened the passenger door to the wrecker and paused before getting in.

'Y'all can rake spinach out of that ditch all you want,' he said. 'I ran a metal detector over it last night. There's no gun in it. So don't go back to New Iberia and be tellin' people you got a bad shake over here.'

'Y'all gonna do somet'ing 'bout my garden, you?' the woman shouted off the porch.

The wrecker drove off with the Buick wobbling on the winch cable behind it. At the corner the wrecker turned and a hubcap popped off the Buick and bounced on its own course down the empty dirt road.

'My, what a nasty little man,' Rosie said.

I looked back at the footprints in the vegetable patch. They exited in the Johnson grass and disappeared completely. We walked into the shade of the oaks and looked back at the road, the bits of broken glass that glinted in the dirt, the brilliant glare of sunlight on the white shell parking lot. I felt a weariness that I couldn't find words for.

'Let's talk to some of the neighbors, then pack it in,' I said.

We didn't have to go far. The elderly woman whom we had been ignoring labored down her porch steps with a cane and came toward us like a determined crab. Her legs were bowed and popping with varicose veins, her body ringed with fat, her skin gold and hairless, her turquoise eyes alive with indignation.

'Where that other one gone?' she said.

'Which one?' I said.

'That po-liceman you was talkin' to.'

'He went back to his office.'

'Who gonna pay for my li'l garden?' she asked. 'What I gone do wit' them smush tomato? What I gone do wit' them smush eggplant, me?'

'Did you see something last night, auntie?' I said.

'You ax me what I seen? Go look my li'l garden. You got eyes, you?'

'No, I mean did you see the shooting last night?'

'I was in the bat'room, me.'

'You didn't see anything?' Rosie said.

The woman jabbed at a ruined eggplant with her cane.

'I seen *that*. That look like a duck egg to you? They don't talk English where y'all come from?'

'Did you see a woman in a white car outside your house?' I said.

'I seen her. They put her in an ambulance. She was dead.'

'I see,' I said.

'What you gone do 'bout my garden?'

'I'm afraid I can't do anything,' I said.

'He can put his big feet all over my plants and I cain't do nothin' 'bout it?'

'Who?' I said.

'The man that run past my bat'room. I just tole you. You hard of hearin' just like you hard of seein'? I got up to go to the bat'room.'

My head was swimming.

'Listen, auntie, this is very important,' I said. 'You're telling me you saw a man run past your window?'

'That's right. I seen him smush my li'l plants, break down my tomato pole, keep on runnin' right out yonder t'ro them tree, right on 'cross the tracks till he was gone. I seen the light on that li'l gun in his hand, too.'

Rosie and I looked at each other.

'Can you describe this fellow, auntie?' I said.

'Yeah, he's a white man who don't care where he put his big muddy feet.'

'Did the gun look like this one?' Rosie said, opened her purse, and lifted out her .357 magnum.'

'No, it mo' li'l than that.'

'Why didn't you tell this to the police last night?' I asked.

'I tole them. I be talkin' and they be carryin' on with each other like I ain't here, like I some old woman just in they way. It ain't changed, no.'

'What hasn't?' I said.

'When the last time white people 'round here ax us what we t'ink about anyt'ing? Ain't nobody ax me if I want that juke 'cross from my li'l house, no. Ain't nobody worried 'bout my li'l garden. Black folk still black folk, livin' out here without no pave, with dust blowin' off the road t'rough my screens. Don't be pretendin' like it ain't so.'

'You've helped us a great deal, auntie,' I said.

She leaned over on her cane, wrapped a tangle of destroyed tomato vines around her hand, and flung them out into the grass. Then she began walking back toward her porch, the folds of skin in her neck and shoulders creasing like soft tallow.

'Would you mind if we came to see you again?' I asked.

'Waste mo' of my day, play like you care what happen down here on the dirt road? Why you ax me? You comin' when you want, anyway, ain't you?'

Her buttocks swelled like an elephant's against her dress when she worked her way up the steps. On the way out of town we stopped at a nursery and I paid cash to have a dozen tomato plants delivered to her address.

'Not smart giving anything to a potential witness, Slick,' Rosie said when we were back on the highway.

'You're used to operating in the normal world, Rosie. Did you hear what Doobie Patout said? Lafayette Homicide has given that girl's death the priority of a hangnail. Welcome to the New South.'

When I got back home I turned on the window fan in the bedroom, undressed, and lay down on top of the sheets with my arm across my eyes. The curtains, which were printed with small pink flowers, lifted and fell in the warm breeze, and I could hear Tripod running back and forth on his chain in the dead leaves under the pecan trees.

In my sleep I thought I could feel the .45 jumping in my palm, the slide slamming down on a fresh cartridge, the recoil climbing up my fore-arm like the reverberation from a jackhammer. Then, as though in slow motion, I saw a woman's face bursting apart; a small black hole appeared right below the mouth, then the fragile bone structure caved in upon itself, like a rubber mask collapsing, and the back of her head suddenly erupted in a bloody mist.

I wanted to wake from my dream, force myself even inside my sleep to realize that it was indeed only a dream, but instead the images changed and I heard the ragged popping of small-arms and saw the border of a hardwood forest in autumn, the leaves painted with fire, and a contingent of Confederate infantry retreating into it.

No, I didn't simply see them; I was in their midst, under fire with them, my throat burning with the same thirst, my hands trembling as I tried to reload my weapon, my skin twitching as though someone were about to peel it away in strips. I heard a toppling round *throp* close to my ear and whine away deep in the woods, saw the long scarlet streaks in the leaves where the wounded had been dragged behind tree trunks, and was secretly glad that someone else, not me, had crumpled to his knees, had cried out for his mother, had tried futilely to press his blue nest of entrails back inside his stomach.

The enemy advanced across an open field out of their own cannon smoke, their bayonets fixed, their artillery arching over their heads and exploding behind us in columns of dirt and flame. The light was as soft and golden as the season, but the air inside the woods was shifting, filled with dust and particles of leaves, the smell of cordite and bandages black with gangrene, the raw odor of blood.

Then I knew, even in sleep, what the dream meant. I could see the faces of the enemy now, hear the rattle of their equipment, their officers yelling, 'Form up, boys, form up!' They were young, frightened, un-knowledgeable of politics or economics, trembling as much as I was, their mouths too dry now even to pray, their sweaty palms locked on the stocks of their rifles. But I didn't care about their innocence, their beardless faces, the crimson flowers that burst from their young breasts. I just wanted to live. I wanted every round we fired to find a target, to buckle bone, to shatter lungs and explode the heart; I wanted their ranks to dissolve into a cacophony of sorrow.

My head jerked erect on the pillow. The room was hot and close and motes of dust spun in the columns of weak light that shone through the curtains. My breath rasped in my throat, and my chest and stomach were slick with perspiration.

The general sat in a straight-backed chair by the foot of my bed, with his campaign hat resting on one knee. His beard was trimmed and he wore a brushed gray coat with a high gold collar. He was gazing out the window at the shifting patterns of light made by the pecan and oak trees.

'*You!*' I said.

'*I hope you don't mind my being here.*'

'*No, I – you simply surprised me.*'

'*You shouldn't have remorse about the kinds of feelings you just experi-enced, Mr Robicheaux. A desire to live doesn't mean you lack humanity.*'

'*I opened up on the Buick too soon. I let off the whole magazine without seeing what I was shooting at.*'

'*You thought your life was at risk, suh. What were you supposed to do?*'

'*They say I killed an unarmed woman, general.*'

'*Yes, I think that would probably trouble me, too.*' He turned his hat in a circle on his knee. '*I have the impression that you were very fond of your father, the trapper.*'

'*Excuse me?*'

'*Didn't he once tell you that if everyone agrees on something, it's probably wrong?*'

'*Those were his words.*'

'*Then why not give them some thought?*'

'General, somebody has done a serious mind fuck on me. I can't trust what I see or hear anymore.'

'I'm sorry. Someone has done what?'

'It's the same kind of feeling I had once in Golden Gloves. A guy hooked me after the bell, hard, right behind the ear. For two or three days I felt like something was torn loose from the bone, like my brain was floating in a jar.'

'Be brave.'

'I see that woman, the back of her head . . . Her hair was glued to the carpet with her own blood.'

'Think about what you just said.'

'What?'

'You're a good police officer, an intelligent man. What does your eye tell you?'

'I need some help, general.'

'You belong to the quick, you wake in the morning to the smell of flowers, a woman responds to the touch of your fingers, and you ask help of the dead, suh?'

He lifted himelf to his feet with his crutch.

'I didn't mean to offend you,' I said.

'In your dream you saw us retreating into a woods and you saw the long blue line advancing out of the smoke in the field, didn't you?'

'Yes.'

'Were you afraid?'

'Yes.'

'Because you thought time had run out for you, didn't you?'

'Yes, I knew it had.'

'We should have died there but we held them. Our thirst was terrible. We drank rainwater from the hoof prints of livestock. Then that night we tied sticks in the mouths of our wounded so they wouldn't cry out while we slipped out of the woods and joined the rest of our boys.'

The wind began blowing hard in the trees outside the window. Last fall's leaves swirled off the ground and blew against the house.

'I sense resentment in you,' he said.

'I already paid my dues. I don't want—'

'You don't want what?' He pared a piece of dirt from under his fingernail.

'To be the only man under a flag.'

'Ah, we never quit paying dues, my friend. I must be going now. The wind's out of the south. There'll be thunder by this afternoon. I always have a hard time distinguishing it from Yankee cannon.'

He made a clucking sound with his tongue, fitted his campaign hat on his head, took up his crutch, and walked through the blades of the window fan into a spinning vortex of gold and scarlet leaves.

629

When I finally woke from my sleep in midafternoon, like rising from the warm stickiness of an opium dream, I saw Alafair watching me through the partly opened bedroom door. Her lips were parted silently, her round, tan face wan with incomprehension. The sheets were moist and tangled around my legs. I tried to smile.

'You okay, Dave?'

'Yeah, I'm fine.'

'You were having a dream. You were making all kinds of sounds.'

'It's probably not too good to sleep in the daytime, little guy.'

'You got malaria again?'

'No, it doesn't bother me much anymore.'

She walked into the room and placed one hand on the bedstead. She looked at the floor.

'What's the matter, Alf?' I said.

'I went to the grocery down at the four-corners with Bootsie. A man had the newspaper open on the counter and was reading something out loud. A lady saw us and touched the man on the arm. Then both of them just stared at us. Bootsie gave them a real mean look.'

'What was the man saying?'

'A lady got shot.' Her palm was cupped tightly on the knob of the bedstead. She stared at the floor, and there was small white discolorations in her cheeks like slivers of ice. 'He said you shot the lady. You shot the lady, Dave.'

I sat up on the edge of the bed.

'I had some trouble last night, Alafair. Somebody fired a pistol at me and I shot back. I'm not sure who fired at me or what this lady was doing there. But the situation is a lot more complex than maybe some people think. The truth can be real hard to discover sometimes, little guy.'

'Did you do what they say, Dave?' I could see the shine of fear in her brown eyes.

'I don't know. But I never shot at anybody who didn't try to hurt me first. You have to believe me on that, Alf. I'm not sure what happened last night, but sooner or later I probably will. In the meantime, guys like you and me and Bootsie have to be standup and believe in each other.'

I brushed her bangs away from her eyes. She looked for a long time at the whirling blades of the window fan and the shadows they made on the bed.

'They don't have any right,' she said.

'Who?'

'Those people. They don't have the right to talk about you like that.'

'They have the right to read what's in the newspaper, don't they?'

'The lady at the counter was saying something just before we walked in. I heard her through the screen. She said, "If he's gone back to drinking, it don't surprise me he done that, no." That's when the man started reading out loud from the newspaper.'

I picked her up by the waist and sat her on the bed. Her muscular body felt as compact as a small log.

'Look, little guy,' I said, 'drinking isn't part of my life anymore. I gave it to my Higher Power.'

I stroked her hair and saw a smile begin to grow at the edge of her mouth and eyes.

'Dave?'

'What?'

'What's it mean when you say somebody's got to be standup?'

'No matter what the other side does to you, you grin and walk through the cannon smoke. It drives them crazy.'

She was grinning broadly now, her wide-set teeth white in the shadows of the room.

'Where's Bootsie?' I asked.

'Fixing supper.'

'What are we having?'

'*Sac-a-lait* and dirty rice.'

'Did you know they run freight trains on that in Louisiana?'

She started bouncing on the edge of the bed, then my words sank in. 'What? Freight . . . what?' she said.

'Let me get dressed, little guy, then we'll check out the food situation.'

My explanation to Alafair was the best I could offer, but the truth was I needed to get to an AA meeting. Since the night I had seen the general and his soldiers in the mist, I had talked once over the phone to my AA sponsor but had not attended a meeting, which was the place I needed to be most. What might be considered irrational, abnormal, aberrant, ludicrous, illogical, bizarre, schizoid, or schizophrenic to earth people (which is what AAs call nonalcoholics) is usually considered fairly normal by AA members.

The popular notion exists that Catholic priests become privy to the darkest corners of man's soul in the confessional. The truth is otherwise. Any candid Catholic minister will tell you that most people's confessions cause eye-crossing boredom in the confessor, and the average weekly penitent usually owns up to a level of moral failure on par with unpaid parking violations and overdue library books.

But at AA meetings I've heard it all at one time or another: extortion, theft, forgery, armed robbery, child molestation, sodomy with animals, arson, prostitution, vehicular homicide, and the murder of prisoners and civilians in Vietnam.

I went to an afternoon meeting on the second floor of an Episcopalian church. I knew almost everyone there: a few housewives, a black man who ran a tree nursery, a Catholic nun, an ex-con bartender named Tee

Neg who was also my sponsor, a woman who used to hook in the Column Hotel Bar in Lafayette, a psychologist, a bakery owner, a freight conductor on the Southern Pacific, and a man who was once a famous aerialist with Ringling Brothers.

I told them the whole story about my psycho-historical encounters and left nothing out. I told them about the electricity that snapped and flickered like serpents' tongues in the mist, my conversations with the general, even the unwashed odor that rose from his clothes, the wounds in his men that maggots had eaten as slick as spoons.

As is usual with one's dramatic or surreal revelations at an AA meeting, the response was somewhat humbling. They listened attentively, their eyes sympathetic and good-natured, but a number of the people there at one time or another had ripped out their own wiring, thought they had gone to hell without dying, tried to kill themselves, or been one step away from frontal lobotomies.

When I had finished, the leader of the meeting, a pipeline welder, said, 'Damn, Dave, that's the best endorsement of Dr Pepper I ever heard. You ought to call up them sonsofbitches and get that one on TV.'

Then everyone laughed and the world didn't seem so bad after all.

When I left the meeting I bought a spearmint snowball in the city park at Bayou Teche and used the outdoor pay phone by the recreation building. Through the moss-hung oak trees I could see kids diving into the public pool, their tan bodies glistening with water in the hot sunlight.

It took a couple of minutes to get the Lafayette coroner on the line. He was a hard-nosed choleric pathologist named Sollie Rothberg, whom cops quickly learned to treat diplomatically.

'I wondered what you had on the Amber Martinez shooting,' I said.

I could hear the long-distance wires humming in the receiver.

'Robicheaux?' he said.

'That's right.'

'Why are you calling me?'

'I just told you.'

'It's my understanding you're suspended.'

'So what? Your medical findings are a matter of public record, aren't they?'

'When they become public they are. Right now they aren't public.'

'Come on, Sollie. Somebody's trying to deep-fry my *cojones* in a skillet.'

In my mind's eye I could see him idly throwing paper clips at his wastebasket.

'What's the big mystery I can clear up for you?' he said.

'What caliber weapon killed her?'

'From the size of the wound and the impact of the round, I'd say a .45.'

'What do you mean "size"?'

'Just what I said.'

'What about the round?'

'It passed through her. There wasn't much to recover. It was a clean exit wound.'

'It was a copper-jacketed round?'

'That's my opinion. In fact, I know it was. The exit hole wasn't much larger in diameter than the entry.'

I closed and opened my eyes. I could feel my heart beating in my chest.

'You there?' he said.

'Yes.'

'What's wrong?'

'Nothing, Sollie. I use hollow-points.'

I could hear birds singing in the trees, and the surface of the swimming pool seemed to be dancing with turquoise light.

'Anything else?' he asked.

'Yeah, time of death.'

'You're crowding me.'

'Sollie, I keep seeing the back of her head. Her hair stuck to the carpet. The blood had already dried, hadn't it?'

'I can't tell you about that because I wasn't there.'

'Come on, you know what I'm asking you.'

'Did she die earlier, you want to know?'

'Look partner, you're my lifeline. Don't be jerking me around.'

'How about I go you one better? Did she die in that car, you want to ask me?'

I had learned long ago not to interfere with or challenge Sollie's moods, intentions, or syntax.

'It's gravity,' he said. 'The earth's always pulling on us, trying to suck us into the ground.'

'What?'

'It's what the shooter didn't think about,' he said. 'Blood's just like anything else. It goes straight down. You stop the heart, in this case the brain and then the heart, and the blood takes the shortest course to the ground. You with me?'

'Not quite.'

'The blood settles out in the lowest areas of where the body is lying. The pictures show the woman curled up on her side on the floor of the Buick. Her head was higher than her knees. But the autopsy indicates that she was lying full length on her back at the time of death. She also had high levels of alcohol and cocaine in her blood. I suspect she may have been passed out when she died.'

'She was shot somewhere else and moved?'

'Unless the dead are walking around on their own these days.'

'You've really been a friend, Sollie.'

'Do you ever carry anything but a .45? A nine-millimeter or a .357 sometimes?'

'No, I've always carried the same Colt .45 auto I brought back from Vietnam.'

'How many people know that?'

'Not many. Mostly cops, I guess.'

'That thought would trouble me. So long, Robicheaux.'

But the moment was not one for brooding. I walked back to the hot-dog stand and bought snowballs for a half-dozen kids. When a baseball bounced my way from the diamond, I scooped it up in my palms, rubbed the roughness of the horse hide, fitted my fingers on the stitches, and whipped a side-arm slider into the catcher's glove like I was nineteen years old and could blow a hole through the backstop.

That night I called Lou Girard at his home in Lafayette, told him about my conversations with the coroner and the mulatto woman across from the bar, and asked him if anyone had vacuumed the inside of the Buick.

'Dave, I'm afraid this case isn't the first thing on everybody's mind around here,' he said.

'Why's that?'

'The detective assigned to it thinks you're a pain in the ass and you should have stayed in your own territory.'

'When's the last time anyone saw Amber Martinez?'

'Three or four days ago. She was a bender drinker and user. She was supposed to be getting out of the life, but I think she'd work up a real bad Jones and find a candy man to pick up her tab until she ended up in a tank or a detox center somewhere.'

'Who was her pimp?'

'Her husband. But he's been in jail the last three weeks on a check-writing charge. Whoever killed her probably got her out of a bar someplace.'

'Yeah, but he knew her before. He used another woman to keep leaving Amber's name on messages at my office.'

'If I can get the Buick vacuumed, what are we looking for?'

'I know I saw gun flashes inside the car. But there weren't any holes in the front of the bar. See what you come up with.'

'Like what?'

'I don't know.'

'Why don't you forget the forensic bullshit and concentrate on what your nose tells you?'

'What's that?'

'This isn't the work of some lone fuckhead running around. It has the smell of the greaseballs all over it. One smart greaseball in particular.'

'You think this is Julie's style?'

'I worked two years on a task force that tried to get an indictment on the Bone. When he gets rid of a personal enemy, he puts a meat hook up the guy's rectum. If he wants a cop or a judge or a labor official out of the way, he does it long distance, with a whole collection of lowlifes between him and the target.'

'That sounds like our man, all right.'

'Can I give you some advice?'

'Go ahead.'

'If Balboni is behind this, don't waste your time trying to make a case against him. It doesn't work. The guy's been oiling jurors and judges and scaring the shit out of witnesses for twenty years. You wait for the right moment, the right situation, and you smoke him.'

'I'll see you, Lou. Thanks for your help.'

'All right, excuse me. Who wants to talk about popping a cap on a guy like Balboni? Amber Martinez probably did herself. Take it easy, Dave.'

At six the next morning I took a cup of coffee and the newspaper out on the gallery and sat down on the steps. The air was cool and blue with shadow under the trees and the air smelled of blooming four o'clocks and the pecan husks that had moldered into the damp earth.

While I read the paper I could hear boats leaving my dock and fishermen's voices out on the water. Then I heard someone walking up the incline through the leaves, and I lowered the newspaper and saw Mikey Goldman striding toward me like a man in pursuit of an argument.

He wore shined black loafers with tassels on them, a pink polo shirt that hung out of his gray slacks, and a thick gold watch that gleamed like soft butter on his wrist. His mouth was a tight seam, down-turned at the corners, his jaw hooked forward, his strange, pale, bulging eyes flicking back and forth across the front of my house.

'I want a word with you,' he said.

'How are you today, Mr Goldman?' I said.

'It's 6 A.M., I'm at your house instead of at work; I got four hours sleep last night. Guess.'

'Do I have something to do with your problem?'

'Yeah, you do. You keep showing up in the middle of my problem. Why is that, Mr Robicheaux?'

'I don't have any idea.'

'I do. It's because Elrod has got some kind of hard-on for you and it's about to fuck my picture in a major way.'

'I'd appreciate it if you didn't use that kind of language around my home.'

'You got a problem with language? That's the kind of stuff that's on your mind? What's wrong with you people down here? The mosquitoes pass around clap of the brain or something?'

'What is it you want, sir?'

'He asks me what *I* want?' he said, looking around in the shadows as though there were other listeners there. 'Elrod doesn't like to see you get taken over the hurdles. Frankly I don't either. Maybe for other reasons. Namely nobody carries my load, nobody takes heat for me, you understand what I'm saying?'

'No.'

He cleared something from a nostril with his thumb and forefinger.

'What is it with you, you put your head in a bucket of wet cement every morning?' he asked.

'Can I be frank, too, Mr Goldman?'

'Be my guest.'

'A conversation with you is a head-numbing experience. I don't think any ordinary person is ready for it.'

'Let me try to put it in simple words that you can understand,' he said. 'You may not know it, but I try to be a fair man. That means I don't like somebody else getting a board kicked up his ass on my account. I'm talking about you. Your own people are dumping on you because they think you're going to chase some big money out of town. I leave places or I stay in places because I want to. Somebody gets in my face, I deal with it, personal. You ask anybody in the industry. I don't rat-fuck people behind their back.'

I set down my coffee cup, folded the newspaper on the step, and walked out into the trees toward his parked automobile. I waited for him to follow me.

'Is there anything else you wanted to tell me?' I said.

'No, of course not. I'm just out here to give you my personal profile. Listen to me, I'm going to finish this picture, then I'm never coming back to this state. In fact, I'm not even going to fly over it. But in the meantime no more of my people are going to the hospital.'

'What?'

'Good, the flashbulb went off.'

'What happened?' I said.

'Last night we'd wrapped it up and everybody had headed home. Except Elrod and this kid who does some stunt work got loaded and Elrod decides he's going to 'front Julie Balboni. He picks up a Coke bottle and starts banging on Julie's trailer with it. Julie opens the door in his jockey undershorts, and there's a twenty-year-old local broad trying to put on her clothes behind him. So Elrod calls him a coward and a dago bucket of shit and tells him he can fix him up in LA with Charlie Manson's chippies, like they got hair under their arms and none on their heads and they're more Julie's speed. Then El tells him that Julie had better not cause his buddy Robicheaux any more grief or El's going to punch his ticket for him, and if he finds out Julie murdered Kelly he's going to do it anyway, big time, with a shotgun right up Balboni's cheeks.

'I don't know what Balboni was doing with the broad, but he had some handcuffs. He walked outside, clamped one on El's wrist, the other on a light pole, and said, "You're a lucky man, Elrod. You're a valuable piece of fruit. But your friend there, he don't have any luck at all." Then he stomped the shit out of the stunt kid. "Stomped" is the word, Mr Robicheaux, I mean with his feet. He busted that kid's nose, stove in his ribs, and ripped his ear loose from his head.'

'Why didn't you stop it?'

'I wasn't there. I got all this from the kid at the hospital. That's why I didn't get any sleep last night.'

'Is the kid pressing charges?'

'Get real. He was on a flight back to Los Angeles this morning with enough dope in him to tranquilize a rhinoceros.'

'What do you want with me?'

'I want you to take care of Elrod. I don't want him hurt.'

'Tell me the truth. Do you have any concerns at all except making your pictures?'

'Yeah, human beings. If you don't accept that, I say fuck you.'

His tense, protruding eyes reminded me of hard-boiled eggs. I looked away from him, felt my palm close and unclose against my trousers. The sunlight on the bayou was like a yellow flare burning under the water.

'I'm not in the baby-sitting business, Mr Goldman,' I said. 'My advice is that you tell all this to the sheriff's department. Right now I'm still suspended. I'm going back to finish my coffee now. We'll see you around.'

'It's Dog Patch. I'm in a cartoon. I talk, nobody hears me.' He tapped himself on the cheek. 'Maybe I'm dead and this is hell.'

'What else do you want to say?' I heard the heat rising in my own voice.

'You accuse me of not having any humanity. Then I tell you Elrod's striking matches on Balboni's balls on your account and you blow me off. You want Balboni to put his foot through El's face?'

'He's your business partner. You brought him here. You didn't worry about the origins of his money till you—'

'That's all true. The question is what do we do now?'

'*We?*'

'Right. I'm getting through. Everybody around here doesn't have meatloaf for brains after all.'

'There's no *we* in this. I'll talk to Elrod, I'll take him to AA meetings, but he's not my charge.'

'Good. Tell him that. I'm on my way to work. Dump him in a cab.'

'What?'

'He's down there in your bait shop. Drunk. I think you have a serious hearing problem. Get some help.'

He stuck a peppermint candy cane in the corner of his mouth and walked back down the slope to his automobile, his shoulders rolling under his polo shirt, his jaws cracking the candy between his teeth, his profile turned into the freshening breeze like a gladiator's.

14

'You did what?' Bootsie said. She stared at me open-mouthed across the kitchen table.

I told her again.

'You *threw* him in the bayou? I don't believe it,' she said.

'He's used to it. Don't worry about him.'

'Mr Sykes started fighting with Dave on the dock, Bootsie,' Alafair said. 'He was drunk and making a lot of noise in front of the customers. He wouldn't come up to the house like Dave told him.'

Way to go, Alf, I thought.

'Where is he now?' Bootsie said, wiping her mouth with her napkin and starting to rise from her chair.

'Throwing up on the rose bushes the last I saw him.'

'Dave, that's disgusting,' she said, and sat back down.

'Tell Elrod.'

'Batist said he drank five beers without paying for them,' Alafair said.

'What are you going to do about him?' Bootsie said. Then she turned her head and looked out the back screen. 'Dave, he just went across the backyard.'

'I think El has pulled his suction cups loose for a while, Boots.'

'Suction cups?' Alafair said, her cereal spoon poised in front of her mouth.

'He's crawling around on his hands and knees. Do something,' Bootsie said.

'That brings up a question I was going to ask you.'

I saw the recognition grow in her eyes.

'The guy went up against Julie Balboni because of me,' I said. 'Or at least partly because of me.'

'You want him to stay *here*? Dave, this is our home,' she said.

'The guy's in bad shape.'

'It's still our home. We can't open it up to every person who has a problem.'

'The guy needs an AA friend or he's not going to make it. Look at him. He's pitiful. Should I take him down to the jail?'

Bootsie rested her fingers on her temples and stared at the sugar container.

'I'll make him a deal,' I said. 'The first time he takes a drink, he gets eighty-sixed back to Spanish Lake. He pays his share of the food, he doesn't tie up the telephone, he doesn't come in late.'

'Why's he squirting the hose in his mouth?' Alafair said.

'All right, we can try it for a couple of days,' Bootsie said. 'But, Dave, I don't want this man talking anymore about his visions or whatever it is he thinks he sees out on the lake.'

'You think that's where I got it from, huh?' I smiled.

'In a word, yes.'

'He's a pretty good guy when he's not wired. He just sees the world a little differently than some.'

'Oh, wonderful.'

Alafair got up from her chair and peered at an angle through the screen into the backyard.

'Oooops,' she said, and put her hand over her mouth.

'What is it?' Bootsie said.

'Mr Sykes just did the rainbow yawn.'

'What?' I said.

'He vomited on the picnic table,' Alafair said.

I waited until Bootsie and Alafair had driven off to the grocery store in town, then I went out into the backyard. Elrod's slacks and shirt were pasted to his skin with water from the bayou and grimed with mud and grass stains. He had washed down the top of the picnic table with the garden hose, and he now sat slack-jawed on the bench with his knees splayed, his shoulders stooped, his hands hanging between his thighs. His unshaved face had the gray colour of spoiled pork.

I handed him a cup of coffee.

'Thanks,' he said.

I winced at his breath.

'If you stay on at our house, do you think you can keep the cork in the jug?' I said.

'I cain't promise it. No, sir, I surely cain't promise it.'

'Can you try?'

He lifted his eyes up to mine. The iris of his right eye had a clot of blood in it as big as my fingernail.

'Nothing I ever tried did any good,' he said. 'Antabuse, psychiatrists, a dry-out at the navy hospital, two weeks hoeing vegetables on a county P-farm. Sooner or later I always went back to it, Mr Robicheaux.'

'Well, here's the house rules, partner,' I said, and I went through them one at a time with him. He kept rubbing his whiskers with the flat of his hand and spitting between his knees.

'I guess I look downright pathetic to you, don't I?' he said.

'Forget what other people think. Don't drink, don't think, and go to meetings. If you do that, and you do it for yourself, you'll get out of all this bullshit.'

'I got that kid beat up real bad. It was awful. Balboni kept jumping up in the air, spinning around, and cracking the sole of his foot across the kid's head. You could hear the skin split against the bone.'

He placed his palms over his ears, then removed them.

'You stay away from Balboni,' I said. 'He's not your problem. Let the law deal with him.'

'Are you kidding? The guy does whatever he wants. He's even getting his porno dirt bag into the film.'

'What porno dirt bag?'

'He brought up some guy of his from New Orleans, some character who thinks he's the new Johnny Wadd. He's worked the guy into a half-dozen scenes in the picture. Look, Mr Robicheaux, I'm getting the shakes. How about cutting me a little slack? Two raw eggs in a beer with a shot on the side. That's all I'll need. Then I won't touch it.'

'I'm afraid not, partner.'

'Oh man, I'm really sick. I've never been this sick. I'm going into the DTs.'

I put my hand on his shoulder. His muscles were as tight and hard as cable wire and quivering with anxiety. Then he covered his eyes and began weeping, his wet hair matted with dirt, his body trembling like that of a man whose soul was being consumed by its own special flame.

I drove out to Spanish Lake to find Julie Balboni. No one was in the security building by the dirt road that led into the movie location, and I dropped the chain into the dirt and parked in the shade, close by the lake, next to a catering truck. The sky was darkening with rain clouds, and the wind off the water blew leaves across the ground under the oak trees. I walked through a group of actors dressed as Confederate infantry. They were smoking cigarettes and lounging around a freshly dug rifle pit and ramparts made out of huge stick-woven baskets filled with dirt. Close by, a wheeled cannon faced out at the empty lake. I could smell the drowsy, warm odor of reefer on the breeze.

'Could y'all tell me where to find Julie Balboni?' I said.

None of them answered. Their faces had turned dour. I asked again.

'We're just the hired help,' a man with sergeant's stripes said.

'If you see him, would you tell him Dave Robicheaux is looking for him?'

'You'd better tell him yourself,' another actor said.

'Do you know where Mr Goldman is?'

'He went into town with some lawyers. He'll be back in a few minutes,' the sergeant said.

'Thank you,' I said.

I walked back to my truck and had just opened the door when I heard someone's feet in the leaves behind me.

'I need a moment of your time, please,' Twinky Lemoyne said. He had been walking fast, holding his ballpoint pens in his shirt pocket with one hand; a strand of hair hung over his rimless glasses and his face was flushed.

'What can I do for you?'

'I'd like to know what your investigation has found out.'

'You would?'

'Yes. What have you learned about these murders?'

I shouldn't have been surprised at the presumption and intrusiveness of his question. Successful businessmen in any small town usually think of policemen as extensions of their mercantile fraternity, dedicated in some ill-defined way to the financial good of the community. But previously he had stonewalled me, had even been self-righteous, and it was hard to accept him now as an innocuous Rotarian.

'Maybe you should call the sheriff's office or the FBI, Mr Lemoyne. I'm suspended from the department right now.'

'Is this man Balboni connected with the deaths of these women?'

'Did someone tell you he was?'

'I'm asking you an honest question, sir.'

'And I'm asking you one, Mr Lemoyne, and I advise you to take it quite seriously. Do you have some personal knowledge about Balboni's involvement with a murder?'

'No, I don't.'

'You don't?'

'No, of course not. How could I?'

'Then why your sense of urgency, sir?'

'You wouldn't keep coming out here unless you suspected him. Isn't that right?'

'What difference should it make to you?'

The skin of his face was grained and red, and his eyelashes fluttered with his frustration.

'Mr Robicheaux, I think . . . I feel . . .'

'What?'

'I believe you've been treated unfairly.'

'Oh?'

'I believe I've contributed to it, too. I've complained to others about both you and the FBI woman.'

'I think there's another problem here, Mr Lemoyne. Maybe it has to do with the price of dealing with a man like Julie Balboni.'

'I've tried to be honest with you.'

'That's fine. Get away from Balboni. Divest yourself of your stock or whatever it takes.'

'Then maybe he *was* involved with those dead girls?' His eyes were bright and riveted on mine.

'You tell me, Mr Lemoyne. Would you like Julie for your next-door neighbor? Would you like your daughter around him? Would you, sir?'

'I find your remark very offensive.'

'*Offensive* is when a stunt man gets his nose and ribs broken and an ear torn loose from his head as an object lesson.'

I could see the insult and injury in his eyes. His lips parted and then closed.

'Why are you out here, Mr Lemoyne?'

'To see Mr Goldman. To find out what I can.'

'I think your concern is late in coming.'

'I have nothing else to say to you. Good day to you, sir.'

He walked to his automobile and got in. As I watched him turn onto the dirt road and head back toward the security building, I had to wonder at the self-serving naïveté that was characteristic of him and his kind. It was as much a part of their personae as the rows of credit and membership cards they carried in their billfolds, and when the proper occasion arose they used it with a collective disingenuousness worthy of a theatrical award.

At least that was what I thought – perhaps in my own naïveté – about Twinky Hebert Lemoyne at the time.

When I reached the security building Murphy Doucet, the guard, was back inside, and the chain was down in the road. He was bent over a table, working on something. He waved to me through the open window, then went back to his work. I parked my truck on the grass and walked inside.

It was hot and close inside the building and smelled of airplane glue. Murphy Doucet looked up from a huge balsa-wood model of a B-17 Flying Fortress that he was sanding. His blue eyes jittered back and forth behind a pair of thick bifocals.

'How you doing, Dave?' he said.

'Pretty good, Murph. I was looking for Julie Balboni.'

'He's playing ball.'

'Ball?'

'Yeah, sometimes he takes two or three guys into town with him for a pepper game.'

'Where?'

'I think at his old high school. Say, did you get Twinky steamed up about something.'

'Why's that?'

'I saw you talking to him, then he went barreling-ass down the road like his noise was out of joint.'

'Maybe he was late for lunch.'

'Yeah, probably. It don't take too much to get Twinky's nose out of joint, anyway. I've always suspected he could do with a little more pussy in his life.'

'He's not married?'

'He used to be till his wife run off on him. Right after she emptied his bank account and all the money in his safe. I didn't think Twinky was going to survive that one. That was a long time ago, though.'

He used an Exacto knife to trim away a tiny piece of dried glue from one of the motors on his model airplane. He blew sawdust off the wings and held the plane aloft.

'What do you think of it?' he asked.

'It looks good.'

'I've got a whole collection of them. All the planes from World War II. I showed Mikey Goldman my B-17 and he said maybe he could use my collection in one of his films.'

'That sounds all right, Murph.'

'You kidding? He meant I should donate them. I figured out why that stingy Jew has such a big nose. The air's free.'

'He seems like an upfront guy to me,' I said.

'Try working for one of them.'

I looked at him. 'You say Julie's at his old high school?' I said.

'Yeah, him and some actor and that guy named Cholo.'

He set his bifocals on the work table and rubbed his hands on the smooth blond surface of his plane. His skin was wrinkled and brown as a cured tobacco leaf.

'Thanks for your time,' I said.

'Stop by more often and have coffee. It's lonely sitting out here in this shack.'

'By the way, do you know why Goldman might be with a bunch of attorneys?'

'Who knows why these Hollywood sonsofbitches do anything? You're lucky, Dave. I wish I was still a real cop. I do miss it.'

He brushed with the backs of his fingers at the starch-white scar on his throat.

A half hour later, as rain clouds churned thick and black overhead, like curds of smoke from an oil fire, I parked my truck by the baseball diamond of my old high school, now deserted for the summer, where Baby Feet and I had played ball as boys. He stood at home plate, wearing only a pair of spikes and purple gym shorts, the black hair on his enormous body glistening with sweat, his muscles rippling each time he belted a ball deep into the outfield with a shiny blue aluminum bat.

I walked past the oak trees that were carved with the names of high school lovers, past the sagging, paintless bleachers, across the worn infield grass toward the chicken-wire backstop and the powerful swing of his bat, which arched balls like tiny white dots high over the heads of Cholo and a handsome shirtless man whose rhythmic movements and smooth body tone reminded me of undulating water. A canvas bag filled with baseballs spilled out at Julie's feet. There were drops of moisture in his thick brows, and I could see the concentrated, hot lights in his eyes. He bent over effortlessly, in spite of his great weight, picked up a ball with his fingers, and tossed it in the air; then I saw his eyes flick at me, his left foot step forward in the batter's box, just as he swung the aluminum bat and ripped a grounder like a rocket past my ankles.

I watched it bounce between the oak trees and roll into the street.

'Pretty good shot for a foul ball,' I said.

'It looked right down the line to me.'

'You were never big on rules and boundaries, Feet.'

'What counts is the final score, my man.'

Another ball rang off his metal bat and arched high into the outfield. Cholo wandered around in a circle, trying to get under it, his reddish-gray curls glued to his head, his glove outstretched like an amphibian's flipper. The ball dropped two feet behind him.

'I hear you've been busy out at the movie set,' I said.

'How's that?'

'Tearing up a young guy who didn't do anything to you.'

'There's two sides to every story.'

'This kid hurt you in some way, Julie?'

'Maybe he keeps bad company.'

'Oh, I see. Elrod Sykes gave you a bad time? He's the bad company? You're bothered by a guy who's either drunk or hungover twenty-four hours a day?'

'Read it like you want.' He flipped a ball into the air and lined it over second base. 'What's your stake in it, Dave?'

'It seems Elrod felt he had to come to my defense with you. I wish he hadn't done that.'

'So everybody's sorry.'

'Except it bothers me that you seriously hurt a man, maybe because of me.'

'Maybe you flatter yourself.' He balanced himself on one foot and began tapping the dirt out of his spikes with his bat.

'I don't think so. You've got a big problem with pride, Julie. You always did.'

'Because of you? If my memory hasn't failed me, some years ago a colored shoe-shine man was about to pull real hard on your light chain. I don't remember you minding when I pulled your butt out of the fire that night.'

'Yesterday's box score, Feet.'

'So don't take everything so serious. There's another glove in the bag.'

'The stunt man left town. He's not going to file charges. I guess you already know that.'

He rubbed his palm up and down the tapered shank of the bat.

'It was a chicken-shit thing to do,' I said.

'Maybe it was. Maybe I got my point of view, too. Maybe like I was with a broad when this fucking wild man starts beating on the side of my trailer.'

'He's staying at my house now, Julie. I want you to leave him alone. I don't care if he gets in your face or not.'

He flipped another ball in the air and *whanged* it to the shirtless man deep in left field. Then he took a hard breath through his nostrils.

'All right, I got no plans to bother the guy,' he said. 'But not because you're out here, Dave. Why would I want to have trouble with the guy who's the star of my picture? You think I like headaches with these people, you think I like losing money? . . . We clear on this now? . . . Why you keep staring at me?'

'A cop over in Lafayette thinks you set me up.'

'You mean that shooting in front of Red's Bar? Get serious, will you?' He splintered a shot all the way to the street, then leaned over and picked up another ball, his stomach creasing like elephant hide.

'It's not your style, huh?' I said.

'No, it's not.'

'Come on, Julie, fair and square – look back over your own record. Even when we were kids, you always had to get even, you could never let an insult or an injury pass. Remember the time you came down on that kid's ankle with your spikes?'

'Yeah, I remember it. I remember him trying to take my eyes out with *his*.'

The sky had turned almost black now, and the wind was blowing dust across the diamond.

'You're a powerful and wealthy man. Why don't you give it up?'

'Give what up? What the fuck are you talking about?'

'Carrying around all that anger, trying to prove you're big shit, fighting with your old man, whatever it is that drives you.'

'Where do you think you get off talking to me like this?'

'Come on, Julie. We grew up together. Save the hand job for somebody else.'

'That's right. That's why maybe I overlook things from you that I don't take from nobody else.'

'What's to take? Your father used to beat you with a garden hose. I didn't make that up. You burned down his nightclub.'

'It's starting to rain. I think it's time for you to go.' He picked up another ball and bounced it in his palm.

'I tried, partner.'

'Oh, yeah? What's that mean?'

'Nothing.'

'No, you mean you came out here and gave me a warning.'

'Why do you think every pitch is a slider, Julie?'

He looked away at the outfield, then back at me.

'You've made remarks about my family. I don't like that,' he said. 'I'm proud to be Italian. I was even proud of my old man. The people who ran this town back then weren't worth the sweat off his balls. In New Iberia we were always "wops," "dagos," and "guineas" because you coonasses were too fucking stupid to know what the Roman Empire was. So you get your nose out of the air when you talk about my family, or about my problems, or anything about my life, you understand what I'm saying, Dave?'

'Somebody made you become a dope dealer? That's what you're telling me?'

'I'm telling you to stay the fuck away from me.'

'You don't make a convincing victim, Julie. I'll see you around. Tell your man out there not to spit on the ball.'

'What?'

'Isn't that your porno star? I'd be careful. I think AIDS is a lot more easily transmitted than people think.'

I saw the rain pattering in the dust as I walked away from him toward the bleachers behind first base. Then I heard a ball ring off the aluminum bat and crash through the tree limbs overhead. I turned around in time to see Julie toss another ball into the air and swing again, his legs wide spread, his torso twisting, his wrists snapping as the bat bit into the ball and laced it in a straight white line toward my face.

When I opened my eyes I could see a thick layer of black clouds stretched across the sky from the southern horizon to a silken stretch of blue in the north. The rain had the warm amber color of whiskey, but it made no sound and it struck against my skin as dryly as flower petals in a windstorm.

The general sat on the bottom bench in the bleachers, coatless, the wind flowing through his shirt, a holstered cap-and-ball revolver hanging loosely from his right shoulder. The polished brass letters CSA gleamed softly on the crown of his gray hat. I could smell horses and hear teamsters shouting and wagons creaking in the street. Two enlisted men separated themselves from a group in the oak trees, lifted me to my feet, and sat me down on the wood plank next to the general.

He pointed toward first base with his crutch. My body lay on its side in the dirt, my eyes partially rolled. Cholo and the pornographic actor were running toward home plate from the outfield while Julie was fitting the aluminum bat back in the canvas ball bag. But they were all moving in slow motion, like creatures that were trying to burst free from an invisible gelatinous presence that encased their bodies.

The general took a gold watch as thick as a buttermilk biscuit from his pants pocket, snapped open the cover, glanced at the time, then twisted around in his seat and looked at the soldiers forming into ranks in the street. They were screwing their bayonets on the ends of their rifles, sliding their pouches of paper cartridges and minié balls to the centers of their belts, tying their haversacks and rolled blankets across their backs so their arms would be unencumbered. I saw a man put rolls of socks inside his coat and over his heart. I saw another man put a Bible in the same place. A boy, not over sixteen, his cap crimped tightly on his small head, unfurled the Stars and Bars from its wooden staff and lifted it popping into the wind.

Then in the north, where the sky was still blue and not sealed by storm clouds, I saw bursts of black smoke, like birds with ragged wings, and I heard thunder echoing in the trees and between the wooden buildings across the street.

'What's that?' I asked him.

'You've never heard that sound, the electric snap, before?'

'They're air bursts, aren't they?'

'It's General Banks's artillery firing from down the Teche. He's targetted the wrong area, though. There's a community of darkies under those shells. Did you see things like that in your war?'

'Yes, up the Mekong. Some villagers tried to run away from a barrage. They got caught out in the rice field. When we buried them, their faces all looked like they had been inside a terrible wind.'

'Then you know it's the innocent about whom we need to be most concerned?'

Before I could answer I saw Cholo and the man without a shirt staring down at my body, their faces beaded with rain. Julie pulled the draw-string tight on the ball bag and heaved it over his shoulder.

'Get in the Caddy, you guys,' he said.

'What happened, Julie?' Cholo said. He wore tennis shoes without socks, a tie-dyed undershirt, and a urine-yellow bikini knotted up tightly around his scrotum. Hair grew around the edges of his bikini like tiny pieces of copper wire.

'He got in the way of the ball,' Julie said.

'The guy's got a real goose egg in his hair,' the shirtless man said. 'Maybe we ought to take him to a hospital or something.'

'Leave him alone,' Julie said.

'We just gonna leave him here?' Cholo said.

'Unless you want to sit around out here in the rain,' Julie said.

'Hey come on, Feet,' Cholo said.

'What's the problem?' Julie said.

'He's not a bad guy for a cop. Y'all go back, right?'

'He's got diarrhea of the mouth. Maybe he learned a lesson this time,' Julie said.

'Yeah, but that don't mean we can't drop the guy off at the hospital. I mean, it ain't right to leave him in the fucking rain, Julie.'

'You want to start signing your own paychecks? Is that what you're telling me, Cholo?'

'No, I didn't say that. I was just trying to act reasonable. Ain't that what you're always saying? Why piss off the locals?'

'We're not pissing off anybody. Even his own department thinks he's a drunk and a pain in the ass. He got what he deserved. Are you guys coming or not?' Julie said.

He opened the trunk of the purple Cadillac limousine and threw the ball bag clattering inside. The porn actor followed him, wiping his chest and handsome face with his balled-up shirt. Cholo hesitated, stared after them, then pulled the first-base pad loose from its anchor pins and rested it across the side of my face to protect it from the rain. Then he ran after the others.

The blue strip of sky in the north was now filled with torn pieces of smoke. I could hear a loud *snap* each time a shell burst over the distant line of trees.

'What were you going to tell me?' I said to the general.

'That it's the innocent we need to worry about. And when it comes to their protection, we shouldn't hesitate to do it under a black flag.'

'I don't understand.'

'I feel perhaps I've deceived you.'

'How?'

'Perhaps I gave you the indication that you had been chosen as part of some chivalric cause.'

'I didn't think that, general.'

His face was troubled, as though his vocabulary was inadequate to explain what he was thinking. Then he looked out into the rain and his eyes became melancholy.

'My real loss wasn't in the war,' he said. *'It came later.'*

He turned slowly and looked into my face. *'Yellowjack took not only my life but also the lives of my wife and daughter, Mr Robicheaux.'*

He waited. The rain felt like confetti blowing against my skin. I searched his eyes, and my heart began to beat against my ribs.

'My family?' I said.

'If you're brave and honorable and your enemies can't destroy you personally, they'll seek to destroy what you love.'

He gestured with his crutch to a sergeant, who led a saddled white gelding around the side of the bleachers.

'Wait a minute, general. That's not good enough,' I said.

'It's all I have,' he answered, now seated in the saddle, his back erect, the reins wrapped around his gloved fist.

'Who would try to hurt them? What would they have to gain?'

'I don't know. Keep the Sykes boy with you, though. He's a good one. You remember what Robert Lee once said? "Texans move them every time." Good day to you, lieutenant. It's time we go give Bonnie Nate Banks his welcome to southwestern Louisiana.' Then he cut the spur on his left boot into his horse's flank, galloped to the head of his infantry, and hollered out brightly, *'Hideeho, boys! It's a fine day for it! Let's make religious fellows of them all!'*

Sometime later, I sat up on the ground in the rain, my clothes soaked, the base pad in my lap, a knot as hard and round as a half-dollar throbbing three inches behind my ear. An elderly black yardman bent over me, his face filled with concern. Down the street I could see an ambulance coming toward me through the rain.

'You okay, mister?' the black man said.

'Yes, I think so.'

'I seen you there and I t'ought you was drunk. But it look like somebody done gone upside yo' head.'

'Would you help me up, please?'

'Sho. You all right?'

'Why, yes, I'm sure I am. Did you see a man on horseback?'

'The Popsicle man gone by. His li'l cart got a horse. That's what you talkin' about?'

The black man eased me down on the bottom plank of the bleachers. It was starting to rain hard now, but right next to me, where the general had been sitting, was a pale, dry area in the wood that was as warm to the touch as living tissue.

15

The sky was clear when I woke in the morning, and I could hear gray squirrels racing across the bark of the trees outside the window. The icebag I had put on the lump behind my ear fell to the floor when I got out of bed to answer the phone.

'I called your office and found out you're still suspended,' Lou Girard said. 'What's going on over there?'

'Just that. I'm still suspended.'

'It sounds like somebody's got a serious bone on for you, Dave. Anyway, I talked to this FBI agent, what's her name, Gomez, as well as your boss. We vacuumed the Buick. Guess what we found?'

'I don't know.'

'Paper wadding. The kind that's used to seal blank cartridges. It looks like somebody fired a starter's gun at you. He probably leaned down through the passenger window, let off a couple of rounds, then bagged out.'

'What'd the sheriff have to say when you told him?'

'Not much. I got the feeling that maybe he was a little uncomfortable. He doesn't look too good, right, when one of his own men has to be cleared by a cop and a pathologist in another parish? I thought I could hear a little Pontius Pilate tap water running in the background.'

'He's always been an okay guy. He just got too close to a couple of the oil cans in the Chamber of Commerce.'

'Your friends don't stand around playing pocket pool while civilians kick a two-by-four up your butt, either.'

'Anyway, that's real good news, Lou. I owe you a redfishing trip out to Pecan Island.'

'Wait a minute, I'm not finished. That Gomez woman has some interesting theories about serial killers. She said these guys want control and power over people. So I got to thinking about the LeBlanc girl. If your FBI friend is right and the guy who killed her is from around here, what kind of work would he be in?'

'He may be just a pimp, Lou.'

'Yeah, but she got nailed on a prostitution charge when she was

651

sixteen, right? That means the court gave somebody a lot of control over her life. What if a probation or parole officer had her selling out of her pants?'

'I saw the body. I think the guy who mutilated her has a furnace instead of a brain. I think he'd have a hard time hiding inside a white-collar environment.'

'It was the pencil pushers who gave the world Auschwitz, Dave. Anyway, her prostitution bust was in Lafayette. I'll find out if her PO or social worker is still around.'

'Okay, but I still believe we're after a pimp of some kind.'

'Dave, if this guy's just a pimp, particularly if he's mobbed-up, he would have been in custody a long time ago. These are dumb guys. That's why they do what they do. Most of them couldn't get jobs cleaning gum off movie seats.'

'So maybe Balboni's got a smart pimp working for him.'

'No, this guy knows how things work from the inside. He sucked us both in on that deal at Red's Bar.'

Lou had never gotten along with white-collar authority, in fact, was almost obsessed about it, and I wasn't going to argue with him.

'Let me know what you come up with,' I said.

But he wasn't going to let it drop that easily.

'I've been in law enforcement for thirty-seven years,' he said. 'I've lost count of the lowlifes I've helped send up the road. Is Louisiana any better for it? You know the answer to that one. Face it. The real sonsofbitches are the ones we don't get to touch.'

'Don't be too down, Lou.' I told him about Julie line-driving a ball off the side of my head. Then I told him the rest of it. 'I asked the paramedics who called in the report. They said it was anonymous. So I went down later and listened to the 911 tapes. It was a guy named Cholo Manelli. He's a—'

'Yeah, I know who he is. Cholo did that?'

'There's no mistaking that broken-nose Irish Channel accent.'

'He owes you or something?'

'Not really. But he's an old-time mob soldier. He knows you don't antagonize cops unnecessarily. Maybe Julie's starting to lose control of his people.'

'It's a thought. But stay away from Balboni till you get your shield back. Stay off baseball diamonds, too. For a sober guy you sure have a way of spitting in the lion's mouth.'

After I hung up the phone I showered, dressed in a pair of seersucker slacks, brown loafers, a charcoal shirt with a gray and red striped tie, and got a haircut and a shoe shine in town. My scalp twitched when the barber's scissors clipped across the lump behind my ear. Through the front window I saw Julie Balboni's purple limo drive down Main

Street. The barber stopped clipping. The shop was empty except for the shoe-shine man.

'Dave, how come that man's still around here?' the barber said. His round stomach touched lightly against my elbow.

'He hasn't made the right people mad at him.'

'He ain't no good, that one. He don't have no bidness here.'

'I think you're right, Sid.'

He started clipping again. Then, almost as a casual afterthought, he said, 'Y'all gonna get him out of town?'

'There're some business people making a lot of money off of Julie. I think they'd like to keep him around awhile.'

His hands paused again, and he stepped around the side of the chair so I could see his face.

'That ain't the rest of us, no,' he said. 'We don't like having that man in New Iberia. We don't like his dope, we don't like his criminals he bring up here from New Orleans. You tell that man you work for we gonna 'member him when we vote, too.'

'Could I buy you a cup of coffee and a doughnut this morning, Sid?'

A little later, with my hair still wet and combed, I walked out of the heat into the air-conditioned coolness of the sheriff's department and headed toward the sheriff's office. I glanced inside my office door as I passed it. Rosie was not inside but Rufus Arceneaux was, out of uniform now, dressed in a blue suit and tie and a silk shirt that had the bright sheen of tin. He was sitting behind my desk.

I leaned against the door jamb.

'The pencil sharpener doesn't work very well, but there's a penknife in my drawer that you can use,' I said.

'I wasn't bucking for plainclothes. The old man gave it to me,' he said.

'I'm glad to see you're moving on up, Rufe.'

'Look, Dave, I'm not the one who went out and got fucked up at that movie set.'

'I hear you were out there, though. Looking into things. Probably trying to clear me of any suspicion that I got loaded.'

'I got a GED in the corps. You're a college graduate. You were a homicide lieutenant in New Orleans. You want to blame me for your troubles?'

'Where's Rosie?'

'Down in Vermilion Parish.'

'What for?'

'How would I know?'

'Did she say anything about Balboni having legal troubles with Mikey Goldman?'

'What legal—' His eyes clouded, like silt being disturbed in dark water.

'When you see her, would you ask her to call me?'

'Leave a message in her box,' he said, positioned his forearms on my desk blotter, straightened his back, and looked out the window as though I were not there.

When I walked into the sheriff's office he was pouring a chalky liquid from a brown prescription bottle into a water glass. A dozen sheets of paper were spread around on his desk. The 'hold' light was flashing on his telephone. He didn't speak. He drank from the glass, then refilled it from the water cooler and drank again, his throat working as though he were washing out an unwanted presence from his metabolism.

'How you doin', podna?' he said.

'Pretty good now. I had a talk with Lou Girard this morning.'

'So did I. Sit down,' he said, then picked up the phone and spoke to whoever was on hold. 'I'm not sure *what* happened. When I am, I'll call you. In the meantime, Rufus is going to be suspended. Just hope we don't have to pass a sales tax to pay the bills on this one.'

He hung up the phone and pressed the flat of his hand against his stomach. He made a face like a small flame was rising up his windpipe.

'Did you ever have ulcers?' he asked.

'Nope.'

'I've got one. If this medicine I'm drinking doesn't get rid of it, they may have to cut it out.'

'I'm sorry to hear that.'

'That was the prosecutor's office I was talking to. We're being sued.'

'Over what?'

'A seventy-six-year-old black woman shot her old man to death last night, then killed both her dogs and shot herself through the stomach. Rufus in there handcuffed her to the gurney, then came back to the office. He didn't bother to give the paramedics a key to the cuffs, either. She died outside the emergency room.'

I didn't say anything.

'You think we got what we deserved, huh?' he said.

'Maybe he would have done it even if he hadn't been kicked up to plainclothes, sheriff.'

'No, he wouldn't have been the supervising officer. He wouldn't have had the opportunity.'

'What's my status this morning?'

He brushed at a nostril with one knuckle.

'I don't know how to say this,' he said. 'We messed up. No *I* messed up.'

I waited.

'I did wrong by you, Dave,' he said.

'People make mistakes. Maybe you made the best decision you could at the time.'

He held out his hands, palms front.

'Nope, none of that,' he said. 'I learned in Korea a good officer takes care of his men. I didn't get this ulcer over Rufus Arceneaux's stupidity. I got it because I was listening to some local guys I should have told to butt out of sheriff's department business.'

'Nobody's supposed to bat a thousand, sheriff.'

'I want you back at work today. I'll talk to Rufus about his new status. That old black woman is part my responsibility. I don't know why I made that guy plainclothes. You don't send a warthog to a beauty contest.'

I shook hands with him, walked across the street to a barbecue stand in a grove of live oaks, ate a plate filled with dirty rice, pork ribs, and red beans, then strolled back to the office, sipping an ice-cold can of Dr Pepper. Rufus Arceneaux was gone. I clipped my badge on my belt, sat in the swivel chair behind my desk, turned the air-conditioner vents into my face, and opened my mail.

Rosie was beaming when she came through the office door an hour later.

'What's that I see?' she said. 'With a haircut and a shoe shine, too.'

'How's my favorite Fed?'

'Dave, you look wonderful!'

'Thanks, Rosie.'

'I can't tell you how fine it is to have you back.'

Her face was genuinely happy, to such an extent that I felt vaguely ill at ease.

'I owe you and Lou Girard a lot on this one,' I said.

'Have you had lunch yet?'

'Yeah, I did.'

'Too bad. Tomorrow I'm taking you out, though. Okay?'

'Yeah, that'd be swell.'

She sat down behind her desk. Her neck was flushed and her breasts rose against her blouse when she breathed. 'I got a call this morning from an old Frenchman who runs a general store on Highway 35 down in Vermilion Parish. You know what he said? "Hey, y'all catch the man put dat young girl in dat barrel?"'

I filled a water glass for her and put it on her desk.

'He knows something?' I said.

'Better than that. I think he saw the guy who did it. He said he remembers a month or so ago a blonde girl coming in his store at night in the rain. He said he became worried about her because of the way a man in the store was watching her.' She opened her notebook pad and looked at it. 'These are the old fellow's words: "You didn't need but look at that man's face to know he had a dirty mind." He said the girl had a convas backpack and she went back out in the rain to the highway with it. The man followed her, then he came back in a few minutes and asked the old fellow if he had any red balloons for sale.'

'Balloons?'

'If you think that sounds weird, how about this? When the old fellow said no, the man found an old box of Valentine candy on the back shelf and said he wanted that instead.'

'I'm not making connections here,' I said.

'The store owner watched the man with the candy box through the window. He said just before he pulled out of the parking lot he threw the candy box in the ditch. In the morning the old fellow went out and found it in the weeds. The cellophone wrapping was gone.' She watched my face. 'What are you thinking?'

'Did he see the man pick up the girl?'

'He's not sure. He remembers the man was in a dark-blue car and he remembers the brake lights going on in the rain.' She continued to watch my face. 'Here's the rest of it. I looked around on the back shelves of the store and found another candy box that the owner says is like the one the man in the blue car bought. Guess what tint the cellophane was.'

'Red or purple.'

'You got it, slick,' she said, and leaned back in her chair.

'He wrapped it around a spotlight, didn't he?'

'That'd be my bet.'

'Could the store owner describe this guy?'

'That's the problem.' She tapped a ballpoint pen on her desk blotter. 'All the old fellow remembers is that the man had a rain hood.'

'Too bad. Why didn't he contact us sooner?'

'He said he told all this to somebody, he doesn't know who, in the Vermilion Parish Sheriff's Department. He said when he called again yesterday, they gave him my number. Is your interagency cooperation always this good?'

'Always. Does he still have the candy box?'

'He said he gave the candy to his dog, then threw the box in the trash.'

'So maybe we've got a guy impersonating a cop?' I said.

'It might explain a lot of things.'

Unconsciously I fingered the lump behind my ear.

'What's the matter?' she said.

'Nothing. Maybe our man is simply a serial killer and psychopath after all. Maybe he doesn't have anything to do with Julie Balboni.'

'Would that make you feel good or bad?'

'I honestly can't say, Rosie.'

'Yeah, you can,' she said. 'You're always hoping that even the worst of them has something of good in him. Don't do that with Balboni. Deep down inside all that whale fat is a real piece of shit, Dave.'

Outside, a jail trusty cutting the grass broke the brass head off a sprinkler with the lawnmower. A violent jet of water showered the wall and ran down the windows. In the clatter of noise, in the time it takes the mind's eye to be distracted by shards of wet light, I thought of horses fording a stream, of sun-browned men in uniform looking back over their shoulders at the safety of a crimson and gold hardwood forest, while ahead of them dirty puffs of rifle fire exploded from a distant treeline that swarmed with the shapes of the enemy.

It's the innocent we need to worry about, he had said. And when it comes to their protection we shouldn't hesitate to do it under a black flag.

'Are you all right?' she said.

'Yeah, it's a fine day. Let's go across the street and I'll buy you a Dr Pepper.'

That evening, at sunset, I was sprinkling the grass and the flower beds in the backyard while Elrod and Alafair were playing with Tripod on top of the picnic table. The air was cool in the fading light and smelled of hydrangeas and water from the hose and the fertilizer I had just spaded into the roots of my rosebushes.

The phone rang inside, and a moment later Bootsie brought it and the extension cord to the back screen. I sat down on the step and put the receiver to my ear.

'Hello,' I said.

I could hear someone breathing on the other end.

'Hello?'

'I want to talk to you tonight.'

'Sam?'

'That's right. I'm playing up at the black juke in St Martinville. You know where that's at?'

'The last time I had an appointment with you, things didn't work out too well.'

'That was last time. I was drinkin' then. Then them womens was hangin' around, made me forget what I was supposed to do.'

'I think you let me down, partner.'

He was quiet except for the sound of his breathing.

'Is something wrong?' I said.

'I got to tell you somet'ing, somet'ing I ain't tole no white man.'

'Say it.'

'You come up to the juke.'

'I'll meet you at my office tomorrow morning.'

'What I got to say can put me back on the farm. I sure ain't gonna do it down there.'

Elrod picked Tripod up horizontally in his arms, then bounced him up and down by tugging on his tail.

'I'll be there in an hour or so,' I said. 'Don't jerk me around again, Sam.'

'You might be a po-liceman, you might even be different from most white folks, but you still white and you ain't got no idea 'bout the world y'all give people of color to live in. That's a fact, suh. It surely is,' he said, and hung up.

I should have known that Hogman would not be outdone in eloquence.

'Don't pull his tail,' Alafair was saying.

'He likes it. It gets his blood moving,' Elrod said.

She sighed as though Elrod were unteachable, then took Tripod out of his arms and carried him around the side of the house to the hutch.

'Can you take yourself to the meeting tonight?' I asked Elrod.

'You cain't go?'

'No.'

'How about I just wait till we can go together?' He rubbed the top of the table with his fingers and didn't look up.

'What if I drop you off and then come back before the meeting's over?'

'Look, this is a, what do you call it, a step meeting?'

'That's right.'

'You said it's about amends, about atoning to people for what you did wrong?'

'Something like that.'

'How do I atone for Kelly? How do I make up for that one, Dave?' He stared out at the late red sun over the canefield so I couldn't see his eyes.

'You get those thoughts out of your head. Kelly's dead because we have a psychopath in our midst. Her death doesn't have anything to do with you.'

'You can say that all you want, but I know better.'

'Oh, yeah?'

'Yeah.'

I could see the clean, tight line of his jaw and a wet gleaming in the corner of his eye.

'Tell me, did you respect Kelly?' I asked.

He swiveled around on the picnic bench. 'What kind of question is that?'

'I'm going to be a little hard on you, El. I think you're using her death to feel sorry for yourself.'

'What?' His face was incredulous.

'When I lost my wife I found out that self-pity and guilt could be a real rush, particularly when I didn't have Brother Jim Beam to do the job.'

'That's a lousy fucking thing to say.'

'I was talking about myself. Maybe you're different from me.'

'What the hell's the matter with you? You don't think it's natural to feel loss, to feel grief, when somebody dies? I tried to close the hole in her throat with my hands, her blood was running through my fingers. She was still alive and looking straight into my eyes. Like she was drowning and neither one of us could do anything about it.' He pressed his forehead against his fist; his flexed thigh trembled against his slacks.

'I got four of my men killed on a trail in Vietnam. Then I got drunk over it. I used them, I didn't respect them for the brave men they were. That's the way alcoholism works, El.'

'I'd appreciate it if you'd leave me be for a while.'

'Will you go to the meeting?'

He didn't answer. There was a pained light in his eyes like someone had twisted barbed wire around his forehead.

'You don't have to talk, just listen to what these guys have to say about their own experience,' I said.

'I'd rather pass tonight.'

'Suit yourself,' I said.

I told Bootsie where I was going and walked out to the truck. The cicadas droned from horizon to horizon under the vault of plum-colored sky. Then I heard Elrod walking through the leaves and pecan husks behind me.

'If I sit around here, I'll end up in the beer joint,' he said, and opened the passenger door to the truck. Then he raised his finger at me. 'But I'm going to ask you one thing, Dave. Don't ever accuse me of using Kelly again. If you do, I'm going to knock your teeth down your goddamn throat.'

There were probably a number of things I could have said in reply; but you don't deny a momentary mental opiate to somebody who has made an appointment in the garden of Gethsemane.

The black jukejoint in St Martinville was set back in a grove of trees off a yellow dirt road not far from Bayou Teche. It was one of those places that could be dropped by a tornado in the middle of an Iowa cornfield and you would instantly know that its origins were in the Deep South. The plank walls and taped windows vibrated with noise from Friday afternoon until late Sunday night. Strings of Christmas-tree lights rimmed the doors and windows year round; somebody was barbecuing ribs on top of a tin barrel, only a few feet from a pair of dilapidated privies that were caked under the eaves with yellow-jacket and mud-dauber nests; people copulated back in the woods against tree trunks and fought in the parking lot with knives, bottles, and razors. Inside, the air was always thick with the smell of muscatel, smoke, cracklings, draft beer and busthead whiskey, expectorated snuff, pickled hogs' feet, perfume, body powder, sweat, and home-grown reefer.

Sam Patin sat on a small stage with a canopy over it hung with red tassels and miniature whiskey bottles that clinked in the backdraft from a huge ventilator fan. His white suit gleamed with an electric purple glow from the floor lamps, and the waxed black surfaces of his twelve-string guitar winked with tiny lights. The floor in front of him was packed with dancers. When he blew into the harmonica attached to a wire brace on his neck and began rolling the steel picks on his fingers across an E-major blues run, the crowd moaned in unison. They yelled at the stage as though they were confirming a Biblical statement he had made at a revival, pressed their loins together with no consciousness of other people around them, and roared with laughter even though Hogman sang of a man who had sold his soul for an ox-blood Stetson hat he had just lost in a crap game:

> *Stagolee went runnin'*
> *In the red-hot boilin' sun,*
> *Say look in my chiffro drawer, woman,*
> *Get me my smokeless .41.*
> *Stagolee tole Miz Billy,*
> *You don't believe your man is dead,*
> *Come down to the barroom,*
> *See the .41 hole in his head.*
> *That li'l judge found Stagolee guilty*
> *And that li'l clerk wrote it down,*
> *On a cold winter morning,*
> *Stagolee was Angola bound.*
> *Forty-dollar coffin,*
> *Eighty-dollar hack,*
> *Carried that po' man to the burying ground,*
> *Ain't never comin' back.*

Two feet away from me the bartender filled a tray with draft beers without ever looking at me. He was bald and had thick gray muttonchop sideburns that looked like they were pasted on his cheeks. Then he wiped his hands on his apron and lit a cigar.

'You sho' you in the right place?' he said.

'I'm a friend of Hogman's,' I said.

'So this is where you come to see him?'

'Why not?'

'What you havin', chief?'

'A 7 Up.'

He opened a bottle, placed it in front of me without a glass, and walked away. The sides of the bottle were warm and filmed with dust. Twenty minutes later Hogman had not taken a break and was still playing.

'You want another one?' the bartender said.

'Yeah, I would. How about some ice or a cold one this time?' I said.

'The gentleman wants a cold one,' he said to no one in particular. Then he filled a tall glass with cracked ice and set it on the bar with another dusty bottle of 7 Up. 'Why cain't y'all leave him alone? He done his time, ain't he?'

'I look like the heat?' I said.

'You *are* the heat, chief. You and that other one out yonder.'

'What other one? What are you talking about, partner?'

'The white man that was out yonder in that blue Mercury.'

I got off the stool and looked into the parking lot through the Venetian blinds and the scrolled neon tubing of a Dixie beer sign.

'I don't see any blue Merc,' I said.

''Cause he gone now, chief. Like it's a black people's club, like he figured that out, you understand what I'm sayin'?'

'What'd this guy look like?' I said.

'White. He look white. That he'p you out?' he said. He tossed a towel into the tin sink, and walked down the duckboards toward the far end of the bar.

Finally Hogman slipped his harmonica brace and guitar strap off his neck, looked directly at me, and went through a curtained door into a back storage room. I followed him inside. He sat on a wood chair, among stacks of beer cases, and had already started eating a dinner of pork chops, greens, and cornbread from a tin plate that rested on another chair.

'I ain't had a chance to eat today. This movie-star life is gettin' rough on my time. You want some?' he said.

'No, thanks.' I leaned against a stack of beer cartons.

'The lady fix me these chops don't know how to season, but they ain't too bad.'

'You want to get to it, Sam?'

'You t'ink I just messin' with you, huh? All right, this is how it play. A long time ago up at Angola I got into trouble over a punk. Not my punk, you understand, I didn't do none of that unnatural kind of stuff, a punk that belong to a guy name Big Melon. Big Melon was growin' and sellin' dope for a couple of the hacks. Him and his punk had a whole truck patch of it behind the cornfield.'

'Hogman, I'm afraid this sounds a little remote.'

'You always *know*, you always got somet'ing smart to say. That's why you runnin' around in circles, that's why them men laughin' at you.'

'Which men?'

'The ones who killed that nigger you dug up in the Atchafalaya. You gonna be patient now, or you want to go back to doin' it your way?'

'I'm looking forward to hearing your story, Hogman.'

'See, these two hacks had them a good bidness. Big Melon and the punk growed the dope, cured it, bagged it all up, and the hacks sold it in Lafayette. They carried it down there themselves sometimes, or the executioner and another cop picked it up for them. They didn't let nobody get back there by that cornfield. But I was half-trusty then, livin' in Camp I, and I used to cut across the field to get to the hog lot. That's how come I found out they was growin' dope back there. So Big Melon tole the hack I knowed what they was doin', that I was gonna snitch them off, and then the punk planted a jar of julep under my bunk so I'd lose my trusty job and my good-time.

'I tole the hack it ain't right, I earn my job. He say, "Hogman, you fuck with the wrong people in here, you goin' in the box and you goin' stay in there till you come out a white man." That's what the bossman say. I tole him it don't matter how long they keep me in there, it still ain't right. They wrote me up for sassin' and put me to pickin' cotton. When I get down in a thin patch and come up short, they make me stand up all night on an oil barrel, dirty and smellin' bad and without no supper.

'I went to the bossman in the field, say I don't care what Big Melon do, what them hacks do, it ain't my bidness, I just want my job back on the hog lot. He say, "You better keep shut, boy, you better fill that bag, you better not put no dirt clods in it when you weigh in, neither, like you tried to do yesterday." I say, "Boss, what's I gonna do? I ain't put no dirt clods in my bag, I ain't give nobody trouble, I don't be carin' Big Melon want to grow dope for the hacks." He knock me down with a horse quirt and put me in the sweatbox on Camp A for three days, in August, with the sun boilin' off them iron sides, with a bucket between my knees to go to the bat'room in.'

He had stopped eating now and his face looked solitary and bemused, as though his own experience had become strange and unfamiliar in his recounting of it.

'You were a standup guy, Hogman. I always admired your courage,' I said.

'No, I was scared of them people, 'cause when I come out of the box I knowed the gunbulls was gonna kill me. I seen them do it befo', up on the levee, where they work them Red Hat boys double-time from cain't-see to cain't-see. They shot and buried them po' boys without never missin' a beat, just the way somebody run over a dog with a truck and keep right on goin'.

'I had me a big Stella twelve-string guitar, bought it off a Mexican on Congress Street in Houston. I used to keep it in the count-man's cage so nobody wouldn't be foolin' with it while I was workin' or sleepin'. When I come out of the box and taken a shower and eat a big plate of rice and beans, I ax the count-man first thing for my guitar. He say, "I'm sorry, Sam, but the bossman let Big Melon take it while you was in the box."

'I waited till that night and went to Big Melon's "hunk," that's what we call the place where a wolf stay with his punk. There's that big fat nigger sittin' naked on his mattress, like a big pile of black inner tubes, while the punk is playin' my guitar on the floor, lipstick and rouge all over his face and pink panties on his li'l ass.

'I say, "Melon, you or your punk fuck wit' my guitar again and I gone cut that black dick off. It don't matter if I go to the electric chair for it or not. I'm gonna joog you in the shower, in the chow line, or while you pumpin' your poke chops here. They's gonna be one fat nigger they gonna have to haul in a piano crate down to the graveyard."

'Melon smile at me and say, "We just borrowed it, Hogman. We was gonna give it back. Here, you want Pookie to rub your back for you?"

'But I knowed they was comin'. Two nights later, right befo' lockup, I was goin' to the toilet and I turn around and his punk is standin' in the do'. I say, "What you want, Pookie?" He say, "I'm sorry I was playin' your guitar, Hogman. I wanta be yo' friend, maybe come stay up at your hunk some nights."

'When I reached down to pull up my britches, he come outta his back pocket with a dirk and aim it right at my heart. I catched him around the neck and bent him backwards, then I kept bendin' him backwards and squeezin' acrost his windpipe, and he was floppin' real hard, shakin' all over, he shit in his pants, 'cause I could smell it, then it went *snap*, just like you bust a real dry piece of firewood acrost your knee.

'I look up and there's one of the hacks who's selling the dope. He say, "Hogman, we ain't gonna let this be a problem. We'll just stuff this li'l bitch out yonder in the levee with them others. Won't nobody care, won't make no difference to nobody, not even to Big Melon. It'll just be our secret."

'All that time they'd been smarter than me. They sent Pookie to joog me, but they didn't care if he killed me or if I killed him. It worked out for them just fine. They knew I'd never cause them no trouble. They was right, too. I didn't sass, I done what they tole me, I even he'ped hoe them dope plants a couple of times.'

'I don't understand, Sam. You're telling me that the lynched black man was killed by one of these guards?'

'I ain't said that. I said they was a bunch of them sellin' that dope. They was takin' it out of the pen in a police car. What was the name of that nigger you dug out of the sandbar?'

'DeWitt Prejean.'

'I'll tell you this. He was fuckin' a white man's wife. Start axin' what he done for a livin', you'll find the people been causin' you all this grief.'

'Who's the guy I'm looking for?'

'I said all I can say.'

'Look, Sam, don't be afraid of these gunbulls or cops from years ago. They can't harm you now.'

He put a toothpick in the corner of his mouth, then took a pint bottle of rum from his coat pocket and unscrewed the cap with his thumb. He held the bottle below his mouth. His long fingers were glistening with grease from the pork chops he had eaten.

'This still the state of Lou'sana, or are we livin' somewhere else these days?' he said.

I couldn't sleep that night. I poured a glass of milk and walked down by the duck pond in the starlight. A pair of mudhens spooked out of the flooded reeds and skittered across the water's surface toward the far bank. The pieces of the case wouldn't come together. Were we looking for a serial killer who had operated all over the state, a local psychopath, a pimp, or perhaps even a hit man from the mob? Were cops involved? Hogman thought so, and even believed there was someone out there with the power to send him back to prison. But his perspective was colored by his own experience as a career recidivist. And what about the lynched black man, DeWitt Prejean? Would the solution to his murder in 1957 lead us to the deviate who had mutilated Cherry LeBlanc?

No, the case was not as simple as Hogman had wanted me to think, even though he was obviously sincere and his fears about retribution were real. But I had no answers, either.

Unfortunately, they would come in a way that I never anticipated. I saw Elrod come out of the lighted kitchen and walk down the slope toward the pond. He was shirtless and barefoot and his slacks were unbuttoned over his skivvies. He clutched a sheet of lined notebook paper in his right hand. He looked at me uncertainly, and his lips started to form words that obviously he didn't want to speak.

'What's wrong?' I said.

'The phone rang while I was in the kitchen. I answered it so y'all wouldn't get woke up.'

'Who was it? What's that in your hand?'

'The sheriff . . .' He straightened the piece of paper in his fingers and read the words to himself, then looked up into my face. 'It's a friend of yours, Lou Girard, Dave. The sheriff says maybe you should go over to Lafayette. He says, I'm sorry, man, he says your friend got drunk and killed himself.'

Elrod held the sheet of paper out toward me, his eyes looking askance at the duck pond. The moonlight was white on his hand.

16

He did it with a dogleg twenty-gauge in his little garage apartment, whose windows were overgrown with bamboo and banana trees. Or at least that's what the investigative officer, Doobie Patout, was telling me when I got there at 4 A.M., just as the photographer was finishing and the paramedics were about to lift Lou's body out of a wide pool of blood and zipper it inside a black bag.

'There's a half-empty bottle of Wild Turkey on the drainboard and a spilled bottle of Valium on the coffee table,' Doobie said. 'I think maybe Lou just got real down and decided to do it.'

The single-shot twenty-gauge lay at the foot of a beige-colored stuffed chair. The top of the chair, the wall behind it, and the ceiling were streaked with blood. One side of Lou's face looked perfectly normal, the eye staring straight ahead like a blue marble pressed into dough. The opposite side of his face, where the jawbone should have been, had sunk into the rug like a broken pomegranate. Lou's right arm was pointed straight out onto the wood floor. At the end of his fingers, painted in red, were the letters *SI*.

'You guys are writing it off as suicide?' I said.

'That's the way it looks to me,' Doobie said. The tops of his jug ears were scaled with sunburn. 'He was in bad shape. The mattress is covered with piss stains, the sink's full of raw garbage. Go in the bedroom and take a whiff.'

'Why would a suicide try to write a note in his own blood?'

'I think they change their minds when they know it's too late. Then they want to hold on any way they can. They're not any different from anybody else. It was probably for his ex-wife. Her name's Silvia.'

'Where's his piece?'

'On his dresser in the bedroom.'

'If Lou wanted to buy it, why wouldn't he use his .357?' I said. I scratched at a lead BB that had scoured upward along the wallpaper. 'Why would he do it with twenty-gauge birdshot, then botch it?'

'Because he was drunk on his ass. It wasn't an unusual condition for him.'

'He was helping me on a case, Doobie.'

'And?'

'Maybe he found out something that somebody didn't want him to pass along.'

The paramedics lifted Lou's body off the rug, then lowered it inside the plastic bag, straightened his arms by his sides, and zipped the bag over his face.

'Look, his career was on third base,' Doobie said, as the medics worked the gurney past him. 'His wife dumped him for another dyke, he was getting freebies from a couple of whores down at the Underpass, he was trembling and eating pills in front of the whole department every morning. You might believe otherwise, but there's no big mystery to what happened here tonight.'

'Lou had trouble with booze, but I think you're lying about his being on a pad with hookers. He was a good cop.'

'Think whatever you want. He was a drunk. That fact's not going to go away. I'm going to seal the place now. You want to look at anything else?'

'Is it true you were an executioner up at Angola?'

'None of your goddamn business what I was.'

'I'm going to look around a little more. In the meantime I want to ask you a favor, Doobie. I'd appreciate your waiting outside. In fact, I'd really appreciate your staying as far away from me as possible.'

'You'd appreciate it—'

'Yes. Thanks very much.'

His breath was stale, his eyes liquid and resentful. Then the interest went out of them and he glanced outside at the pale glow of the sun on the eastern horizon. He stuck a cigarette in the corner of his mouth, walked out onto the porch, and watched the paramedics load Lou's body into the back of the ambulance, not out of fear of me or even personal humiliation; he was simply one of those law officers for whom insensitivity, cynicism, cruelty, and indifference toward principle eventually become normal and interchangeable attitudes, one having no more value or significance than another.

In the sink, on top of a layer of unwashed dishes, was a pile of garbage – coffee grounds, banana peels, burned oatmeal, crushed beer cans, cigarette butts, wadded newspapers. The trash can by the icebox was empty, except for a line of wet coffee grinds that ran from the lip of the can to the bottom, where a solitary banana peel rested.

In the bedroom one drawer was open in the dresser. On top of the dresser were a roll of white socks, a framed photograph of Lou and his wife at a Las Vegas wedding chapel, Lou's holstered revolver, and the small notebook with a pencil attachment that he always carried in his shirt pocket. The first eight pages were filled with notes about an accidental drowning and a stabbing in a black nightclub. The next few pages had been torn out. Tiny bits of paper clung to the wire spirals, and the first blank page had no pencil impressions on it from the previous one.

In his sock drawer I found a bottle of vodka and his 'throw-down,' an old .32 revolver with worn bluing, taped wooden grips, and serial numbers that had been eaten and disfigured with acid. I flipped open the cylinder. Five of the chambers were loaded, and the sixth had been left empty for the hammer to rest on.

I started to replace the revolver in the drawer; instead, I pushed the drawer shut and dropped the revolver into my pants pocket.

On the way out of the apartment I looked again at Lou's blood on the floor. Doobie Patout's shoes had tracked through the edge of it and printed the logo of his rubber heel brightly on the wood.

What a way to exit thirty-seven years of law enforcement, I thought. You died face down in a rented garage apartment that wouldn't meet the standards of public housing; then your colleagues write you off as a drunk and step in your blood.

I looked at the smudged letters *SI* again. What were you trying to tell us, Lou?

Doobie Patout locked the door behind me when I walked outside. A red glow was spreading from the eastern horizon upward into the sky.

'This is what I think happened, Doobie. You can do with it what you want,' I said. 'Somebody found Lou passed out and tossed the place. After he ripped some pages out of Lou's notebook, he put Lou's twenty-gauge under his chin.'

'If he tossed the place first, he would have found Lou's .357, right? Why wouldn't he use it? That's the first thing you jumped on, Robicheaux.'

'Because he would have had to put it in Lou's hand. He didn't want to wake him up. It was easier to do it with the shotgun.'

His eyes fixed on mine; then they became murky and veiled as they studied a place in the air about six inches to the right of my face. A dead palm tree in the small yard clattered in the warm morning breeze.

It was Saturday, and I didn't have to go to the office, but I called Rosie at the motel where she was living and told her about Lou's death.

At noon of the same day Cholo Manelli drove a battered fire-engine-red Cadillac convertible down the dirt road by the bayou and parked by the dock just as I was headed up to the house for lunch. The left front fender had been cut away with an acetylene torch and looked like an empty eye socket. The top was down, and the back seat and the partly opened trunk were filled with wrought-iron patio furniture, including a glass-topped table and a furled beach umbrella.

He wore white shorts and a green Hawaiian shirt with pink flamingoes printed on it. He squinted up at me from under his white golf cap, which was slanted over one eye. When he grinned I saw that an incisor tooth was broken off in his lower mouth and there was still blood in the empty space above his gum.

'I wanted to say good-bye,' he said. 'Give you something, too.'

'Where you going, Cholo?'

'I thought I might go to Florida for a while, take it easy, maybe open up a business like you got. Do some marlin fishing, stuff like that. Look, can we talk someplace a minute?'

'Sure. Come on inside the shop.'

'No, you got customers around and I got a bad problem with language. It don't matter what I say, it comes out sounding like a toilet flushing. Take a ride with me, lieutenant.'

I got into the passenger's seat, and we drove down to the old grocery store with the wide gallery at the four-corners. The white-painted iron patio furniture vibrated and rattled in the back seat. On the leg of one chair was the green trademark of Holiday Inn. Cholo parked in the shade of the huge oak tree that stretched over the store's gallery.

'What's with the furniture?' I said.

'The owner wanted me to take it when I checked out. He said he's been needing some new stuff, it's a write-off, anyway, and I'm kind of doing him a favor. They got po'-boys in here? It's on me.'

Before I could answer he went inside the store and came back with two shrimp-and-fried-oyster sandwiches dripping with mayonnaise, lettuce, and sliced tomatoes. He unwrapped the wax paper on his and chewed carefully on one side of his mouth.

'What's going on, Cholo?' I said.

'Just like I said, it's time to hang it up.'

'You had some problems with Baby Feet?'

'Maybe.'

'Because you called an ambulance for me?'

He stopped chewing, removed a piece of lettuce from his teeth, and flicked it out onto the shell parking lot.

'Margot told him. She heard me on the phone,' he said. 'So last night we was all having dinner at this class place out on the highway, with some movie people there, people who still think Julie's shit don't stink, and Julie says, "Did y'all know Cholo thinks he's Florence Nightingale? That it's his job to take care of people who get hurt on ball fields, even though that means betraying his old friends?"

'I say, "What are you talking, Julie? Who's fucking Florence Nightingale or whatever?"

'He don't even look at me. He says to all the others, "So, we're gonna get Cholo another job 'cause he don't like what he's doing now. He's gonna start work in one of my restaurants, down the street from the Iberville project. Bus dishes for a little while, get the feel of things, make sure the toilets are clean, 'cause a lot of middle-class niggers eat in there and they don't like dirty toilets. What d'you say, Cholo?"

'Everybody at the table's grinning and I go, "I ain't done anything wrong, Julie. I made a fucking phone call. What if the guy'd died out there?"

'Julie goes, "There you go again, Cholo. Always opening your face when you ain't supposed to. Maybe you ought to leave the table. You got wax in your ears, you talk shit, you rat-fuck your friends. I don't want you around no more."

'When I walked out, everybody in the restaurant was looking at me, like I was a bug, like I was somebody didn't have no business around regular people. Nobody ever done anything like that to me.'

His face was bright with perspiration in the warm shade. He rubbed his nose on the back of his wrist.

'What happened to your tooth, Cholo?' I asked.

'I went down to Julie's room last night. I told him that he was a douche bag. I wouldn't work for him again if he begged me, that just like Cherry LeBlanc told him, he's a needle-dick and the only reason a broad like Margot stays with him is because what she's got is so wore out it's like the Grand Canyon down there and it don't matter if he's a needle-dick or not. That's when he come across my mouth with this big glass ashtray, the sonofabitch.

'Here, you want to see what he's into, lieutenant,' he said, pulled a video cassette out of the glove box, and put it in my hand. 'Go to the movies.'

'Wait a minute. What's this about Cherry LeBlanc?'

'If he tells you he never knew her, ask him about this. Julie forgot he told me to take some souvenir pictures when we drove over to Biloxi once. Is that her or not?'

He slipped a black-and-white photograph from his shirt pocket and placed it in my hand. In it, Julie and Cherry LeBlanc sat at an outdoor table under an umbrella. They wore swimsuits and held napkin-wrapped drinks in their hands; both were smiling. The background was hazy with sunshine and out of focus. An indistinct man at another table read a newspaper; his eyes looked like diamonds embedded in his flesh.

'I want you to be straight with me, Cholo. Did Feet kill her?' I said.

'I don't know. I'll tell you what happened the night she got killed, though. They had a big blowup in the motel room. I could hear it coming through the walls. She said she wasn't nobody's chicken, she wanted her own action, her own girls, a place out on Lake Pontchartrain, maybe a spot in a movie. So he goes. "There's broads who'd do an awful lot just to be in the same room with me, Cherry. Maybe you ought to count your blessings." That's when she started to make fun of him. She said he looked like a whale with hair on it, and besides that, he had a putz like a Vienna sausage.

'The next thing I know she's roaring out of the place and Julie's yelling into the phone at somebody, I don't know who, all I heard him say was

Cherry is a fucking nightmare who's snorting up six hundred dollars' worth of his coke a day and he don't need any more nightmares in his life, particularly a teenage moron who thinks she can go apeshit any time she feels like it.'

'Who killed her, Cholo?'

He tossed his unfinished po'-boy sandwich at a rusted trash barrel. He missed, and the bread, shrimp, and oysters broke apart on the ground.

'Come on, lieutenant, You know how it works. A guy like Julie don't do hits. He says something to somebody, then he forgets it. If it's a special kind of job, maybe somebody calls up a geek, a guy with real sick thoughts in his head.

'Look, you remember a street dip in New Orleans named Tommy Figorelli, people used to call him Tommy Fig, Tommy Fingers, Tommy Five? Used to be a part-time meat cutter in a butcher shop on Louisiana Avenue? He got into trouble for something besides picking pockets, he molested a couple of little girls, and one of them turned out to be related to the Giacano family. So the word went out that Tommy Fig was anybody's fuck, but it wasn't supposed to be no ordinary hit, not for what he done. Did I ever tell you I worked in the kitchen up at Angola? That's right. So when Tommy got taken out, three guys done it, and when that butcher shop opened on Monday morning, it was the day before Christmas, see, Tommy was hung in parts, freeze-dried and clean, all over the shop like tree ornaments.

'That sounds sick, don't it, but the people who ran the shop didn't have no use for a child molester, either, and to show how they felt, they called up some guys from the Giacano family and they had a party with eggnog and fruitcake and music and Tommy Fig twirling around in pieces on the blades of the ceiling fan.

'What I'm saying, lieutenant, is I ain't gonna get locked up as a material witness and I ain't going before no grand jury, I been that route before, eight months in the New Orleans city prison, with a half-dozen guys trying to whack me out, even though I was standup and was gonna take the fall for a couple of guys I wouldn't piss on if they was burning to death.'

'You're sure Julie didn't catch up with Cherry LeBlanc later that same night?'

'It ain't his style. But then—' He poked his tongue into the space where his incisor tooth was broken off— 'who knows what goes on in Julie's head? He had the hots for the LeBlanc broad real bad, and she knew how to kick a Coke bottle up his ass. Go to the movies, lieutenant, make up your own mind. Hey, but remember something, okay? I didn't have nothing to do with this movie shit. You seen my rap sheet. When maybe I done something to somebody, I ain't saying I did, the guy had it coming. The big word there is the *guy*, lieutenant, you understand what I'm saying?'

I clicked my nails on the plastic cassette that rested on my thigh.

'A Lafayette detective named Lou Girard was killed last night. Did you hear anything about it?' I said.

'Who?' he said.

I said Lou's name again and watched Cholo's face.

'I never heard of him. Was he a friend of yours or something?'

'Yes, he was.'

He yawned and watched two black children sailing a Frisbee on the gallery of the grocery store. Then the light of recognition worked its way into his eyes and he looked back at my face.

'Hey, Loot, old-time lesson from your days at the First District,' he said. 'Nobody, and I mean *nobody*, from the New Orleans families does a cop. The guy who pulls something like that ends up a lot worse than Tommy Fig. His parts come off while he's still living.'

He nodded like a sage delivering a universal truth, then hawked, sucked the saliva out of his mouth, and spat a bloody clot out onto the shell.

A half hour later I closed the blinds in the sheriff's empty office and used his VCR to watch the cassette that Cholo had given me. Then I clicked it off, went to the men's room, rinsed my face in the lavatory, and dried it with paper towels.

'Something wrong, Dave?' a uniformed deputy standing at the urinal said.

'No, not really,' I said. 'I look like something's wrong?'

'There's some kind of stomach flu going around. I thought you might have a touch of it, that's all.'

'No, I'm feeling fine, Harry.'

'That's good,' he said, and glanced away from my face.

I went back inside the sheriff's office, opened the blinds, and watched the traffic on the street, the wind bending the tops of some myrtle trees, a black kid riding his bike down the sidewalk with a fishing rod propped across his handlebars.

I thought of the liberals I knew who spoke in such a cavalier fashion about pornography, who dismissed it as inconsequential or who somehow associated its existence with the survival of the First Amendment. I wondered what they would have to say about the film I had just watched. I wondered how they would like a theater that showed it to be located in their neighborhoods; I wondered how they would like the patrons of that theater to be around their children.

Finally I called Rosie at her motel. I told her where I was.

'Cholo Manelli gave me a pornographic film that you need to know about,' I said. 'Evidently Julie has branched out into some dark stuff.'

'What is it, what do you mean?'

671

'It's pretty sadistic, Rosie. It looks like the real thing, too.'

'Can we connect it to Balboni?'

'I doubt if Cholo would ever testify, but maybe we can find some of the people who made the film.'

'I'll be over in a few minutes.'

'Rosie, I—'

'You don't think I'm up to looking at it?'

'I don't know that it'll serve any purpose.'

'If you don't want to hang around, Dave, just stick the tape in my mailbox.'

Twenty minutes later she came through the door in a pair of blue jeans, tennis shoes, and a short-sleeve denim shirt with purple and white flowers sewn on it. I closed the blinds again and started the film, except this time I used the fast-forward device to isolate the violent scenes and to get through it as quickly as possible.

When the screen went blank I pulled the blinds and filled the room with sunlight. Rosie sat very still and erect, her hands in her lap. Her nostrils were pinched when she breathed. Then she stood and looked out the window a moment.

'The beating of those girls . . . I've never seen anything like that,' she said.

I heard her take a breath and let it out, then she turned back toward me.

'They weren't acting, were they?' she said.

'I don't think so. It's too convincing for a low-rent bunch like this.'

'Dave, we've got to get these guys.'

'We will, one way or another.'

She took a Kleenex out of her purse and blew her nose. She blinked, and her eyes were shiny.

'Excuse me, I have hay fever today,' she said.

'It's that kind of weather.'

Then she had to turn and look out the window again. When she faced me again, her eyes had become impassive.

'What's the profit margin on a film like this?' she said.

'I've heard they make an ordinary porno movie for about five grand and get a six-figure return. I don't know about one like this.'

'I'd like to lock up Cholo Manelli as a material witness.'

'Even if we could do it, Rosie, it'd be a waste of time. Cholo's got the thinking powers of a cantaloupe but he doesn't roll over or cop pleas.'

'You seem to say that almost with admiration.'

'There're worse guys around.'

'I have difficulty sharing your sympathies sometimes, Dave.'

'Look, the film was made around New Orleans somewhere. Those were the docks in Algiers in the background. I'd like to make a copy and send it to NOPD Vice. They might recognize some of the players. This kind of stuff is their bailiwick, anyway.'

'All right, let's get a print for the Bureau, too. Maybe Balboni's going across state lines with it.' Then she picked up her purse and I saw a dark concern come into her face again.

'I'll buy you a drink,' I said.

'Of what?'

'Whatever you like.'

'I'm all right, Dave. We don't need to go to any bars.'

'That's up to you. How about a Dr Pepper across the street or a spearmint snowball in the park?'

'That sounds nice.'

We drove in my truck to the park. The sky was filling with afternoon rain clouds that had the bright sheen of steam. She tried to pretend that she was listening to my conversation, but her eyes seemed locked on a distant spot just above the horizon, as though perhaps she were staring through an inverted telescope at an old atrocity that was always a-borning at the wrong moment in her mind.

I had tried several times that day to pursue Hogman's peculiar implication about the type of work done by DeWitt Prejean, the chained black man I had seen shot down in the Atchafalaya marsh in 1957. But neither the Opelousas chief of police nor the St Landry Parish sheriff knew anything that was helpful about DeWitt Prejean, and when I finally reached the old jailer at his house he hung up the phone on me as soon as he recognized my voice.

Late that afternoon the sleeplessness of the previous night finally caught up with me, and I lay down in the hammock that I had stretched between two shade trees on the edge of the coulee in the backyard. I closed my eyes and tried to listen to the sound of the water coursing over the rocks and to forget the images from Lou's apartment that seemed to live behind my eyelids like red paint slung from a brush. I could smell the ferns in the coulee, the networks of roots that trailed in the current, the cool odor of wet stone, the periwinkles that ruffled in the grass.

I had never thought of my coulee as a place where members of the Confederate Signal Corps would gather for a drink on a hot day. But out of the rain clouds and the smell of sulfur and the lightning that had already begun to flicker in the south, I watched the general descend, along with two junior officers, in the wicker basket of an observation balloon, one that looked sewn together from silk cuttings of a half-dozen colors. Five enlisted men moored the basket and balloon to the earth with ropes and helped the general down and handed him a crutch. By the mooring place were a table and chair and telegraph key with a long wire that was attached to the balloon's basket. The balloon tugged upward against its ropes and bobbled and shook in the wind that blew across my neighbor's sugarcane field

One of the general's aides helped him to a canvas lawn chair by my hammock and then went away.

'*Magnificent, isn't it?*' he said.

'It surely is,' I said.

'*Ladies from all over Louisiana donated their silk dresses for the balloon. The wicker basket was made by an Italian pickle merchant in New Orleans. The view's extraordinary. In the next life I'm coming back as a bird. Would you like to take a ride up?*'

'*Not right now, thanks.*'

'*A bad day for it?*'

'*Another time, general.*'

'*You grieve for your friend?*'

'*Yes.*'

'*You plan revenge, don't you?*'

'*The Lafayette cops are putting it down as a suicide.*'

'*I want you to listen to me very carefully, lieutenant. No matter what occurs in your life, no matter how bad the circumstances seem to be, you must never consider a dishonorable act as a viable alternative.*'

'*The times you lived in were different, general. This afternoon I watched a film that showed young women being beaten and tortured, perhaps even killed, by sadists and degenerates. This stuff is sold in stores and shown in public theaters. The sonsofbitches who make it are seldom arrested unless they get nailed in a mail sting.*'

'*I'm not quite sure I follow all your allusions, but let me tell you of an experience we had three days ago. My standard-bearer was a boy of sixteen. He got caught in their crossfire in a fallow cornfield. There was no place for him to hide. He tried to surrender by waving his shirt over his head. They killed him anyway, whether intentionally or by accident, I don't know.*'

'*By evening we retook the ground and recovered his body. It was torn by miniés as though wild dogs had chewed it. He was so thin you could count his bones with your fingers. In his haversack was his day's ration – a handful of black beans, some roasted acorns, and a dried sweet potato. That's the only food I could provide this boy who followed me unto the death. What do you think I felt toward those who killed him?*'

'*Maybe you were justified in your feelings.*'

'*Yes, that's what I told myself throughout the night or when I remembered the bloodless glow that his skin gave off when we wrapped him for burial. Then an opportunity presented itself. From aloft in our balloon I looked down upon a copse of hackberry trees. Hard by a surgeon's tent a dozen federals were squatting along a latrine with their breeches down to their ankles. Two hundred yards up the bayou, unseen by any of them, was one of our boats with a twelve-pounder on its bow. I simply had to tap the order on the telegrapher's key and our gunners would have loaded with grape and raked those poor devils through their own excrement. But that's not our way, is it?'*

'Speak for yourself.'

'Your pretense as cynic is unconvincing.'

'Let me ask you a question, general. The women who donated their dresses and petticoats for your balloon . . . what if they were raped, sodomized, and methodically beaten and you got your hands on the men who did it to them?'

'They'd be arrested by my provost, tried in a provisional court, and hanged.'

'You wouldn't find that the case today.'

His long, narrow face was perplexed.

'Why not?' he said.

'I don't know. Maybe we have so much collective guilt as a society that we fear to punish our individual members.'

He put his hat on the back of his head, crossed his good leg across his cork knee, and wet the end of a cheroot. Several of his enlisted men were kneeling by my coulee, filling their canteens. Their faces were dusty, their lips blackened with gunpowder from biting through cartridge papers. The patchwork silk balloon shuddered in the wind and shimmered with the silvery light of the coming rainstorm.

'I won't presume to be your conscience,' the general said. *'But as your friend who wishes to see you do no harm to yourself, I advise you to give serious thought about keeping your dead friend's weapon.'*

'I have.'

'I think you're making a serious mistake, suh. You disappoint me, too.'

He waved his hand impatiently at his aides, and they helped him to his feet.

'I'm sorry you feel that way,' I said.

But the general was not one given to debate. He stumped along on his crutch and cork leg toward the balloon's basket, his cigar clenched at an upward angle in his teeth, his eyes flicking about at the wind-torn clouds and the lightning that trembled whitely like heated wires out on the Gulf.

The incoming storm blew clouds of dust out of my neighbor's cane-field just as the general's balloon lifted him and his aides aloft, their telegraph wire flopping from the wicker basket like an umbilical cord.

When I woke from my dream, the gray skies were filled with a dozen silken hot-air balloons, painted in the outrageous colors of circus wagons, their dim shadows streaking across barn roofs, dirt roads, clapboard houses, general stores, clumps of cows, winding bayous, until the balloons themselves were only distant specks above the summer-green horizon outside Lafayette.

17

On Monday morning I went to Lou Girard's funeral in Lafayette. It was a boiling green-gold day. At the cemetery a layer of heat seemed to rise off the spongy grass and grow in intensity as the white sun climbed toward the top of the sky. During the graveside service someone was running a power mower behind the brick wall that separated the crypts from a subdivision. The mower coughed and backfired and echoed off the bricks like someone firing rounds from a small-caliber revolver. The eyes of the cops who stood at attention in full uniform kept watering from the heat and the smell of weed killer. When the police chief and a captain removed the flag from Lou's casket and folded it into a military square, there was no family member there to receive it. The casket remained closed during the ceremony. Before the casket was lowered into the ground, the department chaplin removed a framed picture of Lou in uniform from the top and set it on a folding table under the funeral canopy. Accidentally he tipped it with the back of his hand so that it fell face down on the linen.

I drove back home for lunch before heading for the office. It was cool under the ceiling fan in the kitchen, and the breeze swayed the baskets of impatiens that hung on hooks from the eave of the back porch. Bootsie set a glass of iced tea with mint leaves and a plate of ham-and-onion sandwiches and deviled eggs in front of me.

'Where's Alafair?' I said.

'Elrod took her and Tripod out to Spanish Lake,' she said from the sink.

'To the movie location?'

'Yes, I think so.'

When I didn't speak, she turned around and looked at me.

'Did I do something wrong?' she asked.

'Julie Balboni's out there, Boots.'

'He lives here now, Dave. He's lots of places. I don't think we should start choosing where we go and don't go because of a man like that.'

'I don't want Alafair around him.'

'I'm sorry. I didn't know you'd object.'

'Boots, there's something I didn't tell you about. Saturday a hood named Cholo Manelli gave me a pornographic video that evidently Balboni and his people made. It's as dark as dark gets. There's one scene where it looks like a woman is actually beaten to death.'

Her eyes blinked, then she said, 'I'll go out to Spanish Lake and bring her home. Why don't you finish eating?'

'Don't worry about it. There's no harm done. I'll go get her before I go to the office.'

'Can't somebody do something about him?'

'When people make a contract with the devil and give him an air-conditioned office to work in, he doesn't go back home easily.'

'Where did you get that piece of Puritan theology?'

'It's not funny. The morons on the Chamber of Commerce who brought this guy here would screw up the recipe for ice water.'

I heard her laugh and walk round behind me. Then I felt her hands on my shoulders and her mouth kiss the top of my head.

'Dave, you're just too much,' she said, and hugged me across the chest.

I listened to the news on the radio as I drove out to Spanish Lake. A tropical storm off Cuba was gaining hurricane status and was expected to turn northwest toward the gulf coast. I glanced to the south, but the sky was brassy and hot and virtually free of clouds. Then as I passed the little watermelon and fruit stand at the end of West Main and headed out into the parish, my radio filled with static and my engine began to misfire.

The truck jerked and sputtered all the way to the entrance of the movie location at the lake. I pulled off the dirt road onto the grass by the security building where Murphy Doucet worked and opened the hood. He stepped out the door in his gray uniform and bifocals.

'What's wrong, Dave?' he asked. His glasses had half-moons of light in them. His blue eyes jittered back and forth when he looked at me.

'It looks like a loose wire on the voltage regulator.' I felt at my pants pocket. 'Do you have a knife I could use?'

'Yeah, I ought to have something.'

I followed him inside his office. His work table was covered with the balsa-wood parts of an amphibian airplane. In the middle of the blue-prints was a utility knife with a detachable blade inset in the aluminum handle. But his hand passed over it and opened a drawer and removed a black-handled switchblade knife. He pushed the release button and the blade leaped open in his hand.

'This should do it,' he said. 'A Mexican pulled this on me in Lake Charles.'

'I didn't know you were a cop in Lake Charles.'

'I wasn't. I was out on the highway with the State Police. That's what I retired from last year.'

'Thanks for the loan of the knife.'

I trimmed the insulation away from the end of the loose wire and reattached it to the voltage regulator, then returned the knife to Murphy Doucet and drove into the grove of oak trees by the lake. When I looked in the rearview mirror Doucet was watching me with an unlit cigarette in his mouth.

The cast and crew were just finishing lunch by the water's edge at picnic tables that were spread with checkered cloths and buckets of fried chicken, potato salad, dirty rice, cole slaw, and sweating plastic pitchers of iced tea and lemonade. Alafair sat on a wood bench in the shade, next to Elrod, the lake shimmering behind her. She was dressed like a nineteenth-century street urchin.

'What happened to your clothes?' I said.

'I'm in the movie, Dave!' she said. 'In this scene with Hogman and Elrod. We're walking down the road with a plantation burning behind us and the Yankees are about to take over the town.'

'I'm not kidding you, Dave,' Elrod said. He wore a collarless gray shirt, officer's striped trousers, and black suspenders. 'She's a natural. Mikey said the same thing. She looks good from any camera angle. We worked her right into the scene.'

'What about Tripod?' I said.

'He's in it, too,' Alafair said.

'You're kidding?'

'We're getting him a membership in the Screen Actors Guild,' Elrod said.

Elrod poured a paper cup of iced tea for me. The wind blew leaves out of the trees and flapped the corners of the checkered table covers. For the first time that day I could smell salt in the air.

'This looks like the good life,' I said.

'Don't be too quick to judge,' Elrod said. 'A healthy lifestyle in southern California means running three miles on the beach in the morning, eating bean sprouts all day, and shoving five hundred bucks' worth of coke up your nose at night.'

The other actors began drifting away from the table to return to work. Tripod was on his chain, eating a drumstick by the trunk of a tree. On the grass next to him was a model of a German Messerschmitt, its wooden fuselage bright with silver paint, its red-edged iron crosses and Nazi swastikas as darkly beguiling as the light in a serpent's eye.

'I gave her that. I hope you didn't mind,' Elrod said.

'Where'd you get it?'

'From Murph, up there at the security building. I'm afraid he thinks I can get him on making props for Mikey or something. I think he's kind of a lonely guy, isn't he?'

'I don't know much about him.'

'Alafair, can you go find Hogman and tell him we need to do that scene again in about fifteen minutes?' Elrod said.

'Sure, El,' she said, swung her legs over the bench, scooped Tripod over her shoulder, and ran off through the trees.

'Look, El, I appreciate your working Alafair into your movie, but frankly I don't want her out here as long as Julie Balboni's around.'

'I thought you heard.'

'What?'

'Mikey's filing Chapter Eleven bankruptcy. He's eighty-sixing the greaseballs out of the corporation. The last thing those guys want is the court examining their finances. He told off Balboni this morning in front of the whole crew.'

'What do you mean he told him off?'

'He said Balboni was never going to put a hand on one of Mikey's people again. He told him to take his porno actor and his hoods and his bimbos and haul his ass back to New Orleans. I was really proud of Mikey . . . What's the matter?'

'What did Julie have to say?'

'He cleaned his fingernails with a toothpick, then walked out to the lake and started talking to somebody on his cellular phone and skipping rocks across the water at the ducks.'

'Where is he now?'

'He drove off with his whole crew in his limo.'

'I'd like to talk with Mr Goldman.'

'He's on the other side of the lake.'

'Ask him to call me, will you? If he doesn't catch me at the office, he can call me at home tonight.'

'He'll be back in a few minutes to shoot the scene with me and Hogman and Alafair.'

'We're not going to be here for it.'

'You won't let her be in the film?'

'Nobody humiliates Julie Balboni in front of other people, El. I don't know what he's going to do, but I don't want Alafair here when he does it.'

The wind had turned out of the south and was blowing hotly through the trees when we walked back toward my truck. The air smelled like fish spawning, and clouds with the dark convolutions of newly opened purple roses were massing in a long, low humped line on the southern horizon.

Later, after I had taken Alafair home and checked in at the office, I drove to Opelousas to talk once again with the old jailer Ben Hebert. A black man raking leaves in Hebert's yard told me where I could find him on a bayou just outside of town.

He sat on top of an inverted plastic bucket under a tree, his cane pole extended out into the sunlight, his red bobber drifting on the edge of the reeds. He wore a crushed straw hat on the side of his head and smoked a hand-rolled saliva-soaked cigarette without removing it from the corner of his mouth. The layers of white fat on his hips and stomach protruded between his shirt and khakis like lard curling over the edges of a washtub.

Ten feet down from him a middle-aged mulatto woman with a small round head, a perforated dime tied on her ankle, was also fishing as she sat on top of an inverted bucket. The ground around her was strewn with empty beer cans. She spit snuff to one side and jigged her line up and down through a torn hole in a lily pad.

Ben Hebert pitched his cigarette out onto the current, where it hissed and turned in a brown eddy.

'Why you keep bothering me?' he said. There was beer on his breath and an eye-watering smell in his clothes that was like both dried sweat and urine.

'I need to know what kind of work DeWitt Prejean did,' I said.

'You what?' His lips were as purple as though they had been painted, his teeth small and yellow as pieces of corn.

'Just what I said.'

'You leave me the hell alone.'

I sat down on the grass by the edge of the slope.

'It's not my intention to bother you, Mr Hebert,' I said. 'But you're refusing to cooperate with a police investigation and you're creating problems for both of us.'

'He done . . . I don't know what he done. What difference does it make?' His eyes glanced sideways at the mulatto woman.

'You seem to have a good memory for detail. Why not about DeWitt Prejean?'

The woman rose from her seat on the bucket and walked farther down the bank, trailing her cork bobber in the water.

'He done nigger work,' Hebert said. 'He cut lawns, cleaned out grease traps, got dead rats out from under people's houses. What the fuck you think he did?'

'That doesn't sound right to me. I think he did some other kind of work, too.'

His nostrils were dilated, as though a bad odor were rising from his own lap.

'He was in bed with a white woman here. Is that what you want to know?'

'Which woman?'

'I done tole you. The wife of a cripple-man got shot up in the war.'

'He raped her?'

'Who gives a shit?'

'But the crippled man didn't break Prejean out of jail, Mr Hebert.'

'It wasn't the first time that nigger got in trouble over white women. There's more than one man wanted to see him put over a fire.'

'Who broke him out?'

'I don't know and I don't care.'

Mr LeBlanc, you're probably a good judge of people. Do I look like I'm just going to go away?'

The skin of his chest was sickly white, and under it were nests of green veins.

'It was better back then,' he said. 'You know it was.'

'What kind of work did he do, Ben?'

'Drove a truck.'

'For whom?'

'It was down in Lafayette. He worked for a white man there till he come up here. Don't know nothing about the white man. You saying I do, then you're a goddamn liar.' He leaned over to look past me at the mulatto woman, who was fishing among a group of willows now. Then his face snapped back at me. 'I brung her out here 'cause she works for me. 'Cause I can't get in and out of the car good by myself.'

'What kind of truck did he drive?' I asked.

'Beer truck. No, that wasn't it. Soda pop. Sonofabitch had a soda-pop truck route when white people was making four dollars a day in the rice field.' He set down his cane pole and began rolling a cigarette. His fingernails looked as thick and horned as tortoise-shell against the thin white square of paper into which he poured tobacco. His fingers trembled almost uncontrollably with anger and defeat.

I drove to Twinky Lemoyne's bottling works in Lafayette, but it was closed for the day. Twenty minutes later I found Lemoyne working in his yard at home. The sky was the pink of salmon eggs, and the wind thrashed the banana and lime trees along the side of his house. He had stopped pruning the roses on his trellis and had dropped his shears in the baggy back pocket of his faded denim work pants.

'A lot of bad things happened back in that era between the races. But we're not the same people we used to be, are we?' he said.

'I think we are.'

'You seem unable to let the past rest, sir.'

'My experience has been that you let go of the past by addressing it, Mr Lemoyne.'

'For some reason I have the feeling that you want me to confirm what so far are only speculations on your part.' There were tiny pieces of grit in his combed sandy hair and a film of perspiration and rose dust on his glasses.

'Read it like you want. But somehow my investigation keeps winding its way back to your front door.'

He began snipping roses again and placing them stem down in a milk bottle full of green water. His two-story peaked white house in an old residential neighborhood off St Mary Boulevard in Lafayette was surrounded by spectacular moss-hung oak trees and walls of bamboo and soft pink brick.

'Should I call my lawyer? Is that what you're suggesting?'

'You can if you want to. I don't think it'll solve your problem, though.'

'I beg your pardon.' His shears hung motionlessly over a rose.

'I think you committed a murder back in 1957, but in all probability you don't have the psychology of a killer. That means that you probably live with an awful guilt, Mr Lemoyne. You go to bed with it and you wake with it. You drag it around all day long like a clanking chain.'

'Why is it that you seem to have this fixation about me? At first you accused me of being involved with a New Orleans gangster. Now this business about the murdered Negro.'

'I saw you do it.'

His egg-shaped face was absolutely still. Blood pooled in his cheeks like pink flowers.

'I was only nineteen,' I said. 'I watched y'all from across the bay. The black man tried to run, and one of you shot him in the leg, then continued shooting him in the water. You didn't even think me worthy of notice, did you? You were right, too. No one ever paid much attention to my story. That was a hard lesson for a nineteen-year-old.'

He closed the shears, locked the clasp on the handles, and set them down on a glass-topped patio table. He poured two inches of whiskey into a glass with no ice and squeezed a lemon into it. He seemed as solitary as a man might who had lived alone all his life.

'Would you care for one?' he said.

'No, thank you.'

'I have high blood pressure and shouldn't drink, but I put lemon in it and convince myself that I'm drinking something healthy along with the alcohol. It's my little joke with myself.' He took a deep breath.

'You want to tell me about it?'

'I don't think so. Am I under arrest?'

'Not right now. But I think that's the least of your problems.'

'You bewilder me, sir.'

'You're partners in a security service with Murphy Doucet. A fellow like that doesn't fit in the same shoe box with you.'

'He's an ex-police officer. He has the background that I don't.'

'He's a resentful and angry man. He's also anti-Semitic. One of your black employees told me you're good to people of color. Why would a man such as yourself go into business with a bigot?'

'He's uneducated. That doesn't mean he's a bad person.'

'I believe he's been blackmailing you, Mr Lemoyne. I believe he was the other white man I saw across the bay with DeWitt Prejean.'

'You can believe whatever you wish.'

'We still haven't gotten to what's really troubling you, though, have we? It's those young women, isn't it?'

His eyes closed and opened, and then he looked away at the south where lightning was forking into the Gulf and the sky looked like it was covered with the yellow-black smoke from a chemical fire.

'I don't . . . I don't . . .' he began, then finished his whiskey and set his glass down. He wiped at the wet ring with the flat of his hand as though he wanted to scrub it out of the tabletop.

'That day you stopped me out under the trees at the lake,' I said, 'you wanted assurance that it was somebody else, somebody you don't know, who mutilated and killed those girls, didn't you? You didn't want that sin on your conscience as well as Prejean's murder.'

'My God, man, give some thought to what you're saying. You're telling me I'm responsible for a fiend being loose in our midst.'

'Call your attorney and come into the office and make a statement. End it now, Mr Lemoyne. You'll probably get off with minimum time on Prejean's death. You've got a good reputation and a lot of friends. You might even walk.'

'Please leave.'

'It won't change anything.'

He turned away from me and gazed at the approaching storm. Leaves exploded out of the trees that towered above his garden walls.

'Go do what you have to do, but right now please respect my privacy,' he said.

'You strayed out of the gentleman's world a long time ago.'

'Don't you have any sense of mercy?'

'Maybe you should come down to my office and look at the morgue photographs of Cherry LeBlanc and a girl we pried out of an oil barrel down in Vermilion Parish.'

He didn't answer. As I let myself out his grden gate I glanced back at him. His cheeks were red and streaked with moisture as though his face had been glazed by freezing winds.

That evening the weatherman said the hurricane had become stationary one hundred miles due south of Mobile. As I fell asleep later with the window open on a lightning-charged sky, I thought surely the electricity would bring the general back in my dreams.

Instead, it was Lou Girard who stood under the wind-tormented pecan trees at three in the morning, his jaw shot away at the hinge, a sliver of white bone protruding from a flap of skin by his ear.

He tried to speak, and spittle gurgled on his exposed teeth and tongue and dripped off the point of his chin.

'*What is it, Lou?*'

The wind whipped and molded his shapeless brown suit against his body. He picked up a long stick that had been blown out of the tree above him and began scratching lines in the layers of dead leaves and pecan husks at his feet. He made an *S*, and then drew a straight line like an *I* and then put a half bubble on it and turned it into a *P*.

He dropped the stick to the ground and stared at me, his deformed face filled with expectation.

18

The connection had been there all along. I just hadn't looked in the right place. As soon as I went into the office at 8 A.M. the next morning I called the probation and parole office in Lafayette and asked the supervising PO to pull the file on Cherry LeBlanc.

'Who busted her on the prostitution charge?' I said.

I heard him leafing back and forth through the pages in the file.

'It wasn't one officer. There was a state-police raid on a bar and some trailers out on the Breaux Bridge highway.'

SP. Yes, the state police. Thanks, Lou, old friend.

'Who signed the arrest report?' I asked.

'Let's see. It's pretty hard to read. Somebody set a coffee cup down on the signature.'

'It's real important, partner.'

'It could be Doucet. Wasn't there a state policeman around here by that name? Yeah, I'd say initial M., then Doucet.'

'Can you make copies of her file and lock them in separate places?'

'What's going on?'

'It may become evidence.'

'No, I mean Lou Girard was looking at her file last week. What's the deal?'

'Do this for me, will you? If anybody else tries to get his hands on that file, you call me, okay?'

'There's an implication here that I think you should clarify.'

Outside, the skies were gray, and dust and pieces of paper were blowing in the street.

'Maybe we have a fireman setting fires,' I said.

He was quiet a moment, then he said, 'I'll lock up the file for you, detective, and I'll keep your call confidential. But since this may involve a reflection on our office, I expect a little more in the way of detailed information from you in the next few days.'

After I hung up, I opened my desk drawer and took out the black-and-white photograph that Cholo Manelli had given me of Cherry LeBlanc and Julie Balboni at the beach in Biloxi. I looked again at the man who

685

was reading a newspaper at another table. His face was beyond the field of focus in the picture, but the light had struck his glasses in such a way that it looked as if there were chips of crystal where his eyes should have been, and my guess was that he was wearing bifocals.

As with most police investigations, the problem had now become one of the time lag between the approaching conclusion of an investigation and the actual arrest of a suspect. It's a peculiar two-way street that both cops and criminals live on. As a cop grows in certainty about the guilt of a suspect and begins to put enough evidence together to make his case, the suspect usually becomes equally aware of the impending denouement and concludes that midsummer isn't a bad time to visit Phoenix after all.

The supervising PO in Lafayette now knew my suspicions about Doucet, so did Twinky Hebert Lemoyne, and it wouldn't be long before Doucet did, too.

The other problem was that so far all the evidence was circumstantial.

When Rosie came in I told her everything I had.

'Do you think Lemoyne will make a confession?' she said.

'He might eventually. It's obvious he's a tormented man.'

'Because I don't think you'll ever get an indictment on the lynching unless he does.'

'I want to get a search warrant and toss everything Doucet owns, starting with the security building out at Spanish Lake.'

'Okay, Dave, but let me be honest with you. So far I think what we've got is pretty thin.'

'I didn't tell you something else. I already checked Doucet's name through motor vehicle registration in Baton Rouge. He owns a blue 1989 Mercury. I'll bet that's the car that's been showing up through the whole investigation.'

'We still don't have enough to start talking to a prosecutor, though, do we?'

'That's what a search warrant is for.'

'What I'm trying to say is we don't have witnesses, Dave. We're going to need some hard forensic evidence, a murder weapon, clothing from one of the victims, something that will leave no doubt in a jury's mind that this guy is a creature out of their worst nightmares. I just hope Doucet hasn't already talked to Lemoyne and gotten rid of everything we could use against him, provided there is anything.'

'We'll soon find out.'

She measured me carefully with her eyes.

'You seem a little more confident than you should be,' she said.

'It all fits, Rosie. A black pimp in the New Orleans bus depot told me about a white man selling dirty pictures. I thought he was talking about photographs or postcards. Don't you see it? Doucet's probably been delivering girls to Balboni's pornographic film operation.'

'The only direct tie that we have is the fact that Doucet arrested Cherry LeBlanc.'

'Right. And even though he knew I was investigating her murder, he never mentioned it, did he? He wasn't even curious about how the investigation was going. Does that seem reasonable to you?'

'Well, let's get the warrant and see what Mr Doucet has to say to us this morning.'

We had it in thirty minutes and were on our way out of the office when my extension rang. It was Bootsie. She said she was going to town to buy candles and tape for the windows in case the hurricane turned in to the coast and I would find lunch for me and Alafair in the oven.

Then she said, 'Dave, did you leave the house last night?'

'Just a second,' I said, and took the receiver away from my ear. 'Rosie, I'll be along in just a minute.'

Rosie went out the door and bent over the water cooler.

'I'm sorry, what did you say?'

'I thought I heard your truck start up in the middle of the night. Then I thought I just dreamed it. Did I just dream it?'

'I had to take care of something. I left a note on the lamp for you in case you woke up, but you were sound asleep when I came back.'

'What are you doing, Dave?'

'Nothing. I'll tell you about it later.'

'Is it those apparitions in the marsh again?'

'No, of course not.'

'Dave?'

'It's nothing to worry about. Believe me.'

'I *am* worried if you have to conceal something from me.'

'Let's go out to eat tonight.'

'I think we'd better have a talk first.'

'A very bad guy is about to go off the board. That's what it amounts to. I'll explain it later.'

'Does the sheriff know what you're doing?'

'He didn't ask. Come on, Boots. Let's don't be this way.'

'Whatever you say. I'm sorry I asked. Everybody's husband goes in and out of the house in the middle of the night. I'll see you this afternoon.'

She hung up before I could speak again; but in truth I didn't know how to explain to her the feelings I had that morning. If Murphy Doucet was our serial killer, and I believed he was, then with a little luck we were about to throw a steel net over one of those pathological and malformed individuals who ferret their way among us, occasionally for a lifetime, and leave behind a trail of suffering whose severity can only be appreciated by the survivors who futilely seek explanations for their loss the rest of their lives.

I lost my wife Annie to two such men. A therapist told me that I would never have any peace until I learned to forgive not only myself for her death but the human race as well for producing the men who killed her. I didn't know what he meant until several months later when I remembered an event that occurred on a winter afternoon when I was seven years old and I had returned home early, unexpectedly, from school.

My mother was not at work at the Tabasco bottling plant, where she should have been. Instead, I looked from the hallway through the bedroom door and saw a man's candy-striped shirt, suspenders, and sharkskin zoot slacks and panama hat hung on the bedpost, his socks sticking out of his two-tone shoes on the floor. My mother was naked, on all fours, on top of the bedspread, and the man, whose name was Mack, was about to mount her. A cypress plank creaked under my foot, and Mack twisted his head and looked at me, his pencil mustache like a bird's wings above his lip. Then he entered my mother.

For months I had dreams about a white wolf who lived in a skeletal black tree on an infinite white landscape. At the base of the tree was a nest of pups. In the dream the wolf would drop to the ground, her teats sagging with milk, and eat her young one by one.

I would deliberately miss the school bus in the afternoon and hang around the playground until the last kids took their footballs or kites and walked off through the dusk and dead leaves toward lighted houses and the sound of *Jack Armstrong* or *Terry and the Pirates* through a screen door. When my father returned home from trapping on Marsh Island, I never told him what I had seen take place in their bedroom. When they fought at night, I sat on the back steps and watched the sugarcane stubble burning in the fields. The fires looked like thousands of red handkerchiefs twisting in the smoke.

I knew the wolf waited for me in my dreams.

Then one afternoon, when I started walking home late from school, I passed an open door in the back of the convent. It was the music room, and it had a piano in it, a record player, and a polished oak floor. But the two young nuns who were supposed to be waxing the floor had set aside their mops and rags, turned on a radio, and were jitterbugging with each other in their bare feet, their veils flying, their wooden rosary beads swirling on their waists.

They didn't see me, and I must have watched them for almost five minutes, fascinated with their flushed faces inside their wimples and the laughter that they tried to hide behind their hands when it got too loud.

I could not explain it to myself, but I knew each night thereafter that if I thought of the dancing nuns before I fell asleep, I would not dream about the white wolf in the tree.

I wondered what kind of dreams Murphy Doucet had. Maybe at one time they were the same as mine. Or maybe it was better not to know.

I had no doubt, though, that he was ready for us when we arrived at the security building at Spanish Lake. He stood with his legs slightly spread, as though at parade rest, in front of the door, his hands propped on his gunbelt, his stomach flat as a plank, his eyes glinting with a cynical light.

I unfolded the search warrant in front of him.

'You want to look it over?' I said.

'What for? I don't give a good fuck what y'all do here,' he replied.

'I'd appreciate it if you'd watch your language,' I said.

'She can't handle it?' he said.

'Stand over by my truck until we're finished,' I said.

'What do you think y'all gonna find?' he said.

'You never know, Murph. You were a cop. People get careless sometimes, mess up in a serious way, maybe even forget they had their picture taken with one of their victims.'

Tiny webs of brown lines spread from the corners of his eyes.

'What are you talking about?'

'If I'd been you, I wouldn't have let Cholo take my picture with Baby Feet and Cherry LeBlanc over in Biloxi.'

His blue eyes shuttered back and forth; the pupils looked like black pinheads. The point of his tongue licked across his bottom lip.

'I don't want *her* in my stuff,' he said.

'Would you like to prevent me from getting in your "stuff," Mr Doucet?' Rosie said. 'Would you like to be charged this morning with interfering with a federal officer in the performance of her duty?'

Without ever removing his eyes from her face, he lifted a Lucky Strike with two fingers from the pack in his shirt pocket and put it in the corner of his mouth. Then he leaned back against my truck, shook open his Zippo lighter, cupped the flame in his hands, sucked in on the smoke, and looked away at the pecan trees bending and straightening in the wind and an apple basket bouncing crazily across a field.

On his work table were a set of Exacto knives, tubes of glue, small bottles of paint, tiny brushes, pieces of used sandpaper, and the delicate balsa-wood wing struts of a model airplane pinned to a blueprint. Outside, Doucet smoked his cigarette and watched us through the door and showed no expression or interest when I dropped his Exacto knives into a Ziploc bag.

His desk drawers contained *Playboy* magazines, candy wrappers, a carton of Lucky Strikes, a thermos of split pea soup, two ham sandwiches, paper clips, eraser filings, a brochure advertising a Teamster convention in Atlantic City, a package of condoms.

I opened the drawer of his work table. In it were more sheets of sandpaper, an unopened model airplane kit, and the black-handled switchblade knife he had lent me to trim back the insulation on an electrical wire in my truck. I put it in another Ziploc bag.

Doucet yawned.

'Rosie, would you kick over that trash basket behind his desk, please?' I said.

'There's nothing in it,' she said, leaning over the corner of the desk.

My back was turned to both her and Doucet when I closed the drawer to the work table and turned around with an aluminum-handled utility knife in my fingers. I dropped it into a third plastic bag.

'Well, I guess this covers it,' I said.

Through the door I saw his hand with the cigarette stop in midair and his eyes lock on the utility knife.

He stepped toward us as we came out of the building.

'What do you think you're doing?' he said.

'You have a problem with something that happened here?' I said.

'You planted that,' he said, pointing at the bag with the utility knife in it. 'You sonofabitch, you planted it, you know you did.'

'How could I plant something that belongs to you?' I said. 'This is one of the tools you use on your airplane models, isn't it?'

Rosie was looking at me strangely.

'This woman's a witness,' he said. 'You're salting the shaft. That knife wasn't there.'

'I say it was. I say your fingerprints are all over it, too. It's probably going to be hard to prove it's not yours, Murph.'

'This pepper-belly bitch is in on it, isn't she?' he said.

I tapped him on the cheek with the flat of my hand. 'You say anything else, your day is going to deteriorate in a serious way,' I said.

Mistake.

He leaped into my face, his left hand like a claw in my eyes, his right fist flailing at my head, his knees jerking at my groin. I lost my balance, tried to turn away from him and raise my arm in front of my face; his fists rained down on the crown of my skull.

Rosie pulled her .357 from her purse, extended it straight out with both hands, and pointed the barrel into his ear.

'Down on the ground, you understand me?' she shouted. 'Do it! Now! Don't look at me! Get your face on the ground! Did you hear me? Don't look at me! Put your hands behind your head!'

He went to his knees, then lay prone with the side of his face in the grass, his lined, deeply tanned neck oozing sweat, his eyes filled with the mindless light that an animal's might have if it were pinned under an automobile tire.

I slipped my handcuffs from the back of my belt and snipped them onto his wrists. I pulled his revolver and can of Mace from his gunbelt, then raised him to his feet. His arm felt like bone in my hand.

'You're under arrest for assaulting an officer of the law, Murph,' I said.

He turned toward me. The top button of his shirt was torn and I could see white lumps of scar tissue on his chest like fingers on a broken hand.

'It won't stick. You've got a bum warrant,' he said.

'That knife is the one you used on Cherry LeBlanc, isn't it?' I said.

Rosie walked behind me into his office and used his phone to call for a sheriff's car. His eyes watched her, then came back onto me. He blew pieces of grass out of his mouth.

'She let you muff her?' he said.

We brought him in through the back door of the sheriff's department, fingerprinted and booked him, let him make a phone call to an attorney in Lafayette, then took him down to our interrogation room. Personnel from all over the building were finding ways to get a look at Murphy Doucet.

'You people get back to work,' the sheriff said in the hallway. 'This man is in for assaulting an officer. That's all he's charged with. Have y'all got that?'

'There's three news guys outside your office, sheriff,' a deputy said.

'I'd like to know who called them down here, please,' he said.

'Search me,' the deputy said.

'Will you people get out of here?' he said again to the crowd in the hall. Then he pushed his fingers though his hair and turned to me and Rosie. 'I've got to talk to these reporters before they break a Jack the Ripper story on us. Get what you can from this guy and I'll be right back. Who's his lawyer?'

'Jeb Bonin,' I said.

'We'll still have Doucet till his arraignment in the morning. When are y'all going to search his place?'

'This afternoon,' Rosie said. 'We already sent a deputy over there to sit on it for us.'

'Was the blue Merc out at Spanish Lake?' the sheriff said.

'No, he drives a pickup to work. The Merc must be at his house,' I said.

'All right, get on it. Do it by the numbers, too. We don't want to blow this one.'

The sheriff walked back toward his office. Rosie touched me lightly on the arm.

'Dave, talk with me a second before we go inside,' she said.

'What is it?'

She didn't reply. She went inside our office and waited for me.

'That utility knife you took out of his drawer,' she said. 'He was completely surprised when you found it. That presents a troubling thought for me.'

'It's his knife, Rosie. There's no question about it.'

'Why was he so confident up until that moment?'

'Maybe he just forgot he'd left it there.'

'You got into that security building during the night, removed the knife, then replaced it this morning, didn't you?'

'Time's always on the perp's side, Rosie. While we wait on warrants, they deep-six the evidence.'

'I don't like what I'm hearing you say, Dave.'

'This is our guy. You want him to walk? Because without that knife, he's sure going to do it.'

'I see it differently. You break the rules, you arm the other side.'

'Wait till you meet his lawyer. He's the best in southwest Louisiana. He also peddles his ass to the Teamsters, the mob, and incinerator outfits that burn PCBs. Before he's finished, he'll turn Doucet into a victim and have the jury slobbering on their sleeves.'

Her eyes went back and forth thoughtfully, as though she were asking herself questions and answering them. Then she raised her chin.

'Don't ever do anything like this again, Dave. Not while we're partners,' she said, and walked past me and into the interrogation room, where Murphy Doucet sat in a straight-backed chair at a small table, surrounded by white walls, wreathed in cigarette smoke, scratching at whiskers that grew along the edges of the white chicken's foot embossed on his throat.

I stepped inside the room behind Rosie and closed the door.

'Where's my lawyer at?' he asked.

I took the cigarette from his fingers and mashed it out on the floor.

'You want to make a statement about Cherry LeBlanc?' I said.

'Yeah. I've given it some thought. I remember busting a whore by that name three years ago. So now y'all can tell me why I'd wait three years to kill somebody who'd been in my custody.'

'We think you're a pimp for Julie Balboni, Mr Doucet,' Rosie said. 'We also think you're supplying girls for his pornography operation.'

His eyes went up and down her body.

'Affirmative action?' he said.

'There's something else you don't know about, Murph,' I said. 'We're checking all the unsolved murders of females in areas around highways during the time you were working for the state police. I have a feeling those old logs are going to put you in the vicinity of some bodies you never thought would be connected to you.'

'I don't believe this,' he said.

'I think we've got you dead-bang,' I said.

'You've got a planted knife. This girl here knows it, too. Look at her face.'

'We've not only got the weapon and the photo of you with the victim, we know how it happened and why.'

'What?'

'Cherry LeBlanc told Julie he was a tub of guts and walked out on him.

But people don't just walk out on Julie. So he got on the phone and called you up from the motel, didn't he, Murph? You remember that conversation? Would you like me to quote it to you?'

His eyebrows contracted, then his hand went into his pocket for a cigarette.

'No. You can't smoke in here,' I said.

'I got to use the can.'

'It's unavailable now,' I said.

'*She's* here for another reason. It ain't because of a dead hooker,' he said.

'We're all here because of you, Murph. You're going down hard, partner. We haven't even started to talk about Kelly Drummond yet.'

He bit a piece of skin off the ball of his thumb.

'What's the bounce on the pimp beef?' he said.

'You think you're going to cop to a procuring charge when you're looking at the chair? What world are you living in?' I said.

'Ask her. She's here to make a case on Balboni, not a security guard, so clean the shit out of your mouth. What kind of bounce am I looking at?'

'Mr Doucet, you're looking at several thousand volts of electricity cooking your insides. Does that clarify your situation for you?' Rosie said.

He looked into her face.

'Go tell your boss I can put that guinea away for twenty-seven years,' he said. 'Then come back and tell me y'all aren't interested in a deal.'

The sheriff opened the door.

'His lawyer's here,' he said.

'We're going to your house now, Murph,' I said. 'Is there anything else you want to tell us before we leave?'

The attorney stepped inside the room. He wore his hair shaved to the scalp, and his tie and shirt collar rode up high on his short neck so that he reminded you of a light-brown hard-boiled egg stuffed inside a business suit.

'Don't say anything more to these people, Mr Doucet,' he said.

I leaned on the table and stared into Murphy Doucet's face. I stared at his white eyebrows, the jittering of his eyeballs, the myriad lines in his skin, the slit of a mouth, the white scar on his throat that could have been layered there with a putty knife.

'What? What the fuck you staring at?' he said.

'Do you remember me?' I said.

'Yeah. Of course. When you were a cop in New Orleans.'

'Look at me. Think hard.'

His eyes flicked away from my face, fastened on his attorney.

'I don't know what he's talking about,' he said.

'Do you have a point, detective?' the attorney said.

'Your hired oil can doesn't have anything to do with this, Murph,' I said. 'It's between me and you now. It's 1957, right after Hurricane Audrey hit. You could smell dead animals all over the marsh. You remember? Y'all made DeWitt Prejean run with a chain locked around his chest, then you blew his leg out from under him. Remember the kid who saw it from across the bay? Look at my face.'

He bit down on his lip, then fitted his chin on top of his knuckles and stared disjointedly at the wall.

'The old jailer gave you guys away when he told me that DeWitt Prejean used to drive a soda-pop truck. Prejean worked for Twinky Lemoyne and had an affair with his wife, didn't he? It seems like there's always one guy still hanging around who remembers more than he should,' I said. 'You still think you're in a seller's market, Murph? How long do you think it's going to be before a guy like Twinky cracks and decides to wash his sins in public?'

'Don't say anything, Mr Doucet,' the attorney said.

'He doesn't have to, Mr Bonin,' I said. 'This guy has been killing people for thirty-five years. If I were you, I'd have some serious reservations about an ongoing relationship with your client. Come on, Rosie.'

The wind swirled dust and grit between the cars in the parking lot, and I could smell rain in the south.

'That was Academy Award stuff, Dave,' Rosie said as we got in my truck.

'It doesn't hurt to make the batter flinch once in a while.'

'You did more than that. You should have seen the lawyer's face when you started talking about the lynching.'

'He's not the kind who's in it for the long haul.'

As I started the truck a gust of wind sent a garbage can clattering down the sidewalk and blew through the oak grove aross the street. A solitary shaft of sunlight broke from the clouds and fell through the canopy, and in a cascade of gold leaves I thought I saw a line of horsemen among the tree trunks, their bodies as gray as stone, their shoulders and their horses' rumps draped with flowing tunics. I pinched the sweat out of my eyes against the bridge of my nose and looked again. The grove was empty except for a black man who was putting strips of tape across the windows of his barbecue stand.

'Dave?' Rosie said.

'Yes?'

'Are you all right?'

'I just got a piece of dirt in my eye.'

When we pulled out on the street I looked into the rearview mirror and saw the detailed image of a lone horseman deep in the trees, a plum-colored plume in his hat, a carbine propped on his thigh. He pushed up the brim of his hat with his gun barrel and I saw that his face was pale and siphoned of all energy and the black sling that held his left arm was sodden with blood.

'*What has opened your wounds, general?*'

'What'd you say?' Rosie asked.

'Nothing. I didn't say anything.'

'You're worried about what Doucet said, aren't you?'

'I'm not following you.'

'You think the Bureau might cut a deal with him.'

'It crossed my mind.'

'This guy's going down, Dave. I promise you.'

'I've made a career of discovering that my priorities aren't the same as those of the people I work for, Rosie. Sometimes the worst ones walk and cops help them do it.'

She looked out the side window, and now it was she whose face seemed lost in an abiding memory or dark concern that perhaps she could never adequately share with anyone.

Murphy Doucet lived in a small freshly-painted white house with a gallery and a raked, tree-shaded lawn across from the golf course on the north side of Lafayette. A bored Iberia Parish deputy and a Lafayette city cop sat on the steps waiting for us, flipping a pocket knife into the lawn. The blue Mercury was parked in the driveway under a chinaberry tree. I unlocked it from the key ring we had taken from Doucet when he was booked; then we pulled out the floor mats, laid them carefully on the grass, searched under the seats, and cleaned out the glove box. None of it was of of any apparent value. We picked up the floor mats by the corners, replaced them on the rugs, and unlocked the trunk.

Rosie stepped back from the odor and coughed into her hand.

'Oh, Dave, it's—' she began.

'Feces,' I said.

The trunk was bare except for a spare tire, a jack, and a small cardboard carton in one corner. The dark-blue rug looked clean, vacuumed or brushed, but twelve inches back from the latch was a dried, tea-colored stain with tiny particles of paper towel embedded in the stiffened fabric.

I took out the cardboard carton, opened the top, and removed a portable spotlight with an extension cord that could be plugged into a cigarette lighter.

'This is what he wrapped the red cellophane around when he picked up the girl hitchhiking down in Vermilion Parish,' I said.

'Dave, look at this.'

She pointed toward the side wall of the trunk. There were a half-dozen black curlicues scotched against the pale blue paint. She felt one of them with two fingers, then rubbed her thumb against the ends of the fingers.

'I think they're rubber heel marks,' she said. 'What kind of shoes was Cherry LeBlanc wearing?'

'Flats with leather soles. And the dead girl in Vermilion didn't have on anything.'

'All right, let's get it towed in and start on the house. We really need—'

'What?'

'Whatever he got careless about and left lying around.'

'Did you call the Bureau yet?'

'No. Why?'

'I was just wondering.'

'What are you trying to say, Dave?'

'If you want a handprint set in blood to make our case, I don't think it's going to happen. Not unless there's some residue on that utility knife we can use for a DNA match. The photograph is a bluff, at least as far as indicting Doucet is concerned. Like you said earlier, everything else we've got so far isn't real strong.'

'So?'

'I think you already know what your boss is going to tell you.'

'Maybe I don't care what he says.'

'I don't want you impairing your career with Fart, Barf, and Itch because you think you have to be hard-nosed on my account, Rosie. Let's be clear on that.'

'Cover your own butt and don't worry about mine,' she said, took the key ring out of my hand, and walked ahead of me up the front steps of the house and unlocked the door.

The interior was as neat and squared away as a military barracks. The wood floors were waxed, the stuffed chairs decorated with doilies, the window plants trimmed and watered, the kitchen sink and drainboards immaculate, the pots and pans hung on hooks, the wastebaskets fitted with clean plastic liners, his model planes dusted and suspended on wires from the bedroom ceiling, his bedspread tucked and stretched so tightly that you could bounce a quarter off it.

None of the pictures on the walls dealt with human subjects, except one color photograph of himself sitting on the steps of a cabin with a dead eight-point deer at his feet. Doucet was smiling; a bolt-action rifle with iron sights and a sling lay across his lap.

We searched the house for an hour, searched the garage, then came back and tossed the house again. The Iberia Parish deputy walked through the front door with an ice-cream cone in his hand. He was a dark-haired, narrow-shouldered, wide-hipped man who had spent most of his five years with the department as a crosswalk guard at elementary schools or escorting misdeameanor prisoners to morning arraignment. He stopped eating and wiped the cream out of his mustache with the back of his wrist before he spoke.

'Jesus Christ, Dave, y'all tore the place apart,' he said.

'You want to stay behind and clean it up?' I said.

'Y'all the ones done it, not me.'

'That's right, so you don't have to worry about it,' I said.

'Boy, somebody didn't get enough sleep last night,' he said. When I didn't answer he walked into the center of the room. 'What y'all found in that trunk?'

When I still didn't answer, he peered over my shoulder.

'Oh man, that's a bunch of little girl's underwear, aint it?' he said.

'Yes, it is,' I said.

The deputy cleared his throat.

'That fella been doin' that kind of stuff, too, Dave?'

'It looks like it.'

'Oh, man,' he said. Then his face changed. 'Maybe somebody ought to show him what happens when you crawl over one of them high barbed wire fences.'

'I didn't hear you say that, deputy,' Rosie said.

'It don't matter to me,' he said. 'A fella like that, they's people 'round here get their hands on him, you ain't gonna have to be worryin' about evidence, no. Ax Dave.'

In the trunk we had found eleven small pairs of girls' underwear, children's socks, polka-dot leotards, training bras, a single black patent-leather shoe with a broken strap, a coloring book, a lock of red hair taped to an index card, torn matinee tickets to a local theater, a half-dozen old photographs of Murphy Doucet in the uniform of a Jefferson Parish deputy sheriff, all showing him with children at picnics under moss-hung trees, at a Little League ball game, at a swimming pool filled with children leaping into the air for the camera. All of the clothing was laundered and folded and arranged in a neat pink and blue and white layer across the bottom of the trunk.

After a moment, Rosie said, 'It's his shrine.'

'To *what*?' I said.

'Innocence. He's a psychopath, a rapist, a serial killer, a sadist, maybe a necrophiliac, but he's also a pedophile. Like most pedophiles, he seeks innocence by being among children or molesting them.'

Then she rose from her chair, went into the bathroom, and I heard the water running, heard her spit, heard the water splashing.

'Could you wait outside a minute, Expidee?' I said to the deputy.

'Yeah, sure,' he said.

'We'll be along in a minute. Thanks for your help today.'

'That fella gonna make bail, Dave?'

'Probably.'

'That ain't right,' he said, then he said it again as he went out the door, 'Ain't right.'

The bathroom door was ajar when I tapped on it. Her back was to me, her arms propped stiffly on the basin, the tap still running. She kept trying to clear her throat, as though a fine fish bone were caught in it.

I opened the door, took a clean towel out of a cabinet, and started to blot her face with it. She held her hand up almost as though I were about to strike her.

'Don't touch me with that,' she said.

I set the towel on the tub, tore the top Kleenex from a box, dropped it in the waste can, then pulled out several more, balled them up, and touched at her face with them. She pushed down my wrist.

'I'm sorry. I lost it,' she said.

'Don't worry about it.'

'Those children, that smell in the trunk of the car.'

She made her eyes as wide as possible to hold back the tears, but it didn't work. They welled up in her brown eyes, then rolled in rivulets down her cheeks.

'It's okay, Rosie,' I said, and slipped my arms around her. Her head was buried under my chin. I could feel the length of her body against mine, her back rising and falling under my palms. I could smell the strawberry shampoo in her hair, a heated fragrance like soap in her skin.

The window was open, and the wind blew the curtain into the room. Across the street on a putting green, a red flag snapped straight out on a pole that vibrated stiffly in the cup. In the first drops of rain, which slanted almost parallel to the ground, I saw a figure standing by a stagnant reed-choked pond, a roiling myrtle bush at his back. He held himself erect in the wind with his single crutch, his beard flying about his face, his mouth an **O**, his words lost in distant thunder. The stump of his amputated right leg was wrapped with fresh white bandages that had already turned scarlet with new bleeding.

'What are you trying to warn me of, general? Why has so much pain come back to you, sir?'

I felt Rosie twist her face against my chest, then step away from me and walk quickly out the door, picking up her handbag from a chair in one smooth motion so I could not see her face. The screen door slammed behind her.

I put everything from Doucet's trunk into evidence bags, locked the house, and got into the pickup just as a storm of hailstones burst from the sky, clattered on the cab, and bounced in tiny white geysers on the slopes of the golf course as far as the eye could see.

That night the weatherman on the ten o'clock news said that the hurricane was moving again in a northwesterly direction and would probably make landfall sometime late tomorrow around Atchafalaya Bay, just to the east of us. Every offshore drilling rig in the Gulf had shut down, and the low-lying coastal areas from Grand Isle to Sabine Pass were being evacuated.

At eleven the sheriff called.

'Somebody just torched Mikey Goldman's trailer out at Spanish Lake. A gallon milk bottle of gasoline through the window with a truck flare right on top of it,' he said. 'You want to go out there and have a look?'

'Not really. Who's that yelling in the background?'

'Guess. I can't convince him he's lucky he wasn't in the trailer.'

'Let me guess again. He wants Julie Balboni in custody.'

'You must be psychic,' the sheriff said. He paused. 'I've got some bad news. The lab report came in late this evening. That utility knife's clean.'

'Are they sure?'

'They're on the same side as we are, Dave.'

'We can use testimony from the pathologist about the nature of the wounds. We can get an exhumation order if we have to.'

'You're tired. I shouldn't have called tonight.'

'Doucet's a monster, sheriff.'

'Let's talk about it in the morning.'

A sheet of gray rain was moving across my neighbor's sugarcane field toward the house and lightning was popping in the woods behind it.

'Are you there?' he said through the static.

'We've got to pull this guy's plug in a major way.'

'We'll talk with the prosecutor in the morning. Now go to bed, Dave.'

After I replaced the receiver in the cradle I sat for a long time in the chair and stared out the open back door at the rain falling on the duck pond and cattails at the foot of my property. The sky seemed filled with electric lights, the wind resonant with the voices of children.

19

The rain was deafening on the gallery in the morning. When I opened the front door, islands of pecan leaves floated in muddy pools in the yard, and a fine, sweet-smelling, cool mist blew inside the room. I could barely make out the marsh beyond the curtain of rain dancing in a wet yellow light on the bayou's surface. I put on my raincoat and hat and ran splashing through the puddles for the bait shop. Batist and I stacked all the tables, chairs, and umbrellas on the dock in the lee of the building, roped them down, hauled our boats out of the water, and bolted the shutters on the windows. Then we drank a cup of coffee and ate a fried pie together at the counter inside while the wind tried to peel the tin roof off the joists.

In town, Bayou Teche had risen high up on the pilings of the draw-bridges and overflowed its banks into the rows of camellia bushes in the city park, and passing cars sent curling brown waves of water and street debris sliding across curbs and lawns all the way to the front steps of the houses along East Main. The air smelled of fish and dead vegetation from storm drains and was almost cold in the lungs, and in front of the courthouse the rain spun in vortexes that whipped at the neck and eyes and seemed to soak your clothes no matter how tightly your raincoat was buttoned. Murphy Doucet arrived at the courthouse in a jail van on a wrist chain with seven other inmates, bare-headed, a cigarette in the center of his mouth, his eyes squinted against the rain, his gray hair pasted down on his head, his voice loud with complaint about the manacle that cut into his wrist.

A black man was locked to the next manacle on the chain. He was epileptic and retarded and was in court every three or four weeks for public drunkenness or disturbing the peace. Inside the foyer, when the bailiff was about to walk the men on the chain to the front of the court room, the black man froze and jerked at the manacle, made a gurgling sound with his mouth while spittle drooled over his bottom lip.

'What the hell's wrong with you?' the bailiff said.

'Want to be on the end of the chain. Want to set on the end of the row,' the black man said.

'He's saying he ain't used to being in the front of the bus,' Doucet said.

'This man been bothering you, Ciro?' the bailiff said.

'No, suh. I just want to set on the end this time. Ain't no white peoples bothered me. I been treated just fine.'

'Hurry up and get this bullshit over with,' Doucet said, wiping his eyes on his sleeve.

'We aim to please. We certainly do,' the bailiff said, unlocked the black man, walked him to the end of the chain, and snapped the last manacle on his wrist.

A young photographer from the *Daily Iberian* raised his camera and began focusing through his lens at Doucet.

'You like your camera, son? . . . I thought so. Then you just keep it poked somewhere else,' Doucet said.

It took fifteen minutes. The prosecutor, a high-strung rail of a man, used every argument possible in asking for high bail on Doucet. Over the constant interruptions and objections of Doucet's lawyer, he called him a pedophile, a psychopath, a menace to the community, and a ghoul.

The judge had silver hair and a profile like a Roman soldier. During World War II he had received the Congressional Medal of Honor and at one time had been a Democratic candidate for governor. He listened patiently with one hand on top of another, his eyes oblique, his head tilted at an angle like a priest feigning attentiveness to an obsessed penitent's ramblings.

Finally the prosecutor pointed at Doucet, his finger trembling, and said, 'Your honor, you turn this man loose, he kills somebody else, goddamn it, the blood's going to be on our hands.'

'Would counsel approach the bench, please? You, too, Detective Robicheaux,' the judge said. Then he said, 'Can you gentlemen tell me what the hell is going on here?'

'It's an on-going investigation, your honor. We need more time,' I said.

'That's not my point,' the judge said.

'I object to the treatment of my client, your honor. He's been bullied, degraded in public, slandered by these two men here. He's been—' Doucet's lawyer said.

'I've heard enough from you today, sir. You be quiet a minute,' the judge said. 'Is the prosecutor's office in the process of filing new charges against the defendant?'

'Your honor, we think this man may have been committing rape and homicide for over three decades. Maybe he killed a policeman in Lafayette. We don't even know where to begin,' the prosecutor said.

'Your sincerity is obvious, sir. So is your lack of personal control,' the judge said. 'And neither is solving our problem here. We have to deal with the charge at hand, and you and Detective Robicheaux both know it.

Excuse my impatience, but I don't want y'all dragging "what should be" in here rather than "what is." Now all of you step back.'

Then he said, 'Bail is set at ten thousand dollars. Next case,' and brought his gavel down.

A few minutes later I stood on the portico of the courthouse and watched Murphy Doucet and his lawyer walk past me, without interrupting their conversation or registering my presence with more than a glance, get into the lawyer's new Chrysler, and drive away in the rain.

I went home for lunch but couldn't finish my plate. The back door was opened to the small screened-in porch, and the lawn, the mimosa tree, and the willows along the coulee were dark green in the relentless downpour, the air heavy and cold-smelling and swirling with mist.

Alafair was looking at me from across the table, a lump of unchewed sandwich in her jaw. Bootsie had just trimmed her bangs, and she wore a yellow T-shirt with a huge red and green Tabasco bottle on the front. Bootsie reached over and removed my fingers from my temple.

'You've done everything you could do,' she said. 'Let other people worry about it for a while.'

'He's going to walk. With some time we can round up a few of his girls from the Airline Highway and get him on a procuring beef, along with the resisting arrest and assault charge. But he'll trade it all off for testimony against Julie Balboni. I bet the wheels are already turning.'

'Then that's their decision and their grief to live with, Dave,' Bootsie said.

'I don't read it that way.'

'What's wrong?' Alafair said.

'Nothing, little guy,' I said.

'Is the hurricane going to hit here?' she said.

'It might. But we don't worry about that kind of stuff. Didn't you know coonasses are part duck?'

'My teacher said "coonass" isn't a good word.'

'Sometimes people are ashamed of what they are, Alf,' I said.

'Give it a break, Dave,' Bootsie said.

The front door opened suddenly and a gust of cool air swelled through the house. Elrod came through the hallway folding an umbrella and wiping the water off his face with his hand.

'Wow!' he said. 'I thought I saw Noah's ark out there on the bayou. It could be significant.'

'Ark? What's an ark?' Alafair said.

'El, there's a plate for you in the icebox,' Bootsie said.

'Thanks,' he said, and opened the icebox door, his face fixed with a smile, his eyes studiously carefree.

'What's an ark?' Alafair said.

'It's part of a story in the Bible, Alf,' I said, and watched Elrod as he sat down with a plate of tuna-fish sandwiches and potato salad in his hand. 'What's happening out at the lake, El?'

'Everything's shut down till this storm blows over,' he said. He bit into his sandwich and didn't look up from his plate.

'That'd make sense, wouldn't it?' I said.

He raised his eyes.

'I think it's going to stay shut down,' he said. 'There's only a couple of scenes left to shoot. I think Mikey wants to do them back in California.'

'I see.'

Now it was Alafair who was watching Elrod's face. His eyes focused on his sandwich.

'You leaving, Elrod?' she asked.

'In a couple of days maybe,' he answered. 'But I'm sure I'll be back this way. I'd really like to have y'all come visit, too.'

She continued to stare at him, her face round and empty.

'You could bring Tripod,' he said. 'I've got a four-acre place up Topanga Canyon. It's right up from the ocean.'

'You said you were going to be here all summer,' she said.

'I guess it just hasn't worked out that way. I wish it had,' he said. Then he looked at me. 'Dave, maybe I'm saying the wrong thing here, but y'all come out to LA, I'll get Alafair cast in five minutes. That's a fact.'

'We'll talk it over,' Bootsie said, and smiled across the table at him.

'I could be in the movies where you live?' Alafair said.

'You bet,' Elrod said, then saw the expression on my face. 'I mean, if that's what you and your family wanted.'

'Dave?' She looked up at me.

'Let's see what happens,' I said, and brushed at her bangs with my fingers. Elrod was about to say something else, but I interrupted him. 'Where's Balboni?'

'He doesn't seem to get the message. He keeps hanging around his trailer with his greaseballs. I think he'll still be sitting there when the set's torn down,' Elrod said.

'His trailer might get blown in the lake,' I said.

'I think he has more than one reason for being out there,' Elrod said.

I waited for him to finish, but he didn't. A few minutes later we went out on the gallery. The cypress planks of the steps and floor were dark with rain that had blown back under the eaves. Across the bayou the marsh looked smudged and indistinct in the gray air. Down at the dock Batist was deliberately sinking his pirogue in the shallows so it wouldn't be whipped into a piling by the wind.

'What were you trying to tell me about Balboni?' I said.

'He picks up young girls in town and tells them he's going to put them in a movie. I've heard he's had two or three in there in the last couple of days.'

'That sounds like Julie.'

'How's that?'

'When we were kids he never knew who he was unless he was taking his equipment out of his pants.'

He stared at the rain.

'Maybe there's something I ought to tell you, Dave, not that maybe you don't already know it,' he said. 'When people like us, I'm talking about actors and such, come into a community, everybody gets excited and thinks somehow we're going to change their lives. I'm talking about romantic expectations, glamorous relationships with celebrities, that kind of stuff. Then one day we're gone and they're left with some problems they didn't have before. What I'm saying is they become shamed when they realize how little they always thought of themselves. It's like turning on the lights inside the theater when the matinee is over.'

'Our problems are our own, El. Don't give yourself too much credit.'

'You cut me loose on a DWI and got me sober, Dave. Or at least I got a good running start at it. What'd you get for it? A mess of trouble you didn't deserve.'

'Extend a hand to somebody else. That way you pass on the favor,' I said.

I put my hand on the back of his neck. I could feel the stiff taper of his hair under my palm.

'I think about Kelly most when it rains. It's like she was just washed away, like everything that was her was dissolved right into the earth, like she wasn't ever here,' he said. 'How can a person be a part of your life twenty-four hours a day and then just be gone? I can't get used to it.'

'Maybe people live on inside of us, El, and then one day we get to see them again.'

He leaned one hand against a wood post and stared at the rain. His face was wet with mist.

'It's coming to an end,' he said. 'Everything we've been doing, all the things that have happened, it's fixing to end,' he said.

'You're not communicating too well, partner.'

'I saw them back yonder in that sugarcane field last night. But this time it was different. They were furling their colors and loading their wagons. They're leaving us.'

'*Why now?*' I heard my voice say inside myself.

He dropped his arm from the post and looked at me. In the shadows his brown skin was shiny with water.

'Something bad's fixing to happen, Dave,' he said. 'I can feel it like a hand squeezing my heart.'

He tapped the flat of his fist against the wood post as though he were trying to reassure himself of its physical presence.

Late that afternoon the sheriff called me on my extension.

'Dave, could you come down to my office and help me with something?' he said.

When I walked through his door he was leaned back in his swivel chair, watching the treetops flattening the wind outside the window, pushing against his protruding stomach with stiffened fingers as though he were discovering his weight problem for the first time.

'Oh, there you are,' he said.

'What's up ?'

'Sit down.'

'Do we have a problem?'

He brushed at his round, cleft chin with the backs of his fingers.

'I want to get your reaction to what some people might call a developing situation,' he said.

'Developing situation?'

'I went two years to USL, Dave. I'm not the most articulate person in the world. I just try to deal with realities as they are.'

'I get the feeling we're about to sell the ranch.'

'It's not a perfect world.'

'Where's the heat coming from?' I said.

'There're a lot of people who want Balboni out of town.'

'Which people?'

'Business people.'

'They used to get along with him just fine.'

'People loved Mussolini until it came time to hang him upside down in a filling station.'

'Come on, cut to it, sheriff. Who are the other players?'

'The feds. They want Balboni bad. Doucet's lawyer says his client can put Julie so far down under the penal system they'll have to dig him up to bury him.'

'What's Doucet get?'

'He cops to resisting arrest and procuring, one year max on an honor farm. Then maybe the federal witness protection program, psychological counseling, ongoing supervision, all that jazz.'

'Tell them to go fuck themselves.'

'Why is it I thought you might say that?'

'Call the press in. Tell them what kind of bullshit's going on here. Give them the morgue photos of Cherry LeBlanc.'

'Be serious. They're not going to run pictures like that. Look, we can't indict with what we have. This way we get the guy into custody and permanent supervision.'

'He's going to kill again. It's a matter of time.'

'So what do you suggest?'

'Don't give an inch. Make them sweat ball bearings.'

'With what? I'm surprised his lawyer even wants to accept the procuring charge.'

'They think I've got a photo of Doucet with Balboni and Cherry LeBlanc in Biloxi.'

'Think?'

'Doucet's face is out of focus. The man in the picture looks like bread dough.'

'Great.'

'I still say we should exhume the body and match the utility knife to the slash wounds.'

'All an expert witness can do is testify that the wounds are consistent with those that might have been made with a utility knife. At least that's what the prosecutor's office says. Doucet will walk and so will Balboni. I say we take the bird in hand.'

'It's a mistake.'

'You don't have to answer to people, Dave. I do. They want Julie out of this parish and they don't care how we do it.'

'Maybe you should give some thought about having to answer to the family of Doucet's next victim, sheriff.'

He picked up a chain of paper clips and trailed them around his blotter.

'I don't guess there's much point in continuing this conversation, is there?' he said.

'I'm right about this guy. Don't let him fly.'

'Wake up, Dave. He flew this morning.' He dropped the paper clips into a clean ashtray and walked past me with his coffee cup. 'You'd better take off a little early this afternoon. This hurricane looks to be a real frog stringer.'

It hit late that evening, pushing waves ahead of it that curled over houseboats and stilt cabins at West Cote Blanche Bay and flattened them like a huge fist. In the south the sky was the color of burnt pewter, then rain-streaked, flumed with thunderheads. You could see tornadoes dropping like suspended snakes from the clouds, filling with water and splintered trees from the marshes, and suddenly breaking apart like whips snapping themselves into nothingness.

I heard canvas popping loose on the dock, billowing against the ropes Batist and I had tried to secure it with, then bursting free and flapping end over end among the cattails. The windows swam with water, lightning exploded out of the gray-green haze of swamp, and in the distance, in the roar of wind and thunder that seemed to clamp down on us like an enormous black glass bell, I thought I could hear the terrified moaning of my neighbor's cattle as they fought to find cover in a woods where mature trees were whipped out of the soft ground like seedlings.

By midnight the power was gone, the water off, and half the top of an oak tree had crashed on the roof and slid down the side of the house, covering the windows with tangles of branches and leaves.

I heard Alafair cry out in her sleep. I lit a candle, placed it in a saucer on top of her bookcase which was filling with her collection of Curious George and Baby Squanto Indian books, and got in bed beside her. She wore her Houston Astros baseball cap and had pulled the sheet up to her chin. Her brown eyes moved back and forth as though she were searching out the sounds of the storm that seeped through the heavy cypress planks in the roof. The candlelight flickered on all the memorabilia she had brought back from our vacations or that we had saved as private sign-posts of the transitions she had made since I had pulled her from the submerged upside-down wreck of a plane off Southwest Pass: conch shells and dried starfish from Key West, her red tennis shoes embossed with the words *Left* and *Right* on the toes, a Donald Duck cap with a quacking bill from Disneyworld, her yellow T-shirt printed with a smiling purple whale on the front and the words *Baby Orca* that she had fitted over the torso of a huge stuffed frog.

'Dave, the field behind the house is full of lightning,' she said. 'I can hear animals in the thunder.'

'It's Mr Broussard's cattle. They'll be all right, though. They'll bunch up in the coulee.'

'Are you scared?'

'Not really. But it's all right to be scared a little bit if you want to.'

'If you're scared, you can't be standup.'

'Sure you can. Standup people don't mind admitting they're scared sometimes.'

Then I saw something move under the sheet by her feet.

'Alf?'

'What?' Her eyes flicked about the ceiling as though she were watching a bird fly from wall to wall.

I worked the sheet away from the foot of the bed until I was staring at Tripod's silver-tipped rump and black-ringed tail.

'I wonder how this fellow got in your bed, little guy,' I said.

'He probably got out of his cage on the back porch.'

'Yeah, that's probably it. He's pretty good at opening latched doors, isn't he?'

'I don't think he should go back out there, do you, Dave? He gets scared in the thunder.'

'We'll give him a dispensation tonight.'

'A dis— What?'

'Never mind. Let's go to sleep, little guy.'

'Goodnight, big guy. Goodnight, Tripod. Goodnight, Frogger. Goodnight, Baby Squanto. Goodnight, Curious George. Goodnight, Baby Orca. Goodnight, sea shells. Goodnight—'

'Cork it, Alf, and go to sleep.'

'All right. Goodnight, big guy.'

'Goodnight, little guy.'

In my sleep I heard the storm pass overhead like freight trains grinding down a grade, then suddenly we were in the storm's eye, the air as still as if it had been trapped inside a jar; leaves drifted to the ground from the trees, and I could hear the cries of seabirds wheeling overhead.

The bedroom windows shine with an amber light that might have been aged inside oak. I slip on my khakis and loafers and walk out into the cool air that smells of salt and wet woods, and I see the general's troops forming into long columns that wind their way into other columns that seem to stretch over an infinitely receding landscape of hardwood forests fired with red leaves, peach orchards, tobacco acreage, rivers covered with steam, purple mountain ridges and valleys filled with dust from ambulance and ammunition wagons and wheeled artillery pieces, a cornfield churned into stubble by horses' hooves and men's boots, a meandering limestone wall and a sunken road where wild hogs graze on the bodies of the dead.

The general sits on a cypress stump by my coulee, surrounded by enlisted men and his aides. A blackened coffeepot boils amidst a heap of burning sticks by his foot. The officers as well as enlisted men are eating honeycombs peeled from inside a dead oak tree. The general's tunic is buttoned over his bad arm. A civilian in checkered trousers, high-top shoes, braces, and a straw hat is setting up a big box camera on a tripod in front of the group.

The general tips his hat up on his forehead and waves me toward him.

'A pip of a storm, wasn't it?' he says.

'Why are you leaving?'

'Oh, we're not gone just yet. Say, I want to have your photograph taken with us. That gentleman you see yonder is the correspondent for the Savannah Republican. *He writes an outstanding story, certainly as good as this Melville fellow, if you ask me.'*

'I don't understand what's happening. Why did your wounds open, what were you trying to warn me of?'

'It's my foolishness, son. Like you, I grieve over what I can't change. Was it Bacon that talked about keeping each cut green?'

'Change what?'

'Our fate. Yours, mine. Care for your own. Don't try to emulate me. Look at what I invested my life in. Oh, we were always honorable – Robert Lee, Jackson, Albert Sidney Johnston, A. P. Hill – but we served venal men and a vile enterprise. How many lives would have been spared had we not lent ourselves to the defense of a repellent cause like slavery?'

'*People don't get to choose their time in history, general.*'

'*Well said. You're absolutely right.*' *He swings the flat of his right hand and hits me hard on the arm, then rises on his crutch and straightens his tunic.* '*Now, gentlemen, if y'all will take the honeycombs out of your faces, let's be about this photographing business. I'm amazed at what the sciences are producing these days.*'

We stand in a group of eight. The enlisted men have Texas accents, powder-blackened teeth, and beards that grow like snakes on their faces. I can smell horse sweat and wood smoke on their clothes. Just as the photographer removes his straw hat and ducks his head under a black cloth at the back of the camera, I look down the long serpentine corridor of amber light again and see thousands of troops advancing on distant fields, their blue and red and white flags bent into the fusillade, their artillery crews laboring furiously at the mouths of smoking cannon, and I know the place names without their ever being spoken – Culp's Hill, Corinth, the Devil's Den, Kennesaw Mountain, the Bloody Lane – and a collective sound that's like no other in the world rises in the wind and blows across the drenched land.

The photographer finishes and stoops under his camera box and lifts the tripod up on his shoulder. The general looks into the freshening breeze, his eyes avoiding me.

'*You won't tell me what's at hand, sir?*' *I say.*

'*What does it matter as long as you stay true to your principles?*'

'*Even the saints might take issue with that statement, general.*'

'*I'll see you directly, lieutenant. Be of good heart.*'

'*Don't let them get behind you,*' *I say.*

'*Ah, the admonition of a veteran.*' *Then his aides help him onto his horse and he waves his hat forward and says,* '*Hideeho, lads,*' *but there is no joy in his voice.*

The general and his mounted escort move down the incline toward my neighbor's field, the tails of their horses switching, the light arcing over them as bright and heated and refractive as a glass of whiskey held up to the sun.

When I woke in the morning the rain was falling evenly on the trees in the yard and a group of mallards were swimming in the pond at the foot of my property. The young sugarcane in my neighbor's field was pounded flat into the washed-out rows as though it had been trampled by livestock. Above the treeline in the north I saw a small tornado drop like a spring from the sky, fill with mud and water from a field, then burst apart as though it had never been there.

I worked until almost eight o'clock that evening. Power was still off in parts of the parish; traffic signals were down; a rural liquor store had been burglarized during the night; two convenience stores had been held up; a drunk set fire to his own truck in the middle of a street; a parolee two days out of Angola beat his wife almost to death; and a child drowned in a storm drain.

Rosie had spent the day with her supervisor in New Orleans and had come back angry and despondent. I didn't even bother to ask her why. She had the paperwork on our case spread all over her desk, as though somehow rereading it and rearranging it from folder to folder would produce a different result, namely, that we could weld the cell door shut on Murphy Doucet and not have to admit that we were powerless over the bureaucratic needs of others.

Just as I closed the drawers in my desk and was about to leave, the phone rang.

'Dave, I think I screwed up. I think you'd better come home,' Elrod said.

'What's wrong?'

'Bootsie went to town and asked me to watch Alafair. Then Alafair said she was going down to the bait shop to get us some fried pies.'

'Get it out, Elrod. What is it?' I saw Rosie looking at me, her face motionless.

'I forgot Batist had already closed up. I should have gone with her.'

I tried to hold back the anger that was rising in my throat.

'Listen, Elrod—'

'I went down there and she was gone. The door's wide open and the key's still in the lock—'

'How long's it been?'

'A half hour.'

'*A half hour?*'

'You don't understand. I checked down at Poteet's first. Then I saw Tripod running loose on his chain in the road.'

'What was she wearing?'

'A yellow raincoat and a baseball cap.'

'Where's Bootsie?'

'Still in town.'

'All right, stay by the phone and I'll be there in a few minutes.'

'Dave, I'm sorry, I don't know what to say, I—'

'It's not your fault.' I replaced the phone receiver in the cradle, my ears whirring with a sound like wind inside a sea shell, the skin of my face as tight as a pumpkin's.

20

Before Rosie and I left the office I told the dispatcher to put out an all-car alert on Alafair and to contact the state police.

All the way to the house I tried to convince myself that there was an explanation for her disappearance other than the one that I couldn't bear to hold in the center of my mind for more than a few seconds. Maybe Tripod had simply gotten away from her while she was in the bait shop and she was still looking for him, I thought. Or maybe she had walked down to the general store at the four-corners, had forgotten to lock the door, and Tripod had broken loose from the clothesline on his own.

But Alafair never forgot to lock up the bait shop and she wouldn't leave Tripod clipped to the clothesline in the rain.

Moments after I walked into the bait shop, all the images and fears that I had pushed to the edges of my consciousness suddenly became real and inescapable, in the same way that you wake from a nightmare into daylight and with a sinking of the heart realize that the nightmare is part of your waking day and has not been manufatured by your sleep. Behind the counter I saw her Astros baseball cap, where it had been flattened into the duckboards by someone's muddy shoe or boot. Elrod and Rosie watched me silently while I picked it up and placed it on top of the counter. I felt as though I were deep under water, past the point of depth tolerance, and something had popped like a stick and pulled loose in my head. Through the screen I saw Bootsie's car turn into the drive and park by the house.

'I should have figured him for it,' I said.

'Doucet?' Rosie said.

'He was a cop. He's afraid to do time.'

'We're not certain it's Doucet, Dave,' she said.

'He knows what happens to cops inside mainline jails. Particularly to a guy they make as a short-eyes. I'm going up to talk to Bootsie. Don't answer the phone, okay?'

Rosie's teeth made white marks on her bottom lip.

'Dave, I want to bring in the Bureau as soon as we have evidence that it's a kidnapping,' she said.

'So far nothing official we do to this guy works. It's time both of us hear that, Rosie,' I said, and went out the screen door and started up the dock.

I hadn't gone ten yards when I heard the telephone ring behind me. I ran back through the rain and jerked the receiver out of the cradle.

'You sound out of breath,' the voice said.

Don't blow this one.

'Turn her loose, Doucet. You don't want to do this,' I said. I looked into Rosie's face and pointed toward the house.

'I'll make it simple for both of us. You take the utility knife and the photo out of the evidence locker. You put them in a Ziploc bag. At eight o'clock tomorrow morning you leave the bag in the trash can on the corner of Royal and St Ann in New Orleans. I don't guess you ought to plan on getting a lot of sleep tonight.'

Rosie had eased the screen door shut behind her and was walking fast up the incline toward the house in the fading light.

'The photo's a bluff. It's out of focus,' I said. 'You can't be identified in it.'

'Then you won't mind parting with it.'

'You can walk, Doucet. We can't make the case on you.'

'You lying sonofabitch. You tore up my house. Your tow truck scratched up my car. You won't rest till you fuck me up in every way you can.'

'You're doing this because your *property* was damaged?'

'I'll tell you what else I'm going to do if you decide to get clever on me. No, that's not right. It won't be me, because I never hurt a child in my life. You got that?'

He stopped speaking and waited for me. then he said it again: 'You got that, Dave?'

'Yes,' I said.

'But there's a guy who used to work in Balboni's movies, a guy who spent eleven years in Parchman for killing a little nigger girl. You want to know how it went down?'

Then he told me. I stared out the screen door at my neighbor's dark green lawn, at his enormous roses that had burst in the rain and were now scattered in the grass like pink tear drops. A dog began barking, and then I heard it cry out sharply as though it had been whipped across the ribs with a chain.

'Doucet—' I broke in. My voice was wet, as though my vocal cords were covered with membrane.

'You don't like my description? You think I'm just trying to scare you? Get a hold of one of his snuff films. You'll agree he's an artist.'

'Listen to me carefully. If you hurt my daughter, I'll get to you one way or another, in or out of jail, in the witness protection program, it won't matter, I'll take you down in pieces, Doucet.'

'You've said only one thing right today. I'm going to walk, and you're going to help me, unless you've let that affirmative-action bitch fuck most of your brains out. By the way, forget the trace. I'm at a phone booth and you've got shit on your nose.'

The line went dead.

I was trembling as I walked up the slope to the house. Rosie opened the screen door and came out on the gallery with Bootsie behind her. The skin of Bootsie's face was drawn back against the bone, her throat ruddy with color as though she had a windburn.

'He hung up too soon. We couldn't get it,' Rosie said.

'Dave, my God. What—' Bootsie said. Her pulse was jumping in her neck.

'Let's go inside,' I said, and put my arm around her shoulder. 'Rosie, I'll be out in just a minute.'

'No, talk to me right here,' Bootsie said.

'Murphy Doucet has her. He wants the evidence that he thinks can put him in jail.'

'What for?' she said. 'You told me yesterday that he'll probably get out of it.'

'He doesn't know that. He's not going to believe anybody who tells him that, either.'

'Where is she?'

'I don't know, Boots. But we're going to get her back. If the sheriff calls, don't tell him anything. At least not right now.'

I felt Rosie's eyes on the side of my face.

'What are you doing, Dave?' Bootsie said.

'I'll call you in a little while,' I said. 'Stay with Elrod, okay?'

'What if that man calls back?'

'He won't. He'll figure the line's open.'

Before she could speak again, I went inside and opened the closet door in the bedroom. From under some folded blankets on the top shelf I took out a box of twelve-gauge shells and the Remington pump shotgun whose barrel I had sawed off in front of the pump handle and whose sportsman's plug I had removed years ago. I shook the shells, a mixture of deer slugs and double-ought buckshot, out on the bed and pressed them one by one into the magazine until I felt the spring come snug against the fifth shell. I dropped the rest of the shells into my raincoat pockets.

'Call the FBI, Dave,' Bootsie said behind me.

'No,' I said.

'Then I'll do it.'

'Boots, if they screw it up, he'll kill her. We'll never even find the body.'

Her face was white. I set the shotgun down and pulled her against me. She felt small, her back rounded, inside my arms.

'We've got a few hours,' I said. 'If we can't get her back in that time, I'm going to do what he wants and hope that he turns her loose. I'll bring the sheriff and the FBI in on it, too.'

She stepped back from me and looked up into my face.

'Hope that he—' she said.

'Doucet's never left witnesses.'

She wanted to come with us, but I left her on the gallery with Elrod, staring after us with her hands clenching and unclenching at her sides.

It was almost dark when we turned off the old two-lane highway onto the dirt road that led to Spanish Lake. The rain was falling in the trees and out on the lake and I could see the lights burning in one trailer under the hanging moss by the water's edge. All the way out to the lake Rosie had barely spoken, her small hands folded on top of her purse, the shadows washing across her face like rivulets of rain.

'I have to be honest with you, Dave. I don't know how far I can go along with this,' she said.

'Call in your people now and I'll stonewall them.'

'Do you think that little of us?'

'Not you I don't. But the people you work for are pencil pushers. They'll cover their butts, they'll do it by the numbers, and I'll end up losing Alafair.'

'What are you going to do if you catch Doucet?'

'That's up to him.'

'Is that straight, Dave?'

I didn't answer.

'I saw you put something in your raincoat pocket when you were coming out of the bedroom,' she said. 'I got the impression you were concealing it from Bootsie. Maybe it was just my imagination.'

'Maybe you're thinking too much about the wrong things, Rosie.'

'I want your word this isn't a vigilante mission.'

'You're worried about *procedure* . . . In dealing with a man like this? What's the matter with you?'

'Maybe you're forgetting who your real friends are, Dave.'

I stopped the truck at the security building, rolled down my window, and held up my badge for the man inside, who was leaned back in his chair in front of a portable television set. He put on his hat, came outside, and dropped the chain for me. I could hear the sounds of a war movie through the open door.

'I'll just leave it down for you,' he said.

'Thanks. Is that Julie Balboni's trailer with the lights on?' I said.

'Yeah, that's it.'

'Who's with him?'

The security guard's eyes went past me to Rosie.

'His reg'lar people, I guess,' he said. 'I don't pay it much mind.'

'Who else?'

'He brings out guests from town.' His eyes looked directly into mine.

I rolled up the window, thumped across the chain, and drove into the oak grove by the lake. Twenty yards from Balboni's lighted trailer was the collapsed and blackened shell of a second trailer, its empty windows blowing with rain, its buckled floor leaking cinders into pools of water, the tree limbs above it scrolled with scorched leaves. To one side of Balboni's trailer a Volkswgen and the purple Cadillac with the tinted black windows were parked between two trees. I saw someone light a cigarette inside the Cadillac.

I stepped out of the truck with the shotgun hanging from my right arm and tapped with one knuckle on the driver's window. He rolled the glass down, and I saw the long pink scar inside his right forearm, the boxed hairline on the back of his neck, the black welt like an angry insect on his bottom lip where I had broken off his tooth in the restaurant on East Main. The man in the passenger's seat had the flattened eyebrows and gray scar tissue around his eyes of a prizefighter; he bent his neck down so he could look upward at my face and see who I was.

'What d'you want?' the driver said.

'Both of you guys are fired. Now get out of here and don't come back.'

'Listen to this guy. You think this is Dodge City?' the driver said.

'Didn't you learn anything the first time around?' I said.

'Yeah, that you're a prick who blindsided me, that I can sue your ass, that Julie's got lawyers who can—'

I lifted the shotgun above the window ledge and screwed the barrel into his cheek.

'Do yourself a favor and visit your family in New Orleans,' I said.

His knuckles whitened on the steering wheel as he tried to turn his head away from the pressure of the shotgun barrel. I pressed it harder into the hollow of his cheek.

'Fuck it, do what the man says. I told you the job was turning to shit when Julie run off Cholo,' the other man said. 'Hey, you hear me, man, back off. We're neutral about any personal beefs you got, you understand what I'm saying? You ought to do something about that hard-on you got, knock it down with a hammer or something, show a little fucking control.'

I stepped back and pulled the shotgun free of the window. The driver stared at my hand wrapped in the trigger guard.

'You crazy sonofabitch, you had the safety off,' he said.

'Happy motoring,' I said.

I waited until the taillights of the Cadillac had disappeared through the trees, then I walked up onto the trailer's steps, turned the door knob, and flung the door back into the wall.

A girl not over nineteen, dressed only in panties and a pink bra, was wiggling into a pair of jeans by the side of two bunk beds that had been pushed together in the middle of the floor. Her long hair was unevenly peroxided and looked like twisted strands of honey on her freckled shoulders; for some reason the crooked lipstick on her mouth made me think of a small red butterfly. Julie Balboni stood at an aluminum sink, wearing only a black silk jockstrap, his salt-and-pepper curls in his eyes, his body covered with fine black hair, a square bottle of Scotch poised above a glass filled with cracked ice. His eyes dropped to the shotgun that hung from my right hand.

'You finally losing your mind, Dave?' he said.

I picked up the girl's blouse from the bed and handed it to her.

'Are you from New Iberia?' I asked.

'Yes, sir,' she said, her eyes fastened on mine as she pushed her feet into a pair of pumps.

'Stay away from this man,' I said. 'Women who hang around him end up dead.'

Her frightened face looked at Julie, then back at me.

Rosie put her hands on the girl's shoulders and turned her toward the door.

'You can go now,' she said. 'Listen to what Detective Robicheaux tells you. This man won't put you in the movies, not unless you want to work in pornographic films. Are you okay?'

'Yes, ma'm.'

'Here's your purse. Don't worry about what's happening here. It doesn't have anything to do with you. Just stay away from this man. He's in a lot of trouble,' Rosie said.

The girl looked again at Julie, then went quickly out the door and into the dark. Julie was putting on his trousers now, with his back to us. The walls were covered with felt paintings of red-mouthed tigers and boa constrictors wrapped around the bodies of struggling unicorns. By the door was the canvas bag filled with baseballs, gloves, and metal bats. Julie's skin looked brown and rubbed with oil in the glow from a bedside lava lamp.

'It looks like you did a real number on Mikey Goldman's trailer,' I said.

He zipped his fly. 'Like most of the time, you're wrong,' he said. 'I don't go around setting fires on my own movie set. That's Cholo Manelli's work.'

'Why does he want to hurt Mikey Goldman?'

'He don't. He thought it was my trailer. He's got his nose bent out of joint about some imaginary wrong I done to him. The first thing Cholo does in the morning is stick his head up his hole. You guys ought to hang out together.'

'Why do you think I'm here, Julie?'

'How the fuck should I know? Nothing you do makes sense to me anymore, Dave. You want to toss the place, see if that little chippy left a couple of 'ludes in the sheets?'

'You think this is some chickenshit roust, Julie?'

He combed his curls back over his head with his fingers. His navel looked like a black ball of hair above his trousers.

'You take yourself too serious,' he said.

'Murphy Doucet has my daughter.' I watched his face. He put his thumbnail into a molar and picked out a piece of food with it. 'Did you hear what I said?'

He poured three fingers of scotch into his glass, then dropped a lemon rind into the ice, his face composed, his eyes glancing out the window at a distant flicker of lightning.

'Too bad,' he said.

'Too bad, huh?'

'Yeah. I don't like to hear stuff like that. It upsets me.'

'Upsets you, does it?'

'Yeah. That's why I don't watch that show *Unsolved Mysteries*. It upsets me. Hey, maybe you can get her face on one of those milk cartons.'

As he drank from his highball, I could see the slight tug at the corner of his mouth, the smile in his eyes. He picked up his flowered shirt from the back of a chair and began putting it on in front of a bathroom door mirror as though we were not there.

I handed Rosie the shotgun, put my hands on my hips, and studied the tips of my shoes. Then I slipped an aluminum bat out of the canvas bag, choked up on the taped handle, and ripped it down across his neck and shoulders. His forehead bounced off the mirror, pocking and spiderwebbing the glass like it had been struck with a ball bearing. He turned back toward me, his eyes and mouth wide with disbelief, and I hit him again, hard, this time across the middle of the face. He crashed headlong into the toilet tank, his nose roaring blood, one side of his mouth drooping as though all the muscle endings in it had been severed.

I leaned over and cuffed both of his wrists around the bottom of the stool. His eyes were receded and out of focus, close-set like a pig's. The water in the bowl under his chin was filling with drops of dark color like pieces of disintegrating scarlet cotton.

I nudged his arm with the bat. His eyes clicked up into my face.

'Where is she, Julie?' I said.

'I cut Doucet loose. I don't have nothing to do with what he does. You get off my fucking case or I'm gonna square this, Dave. It don't matter if you're a cop or not, I'll put out an open contract, I'll cowboy your whole fucking family. I'll—'

I turned around and took the shotgun out of Rosie's hands. I could see words forming in her face, but I didn't wait for her to speak. I bent down on the edge of Julie's vision.

'Your window of opportunity is shutting down, Feet.'

He blew air out of his nose and tried to wipe his face on his shoulder.

'I'm telling you the truth. I don't know nothing about what that guy does,' he said. 'He's a geek . . . I don't hire geeks, I run them off . . . I got enough grief without crazy people working for me.'

'You're lying again, Julie,' I said, stepped back, leveled the shotgun barrel above his head, and fired at an angle into the toilet tank. The double-ought buckshot blew water and splintered ceramic all over the wall. I pumped the spent casing out on the floor. Julie jerked the handcuffs against the base of the stool, like an animal trying to twist itself out of a metal trap.

I touched the warm tip of the barrel against his eyebrow.

'Last chance, Feet.'

His eyes closed; he broke wind uncontrollably in his pants; water and small chips of ceramic dripped out of his hair.

'He's got a camp south of Bayou Vista,' he said. 'It's almost to Atchafalaya Bay. The deed ain't in his name, nobody knows about it, it's like where he does all his weird stuff. It's right where the dirt road ends at the salt marsh. I seen it once when we were out on my boat.'

'Is my daughter there?' I said quietly.

'I just told you, it's where he goes to be weird. You figure it out.'

'We'll be back later, Feet. You can make a lot of noise, if you like, but your gumbals are gone and the security guard is watching war movies. If I get my daughter back, I'll have somebody from the department come out and pick you up. You can file charges against me then or do whatever you want. If you've lied to me, that's another matter.'

Then I saw a secret concern working in his eyes, a worry, a fear that had nothing to do with me or the pain and humiliation that I had inflicted upon him. It was the fear that you inevitably see in the eyes of men like Julie and his kind when they realize that through an ironic accident they are now dealing with forces that are as cruel and unchecked by morality as the energies they'd awakened with every morning of their lives.

'Cholo—' he said.

'What about him?' I said.

'He's out there somewhere.'

'I doubt it.'

'You don't know him. He carries a barber's razor. He's got fixations. He don't forget things. He tied parts of a guy all over a ceiling fan once.'

His chest moved up and down with his breathing against the rim of the toilet bowl. His brow was kneaded with lines, his nose a wet red smear against his face, his eyes twitching with a phlegmy light.

I shut off the valve that was spewing water upward into the shattered tank, then found a quilt and a pile of towels in a linen closet and placed the towels under Julie's forearms and the quilt between his knees and the bottom of the stool.

'That's about all I can do for you, Feet. Maybe it's the bottom of the ninth for both of us,' I said.

The front wheels of the truck shimmied on the cement as I wound up the transmission on Highway 90 southeast of town. It had stopped raining, the oaks and palm trees by the road's edge were coated with mist, and the moon was rising in the east like a pale white and mottled-blue wafer trailing streamers of cloud torn loose from the Gulf's horizon.

'I think I'm beyond all my parameters now, Dave,' Rosie said.

'What would you do differently? I'd like for you to tell me that, Rosie.'

'I believe we should have Balboni picked up – suspicion for involvement in a kidnapping.'

'And my daughter would be dead as soon as Doucet heard about it. Don't tell me that's not true, either.'

'I'm not sure you're in control any more, Dave. That remark about the bottom of the ninth—'

'What about it?'

'You're thinking about killing Doucet, aren't you?'

'I can put you down at the four-corners up there. Is that what you want?'

'Do you think you're the only person who cares about your daughter? Do you think I want to do anything that would put her in worse jeopardy than she's already in?'

'The army taught me what a free-fire zone is, Rosie. It's a place where the winners make up the rules after the battle's over. Anyone who believes otherwise has never been there.'

'You're wrong about all this, Dave. What we don't do is let the other side make us be like them.'

Ahead I could see the lighted, tree-shadowed white stucco walls of a twenty-four-hour filling station that had been there since the 1930s. I eased my foot off the gas pedal and looked across the seat at Rosie.

'Go on,' she said. 'I won't say anything else.'

We drove through Jeanerette and Franklin into the bottom of the Atchafalaya Basin, where Louisiana's wetlands bled into the Gulf of Mexico, not far from where this story actually began with a racial lynching in the year 1957. Rosie had fallen asleep against the door. At Bayou Vista I found the dirt road that led south to the sawgrass and Atchafalaya

Bay. The fields looked like lakes of pewter under the moon, the sugarcane pressed flat like straw into the water. Wood farmhouses and barns were cracked sideways on their foundations, as though a gigantic thumb had squeezed down on their roofs, and along one stretch of road the telephone poles had been snapped off even with the ground for a half mile and flung like sticks into distant trees.

Then the road entered a corridor of oaks, and through the trunks I saw four white horses galloping in circles in a mist-streaked pasture, spooking against the barbed-wire fences, mud flying from their hooves, their nostrils dilated, their eyes bright with fear against a backdrop of dry lightning, their muscles rippling under their skin like silvery water sliding over stone. Then I was sure I saw a figure by the side of the road, the palmetto shadows waving behind him, his steel-gray tunic buttoned at his throat, a floppy campaign hat pulled over his eyes.

I hit my bright lights, and for just a moment I saw his elongated milk-white face as though a flashbulb had exploded in front of it. *'What are you doing here?'* I said.

'Don't use those whom you love to justify a dishonorable cause.'

'That's rhetoric.'

'You gave the same counsel to the Sykes boy.'

'It was you who told me to do it under a black flag. Remember? We blow up their shit big time, general.'

'Then you will do it on your own, suh, and without me.'

The truck's front springs bounced in a chuckhole and splashed a sheet of dirty water across the window; then I was beyond the pasture and the horses that wheeled and raced in the moonlight, traveling deep into the tip of the wetlands, with flooded woods on each side of me, blue herons lifting on extended wings out of the canals, the moist air whipped with the smell of salt and natural gas from the oil platforms out in the swamp.

The road bent out of the trees, and I saw the long expanses of sawgrass and mudflats that spread out into the bay, and the network of channels that had been cut by the oil companies and that were slowly poisoning the marshes with salt water. Rosie was awake now, rubbing her eyes with one knuckle, her face still with fatigue.

'I'm sorry. I didn't mean to fall asleep,' she said.

'It's been a long day.'

'Where's the camp?'

'There's some shacks down by the flats, but they look deserted.'

I pulled the truck to the side of the road and cut the lights. The tide was out, and the bay looked flat and gray and seabirds were pecking shellfish out of the wet sand in the moonlight. Then a wind gusted out of the south and bent a stand of willow trees that stood on a small knoll between the marsh and the bay.

'Dave, there's a light back in those trees,' Rosie said.

Then I saw it, too, at the end of a two-lane sandy track that wound through the willows and over the knoll.

'All right, let's do it,' I said, and pushed down on the door handle.

'Dave, before we go in there, I want you to hear something. If we find the wrong thing, if Alafair's not all right, it's not because of anything you did. It's important for you to accept that now. If I had been in your place, I'd have done everything the same way you have.'

I squeezed her hand.

'A cop couldn't have a better partner than Rosie Gomez,' I said.

We got out of the truck and left the doors open to avoid making any unecessary sound, and walked up the sandy track toward the trees. I could hear gulls cawing and wheeling overhead and the solitary scream of a nutria deep in the marsh. Humps of garbage stood by the sides of the track, and then I realized that it was medical waste – bandages, hypodermic vials, congealed bags of gelatin, sheets that were stiff with dried fluids.

We moved away from the side of the road and into the trees. I walked with the shotgun at port arms, the .45 heavy in the right-hand pocket of my raincoat. Rosie had her chrome-plated .357 magnum gripped with both hands at an upward angle, just to the right of her cheek. Then the wind bent the trees again and blew a shower of wet leaves into a clearing, where we could see a tin-roofed cabin with a small gallery littered with cane poles, crab traps, and hand-throw fishnets, and a Coleman lantern hissing whitely on a wood table in the front room. In the back were an outhouse and a pirogue set up on sawhorses, and behind the outhouse was Murphy Doucet's blue Mercury.

A shadow moved across the window, then a man with his back to us sat down at the table with a coffee pot and a thick white mug in his hands. Even through the rusted screen I could see his stiff, gray military haircut and the deeply tanned skin of his neck whose tone and texture reminded me of a cured tobacco leaf.

We should have been home free. But then I saw the moonlight glint on the wire that was stretched across the two-lane track, three inches above the sand. I propped the shotgun against a tree, knelt down in the wet leaves, and ran my fingers along the wire until I touched two empty Spam cans that were tied with string to the wire, then two more, then two more after that. Through the underbrush, against the glow of moonlight in the clearing, I could make out a whole network of nylon fishing line strung between tree trunks, branches, roots, and underbrush, and festooned with tin cans, pie plates, and even a cow bell.

I was sweating heavily inside my raincoat now. I wiped the salt out of my eyes with my hand.

One lung-bursting rush across the clearing, I thought. *Clear the gallery in one step, bust the door out of the jamb, then park a big one in his brisket and it's over.*

But I knew better. I would sound like a traveling junkyard before I ever made the gallery, and if Alafair was still alive, in all probability he would be holding a pistol at her head.

'We have to wait until it's light or until he comes out,' I whispered to Rosie.

We knelt down in the trees, in the damp air, in the layered mat of black and yellow willow leaves, in the mosquitoes that rose in clouds from around our knees and perched on our faces and the backs of our hands and necks. I saw him get up once, walk to a shelf, then return to the table and read a magazine while he ate soda crackers out of a box. My thighs burned and a band of pain that I couldn't relieve began to spread slowly across my back. Rosie sat with her rump resting on her heels, wiping the mosquitoes off her forearms, her pink skirt hiked up on her thighs, her .357 propped in the fork of a tree. Her neck was shiny with sweat.

Then at shortly after four I could hear mullet jumping in the water, a 'gator flop his tail back in the marsh, a solitary mockingbird singing on the far side of the clearing. The air changed; a cool breeze lifted off the bay and blew the smell of fish and grass shrimp across the flats. Then a pale glow, like cobalt, like the watery green cast of summer light right before a rain, spread under the rim of banked clouds on the eastern horizon, and in minutes I could see the black shapes of jetties extending far out into the bay, small waves white-capping with the incoming tide, the rigging of a distant shrimp boat dropping below a swell.

Then Murphy Doucet wrote the rest of the script for us. He turned down the Coleman lantern, stretched his back, picked up something from the table, went out the front door, and walked behind our line of vision on the far side of the cabin toward the outhouse.

We moved out of the trees into the clearing, stepping over and under the network of can-rigged fishline, then divided in two directions at the corner of the gallery. I could smell a fecund salty odor like dead rats and stagnant water from under the cabin.

The rear windows were boarded with slats from packing boxes and I couldn't see inside or hear any movement. At the back of the cabin I paused, held the shotgun flat against my chest, and looked around the corner. Murphy Doucet was almost to the door of the outhouse, a pair of untied hunting boots flopping on his feet, a silvery object glinting in his right hand. Beyond the outhouse, by the marsh's edge, a bluetick dog was tied to a post surrounded by a ring of feces.

I stepped out from the lee of the cabin, threw the stock of the shotgun to my shoulder, sighted between Doucet's neck and shoulder blades, and felt the words already rising in my throat, like bubbles out of a boiling pot, *Surprise time, motherfucker! Throw it away! Do it now!* when he heard Rosie trip across a fishline that was tied to a cow bell on the gallery.

He looked once over his shoulder in her direction, then leaped behind the outhouse and ran toward the marsh on a long green strip of dry ground covered with buttercups. But five yards before he would have splashed into the willows and dead cypress and perhaps out of our field of fire, his untied boots sank into a pile of rotting medical waste that was matted with the scales of morning-glory vines. A wooden crutch that looked hand-hewn, with a single shaft that fitted into the armrest, sprang from under his boot and hung between his legs like a stick in bicycle spokes.

He turned around helplessly toward Rosie, falling backward off balance now, his blue eyes jittering frantically, his right arm extended toward her, as though it were not too late for her to recognize that his hand held a can of dog food rather than a weapon, just as she let off the first round of her .357 and caught him right in the sternum.

But it didn't stop there. She continued to fire with both hands gripped on the pistol, each soft-nosed slug knocking him backward with the force of a jackhammer, his shirt exploding with scarlet flowers on his bony chest, until the last round in the cylinder hit him in the rib cage and virtually eviscerated him on the water's edge. Then he simply sat down on top of his crumpled legs as though all the bones in his body had been surgically removed.

When she lowered the weapon toward the ground, her cheeks looked like they contained tiny red coals, and her eyes were frozen wide, as though she were staring into a howling storm, one that was filled with invisible forces and grinding winds only she could hear.

But I didn't have time to worry about the line that Rosie had crossed and the grief and knowledge that dark moment would bring with it.

Behind me I heard wood slats breaking loose from the back of the cabin, then I saw metal chair legs crash through the window, and Alafair climbing over the windowsill, her rump hanging in midair, her pink tennis shoes swinging above the damp earth.

I ran to her, grabbed her around the waist, and held her tightly against me. She buried her head under my chin and clamped her legs on my side like a frog, and I could feel the hard resilience of her muscles, the heat in her hands, the spastic breathing in her throat as though she had just burst from deep water into warm currents of salt air and a sunlit day loud with the sound of seabirds.

'Did he hurt you, Squanto?' I said, my heart dropping with my own question.

'I told him he'd better not. I told him what you'd do. I told him you'd rip his nuts out. I told him—'

'Where'd you get this language, Alf?'

A shudder went through her body, as though she had just removed her hand from a hot object, then her eyes squeezed shut and she began to cry.

'It's all right, Baby Squanto. We're going back home now,' I said.

I carried her on my hip back toward the truck, her arms around my neck, her face wet against my shirt.

I heard Rosie walking in the leaves behind me. She dumped the spent brass from the cylinder of her .357 into her palm, looked at them woodenly, then threw them tinkling into the trees.

'Get out of it, Rosie. That guy dealt the play a long time ago.'

'I couldn't stop. Why didn't I stop shooting? It was over and I kept shooting.'

'Because your mind shuts down in moments like that.'

'No, he paid for something that happened to me a long time ago, didn't he?'

'Let the Freudians play with that stuff. They seldom spend time on the firing line. It'll pass. Believe me, it always does.'

'Not hitting a man four times after he was going down. A man armed with a can of dog food.'

I looked at the spreading glow out on the bay and the gulls streaking over the tide's edge.

'He had a piece on him, Rosie. You just don't remember it right now,' I said, and handed Alafair to her.

I went back into the trees, found my raincoat, and carried it over my arm to the place where Murphy Doucet sat slumped among the butter-cups, his torn side draining into the water. I took Lou Girard's .32 revolver from my raincoat pocket, wiped the worn bluing and the taped wooden grips on my handkerchief, fitted it into Doucet's hand, and closed his stiffened fingers around the trigger guard.

On his forearm was a set of teethmarks that looked like they had been put there by a child.

Next time out don't mess with Alafair Robicheaux or the Confederate army, Murph, I thought.

Then I picked up the crutch that had caught between his legs. The wood was old, weathered gray, the shaft shaved and beveled by a knife, the armrest tied with strips of rotted flannel.

The sun broke through the clouds overhead, and under the marsh's green canopy I could see hammered gold leaf hanging in the columns of spinning light, and gray shapes like those of long-dead sentinels, and like a man who has finally learned not to think reasonably in an unreasonable world, I offered the crutch at the air, at the shapes in the trees and at the sound of creatures moving through the water, saying *Don't you want to take this with you, sir?*

But if he answered, I did not hear it.

Epilogue

I'd like to tell you that the department and the local prosecutor's office finally made their case against Julie Balboni, that we cleaned our own house and sent him up the road to Angola in waist and leg chains for a twenty- or thirty-year jolt. But that's not what happened. How could it? In many ways Julie was us, just as his father had been when he provided the town its gambling machines and its rows of cribs on Railroad and Hopkins avenues. After Julie had left town on his own to become a major figure in the New Orleans mob, we had welcomed him back, winking our eyes at his presence and pretending he was not what or who he was.

I believe Julie and his father possessed a knowledge about us that we did not possess about ourselves. They knew we were for sale.

Julie finally went down, but in a way that no one expected – in a beef with the IRS. No, that's not quite right, either. That ubiquitous federal agency, the bane of the mob, was only a minor footnote in Julie's denouement. The seed of Julie's undoing was Julie. And I guess Julie in his grandiosity would not have had it any other way.

He should have done easy time, a three-year waltz on a federal honor farm in Florida, with no fences or gunbulls, with two-man rooms rather than cells, tennis courts, and weekend furloughs. But while in federal custody in New Orleans he spit in a bailiff's face, tore the lavatory out of his cell wall, and told an informant planted in his cell that he was putting a hit out on Cholo Manelli, who he believed had turned over his books to the IRS (which I heard later was true).

So they shipped Baby Feet up to a maximum-security unit at Fort Leavenworth, Kansas, a place that in the wintertime makes you believe that the earth has been poisoned with Agent Orange and the subzero winds blow from four directions simultaneously.

Most people are not aware of who comprises the population of a maximum-security lockup. They are usually not men like Baby Feet, who was intelligent and fairly sane for a sociopath. Instead, they are usually psychotic meltdowns, although they are not classified as such, otherwise they would be sent to mental institutions from which they would probably be released in a relatively short time. Perhaps they have the intelligence levels of battery-charged cabbages, housed in six-and-one-half-foot bodies that glow with rut. Often they're momma's boys who wear horn-rimmed glasses and comb their hair out on their frail shoulders like girls, murder whole families, and can never offer more in the way of explanation than a bemused and youthful smile.

But none was a match for Julie. He was a made guy, connected both on the inside and outside, a blockhouse behemoth whose whirling feet could make men bleed from every orifice in their bodies. He took over the dope trade, broke heads and groins in the shower, paid to have a rival shanked in the yard and a snitch drowned in a toilet bowl.

He also became a celebrity wolf among the punk population. They ironed his clothes, shampooed his hair, manicured his nails, and asked him in advance what kind of wigs and women's underthings they should wear when they came to his bunk. He encouraged jealousies among them and watched as an amused spectator while they schemed and fought among themselves for his affections and the reefer, pills, and prune-o he could provide to his favorites.

Perhaps he even found the adoration and submission that had always eluded him from the time he used to visit Mabel White's mulatto brothel in Crowley until he had Cherry LeBlanc murdered.

At least the psychologist at Fort Leavenworth who told me this story thought so. He said Julie actually seemed happy his first and final spring on the yard, hitting flyballs to his boys in the outfield, ripping the bat from deep in the box with the power and grace of a DiMaggio, the fine black hair on his shoulders glazed with sweat, his black silk shorts hanging on his hips with the confident male abandon of both a successful athlete and lover, snapping his wrists as he connected with the ball, lifting it higher into the blue sky than anyone at Leavenworth had ever done before, while all around him other cons touched themselves and nodded with approval.

Maybe he was still thinking about these things on the Sunday evening he came in from the diamond, showered, and went to the empty cell of his current lover to take a nap under a small rubber-bladed fan with the sheet over his head. Maybe in his dreams he was once again a movie producer on the edge of immense success, a small-town boy whose story would be recreated by biographers and become the stuff of legends in Hollywood, a beneficient but feared mogul in sunglasses and a two-thousand-dollar white tropical suit who strolled with elegance and grace through the bougainvillea and palm trees and the clink of champagne glasses at Beverly Hills lawn parties.

Or maybe, for just a moment, when a pain sharper than any he had ever thought possible entered his consciousness like a red shard of glass, he saw the face of his father contorted like a fist as the father held him at gunpoint and whipped the nozzle end of a garden hose across Julie's shivering back.

The Molotov cocktail thrown by a competitor for Julie's affections burst on the stone wall above the bunk where Julie was sleeping and covered his entire body with burning paraffin and gasoline. He erupted from the bunk, flailing at the air, the sheet dissolving in black holes against his skin. He ran blindly through the open cell door, wiping at his eyes and mouth, his disintegrating shape an enormous cone of flame now, and with one long bellowing cry he sprang over the rail of the tier and plunged like a meteor three stories to the cement floor below.

What happened to Twinky Hebert Lemoyne?

Nothing. Not externally. He's still out there, a member of a generation whose metamorphosis never quite takes place.

Sometimes I see his picture on the business page of the Lafayette newspaper. You can count on him to be at fund-raiser kick-off breakfasts for whatever charity is in fashion with the business community. In all probability he's even sincere. Once or twice I've run into him at a crab boil or fish fry in New Iberia. He doesn't do well, however, in a personal encounter with the past. His manners are of course gentlemanly, his pink skin and egg-shaped head and crinkling seersucker suit images that you associate with a thoughtful and genteel southern barrister but in the steady and trained avoidance that his eyes perform when you look into his face, you see another man, one whose sense of self-worth was so base that he would participate in a lynching because he had been made a cuckold by one of his own black employees.

No, that's not quite fair to him.

Perhaps, just like Julie Balboni, Twinky Hebert is us. He loathed his past so much that he could never acknowledge it, never expiate his sin, and never forgive himself, either. So, like Proteus rising from the sea and forever reshaping his form, Twinky Hebert Lemoyne made a contract of deceit with himself and consequently doomed himself to relive his past every day of his life.

At the crab boil in the park on Bayou Teche he inadvertently sat down at a wood table under the pavilion not three feet away from me, Bootsie, and Alafair. He had just started to crack the claws on a crab when he realized who sat across from him.

'What are *you* doing here?' he asked, his mouth hanging open.

'I live in New Iberia. I was invited to attend.'

'Are you trying to harass me?'

'I closed the file on the summer of 1957, Mr Lemoyne. Why don't you?'

There was a painful light, like a burning match, deep in his eyes. He tried to break open a crab claw with a pair of nutcrackers, then his hand slipped and sprayed juice on his shirt front.

'Tell a minister about it, tell a cop, get on a plane and tell somebody you never saw before,' I said. 'Just get rid of it once and for all and lose the Rotary Club doodah.'

But he was already walking rapidly toward the men's room, scrubbing at his palms with a paper towel, his change rattling in his pants' pockets, twisting his neck from side to side as though his tie and stiff collar were a rope against his skin.

We took our vacation that year in California and stayed with Elrod in his ranch home built on stilts high up on a cliff in Topanga Canyon, overlooking the Pacific Coast Highway and the ocean that was covered each morning with a thick bluish-white mist, inside which you could hear the waves crashing like avalanches into the beach.

For two weeks Alafair acted in a picture out at Tri-Star with Mikey Goldman and Elrod, and in the evenings we ate cherrystone clams at Gladstone's on the beach and took rides in Mikey Goldman's pontoon plane out to Catalina Island. As the late sun descended into the ocean, it seemed to trail ragged strips of black cloud with it, like a burning red planet settling into the Pacific's water green rim. When the entire coastline was awash in a pink light you could see almost every geological and floral characteristic of the American continent tumbling from the purple crests of the Santa Monica Mountains into the curling line of foam that slid up onto the beaches: dry hills of chaparral, mesquite and scrub oak, clumps of eucalyptus and bottlebrush trees, torrey and ponderosa pine growing between blue-tiled stucco houses, coral walls overgrown with bougainvillea, terraced hillside gardens filled with oleander, yucca plants, and trellises dripping with passion vine, and orange groves whose irrigation ditches looked like quicksilver in the sun's afterglow.

Then millions of lights came on in the canyons, along the freeways, and through the vast sweep of the Los Angeles basin, and it was almost as if you were looking down upon the end point of the American dream, a geographical poem into which all our highways eventually led, a city of illusion founded by conquistadors and missionaries and consigned to the care of angels, where far below the spinning propellers of our seaplane black kids along palm-tree-lined streets in Watts hunted each other with automatic weapons.

I thought in the morning mists that rolled up the canyon I might once again see the noble and chivalric John Bell Hood. Just a glimpse, perhaps, a doff of his hat, the kindness of his smile, the beleaguered affection that always seemed to linger in his face. Then as the days passed and I began to let go of all the violent events of that summer, I had to accept the fact that the general, as Bootsie had said, was indeed only a hopeful figment of my fantasies, a metaphorical and mythic figure probably created as much by the pen of Thomas Mallory or Walter Scott as the LSD someone had put in my drink out at Spanish Lake.

Then two nights before we returned home, Alafair was sitting on the coral wall that rimmed Elrod's terrace, flipping the pages in one of the library books Bootsie had checked out on the War Between the States.

'What you doing in here, Dave?' she said.

'In what? What are you talking about, little guy?'

She continued to stare down at a page opened in her lap.

'You're in the picture. With that old man Poteet and I saw in the corn patch. The one with BO,' she said, and turned the book around so I could look at it.

In the photograph, posed in the stiff attitudes of nineteenth-century photography, were the general and seven of his aides and enlisted men.

'Standing in the back. The one without a gun. That's you, Dave,' she said. Then she stared up at me with a confused question mark in the middle of her face. 'Ain't it?'

'Don't say "ain't," little guy.'

'What are you doing in the picture?'

'That's not me, Alf. Those are Texas soldiers who fought alongside John Bell Hood. I bet they were a pretty good bunch,' I said, and rubbed the top of her head.

'How do you know they're from Texas? It doesn't say that here.'

'It's just a guess.'

She looked at the photograph again and back at me, and her face became more confused.

'Let's get Elrod and Bootsie and go down to the beach for some ice cream,' I said.

I slipped the book from her hand and closed it, picked her up on my hip, and walked through the canopy of purple trumpet vine toward the patio behind the house, where Bootsie and Elrod were clearing off the dishes from supper. Down the canyon, smoke from meat fires drifted through the cedar and mesquite trees, and if I squinted my eyes in the sun's setting, I could almost pretend that Spanish soldiers in silver chest armor and bladed helmets or a long-dead race of hunters were encamped on those hillsides. Or maybe even old compatriots in butternut brown wending their way in and out of history – gallant, Arthurian, their canister-ripped colors unfurled in the roiling smoke, the fatal light in their faces a reminder that the contest is never quite over, the field never quite ours.